There was a bang.

Loud enough to get his attention above the raging water. Someone in the trunk screamed for help. Charlotte was still alive.

"I'm coming! Hang on!" He grabbed the latch on the back.

"Hurry, we don't have much time," she called.

We? She wasn't alone. Jonas struggled with the handle while watching the rising water claim more of the sinking vehicle.

When the door finally released, the deputy's huge green eyes met Jonas's. "Help me get her out before it goes under. She's been shot."

"I've got her." But getting the injured woman from the Jeep wasn't easy. The fear in the young woman's eyes urged him on.

"The Jeep is going to take us down with it," Charlotte said. "We've got to get away."

"*Jah*...yes," he corrected quickly. Even though he wasn't Amish anymore, Jonas had gotten accustomed to using Pennsylvania Dutch in his thoughts. Letting go of the old ways was hard.

"Let's try to make it to the bank." Charlotte swam out in front of him. From where he was now, the riverbank appeared miles away.

Mary Alford was inspired to become a writer after reading romantic suspense greats Victoria Holt and Phyllis A. Whitney. Soon, creating characters and throwing them into dangerous situations that tested their faith came naturally for Mary. In 2012, Mary entered the speed dating contest hosted by Love Inspired Suspense and later received "the call." Writing for Love Inspired Suspense has been a dream come true for Mary.

Books by Mary Alford

Love Inspired Suspense

Forgotten Past
Rocky Mountain Pursuit
Deadly Memories
Framed for Murder
Standoff at Midnight Mountain
Grave Peril
Amish Country Kidnapping
Amish Country Murder
Covert Amish Christmas
Shielding the Amish Witness
Dangerous Amish Showdown
Snowbound Amish Survival
Amish Wilderness Survival
Amish Country Ransom
Deadly Mountain Escape

Visit the Author Profile page at LoveInspired.com.

DEADLY MOUNTAIN ESCAPE

MARY ALFORD

LOVE INSPIRED SUSPENSE

INSPIRATIONAL ROMANCE

LOVE INSPIRED® SUSPENSE
INSPIRATIONAL ROMANCE

ISBN-13: 978-1-335-59788-5

Recycling programs
for this product may
not exist in your area.

Deadly Mountain Escape

For questions and comments about the quality of this book, please contact us at CustomerService@Harlequin.com.

Love Inspired
22 Adelaide St. West, 41st Floor
Toronto, Ontario M5H 4E3, Canada
www.LoveInspired.com

Printed in U.S.A.

And God shall wipe away all tears from their eyes;
and there shall be no more death, neither sorrow,
nor crying, neither shall there be any more pain:
for the former things are passed away.
—*Revelation* 21:4

To my mom and dad.
Thank you for starting me on this amazing journey.

ONE

Deputy Charlotte Walker stepped out onto the porch. Her neighbor Dottie Marques turned troubled eyes her way. "I know it's hard, but please try not to worry," Charlotte said. "I'm sure there's a valid explanation for why she didn't come home after work last night." Yet the pit in Charlotte's stomach disagreed with those words.

"Thank you," Dottie said. "I know I'm probably being an overprotective grandmother, but Lainey is the only family I have, and she wouldn't stay away so long without calling." The older woman shuddered. "I'm so afraid. I can't lose her."

"This will help." Charlotte held up the pink argyle garment that belonged to Lainey. "Annie should be able to get Lainey's scent from it."

Dottie's eyes were red and swollen from crying. "You'll call as soon as you know anything?"

Charlotte nodded. "I'll start at the Christian youth camp you said Lainey likes to visit. She may very well be there and can't get service enough to check in with you. That part of the county is remote."

Dottie clutched Charlotte's hands. "From your lips to God's ears."

Charlotte's family and the Marques family had owned

neighboring ranches in the Ruby Valley of Montana for several generations. After Dottie's husband died, she'd managed the ranch on her own until Lainey came to live with her a few years back. When Charlotte's parents both died soon after each other, she wouldn't have gotten through without Dottie. The woman was forged in steel and Montana strong.

"Stay close to the phone in case Lainey calls. If you do hear from her, let me know."

"Find her, Charlotte. Please."

"I will. I promise." With a heartbreaking plea from a desperate grandmother still ringing in her ears, Charlotte prayed she'd be able to back it up. "Stay strong. For Lainey."

When Dottie called for help, Charlotte couldn't refuse. So, off duty and out of uniform, she headed for her bright yellow Jeep parked in the drive. Annie, her K-9 partner, waited in the passenger seat, eyes glued to Charlotte.

Annie was a bluetick coonhound with a unique tri-colored coat that was predominately dark blue in color. She had black spots on her back, ears and sides known as ticking. Charlotte placed Lainey's sweater on the center console and waved to Dottie as she drove away.

Annie sniffed the sweater as if sensing her skills were about to be put to the test.

"Are you ready to get to work? Dottie needs our help." Annie's enthusiastic woof had Charlotte smiling despite her pressing concern for Lainey's safety. Lainey might be twenty and an adult, but she would never do anything to cause her grandmother undue worry. Disappearing for any length of time without calling wasn't like her.

Charlotte drove toward the deserted place in the wilderness where the Christian camp was located, not far from the Tobacco Root Mountains. Memories of the last missing person case she'd worked on in that area came to mind. Michaela Reagan's case had cost Charlotte personally. She'd lost her fiancé, Ryan—a K-9 trainer and member of the county's search and rescue team—when Ryan fell to his death while assisting with Michaela's search.

Law enforcement, along with the county's SAR team, had searched tirelessly throughout the night only to find the missing teen dead at the base of Hollowtop Mountain. She'd been shot once in the head. The gun was found lying near her body. The cause of death was ruled suicide, yet many believed the scene was staged.

Charlotte was among them. Michaela was a well-liked teen from a prominent and loving family. Why would she shoot herself? Could her death have anything to do with the mysterious call Charlotte had gotten a week before?

Something deep inside her itched for more answers about her fiancé's death, too. But she never allowed herself to think on it too long. Too painful.

She would never forget Ryan's funeral. Even after hearing Ryan's best friend, Phillip, give the eulogy—watching as the dirt was placed over Ryan's coffin at the graveyard—Charlotte still hadn't been able to grasp the reality that he was really gone until much later.

Charlotte glanced briefly at her partner. Annie was the last dog Ryan had ever trained and more than a friend for Charlotte. She and Annie had continued to grieve Ryan's death throughout this past year he'd been gone. The winter months had been the hardest. She had too much time on her hands. Work helped. Still, each day came with its own pain. Every step forward hurt; Ryan still claimed her heart.

Charlotte turned onto the small dirt road that headed toward the Christian camp. After the camp's closure several years back, the woods had slowly been reclaiming the small lane used to access the site. Lainey would have had to park on the side of this road and hike in.

A strange place for a young woman to go alone, yet Dottie had told her that Lainey went there to get closer to God.

As Charlotte passed the first house down the road, she spotted a man she'd met on a couple different occasions repairing his fence. Jonas Knowles's dark blond hair was covered by a straw hat that looked as if it had seen better days. He wore a dark blue shirt, jeans and suspenders. She remembered Jonas in particular because he had the most unusual shade of blue eyes. Ice blue. The kind you didn't forget.

She waved. Jonas removed his hat and scraped back his hair before returning her greeting.

Living in the shadow of the Tobacco Root Mountains, her family's ranch in the Ruby Valley had been Charlotte's home all her life. She was familiar with just about everyone in the county where she served as a deputy. Her parents had raised her to have faith and be strong. Her dad had been sheriff here for almost five years before he'd retired to care for his ailing wife. Dad had survived countless attacks from both knives and guns, but losing his wife of forty years was something he couldn't overcome. He'd died a few months after his wife.

Even though almost five years had passed, the pain of their deaths was always close, yet something her father told her shortly before his death came to mind. He'd told her focusing on the past was the surest way to stop moving forward. She'd tried to abide by those words, but this past year had been hard.

As she neared the place where the former camp road had been, an uneasy feeling grasped Charlotte and wouldn't let go. Past Jonas Knowles's place, the trees appeared to grow closer to the road, giving the area a sinister look. The perfect place to cover up a crime if one was looking to do so. Madison County had its share of unsavory suspects who would do whatever was necessary to stay out of prison.

The Christian campsite was a few miles in and on privately owned land. The rest of the property on the right of the road was all national forest. Following an instinct Charlotte couldn't explain, she pulled over onto the edge of the road and grabbed her Kevlar vest from the back seat. Once it was secured in place, she held the sweater out for Annie to get a scent.

As soon as she opened the Jeep's door, Charlotte noticed a set of tire tracks near where she'd parked. Someone had been here at one time. Before she could investigate, Annie bounded from the vehicle. After a few sniffs on the ground, she had her scent and was running with it.

Charlotte scrambled after her partner. Annie moved quickly when on a scent. There was no time to hesitate if Charlotte wanted to keep up with the dog.

Her bright orange K-9 vest made her easy to spot most times, except when traveling through thick brush like now—most of it was taller than the dog.

It took a moment to home in on Annie's direction through the undergrowth. She was heading away from the campsite. Why would Lainey have gone this way?

Charlotte picked up the trail and raced after her partner while her fear for Lainey's safety grew. Even if Lainey had intended to spend some time at the camp, she recognized the area well enough not to get this far off trail.

Yet Lainey had definitely been down this way at some point recently, either by her own volition or by someone else's. Charlotte's shoulders grew tense at the thought of her friend being taken against her will.

Once more she lost track of Annie in the thigh-deep brush. Charlotte stopped and spun around while a sliver of fear wound itself tight in her head. She'd come here alone with only her K-9 partner. Charlotte should have called someone to let them know her location. Dottie knew about the Christian campsite, but as she recalled, there was more than one way to reach it, so it might take searchers longer to find her.

She pulled her phone from her jeans pocket and checked. The no service indicator mocked her mistake. As a deputy for the Madison County Sheriff's Department, the right thing to do was to backtrack until she was able to call her dispatcher and apprise her of what was happening just in case.

But Annie was on track…

Charlotte picked up the dog's location once more and made the decision to keep going. As she walked, she shoved back brush that made moving through it nearly impossible.

After several miles of fast-paced moving, she noticed the woods ahead had been cleared away around a run-down piece of property. It took Charlotte a second to gain her bearings but when she did, she realized she knew the house and its owner quite well. A man by the name of Harley Owens had been in and out of jail for abusing his wife since Charlotte had joined the force.

On multiple occasions Charlotte been called out here on domestic abuse reports…and then his wife would refuse to press charges, claim to have fallen down the steps or something similar.

Tension coiled down deep in her body. Charlotte immediately unholstered her weapon. Harley was dangerous and had gone on record many times bragging about the number of weapons he owned. He'd managed to beat all charges brought against him. Partly because his wife refused to testify, but mostly because Phillip Hollins, the county's district attorney, had said they didn't have enough evidence to convict Harley.

If Lainey's trail led here, there was reason to be concerned.

She approached the dilapidated, peeling white house with caution. Annie had disappeared around the corner of the structure.

An out of place noise coming from the direction Annie had disappeared had Charlotte slowly advancing. She flattened herself against the wall of the house and peeked around, her heart in her throat. Where was Harley? She hadn't seen his beat-up pickup truck parked in the front yard like normal. She listened carefully. No sound came from inside the house. Harley's wife, Betty, didn't work to Charlotte's knowledge. Where was she?

Charlotte dialed 9-1. Before she hit the last 1, a sound almost too faint to hear had her whipping around. She caught sight of a man in a mask before something was shoved against her side. A sharp electrical current sent her to her knees. She'd been Tased. Her attacker snatched her weapon and phone away from her unresisting hands. Another fierce blast from the Taser proved this was deadly serious. She had to get away if she stood a chance at surviving. Charlotte began crawling away from her attacker, but she was weak and barely able to move. She was now in a fight for her life to survive a man who clearly had everything to lose.

Jonas Knowles wiped his forehead as he surveyed the fence line. As much as he wanted to get it finished today, the woman he'd recognized as a deputy for the county wouldn't get out of his head. It had been several hours since she'd passed his place. The only other residence down the dead-end road was Harley's. She hadn't been going there on official business because she was in her personal vehicle. Why had she come down this way in the first place?

He'd spotted the dog with her. Jonas recalled she was part of the sheriff's K-9 unit.

It didn't matter what her business was; it didn't concern him. He jabbed the post hole digger into the earth as her name teased around the edges of his memory. Walker. Charlotte Walker. She'd stopped by to ask Jonas questions about Harley the couple of times she'd been out here. She'd seemed nice enough. Efficient. Though she was petite, he had no doubt she could handle herself. Her sharp green eyes seemed to key in on him. He had no doubt she'd seen the guilt Jonas harbored in his heart.

After he finished the post he'd been working on, Jonas stabbed the post hole digger into the next spot and then headed up to his house for a drink.

Though it was technically springtime in the shadow of the Root Mountains, today had been a hot one.

Jonas reached the porch and opened the screen door. He let it slam behind him. In the kitchen, he poured cold water from the pitcher chilling in the battery-powered fridge and stared out the window toward Harley's place.

In the six years he'd lived here, Jonas had seen things that didn't sit right with him. More than once, he'd come to the defense of Harley's wife, Betty, after he'd heard screaming coming from their house. He'd tried to get Betty to leave her abusive husband, but she was more afraid of what Harley would do to her if she did leave than if she stayed. Harley never seemed to end up in jail for long. And there were all sorts of strange comings and goings at the place all hours of the night.

For someone who had lived twenty-six years of his life as Amish, the activity coming from Harley's was troubling. More than once, Jonas had debated selling his home, even if it meant taking a loss, and finding another piece of property as far away from Harley as possible.

Each time he considered it, he remembered Betty and realized he couldn't abandon her to Harley's violence. Even if she wouldn't accept his help, he'd be there for her. When she fled her house to get away from her husband, Jonas offered her a safe place to stay and volunteered to ride to the nearest neighbor and call for help. Though Betty declined, he had no doubt that, at some point in the future, everything was going to come to a head. He'd be there to help Betty like he hadn't been for his wife.

Jonas set his glass down and stepped out onto the front porch once more. Best get back to work. The fence had needed repairing for a while now. He'd waited through winter because the ground was frozen. Thankfully, the handful of cows he owned were in the back pasture and he hadn't been worried about them escaping through the missing posts and wire out front. Now it was time to move the animals for better grazing. Fixing the fence was critical.

A noise caught his attention—a scream perhaps—gone before he could be sure. Jonas shielded his eyes against the afternoon glare and listened. Nothing but silence and then…a vehicle's engine firing down the road. He left the porch, his footsteps sure. Something wasn't right, and Charlotte was familiar enough with what Harley was capable of.

The frantic sound of a dog barking stopped him cold. Harley didn't own a dog. This one had to belong to Charlotte. Had the scream he heard been hers?

Something inside warned that his concern was well

justified. He didn't care if he had to fight Harley—he'd make sure Betty and Charlotte were okay.

Cutting across the property would be faster, but Harley had all sorts of booby traps set up along his property line.

Before Jonas reached the road, patches of bright yellow appeared through the leaves. The quiet of the countryside was broken by an approaching vehicle. Jonas ducked out of sight as the yellow Jeep eased past his position. Relief flooded him briefly before he spotted the driver. It wasn't Charlotte but Harley behind the wheel, an angry scowl on his face as he glanced over at Jonas's place.

Where was Charlotte? Jonas tried to untangle the truth as he watched the vehicle move out of sight. If Harley was driving the Jeep, he'd done something to the deputy. He wouldn't be driving her vehicle now unless he was trying to get rid of evidence of foul play.

Jonas ran toward the barn. He had to go after Harley and try to save Charlotte.

Though he hadn't been Amish in six years, Jonas still kept the ways, mostly because it was hard to give them up and he found comfort there. He didn't own a car. His only means of transportation was the horse and the buggy he used for longer trips to town.

He yanked the barn door open. Sandy, the mare that had been with him since the move six years earlier, glanced up at the commotion. The buggy would draw too much attention.

"Come on, girl. Time for a ride." Jonas worked quickly to get the saddle in place. Once he had it, he grabbed the rifle he kept in the barn and nudged the horse into action.

Sandy shot from the structure. Under Jonas's guidance, she galloped toward the road and didn't slow once they'd reached it.

A cloud of dust followed the vehicle. Through it, Jonas

was able to see glimpses of taillights. He followed at a safe distance.

Harley had reached the road's intersection. Instead of turning, he kept going straight. The direction he was heading would lead deeper into the Beaverhead-Deerlodge National Forest, which was over three million acres, many of them isolated and uninhabited where few people ever went. Harley wanted to erase all evidence that the deputy had been to his place.

Jonas kept Sandy in the trees along the road. It made traveling slower, but he wouldn't be any good to Charlotte if he ended up dead.

The dirt road turned into little more than a path, yet Harley didn't slow down. He was driving deeper into the woods. The sunny afternoon was all but eclipsed by the trees, making it hard to see much. If it weren't for the taillights, Jonas wasn't so sure he could find the way.

After Jonas had followed Harley for a while, the Jeep left the path they were on. Jonas's bad feeling doubled. The route they were on led to a river that would feed into the much larger Madison River at some point. This was bad.

Harley drove the Jeep right up to the water's edge. The sound of another vehicle coming had Jonas urging the mare out of sight. A second later, the other vehicle, a small silver car, stopped a little way from the Jeep.

As soon as it arrived Harley swung the door open and got out of the Jeep. He didn't waste time rounding to the trunk. Jonas dismounted and moved close to get a better view.

Harley opened the hatch. Someone was in there. He had no doubt it was the deputy. A struggle took place as the female officer seemed to fight for her life. Jonas watched in horror as Harley pulled out a weapon and fired two shots. The fight ended.

Jonas stumbled backward and dropped to his knees. Had he just watched a murder? He gathered breath and realized if he could get to Charlotte in time, he might be able to save her life.

He prepared to remount and ride to her rescue. Harley slammed the hatch shut and returned to the driver's side. It soon became apparent what he intended when he shoved the Jeep into the water.

An instinct Jonas imagined came straight from *Gott* warned him not to leave his coverage until Harley was gone, yet the Jeep was now drifting away from the shore. The spring melts had the river rising. It wouldn't take long for the vehicle to be swept under the current and down to the bottom.

With his heart racing in his chest, Jonas watched Harley climb inside the second car. The driver reversed and drove quickly past Jonas's hiding place.

Jonas jumped into the saddle and dug his heels into the mare's sides. Sandy sensed the urgency and raced toward the river.

At this point, Jonas was almost certain he'd find Charlotte dead inside, yet he had to try to save her.

Jonas leaped from the mare and dove into the river that was close to overflowing its banks. The current was so strong it took all his strength to swim to the Jeep, which was being swept away.

A banging sound caught his attention above the raging water. Someone screamed for help inside. Charlotte was still alive.

"I'm coming. Hang on!" He grabbed the latch on the back.

"Hurry! We don't have much time."

We? She wasn't alone. Jonas thought about Betty and struggled with the latch while fearfully watching the rising water claim more of the vehicle.

When the door finally released, the relief was physical. The deputy's huge green eyes fixed on Jonas's. To his surprise she wasn't bleeding. Impossible. Had Harley missed in the struggle?

She climbed from the back of the vehicle and quickly went under. Before he could assist, she'd fought her way back to the surface and grabbed hold of the Jeep to keep from being swept away. "Help me get her out before it goes under. She's been shot."

Jonas' eyes widened when he realized the other woman wasn't Betty, but she was bleeding.

"I've got her." Yet getting the injured woman from the Jeep, which was now almost completely submerged, wasn't easy. The fear in the young woman's eyes urged him on. Despite being shot in the shoulder, she practically launched herself into his arms. Jonas dragged her the rest of the way from the vehicle, and she clung to him as he struggled to keep above the water while holding on to the Jeep that was quickly moving downstream. He could sense her trembling and held on tight.

The Jeep groaned as it shifted in the water and continued to sink beneath the surface.

"We've got to get her help. Do you have a phone?" Charlotte asked. "Mine was taken… I'm Deputy Charlotte Walker by the way, and this is Lainey." She indicated the woman in Jonas's arms.

"I remember you, Deputy Walker. I'm Jonas Knowles."

"It's Charlotte, and I remember. You're Harley's neighbor. The sinking Jeep is going to take us down with it. We've got to get away."

"*Jah*…yes," he corrected quickly. Even though he wasn't

Amish anymore, Jonas rarely spoke to anyone. He'd gotten accustomed to using Pennsylvania Dutch in his thoughts and with his occasional conversations with Sandy. Letting go of the old ways was hard. "I'm sorry, I don't own a phone."

Lainey's hold on him loosened and she almost slipped into the raging water. Jonas grabbed her tighter, his attention on her face. "She's unconscious."

"Let's try to make it to the bank." Charlotte swam out in front of him. From where he was now, the riverbank appeared miles away.

"Did you see Annie?" Charlotte asked, glancing back at him. She seemed to be testing the depth to the bottom. "I believe I can stand up now. It might help fight the current." She appeared to plant her feet on the muddy bottom and he did the same. The water went up past her chest. Swimming against the flow of the water had been hard enough. Would walking be any better? He sure hoped so. They began to stagger forward.

Jonas realized what he'd been too frightened to see before. Charlotte had been through a battle, and it showed on her face. Harley had beaten her badly. Her eyes were swollen. Her auburn hair was pulled loose from her ponytail and soaked from the water. She'd taken a blow to the head. Blood matted the hair at her temple.

Anger rose inside at what Harley had done to her. He'd proven multiple times that he had no qualms about raising his hand to a woman.

Through his anger, Jonas remembered she'd asked about someone. Annie. Was there another woman missing? "Who's Annie?"

"My K-9 partner. She led me to Harley's."

Jonas recalled hearing the dog barking and told her, "She wasn't in the Jeep." He could see Charlotte was worried about her partner. After what Harley had done to her, Jonas could certainly understand why.

"What happened?" Jonas asked while keeping a close eye on the direction Harley and his associate had disappeared. He took another step, trying to keep his balance while holding Lainey.

"I went looking for Lainey after her grandmother became worried about her. Dottie told me she liked to go to the Christian camp off your road."

He was familiar with the camp. Jonas spent plenty of time there pouring out his anger to *Gott*. "Dottie is Lainey's grandmother?"

Charlotte nodded. "Annie led me to Harley's house where I was attacked by a man in a mask." She told him about the Taser and then the beating. "The last thing I remember was being struck in the head." She touched the spot on her temple and winced. "From the glimpse I got of my attacker, I don't believe it was Harley, but I have no doubt Harley's in cahoots with my attacker somehow."

"There was another man who picked Harley up just now." Jonas hadn't been able to see him since he'd remained in the car while Harley did the dirty work. Jonas described the car.

Charlotte frowned. "It wasn't at Harley's house as far as I could tell. What's he up to?"

In the trees beyond the water's edge, a flash caught Jonas's attention, followed by rapid gunfire. The shots came from the trees near where Jonas had left his mare. Soon, galloping could be heard. Sandy was on the run, along with his weapon.

"Dive underwater fast—before we're hit. Go, go, go." Charlotte dipped beneath the surface. Bullets peppered the space around him as they swam away. Jonas quickly lowered himself and Lainey into the water and wrapped his arm around her waist. The frigid water woke her immediately. She fought to free herself while holding her breath. It took everything he could muster not to lose his grip on her. If she got free, she'd be swept away. And if he couldn't reach her in time, Lainey might die.

TWO

Charlotte spun in the water at the struggle taking place. Lainey had panicked. Charlotte swam back to the young woman and tried to calm her, but she was all too familiar with the cause of Lainey's terror. The younger woman had almost drowned as a little girl and had been terrified of water ever since.

Jonas pointed to the surface, and she nodded. Hopefully, they were far enough from the shooting to be protected from the bullets.

As she broke the surface, Charlotte searched around until she'd gained her bearings. The shots continued to pellet the water a short distance from her current location.

Jonas popped up, still holding on to Lainey. The young woman's fear didn't ease any by being above water.

"Look at me, Lainey." Charlotte got into Lainey's line of sight. The younger woman's breathing came in rapid gasps. She was close to hyperventilating. Lainey's frightened eyes latched on to Charlotte. "You're going to be okay. We're not going to let you drown."

Lainey slowly stopped struggling, her eyes huge and filled with tears. "He hurt you. He said you'd come to get me, and he hurt you."

Charlotte jerked back. Lainey had knowledge of her

attack. A dozen different questions flew through Charlotte's head, but right now, keeping them all alive was her only concern.

"We'll have to make it to the other side." Which meant swimming across the river against the current.

Lainey immediately rejected the notion. "I can't. It's too far. I'm scared."

"You can because we'll help you." Charlotte glanced toward Jonas who nodded in agreement. "Let's get started." She searched behind them and saw that the car was now approaching the water. "Hurry." Jonas followed her line of sight. "They're going to try to get close enough to shoot us, and if they reach the shore, they just might accomplish it."

Charlotte carefully grabbed hold of Lainey's waist, avoiding her injured left shoulder. Jonas placed his arm above Charlotte's. Together, they swam for shore.

Charlotte's chest hurt like crazy where the bullet had lodged into her vest and would no doubt leave a nasty bruise.

Car doors slammed behind them, the sound reaching past her labored breathing.

"Hurry, Jonas," she said.

He jerked toward the sound of weapons being fired once more. Lainey screamed as several bullets came far too close to their location.

"We'll have to go under again." Charlotte didn't give her friend time to protest. Jonas released his hold on Lainey while Charlotte dove beneath the surface with her. While Charlotte was a strong swimmer, it took everything she could muster to fight her way to the opposite side after being injured.

She and Lainey resurfaced, both coughing up water. Charlotte searched the river for Jonas. He'd been right beside her when she'd gone down. Her heartbeat ticked off every second he was under and there were far too many.

Charlotte hauled Lainey to the shore. "Wait here." She dove back in and swam toward Jonas's last location. Before she reached it, Jonas called out. He was some distance from his previous spot, holding on to a tree that had gone into the water. She reached his side. They could exit the river here and walk back to Lainey.

Jonas swept back dark blond hair from his face.

"Are you hurt?" Charlotte asked as she skimmed his face and realized this was the first time she'd really looked at him. His square jaw was covered in a beard only slightly darker than his hair. While he dressed Amish, she knew very little about them, or Jonas, except that the Amish settlement was some distance away and near the mountains. He didn't live there. She wondered why.

Once her parents had visited one of the Montana communities when she was a teen. They'd been told a beard indicated a married man, yet there hadn't been anyone at Jonas's house when she'd questioned him. Perhaps he'd simply grown the beard for protection against the cold.

"I'm fine," he murmured, his ice-blue eyes reminding her of the Montana skies on a snowy day. "I just had a cramp. Go ahead. I'll be right behind you."

Charlotte wanted to believe him, but the look of exhaustion clung to him. She spotted Harley wading out into the water. "They're looking for a place to get off a better shot." She found her footing in the water and helped Jonas out. Together, they hurried to where she'd left Lainey.

Charlotte dropped down beside the younger woman on the riverbank. Lainey held her shoulder and she looked as pale as a sheet.

Jonas sank to his knees near them.

Once she'd made sure of Harley's position, Charlotte leaned over to examine Lainey's injury.

"No, it hurts too much," Lainey moaned when Charlotte's fingers connected with the wound.

"I know it does, but I need to assess the damage." She glanced around. They were miles away from anyone who could help. It would be up to her to protect Lainey and get them all to safety.

Charlotte gently unbuttoned Lainey's shirt and pushed it aside so she could see the wound. Whether it was the cold water or something else, the bleeding had slowed. Still, the young woman needed more medical attention than Charlotte could give her. The medical kit she carried with her everywhere was in the back of the submerged Jeep.

She glanced down at her vest. It might help protect Lainey's injury from greater damage at least.

Charlotte quickly removed the Kevlar vest. The bullet lodged there was a reminder of how differently things could have turned out. Charlotte dug out the bullet and stuck it in her pocket to be used as evidence against Harley.

She explained what she was going to do, and Lainey slowly nodded. Charlotte cinched the vest as tight as Lainey could handle. "How's that?"

Lainey tested it out. "It feels better."

Charlotte smiled reassuringly. "Good."

"Did my grandmother send you?"

"Yes, she did. Dottie was worried about you."

Lainey nodded. "I'm glad she called you. If you hadn't found me, I'm not sure what they would have done to me."

Before Lainey could tell her what happened, Charlotte noticed Jonas searching the opposite riverbank.

She hurried over. "What is it?"

"I don't see them," he said.

Charlotte shielded her eyes and scanned the bank. "The vehicle's gone, too. We can't stay here, Jonas. They'll keep coming and eventually they'll find us."

This part of the landscape was at the far edge of the vast county she protected. Charlotte hadn't been to this area before, but Jonas lived close by. Maybe he understood better how to hike out.

"Is there a way back to the main road from here?" she asked him. They were all soaked. Even though it was springtime, the chill of winter still clung to the air. If they could keep moving, it would help put space between themselves and Harley, as well as fend off the onset of hypothermia with the chilly temperatures.

The taut set of Jonas's jaw was discouraging. "Not without crossing the river again, and that would be too risky." He glanced at Lainey to make a point. "Or walking for hours. If we had a vehicle, perhaps we could make it sooner." He shrugged. "There's a small group of Amish families who settled in the valley many years back. They won't have a phone, but I can borrow a horse and ride the five miles to the town of Elk Ridge."

Not the news she wanted to hear but their only option. No one was looking for her. She tried to recall how much time had passed since she'd left Lainey's home. Several hours. But not enough for Dottie to have contacted the sheriff's department yet. Dottie would be expecting Charlotte to call. It could be hours before she reached out to law enforcement.

The exhaustion on Lainey's face confirmed she was in no condition to be exposed to the dipping temperatures that would come with the approaching nightfall. Charlotte wasn't in the best shape, either.

"Lainey's grandmother is the only person who knows

I'm out here and she won't call anyone for a while," she told him without trying to sugarcoat their situation. "What about you?"

"There's no one." His voice came out too sharp. She focused on his closed-off expression that warned her not to pry too deeply. There was a story there that Charlotte wanted to hear, but right now their lives were in danger.

"You don't live in the Amish settlement anymore." She'd taken a guess he'd once been part of it. The deepening frown on his face confirmed she'd guessed correctly. He didn't own a car or a phone. Why was Jonas—who clearly still dressed and lived like the Amish—not residing with those of his own faith? Had he been shunned?

"I'm no longer Plain." His chilly eyes warned he didn't want to talk about the reasons why.

Charlotte took stock on their current position. They had no weapons should Harley and his friend catch up with them. If they managed to reach the Amish community, at least there might be something useful to protect themselves.

"Let's head to the settlement. Is there someone there who would be willing to help?" The length of time it took for him to answer sent up plenty of warning signals. Something had happened to him.

"There is someone." He didn't elaborate, which added to her feeling that Jonas was hiding some guilt of his own. She of all people understood how hard it was to overcome, especially when it resulted in the loss of someone important…like losing Ryan.

Stop! Don't go there again.

She'd barely survived this last year while carrying the guilt that his death was on her. Ryan hadn't felt a hundred percent, but she'd asked him to help find Michaela and he had.

Charlotte pulled in a breath and let the anger and guilt—the self-loathing—go.

This situation was what she had to focus on. Getting Lainey safely back to her grandmother would only happen if she didn't allow herself to go down into a dark place again.

She thought about the attack at Harley's house and wondered who the man responsible for it was.

She turned back to Lainey, drawing the young woman's attention her way. "You said you saw the attack on me. How did you end up at Harley Owens's place to begin with?"

"It was awful. I was so scared." Lainey shuddered visibly at the memory.

Charlotte nodded. "I know it's hard, but I need to hear everything."

"It all happened so quickly," Lainey said, apparently struggling to keep it together. "Right after I'd left work." Her voice shook so much she was hard to understand. "I'd been driving down the road in front of the Quicken Mart when someone came out of nowhere and rammed me."

The accident was staged to kidnap Lainey. That stretch of road was pretty isolated with the exception of the Quicken Mart. Her kidnapper had probably been watching Lainey's movements for a while and figured out the best way to take her.

"He wore a mask," Lainey continued, "but I'd seen a man with the same build in the store before—several times, in fact."

"What did the man in the store look like?" Harley was well past fifty and overweight. His normal dress code was a stained white T-shirt and grimy jeans.

"Older. And he smelled. I was shaken up from the crash and disoriented. He came up to my door and opened it.

The mask scared me. I knew something was dreadfully wrong." Lainey's voice sounded strained. "Before I had the chance to scream, he covered my mouth with his hand and jabbed something in my neck. I don't remember anything else until I woke up in a basement chained to the wall." Her eyes held tears. "And there's something else. I wasn't the only woman being held there."

There were other women trapped in Harley's house. The notion washed over Jonas like a nightmare he couldn't wake up from. Women were being kept prisoner right next to his place and Jonas had had no idea.

"Why do you suppose there were others?" Charlotte was asking.

Lainey wiped at her face. "Because I heard their whispers and then someone yelling. After that it got really quiet."

Jonas had no doubt Harley was involved in something far more sinister than abusing Betty, which was dreadful enough.

"Then, another man came in. I didn't recognize him." She shook her head. "The new guy and the one who took me got into an awful argument. The second person was young and really mad. I believe he was in charge. I was so certain they were going to kill me right then except the one in charge heard a noise outside and went to investigate. When he returned, he said someone—a deputy—had come looking for me, and they had to get rid of us both. He apparently recognized you, Charlotte. The older man stuck something in my neck again. I woke up in the back of your Jeep next to you right before we went into the water."

And that's where Jonas had come in. He'd followed Harley and come across two attempted murders.

Though injured, both Lainey and Charlotte were

blessed to be alive, but there were others in the house who might not be as fortunate.

Jonas couldn't believe he hadn't seen the truth that was right under his nose…just like he hadn't seen the seriousness of his *fraa* Ivy's condition until it was too late.

He should never have gone up to the mountain to trap on that final occasion. The baby was due in less than two weeks. He'd told himself Ivy and the baby would be fine without him for a few days. But she wasn't. Ivy had been forced to harness the buggy alone in a snowstorm and drive it the five miles to her parents' homestead. By the time they reached the hospital, it was too late to save her and their unborn child.

Ivy's *bruder* had tracked Jonas down and taken him to the hospital, but they were both gone.

Losing her and their child had destroyed his faith and caused him to leave the Plain life behind for good. It was just too hard to live amongst his people and not see Ivy everywhere. Or endure the accusations from Samuel, his father-in-law, that were justified.

"Wait—did you hear something?" Charlotte was no longer pacing but listening intently.

Jonas stopped dead. It didn't take long to hear what she did. Someone was coming.

"They must have gotten across the river somehow. Quick—take cover." Charlotte urged Lainey behind some trees while Jonas looked for a sturdy enough tree limb to use as a weapon.

Soon, the noise became amplified around them. Multiple footsteps were moving through the area near their hiding spot. There were more than just Harley and the other man. Many more.

"Are you sure they came this way?" A male voice was close enough to hear clearly.

"That's what Harley said," another replied. "He warned we'd better not let them get away or it will be all our lives at stake. One of them is a cop. Someone really screwed up by nabbing the girl."

"You know why he took her—she's pretty." Laughter followed. "He didn't realize she was friends with a deputy. He had a quota to fill."

Charlotte's gaze homed in on Jonas while disgust rose in his throat. They spoke of the young women they'd kidnapped as if their lives meant nothing.

"Yeah, well, because of his carelessness, we have to trudge through this stuff looking for them and it's going to get dark soon. You understand what we'll have to do when we find them."

"I, for one, don't like the idea of killing a cop."

Jonas's hand tightened on the branch. Despite everything they'd survived he hadn't wanted to consider that Harley was capable of murder, but these men hadn't held anything back. Once more, Jonas wondered what Harley was involved in and why he hadn't had some inkling on what was happening in his own backyard.

"Hey, it's us or them," one of their pursuers said. "I'm not going to die because Harley screwed up, and I sure don't want to end up in jail. If that happens, we're all dead men."

Jonas held back his shock somehow as the men began to clear out of the area. His hand ached from clutching the tree limb so tight he wondered if it might snap in two.

"I'm sure it's safe to move now," Charlotte whispered after what felt like an eternity. Lainey clung to her side, probably terrified those men would find her again.

Jonas slowly stepped from his hiding spot. The men were no longer visible. He'd heard two speaking but there were far more from the sound of them trudging through the woods.

"Which way?" Charlotte's question pulled him back.

Jonas could find the way to the Amish settlement with his eyes closed. He'd hunted this land since he'd moved here from Virginia in his late teens. After he and Ivy married, they'd settled into a little house he'd built for them some way from the nearest Amish neighbor because he'd been a loner at heart most of his life.

"This way." He pointed up ahead, grateful that they'd be heading in a different direction from those men.

Taking the lead, Jonas thought about what those men had said and couldn't imagine what terrible things Harley had going on at his house.

When Charlotte and Lainey caught up, Jonas voiced his concerns. "My guess is Harley is involved in trafficking young women."

Charlotte's lips thinned. "It's terrible to consider such things happening in our county, but I'm not naive enough to think it doesn't."

When he'd been part of the Amish community, he'd felt insulated from such things. Sure, they had their share of mishaps, usually involving the young people who went out on their *Rumspringa* getting into trouble, but there hadn't been any murders or taking of young women.

"I can't understand why I didn't see this," he muttered angrily. "I've lived next to Harley for six years now and I've seen the evidence he beats his wife—I've gone to the local police and reported it in the past many times— but I never thought…"

Charlotte tentatively touched his arm. "Why would you? These people are good at keeping secrets." She looked in the direction the men had gone. "What I don't understand is, why involve Harley? He's not the brightest person around and he's gotten into trouble in the past. He's on law enforcement's radar."

This was something Jonas didn't understand, either. He stopped suddenly as he recalled an incident that happened with Betty some time back. Jonas had heard screams coming from the house and had gone there with his rifle, determined to get Betty out of there.

She'd answered the door without a mark on her and claimed she'd seen a snake in the house. When he'd offered to help her remove the reptile, she'd stopped him from coming inside. It was then he'd seen a man standing behind Betty. She'd claimed he was her nephew but there was something disturbing about him that assured Jonas this was no family member. Maybe the real reason Betty refused to leave was only in part her fear of Harley… Maybe she was more afraid of the man running the trafficking ring.

THREE

Charlotte tried to ignore the bitter cold settling in past her damp green sweater and jeans. It would only get worse with the coming darkness. She looked at Lainey who was shivering, her teeth chattering. Every little sound had Lainey jerking toward it.

"I hear something," Lainey said, her frightened eyes finding Charlotte's. "They're coming after us again."

At first, Charlotte thought it was just Lainey panicking until the snap of a twig beneath a footstep confirmed someone was close.

"She's right. Take her with you," Charlotte told Jonas and pushed them both behind a tree. There was just enough time to grab the nearest log before someone barreled from the woods and straight for her. Charlotte wielded the heavy log over her head and prepared to strike.

A man slammed into her before she could make contact. The force of his weight had her hitting the ground hard. Her head bounced off it several times. The log flew from her grasp. She was now in a hand-to-hand fight for her life.

"Where's the others?" The man straddled her before she could get on her feet.

Charlotte caught movement behind her attacker. Jonas grabbed hold of the man's collar and pulled him off her.

"He has a gun," she yelled and scrambled to her feet as Jonas and the other man struggled for the weapon. The unknown assailant shoved Jonas, forcing him backward. As he prepared to shoot, Charlotte leaped into action and struck his arm holding the weapon. The gun fired, missing Jonas by inches. If he got another clear shot, Jonas would be dead.

Charlotte grabbed the log and struck the shooter's midsection. He doubled over. She dropped the log and went for the gun, but her attacker wasn't letting it go. He struggled to get it into position to fire at her. In her peripheral vision Jonas had grabbed the log. He slammed it against the man's head before he had time to react. A look of surprise crossed the perp's face before he went down hard. The gun dropped free. Another blow to the head had him falling forward, unconscious.

Scrambling for the weapon, Charlotte grasped it and tucked it in her waistband before searching the man's pockets. He didn't have a cell phone, which wasn't a huge surprise. Many times, criminal elements weren't allowed to carry phones. Those in charge didn't trust the ones who worked for them not to be snitches.

She rose and faced Jonas. "Thank you for saving my life—again." A shuddering breath escaped her as another disturbing thought nudged at her to hurry. "There are others out here. They'll have heard the shots. We'd better get out of here before they come looking."

Jonas kept hold of the log while Charlotte went to retrieve Lainey, whose terror was written on her face as she stared at the person on the ground. "Is he dead?"

"No, just unconscious." Charlotte looped her arm with Lainey's and urged her away from the area as quickly as possible. "You should take the lead," she told Jonas. Almost like flipping a switch, the darkness of night descended. It would work in their favor to stay hidden but make it harder to see where they were going.

She worried about Annie. Was she safe? The last time she'd seen her partner was at Harley's. Had Annie managed to escape?

Jonas stepped out in front and started down the path, which was continuously rising as they neared the Roots— what the locals referred to as the mountain range that rose between the Jefferson and Madison Rivers.

"I'm so scared. I want to go home." Lainey gulped the words.

"I know, sweetie," Charlotte said softly. "I want to get you home, too. Right now, we keep moving."

Lainey tilted her head sideways. "I get so upset when my grandmother still sees me as a little girl, and yet now I realize how precious it is to have someone there for you."

Charlotte flinched as if she'd taken another blow. "You're right, it is." She thought about how hard it had been losing both her parents so close together. She'd found herself suddenly twenty-five and alone. Before their deaths, Charlotte had planned to continue her education and become a lawyer, but after her dad's death she'd needed to come home to the one tangible place left in a world crumbling around her.

After a while, Sheriff Wyatt McCallister, a family friend, came to her with a proposition. Join the sheriff's department and head up their K-9 unit because she'd helped her dad train dogs as a teen. At the time, she'd just been doing the next necessary thing, not realizing that setting up the newly formed unit would be the healing her heart needed. She'd gone through intensive training and then she and Wyatt had gone to an expert dog trainer, and she'd met Ryan.

She blinked back tears. Ryan's love had made her not

feel so alone. He'd given her something to look forward to. And slowly, she'd begun to dig her way out of the depression that grief had left behind.

Charlotte had a purpose—someone to care for her—life was back on track.

She'd taken charge of the K-9 unit and had loved everything about it. She and her then K-9 partner, Sage, worked well together. Charlotte had trained the other member of the team, Drew Hathaway. Sage partnered with Drew and Annie joined Charlotte...

And then Ryan died.

Up ahead, Jonas had stopped. Charlotte released Lainey and hurried to his side. "Do you see something?"

He turned those startling blue eyes her way. Instantly, Charlotte lost her equilibrium. The storm of hurt in his eyes, she was familiar with.

"No, it's just..." She stood even with him. He'd lost someone, too. She felt an instant connection with Jonas because of the pain.

At times, she'd wake up and think for a moment that Ryan was still alive, and she'd be happy. And then she'd remember, and the darkness would descend like a heavy cloud. Work helped. Annie was a huge blessing.

Charlotte jerked around and pretended to survey the settling darkness behind them. She wanted to look anywhere but at him, because like her, Jonas had to be seeing the depth of her hurt as well.

Lainey had sunk down beside a tree and was resting out of earshot, and Charlotte wanted to understand what happened to bring him to this point.

"Who did you lose?" she said softly.

He stared ahead. "My wife and child," he said in a rough voice. "I killed them."

She searched his face as a sliver of something unsavory crawled down her spine. "What do you mean you killed them?" Though she didn't know Jonas very well, she couldn't see him capable of murder.

"I was too busy being the adventurer to see Ivy was struggling with the pregnancy and needed me home until it was too late."

Relief swept through her body, replacing the unease. But it was followed by sadness for Jonas. "I'm sure you were only doing the best you could."

The smile that curled the corner of his lip held no real humor. "*Nay*—I enjoyed the solitude and the challenge of trapping. I told myself Ivy understood, but she didn't really. She needed me and I let her down." He nodded toward the settlement. "Her parents still live there. They've never forgiven me for what happened."

Now she understood why he'd stopped in his tracks. Why he was reluctant to return to the place where there were so many bad memories. Facing loved ones who blamed you for the death of your wife couldn't be easy.

She touched his arm. Felt the muscles beneath her fingers clench before he stepped back.

Charlotte cleared her throat. She'd crossed some line. "Sorry."

He dragged in a breath. "Abram, Ivy's younger *bruder*, lives in…" He stopped and gathered himself. "Abram and I were always close, but it has been years. Still, he was kind to me following Ivy's passing. Abram is a *gut* man."

Charlotte wondered about what he hadn't said, but now was not the time for questions when all their lives were in danger. "Then let's go to Abram's place." At least it might give them shelter from the weather and cover from Harley's men.

She motioned Lainey over and the three continued down the path. As they walked, Charlotte placed a protective arm around Lainey's shoulders. When she thought about what might have happened if Annie hadn't tracked Lainey's scent... If Dottie hadn't called.

Though she was worried about her partner, Annie could handle herself in just about any situation. But they were in real danger, and Harley was highly motivated to make sure they didn't walk out of these woods alive.

Everywhere he looked, he saw Ivy's smiling face. Six years hadn't been long enough to erase the good memories, or the heartbreaking ones that had destroyed the rest. Jonas had stood over his wife's body in the morgue and wept for the loss of the love of his life. That day, his life ended. He was putting one foot in front of the other—taking care of what needed to be done—but he was a dead man existing in a world he no longer recognized. He'd never share with someone else the love he had with Ivy.

When he'd first come to the Ruby Valley of Montana from Virginia, it was because he hadn't wanted to follow in his *daed*'s footsteps and become a beekeeper. Jonas craved adventure. Moving cross-country to the rugged land surrounding the Tobacco Root Mountains had certainly offered adventure and much more. He'd fallen in love with the remote community even though he'd only heard rumors about it.

The small Amish settlement, which butted up against the mountain, had lived up to everything he'd heard about it.

"How much farther?" Lainey whispered, breaking the past's hold. "I don't think I can go on any longer."

"She needs to catch her breath," Charlotte told him. "Let's stop for a second."

Lainey dropped down to the ground and placed her head in her hands.

The night made it impossible to see much more than his hand in front of him.

"How far are we from the settlement?" Charlotte asked from close by.

Jonas hadn't realized she was near until she spoke. There was something about this woman that made him uneasy. Not so much because she was in law enforcement. No, what troubled him about her was much more personal and something he wasn't prepared for.

"Still some distance. Abram's place is closer," he said in a gruff tone, then pointed down the slope they'd been hiking along. "Over there."

She followed his direction. A faint light, as if from a lantern, blinked in the darkness.

"How many families live here?" When he didn't answer, she prompted. "Jonas?"

He cleared his throat. "Five, at least, was the count the last time I was there. It may have changed."

Charlotte stared at him for a long moment before she said, "We'd better get going."

He shouldered past her without another word. A second later, Charlotte helped Lainey to her feet and followed.

As he neared the house that had once been his home, a lump formed in his throat that wouldn't go away. The lantern grew brighter in the window facing them. Abram was awake, but then again, it was still quite early. Darkness made it hard to determine time.

The last conversation he'd had with Abram stuck in his head through the years. Abram had asked him not to go. Give it time. Eventually Ivy's *mamm* and *daed* would see the truth. But Jonas had realized he wouldn't be able to stay there and carve out some semblance of a life without Ivy.

From near the barn, a dog barked. Jonas jerked toward the sound with his heart in his throat. Charlotte drew the weapon she'd taken from their last attacker and urged Lainey around the side of the house as the dog continued to bark, probably at their intrusion.

Footsteps came from inside the house. Jonas braced himself for the awkward reunion he'd never wanted.

The front door squeaked open—a reminder of the many times he'd promised Ivy he'd fix it. Some things never changed.

A lantern breached the door frame first, followed by a man. A man! The last time Jonas had seen Abram he'd been a gangly fourteen-year-old. This was no boy searching the darkness.

"Is anyone out here?" Abram's voice had gotten deeper as well.

Jonas stepped from the shadows. "It's me, Abram. Jonas." He reluctantly stepped up on the porch. The shock on Abram's face was no surprise. Jonas had told him he'd never come back here again.

Abram covered the space between them swiftly, holding the lantern high. "Jonas? I—I can't believe it's you."

Jonas wasn't sure what he expected, but when Abram enveloped him in a tight hug, it left him frozen in place.

"It's *gut* to see you," Ivy's *bruder* said.

Jonas slowly untangled himself. "You, too. I wish it were under different circumstances." He turned toward Charlotte and Lainey, who had emerged from the shadows, too. "We need your help." He introduced the two women. "Can we come inside?" Jonas glanced around uncomfortably as the dog continued to bark.

"*Jah*, come in and warm up." Abram's gaze swept over his disheveled appearance and then to the two women.

Charlotte and Lainey went on ahead while Jonas followed Abram inside.

His brother-in-law strode to the woodstove and stoked the fire before tossing some logs on top. He straightened. Jonas noticed again how Abram had gotten taller and more filled out.

"I'm glad you're here, but curious as to what this is about," the younger man said.

Where did Jonas even start? It really wasn't his story to tell even. He faced Charlotte. "Perhaps you should explain. I still don't fully understand what we're up against."

She slowly nodded.

"Please—sit," Abram told them all. "You look ready to drop."

Jonas pulled up two of the rockers close to the fire and waited for Charlotte and Lainey to sit. He couldn't. Everything about the house remained pretty much the same as when he'd walked away from it, his life collapsing around him. He hadn't known where he'd go, only that he couldn't stay here any longer.

Outside, the dog had quieted. Charlotte's sweet voice filled the room. As she explained the twisted nightmare they'd gone through so far, Jonas leaned against the wall and found himself wondering about Abram's life. He'd be around twenty by now. Was he married? If so, where was his wife?

The expression on Abram's face once Charlotte finished reinforced how frightening the story was.

"This man Harley—he's selling people," his brother-in-law said. The idea would seem horrific for someone like Abram, who lived a simple life filled with hard work and had only rare exposure to the unsavory world that existed beyond the settlement. One of the many things

Jonas missed about this small, isolated settlement in the woods. That and the life he'd once had here.

Abram's troubled gaze found him. "What can I do to help?"

Jonas shoved off the wall and came to where Abram stood. "We need whatever weapons you can spare." In the light from the fire and the lanterns placed around the house, he noticed Charlotte's injuries, and Lainey's gunshot wound would need attending to. "Do you have something to bandage up their wounds?"

Abram swung toward Lainey. "You're hurt, too."

She managed a smile and told him what happened.

The horror on Abram's face was undeniable. "There are supplies in the kitchen and I have an extra rifle."

Jonas inclined his head. "Much appreciated."

Abram led him through to the kitchen where memories of the many meals he'd shared with Ivy crowded in.

"I heard you moved across the valley," Abram asked, pulling Jonas's attention away from the table he'd built for his wife. It wasn't much to look at but there were memories.

"*Jah*. I have a small spread across the lake. A few cattle." He shrugged.

"You always were *gut* with the animals." Abram brought out bandages and some strips of cloth. "You never remarried?"

Jonas flinched at the suggestion but managed an answer.

"She wouldn't want you to be alone, Jonas. You need someone in your life."

Jonas's jaw clenched. When he'd left Virginia, he'd been positive he'd live a solitary life filled with adventure until Ivy came along.

He stepped past Abram, breaking eye contact, and snatched up the supplies. "You haven't wed?"

"*Nay.* The settlement is small. There aren't many young women here. *Daed* tells me I should visit one of the other communities in the state. We have some cousins near West Kootenai."

Before Jonas could respond, Charlotte rushed into the room. "The dog is barking again." Her worried eyes locked with Jonas's.

Abram hurried past her. "I'll check it out. Lobo barks a lot. There are many wild animals in the area. It could be nothing."

Or it could be the danger they'd barely escaped closing in.

FOUR

The minute Charlotte returned to the living room, Lainey rushed to her side. "I'm scared, Charlotte. I can't go through that again." The fear in Lainey's eyes backed up those words. The terror she'd gone through at Harley's hands would brand her for life.

"You won't. I'm going to protect you."

Charlotte stopped Abram before he could leave. "The dog's barking might be him picking up the scent of another animal nearby, but we can't take such a chance." She looked to Jonas. "What if those men tracked us here? Can you and Abram stay with Lainey while I check around?" From the looks on their faces, no one in the room was convinced Lobo was worked up about a wild animal.

"Those men are heavily armed and it's obvious they want us dead," Jonas said. "If they're out there somewhere, you can't take them on alone. Abram will protect Lainey. I'm coming with you." The look of determination on his face assured her it would be useless to point out that she was the one sworn to protect those in this room.

Abram moved to Lainey's side when a noise outside came from close to the barn where Lobo was.

Charlotte trusted Jonas's skills and he'd saved her life more than once already. "We can't go out the front without being spotted. Is there a back entrance?"

Abram silently pointed to the kitchen and Jonas hurried toward it. Charlotte grabbed his arm before he could charge out into the night. He gave her a questioning look.

"We don't fully understand what we're up against. There's a lot of Harley's people looking for us. It's more than just our lives at stake." She tilted her head toward where Abram and Lainey stood watching.

"You're right," Jonas said with a shake of his head.

Charlotte slowly opened the door and listened. Nothing came from the barn, and she wondered if the noise they'd heard had been the animals stationed inside.

Jonas followed closely behind as she stepped outside. Charlotte edged toward the side of the house facing the barn while trying to keep the noise to a minimum. The pitch-dark and fog that had been gathering made it hard to see anything.

Keeping close to the side of the house, she eased to the front with Jonas at her six. There was nothing but yard between them and the barn now—a whole lot of open space should someone be hiding inside.

Charlotte pointed to the back of the structure. "On my word."

Jonas confirmed he understood while Charlotte counted off three in her head and prepared to cover the space that seemed miles away. "Go," she said and ran toward the back of the barn with Jonas attached to her hip. They'd barely made it a quarter of the way before multiple shots came from the front of the barn.

"Go back!" Charlotte yelled over the noise and slammed into Jonas as she turned to run. She fired several rounds, hoping to force the shooters back into hiding.

She and Jonas reached the side of the house safely and hurried along it.

"I counted three shooters," Jonas said, his intense gaze

on her. "By now, however many others are out there will have heard the shots and come to assist."

Every word of what he said was true. But they were pinned down. The only way to get themselves, Abram and Lainey out safely was to take out the shooters.

She told him as much and waited for the truth to sink in. Charlotte understood about the Amish being pacifists who shunned violence, but Jonas was no longer Amish. Did he still hold to their values?

"It will take both of us to manage this."

Despite their desperate situation, and no matter what Jonas's story might be, he had come after her when it meant risking his own life, and he hadn't backed down from the danger they'd gone through.

"I can't ask you to risk your life any more than you already have. You're a civilian, Jonas."

His chin lifted. "And you're alone without backup. I've come this far with you. Let me help you. You can't do this alone."

As another round of shots confirmed the shooters were advancing on their location, the decision was made for her. Jonas was right. It would take everything they could throw at the bad guys to get through this.

Sounds coming from the front of the house had her spinning toward it. Gun barrel flashes helped her pinpoint their location. She pushed Jonas behind the cover of the house and returned fire. "They're closing in for the kill."

"I'll circle around and see if I can sneak up on them from behind."

"No, Jonas." Before she could stop him, he'd disappeared.

Her attention was riveted back to the sound of multiple footsteps coming at them. Abram and Lainey were still inside. Should she try and get them out of the house?

A heartbeat later, it became apparent that the men were

almost right on top of them. There wouldn't be time to get Abram and Lainey out.

Please *keep them safe...*

She glanced around the darkness for someplace to hide to give her the advantage. She spotted a small shed at the edge of the property and ran toward it. With her heart drumming in her ears, she half expected to be shot before reaching the shed.

Slipping to the back of the shed, she gathered in several breaths before peeking around the side. One armed man was followed by another. Where was the third?

The lead looked through his scope on the ground and Charlotte's heart sank. He had thermal vision capability on that scope. He pointed to Charlotte and Jonas's footprints.

"They split up," the lead said and then leveled the weapon toward the shed. Charlotte ducked out of sight. One or both were coming her way.

Lord, please help us...

The frantic prayer slipped through her head as footsteps crunched closer. She'd have to take her pursuers by surprise to stand a chance at surviving.

Charlotte kept her attention on the side of the shed. A shoe appeared. Time was running out. She had to act.

When the rest of the man's body appeared, Charlotte slammed into him with her full weight, taking him by surprise. She took advantage and smashed her handgun against his temple. He didn't have time to react before dropping.

The struggle captured the attention of his partner immediately. Charlotte grabbed the unconscious man's weapon in case he woke. She scrambled out of sight and prepared for another hand-to-hand struggle that didn't come. She heard a small yelp followed by a thud.

Her mind froze. Was it a trap?

"Charlotte, are you okay?" Jonas!

She slipped from her hiding place as Jonas came her way.

"What happened?"

He indicated the second man on the ground. "This one was coming for you. I was able to stop him before he could see me. The third man is gone."

"If I had to guess, he's probably warning the rest of his team. Which means we won't have long to get out of here." She looked back at the man lying near the shed. "We need to get these two tied up and out of sight in the barn."

Jonas approached the man he'd taken down. "Can you take his feet?"

Working together, they carried the unconscious man to the barn. Jonas found rope and secured him inside an empty stall. The man near the shed hadn't regained consciousness. Once he was tied up with his buddy, Charlotte hurried back to the house with Jonas.

"What happened?" Abram asked when he met them at the back door. "We heard shooting."

Charlotte explained about the two men in the barn and the third who had escaped. "We've got to get out of here before anyone returns."

"We can't leave them," Lainey exclaimed, and her troubled expression had Charlotte stepping toward her.

"Who are you talking about?"

Lainey was shaking. "The women that are being held." She was worried about the others. Lainey squared her shoulders. "Charlotte, I want to go back for them. I won't leave them to whatever fate Harley has planned."

Charlotte's first thought was to get Lainey, Abram and Jonas to Elk Ridge and the sheriff's office.

"Please," she pleaded. "They're scared."

Charlotte couldn't ignore those women or Lainey's pleas. "I'll go back for them," she decided. She turned to Jonas. "Can you and Abram take the buggy to Elk Ridge? Go to the sheriff's station and explain what's happened."

Jonas shook his head. "Abram, take Lainey and go for help. I'm going with Charlotte."

"No," Charlotte said firmly, "it's too dangerous." Though she didn't relish the thought of the miles of woods that stood between her and Harley's place, which posed all sorts of danger. There were people in them who wanted to silence her and anyone with her to cover up their crimes.

"I'm going," Jonas insisted.

Abram glanced between them before he went over to Lainey. "I can get Lainey to Elk Ridge safely." He smiled down at her. "I have an extra coat you can use for warmth."

Lainey nodded. "Thank you." Turning, she said, "And thank you, Charlotte."

"You're welcome. As soon as you reach town, call the sheriff and tell them what's happening and where we're headed."

"I will," Lainey assured her.

Abram added, "There are flashlights in the kitchen, and I do have some extra jackets in the closet. Take whatever you need." He slipped on his jacket, helped Lainey into one and ushered her outdoors.

Charlotte faced Jonas, saying, "I'll get the flashlights if you grab the jackets." He agreed and went to the kitchen and opened drawers.

Charlotte found a couple of extra coats in the closet. They'd help keep the cold and dampness away.

In the kitchen, Jonas held up two flashlights. They had both the shooters' weapons—she wished one of them had been carrying a phone, but she knew from past cases that only those in charge did.

Charlotte handed Jonas one of the jackets. He slipped it on and gave her a flashlight. Using them would draw attention to their location, but they'd still come in handy.

Outside, the sound of a buggy heading away from the house was a welcome one. She prayed Lainey and Abram would make it safely to Elk Ridge without running into trouble.

With Jonas close, Charlotte slipped out the back door and into the night. As hard as it was, she took a second to listen for any sound out of the ordinary.

"What's the best way to get back to Harley's from here? We can't cross the river again." At night and under the current conditions they'd both die.

"Give me a second. I'm a little turned around." He spun around while searching the darkness to get his bearings. Jonas pointed to the right of the house. "This way."

Together, they started walking.

"It's too risky to use the flashlights unless we need them," Charlotte explained, heading into the woods. "How long will it take Abram and Lainey to reach Elk Ridge?"

Jonas turned his head toward a sound in the trees. Once he was satisfied it was nothing, he said, "Probably a couple of hours if everything goes well."

Charlotte understood what he hadn't said. There could be far more people out there looking for them. If Lainey and Abram ran into them…

"I hope that doesn't happen." She settled into his pace. "How long has it been since you left the Amish way of life?"

Charlotte glanced his way when he didn't answer. She was curious about him. Had she overstepped her boundaries once more? "Sorry, forget I asked. It's none of my business." She of all people understood some things were best left unsaid.

Jonas's clenched hand slowly relaxed. "No, it's okay. I left six years ago. Right after my wife died."

He'd mentioned his wife dying before. Charlotte's thoughts went to Ryan. She hadn't told anyone about her part in his death—that they'd needed his experience in mountain tracking to find a missing teen, Michaela Reagan. She'd called him out despite that he'd been sick and needed rest. He wasn't himself, and he'd taken a fatal fall.

Because of her, Ryan died.

"Ivy had complications with the pregnancy, and I wasn't around when she needed me." His quiet words pulled Charlotte from her own misery. He'd lost a wife and child. She couldn't imagine the torment he'd gone through.

"You couldn't have known she would have complications."

His laugh was bitter. "Regardless, I should have been there. She was noticeably frightened in the weeks before. This was our first child and she was scared, and I didn't do anything to help her. Instead of remaining at home, I just took off to the mountains to trap."

It was a useless and destructive game to look back and wonder what might have happened if one thing went differently. She of all people understood this. "Jonas, sometimes you can't help what happens. And regret will drive you mad…" Here she was telling Jonas it was useless to blame himself for what happened when she'd been doing the same things. Maybe it was time to accept Ryan's death wasn't her fault.

He looked her way. "That sounds awfully personal."

He'd shared about his wife. "It is. My fiancé, Ryan, died

last year. It was my fault." She told him about the search for Michaela and her call to Ryan.

"I'm sorry. I remember when the young woman went missing, and later hearing about her death along with the death of one of the search and rescue workers. I didn't realize he was your fiancé."

Charlotte swallowed multiple times before she could speak. "Yes, Ryan's death was an accident, but Michaela's..." She shook her head, still refusing to accept the coroner's decision. "Her death was ruled a suicide, but I never supported it. According to Michaela's parents, she'd been looking forward to graduating soon."

"You believe someone killed her?" The surprise in his voice was evident.

She thought about what Lainey had gone through and stopped suddenly. "Lainey described Harley as the person who took her. She said there were other girls being held at his place. What if...?" She didn't finish because it was just too awful to consider. Was it possible that what happened to Michaela was connected to what Lainey and the other women had gone through?

Michaela's parents had mentioned she'd been scared of something before her death. If so, Charlotte was confident Harley was involved somehow.

She told her fears to Jonas.

"If this is the case, and Harley and whoever he's working for realize we've gotten away, he'll realize our first move is to call the police. Those women are in real danger. If he thinks the police are coming..."

Harley might choose to kill the women rather than have them implicate him and his crew. Charlotte started walking faster. "We can't let that happen." The guilt of not reaching Michaela in time still haunted her. They'd been only a matter of minutes away when she'd died.

Jonas's jaw tightened. "Harley's done a lot of bad things, but murder? I never thought he'd go so far."

"He's a dangerous man, no doubt. Still, I can't imagine he's the one in charge." In her opinion, Harley wasn't smart enough to run a human trafficking ring.

Jonas stopped suddenly and her thoughts shut off. "What is it?" she asked.

He faced her. "I heard something."

She focused on the darkness around them and heard it, too. Something was with them in the woods. Was it an animal or another type of predator?

He couldn't tell the direction it came from at first. The fog had everything distorted. "Whatever it is, there's more than one of them," he whispered in Charlotte's ear. In his mind that meant it probably wasn't an animal. "Let's head away from whatever is out there." He urged her along with him while praying the sound of their footsteps would not be as easily heard. At least the fog might help to distort the direction he and Charlotte were going.

They continued walking while he kept track of the noise. It was heading in the same direction as them.

"They're still coming," Charlotte observed. "We can't keep going this way." She turned to the left and kept walking. Jonas followed. The woods were thicker here. With the darkness and the fog added to the mix it was impossible to see where they were going.

Charlotte tucked behind a tree and pulled Jonas with her. When he would have questioned the move, she held her finger up to her lips and pointed to the direction of the sound.

Through the limited conditions, Jonas picked up movement. Dark shapes heading through the woods.

He strained and counted at least three figures. None of

the men spoke. Had they been tracking Jonas and Charlotte all along? The thought was chilling.

The people he was observing suddenly stopped. He grabbed Charlotte's arm but there was no need. She'd seen it, too.

Both ducked out of sight. Jonas's heart pounded in his ears. Had they been spotted? He didn't even realize he was holding Charlotte close. It was just an instinctual gesture of protectiveness.

Seconds dragged by and then the sound of walking continued. He released a silent breath. Their pursuers were on the move.

He waited until nothing could be heard before he let Charlotte go.

She stepped back, searching his face. "We should be safe to move on." Her voice was somewhat higher than normal.

Jonas hadn't held a woman since he'd lost Ivy. That last time stood out like a painful reminder of all his mistakes. He'd held his *fraa*'s body at the morgue and cried until he hadn't been able to shed another tear.

And he hadn't since.

"I'm turned around. Do you remember the way?"

Jonas shoved his last images of Ivy back down where he kept his grief locked away and studied their surroundings. "This way."

As they started walking again, Jonas's thoughts ran rampant. He'd trapped the Roots during some of the worst winter weather ever. He'd been attacked by a brown bear and had a run-in with a mountain lion. Jonas had thought he'd seen it all. But what was happening now went beyond anything he could imagine.

FIVE

"Do you believe Harley has moved the girls by now?" Jonas voiced Charlotte's greatest fear aloud. "If he thinks the police will come looking for you, he might want to get them as far away from his place as possible."

Charlotte searched the darkness around them while suppressing a shiver. "I sure hope not. If we lose them, those girls could end up anywhere. Another state or worse—another country. These trafficking rings pick up and move quickly. Staying in one place for long means risking getting caught if someone notices an unusual amount of activity taking place where it shouldn't."

When she realized what she'd said, Charlotte turned his way. "You can't blame yourself for this, Jonas. Harley and his team are good at staying in the shadows. Not calling attention to themselves. Finding remote locations to hide the girls, like his house. You would have no way of knowing what was happening inside those four walls."

Jonas sighed. "Still, in hindsight, I should have figured out that all those vehicles I'd seen driving by my place at night weren't normal. If I'd investigated, I could have prevented what happened to Lainey or even Michaela. The thought that Harley might have killed the young woman turns my stomach."

"Don't take on the blame." Though Charlotte certainly understood the driving force behind his guilt. She'd been to speak to Harley multiple times. She was a trained officer of the law, yet nothing that would indicate a trafficking ring was evident during her visits.

"Does this stuff ever get to you?" Jonas asked quietly.

"Oh, yes. It's hard not to make it personal, especially when it is." Bitterness she couldn't stop crept into her voice.

"It must have been hard losing him in such a way."

She could sense him studying her profile, probably noticing the way her entire body tensed every time Ryan's name came up in conversation. The events of that day were still as fresh as if it had just happened. She wondered if they would ever fade enough where the good things—the sweet memories she and Ryan shared—could wipe away the hurt of all she'd lost.

"Ryan was the one person who helped me over the pain of losing my parents so closely together." She told him about how both had died within a matter of months of each other.

"When I called Ryan to assist," she continued, "he'd been sick for a few days, but we needed his help with the search to locate Michaela." Charlotte was no longer aware of Jonas. It was just her and her memories. "I talked him into coming out and bringing his dogs because he was one of the best SAR trainers around and he understood how to work the dogs in the mountains." She stopped for a breath. Going on was hard.

"Ryan's last transmission was barely distinguishable. He mentioned he'd spotted Michaela—"

Getting the rest of the story out was hard.

"And then we heard his scream," she said in a voice

barely audible. "We were able to pinpoint his location from the dogs' collars."

"I remember," Jonas said. "The incident was a tragedy only intensified by the death of Michaela Reagan."

"Yes. I never understood how someone as experienced as Ryan could make such an easy misstep like he did." She wrapped her arms around herself. "Ryan knew those mountains like the back of his hand. He could maneuver through them under any weather conditions or in the dark."

A pause. "Are you saying it wasn't an accident?"

Never once had she voiced her worst nightmare aloud to another soul before Jonas. The SAR team lead suggested Ryan's death was due to a mistake on his part because he'd been sick and not himself.

But what if it wasn't?

"I never believed Michaela took her own life." Yet she'd convinced herself Ryan's death came as a mistake because it was easier to believe an accident over something far more sinister.

Michaela was popular and well-liked. She was the star athlete on the basketball team, and her parents were loving. The only thing that stood out as odd was what happened about a week before her death.

"Michaela had called the station to report something strange a short time before her death," Charlotte said. "I was the one who was dispatched to take her statement."

Jonas's attention remained on her. "What happened?"

"This was about a few weeks before her death. Michaela called to report her friend Sasha missing. She didn't remember Sasha's last name but said the girl had invited her to a party at a ranch. They'd only met a few days before. Michaela said Sasha was friends with the owner. It was at night and of course there was drinking involved. Michaela swore she'd stuck to soda." She looked his way and saw the same doubts she'd had.

"Anyway," she continued, "there were lots of young girls there around Michaela's age but a few older men as well. Michaela said she got a bad inclination right away, and several of the men kept looking at her strangely. Before she could ask Sasha to leave, another girl came and got Sasha and that was the last Michaela saw of her. While Michaela tried to figure out what to do, she said she sipped on her soda and started to feel odd. Apparently, she passed out. When she woke up, she was alone. She looked everywhere for Sasha but couldn't find her."

"What happened next?" Jonas asked while keeping a careful eye on their surroundings.

"Michaela, though groggy, walked home and reported the incident. The ranch where she was taken had been abandoned for years and proved a dead end. Michaela did say something interesting, though. Sasha claimed to be seventeen—like Michaela—but she lived on her own."

"She was lying about her age. Why?"

Charlotte shrugged. "In light of what's happened, I hate to say it, but Sasha was probably working for the traffickers and brought Michaela there so she could be taken. Which was probably what happened to the other girls."

"This just keeps getting uglier." Jonas was clearly disgusted by what he'd heard.

She smiled gently. "It happens sometimes. The young women are older and not what their clients want anymore. Their handlers convince them to recruit more girls, probably in order to stay alive themselves."

"So why not take Michaela?"

"Because someone probably recognized her as being from a prominent family in Elk Ridge and figured if she disappeared there would be a massive search. Still, whatever happened that night set in motion the events that cost Michaela and Ryan their lives."

Jonas's jaw flexed. "I sure hope you're wrong about their deaths being intentional, because if not, then we have two murders associated with Harley so far." He stopped talking for a moment to listen before asking her about the day Ryan died.

Every second of that day was tattooed on her brain. She didn't even have to close her eyes to recall it. "When we reached the place where Ryan had fallen, the dogs were standing guard. They were faithful to him. Annie was one of them." Her voice became unsteady, and she swallowed several times. "She was the last dog Ryan trained and has been my partner ever since." She took a deep breath. "Anyway, while we were trying to bring Ryan up, there was a gunshot. I couldn't leave Ryan…" Sheriff Wyatt McCallister and several members of his team had gone. "They found Michaela nearby. Dead from a single gunshot wound to the temple." She pointed to the spot on her head without thinking. "The handgun was still in her right hand. There was gunshot residue of course. It was soon deemed a suicide."

"But you don't agree with the conclusion," Jonas stated. She shook her head. "If not, then someone made the scene appear like it was. Someone was up there with Ryan and Michaela."

"Exactly." Charlotte stopped walking. "I'm so turned around. Do you have any idea where we are?"

Jonas looked around for any landmarks and gestured where they needed to go. "I've spent a lot of time wandering the woods and countryside around my place over the past six years. I rarely sleep. At times I feel like a ghost flitting around searching for the person I used to be."

Charlotte felt like she'd found a kindred spirit in him.

"I'm so sorry about your wife and child. Is this the reason why you left the Amish faith?"

Immediately, Jonas's guard returned, and she saw it on his face. The breakthrough they seemed to have made before vanished and she felt like a heel.

He cleared his throat. "We're not too far from the Christian camp," he said without answering her question. She understood he didn't want to talk about the past. Talking about it was like reliving everything and she'd done that enough on her own.

This was the place where Lainey liked to visit. Charlotte remembered it vaguely from the one time she'd stayed there as a kid. "The fog makes it hard to tell where anything is until we're right on top of it." The damp from the fog also made the cold bone-chilling.

"Do you think Abram has reached Elk Ridge yet?" Charlotte asked because every second they were out here alone they were a target for Harley's people. By now, she was almost certain Harley's men would have found those three guys they'd taken down at Abram's place.

"He would have to stick to the buggy paths, which will slow them down. Still, we've been walking for several hours."

Charlotte checked her watch. "Exactly two hours and twenty minutes."

Jonas smiled. "Got it. They're close. If they haven't come across any trouble, they should be there in another fifteen minutes or so. At this time of the night, will there be anyone at the sheriff's office to help?"

"Oh, yes. Though Elk Ridge is small, Deputy Peter Sorrels is on duty along with the night dispatcher. They can have the sheriff and the rest of the team ready to roll out in minutes."

Jonas captured her gaze with a curious look. "You sound like you're proud of the work you do."

"I am. And I was so proud of my dad and the work he did in law enforcement."

An out of place noise had her stopping. "Did you hear something?" she asked. Her eyes darted through the darkness looking for danger.

Jonas glanced around. "I did. It's coming from behind us."

A second later, another sound was to their left, then to their right. With a sinking sensation, Charlotte realized they were being surrounded. The enemy had found them, and they were closing in.

"We need to get to the camp," Jonas whispered. "It's the only direction that appears clear right now. At least it will give us some amount of protection." Jonas leaned closer. "Whatever happens, we can't get separated."

She searched his face before nodding. "I understand."

Something he hadn't felt in a long time forced its way past the indifference Jonas normally used as a self-protective shield. He clasped her hand because he meant what he'd said about not getting separated. Together they ran in the direction he estimated the camp to be.

There was no hiding the disturbance their racing through the woods made or their labored breathing. They had to dodge trees that were impossible to see because of the fog. At any moment, Jonas expected to slam face-first into one.

As they ran, another far more dangerous sound had him jerking his head toward it. Gunshots. The enemy wasn't taking any chances of them getting away.

Both he and Charlotte ducked low. Keeping their feet

beneath them with the momentum of running in a low-ered position was nearly impossible.

After what his panicked heart deemed a lifetime, the shooting halted. The shooters either needed to reload or perhaps they thought they'd hit their target.

Jonas straightened along with Charlotte. As much as he wanted to ask her if she was okay, the sound of their voices would alert the enemy that they were still alive. He took stock of their surroundings and realized they were no longer heading for the camp. Jonas stepped behind a tree and whispered that they had to shift their direction slightly.

Charlotte pulled in several deep breaths before agreeing. "I'm ready." She spoke softly. "Let's keep moving before they find us." She'd told him about the thermal vision capability she thought those men were using.

If that were the case, then it wouldn't matter how far they ran, they'd be easy to track.

Stepping away from the protection of the tree and into the unknown was hard, but somehow holding Charlotte's hand made it easier.

So far, it didn't appear the shooters had caught their change of direction.

After covering some space, Jonas slowed to a fast walk.

Charlotte glanced behind them. "I believe we're too far away for their night vision capability to pick us up."

Still, Jonas couldn't get over the sensation of being hunted. Each step mirrored by the enemy.

Charlotte pointed. "I see something up ahead."

Jonas followed the direction of her finger. Several buildings emerged from the fog. He breathed out a huge sigh. The camp. Knowing there was a place to get out of the weather and take cover was comforting.

He remembered the place by heart. The first set of buildings were cabins where the campers bunked.

"Hopefully, we can find something to dry off with inside," Charlotte whispered. Both were soaked. Jonas stepped up on the porch of the first cabin and opened the door. The last time he'd been to the camp had been a few months back. He rarely went inside the buildings apart from the sanctuary that was in the middle of the site.

The electricity had long since been disabled. The camp had been closed for years.

Jonas clicked on the flashlight he'd taken from Abram's house. A half dozen bunk beds.

"There's nothing useful here," Charlotte said. "But on a positive note, there's no bad guys, either."

Jonas smiled. "We might be better off checking the dining hall."

She looked at him curiously. "You've been there?"

He nodded. "I've spent a lot of time here," he said in way of answer to her arched brows. "It's a little distance from here."

Jonas shut off the flashlight before stepping outside once more. The darkness descending almost felt physical. He listened for anything strange but heard nothing. If their stalkers didn't pick up on the change in direction and weren't familiar with the area, they might miss the camp entirely.

"I sure hope Abram and Lainey have arrived safely by now. We need them to bring help as soon as possible." Charlotte rubbed her hands over her arms. The cold seemed to pierce through the jackets they wore. "I hate being out here like this. It's impossible to see anything and we can't say how many men are out here looking for us."

The thought settled uncomfortably between them as

Jonas kept close to Charlotte. They reached the large building that was the dining hall.

"The owners appear to have left a lot of the stuff behind when they closed the camp." He recalled the sanctuary was still intact. "Perhaps they hoped to reopen it sometime in the future."

Inside the dining hall were more than a dozen tables set up around the large room.

"The kitchen's through here." He'd explored all the buildings on his first visit. Jonas stepped through a set of swinging doors and into the kitchen.

Charlotte shone the flashlight around the space. "I could use something to dry off a bit." She began opening cabinets.

"There's some plastic containers over here." Jonas opened several before he found a roll of paper towels. "Here." He handed her several.

"Thanks." She dried off her face and hair. "I'm hoping those men won't be able to follow us, but if they do, they may realize we're heading back to Harley's. If the girls are still at the house, they won't be long."

He couldn't allow that to happen. "Let's see if there's anything useful here."

A thorough search of the rest of the structures produced nothing. The last building at the center of the clearing was the sanctuary. The minute he stepped inside, a sense of peace that had alluded him for so long returned. It was here every time he visited the sanctuary, which he'd done occasionally since moving to the area.

"I remember this place," Charlotte told him with a hint of surprise in her tone. She headed to the front where the altar beckoned. He followed. "I came here with a friend one summer when I was around eight. We had so much fun, but the best part was the final service. It was so moving. There were several kids who became Christians." A smile curled the corners of her mouth at the memory. Jonas couldn't take his eyes off her. She had a pretty smile. The thought was so out of place for him that it had him recoiling.

Ivy had been the only woman he'd thought pretty. He could still call up her face whenever he chose. Beautiful Ivy. Their courtship had been a time of getting to know each other, leading to a marriage of adventure he so craved…or so he thought. Looking back, he wondered if Ivy enjoyed all the adventures into the mountains he took her on as much as she claimed, or if she only wanted to please him.

When the baby came along, things changed. He'd had to grow up quickly. But he hadn't really. If he had, he would never have left Ivy alone so late in the pregnancy.

If he'd been there, he could have gotten Ivy to the hospital in time…his life would have turned out so differently. Instead, he'd had to bury his wife and his first child. As he'd stood over their graves, something had died in him that day. He'd left the cemetery a different person. Hope was no longer part of his world. Surviving each day without falling apart became his only goal. "Jonas?"

He realized Charlotte had asked him something. "I'm sorry."

Sympathy softened her face. "It doesn't matter. We should probably keep moving. I don't want to get caught here. I'd rather take my chances in the woods."

They reached the back of the sanctuary once more.

Before he could step outside, Charlotte barred his way. "Did you hear that?"

He did. Another heartbeat confirmed the truth. It was too late to leave the camp. The enemy had arrived.

SIX

Their only chance at surviving lay in their ability to stay hidden.

"Up front. There's a crawl space back behind the baptistery." Charlotte glanced down at her muddy shoes. "We have to take off our shoes. They'll follow our muddy tracks otherwise."

Charlotte slipped out of her shoes and waited for Jonas to do the same before heading to the front of the sanctuary. Two sets of doors on either side of the pulpit led to the baptistery, which could be reached by a set of stairs.

Charlotte chose the left-side door because if her memory served her correctly, it was the one that would take them to the crawl space. Her heart drummed its frantic beat into her ears. If they were caught, Harley's people would make them disappear just as assuredly as they would the young women she and Jonas were trying to rescue. To save their lives, they'd be forced to face those coming after them, and Charlotte had no idea how many there were.

She opened the door and went in with Jonas before carefully closing it without making a sound.

"There are the stairs to the baptistery," she said lowly. "The crawl space for doing repairs is past them. If you're not looking for it, you wouldn't realize it's there."

"How do you know this?" he asked, a frown wrinkling the spot between his eyes.

"My friend and I explored the sanctuary when we were here. If I remember correctly, it's creepy back there." Hopefully, too creepy for those coming after them to give it more than a cursory search.

Charlotte climbed up the set of stairs quickly. Once on the landing, the steps to the baptistery were right there. "This way." A thick green velvet curtain hid the crawl space where the plumbing could be accessed.

The space was small. Barely room for two people crammed in. If discovered…she didn't want to think about what would happen.

"I don't like it," Charlotte told Jonas.

"I agree. What's down there?" Jonas pointed to a ladder that appeared to lead down into nothingness.

She shrugged. "Becky and I were too afraid to investigate."

Jonas clicked on the flashlight and searched the shadows below. "It seems to be heading straight beneath the building." He turned her way. Saw the fear she couldn't hide. Dark spaces like what she'd glimpsed below were her phobia. "I'll go first," he said with a hint of compassion in his tone. "Will you hold the light for me? I can't see anything."

She took the light from him. "Go, I've got it."

Jonas tossed his shoes down and swung around on the ladder while Charlotte kept the light down and out of his eyes, directed at the rungs in front of him.

He slowly descended some fifteen feet until he was on the ground.

Before Charlotte worked up the courage to follow, the double doors at the back of the sanctuary were shoved open—with enough force to slap the walls. Charlotte jerked toward the noise. "They're coming."

"Hurry, Charlotte. It won't take them long to search the building."

She swallowed deeply and tossed the flashlight down first followed by her shoes. She swung her legs onto the ladder. The next rung was hidden by darkness and she froze. "I can't see my next step." Her voice rose an octave while her heart rate soared.

Jonas quickly corrected the issue.

Don't dwell on the darkness...

At the sound of Harley's troops storming the sanctuary, Charlotte carefully made her way down to the last rung. Jonas helped her off and she stood beside him breathing deeply to keep from hyperventilating.

Her attention went back to the ladder. "We need to get it down. If they find it, they'll surely search here."

"You're right." With Jonas's help, the ladder was pulled away from its resting place and laid out of sight. Both slipped into their shoes once more.

Noises from above told them that the intruders had reached the front of the sanctuary.

Jonas killed the flashlight and they stepped into the shadows, away from the opening overhead. Immediately, Charlotte took a step closer to him. The place gave her the creeps. She had disliked damp, dark spaces since she was a child, when she and a friend had gotten locked in her family's root cellar.

"I see something over there." Jonas held her hand as they moved farther along one of the walls. A small opening to the outside world had been blocked by a stack of bricks.

Before Jonas had the chance to grab the first brick, she said, "What if they're out there waiting for us?"

He stopped immediately. "You're right. It could be a trap. Let's wait for them to leave first."

Voices drifted their way. Charlotte couldn't make out what was said.

"Let's cover up our footprints so they aren't visible in case those men find the opening and look down."

"Good thinking." Charlotte helped him smudge their footprints.

While they worked, a door opened. Their pursuers were near the baptistery.

Both she and Jonas moved as far away from the entrance as possible. Soon, a light was flashed around the ground below and Charlotte prayed they'd done an efficient job hiding their footprints.

The light eventually disappeared. Darkness reclaimed the space. Once more, Charlotte edged closer to Jonas and waited.

"I believe they're leaving," Jonas whispered.

A light swept through the space between the bricks penetrating the darkness. Charlotte jumped back when it appeared to come close to their hiding place. After a moment, it disappeared.

Soon, there was no sound at all.

"I'm almost afraid to leave," she told Jonas.

"I feel the same way. Hopefully, they'll think we left the sanctuary and the camp."

She hoped for the same thing. They'd have to be careful—Harley's people would know Jonas lived near the camp.

"Shall we move the bricks?" Jonas asked softly.

"Yes, I've had enough of this place." She shuddered. Clearing a way out didn't take too long. When the final brick was gone, there was enough room to move through the opening.

"Let me go first," Jonas said. He was being protective

of her, and her heart softened in gratitude. But she couldn't let him. She was, after all, the one carrying the badge.

"I'm the deputy. I'll go first." Charlotte got down on her hands and knees and crawled out into the foggy night. She rose and scanned her surroundings. There was no sign of anyone close by. "It's safe."

Jonas followed her example then stood up, dusting off his clothes.

As they moved to the center of the camp, Charlotte spotted lights at the edge of the area. "Oh no." Her heart sank. She ran a frustrated hand through her hair. "We have to get out of sight." Using one of the cabins as cover, she and Jonas inched closer. "What are they doing?" she wondered aloud.

They appeared to have gathered there and were waiting for someone. "I can't tell." Jonas was close enough for her to feel the breath in which those words were carried. "But I don't like it."

She didn't, either. "I want to get closer and see if I can hear what they're saying," she said.

Jonas looked at her incredulously. "No, Charlotte. They want us dead."

She understood the risk but there was something more going on that she had to uncover. "I'll be okay. I'm a deputy. This is what I do." She searched his beautiful eyes before adding, "Wait for me here."

The words barely cleared her lips before he rejected the idea. "I'm going with you. We've come this far together. No matter what, we stick together."

Jonas witnessed the struggle taking place in Charlotte. She was worried about him.

"I can take care of myself, Charlotte, and those men are dangerous."

She slowly smiled. "You're right. We stick together." As she looked into his eyes, her smile faded.

Just for a second, the world around them and the danger close by disappeared and it was just two people looking at each other as if they'd discovered something they'd lost. Jonas wondered why, with this woman he scarcely knew, he felt a spark of something he hadn't felt since Ivy's death.

He stepped back, breaking the spell.

"Follow me and be careful." Her voice came out sounding nothing like her usual confident self.

Jonas managed a nod because his emotions were all over the board and he didn't trust himself to speak.

After another searching look, Charlotte slowly started toward the men while carefully watching each step.

Jonas's heartbeat drowned out all sound around him, and he wasn't sure if it was because of what lay ahead of them or what he'd just experienced with Charlotte.

They reached the back of one of the bunkhouses near the edge of camp. Charlotte held up her hand and stopped. Tilting her head to one side, she listened. "I still can't make out what they're saying." She pointed to a group of trees—all that stood between them and those armed men.

Jonas shook his head. *Too risky*, he mouthed.

But Charlotte was going despite the risk.

Before he could stop her, she ran toward them.

Jonas waited until she was safe before he snatched a breath and followed.

The conversation taking place close by stopped abruptly.

"Did you hear something?" said a voice Jonas recognized. It belonged to one of the men chasing them earlier in the day by the river.

Charlotte's wide eyes latched on to Jonas's.

"I don't hear anything." Another man Jonas didn't recognize sounded skeptical.

"I'm telling you I heard something. Go check it out to be sure." The first person appeared to be calling the shots.

Grumbling was followed by someone moving closer to their location.

Jonas instinctively gathered Charlotte close as if they could make themselves less visible that way.

Footsteps stopped near to the tree they were sheltering behind, and Jonas closed his eyes. *Lord, please keep us hidden.*

He kept his attention on the ground and saw what appeared to be the tip of a boot. *Stop, please, don't come closer.* The boot disappeared. Footsteps faded.

"It must have been an animal," their pursuer said once he'd returned to his people. "How much longer are we going to wait here?" He clearly sounded impatient.

"However long it takes!" the one in charge snapped. "He's supposed to call soon and let us know what to do next." Who was supposed to call, Harley? Or someone else?

"This is a waste of time, in my opinion."

"Yeah, well, there's a lot riding on Harley getting things under control and out of sight at his place. If the police come to investigate, we can't let them find anything."

Harley was moving the women. Would they be too late to save them?

Nearby, a phone rang. The leader spoke to someone briefly.

"Harley's not picking up his phone," the man in charge announced. "Never should have trusted that guy in the first place." A few unsavory words followed. "We still have a job to do. Find the deputy and the others. We don't need them causing a stink right now. Too much is at stake."

A bunch of varying opinions were expressed as the men talked over each other.

"Enough," the leader said. "Let's go. They aren't at the camp. Which means they're still out in the woods somewhere."

Soon the sound of multiple footsteps moving away could be heard. Jonas stood stock-still, too afraid to move in case it was a trap.

"Jonas?" Charlotte looked like she'd been trying to get his attention for a while. "We should be safe to leave now."

He let her go and stepped from the trees. The flashlights were some distance away.

"At least they don't believe we've come this way," Charlotte told him. "I guess that's something."

"Sounds like Harley isn't answering their calls...probably because he's too busy moving the girls." Or worse. At this point, Jonas wouldn't put anything past Harley Owens.

"I sure hope not. Regardless, we must try and save them." She looked back to the flashlights and shivered. "Let's get out of here."

Crossing through the camp, they faced the woods that separated the camp from the road.

Jonas broke the silence, airing his thoughts. "With so many out here looking for us, hopefully we won't face any resistance once we reach Harley's house. Still, I'm worried about Betty. Where is she in all this?"

"A good question. I didn't see her before, but then I didn't make it inside the house. Is it possible she would have gone somewhere?"

Jonas immediately shook his head. "No. I'm certain Harley controls everything she does and who she sees."

Charlotte sighed. "That poor woman. Harley is a terrible person and Betty deserves so much better than him."

Jonas remembered the time when he'd heard Betty scream and gone to her aid. She'd told him there was a snake in the house. There'd been a man there who she claimed to be her nephew. Only Betty seemed almost afraid of him.

He shared the incident with Charlotte.

"Do you remember what the man looked like?" she asked.

"I do. He was close to my age, I'd guess, and he had short, dark hair and eyes."

"From what you've described it could be almost any number of people. And as we've established, this organization is much bigger than Harley. He's just a small cog and it sounds like his own people are turning on him."

Jonas agreed. "You're suggesting this ring is operating outside of Montana as well?"

Charlotte blew out a breath. "Probably all over the country if not internationally. To be able to do this, they'd need to buy off a lot of people in power along the way."

Jonas focused on her face. "You're kidding. It's hard to believe anyone in power would allow such an awful thing to take place."

"It's big business and generates millions of dollars each year. There are trafficking rings that operate within and outside of the US. They move women in and out of the country illegally. Sometimes using mules to cross the border. Other times, they fly them in on the pretense of working. Of course, it's just a cover for what's really happening." Even in the shadows, he saw how her mouth thinned. "I hate that such things happen to so many innocent girls. Even the ones who are saved, their lives are never the same again."

Anger rose inside Jonas. He couldn't imagine treating another human being the way these girls were treated. No matter what it cost him, he was going to do everything in his power to stop Harley and whoever else was involved.

SEVEN

Never should have trusted that guy in the first place...

Charlotte kept replaying those words in her head. It sounded like those in charge were losing patience with Harley. How long before Harley became too much of a liability to keep alive? Her fear escalated for those innocent young women trapped with men whose only concern was greed and keeping their crimes secret at any cost.

She voiced her concern to Jonas. "This has all the makings of a big operation. We can't let the girls get out of the county."

"I still don't understand why they'd enlist Harley's help in the first place. He's always been a loose cannon. It doesn't add up."

He was right. Harley had been in trouble with the law and was on their radar for abuse and petty crimes. She wouldn't have pegged him as being involved in something so much bigger.

Jonas stopped and faced her. "What if we're walking into a setup? Because I have a bad feeling about this."

Fear shot through her limbs. "I hope you're wrong." By now, Lainey and Abram should have contacted the sheriff's department. Help would be on the way soon enough...*if everything went as planned.* Why were there no sirens filling the night with their sounds?

"Let's take a break," she said. Jonas had been with her through some awful things, and she hated that he'd been forced into getting involved. If something were to happen to him, she'd never forgive herself.

Jonas looked around for some place to sit. The only available spot was a downed tree trunk.

The dampness of the log soaked through her jacket and into her jeans. "I'm worried." She shifted toward him. He needed to hear everything on her mind.

"About us walking into an ambush at Harley's?" he asked.

That was part of it but not everything. "It's too quiet," she said, and his frown deepened. "Abram and Lainey should have reached the sheriff's office some time ago. Where are the sirens? We should hear them this close to the road." Where were her people?

"You believe something happened to them?"

"I hope not but we have to accept the fact they may have been delayed or…" She couldn't say the words aloud. Couldn't think about having to tell Dottie she'd failed, and her granddaughter was hurt or worse.

"Which means it's up to us to save those women if they are indeed still there."

"Exactly." Charlotte hesitated. "Jonas, I'm worried about you, too. I've put your life in danger far too many times already. This is my job and I accept the danger, but it isn't yours and—"

"We've been over this already," he cut her off. "I'm not leaving you alone to face whatever might be waiting for us at Harley's. I'm coming with you," he insisted earnestly.

As she looked into his handsome face, something she hadn't experienced in a long time hit her like a storm.

When she and Ryan had first met, there had been an instant awareness. The attraction had grown stronger as they got to know each other. With Ryan's death, she'd felt as if that part of her life had died with him. But the way her heart was racing now just looking into Jonas's eyes… It was nice to have Jonas by her side. She hadn't had anyone to lean on like this since Ryan passed.

"Are you okay?" he asked, likely having seen what she couldn't hide.

Charlotte rose unsteadily and tried to put space between them without being too obvious. "Yes, I'm fine. We should head out, though."

Jonas stood as well. "You're right. We need to hurry."

As they started walking again, the temperatures continued to plummet. "It's freezing out here." Charlotte wrapped her arms around her body for added warmth. It would be so easy to give up and just accept whatever fate that would come their way, but every time she thought about giving up, she remembered Lainey begging her to help the other women. As a deputy, she felt called to investigate.

"We're getting closer," Jonas said. The realization had her on immediate alert. The thought of going through another shootout was hard to consider, but they had to be prepared for anything.

She grabbed his arm as they neared Harley's house. Nothing but darkness appeared in front of them. "Hang on a second."

"Did you see something?" Jonas searched her face.

"No, that's just it. There aren't any lights on inside."

"Almost as if no one's home."

"Exactly. Wouldn't Betty be here?" Charlotte hadn't been conscious long enough to see if Betty was in the house, and Harley probably kept her living in fear and not asking questions. Besides, Harley wasn't the man who'd attacked Charlotte. He'd been much taller and more slender than Harley.

"Stay close to me," she said because her gut warned they could be walking into danger.

Once they reached the structure itself, Charlotte debated on the wisdom of going inside without backup. Should they keep the house under surveillance until the sheriff and his team arrived? What if no one was coming?

She slowly eased onto the porch with Jonas following. A board squeaked beneath her foot, and she cringed before continuing. Jonas carefully avoided the step. With the weapon pointed in front of her, Charlotte moved to the door. Normally, she would announce herself before entering a house but right now they had the element of surprise and Charlotte wasn't officially here on police business.

Charlotte reached for the screen door and eased it open to a screeching noise that grated along her nerves. She tried the doorknob. It turned freely in her hand. Tension flooded her limbs. "I don't like this."

He was right there with her as she slowly stepped inside the house where she'd been a handful of times.

Jonas stepped over the threshold, leaving the door open.

From what Lainey had said, the girls were being held in the basement.

"We need to clear the house first," she told Jonas. "Which means we go through each room to make sure there's no one here."

He confirmed he understood.

Charlotte started on the first floor and checked each room using the flashlight to make sure they were empty. The house was neat and clean, likely thanks to Betty's influence. The kitchen was tidy. She felt the stove top. Nothing had been cooked there in a while. Charlotte couldn't get over the idea that something was terribly wrong, almost as if the house were staged. She'd overheard the men suggesting that the place needed to be scrubbed for evidence. There was no landline. She assumed Harley would have a cell phone, but wouldn't it be risky for connecting with his cohorts?

An uneasy tension settled between her shoulder blades.

Once the second floor was cleared, Charlotte and Jonas went back down to the kitchen where the door to the basement was located.

Outside, nothing but silence. The sirens and flashing lights she'd prayed for didn't come.

His heart echoed every step leading down to the basement. Charlotte held the flashlight, shining it around. The room was surprisingly uncluttered. Only a few pieces of furniture had been stored down here. Nothing more.

Jonas's heart plummeted. "Now what?"

Disappointment was clear on Charlotte's face. "I can't believe it. This is Harley's house. Those men said he was getting the girls out of sight. Where are they?" She spun around the room. "Is there another building we missed?"

"Wait, what's that?" Jonas spotted something over in the corner of the room and picked it up.

"It's a denim jacket." Charlotte took the garment from him. "Betty's?"

"Doubtful. I've never seen her wear anything like it." It had been hand stitched with a flower design in brightly colored threads.

She turned the jacket over and looked inside. "It's a size two. I don't believe it would fit Betty. It could belong to one of the girls. I need Annie. She could help us locate the owner." Her expression saddened. "I hope she's okay."

"She's obviously a smart dog. Is it possible she's still

searching for Lainey?" He could tell she wasn't fully convinced. Charlotte flashed the light all around once more and he followed the beam. "I don't see anything else. Harley doesn't have a garage. The house is it."

"We're too late."

Jonas tried to make sense of it. "This isn't the best spot to hide anyone. If Harley is involved, it's the first place law enforcement would look."

"So, if not here, then where would he take them?"

Realization dawned within him and he slapped his palm against his forehead. "I don't understand why I didn't think of this earlier."

Charlotte stepped forward. "What?"

"I still go trapping in the wintertime. The last time I did—a few months back—I ran into Harley up in the mountains. He seemed surprised to see me."

"What was he doing up there?"

Jonas had wondered as much himself. "He seemed cagey as all get-out."

"He was hiding something," she concluded.

"Those were my thoughts. At the time I had no idea the scope of what Harley was capable of." He shook his head. "Anyway, I asked him why he was in the mountains in the wintertime because Harley isn't a hunter or a trapper."

Charlotte's brow creased. "He was doing something illegal."

"I have no doubt about it now. Harley told me he owned a place up there and came there to get away from time to time."

Charlotte's frown deepened. "That can't be the case."

"My thoughts, too. It could belong to one of his criminal buddies. I'm guessing Harley left the men searching for us and ditched the person who picked him up at the river so he could move the women. He'd certainly have enough time by now."

"You're right. We've been looking at the wrong house." Her shoulders slumped. "And we've wasted valuable time trying to get here."

Jonas felt like a heel for not remembering sooner. "If we don't find those young women soon, I can't even imagine the world they'll be subject to."

She searched his face. "But how? Do you have any idea which place is his?"

He did. "I can find it. There are only a few places on the mountain, and most are used for trapping. Harley couldn't take the girls there because those cabins are usually one room and small." Jonas remembered one house in particular that was much bigger. He told her about it. "I always wondered who it belonged to because it didn't fit with the rest up there. I'm guessing it's the one Harley claimed was his."

"Let's go." Charlotte started up the stairs. A second later, Jonas caught up with her.

Charlotte suggested they find some dry clothes to change into before heading up to the mountains.

"I think I saw some in the bedroom." They returned to the room she assumed Betty shared with Harley, and Charlotte dug through the closet until she found something that would work for both her and Jonas. They changed in separate rooms and stepped into the hallway a couple minutes later. Harley's jeans were too short for him, and Charlotte suppressed a grin.

"Not exactly a good fit, but they're dry," he said in answer to her obvious amusement. They went back downstairs, where Charlotte stuffed their damp clothes in a trash bin.

Before they reached the front door, a set of flashlights appeared in the woods in front of the house.

Charlotte ducked away from the window that ran alongside the door. "Someone's out there."

Jonas watched the lights from the corner of a glass pane. "They're coming this way. The back door."

He ran for the kitchen where he'd noticed a second entrance. Before he stepped out into the darkness, Jonas carefully scanned the surroundings to make sure there was no one coming up on them. He and Charlotte stepped out and closed the door as quietly as possible. He didn't want to give those men approaching a heads-up. Unfortunately, as careful as both were trying to be, Harley's back porch was a mess and several of the boards creaked beneath their feet.

"Run!" Charlotte whispered. Both jumped from the porch and raced toward the woods in front of them.

"That's far enough. Stop where you are." A flashlight beam pinned them in place. Two of Harley's people headed their way.

"Well, well. This is a lucky surprise. Where's Harley?" one man said.

The person without the light immediately sounded the alert to the others who were close.

Shocked, Jonas jerked his head toward Charlotte.

"We can't let them take us," she said under her breath. He understood what she meant. They'd have to fight for freedom.

As the two approached, Jonas whirled around and fired. Both men ducked. Jonas ran after the one with the light and slammed into him hard with all his weight. It took everything Jonas could muster to fend the man off and keep from being shot. Out of the corner of his eye, he saw that Charlotte was struggling with the second man.

Voices of the others who were with them drifted his way. They were almost out of time.

Jonas slugged his attacker hard, but the man just kept coming, matching him fist for fist. Jonas finally managed to get his weapon in a position to strike the man hard. It was enough to drop him to his knees. He fell forward and sprawled on the ground unconscious. Jonas grabbed his weapon.

Charlotte!

The second man was about to shoot. Jonas ran toward the nightmare unfolding. A rustling noise nearby had the shooter pausing.

A dog raced from the woods before he had the chance to react. This was Annie, Charlotte's K-9 partner. The man shot at the animal and missed. Annie grabbed hold of his arm and latched on tight. Cursing, the man tried to shake the dog off but couldn't.

The unconscious man woke and scrambled to his feet then ran toward the woods. Jonas fired but missed.

The second armed soldier kicked Annie hard. The dog let go.

"We have to get out of here," Charlotte yelled to Jonas. "Come, Annie." With the dog leading the way, they all ran for the woods while the remaining attacker shot at them.

By *Gott*'s hand they'd escaped unscathed.

"Don't stop," Charlotte told him as they continued running as fast as possible to put distance between themselves and the house.

Jonas kept careful watch behind. This direction would take them deeper into the woods. There wasn't another house past Harley's. At some point, they'd have to change direction.

"Why aren't they coming after us?" Charlotte slowed to a fast walk with the dog keeping pace.

He stopped and looked the way they'd come. "I can't say. The one guy saw which way we went but didn't follow."

"They weren't there for us."

"Harley." Their attacker had asked where Harley was and, in the woods earlier, Jonas overheard one saying Harley wasn't picking up. "They were sent to find him."

"Exactly. He's really made someone angry." Charlotte focused on the dog and did a quick exam. Jonas noticed blood on Annie's head. "She has a small cut and there's a bump. It looks as if she's been struck by something."

"Probably when you were attacked earlier."

"Possibly." She gave the dog a hug and then brought out the denim jacket. "Search, Annie."

The dog immediately sniffed the ground before picking up a scent. She started for the front of the house. Charlotte stopped her. "We can't risk her running into danger. Would Harley be able to get the women to the house by vehicle?"

"It would have to be four-wheel drive. It's rugged up there." As happy as Jonas was that the dog was found, he still didn't trust those men not to come after them. "Let's keep moving."

Charlotte kept a close eye on the dog as they moved through the woods at the side of the house. "Does Harley own a Jeep or a four-wheeler?"

"Not that I recall. Look." He pointed to the house. "They're inside now." The men didn't appear to be too concerned about Charlotte and Jonas. They'd come for Harley.

Annie sniffed around the ground without picking up a scent.

"After you cross the mountains, there's a valley below that's sparsely populated," Charlotte said. "It would provide a good passage to move the girls without being spotted."

Jonas hadn't thought about it before. "Makes sense. But I wouldn't consider it ideal in the winter months. The snow gets deep up there. You'd have to have a special type of machine in order to travel through it."

"You're right. Unless Harley was up to something besides trafficking young women."

"Like what?" Jonas watched her closely.

"Possibly weapons smuggling or a dozen different scenarios just as bad."

Disgust rose inside Jonas. "I always thought Harley was a bad person, but I had no idea how bad."

Charlotte glanced behind them. "There's no sign we're being followed."

"To be safe, we should avoid the camp. As it is, it will be several hours before we reach the mountains. Avoiding the camp won't cause us much more of a delay. The way I'm going to take us would be accessible by a four-wheel drive vehicle. If we can pick up Harley's trail again, Annie can get back on the kidnapped woman's scent."

"I hope so." Charlotte bit down on her bottom lip. "To be honest, if I never see that camp again, it will be too soon."

Jonas smiled. He certainly understood. Their last visit had been terrifying.

"Still, I'm worried about how we'll let my people know where we are," Charlotte said. "They'll be expecting us at Harley's house, and we have no way of getting word to them about the change in direction. They could be walking into a dangerous situation if those men are still around."

Their attackers were willing to take anyone out to accomplish their mission. If cornered by law enforcement, he couldn't imagine the carnage. "I don't remember any *Englischer* houses between here and the mountains where we can use their phones."

Charlotte frowned. "Annie's collar has a tracking device made into it."

"Would your team automatically consider checking the location of the dog?"

"Probably…but we can't afford to take the chance." She stopped walking. "We need to leave word for them somewhere they'll think to check when they don't find us at Harley's."

"My house," he answered. "It's closer."

"Yes! My place is miles away by vehicle—which we don't have. Abram and Lainey know you're with me. If we circle back to your place and leave a note, perhaps it will be found by the sheriff's department."

"Or by those men. We could be leading them to where we're going."

She didn't deny it. "That's possible, too."

Did they dare take the chance that those at Harley's wouldn't check his home? "We have to try," he told her because he had a bad feeling about Abram and Lainey. With so many men combing the woods, had the two managed to reach help? If so, why was it taking so long for help to reach them?

With Annie glued to Charlotte's side, they made a wide berth around Harley's place. The miles covered since he'd last left his house weighed on his exhausted limbs.

His house appeared through the fog. After checking for any sign of a vehicle moving their way, Jonas crossed the road with Charlotte and the dog.

As he neared the house, the hackles at the back of his neck stood at attention. Something felt off.

"Let's take a detour," he whispered and guided her toward the barn. Once they were inside, his fears didn't ease any by the realization that his horse hadn't returned.

"Sandy's not here."

Charlotte studied his face. "Who's Sandy?"

"My mare. I rode her to the river. The shooting spooked her, but she normally would return home." He turned toward the door he'd left open. "She always comes home."

Charlotte followed his gaze. "You believe someone took her?"

He didn't know what he thought. He faced Charlotte again. "Stay here. Let me slip around the back and see if I can get a good look inside."

Charlotte immediately shook her head. "It's too dangerous. I'm coming with you."

It would be pointless to try and change her mind. Jonas pointed to the side door. "That way."

Annie fell into step while Jonas eased toward the back of the barn and prayed if his hunch was true, those men wouldn't be looking for them.

Once they were even with the house, he quickly crossed around back with Charlotte and the dog.

The window at the back of the house looked out from the kitchen. Inside was darkness. Jonas stepped close and tried to see in.

"Do you see anything?" Charlotte whispered.

He leaned closer. A shadow moved inside, and then he was looking into the face of the enemy.

EIGHT

"Go, go, go!" Jonas yelled. He peeled off around the side when a shot shattered the window they had just been looking through.

Another round of shots followed in rapid succession.

Charlotte charged through the night, grasping for Jonas's hand. She needed to know they were all moving together.

"Which way?" she asked, because in the dark and under these weather conditions everything looked the same.

"Left."

They raced behind the barn and kept going while the sound of pursuit could be heard.

"They're coming. Don't stop," Jonas told her.

He was their only chance at survival. She knew he understood the layout of the land far better than these men after them.

They crossed the road. Charlotte glanced around and was happy to see Annie right at their heels.

Once they reached the other side, Jonas didn't slow down. They charged through the woods, fighting back the dense underbrush Charlotte had faced before. The cold burned her lungs.

Behind them, what sounded like several men were searching Jonas's property. Those at Harley's house would join the search soon enough. They couldn't afford to stop.

Charlotte lost her footing and almost went down. She would have if it weren't for Jonas's hold on her.

After they'd been running for a long time, Jonas stopped long enough to listen. "I don't hear them yet."

Which meant they had the advantage for the moment.

"Let's see if we can get back on the four-wheeler path," Charlotte said, and they started walking at a fast pace. Her worst fear was that the others were heading their way to cut them off. She said as much to Jonas.

"I'm worried, too," he replied. "Yet they don't know where we're going, which will work to our favor." He looked behind them. "If we keep going, we'll reach the camp, which I don't think is wise." He pointed to the left. "Best to take a little longer to get there and get there alive."

A chill sped down her spine at those words. She was struggling to breathe normally after their race for freedom. "Are we safe slowing down a bit?"

Jonas must've noticed her struggle. "We should be." He slowed his steps to match hers. "Why were they at my house?"

Charlotte was convinced they were expecting them to come back to Jonas's at some point and said so.

"Which is probably why they took Sandy," Jonas decided. "To keep me from using her to ride for help."

"Exactly." Charlotte peeked over her shoulder. If Harley's people realized where they were heading, they'd move the girls for sure, if they hadn't already.

Once they had traveled for some time, Jonas stopped and knelt beside a set of tracks. "Look. These appear too small to belong to a Jeep and you'd never get a pickup through here. It could be one of those side-by-sides."

Charlotte glanced at the tracks—they certainly could belong to an off-road utility vehicle. She took out the jacket once more. Annie sniffed the garment and then the air in several directions before taking off. "She's found the scent."

While they followed Annie, her thoughts kept returning to Lainey and Abram. Was she worried for no reason? Perhaps they'd just been delayed.

"Whatever happened, Lainey is with Abram. He'll protect her," Jonas said as if reading her troubled thoughts.

"I hope you're right, but neither of them has been up against anything like this."

"Abram is smart and knows these woods well," Jonas said. "The best way we can help right now is to find those women and get them to a safe location before they're moved or hurt. If Harley and his people were responsible for killing Ryan and Michaela, they must be stopped."

His words had her slowing in her tracks, but he was right. For so long, she hadn't wanted to consider that Ryan might have been met with foul play or was even murdered, but the question was always there in the back of her mind. The thought of someone killing him and Michaela to protect their crimes was unthinkable. "Whatever happened a year ago started with Michaela." Charlotte glanced sideways at Jonas and saw him agree.

"It sounds like it has everything to do with what happened to her friend Sasha and that party."

Charlotte frowned. "Yes. But Michaela didn't recognize any of the men there—at least that's what she claimed."

Jonas shook his head. "It doesn't make sense. Sasha made a mistake with Michaela, just like Harley did with Lainey."

It sickened Charlotte to consider what Harley had

planned for Lainey before she was introduced into the sex trafficking world. "Sasha and now Harley screwed up and put a spotlight on the organization. Ryan's death was made to look like a fall to cover up something he probably saw that night." Her stomach clenched as she said the words aloud. "Michaela's was staged to look like a suicide. I don't know what they'd do to Lainey if they catch her." Or them. All she knew for certain was they wouldn't live to tell their side of the story.

A noise up ahead had Annie investigating. The dog soon lost interest and retraced her tracks.

Charlotte tried to relax. "How long have you lived in this area?" she asked, not only because she was curious about him, but also because she had to find something for her brain to fix on other than the danger all around them.

He lowered his head. "I moved here from Virginia when I was seventeen."

Charlotte was surprised to hear he'd come from out east. "That's a big move for someone so young."

He attempted a smile. "I guess. Strangely, I never hesitated. My father was a beekeeper like his father before him."

She looked at him, silently inviting him to tell her more. "But you didn't want to follow in the family business."

"I didn't. In fact, I couldn't imagine anything more boring to be honest with you." He laughed before continuing. "I'd heard about Montana and the mountains. Seen pictures of them. I couldn't wait to see them for myself."

"And did they live up to what you imagined?" She'd lived here all her life. Most times, the mountains were just something in the distance and easy to take for granted.

"Yes, they did," he said with awe in his voice. "I loved everything about them. For the first year, I traveled around the different communities in Montana before settling here."

"And you found the settlement?" She watched Annie weave her way through the tall brush.

"I did. I went to work for Ivy's *daed*. In my spare time, I taught myself how to trap and made a decent living at it."

"And you and Ivy?" She waited to hear their love story.

"I actually loved her the moment I saw her, only she was fifteen at the time and her *daed* wanted her to wait for a couple of years before marrying." His mouth quirked. "I was happy to wait for her. I loved her so much."

Her thoughts returned to Ryan. She'd felt the same way the first time they met. When he asked her out, she thought she was the luckiest person alive. In typical Ryan fashion, he'd invited her to join in the dog training. She'd gotten to see him in action. The way he interacted with the animals. It was a beautiful thing.

"While I waited, I built the house where Abram now lives."

Charlotte hadn't realized that. No wonder it seemed hard for him to go there. "Abram lives in your old house?"

He jerked his head in answer. "After Ivy died, I could no longer stay Amish. I'd failed Ivy. Let my own desires take precedence over her needs."

"Oh, Jonas." Charlotte hated that he blamed himself. The "what if" game was futile and there were no winners. "I felt the same way about what happened to Ryan," she reminded him softly, capturing his attention.

He shook his head. "Ryan understood the dangers of going up when he wasn't a hundred percent."

She stopped walking and faced him. "Take your own advice, Jonas." He looked deep into her eyes and smiled slightly.

"It's hard. My head tells me I couldn't have predicted what happened to Ivy and yet my heart…"

She stepped closer and placed her hands on his shoulders. "I understand exactly what you mean, but I believe both Ivy and Ryan wouldn't want us to keep blaming ourselves forever for what happened."

His eyes held hope. "I want to let it go. It's such a heavy burden to carry."

She did something that was as much a surprise to her as it was to Jonas. Charlotte wrapped her arms around his waist and tugged him close. She held him and could feel his body quaking.

"This is something we can work on together." She wanted to try to move past the guilt. She had to. If she didn't, she'd spend the rest of her life living in regret.

Jonas pulled away and searched Charlotte's face. For reasons he couldn't let himself explore, going through this with Charlotte made him feel better.

"We should probably keep going," he said softly, but he didn't want to. More than anything he wanted this to be over.

And then…

Best not to go there. He couldn't lose someone else that he cared about. Ivy and the baby had almost broken him.

Charlotte let him go and stepped back. "You're right." She shifted the conversation back to the task at hand. "I promised Lainey's grandmother I would bring her home safely, and I would hate to put Abram's life in jeopardy after he went out of his way to assist us."

"Abram's smart." Jonas searched the woods around them. He couldn't explain why he was so much more on edge than before except because of what they'd gone through.

"I see something up ahead." Charlotte pointed.

Through the darkness and fog he was able to make out a dark shape. "It looks like some type of shelter."

Annie reached the structure when it dawned on Jonas what it was. "That's one of the forest service's lookout stations. They have several around. During the fire season, they're manned to help prevent fires."

The dog waited near the entrance.

Jonas opened the door, and he, Charlotte and the dog went inside. He'd explored this station as well as some of the others before. The building consisted of a circular room and a set of stairs in the middle leading up to the top level where the lookout station was located.

"Wait," he said, remembering. "There's a set of walkie-talkies and binoculars on the top level."

Charlotte clicked on the flashlight and started for the stairs. He went after her and they climbed until they reached the lookout area.

"Over there." Jonas spotted the walkie-talkies the rangers used to communicate during fires. "There's the binoculars."

Charlotte grabbed the walkie-talkie. "This is Deputy Charlotte Walker. Is anyone within range?" She tried several channels without an answer. "We're not close enough to a receiver. Can you see anything through the binoculars?"

He focused below. "Nothing but darkness."

She blew out a sigh. "We'll take the walkie talkies with us and the binoculars. Once this is over, we'll return them to the station."

While it was nice to be out of the dampness and cold, staying in one place for long was a bad idea. Jonas slowly descended the steps with Charlotte right behind him.

On the ground floor, Annie stood alert near the door.

Charlotte went over to the closet and opened it. "There's bottled water." She handed him a water and took one for herself and gave some to the dog. "There are some heavy fireproof jackets inside. They'll keep us warmer."

He drank deep. "I'll take the warmth over the weight any day."

She smiled up at him and slipped on one of the jackets and gave him the other.

Jonas shrugged into the jacket. "Let's get out of here." Jonas slung the binoculars strap around his neck and took up walking in the direction they'd been heading.

Charlotte tried the walkie-talkie once more and shook her head before sticking it into her pocket. "Hopefully we'll get into range soon enough."

Though still some distance from the base of the Root Mountains, the ground beneath their feet had been steadily climbing.

Jonas's skin crawled—he felt as if danger could be coming at them from any direction.

"So, you still enjoy trapping in the mountains?" Charlotte asked him.

"I wasn't so sure I would anymore. Last winter was the first time since…" He hadn't been able to do much trapping before because everywhere he looked, his mistakes taunted him.

"I know what you mean. I haven't been up to the mountain where Ryan fell since his death." She chanced a look his way. "We used to love hiking that mountain. We did it so many times but since then…"

He of all people understood. "It's hard. People expect you to move on and I suppose it's the right thing to do, but it's still hard."

"Yes. My friends have all tried to fix me up with someone new, but I can't." She shook her head.

For some reason, the fact her friends wanted to set Charlotte up didn't sit well with him, but Jonas decided to let it go.

"Did you hear something?" Charlotte asked and he focused on their surroundings.

"No, nothing."

She shook her head. "Perhaps I'm being paranoid, but I thought I heard something."

"It could be an animal, but to be safe, let's keep moving." The tension in his stomach churned out acid when Annie suddenly stopped, the hair on her back raising. The dog let out a low growl.

"What is it?" Charlotte barely got the words out before the woods around them moved. The dog charged forward. A half dozen men stepped from the trees.

NINE

"No, Annie, stop." Charlotte called out to her partner when one of the men aimed his weapon at the charging animal.

Annie halted abruptly. The man lowered his weapon. With an order from someone in charge, the soldiers advanced on them with precision. None appeared concerned about her K-9 partner, but they didn't know Annie. She was a warrior and zealous when it came to defending Charlotte.

"Drop your weapons." The order came from the same person. A tanned man dressed entirely in black wore a knit cap pulled down low. The look on his face was like looking into darkness itself.

The ones surrounding them halted a few feet away, with their weapons trained on Charlotte and Jonas.

Annie moved to Charlotte's side unopposed.

Charlotte's heart sank. This was all on her. She should have gone with Lainey and Abram to the station. If she had, there would be a team to back her up before heading to Harley's. Instead, her actions had led to her and Jonas's capture.

Jonas kept the handgun leveled at the one calling the shots while he glanced her way.

"You'd be foolish to try. Drop it." The man calling out the orders stepped closer to Jonas.

Charlotte slowly lowered her weapon to the ground. "Do as he says. They'll kill us otherwise." While she prayed that wouldn't happen if they surrendered, she and Jonas posed a threat to their illegal operation. They were better off dead.

Jonas slowly lowered his weapon to the ground.

"Get them." The leader ordered one of his people to confiscate their weapons.

The subordinate kept his attention trained on Charlotte and Jonas as he advanced. He grabbed the weapons and retreated to his position.

"Search them. There could be other weapons," the man in charge ordered.

A thorough check gave up the walkie-talkie from Charlotte's pocket. The binoculars were ripped from Jonas's neck.

Once he was certain they were no longer a threat, the boss stepped to within a few inches of them. "Where are they?"

Charlotte recoiled from the anger on his face. "I don't know what you're talking about."

"The girl and the Amish man. They escaped. Where are they?"

Charlotte shot Jonas a look. Abram and Lainey had been captured but managed to get away. If they'd been forced to hide out to avoid being caught, it would explain the delay in them reaching the sheriff.

"I have no idea where they are," Charlotte told him while her brain struggled to come up with a way to escape their captors.

"You're lying." He turned his full attention to her. "The girl was with you—we know that much. You went to the Amish man for help. So, I'll ask you again, where would they go?"

Charlotte held his gaze and tried not to show her fear. "We split up. I have no idea where they are."

"Then you'll help us find them." He motioned to several of the men who grabbed hers and Jonas's arms. "Bring them." She and Jonas were hauled along with the group while Charlotte gave the hand signal to Annie to fall back. She wouldn't put it past these creeps to shoot her partner.

Annie fell back and trotted into the woods while garnering only a passing notice from a few of their captors. Annie would keep following. The first opportunity she got she'd come to Charlotte's aide.

They were heading to the camp. With her and Jonas in custody, there were only two people standing in the way of the crimes committed here being buried forever. She and Jonas didn't have much time to figure out a way to escape.

Charlotte caught Jonas's attention. *We have to escape*, she mouthed and hoped he understood enough. He slowly nodded and she whispered, "As soon as we have the chance."

After walking for some time, the camp came into view.

"Get them inside and watch them," the boss said. "I'm checking in." The leader stopped in front of the dining hall. The two men guarding her and Jonas clutched their arms and headed for it. "You two—go with them."

Charlotte's heart sank. There would be four to overpower.

Inside the dining hall, she and Jonas were forced into chairs.

"Don't try anything," one of their guards barked at them.

The four stepped a little away. Charlotte couldn't believe those men hadn't tied them up. She watched as they walked around the dining room. Most appeared on edge. She leaned over closer to Jonas. "This is our only chance. We won't have long. I have no doubt they'll kill us soon once we can't help them find Lainey and Abram."

"What do you want to do?"

"I'm going to fake becoming ill. When I fall on the floor, call them over. Do whatever is necessary to overpower them quickly."

He swallowed deeply and held her gaze. Both recognized the impossible odds they faced.

Charlotte closed her eyes. *Give us strength, Lord. We need Your help.*

Though she'd grown up in a Christian home and was a Christian, Ryan's passing had shaken her faith. She'd stopped talking to God. If she were being honest, she blamed Him as well as herself for Ryan's death. Now, when she was at the end of her strength, Charlotte realized she and Jonas needed God's help to live.

As soon as the final amen slipped through her head, she went into action and shoved the chair back before dropping to the floor writhing around.

"Help, there's something wrong with her," Jonas called out.

All four men ran their way.

"Get up. What do you think you're doing?" one asked.

While all four looked down at her, Jonas jumped up to his feet and grabbed his chair. He swung it at the nearest man and hit him hard. He fell to the floor, knocked out. The closest man charged for Jonas who wielded the chair again.

Charlotte took advantage of the distraction and snatched the weapon of the man standing closest. She vaulted to her feet and ordered, "Get your hands in the air." Instead of obeying, he dove for her. It was going to be a fight to the end. She didn't want to fire the weapon and alert others. Instead, Charlotte slammed it into his forehead before he grabbed her. A look of surprise was almost comical before his eyes snapped shut and he dropped to the floor near his partner.

"Put it down," the third guard demanded with his gun aimed at Charlotte's head.

"I'm not going to do that." Charlotte was surprised at the steadiness in her voice as she trained her weapon on him.

A crashing sound jerked her opponent's attention away. Jonas was struggling with the second conscious man. It was all she needed to quickly slam the butt of the handgun against his head. With her guy incapacitated, she rushed to assist Jonas.

He was pinned against the table. Charlotte grabbed the perp and pulled him off. Before she could get the weapon into position to threaten, the man whirled and slammed his fist against her jaw, sending her flying backward. Her attacker reached her in two quick steps and grabbed her throat. Desperate, Charlotte's frightened gaze spotted Jonas once more with the chair. *Hold on*, she told herself and tried not to panic.

The chair smashed against the man's back. He fell forward and the weight of the unconscious man drove her to the floor.

Charlotte scrambled out from under him with Jonas's help.

"Check for weapons and phones," she told him and felt inside her perp's pockets. He had a weapon but no phone. After a thorough exam, they had four additional weapons and clips but no cells, which meant no means to communicate with her people, and Charlotte had no idea where Lainey and Abram were.

"Let's get out of here. I don't see how others didn't hear the commotion." Charlotte ran to the rear exit and slowly opened the door. Jonas slipped out behind her. The woods were just a short distance from the back of the dining room.

"Run and don't stop," she told him. "We don't have long before they come after us." They fled.

Annie appeared in the woods in front of them. Charlotte and Jonas reached the trees and kept going.

"We need to get back on track with finding the women, but I'm scared for Lainey and Abram." Charlotte held the denim jacket out to Annie. Her partner detected the trace scent left behind by its owner and veered to the left. Charlotte and Jonas ran after the dog, happy to get as far away from their attackers as possible.

They kept pace with Annie until they'd put a significant amount of space between themselves and the camp. "I believe we can slow down now," Charlotte said. "As happy as I am that Abram and Lainey were able to escape their captors, if they're still in the woods, both are in danger. You've seen the amount of people searching for us." She hated to consider how frightened Lainey must be.

"Abram knows this countryside well," Jonas reminded her. "He will keep them hidden."

Charlotte smiled. She would have to trust Abram to keep them safe, but one thing was glaringly clear. "There's no one coming to help us, Jonas. We're on our own." She looked behind them. Not a single light showed.

His attention went to the dog. "You said Annie's collar has a GPS signal attached to it. Your people might already be tracking us."

He was trying to put a positive spin on the situation, and she was grateful. Charlotte searched his face. If she'd called for backup to search for Lainey instead of going it alone, none of this would be happening.

He must have seen the doubt in her eyes because he said, "This isn't your fault, Charlotte—none of it. You were trying to help a friend in trouble. You saved Lainey's life."

Charlotte wished she felt the same way. "And now Lainey and Abram are both in danger like us."

He stepped closer and brushed his fingers across her cheek, sending a chill trailing after his touch. "We're still alive and fighting. After everything we've gone through, we haven't given up."

She leaned into his hand for a moment. Was it just the circumstances that had thrown them together that was responsible for the way she felt when she looked into his eyes? Honestly, Charlotte barely knew him…except that he was strong and courageous and hadn't left her side despite facing down death multiple times.

This isn't real…

It couldn't be. Because if she were capable of feeling something for Jonas, it meant she'd begun letting go of Ryan and she wasn't ready.

Charlotte reached up and clasped Jonas's hand for a second before letting him go.

"Then it's settled," she said in a breathy voice. "We go after Harley and the women."

Jonas slowly agreed. "We better keep moving," he said in a voice as unsteady as hers. "Annie's getting ahead and there could be more out here looking for us."

She shivered at the thought. It was terrifying that so many were coming after them. How big was this operation and who was the person calling the shots?

For the moment, the bad guys were the last thing on his mind. Jonas kept replaying the tender moment between himself and Charlotte. For the first time since he'd lost Ivy, he had feelings for another woman and it scared him. He'd lived a life of solitude for the past six years, living in self-imposed isolation because he didn't believe himself worthy of being happy again. Yet, despite their circumstances, Charlotte made him smile whenever he glanced at her.

If he let her into his heart—if she became important to him like Ivy and their baby had—could he survive if the relationship didn't work out? His heart was so fragile now. Jonas wasn't so sure he'd recover from another loss.

"I still think we're missing something." The woman dominating his thoughts spoke, giving him the excuse he needed not to examine his heart too closely.

"Such as?" He cleared his throat to cover up the roughness that had everything to do with her.

"Like who is really in charge of this organization because it sure isn't Harley."

Jonas didn't see Harley as a leader, either. The man had a temper and had caused plenty of scenes when things didn't go his way. And the violence he showed toward Betty spoke of someone dangerous.

"I've been thinking about the times Harley has gotten arrested and somehow gotten off. I believe the real person in charge is someone with enough power to get him out of anything."

Jonas stopped at the very idea. "Like someone in law enforcement?"

It was clear she hadn't considered the option. "Oh, no, I sure hope you're wrong. I'm friends with everyone in the sheriff's department, and each is as good as they get. I trust them," she stressed.

"What about the local police?" Jonas heard noises coming from the direction of the camp.

Charlotte froze. "They're coming. Let's go."

They hit a fast pace.

While worrying about those coming after them, Jonas thought on the little he'd heard about the local police. Most seemed nice enough. It was a small department. Was it possible someone from the force was running an illegal trafficking ring?

"Jonas, they're gaining," Charlotte whispered. "We've got to get out of sight." She looked around for someplace to hide.

Charlotte pointed to a spot that was overgrown with brush. With Annie close, they knelt behind the camouflage, huddled close together.

After a handful of tense moments, several sets of footsteps tramped through the woods near them. Jonas clenched his hand and held his breath.

"Any sign of them?" a man whispered almost inaudibly. Jonas recognized the voice of the one calling the shots from earlier.

"Nothing yet but they can't have gotten far," another replied lowly.

"This is the last thing we need," the leader responded. "Especially with the deal almost in place."

Each man's voice was little more than a whisper. Jonas turned his head slightly, uncertain he'd heard correctly until he saw Charlotte's eyes widen. She'd been right. There was something more going on.

"Yeah, well, if this gets out, you can forget about a deal. Harley set all of this in motion," a new man Jonas didn't recognize was now speaking.

"Harley has no business being in any form of leadership and I've told Elliott this for a while. I figured it was only a matter of time before Harley screwed something up and got us all caught." This was the leader again. Jonas strained to hear him clearly. "I tell you what, if those two get to a phone and bring the sheriff's department into this, we'd better clear out quickly and get rid of our weakest link fast, as well as the girls."

No one answered that dreadful claim.

Anger rose inside Jonas.

Everyone involved would disappear into the darkness and probably set up operations in another part of the state.

Conversation ended and soon those following them were on the move. Jonas waited through a long, intense silence before he finally rose and held his hand out to Charlotte.

"It should be safe to start walking again," he told her. "The only problem is, they're heading in the same direction we need to go."

"We'll have to give them a wide berth. We can't afford to get captured again. Too much is at stake."

Jonas replayed the conversation he'd heard in his head. "Are you acquainted with someone by the name of Elliott?" He was surprised one of the men had mentioned a name.

"No..." Charlotte's hand flew to her mouth. "Wait, I am...but it can't be him. He's a police officer and a friend of mine."

Jonas's stomach plummeted. "We said the person in charge could be in law enforcement."

Charlotte clearly didn't want to consider it might be her friend. "But Elliott Shores has a wife and two little girls. It can't be him." Her troubled eyes searched his face hoping he would deny it. For her sake, Jonas hoped he was wrong.

Once more he thought about all the different vehicles he'd seen traveling down his dirt road toward Harley's. Most of the time it was at night. Occasionally during the day.

Jonas recalled one time in particular. He'd stepped out on his porch. A car he didn't know passed by his place just as it was getting dark. There were four men inside. He hadn't recognized any of them.

"I really hope this isn't Elliott, but he was acquainted with Ryan and we can't afford to rule him out at this point. Elliott works in the department's human trafficking task force."

The irony of the statement was not lost on Jonas. "If this is him, then he'd have access to what groups the police are targeting, and he'd understand how to avoid the area where other suspected rings operate."

Charlotte clearly wasn't ready to accept that her friend might be the enemy. "Elliott is more of the type to take orders than give them, although he'd kill me for saying as much." She seemed to realize what she'd said and clamped her hand over her mouth again.

"I guess it's possible there's another side to him you haven't seen," Jonas said gently. "If he's involved in trafficking and has the gall to work on the police department's task force to bring down human trafficking rings, then he's obviously not the person you thought you knew."

She shuddered. "You're right."

Annie kept her nose to the ground, sniffing out the scent belonging to the young woman who possessed the denim jacket.

If this Elliott Shores was involved, perhaps he wasn't the one in charge and just another person in a large organization.

"If he is involved, it's a frightening thought." Charlotte sighed. "How many others in law enforcement are working for this organization?"

The world in which these things took place was one he couldn't imagine. "There are times like this when I miss being Amish," he told her honestly. "They are far from perfect, but it seems like the *Englischer* world is so far removed from those simple ways."

"You're right—it is. Do you think you'd ever return to the faith?" she asked, her attention on his face.

He answered the question honestly. "I am no longer the same person."

"But you still live their way for the most part. You don't own a car or a phone."

He could tell she thought this odd. "I guess it's hard to completely let go of the only way of life I've ever known. I am content with my life as it is." Was he? He had been simply existing for so long. Hiding out on his little piece of property and holding vigil to his dead wife.

Jonas had lost track of how long they'd been on the run. The long time spent moving without rest were taking their toll. He tried to figure out how many hours had passed and couldn't. A guess would be they'd started a new day by now, which meant they may have hours still of walking in the dark before the sun would guide them.

The sudden sound of voices speaking loudly, without trying to disguise their presence, was so strange that it took him a second to figure out it was real.

He and Charlotte found a safe place to hide and headed for it. She gave a hand signal for the dog to follow.

"Where's it coming from?" he whispered close to her ear. The fog that continued to make life miserable also made determining the location of the sounds hard. When she didn't answer, he turned his head her way. "Charlotte?"

Her huge green eyes found him. "It's coming from straight ahead and I recognize one of the voices. It's Elliott Shores." A dirty cop.

TEN

"Let's get out of here. Now." Yet before Charlotte had taken a single step, a snatch of conversation stopped her in her tracks. She grabbed Jonas's arm, keeping him there.

The disbelief on Jonas's face confirmed he'd also heard what was said. "They have Lainey and Abram…"

"I want to get closer to see if we can figure out where they're being held," Charlotte said. "We stand a chance at rescuing them."

Jonas immediately shook his head. "Not a good idea."

"We have to try." Charlotte signaled for Annie to stay while she carefully moved forward one tree at a time, Jonas trailing her, until they were close enough to hear the conversation clearly.

"They're holding the girl and that Amish man at the abandoned Christian camp," Elliott was saying, "I want to speak to them further and see who else they've told about us."

"What about the other two? One's a cop. Shouldn't we be focused on them?" The man in the knit cap who was giving orders before didn't seem to like the change in plans.

"They're not going anywhere," Elliot said. "We have men stationed in the woods and on all the roads leading to town, and there's no houses around for them to call for help." Elliott's annoyed-sounding sigh reached her. Charlotte went emotionally numb. Someone she called a friend was involved in this terrible operation.

"We have far more pressing things to deal with. Harley needs to be found and dealt with," Elliott announced to his people.

They wanted Harley dead.

"You want us to take care of the matter while you take some men and speak to the two at the camp?" the leader from before said without any hint of remorse.

"That's not our place. We'll let him take care of Harley."

Charlotte's attention pivoted to Jonas. Elliott just confirmed he wasn't the one in calling the shots. There was someone bigger heading this up.

Multiple footsteps started toward them.

Charlotte ducked out of sight along with Jonas. Flashlights panned all around while she held her breath and prayed Elliott's people hadn't heard the movement.

While they hunkered down, the number of people with Elliott kept coming. She counted almost a dozen. After the last person passed by, Charlotte let go of her breath. At least they weren't spotted.

Lainey and Abram needed help. Once Elliott's people figured out the two didn't know anything, they'd be dead.

Lord, please keep those young women safe until we can help them.

"Let's give them time to get ahead of us before we follow," Jonas whispered, coming to the same conclusion as Charlotte.

Seconds ticked by. "It should be safe to leave," Charlotte said and called Annie to her side. Keeping her attention on those ahead, a dreadful thought turned Charlotte's stomach. "What if Elliott was the one who ordered Ryan's death? Or worse, what if he killed Ryan and Michaela?" The thought of Ryan being betrayed by someone Charlotte called a friend sickened her. She remembered all the time she and Elliott had discussed what happened. Elliott was a witness to how devastated she was by losing Ryan. He'd been a huge support. Was it all an act?

"We don't know anything for certain yet."

She forced herself to let go of the betrayal she felt toward Elliott. She had a job to do. "I pray Lainey's grandmother decided to call the sheriff's office instead of waiting. If she did, Sheriff McCallister will realize I have Annie with me, and he'll check her GPS."

But she couldn't count on this happening in time to save Lainey and Abram. "I hope she did. There are so many men," Charlotte said. "Our only chance to save Abram and Lainey is to get in and out without the bad guys figuring out we were there. Still, we can't keep wandering through the woods without eventually getting caught."

She couldn't get what Elliott had said out of her head.

"I'm sorry your friend Elliott is involved," Jonas said.

"Me, too." She gave a sad smile. "With Elliott's involvement, we must look at this entire organization differently. There could be more people in the law enforcement community involved." Knowing that someone who had sworn to protect the ones who were being trafficked was involved was a heart-wrenching thought.

Charlotte's heart broke over the decision they were now forced to make, choosing between saving the innocent girls and rescuing her friend and Abram.

"I sure hope we can find Lainey and Abram soon and save them. I have a feeling time is running out on the girls. We won't have long to reach them before they're moved. I wonder if Harley realizes his people have turned on him?"

Jonas nodded. "It would explain why no one's been able to reach him. If Harley is one small cog in this operation, would he be aware of the next step after he'd delivered the girls?"

She thought about his question. "Probably not. It sounds as if Harley is one who kidnaps the girls and from there someone else takes them to another location. From what we've overheard, Harley has been getting sloppy for some time and has become a liability. If he was the one who took Michaela and had to let her go, then I don't understand why they would trust him to keep grabbing girls."

Jonas rubbed his beard thoughtfully. "Unless Harley has something on Elliott, or the real person in charge."

Charlotte hadn't considered it before. "Harley's not above blackmail."

"No, he isn't. Using that theory, I'm wondering if perhaps he wasn't the one who killed Michaela but saw the person who did—Elliott or the one in charge. He might even have evidence against them."

Her eyes widened. "If we can get to Harley and save the women, we might be able to talk him into cooperating." Her thoughts went to Betty. "I can't imagine Betty being aware of what Harley was doing, but she might have seen something useful."

Jonas shook his head. "I guess, but in my opinion, she's another victim like those girls."

Charlotte didn't want to think about Betty paying the price for Harley's crimes with her life. "She wasn't at the house."

"He may have her with him. He may have forced her to go. If so, she's bound to have figured out what Harley's been up to by now. She could be a major witness against him if we can convince her to cooperate."

Charlotte shook her head. So many innocent people's lives were in danger all because of greed.

Since it was dark and Jonas probably hadn't seen Elliott clearly, she described him. Thin, barely five foot eight. His sandy brown hair had been receding for some time. "Was he the one with Betty when you heard her scream?"

The furrow between Jonas's brows deepened. "He doesn't sound like the same man. The person I saw had dark hair and was at least six-two or more."

She sighed. "That's not Elliott. I was hoping we could connect him to Harley and…" And what? She had no idea what Elliott being at Harley's house would prove other than they knew each other.

"It was a good thought." Jonas glanced around at their surroundings. "We have to be getting close to the camp by now."

"I'm not sure what to do once we reach it," she admitted. "Hopefully, we can locate where they're holding Lainey and Abram and find a way to get them out."

They kept moving, Annie at their side, keeping a safe distance from Elliot and the men ahead of them. They'd been walking around in circles for hours since they'd left Abram's house and were no closer to understanding what was happening or escaping than when they'd first begun the trek to Harley's house.

Up ahead, the woods cleared. Charlotte pointed to the back of the closest building. If they could make it there, perhaps they could find a way to get close enough to figure out where Lainey and Abram were being held.

She and Jonas slipped to the back of the building and

then down the side until they were near the front but still hidden.

"I don't see anything," Charlotte whispered. It stood to reason they would have moved Lainey and Abram out of sight.

"Over there." He pointed to the building where she and Jonas had been held before. "There's a bunch of soldiers near the front."

"That's it. Let's circle around behind and see if we can get closer." They started toward the dining hall while doing their best to stay hidden.

Several times, Charlotte halted abruptly when snatches of conversation seemed to indicate the men guarding the building were on high alert.

"They're expecting us," she whispered to Jonas. "We can't get captured." They were Lainey and Abram's only hope in avoiding certain death.

Once they reached the back of the dining hall, Charlotte made sure there wasn't anyone standing guard around back. Advancing to the building, she saw that the windows were too high up to see inside without being on the porch.

She tentatively managed the first step and held her breath when a board creaked under her foot. When the people inside didn't appear to hear she climbed the rest of them until she was standing on the porch.

Jonas avoided the noisy board and traversed the stairs. Edging closer to the windows, Charlotte stood on one side while Jonas moved to the other.

The building was mostly dark. Someone had lit a couple of candles and placed them around to give light.

Charlotte searched the dining room until she spotted Lainey and Abram in the corner and pointed to their location. Both were seated at one of the tables, their arms secured behind them. The men weren't taking any chances of them escaping like Charlotte and Jonas had.

She could see the strain on Lainey's face even from here. Charlotte couldn't imagine the pain she was suffering from the gunshot wound with her hands secured.

She looked around the room. Where were the men watching them?

While she contemplated the best course of action, several men came from the kitchen area. More candles were lit. She recognized Elliott right away and noticed something she hadn't been able to detect before. Elliott was dressed in his police uniform.

He stepped over to where Lainey and Abram were held. "So, we meet again," he said with a smirk on his face.

He'd run into them before.

"You tricked us," Lainey said as she looked at him in fear. "You let us believe you were going to help us."

Charlotte's shoulders slumped. Elliott had used his position as a police officer to lure them into believing he was one of the good guys. He and his people had probably been looking for Lainey and Abram the way they were her and Jonas. Lainey would have trusted Elliott because of the uniform.

"Yes, I did, and you believed me, so we both messed up." Though Elliott wasn't a big man, his current position of authority over these two innocent people probably made him feel important. Charlotte did her best to control her revulsion. Her first instinct was to charge inside and confront Elliott with what she suspected. But if she did, she'd be signing all their death warrants.

He deliberately put pressure on Lainey's wound. She screamed in pain. Elliott seemed pleased. "Where are they going?" Elliott didn't waste time getting to what he wanted to know. "They were with you at one point. They sent you to get help. You have some idea what's planned."

Lainey dropped her eyes to the table without answering. Elliott's face twisted as his anger grew. He grabbed hold of Abram's head and pointed his weapon at his temple. "Speak or he dies."

"No, don't!" Lainey pleaded. "I don't have any idea where they are now. They were supposed to go to Harley's house and..."

Elliott leaned in closer, likely to intimidate. "And what?"

"And they were going to try and get Charlotte's phone back."

Elliott jerked back. After a long minute he let Abram go.

Charlotte bit her lip and prayed Elliott wouldn't realize the real reason why she and Jonas had returned to the place where she'd been taken.

"They needed a way to call for help in case we failed to reach the sheriff's department," Lainey added to make her story believable.

Elliott stared her down for a long moment. "They were at the house but got away. Where would they go from there?"

Lainey stared at him with her eyes filled with tears. "The plan was to get the phone and call for help."

Elliott shook his head. "They didn't. The phone wasn't at the house. Harley has it. So, I'll ask you again, where would they go from there?"

Lainey struggled to come up with an answer. "I don't know," she insisted again.

Her response displeased Elliott. Once more he pushed his fingers onto her gunshot. Lainey bit her bottom lip to keep from screaming again.

One thing became very clear—Elliott wasn't the smartest person. He didn't notice Lainey was making up her answers.

"All right, let's suppose you're telling the truth," he said. "You must have some idea where they'd go?"

Lainey watched him with huge fearful eyes.

When she didn't answer, Elliott stuck his face inches from hers. "Who did *you* tell about what was happening?"

"No one. You found us before we reached a phone."

"Oh, no," Charlotte whispered. If Elliott was convinced no one was coming to assist, he had no reason to keep Lainey and Abram alive.

"Good." Pleased, Elliott stepped away, and Charlotte couldn't hear what he said.

Soon, Elliott and his goons left the dining hall. This was it. She moved to Jonas's side. "We have to act now."

Jonas slipped to the back door. Opening it made only the slightest of sounds, yet both Lainey and Abram heard it.

Charlotte placed her finger to her lips before Lainey could say a word.

Once they reached the table, Jonas examined Lainey and Abram's ties. Their hands were secured behind the chair backs. "We need some way to cut their restraints."

"I have a knife inside my pocket," Abram told them. "No one searched us."

Jonas retrieved it and cut both their restraints away. "We must hurry. They'll come back soon."

Charlotte stayed close to Lainey as they covered the space to the door. Slipping outside, she ran with Lainey toward the trees where Annie waited. A heartbeat later, Jonas and Abram reached the safe spot.

"I'm so happy to see you." Lainey said through tears. "I was afraid they'd killed you."

"I'm happy you're both okay," Charlotte replied, smiling at Abram, too, "How's your shoulder?" Her mouth thinned as she recalled Elliott's actions.

"It's okay," Lainey assured her even though she appeared quite pale from the ordeal.

"We need to keep moving." Charlotte started through the trees, not sure if they were heading anywhere close to the direction of Harley's mountain house.

Jonas kept close attention behind them. "So far, I don't see anyone following yet. As soon as they realize Lainey and Abram are gone, they'll figure we're involved."

"I have something that might help." Lainey dug into her pocket and pulled out a cell phone.

"Where did you get this?" Charlotte asked, unable to accept what she was seeing.

Lainey smiled at her reaction. "One of those men left it on the counter before they tied us up. I grabbed it and stuffed it in my pocket." Charlotte didn't miss how Abram gazed at Lainey with what looked like fondness and admiration as she held the phone out to Charlotte.

"Thank you, Lainey." Charlotte accepted the phone and tried to call 9-1-1. The frustration of the call not going through was enough to double her over. "There's no service here. Let's keep going. Hopefully, we can pick up some along the way."

Flashlights pierced the darkness behind them. "Someone's coming. They'll spread out and search every square inch of this place." Jonas's words reinforced the urgency.

"He's right." Charlotte slipped the cell phone into her pocket and grabbed hold of Lainey's arm once more. Together with Jonas and Abram they ran.

At this point, they were simply trying to survive. She'd figure out the best way to get to the girls after they were safe. For the moment, saving the lives of those with her was the most important thing. Because if they died, the secrets that Elliott and Harley were willing to kill to cover up would die with them.

Jonas studied the lights. "They're going in a different direction. At least that's something. Still, we have no idea how many others are out there and have been alerted to our escape. We need help." And he had no idea how to get it for them.

"Give us a minute," Charlotte told Lainey and Abram. "Annie, stay." She reached for Jonas's arm and tugged him out of earshot. Both Lainey and Abram huddled together, their troubled gazes darting around the darkness.

She tried the cell phone once more before shaking her head. "I'm still not picking up any service. What do you suggest?"

Jonas kept his fading hope to himself. It seemed everything they tried ended badly. He ran his hand through his damp hair and struggled to come up with a plan to get them out of this mess. To pick up service, they'd need to get out of the trees. He could think of only one way. "What about the fire tower from earlier? I don't believe it's that far from here. The service should be better."

Relief flashed across Charlotte's face. "You're right. It's perfect." Her smile disappeared just as quickly. "Jonas, those girls. They're in danger every second Harley has them."

"We have no choice. We can't let them die."

She shook her head. "You should stay with Lainey and Abram. Get to the tower and call for help."

He stepped closer. "I'm not letting you go after Harley alone. We have no idea what kind of state he's in or if there are others with him." And he cared too much about her to let her go it alone.

She didn't look away, and for a long moment their fears slipped into the background and it was just her and him, and he had hope again. Despite facing death and not being sure they were going to make it out of this thing alive, he had hope.

"I don't think it's a good idea for Lainey and Abram to go on alone," she said, breaking the moment.

Jonas held her gaze. "If we want to try and save those girls, I don't think we have a choice. The stakes are higher now. Those men have a deal to make and will try to wrap it up quickly because they think the sheriff has been called. Elliott will contact the people watching the girls soon enough and have them moved. This might be our only chance to rescue them."

She glanced over to where Abram and Lainey stood, obviously trying to make the right decision. He knew she didn't want to make a mistake. "Okay," she said finally. "Do you think Abram will be able to find the tower with Lainey?"

Jonas had no doubt. "Abram is a *gut* hunter. He will be able to locate it. It's best if they stay there at the tower. They'll be out of the elements, and it will make it easier for the sheriff's people to find them. They should be safe enough." Unless Elliott and his people searched the tower.

It wasn't necessary to say the words out loud. Charlotte understood the risks.

"We'd better hurry," she said, breaking the silence he was happy to let go on forever. Here in the small space between them existed nothing dangerous or evil.

But the people coming after them needed to silence them. Even though they didn't fully grasp the truth of how far-reaching this operation was, what he and Charlotte had seen was enough to put people away.

He reluctantly stepped back. Together they told Lainey and Abram the plan.

"What if we're caught?" Lainey asked anxiously. "I'm afraid."

Charlotte reached for her hand. "You'll be okay. Abram will be with you."

Abram nodded. "I'm familiar with where the tower is. I'll get us there safely. And Charlotte is right. We should be secure there."

Jonas prayed that would prove to be the truth.

Charlotte handed the cell phone back to Lainey. "We are counting on you and Abram to reach the tower and call for help."

Lainey slowly accepted it.

"Good," Charlotte said. "Keep trying 9-1-1 along the way, and once you get service, tell them what happened."

"But where will you be?" Lainey asked.

"We're going to try and save the rest of the girls." She turned to Lainey. "Can you tell them we're heading to Harley Owens's house in the mountains so the sheriff and his people can find us?"

Lainey assured her they would.

Jonas clapped his former *bruder*-in-law's shoulder. "Be careful, Abram. If they catch any of us again, they won't hesitate to kill."

Abram's chin rose. "I will be careful. There's a lot at stake." He glanced Lainey's way, and she looked at him as Ivy had once looked at Jonas.

Was there something forming between these two or was it simply the dangerous situation they faced making Abram protective?

"Here, take this," Jonas handed his friend one of the weapons they'd taken.

Charlotte did the same to Lainey, who reluctantly took

the weapon. It was a good thing they'd taken all four guns from the guards the last time they escaped capture. "Just remember what your father taught you about using a weapon."

Lainey nodded.

Abram reached for Lainey's arm and started away.

Charlotte stared after them for a moment. "I sure hope we didn't send them to their deaths."

The reality of those words had him struggling for something positive to say. "Abram is a skilled shot. Although he's Amish and a pacifist, he'll do whatever is necessary to defend Lainey and himself. We made the best decision we could to help everyone involved. We'd better get going. It's not wise to stay in one place for too long."

The flashlights had moved away from their location. If their pursuers kept going the way they were, then Abram and Lainey should be safe.

Charlotte wrapped her arms around herself to stay warm as the cold worked its way down deep past the fireman's jacket she wore.

Jonas gathered his bearings and started walking toward the dark silhouette of the mountain that was in the distance. The biggest thought going through his head was all those innocent girls who were being held by Harley. Were they still alive?

He shared his fears with Charlotte. "Harley is all about protecting himself. He won't think twice about killing them if it means saving himself."

Charlotte was on edge like him and constantly reacting to every little sound in the woods. "This is such a terrible situation. I still can't fathom what's happening now might have ties to Ryan and Michaela's deaths."

He'd never been involved in anything as sinister as

murder before. His part in Ivy's death was bad enough, but he couldn't imagine willingly taking someone's life.

Charlotte rubbed her forehead. "I believe Michaela saw something more than what she told us at the party. Whatever it was, she had to die." She stopped so suddenly it had his full attention. "Oh, no." Startled eyes found him. "I think I know what it was."

The expression on her face confirmed this was going to be bad.

ELEVEN

Why hadn't she remembered this before now? With everything that had happened following Ryan's death, she'd just completely forgot.

"What do you remember?" Jonas frowned as he waited.

"Something Michaela's mother told me after her funeral. She said her daughter was convinced someone was following her after the incident at the party. She was scared. She thought it might have something to do with her friend Sasha's disappearance. Her mother urged her to go to the police. She said Michaela planned to reach out and then she disappeared."

She recalled the conversation. "There was no report made with our people. Wyatt checked with the local police, and they hadn't received one, either."

"Unless she did call the police and somehow spoke to Elliott. I know the department has been short staffed from time to time. Elliott mentioned once he'd been forced to answer dispatch calls."

The reality of those words slapped her in the face. "Oh, no. This must be what happened. Michaela's mother was so sure her daughter had called to report what happened."

"She probably did." Jonas's mouth twisted grimly. "She never stood a chance."

Charlotte's heart broke for Michaela and her family. If only she'd reported the stalking to the sheriff's department. Or if Charlotte had followed up with Michaela about the incident at the ranch. At the time, she'd been so caught up in her own grief over losing Ryan that she hadn't been able to function for a long time. "Michaela's family was devastated by her death. They never considered she would take her own life and they did everything possible to get the coroner to change the cause of death from suicide, but he seemed certain she killed herself."

So many people found Michaela's death suspicious. The scene appeared staged, but they also trusted the system and didn't suspect that dirty cops might be involved.

"Dr. McCarthy is usually a reasonable man and he's been the county's coroner for as long as I can remember. My dad thought very highly of him."

"Has he ever been wrong about a cause of death before?"

Charlotte thought about it for a moment. "I don't believe anyone's ever disputed his ruling before." She'd tried to convince him to do additional testing on Michaela to be certain, but he'd gotten angry and told her the cause of death stood as suicide. He'd ruled Ryan's death an accident. At the time, she'd found his change in temper odd, but he'd been quick to soften toward her, saying they couldn't dispute the science. The deaths had rocked the whole community, certainly her whole world, so she'd understood if he was on edge. "Once this is over, we have to seriously look into both deaths." She paused, trying to get her next words out. "What if Dr. McCarthy's involved in what's happening?"

"Could he be the one in charge?"

"I guess." But she had doubts. "He's the coroner for the county. He might be able to fix the cause of death, but he certainly couldn't keep a human trafficking pipeline hidden from the public."

Jonas nodded. "Obviously there's at least one law enforcement officer involved—probably others. It's possible they have people in various positions of authority to keep things moving smoothly."

Charlotte combed her fingers through her tangled hair. "I believe we're beginning to see bits and pieces of a much bigger picture. I just want to find those women and get them out of there safely before it's too late. And then I want to find the people who are responsible for this and put them all in prison for a very long time. I don't think I'll ever forget this case."

Those words echoed through her head reminding her of the one case that had haunted her father during his career. A child had been taken from her home. Her dad and all the local law enforcement agencies had been called out, but the child was never recovered. Her father had kept a photo of the little girl in his wallet. Through the years until he retired, every chance he got he'd go over her file searching for something he might have missed.

There were cases that haunted a person long after they ended. Michaela's case was like that for Charlotte. She hadn't been able to let it go despite the coroner's ruling. She'd gone over every single piece of evidence, every moment of the time on the mountain, and though she hadn't been able to see it, there was something far more sinister involved than an accidental fall and a suicide.

"I can barely stand up anymore. My legs are like jelly," Charlotte said. "Do you think we can stop for a second? I realize time is critical, but we're not going to be any good to anyone if we don't have the strength to save them."

Like him, the hours of walking, the close calls with the enemy, were taking their toll.

"Yes, that's a good idea. I'm struggling as well." Jonas found a place to sit, and he and Charlotte took a break while Annie sniffed around the ground.

In the rush to escape, they were off target. The path Harley used to travel through the woods was more to their left. After resting, he'd get Annie back on the scent.

Right now, Jonas's brain felt like it was covered in the same fog surrounding them. Thinking clearly was nearly impossible. When the previous day had started, his only concern was getting the fence finished and the cows moved. He had no idea the danger that was about to overtake those plans.

The pit that continued to grow in Jonas's stomach warned him bad people and things were closing in on them and the missing women. "Lainey didn't have any idea how many women were in the basement with her, right?" He and Charlotte could be searching for one, two, or half a dozen or more.

"No." Charlotte shifted toward him with regret on her pretty face.

He wouldn't let her apologize for what wasn't her fault. "I'd do it all over again," he said quietly. "When I saw Harley driving your vehicle, I realized you were in danger, and I couldn't stand by and do nothing."

She reached for his hand and held it between hers. "I'm glad you did. If you hadn't, both me and Lainey would be dead, and this whole thing would be swept under the rug." Her expression held admiration. "I owe you my life."

He swallowed deeply, wishing he felt deserving of her faith in him. By his carelessness, Ivy and his child had died. Helping Charlotte had made him somewhat more redeemed.

As he looked into Charlotte's face, he wondered if she hadn't saved *him* in some way. His feelings for Charlotte were changing and his guilt growing. Every time he thought about the way Ivy had loved him unconditionally, this—whatever it was happening between him and Charlotte—felt wrong. Ivy had taken Jonas how he was and hadn't tried to tame his adventurous nature. She'd encouraged him to go trapping when he should have stayed with her. Ivy had deserved a better husband than him. Finding happiness—having a future beyond Ivy—didn't seem right.

Jonas slowly pulled his hand free and rose. "We still have a long way to go, and the countryside will be rough."

After an awkward moment, Charlotte stood as well.

Jonas dusted himself off and started walking. "If we head to the left, we should intersect with the path Harley used to climb the mountain," he said without looking at her.

He knew he'd hurt her by his abrupt change. Another thing to regret. Jonas did his best to shake off the guilt.

By his calculations, they were getting close to daybreak, which meant they'd be arriving at the house where Harley hopefully had the girls around sunrise. It would be better to see in the mountainous terrain, but also dangerous should anyone follow them up the mountain.

"Look, there are tire tracks. We're back on Harley's trail."

Charlotte held the denim jacket out to Annie. The tracks had the dog's attention right away. Once she had the smell of their anonymous woman, she frantically sniffed the air until getting on the scent. When the dog was on track, she was hard to keep up with. Both Jonas and Charlotte raced to stay with her.

"I don't suppose there's a way to slip up on the house without being spotted?" Charlotte asked.

Jonas tried to recall. "I have only been by the house a couple of times and each one I had no idea anyone lived there… I'm not sure if Harley even owns it. He could have just claimed to. I wouldn't put it past him to not tell the truth."

Charlotte watched Annie work the path in front of them. "We can't let him see we're coming."

Jonas didn't respond. His thoughts kept returning to the tender moment he'd almost shared with Charlotte. Until now, he'd been content with his life. His farm was his world. Though he still prayed from time to time, his faith since losing Ivy and his child wasn't strong. It felt as if he were going through the motions most times during the silent prayers over meals. Reading his Bible was a chore that he sometimes found an excuse to skip. He'd been angry with *Gott* for letting Ivy and the baby die. Now, in the middle of a life and death situation, where more than his life was on the line, he found himself asking *Gott* to help them. He didn't want to make another mistake that would cost lives.

"Jonas?"

He jerked his head toward Charlotte and realized she'd stopped walking. "What's wrong?" Immediately he could tell something was.

She pointed to their right. "Someone's coming."

A single flashlight moved through the woods. These couldn't be the same people who had been at the camp. Whoever it was, they were coming from the wrong direction.

"Hurry, let's get out of sight." He instinctively reached for Charlotte's hand, and together they searched for a place to get out of the path of those moving their way.

She called the dog off the track and Annie followed them to their hideout.

Huddled together with Annie, Jonas could almost sense Charlotte's anxiety matching his.

Soon, it became apparent there was more than one person moving through the underbrush. His heart sank. The noise was magnified. It sounded like a dozen or more people, but it was probably only a handful.

"Do we even have an idea where we're going?" one person spoke with obvious agitation.

"Keep quiet!" another snapped. "They could be close. And if we can't find them before they reach the police, it doesn't matter where we're at. It's all over for us."

The first man clearly wasn't going to be quiet. "Wasn't that supposed to be Elliot's job? To keep this off the police's radar? How did the deputy get involved, anyway?"

The group sounded as if they were right on top of Jonas and Charlotte's location.

"Look." The second man had had enough of the complainer. "None of this is Elliott's fault. He tried to fix what Harley messed up. Besides, D.A. is the one who messed up by not getting control over Harley long ago. The guy is a loose cannon and has been for a while."

D.A.? Jonas looked to Charlotte to see if she recognized the name, but she appeared as confused as he was.

"So, keep your mouth shut and do your job if you don't want to end up in the same predicament as Harley. Understood?"

The first man snorted a response Jonas didn't hear and followed after the others. The sound of tromping through the woods echoed all around them, and Jonas had to wonder how much longer he and Charlotte would be able to stay hidden from so many who were determined they weren't going to walk out of the woods alive.

For a long time after the group had left the area, Jonas remained still, kneeling beside Charlotte.

"This just keeps getting more confusing," he said as he rose and took Charlotte's hand. "Do you recognize the initials D.A.?"

She shook her head. "No, I have no idea who they were talking about."

"You have to wonder how many people are involved in this."

Charlotte gathered her heavy jacket closer. "I'm worried. There are so many. While I'm sure we've run into several of the same people, even so, that's a lot of armed soldiers looking for us. They can't afford to let us live. Especially since there's at least one police officer involved in the trafficking ring and possibly the county coroner."

In other words, even if they were able to escape, there were some powerful people who would do their best to cover up everything, and it would be his and Charlotte's word against theirs.

Jonas tried not to lose hope, yet he wondered if, when they reached the house Harley had claimed was his, they would be walking into a trap they wouldn't be able to escape.

As they reached the mountains' foothills, the trees thinned. At the higher altitude the mountains rose above the tree line, nothing more than dark silhouettes against the night sky.

"I realize it's more dangerous for us in the daylight," Charlotte said unsteadily, "but I'm so tired of walking around in the dark."

Jonas smiled as she voiced his sentiments. "Yeah, me, too." At one time following Ivy's death, he'd practically lived in the darkness. Sleep alluded him. He'd spend hours riding or walking his property in search of some relief from his guilt. Slowly, his time in the darkness had ended. Sleep returned and yet the reprieve from the guilt remained with him still.

"You sure you can find Harley's house again in this weather?" Charlotte squinted through the fog that hung all around them.

He shoved aside the things that couldn't be changed. The life he'd imagined living—the family he and Ivy had planned for—was gone, as was the man who'd envisioned it. This shell of the person left in the wake of losing her was all he had left.

"*Jah*—yes, I believe so." He didn't tell her the many times he'd walked to the mountain and to his trapping cabin.

"How are you holding up?" Charlotte asked. Maybe she'd picked up on the strain in his voice.

"I'm fine. Just mulling everything over, I guess."

"Do you believe they made it to the tower…that they're still alive?" Charlotte asked, and he realized who she was talking about. Abram and Lainey.

"I hope so."

Charlotte looked over her shoulder once more. Both she and Jonas were on edge. "I wonder if Harley realizes they're going to kill him. After all, this was all his fault. By taking Lainey, he brought me to his door."

She was right.

"From what it sounded like," she continued, "they don't have a clue where Harley is. They're looking for him and the girls. That might work in our favor. I just hope this D.A. person doesn't have an inkling about Harley's other house." If D.A. was the actual man in charge, once he found Harley's hideout, he'd kill him and the girls, and they'd move their operation to another location. Hopefully they could get there before any of that happened.

"Me, too." Jonas hoped Harley had taken the girls to the place in the mountains. Because if not, then he had no idea where Harley would go next, and they'd risked their lives and probably Lainey's and Abram's for nothing.

Jonas was familiar with the rugged landscape surrounding the mountains. It would take the dog miles to reach an *Englischer* home with a phone. They'd made the right call sending Lainey and Abram to the fire tower with the cell.

"I sure hope Abram and Lainey were able to reach help." Charlotte stared after Annie. She'd said as much earlier, and yet perhaps repeating that thought gave her comfort. "Because otherwise, it's just us and we're extremely outnumbered."

It wasn't the first time they'd voiced that fear tonight. And yet, those words settled around him like a bad feeling. Two or even four against so many left them at a severe disadvantage, and he wasn't sure he could protect Charlotte. He didn't want Charlotte and Abram and Lainey to sacrifice their lives. He didn't want to die and let these terrible people win. There were more lives at stake than just theirs. Many more. They might not be able to save all the women out there who were already entangled in sex trafficking, but he wanted to try to help those who'd been held with Lainey. Because they didn't deserve the nightmare coming their way.

TWELVE

Annie loped out in front of them once more as they continued walking. Charlotte noticed something she hadn't before. "She's limping. Annie, stop."

The dog immediately obeyed her request. Charlotte moved over to the dog and lifted her leg. Annie whined and Charlotte noticed what was wrong. The dog had a cut on her right front paw.

"We need to wrap the paw to limit the damage." Jonas took out his knife and cut away some of his jacket's lining.

"It's okay, Annie." Charlotte held the dog's paw while Jonas wrapped the injury gently.

"That should keep it from hurting as much." He gave Annie a pat and the dog licked his hand in appreciation.

Charlotte chuckled at Annie's response. "Thank you, Jonas, and Annie thanks you. I wonder what happened?"

"There are all sorts of dangers in the woods. It looks as if she stepped on a sharp rock."

Annie still had a slight limp as she walked but she was able to put pressure on the injured paw.

"I guess none of us are going to get through this unscathed." Charlotte pushed her hair from her face. This night had been a roller coaster ride—one innocent people had been forced upon. Yet through it all, Jonas had been there for her. He'd risked his life so many times, starting with diving into the river to pull her and Lainey from her Jeep. And she couldn't deny that his tender ministrations with her dog melted her heart a bit.

She snuck a look his way. Such a strong profile. He was a good man and yet he blamed himself for his wife's death.

Charlotte of all people understood the devastating effects the blame game could have on a person. She'd blamed herself for Ryan's death. Had allowed herself to be frozen in a moment in time and hadn't really been living at all. When she looked at Jonas, she saw something—felt something—that made her want to try, and yet how could she? Ryan was the love of her life. How could she simply move on as if his life and love meant nothing?

She couldn't. Ryan had to mean more to her than that. Time to keep moving.

Before she had the chance to take another step, Annie growled low, the hair down her back standing at attention.

"She senses something." Dread slithered into the pit of Charlotte's stomach. She heard a sound. She'd been so wrapped up in her own thoughts she must have missed it earlier. She spun around trying to determine the direction of the noise.

"It's straight ahead," Jonas whispered. He touched her arm and motioned toward the closest coverage while Annie continued to growl and stare ahead of them.

"Annie, come." Charlotte tried to be as quiet as possible. The dog followed them over to the trees.

While they huddled together, Charlotte continued to try to place where they'd heard the noise.

"Drop your weapons and get your hands in the air—both of you," came a voice.

The bottom dropped out of Charlotte's stomach. Three armed men drew down on them.

"I said Drop. Your. Weapons."

No matter what, they couldn't surrender their weapons. Their survival was at stake.

"Now!" said the same man, with growing irritation in his tone.

Charlotte held Jonas's gaze and shook her head, praying he understood. Taking down three armed men wouldn't be easy to do, so she'd have to enlist Annie's help.

"Annie, attack." The command barely cleared her lips before Annie charged. The lead gunman tried to fire on the dog.

Charlotte leaped to her feet and threw her weight at him before the shot could hit her partner. He stumbled backward, Annie latching on to his leg. While he screamed in pain, Charlotte wrestled the weapon from the attacker's hand and knocked him unconscious.

Immediately, another man came after Charlotte. When he spotted Annie's bared teeth, he ran. Annie flew through the air, chomping down on his arm and sending him sprawling across the ground. His weapon was shaken free.

While the man tried to push Annie off, Charlotte pinned him down with her weight. "Stop right there. Don't even think about moving." Out of the corner of her eye, she noticed Jonas disarming the final perp.

"We need to secure them to a tree," she said while giving Annie the order to release but remain close.

Jonas ripped off pieces of the inside of his jacket and tied up the man he'd taken down.

"You two are dead!" the guy yelled at him. Jonas ignored him and tore off more strips of cloth. He placed one over the man's mouth to keep him quiet. Charlotte hauled the man she was guarding over to the same tree. With Jonas's help, he was secured without incident.

He pulled at his restraints. "You'll never get out of here alive."

Charlotte stopped what she was doing as a smirk played across his face. She searched his pockets and found a cell phone.

Thank You, God.

The man's smile spread. "You have no idea who you're dealing with. This is so much bigger than anything you can imagine."

Charlotte recoiled at the confirmation of what she and Jonas suspected. "Who are you talking about? Tell us what's going on and we might be able to work out a deal on your behalf."

He laughed in her face. "I won't need a deal, and you can't even save yourselves, much less me."

Charlotte pocketed the phone and found an extra magazine for the weapon in the man's other pocket. "Last chance. Tell us about the organization, and we'll do what we can to help."

She held a strip of cloth in her hand, ready to shut him up if he didn't say what she needed to hear.

"I've got nothing to worry about," he said nonchalantly. "Do what you must. You're no threat to us. We'll still be operating long after you two are gone. It's only a matter of time before you're as dead as your boyfriend."

Jonas's eyes shot to Charlotte. All the color had left her face at that obvious taunt about Ryan.

She stepped inches from his face. "What did you say?"

The man must've realized he'd gotten under her skin because he appeared pleased. They wouldn't be getting anything useful out of him.

Jonas tugged Charlotte back, took the gag from her and secured the jeerer.

While Charlotte couldn't seem to take her eyes off the man, Jonas worked fast to get the final person tied up. He checked pockets without finding another phone. Jonas gathered all the weapons before he returned to Charlotte.

"We have to go." When she didn't move, he clasped her arm and tugged her along with him, giving Annie the command to follow.

"I'm okay," Charlotte said and snapped out of it. "He was talking about Ryan." She sounded stunned. "He all but confirmed Ryan was murdered."

"He did. This is bad on so many levels." A rush of shock raced through his body. Jonas couldn't believe what the man had said.

Charlotte drew in a breath, clearly gathering herself. "We'll get them, and we'll find out who is really in charge, but right now, we can't take a chance Abram and Lainey weren't able to call the sheriff." She brought out the criminal's phone. "It doesn't look as if the phone has been used in a while." She punched in some digits and waited. "I guess I understand why. The service is still sketchy. It could appear once we reach a higher altitude." She hung up and stuffed the phone in her pocket.

"Let's hope." Jonas thought about what the one man had said. "He sure didn't seem too worried about going to jail, even after pretty much admitting Ryan's death wasn't an accident."

Charlotte's mouth hardened. "Almost as if he thought he had a get-out-of-jail-free card."

Jonas tilted his head. "I don't understand."

"It means you don't have to worry about going to jail. It was part of a game called Monopoly. If you had a get-out-of-jail card, you didn't have to worry about going to jail." She looked back in the direction they'd come. "I'm guessing because there are law enforcement officers on his team who will protect him."

"I guess." Jonas believed it went much deeper. "But there's more to this. There must be."

She sighed and watched Annie weave her away along while on the scent. "You're right. I just wish I could figure out the identity of the real person in charge."

"Me, too. Right now, let's keep going. Once we're above the tree line we should be able to pick up service."

He hoped it proved true.

The path continued to rise beneath their feet. The Root Mountains were not all that tall but the weather conditions at the higher altitude were always tricky.

"It feels like it's getting colder," Charlotte said and wrapped her jacket tighter.

"It probably is." He kept going over what the man had said. Was it possible that Elliott had promised those who worked for him safety from prosecution? "This Elliott person isn't very high up in his department?" he asked because he wanted to understand.

"No, he's just a patrol officer."

"So, he would only have so much power." He rubbed a hand over his tired eyes. "Who would he report to?"

Charlotte told him there was a chief of police over the officers. "I'm friends with the chief of police and he wouldn't be involved in such… Then again, I thought the same thing about Elliott. But Chief Harris is a grandfather with three girls of his own and two granddaughters. How could he turn a blind eye to what those women will be facing and still care about his own girls?" She shook her head. "But then, Elliott is married with a couple of young children himself."

"I don't understand any of this. These men are selling women for money." He knew his disgust showed in his voice. "How can anyone with a heart treat another human being in such a way?"

"It's about greed. They might not have meant for it to go this far, or for them to get in so deep. It probably started with taking a bribe to look the other way. And then before long, they were too deep to get out." She pulled in a breath. "These organizations are sometimes connected to other illegal organizations. This one could have originated in another country even."

The ways of the *Englischers* still eluded him, and he was okay with that.

"I'm going to try to call out again." She pulled out the phone and redialed.

Jonas went over to check Annie's bandage. She'd been a fierce protector and had helped save them. He lifted the dog's injured paw. The bandage was still securely in place, but it was dotted with blood. He gently placed the limb on the ground and stroked the dog's head. "You're a trooper, Annie. Hang in there."

The dog gave a low whimper in answer.

"Hello?"

Jonas's attention returned to Charlotte. The call had gone through? He hurried to her side.

"Hello, dispatch, can you hear me?" Her wide eyes found his, and she shook her head in frustration. "There's so much static." She punched end and tried again. "Hello, this is Deputy Charlotte Walker." She succinctly explained what was going on and where she and Jonas were heading. "We need immediate help. We have two civilians in the fire tower east of the Christian camp and they are in danger." She told the dispatcher about her partner's collar. "If you can't track this number, please try to pinpoint Annie's location."

She held the phone away from her ear and made a groaning sound. "I've lost the call." Another try proved futile. "We need to get up higher." She started walking at a fast pace and Jonas scrambled to catch up.

"Do you think they understood anything you said?" His hope was hanging on by a thread.

"Yes, at least part of it. I just hope they'll be able to find us by using Annie's collar because the service on this phone is terrible. It's probably a burner, which means it was prepaid and probably with cash. In other words, it's pretty much untraceable."

The ways of those who did evil were hard to comprehend.

A disturbing thought occurred. The local police were compromised. Was there a chance that there could be a mole in the sheriff's department too? If so, Charlotte had just given away their location as well as Lainey's. He voiced his fears aloud.

Charlotte stopped abruptly and shook her head. "You can trust my team, I promise. The fact that this case seems to trace back to the local police tells me the sheriff's department may be our only hope to set things right. Please trust me, Jonas."

He did trust her. "I do. Always."

She smiled. "I'll keep trying to reach the dispatcher again."

The steep incline of the rising mountain range reminded Jonas of the precarious trek they'd be forced to make. This wasn't the easiest route to reach the location of the house Harley claimed he owned, but with all the activity circling through the woods it was their only choice.

Once they'd cleared most of the trees, the wind whipped around with a force that threatened to knock them over.

But the biggest concern for Jonas was there would be

no place to hide should they come across others from Harley's organization.

Jonas looped his arm through Charlotte's to keep them both from stumbling in the brutal wind. They leaned into it and struggled to move.

Out in front of them, Annie turned her head in the direction they'd come and sniffed the air.

Jonas whipped around. Flashlights appeared. "It looks like it's coming from the location we left those men."

Which meant their partners would have found them and been told the direction he and Charlotte were heading. They were out in the open with no place to hide and a virtual army coming after them.

The phone in Charlotte's pocket chimed an unknown ringtone. Charlotte grabbed it, no doubt thinking the call was from the sheriff. "I don't recognize this number." Her attention shot to Jonas.

"Can Harley's organization track the phone?"

Abruptly the ringtone stopped. "Normally, I'd say no, but this appears to be a sophisticated organization." She stared at the phone in her hand. "We can't afford to keep the phone if there's the slightest chance, they'll be able to track it. I just hope they aren't able to do the same with the phone Lainey and Abram have."

The thought was alarming.

Her gaze slid past Jonas to the flashlights that appeared to be heading straight for their location. "I just hope that Ruby, the dispatcher, was able to understand where Abram and Lainey are, and I hope she heard the part about tracking Annie's GPS collar." She tossed the phone away. It landed some distance down the mountainside. "Is there another path to Harley's?"

"If we head to the right slightly it will be easier going

but we'll have to circle back once we summit, which means it will take us longer to reach the place."

Charlotte watched the lights advancing once more. "Let's do it. I just hope those men have no idea about Harley's mountain place, because if so, they'll come after us there."

Jonas shifted their direction. Something soft and wet fell on his face and he looked up and realized it was snowing. Snow covered the ground at their feet. At this high an elevation, the snow sometimes stuck around into summer.

After they'd traveled for some distance, Jonas stopped her. Charlotte gave the command for Annie to halt.

"What's going on?"

"The last time I was up this way was a while ago. Still, we should be safe to start heading for the mountain summit from here." Jonas started toward the dark shapes looming in the distance while the snow swirled harder around them. Temperatures had plummeted. Both he and Charlotte were exhausted.

"My cabin is close," he said. "We can get out of the weather for a bit before continuing."

Charlotte nodded while huddling under her jacket. "So far, it doesn't appear as if they're tracking us, but with the snow on the ground, if they come this way, they'll see our footprints." She pointed to the clear prints behind them.

She was right, but at this point there wasn't much they could do to cover them. "Let's hope the snow fills them in soon."

The darkness and the weather made each step dangerous. The rocks beneath the snow were slippery. One false move and they could be in trouble.

"Give me your hand," Jonas said, and Charlotte looked at him strangely. He pointed to the rocks. "Just to be safe."

She held her hand out to him and he clasped it. The

fact that it felt right holding her hand was something he refused to think about.

Annie slowly picked her way through the rocks up higher.

Several times he and Charlotte slipped and almost slid backward.

"How much longer?" Charlotte asked once they stopped to catch their breaths.

He tried to gather his bearings. "Another mile or so."

The dejection on her face confirmed she was struggling.

"Over there." He pointed to a group of rocks that they could get behind to act as a barrier from the wind. "It's a bit of protection until we can catch our breaths and keep going."

With her hand still in his they made their way precariously there. Charlotte knelt beside him. The dog came over and sat on her haunches.

Jonas gathered Charlotte close. She tucked her face against his chest. Over the blowing wind, he was content to hold her and listen for any sound above the quick beat of his heart at having her close.

He rested his chin against her auburn hair, needing a moment of comfort during a night that felt neverending. This was wrong. How could he have feelings for this woman in his arms when he missed Ivy with every breath?

THIRTEEN

Amidst the confusion in her head, another sound just about broke her heart. Were those footsteps?

Please, God, no.

She focused intently to confirm the worst possible news and it soon became clear. Someone else was up on the mountain.

Charlotte lifted her head and whispered against Jonas's ear. "There's someone up here."

His eyes locked with hers. "Where?"

Getting a correct bead on the direction was difficult in such weather, but she pointed above them while giving Annie the command of silence.

Charlotte held on to Jonas and prayed with all her heart that they wouldn't be spotted. She wasn't sure how much more she could handle. Above everything she wanted them to live. Wanted to save those women if they could. Wanted to make those who were responsible pay.

Over the rush of the wind, the footsteps sounded closer. She clutched Jonas tighter and looked to Annie who was waiting for her command to attack. Charlotte put her finger on her lips and shook her head. The dog understood. Annie was one of the best K-9 partners she'd ever had, and they worked seamlessly together.

Soon, the noise of crunching footsteps appeared to fade.

Charlotte held Jonas's gaze until the sound was gone completely. "Could you tell how many there were?"

He shook his head.

Pulling in a breath, Charlotte slowly rose. "I don't see anyone."

Jonas stood beside her. "They weren't using flashlights."

"Let's get to your cabin." The cold bored right through to her bones. "Which way?"

Jonas pointed straight ahead. Thankfully, the direction was heading away from whoever was up here on the mountain with them.

Snow mixed with ice fell harder the higher they climbed. Snowflakes clung to Charlotte's lashes, making it hard to see. She brushed a frozen hand across her eyes.

"Over there."

Charlotte squinted through the deluge and spotted the shadow of a structure amongst the darkness. Relief swept through her weakened limbs. If she'd had the strength to run toward it, she would have.

She clutched Jonas's hand and waded through the deep accumulation of snow until they reached the cabin.

Jonas faced her. "Stay here and let me check the cabin out first."

Her teeth were chattering so much it was impossible to get words out.

Jonas shoved the door open and went inside before she could respond. Charlotte wasn't about to let him risk danger alone. She followed him inside the single room and pulled out the flashlight. A cot in the corner. A table and a couple of chairs against one wall. A woodstove proved to be the best thing she'd seen in a while.

"I'll make a fire. It's risky, but we need to warm up.

We're both frozen." Jonas opened the woodstove's door and placed some paper inside before adding some wood from a pile stacked close to the stove. He struck a match and soon the paper caught followed by the logs.

Charlotte stood beside him while Annie roamed around the room sniffing.

Jonas dragged the two chairs over close to the fire. "We can't stay long, but it'll be so nice to rest for a little while and warm up."

"Who do you think was out there?" she asked. She couldn't let go of the sensation that whoever it was, they posed a threat, and if the smoke from the fire was spotted…

"There are other trappers who come up here, but most would use a light to see where they were going."

That point gnawed at her brain. "How close are we to the house?"

"Very, though with the weather, finding it might be difficult. It's in a secluded location."

Of course, Harley would choose a place of isolation. Considering that everything pointed to it being a place for illegal activities…trafficking and who knew what else.

She held her hands close to the fire, basking in the warmth of the flames. "I can feel my hands again."

Jonas turned his head her way and smiled. "Me, too. Neither of us exactly dressed for the things we've gone through today."

Charlotte agreed. "I had no idea when I agreed to help Dottie find her granddaughter that I'd almost die and be thrown into the middle of a trafficking ring." Or that she would be teamed up with Jonas…and that being close to him would bring unwelcome reminders of the things she once had in her life.

His smile suddenly disappeared. "I'm glad I found

you," he said softly. The roughness in his voice sent a shiver through her. She was glad she had him with her, too. Glad…

Jonas leaned closer and brushed back strands of her hair from her face. "This is the first time in a long time I've felt needed."

She reached for his hand and entwined their fingers. "You are needed, Jonas. I couldn't do this without you. I would have died and so would Lainey."

He studied their joined hands. "These past six years, well, I've been living in a state of self-imposed reclusion because I thought I deserved to be punished for not being there for my wife."

She shook her head before he finished. "You didn't do anything wrong. You were trying to provide for your wife and child. Ivy knew this. You couldn't have predicted what happened…" She was ready to accept that truth for herself, too. She'd spent the last year blaming herself for asking Ryan to come out to assist with the search and yet Ryan wasn't the type of man to sit by when he was needed. It didn't matter if he was sick, he would have come to assist. It was just who he was.

"We've both been blaming ourselves for something that wasn't our fault," he said softly, and she couldn't take her eyes off him. Maybe he was ready to accept the truth, too. She'd been living in limbo for so long, wishing for things that were gone forever.

Jonas leaned forward and touched his forehead to hers. "I'm tired of blaming myself."

A tiny sob escaped her. She was, too. So tired. His lips brushed hers. She inched away for a second, lowering her lashes. Jonas's gentle kiss took her by surprise. But then Charlotte leaned into him and kissed him back.

Unfinished business… The words played on a loop

through her mind. She had to uncover the truth. Had to see the face of the person who'd claimed Ryan's life if she were ever going to move forward.

She ended the kiss and straightened. The hurt on Jonas's face confirmed he didn't understand the reason for her sudden change.

He turned away. She tried to come up with the right words to say, but a noise outside had her on sudden alert.

Annie growled and leaped to her feet, moving closer to the door.

Jonas jerked toward the door. There was no lock on it.

Charlotte quieted Annie. "Over there." Charlotte, Jonas and the dog moved to the side of the door. If someone came in, the door would offer them protection and hopefully give them the edge they'd need to overpower the intruder.

Seconds ticked by. Jonas looked her way. She wanted to say so much—to tell him she had feelings for him—yet once more the danger facing them stood in the way.

Someone pounded on the door. "Help me, please. Somebody."

Jonas' eyes widened at the woman's voice. "It's Betty."

He started for the door, but Charlotte stopped him. "What if it's a trick?" she whispered. At this point they couldn't afford to take any chances. Charlotte spotted the back door. "I'll go around and make sure she's alone."

Jonas rejected the idea. "It's too dangerous. Let me."

Though her confidence had taken a beating after everything they'd gone through tonight, she was still a deputy and it fell to her to protect him.

She shook her head. "I'll go. Wait here." Charlotte slipped from the cabin and took a second to listen before proceeding. The person at the front door continued to beg for help. If Betty was alone, Charlotte wanted to get her help as quickly as possible, but she had to make sure Harley—or worse, all those men who had been searching for them—wasn't waiting nearby to ambush.

She slipped quickly around the back to the side of the house and stayed as close to it as she could with the snowdrifts piled up there.

Once Charlotte reached the front of the cabin, she took stock on the limited line of sight. There was a single person huddled near the front door. Nothing else stirred. Betty appeared to be alone.

Charlotte eased toward the woman, trying not to startle her. As she neared, Betty whirled around and screamed. Before she could run away, Charlotte closed the space between them.

"Betty, it's okay," Charlotte said. "I'm a sheriff's deputy. I just had to make sure you were alone."

Betty backed away as she neared. "Why are you up here alone?" Betty was clearly suspicious. The woman didn't have a coat and her feet were bare. She had to be frozen.

"I'm not alone. Jonas Knowles, your neighbor, is inside." Charlotte moved past Betty to the door. "Jonas, it's okay. Betty is alone. We're coming in." She reached for the door, but it opened before she could turn the knob.

Jonas's attention shot between the two women before he stepped back.

Charlotte ushered Betty inside and closed the door. Annie stood in the middle of the room watching with her hackles raised.

"It's okay, Annie. She's a friend." Charlotte put her arm around Betty's shoulders and led her over to one of the chairs. "Sit down and warm yourself. It's freezing outside."

Betty seemed in a state of shock, but she obeyed. "Jonas, why are you here?"

"Never mind that now." Jonas removed his jacket and placed it over Betty's frail shoulders.

Charlotte moved the second chair closer so Betty could put her legs up on it and warm her feet.

As the fire worked its wonders, Betty rocked slightly and moaned. Charlotte found the bottle of water and opened the cap before handing it to Betty. "Here, drink it slowly."

Betty stared at the bottle as if she didn't understand. Charlotte held the bottle to her lips, and she eventually drank a few sips.

Charlotte felt the woman's hands. They were still ice-cold but the heat from the stove was slowly melting the chill away. She took off her firemen's coat and placed it over Betty's legs and feet, noticing there were fresh cut marks on her hands. Charlotte's mouth thinned as she thought about the terrible things Harley had put this innocent woman through. Betty probably didn't have any family to turn to for help, and Harley was good at intimidating those weaker than himself.

Her fear for the young women with Harley grew, and Charlotte wanted to jump in and ask Betty how she'd ended up here on the mountain where they were searching for her husband. Yet the look of bewilderment on Betty's face told her Betty had nothing to do with her husband's crimes.

A deep, gut-wrenching sigh escaped Betty's lips, and she focused on Jonas as if she were really seeing him. "Jonas, I'm glad you're here." A tiny smile hovered at the corners of her lips.

Jonas knelt beside her. "Are you hurt?" he asked gently. Her hands were cut up as if she'd been in a fight.

Betty's eyes filled with tears, but she shook her head.

"I'm okay. I got these running through the underbrush near the cabin."

Jonas frowned. "Near this cabin or…"

The words were barely out before she shook her head. "No, not this cabin. The one Harley just told me about."

Jonas's eyes slid to Charlotte. She appeared just as confused as him.

"You didn't have any idea Harley had a place up here?"

Betty wiped her eyes. "No, he's never said a word about a house in the mountains. I never even realized he came up here."

Charlotte moved to the other side of Jonas, drawing Betty's attention.

"I recognize you," the woman said.

"You do?" Charlotte asked in surprise, and Jonas wondered if Betty had been at the house when Charlotte was attacked.

"Yes, you came to the house before…to talk to Harley."

Jonas remembered the times Charlotte had gone to the house on a domestic violence report.

Charlotte smiled gently. "That's right. I was at your house earlier today—yesterday. In the afternoon. Were you home?"

Betty stared at her with a frown creasing her forehead. "Why, no. Harley sent me to Bozeman for supplies."

Charlotte frowned. Bozeman was over a hundred miles away. Why would Harley send her so far to get supplies…? He wanted her out of the house so he could handle his illegal activity.

"Why were you at my house?"

Charlotte looked at Jonas before answering. "I came there looking for my friend, Lainey Marques. Her grandmother called and asked for mine and Annie's help." She indicated the dog. "Annie followed Lainey's trail to your house."

Betty looked at the animal but still didn't understand. "And you found her there?"

Charlotte shook her head. "She needs to hear the truth," she told Jonas.

Jonas agreed. Betty needed to see what her husband was capable of. "Tell her."

Charlotte drew in a breath and told her about what happened to her after she'd reached Harley's house. "Your husband tried to kill me and Lainey. Since then, we've been trying to escape armed men who are working with Harley." She paused before telling Betty about the young women who Lainey reported being held at their house.

Jonas watched Betty's expression carefully for any sign she might have been involved in her husband's crimes.

Her hand flew up to cover her trembling lips. "They were there—at my house? I had no idea, but it explains why Harley sent me away from the house so often. He must have brought them there while I was away and made sure they were gone before I returned."

Jonas sat back on his haunches and watched Betty's pained reaction. "You know about the girls?" He couldn't accept she was part of Harley's evil plans.

Betty repeatedly shook her head. "No, I didn't, not until Harley brought them up here a little while ago."

"Harley's here with the girls?" Charlotte asked in shock. "When did this happen?"

Betty clutched her hands together in her lap. "About an hour earlier."

Relief sank in quickly. The girls were alive. At least for the moment. "Why don't you start by telling us how you ended up here," Jonas said quietly.

Betty gave a shuddering sigh. "As I said, Harley told me to go to Bozeman to get supplies."

"Does he do this often?" Jonas rarely saw Betty outside the house.

"No," she replied, "usually only a couple of times a month. He sends me there with a list of things he needs, and he tells me not to come back home until I call first."

Harley wanted to make sure Betty wasn't around when he was moving the girls.

"What happened yesterday?" Charlotte glanced at the door as if half expecting Harley to barge in.

"It started early—much earlier than normal. Harley was up before dawn. When I woke up, he told me to head to Bozeman. He didn't even allow me to have my breakfast." Betty rubbed her trembling lips. "He's done something terrible, hasn't he?"

"I'm afraid so," Charlotte said quietly. "Please keep going."

"Well, I left immediately. I knew better than to cross him." She trembled as if the thought terrified her. "Anyway, I got the things he needed and was ready to head home, only Harley told me he would call when I could come."

"And did he?" Jonas still couldn't grasp the events that had taken place.

"Yes, but it was afternoon, and when I got home, he told me I had to leave again."

A strange thing. Probably with everything that happened, Harley didn't want Betty anywhere near the house.

"He told me about the house up here in the mountains." Betty's surprise was clear. "I had no idea he had it. Harley told me how to get here and insisted I should take a side-by-side." Her bottom lip quivered. "I didn't even realize he owned a side-by-side. It was parked near a truck I didn't recognize. When I asked him about it, he hit me here—" she touched her cheek "—and told me to mind my own business and not to try anything or he'd come after me."

Jonas's blood boiled at Harley's cruel treatment of his wife.

"So, you did as he asked," Charlotte prompted when Betty grew quiet.

"Yes. I got here after dark, and I was so scared. I'd never been in the mountains at night. Anyway, as soon as I reached the house, Harley called, checking up on me. He told me to wait there until he told me differently."

She stood suddenly when a sound outside grabbed everyone's attention.

"I'll check it out, but I'm pretty sure it was the wind." Charlotte stepped out into the cold. Both Jonas and Betty didn't take their eyes off the door until she returned.

"There's no sign of anyone. Still, we need to go after the women while we can," Charlotte told Jonas.

"I'm not sure they're still alive," Betty said.

The shock of those words settled uncomfortably around Jonas. "Why do you say such a thing?" Had they risked their lives only to find the women they'd been trying to save were all dead?

FOURTEEN

Charlotte waited with dread for Betty to tell them what she'd witnessed.

"The house was big—bigger than our place. I looked around and realized there were two floors. The one you come in from the front door and then a basement area," Betty explained. "Even though Harley told me not to go downstairs, I did. It was dark and there was a room cluttered with stuff."

"What kind of stuff?" Charlotte asked. She recalled how the basement in the house near Jonas's had been virtually empty.

"All sorts of electronics. Boxes of new cell phones and tablets. Other types of laptops. There were some crates I couldn't open. I have no idea where those things come from. Harley works at the lumber mill from time to time. He insists I stay home and keep the house." Betty lifted her gaze to them. "We live paycheck to paycheck. How was he able to afford all those things?"

Charlotte didn't say as much, but she was pretty sure all those items were stolen. "What happened when Harley arrived?" She hated to push the already shaken Betty, but time was critical, and she and Jonas had to understand what they'd be facing once they reached the house.

"He stormed in and demanded to know what I'd been

up to." Betty's shifting facial expressions showed she was reliving the terror. "I told him nothing. I'm not sure he believed me or not, but he went back outside and brought in four young women."

The girls who had been held with Lainey.

"Did you recognize any of them?" Charlotte asked.

Betty shook her head, her worried eyes holding Charlotte's. "No, I had no idea why they were there. I tried to ask Harley, but he told me to keep my mouth shut and then he took my phone." She wiped at her eyes once more.

"He forced the girls downstairs. When he came back up, he kept muttering something about 'they were going to kill him.' I had no idea what he was talking about but the look on his face scared me. I tried to stay out of his way. He just kept pacing the room and saying he didn't know what to do. After a while, he went outside and was gone for a long time. When he came back in, he stormed back down the stairs and slammed the door. I heard several shots. That's when I ran."

Had Harley murdered those girls? *Please, Lord, let them be alive.*

Another frightening thought occurred. According to the timeline, Harley could have been the one roaming around before she and Jonas reached his cabin.

Clearly, Harley was growing paranoid and worried his people were turning on him—with good reason according to what they'd overheard.

"I tried to use the side-by-side to get away," Betty went on shakily, "only the keys were gone. Harley must have taken them. And there was another side-by-side parked beside it without the key, either."

Harley wanted to make sure she didn't escape. If he killed the young women, he'd do the same to Betty. And when he realized she was gone, he'd come looking for her.

"Betty, you stay here where it's warm. We're going after the women." Charlotte turned to Jonas, beckoning him away. "We need to find a way to secure the doors for her. Just in case," she said in a whisper.

Jonas looked around the cabin. "I can use the table to block the back entrance." He went back to Betty, crouching before her. "Betty, when we step outside, I need you to take one of the chairs and shove it beneath the doorknob. Don't open the door to anyone but us."

Betty grabbed Jonas's arm, her face filled with fear. "He'll kill you if he catches you."

The words had her chest tightening. "We'll be careful. Are you familiar with how to use a weapon?" She moved next to Jonas as he rose.

Betty slowly nodded. "Yes, when I was young, my father taught me."

Charlotte held out one of the handguns. "If someone tries to get in besides us, shoot to kill."

Betty clasped the weapon with a hand that shook. "I almost forgot. I took Harley's phone before I left the house."

"You did?" Jonas said in disbelief.

"Yes. As I was leaving, I grabbed it. He'd left it on the table. Only it wasn't his usual phone. I've never seen this one before." She gave the mobile to Charlotte.

The service indicator confirmed cell reception was nonexistent. The mountain so close was probably blocking any signal.

With Jonas looking over her shoulder, Charlotte scrolled through the numbers called. "Here's one for a D.A. This must be the same D.A. that was mentioned before." Charlotte asked Betty about the person.

Betty shrugged. "I have no idea. I have a suspicion there are lots of things Harley kept from me."

Even if there was no service, the phone could be used

as evidence against Harley. Charlotte shoved it into her pocket. "Are you warm enough?" She and Jonas had the jackets Abram gave them. She'd leave Betty the fire jacket. She'd be okay. Hopefully, the cold would keep them sharp.

Betty nodded. "Yes, I'm fine."

As much as Charlotte wanted to leave Annie there to protect Betty, they'd need her partner's expertise to alert them to danger.

Jonas moved one of the chairs over to the door. "Don't forget to wedge the chair under the doorknob, Betty."

Charlotte checked her magazine. The clip was almost full. "Ready?" she asked him while stuffing the weapon into her pocket. The tension on Jonas's face matched hers.

"We'd better hurry," he said. "If Harley shot those women, then they could be in bad shape."

She stepped past him into the cold weather that had continued to worsen. Once she was sure Betty had secured the door, she and Jonas started walking while Annie took her position as lead.

"How far are we?" Charlotte was on edge, expecting Harley or one of the rest of his crew members to find them. She scanned their surroundings.

"Half an hour under normal circumstances, but in this weather…" He shrugged. It was excruciating to realize the storm berating the mountains would slow them down even more when every second counted. "Harley probably knows Betty escaped by now. He may be out looking for her."

And if he was, with the weather and the darkness, they might not even see him until it was too late.

Jonas replayed every piece of Betty's story in his head. Harley was now desperate and had quite possibly executed the young women he'd brought with him. He wouldn't want to leave any witnesses. Betty was a witness who could not only place the women with Harley but also identify the timeline in which Harley had had her leave the house. Jonas was certain it would match up to when the women had been moved.

"I pray we find them alive." Charlotte voiced the biggest thing on his mind aloud. "Those poor girls. They've been through so much already, and to lose their lives because Harley is worried about getting caught…"

Jonas's hand fisted around his weapon. "Harley is only one man. If we can take him by surprise, we should be able to overpower him. I'm more worried about those other men. If they're tracking Harley's phone, they could be anywhere up here." And Charlotte had the phone. With a virtual army of soldiers bearing down on them, there wouldn't be much time.

"All the more reason to find Harley and subdue him quickly," Charlotte said. "If his back is against the wall then we stand a chance at flipping him."

The Harley Jonas was familiar with wouldn't give in so easily. He'd fight until the bitter end, but he didn't tell Charlotte that.

A sudden unidentified sound had the dog charging ahead.

"Annie, no." Charlotte grabbed the dog's collar before she left their sight. "Come." She and Jonas crouched behind a pile of rocks near the mountainside.

Movement came from nearby. It sounded like more than one person. Were they too late?

"I can't get a read off this thing," a male voice Jonas recognized from one of their previous encounters came from only a few feet away.

"Let me have a look." The second person's voice came closer. "The program's not working. The weather, I'm sure. The last time we were able to get a track on Harley's phone it was somewhere to the left of this location." The man huffed out a breath. "Let's head that way. He told us to take Harley out and then get the girls and evidence Harley has. And I for one don't want to cross him. I've seen what he's capable of with the girl and the dog trainer."

Next to him, Charlotte's shoulders quivered.

Two sets of footsteps carefully shuffled away, the men grumbling at the weather, Harley and what they'd need to do. Soon, the sounds faded.

Annie left her hiding spot and sniffed the ground, picking up the men's scents but not tracking them.

"I'm sorry," Jonas said softly. He brushed her hair away from her face and held her gaze. "But we must hurry, Charlotte. We can't let those men kill Harley and destroy whatever evidence he's been gathering on the person in charge." Jonas rose and pulled her up beside him. "I realize it hurts to hear the truth verified, but those girls are counting on us."

Charlotte drew in a breath and let it go slowly. "You're right." She pulled out Harley's phone. "Right now, they probably aren't able to track the phone due to the weather, but that could change." She turned the phone off. "They shouldn't be able to track it if it's off."

In the distance, daylight lightened the sky. He pointed the dawning out to her.

"As happy as I am to see the sunlight coming, it will make it easier for us to be spotted." She glanced around uneasily. "I sure hope between our call, and Lainey and Abram's, help is on its way. We can't stay hidden much longer."

The edge in her tone confirmed how serious their situation was. The only way out should those men keep coming would be to summit the mountains, and from what Jonas remembered, that would be difficult.

"Hey, I think I see something," Charlotte said. She'd stopped and was leaning forward as if to see better.

Jonas glanced through the troubling weather and saw it, too. "That's the house." He started for it when Charlotte grabbed him.

"What's wrong?"

"Those men are up there somewhere."

What she wasn't saying was the chances were great that he and Charlotte would have to take them down before they were able to search for Harley.

Jonas's blood hummed through his veins, warning him the showdown he'd been expecting for a while was about to take place. They'd survived so much. Could they make it through another battle?

As he looked into her pretty face, there were things he wanted to say. He cupped her shoulders and brought her close. "Charlotte…"

She placed her finger over his lips and didn't let him finish. "We have to end this, Jonas. Nothing else matters. Those girls have families who need to know what happened to them no matter what."

He slowly nodded. She was right. Now was not the time to talk about them. What he'd been about to say could wait.

Slowly they advanced toward the house. The two side-by-sides that Betty had mentioned were parked out front. Why hadn't Harley chosen to flee on one if he suspected those men were searching for him to kill him? Leave the women and use the side-by-side and head over the mountain and out of danger. It didn't make sense unless Harley had been found and killed already.

No.

As bad as Harley was, Jonas wanted him alive to have to pay for what he'd done.

Charlotte pointed to the side of the house. Jonas spotted a man carefully looking around. Was it one of the men they'd overheard earlier? Where was the second man? "We have to take him down as quietly as possible." She held the gun in her hand. "Stay behind me."

She was still trying to protect him.

"Stay, Annie," Charlotte said and moved quickly toward the unsuspecting man. Before they reached his side, he whipped around and opened fire.

Charlotte pulled Jonas behind a nearby tree before returning fire. Shots rang out all around them. She waited until silence followed and shot at her target. The man screamed and hit the ground.

Jonas followed Charlotte over to the perp. She felt for a pulse. "He's gone." Before they had a chance to move, the second man came around the corner, weapon blazing.

Jonas whirled around and fired. The surprise on the shooter's face before he fell would haunt Jonas the rest of his life. The man was dead.

Charlotte squeezed his arm as if reading his distraught thoughts. "There's no way Harley didn't hear what happened."

Jonas forced the regret back and followed her to the back of the house. Betty had been right. There was no rear entrance. The house butted up against the mountainside.

Annie moved closer, likely to protect her partner.

If Harley was inside, he'd have seen their approach through the front windows.

"What do we do?" Jonas asked. He was at a loss and his exhausted brain was making it hard to think clearly.

"Most houses have two entrances. There must be another entrance on the other side."

The question was how they got there without alerting Harley they were coming.

"Follow me," Charlotte said and eased back to the front of the house.

Once they reached it, she pointed to the porch. "If we can duck down low enough, the porch should protect us from anyone inside's line of sight."

It was risky, but everything they'd done up until this point had been risky.

Jonas nodded and bent down low following Charlotte's example.

With his heartbeat drowning out all other sound, he hurried after Charlotte until they reached the other side of the house.

Another door.

Charlotte edged toward the nearby window and looked inside. "It's a kitchen."

Jonas got on the opposite side of the pane and tried to see as much as possible. A small kitchen, then a living room. On the opposite wall of the kitchen was a door. Which must be the door leading downstairs to the basement where Harley had taken the women.

"I don't see anyone." Charlotte waited for him to confirm. "It's possible Harley is searching for Betty and not here. If that's the case, we won't have long." She shifted back to the door and eased toward it.

Jonas's hands were shaking. After everything they'd gone through, it felt as if they were at the end of the road one way or another.

"Annie, stay here and watch." The dog's ears tilted to alert. She understood and would be on guard.

Charlotte tried the doorknob. It turned in her hands. She shot Jonas a look that was filled with apprehension.

She slowly twisted it open and stepped inside with her weapon drawn.

Jonas kept close to her. She might be law enforcement, but he would have her back no matter what.

In the kitchen, Jonas quietly closed the door. The house didn't appear to be occupied. His gut twisted. The girls.

"We have to clear this floor first," Charlotte told him. This was police procedure and part of her training.

They moved through the few rooms on that floor. Living room, kitchen, bedroom and bath. Each room was cluttered and appeared as if the person who was staying there had little regard for neatness.

A reminder of Harley's messy yard. But the house down the mountain had been kept up thanks to Betty. Her touches were not present here. Betty had said she had no idea Harley had a place up on the mountain and that appeared to be true.

"There's no one here," Charlotte confirmed as they returned to the living room. There was a woodstove in the middle of the space. She pointed to it. "That hasn't been used in a while."

"You're right. Probably not in a long time. So, Betty was here for a while with no heat?"

She shrugged. "He may have told her not to use it. But why would he do so unless…" Charlotte hurried over to the stove and opened the door. "The ashes are cold." She dug around. "There's something here." She pulled out a phone. "It's mine and there's another one. This is Lainey's." She turned the phones over. "The batteries have been removed," she said in a dejected tone. "He was making sure they couldn't be tracked." Charlotte handed both phones to Jonas. "There's something else here. A book."

Charlotte pulled it out and flipped through its pages. "It's girls' names, descriptions and dates."

Jonas looked over her shoulder at the names before confirming what she was likely thinking. "He wrote down the captured girls' descriptions and names."

Charlotte flipped through page after page. "This has been going on for at least five years. Probably longer. Harley didn't wise up and start keeping notes until then."

"Too bad he didn't list the names of those involved," Jonas said, recalling the conversation he and Charlotte had overheard.

"This isn't what the person in charge was looking for," she said mostly to herself. "If Harley went to this much trouble to list the names of the girls, why wouldn't he also name his accomplices in case he was caught? He'd have leverage." Understanding dawned on her face. "He took the evidence that the man in charge is worried about with him," Charlotte concluded.

"Perhaps." But why take some and not everything?

Charlotte flipped through the remaining pages. On the inside cover at the back, Harley had taped a key. "Wait, this looks like a safe deposit key or a personal safe. Maybe there's one in the basement?" She faced him. "Stay close." They returned to the kitchen. She placed her ear on the door and listened. "I don't hear anything."

The words held little comfort when the reason they'd come here was to save the young women.

Charlotte's hand hovered over the door handle. "Ready?" she asked him, but he could see that she wasn't nearly ready to face whatever waited for them downstairs.

"Yes, I'm ready," he told her. "It will be okay." He didn't elaborate, likely doing a poor job of reassuring her.

Charlotte nodded and reached for the handle. "It's locked." She shot him a look before focusing on the key-hole in the center of the knob.

If Harley had left to look for Betty, he might have secured the door in case someone was to happen upon the house. But what was he hiding behind the lock?

"Stand back." Charlotte took the butt of her weapon and slammed it against the knob. It took half a dozen tries before the knob broke off. The door still wouldn't open.

"Let me." Jonas put his full weight against the door, and it eventually gave way.

Darkness and bitter cold flew up to greet them.

Jonas tried the light switch without any response. The lights would probably be powered by a generator, which obviously wasn't working.

He pulled out the flashlight and clicked it, shining it down the steps to the floor below. From his limited line of sight, the space appeared cluttered with boxes.

"Stay close," Charlotte repeated and started down the steps, using her flashlight in one hand to guide her and the handgun at the ready in the other.

Jonas glanced over his shoulder, expecting Harley to appear out of the blue and attack them.

He wasn't normally one for jumping at shadows, but the last hours they'd spent trying to allude people who were trying to kill them had taught him that not being aware of his surroundings could cost lives.

Charlotte stopped abruptly when one of the stairs squeaked. She blew out a breath that chilled the air in front of her. "Let's keep going." She slowly covered the remaining steps until she stood on the basement floor.

Jonas stopped next to her. The space was filled with boxes and what appeared to be other types of electronics and expensive phones and tablets like Betty had described.

"Where did he get all of this?" Jonas asked as he flashed the light around the clutter.

"He probably stole it. Or someone else did and it's a form of payment for getting the girls."

Jonas's mouth thinned. Harley had been up to terrible things.

Moving through the clutter was difficult. Jonas shoved boxes out of the way just to have a place to walk.

He and Charlotte slowly fanned out and searched every corner of the room. His worst fear was he'd find the bodies of the young women among the boxes, or that Harley was just waiting for him to make a wrong move to take him out.

Something moved out of the corner of his eye and Jonas whirled toward it. He realized it was a rat the size of a small dog. The sight of the rodent gave him the creeps.

He kept searching until he reached one wall. There was a door. Jonas drew in a breath and slowly pulled the door open. A small closet stuffed with more electronics greeted him. He bent over in relief.

"Anything?" Charlotte called out from beyond the stacks of boxes.

"Nothing but a rat. What about you?"

"There's no sign of them... Wait, I see something."

Jonas hurried over as fast as the clutter would allow. "What is it?"

"Bullet holes." She pointed to the wall. "I count at least three and there are several more lodged in the boxes." She flashed the light all around. "But there's no sign of blood."

Which meant Harley hadn't hit those young women with his shots. Had he been trying to scare them or simply on the verge of a breakdown and out of control?

FIFTEEN

"Where are they?" Charlotte glanced around the crowded space before turning the key over in her hand. "And what does this fit?"

"Whatever it is, I don't believe it's down here. We should head back upstairs. It's freezing down here."

She agreed and started for the steps when a sound caught her attention. "Did you hear that?" The sound came again. "A whimper."

Charlotte hurried toward the noise. "It's coming from inside the wall. Hello?" she called. "Who's there?"

"Help! Please, help us!" A young woman's frantic voice came from nearby.

"I'm Deputy Charlotte Walker. How did you get in there?"

"There's a hidden door," the muffled voice replied. "He tapped the wall and it opened."

Charlotte and Jonas both began knocking on the wall.

"Wait, I have something." Jonas felt around the wide crack in between boards. "Got it." He yanked hard and the hidden door opened.

Four frightened women were tied to hooks on the wall.

"Help us," the same woman cried out while others whimpered, clearly too afraid to speak.

All four shivered from fear and the cold, their eyes huge and terrified.

"We've got you," Charlotte told the vocal woman and, with Jonas's help, worked to untie the leather straps that secured the women to the hooks. "Where did Harley go?" she asked the one who'd spoken before.

Once she was loose, the young woman rubbed her wrists. "I'm not sure. I heard him rummaging around and then he went upstairs but he hasn't returned."

"What's your name?" Charlotte asked.

"I'm Elizabeth. This is Sally, Jennifer and Maria." She pointed to each of the freed women. "Please, you have to get us out of here before he comes back."

Charlotte uttered a silent prayer of thanks that they'd been able to find the women.

"She's right," she told Jonas. "We'll take them to Betty and then return because I can't help but sense there are answers here somewhere."

Charlotte led the way up the stairs all the while expecting Harley to waylay them.

"Did you find the other girl?" Elizabeth asked once they reached the landing and gathered in the kitchen.

"You mean another girl who was with you at the first house?" Charlotte asked.

Elizabeth shook her head. "No, she was here with us earlier. She said her name was Sasha."

Shocked, Charlotte jerked toward Jonas. "That's the name of the girl Michaela reported."

"She showed up here after the older woman left," Elizabeth explained. "I heard her and Harley get into this terrible argument and then I heard her scream."

"He must have taken her with him," Jonas said. "Let's get these women to my cabin and out of danger."

Charlotte slipped outside the side door and checked

to make sure it was safe before ushering the women outside. "Stay close. We have no idea where Harley is," she warned. Charlotte gave the word for Annie to follow.

Every step of the way to Jonas's cabin was filled with apprehension.

As they neared, Charlotte called out to Betty. "It's us, Betty. Open the door." She searched their surroundings to make sure Harley hadn't followed them.

Sounds of the chair being moved were followed by the door opening. When Betty spotted the girls, she clasped her hand over her mouth. "I was so worried…so afraid he'd killed you."

Charlotte followed the women inside with Jonas. "We can't stay." She explained about the key they'd found. "Do you have any idea what it might fit?"

"I'm not sure," Betty told her, "but I do remember Harley kept eyeing the bookcase when he found me down in the basement, as if he didn't want me near it."

Charlotte squeezed Betty's arm. "Thank you. Take care of the girls."

Once the chair was back in place, Charlotte called the dog, and they hiked the distance back to Harley's mountain house. It felt quicker this time, knowing where they were going, and that Harley's captives were safe. She'd even forgotten about the cold, though the snow kept falling.

They were so close to this being over…just a little bit farther.

"I wonder if there's a safe behind the bookcase…or if the key is to a door," Charlotte said. "The way Harley was able to escape with Sasha. What's her part in all this?"

He frowned. "No doubt she was a victim in the beginning, like you said, and probably agreed to help Harley to stay alive."

As they reached Harley's house, the dog served as lookout again as they entered through the side door once more. Charlotte started back downstairs. "We have to find out what's behind the bookcase."

She pulled the key free of its tape and kept the book with names with her as she hurried down the steps once more.

Jonas followed her down the stairs.

Charlotte reached the bookcase, which held a handful of outdated books. "I didn't notice this before. There's a space between the bookcase and the wall. Help me move it."

With Jonas's help, they were able to inch the heavy piece of furniture away enough to see behind it.

"A door!" Jonas exclaimed. It stood slightly ajar as if someone had been in a rush and had forgotten to close it.

Charlotte flashed the light into what appeared to be a tunnel with a low ceiling. "I don't like this," she whispered with trepidation washing over her.

Jonas let out a breath. "If Harley used the tunnel to escape, he could be long gone by now."

Charlotte slipped inside with Jonas right behind her. The space was dank. "These look like footprints." Charlotte zeroed the light in on the ground where multiple prints were embedded in the dust. "Someone's been down this tunnel recently."

She had a bad feeling, and yet if there was a chance at catching Harley, they had to go after him. "Let's keep going." She bent down so that she could move. Jonas remained close behind her. They had only taken a few steps when a noise behind them had Charlotte turning. "Someone's here."

Jonas jerked toward the sound. Something was tossed inside, and the door slammed shut. Charlotte recognized the object immediately. "It's a grenade. Run, Jonas!" She whipped around and started running, Jonas right on top of her.

They'd managed only a handful of steps when an explosion rocked the world around them. Charlotte lost her footing and fell to the dirt. Jonas placed his body over her to protect her as the explosion reduced the tunnel in the direction they'd come to rubble. Ashen dust flew down, covering everything, including them.

Charlotte coughed, trying to clear the dust from her lungs. They both sat up. "Are you okay?" she asked.

He was covered in white, and the dust reduced him to a fit of coughing, which was concerning.

"Jonas?" She couldn't find her flashlight.

"I'm okay," he wheezed and shoved the rubble that had landed on them away. "There's the light." He grabbed it and shone it around to reveal the devastation. Part of the ceiling had collapsed along with half the tunnel. Every second they were here they were in danger of the rest of it collapsing. Somehow, Harley had been able to hide from them until they were inside and then he'd taken advantage of the situation to try to kill them.

"The evidence. I lost it in the collapse."

Jonas flashed the light around until he located the book. "Here." He handed it to Charlotte.

"Thank goodness." She'd tucked both phones and the key into her pocket. They were safe inside—she wouldn't lose track of them until they were in the sheriff's hands.

More rumbling sounded as pieces of the tunnel continued to break away.

"It's not safe here. We need to see where this tunnel leads," Jonas told her. He slowly rose as far as he could and helped Charlotte up.

The ground beneath them shook violently. "This whole

place is going to collapse. We'll need to reach the end before that happens."

Another rumble had her stumbling. She grabbed hold of Jonas and together they held on until the moment passed. A blast of debris flew all around them.

"Run!" Charlotte yelled again when she looked over her shoulder and couldn't see anything but a dust cloud.

She raced down the tunnel with the flashlight's beam picking up nothing but gray.

Over the rumbles of aftershocks, keeping their feet beneath them was next to impossible. She prayed there was a way out at the end of the tunnel, and that Harley hadn't destroyed it before trying to kill them. If so, they'd be buried here along with Harley's secrets.

Jonas couldn't see an end in sight. The dust was so thick, and every breath he took tasted like ash.

"I can't imagine this can go on much farther," Charlotte managed before coughing violently.

"We need to cover our noses and mouths." Jonas ripped off more of his lining and handed her a strip. The inside of his jacket had become completely frayed. "It's not much, but it might help."

Charlotte stopped long enough to tie the cloth over her nose and mouth. "It helps."

Jonas did the same and they started moving again. How had the tunnel come to be in the first place? Though he wasn't acquainted with Harley beyond what he'd seen him do to Betty, and what he'd heard from Charlotte, his neighbor didn't seem the type to put a lot of hard labor into doing something like this.

"Do you suppose Harley built the tunnel?" he asked Charlotte. She had slowed down. Despite covering their noses and mouths, it was still difficult breathing, and the struggle was slowing them down.

"No way. I'm not sure this house even belongs to Harley. It seems likely that this tunnel was made on the orders of whoever's heading up the trafficking ring as a way to move girls." She steadied herself as another blast rocked the ground.

Charlotte breathed deeply. "But who knows… It's hard to think clearly."

He felt the same way. He could feel his body slowing down from the miles of walking and this final blow.

"This place gives me the creeps," Charlotte said with a shudder. "It seems almost as if we're living on borrowed time."

Jonas felt the same way. He prayed they reached the end before the whole thing collapsed.

A crashing noise up ahead had him stopping. "What was that?"

Charlotte stood beside him and waited. "I don't know but I don't like the sound of it."

A few minutes later, the sound of an engine firing overhead could be heard. "It must be Harley. He's leaving."

"Let's keep going," Charlotte said. "The only way to get help is to get out of here alive."

As they continued walking, a scent much stronger than the dust reached them.

"Is it…?" Charlotte whirled around and stared up at him, wide-eyed.

"Smoke." He voiced it in utter disbelief. Harley had set the place on fire. "If the collapsing tunnel isn't enough, he's going to burn us alive."

The terror on her face made him wish he'd chosen his words better. "We still have a chance," he told her and placed his hands on her shoulders. "We keep fighting. We don't give up."

Charlotte slowly nodded. "You're right. This tunnel is safe from the fire, unless it can penetrate the compromised areas…"

"We aren't sure that's happened."

Still, the smoke from above was mingling with the dust and making it impossible to breathe. Soon, it wouldn't matter if the fire could reach them. The smoke they were inhaling would kill them.

They kept moving as fast as they could to stay ahead of the rumbles that continued to shake the collapsing tunnel. Jonas tried not to give in to the fear that gripped him—they just needed to focus on getting out.

"I see something." Jonas focused the light ahead. "That looks like a door." She ran toward it and he followed.

They reached for the door handle and realized it was locked from the outside.

"Oh, no." Charlotte shoved her weight against it. "It won't budge."

Behind them, the smoke grew thicker. "Let's see if we can get the doorknob loose and hopefully the door will open." Jonas followed Charlotte's earlier example and slammed the butt of the handgun against the handle. It gave way eventually, only the door didn't open. He threw his weight against it. "Something's blocking it."

Charlotte took the flashlight and shone it through the hole where the doorknob used to be. "I can't see anything." She straightened. "I'm certain Harley put something in front of the door. Something heavy."

In other words, if they couldn't get the door open, they were stuck here with no way to escape. His chest tightened—they were running out of time.

"Let's see if we can work together and get it open," he

said with a calm he didn't feel. Jonas placed his shoulder against the door and waited for Charlotte to do the same.

"On the count of three." He counted off and they worked together to shove against the door. Nothing happened.

"This isn't working," Charlotte said, her voice rising. "We're stuck, Jonas." She searched his face. "We'll have to try and go back the way we came. Let's see if we can move the debris out of the way."

They both knew the odds of getting through the rubble was next to impossible, but she was right. If they remained here and did nothing, they'd be dead.

SIXTEEN

Charlotte's legs were rubber. Walking took all the strength she could muster, but there wasn't any other option. If they didn't try, death was certain.

She kept close behind Jonas. Every little rumble had her cringing and thinking this could be the one that ended it all.

As they headed back down the tunnel, the smoke grew thicker. Both she and Jonas were coughing hard, their eyes watering so much, it was hard to see.

She tapped his shoulder. "We need to dampen the rags." She pointed to the cloth covering her mouth and nose. "It should help us breathe and keep some of the smoke out."

Charlotte pulled out her bottled water she'd taken from the fire tower from her jacket pocket and wet the cloth while Jonas did the same.

It helped some, or maybe she just wanted it to be better.

They reached the first pile of rubble, which completely blocked the path ahead.

Jonas began moving the rocks. Charlotte moved to his side and assisted until there was enough room to crawl over the remaining rocks.

Jonas went first. Once he'd reached the other side, he held out his hand for Charlotte. "You can do it."

Though it sounded as if Harley was heading away from their location, she was still worried he would somehow find Betty and the girls. They had to make it out of here. Charlotte told Jonas about her fears.

He shook his head. "Harley's too worried about saving himself to go back for them."

She got down on her hands and knees and crawled through the opening with his help.

"One down," she said and attempted a laugh to lighten the moment.

"Let's hope there aren't too many more."

Tension coiled through her body. Having to walk almost doubled over and breathing in a mixture of dust and smoke was taking its toll. Her back ached. Her eyes burned and teared up. And her lungs felt as if they were clogged.

Another pile of debris lay ahead of them. The heat from the fire above had grown intense.

"I sure hope we're not walking into the fire," Jonas said.

So far, the light hadn't picked up any flames, but then she had no idea what would lay on the other side of the debris field.

Charlotte touched her hand to it. "I don't feel heat."

Together they worked to free a space to pass through.

Once they were on the other side, Charlotte shone the light all around. They were close to the door they'd entered.

After working their way around another mountain of rocks, Charlotte stood before the door.

Once more, she felt it to see if it was safe. "It's cool to the touch." She looked under the door but there was no sign of smoke.

"Let's try it," Jonas said. He attempted to push the door open but something was blocking it.

"It's the bookcase." Charlotte joined him and they tried to push the door open.

"This is more than the bookcase," Jonas said. "It's like something has been nailed over the door to prevent it from opening... Harley did this. He wants us to die down here." He stepped back and looked at the path they'd come. "I'm not sure what to do."

Charlotte reached for his hand. "We pray."

His eyes held hers. "You're right. We've done everything we could. *Gott* is the only One who can save us now."

Clutching his hand, Charlotte poured out her heart to God. "We need You, Lord. We're all out of options as far as we can see through human eyes, but we know that You can get us through this. We wait on You, Lord. Please help us. Amen."

Though their circumstances hadn't changed yet, they wouldn't die here. God had a plan for them, and it wasn't to die here in this tunnel.

"There's no way out here, we have to go back," Charlotte said. "We have nothing to lose at this point."

Together she and Jonas scrambled back toward the other end of the tunnel. They knew how to maneuver around the debris this time. As they neared, barking came from beyond the door. Had the fire gone out? The barking was the best sound ever. "That's Annie. She's found her way to the end of the tunnel." Once Charlotte reached the door, she called out to her partner. "Annie, get help. We need you to get help."

The dog barked again but she didn't move.

"She's not responding," Jonas said.

Charlotte's heart sank. Annie wasn't leaving her behind. Her eyes filled with tears, and she sank down to her knees. "Annie, it's okay." She loved the dog and couldn't bear the thought of dying and leaving her alone.

Jonas knelt beside her and took her in his arms.

She wrapped her arms around him and held him tight. "Jonas, I'm so sorry." She was crying but it felt right. The emotions that had been boiling up inside her were finally free.

"Don't…" he murmured and tipped her chin back. "I'd do it all over again."

Charlotte pushed her mask aside and lowered his. If this was the end for them, she wanted to kiss him one more time.

She leaned forward and touched her lips to his. A sob escaped and the dam released. She kissed him with everything in her heart.

Jonas placed his hands on either side of her head and kissed her back.

The dog continued barking and then another sound had them breaking apart.

"What was that?" Charlotte asked.

It took her a few seconds to realize it was the sound of someone near the door.

"There's someone out there," Jonas said.

Would Annie remain there if Harley or his associates had come to do them harm?

"Charlotte, are you in there?" Sheriff Wyatt McCallister called out.

"Yes. I'm here with Jonas Knowles," she replied. "The tunnel is collapsing. We're trapped."

"We're going to get you out of there," Wyatt assured her. "Hold on."

"Hurry," she urged. "There's a fire, and smoke is pouring in."

"We got you, Charlotte. You just stay close to the door where you can get some fresh air."

It was going to be okay. Despite everything Harley and his people had thrown at them, they were going to be okay.

The noise of what sounded like a tool being used to try and pry the door open could be heard over the noise of the fire.

"Wyatt, Harley Owens is behind this." Charlotte told the sheriff all they'd discovered. "He left the area in a side-by-side like the one out front."

The sheriff spoke to one of his people before answering. "We'll get him, Charlotte. The fire has just about burned what's left of the house. When we arrived, we were so afraid until we heard Annie barking."

Annie had saved their lives.

Jonas held Charlotte close as they kept near the door. The door eased open slightly, the fresh air rushing through the hole was pure bliss.

"We're almost there," the sheriff called out. "I've never seen a door like this one before. There's no door handle or lock. It's metal and several inches thick. I'm thinking Harley had some type of remote to close it, which would make it easy to close but without the property tools impossible to open."

Jonas was angry at the lengths Harley was willing to go to save himself and harm others.

Charlotte explained about Betty. "She has the four women who were taken with her."

A pause, then Wyatt said, "I'll send some men to get them and take them to the station. You probably saved their lives."

Charlotte told him about Sasha's role in things, as well. "He has her and she's in danger because she has things on Harley that will incriminate him."

Soon the last obstacle was removed from in front of the door, and it opened.

Jonas, still holding on to Charlotte, stepped from the nightmare of smoke and dust into the cold and snowy morning, and it had never felt more welcoming.

Blankets were placed over their shoulders. "Let's get you into my cruiser to warm up." The man whose voice Jonas recognized as the sheriff led them over to a Jeep bearing the sheriff's insignia on it.

He waited until both Jonas and Charlotte had slipped into the back seat before he got in and cranked the heater up high.

Sheriff Wyatt McCallister turned in his seat so he would see them.

"Sheriff, this is Jonas Knowles," Charlotte said, gesturing to him. "I wouldn't be alive right now if it weren't for him."

"It's nice to meet you, Sheriff," Jonas said. "You and your people are a welcomed sight. Do you have any word on Abram and Lainey?"

The sheriff nodded. "She called earlier, and we picked her and Abram up. She was treated at the hospital. They are both safe at the station."

That was good news indeed.

"Both were too shaken up to make much sense," Sheriff McCallister continued, "but I have a suspicion whatever is happening here is huge."

Charlotte reached for Jonas's hand and explained to her boss what led her to Harley's house in the first place.

The sheriff's brow creased. "So, Harley kidnapped Lainey from near her work?"

"That's correct." Charlotte nodded. "Dottie called me in to help. I thought it would be just a simple matter of

Lainey falling asleep in the camp." She shook her head. "Boy, was I wrong."

Charlotte remembered the ledger and the key she'd placed in her pocket. "There's something else you need to hear." She told him about Elliott Shores's involvement. "He's part of the ring, Wyatt. And there are others in high places involved."

"Like possibly the coroner," Jonas added.

The sheriff's frown deepened. "This is terrible."

"One more thing," Charlotte added. "Elliott and several others referred to the person in charge by the initials D.A." She looked to Jonas. "We haven't been able to figure out his name, though."

The sheriff scanned the tunnel area where his men were examining. "Do you have any idea how many men are in the woods looking for you?"

Jonas shook his head. "We lost track. There were several groups and I'm pretty sure we ran into some more than once. I'd say at least a dozen." Charlotte nodded in agreement.

"Stay put," the sheriff instructed. "I've called in extra manpower. Lainey and Abram told us about Elliott. I've alerted his chief to what he is being accused of. He had no idea one of his officers was involved in a human trafficking ring." Wyatt shook his head.

"I want to be part of the group who goes after Harley and the rest of the men," Charlotte told her superior.

He eyed her carefully. "You're exhausted. You need to go to the hospital and get checked out for smoke inhalation at the very least."

Charlotte shook her head, clearly ready to reject his suggestion. "I'm fine, Wyatt. This is too important. I want to see it through for Michaela and Ryan."

The sheriff's brows rose. "What are you talking about?

Do you believe their deaths had something to do with this?"

"I do." Charlotte told him her suspicions.

McCallister leaned forward in his seat. "I never understood a lot of things about the case starting with Ryan's fall. He'd been through much more difficult situations than what he faced on the mountain that day."

"Exactly," Charlotte said. "I'm certain he spotted Michaela with whoever was trying to kill her and tried to help."

And whoever had Michaela had recognized Ryan, so he'd had to die, too. It sickened Jonas to imagine how many people's lives were sacrificed so they could keep doing what they were doing. How many others in authority were involved in this dreadful crime ring?

"I want to be part of bringing them down, too," Jonas told them both. For Charlotte but also for himself. He wanted to see Harley behind bars and make sure Betty would never have to deal with her abusive husband again. And all those men who had played a part in hurting so many innocents, he wanted them to be brought to justice and made to pay for what they'd done. They'd ruined so many lives because of greed.

"Not going to happen," McCallister said, facing him. "You're a civilian. I understand you're invested in this case, Jonas, but as these men have proven, they're dangerous and have everything to lose."

"Sheriff, come in." The police radio squawked to life.

The sheriff hit the mic attached to his jacket. "Go ahead, Rogers."

"We've spotted the side-by-side."

McCallister sat up straight. "Where?"

The deputy gave the coordinates.

"We're on our way." The sheriff gave the command to

his team and put the Jeep into gear. "Buckle up. There's some rough terrain ahead."

Jonas snapped the seat belt into place and held on tight as the Jeep pulled out and barreled down the mountainside. Jonas prayed Harley would be taken alive. They needed answers that only he could provide.

SEVENTEEN

Wyatt slowed the vehicle to a crawl then stopped.

Charlotte noticed an officer heading their way. "That must be the one who spotted Harley."

The rest of the team pulled in behind Wyatt's vehicle.

"Sheriff," the deputy acknowledged once all three had exited the cruiser. "As far as I can tell, he's held up in a trapper's cabin a quarter of a mile down the mountain. I came across the side-by-side abandoned in the woods just up from here. It looks as if he ran out of fuel."

Wyatt's steely gaze scanned the area. "And how do you know he's still in the cabin?"

"I approached the cabin and saw movement inside. That's when I radioed you."

Wyatt nodded. "Since we don't have an idea of how many others may be in the cabin, we approach cautiously. Harley may be holding up with some people loyal to him." Wyatt directed several of his deputies to circle around behind the cabin. They would come from all directions.

"Jonas, you need to wait for us here," Charlotte told him. They'd gone through so much together. She couldn't bear it if something happened to him when they were so close to finishing this nightmare.

He reluctantly agreed.

She got out and followed Wyatt. As the team of law

enforcement officers approached, Charlotte noticed that the cabin appeared to have only one window.

When they were still some distance away, Wyatt ordered them to halt. He radioed to the deputies around the back. "Any sign of Harley?"

"Negative, Sheriff. There's no window at the back, only a door. Should we keep going?"

"Affirmative."

Charlotte's hands shook on the weapon in her hand as the team edged toward the cabin.

"Take the door," Wyatt ordered the officers around back.

On Wyatt's command, the front entrance was breached. In a matter of seconds, they were inside, and the tense scene unfolded.

The cabin was larger than Jonas's. The team quickly cleared the living room and kitchen. One closed door remained.

Wyatt gestured toward the door. As they neared, a barrage of shots flew through the wooden door, and everyone jumped back.

When silence returned, Wyatt moved to the door. He was a strong man who led by example. Wyatt kicked the door open. It slammed against the wall. Another round of shots had them backing away.

A click, click, click followed. "Go!" Charlotte yelled, and the team poured into the room. Harley held a knife against the throat of a noticeably emaciated woman with purple hair. Michaela had mentioned Sasha had purple hair... This was Sasha.

The young woman's frightened eyes latched on to Charlotte for help.

Wyatt stepped forward. "It's over, Harley. Let her go. There's no getting out of this. Drop the knife and get your hands in the air."

She'd never seen Harley look so freaked out before. "No way," he said while continually shaking his head. "You're going to kill me if I do."

"No one's going to hurt you," Wyatt assured him. "This is your chance to help yourself by bringing in the rest of those men. But you have to let her go."

Harley appeared to lose all color. "They'll kill me."

"We can protect you," Wyatt assured him.

Harley's hand on the knife shook. "You promise you aren't going to shoot me?"

"I'm the sheriff, Harley. I'm not going to let anyone hurt you. You have my word."

Harley's grip on Sasha tightened briefly before he let her go.

"Come to me," Charlotte told Sasha. The woman ran into Charlotte's open arms. "You're safe now." Sasha buried her face against Charlotte's shoulder.

But the situation wasn't over yet.

"Drop the knife, Harley," Wyatt said calmly. "We're almost finished but you need to drop the knife."

Harley stared at it as if he had forgotten he held it. He lowered his hand and placed the knife on the floor.

"Okay, now kick it over to me," Wyatt told him. Charlotte watched him do what he did best. Wyatt could make a victim, or a perp, feel as if they were his best friend.

Once the knife was out of Harley's reach, Wyatt picked it up and handed it to his deputy.

"Okay, I need you to put your hands behind your back, Harley. I'm going to cuff you and then we're taking you back to the station."

"You're going to kill me." Harley was practically in tears.

Wyatt kept eye contact with the man as he said, "Now,

Harley, I gave you my word. I'm not going to let anyone hurt you."

"All right, but I'm trusting you." Harley turned around and Wyatt cuffed him and led him from the room.

As he passed by them, Sasha shrank away.

"You're okay. Is your name Sasha?" Charlotte asked. She needed to be sure.

The young woman's surprise was clear. "Yes. How did you know?"

"Michaela told me."

Sasha flinched then tears filled her eyes. "I didn't mean for her to die. I was just trying to stay alive."

"It's okay," Charlotte said and led her to the living room where EMTs had arrived. "Let them check you out and then you will be transported to the sheriff's station for questioning. Is there someone we can call?"

Sasha's tears fell freely. "M-my parents. I haven't spoken to them in years."

While Sasha was treated, Charlotte stepped outside. Jonas left the vehicle and joined her.

She told him what happened. "I'm so glad Wyatt convinced him to surrender." She held up her shaking hands.

Jonas glanced around at the activity taking place. "I'm glad he's in custody but we still don't have any idea about the others."

"No, we don't." Charlotte looked toward the cruiser where Harley was being held. "Hopefully, he can help unravel the truth, along with Sasha. You're right about her. She's a victim."

Harley on the other hand, well, Charlotte wanted him to get what he deserved. Harley Owens should never see the outside of a prison again.

Wyatt found them. "This is something else," he said. "We have law enforcement agents scouring the woods for the rest of those involved." He glanced back at Harley. "My guess is, they'll hear the news soon enough and scatter."

"We can't let them get away, Wyatt. Every one of them needs to pay for what they've done." Charlotte couldn't imagine how someone sworn to protect the public could get involved in trafficking young women.

"I'm going to run Harley into town and get him processed. By the way, the other young women who were kidnapped are safe at the station and giving their statements." Wyatt blew out a sigh. "I'm guessing you want to be part of Harley's interview?"

"I do, but I want to be part of bringing in the rest of those men, as well, and I'm pretty sure we should start at the camp."

Wyatt nodded. "Let's bring those who hide in darkness to the light and make them show their faces."

The first set of vehicles parked some distance from the Christian camp. According to the team of law officers sitting on the camp, an unknown number of people were holed up inside.

Jonas had never had much dealing with law enforcement except for the occasional visits from Charlotte concerning Harley. Now, he found himself in a manhunt to bring down members of a trafficking ring and he understood the adrenaline rush that came from tracking down a bad guy.

"Are you doing okay?" Charlotte asked. She'd been keeping a close eye on him.

He swung her way. "Just ready to have this finished." Something shifted in her eyes, and she looked sad. Jonas wondered what he'd said to be responsible.

"It's almost over." She nodded. "Soon, you'll be able to return to your life."

Was it his imagination or was there a strain to her voice he hadn't heard before? Before he could ask her, several of her fellow law enforcement officers came over.

Charlotte turned away, and he doubted everything he'd once believed he thought she felt toward him. He'd opened his heart up again after losing Ivy—he'd thought for certain Charlotte returned his feelings—and yet the chilliness in her behavior now had him convinced he'd misread everything. "We have people in place around the camp. No one's getting through," Elliott's boss, Chief Harris, assured her.

Jonas didn't trust the chief fully. After all, Elliott was dirty. What if there were others? She nodded. "Let's hope they're all there."

"Do you trust him?" Jonas asked once the chief disappeared.

She turned to him and Jonas tried to recover from the impression he'd lost her,

"I do," she said quietly. "But I need you to stay here, Jonas." Charlotte drew her weapon and checked the magazine.

"All right." He reluctantly did as she asked but watched the band of law enforcement agents as they advanced toward the camp.

Clearing a place as big as the camp took time. They started with the living quarters and worked their way toward the center of the camp where the dining hall and the chapel were located.

Shots were fired near the dining hall. Jonas's fear for Charlotte's safety had him wanting to rush after her. He squinted through the sea of officers and spotted her. She was okay.

Several armed men appeared to be inside still and doing their best to hold off the police.

The officers exchanged shots with the criminals, peppering the walls of the dining hall until silence returned to the camp.

"Take the building," Chief Harris's command could be heard from where Jonas stood. Officers and deputies stormed it, and he knew Charlotte was among them.

He counted off every tense-filled minute until she and the rest of the officers exited the building. A half dozen cuffed men were led out.

Charlotte found him and came over.

"Was anyone hurt?" he asked.

She shook her head, her attention on the restrained men. "There's Elliott," she said in flat tone.

Shores kept his attention on the ground while his chief secured his hands behind his back.

Charlotte hurried over to the policeman. When Shores saw her, he looked as if he would have backed away if it weren't for Chief Harris holding on to him.

"You were my friend." Charlotte's hands clenched at her sides, her expression tight as she waited for Shores to speak but he didn't.

"You realized how important Ryan was to me, yet all this time you were part of the ones who killed him."

Shores flinched as if she'd struck him. "I don't know what you're talking about. I had nothing to do with Ryan's death."

His nervous denial proved his involvement in Jonas's mind.

"This is all a misunderstanding," Shores said. "I was working undercover to bring down this ring."

"That's not true!" He knew Charlotte wouldn't let him go on. "You're part of it. How could you? You have a wife and little girls." She turned away, a disgusted expression on her face.

"I *am* working undercover," the cop insisted. "I found out about what was happening and decided to go undercover."

Charlotte whirled back to him. "If that's so then why doesn't your chief here have knowledge about your doings?" Shores didn't have an answer.

Jonas watched alongside Charlotte as the guilty were led away.

"We still don't have the one in charge," she said in frustration. "And I have a feeling these men will be too afraid to speak his name."

Jonas couldn't get the key out of his head. "I realize we searched Harley's house before, but we never found a safe. He could have hidden it."

"You're right." Charlotte motioned to one of the deputies. "Brad, can I use your cruiser?" She told him where they were headed.

"Sure." He tossed her the keys. "I can catch a ride. I have a suspicion we're going to be busy booking all these men for a while. Do you need backup?"

The stakes were high. Finding the evidence as quick as possible was imperative. Charlotte looked at Jonas before shaking her head. "We've got this. Do you mind if I take your phone?" she asked Brad. "Mine was destroyed. I'll let Wyatt know where we're going."

"Okay." Brad handed her his phone. "Be careful. Call if you need help."

Charlotte loaded Annie into the back seat of the police car while Jonas got into the passenger side. She fired the engine and slowly eased from the camp while Jonas recalled the terrifying moments they'd gone through here.

"I'm glad Abram and Lainey are safe, as well as those

women," he said. "But there were others who weren't so lucky. If we can save them still…"

"I hope so. Hang on," Charlotte warned as the path in front of them grew rough.

Jonas grabbed the dash as the cruiser rocked over some downed trees.

"Sorry about that." She glanced his way.

More than anything, Jonas wanted to open his heart up and tell her what he felt for her and yet…

If he were to admit his feelings—if he let himself become that vulnerable again and she rejected him, Jonas wasn't sure he'd recover from a blow like that.

EIGHTEEN

Charlotte could almost sense the tension in Jonas. He kept looking her way. He wanted to ask her about the way she'd reacted to him earlier. But how could she answer him when she wasn't sure herself. Why had she hesitated? Every time she looked at Jonas, she thought about Ryan and the unfinished business standing in their way.

She eased the cruiser onto the road that ran past Jonas's house.

"Do you believe we have all the men?" he asked with a hint of uneasiness in his tone.

She blew out a sigh, just happy they were talking again. "I sure hope so. Except for the person who's in charge, but then I doubt he gets his hands dirty, and if he's gotten wind of what's been happening, he could have fled the county by now."

Charlotte prayed that she was wrong about the coroner being involved. It was bad enough Elliott had betrayed his oath.

"I feel sorry for Betty." Jonas sighed. "She doesn't work. How's she going to survive this?"

Charlotte touched his arm. "We'll do what we can to help her. She doesn't deserve to lose everything because of her husband's crimes."

As they reached the spot where she'd begun her search

for Lainey, Charlotte shivered when she thought about how close to death she'd come. Did Elliott have any knowledge she'd been taken, and that Harley was planning to kill her? The betrayal she felt at the thought of Elliott okaying her murder shook her to her core.

She made the bend in the road, and the house sat as another reminder of what had happened.

Charlotte rolled the cruiser to a stop. The darkness of the house gave her the creeps.

"Here, take this...just in case." Charlotte handed him the extra weapon she'd taken from one of Harley's people. She unholstered her weapon and opened the door. Jonas did the same. She carefully closed the door and panned the area looking for anything that might spell trouble. Nothing but silence. She opened the back door and let Annie out. The dog sniffed the ground and headed around the corner of the house like before.

Jonas shot her a look. "Is she on something?"

"I'm not sure." With her weapon drawn and ready, Charlotte eased around the corner of the house with Jonas at her six.

The dog had reached the back porch and was sniffing around. When she spotted Charlotte, Annie wagged her tail and Charlotte relaxed. "She's just following scents— nothing in particular." The relief she felt at not having to face down another bad guy made her knees feel weak.

At the back door, Charlotte glanced through the kitchen and what was visible of the living room. "I don't see anyone." She slowly opened the door and stepped inside.

When they'd come here earlier, she and Jonas were looking for the missing women. They'd searched the place but hadn't been looking for a safe.

"We stay together," Charlotte instructed. Starting in

the kitchen, Charlotte began opening cabinets. "Don't overlook anything. It's possible Harley could have a small lockbox the size of a shoebox or maybe something bigger." And it was possible the key fit a safe-deposit box of something they might never find. She struggled not to give in to the doubts.

Jonas took the opposite side of the kitchen, and they searched through every cabinet and drawer.

"Nothing here." Charlotte placed her hands on her hips. "The laundry room." They'd given it only a cursory look before.

She hurried through the opening off the kitchen, which led to the room containing a washer and dryer, a small sink and several cabinets. "Please be here." Yet after searching the final cabinet, they were no closer to finding the safe than before.

"What about in one of the closets?" Jonas suggested.

"It's possible." There was still lots of house to check. Yet her sinking sensation wouldn't let her go.

In the hall, there were closets on either side. While Jonas checked one, Charlotte opened the door to the other. It was crammed full of junk. She blew out a frustrated sigh and started digging.

"Anything?" Jonas asked once he'd finished his search.

"Not yet."

He came over and knelt beside her. While he worked, she glanced at his strong profile. Exhaustion clung to him as it did her, yet he'd never once faltered in backing her up. He was a strong and handsome man, and she cared deeply for him. She might even... She couldn't let herself say the word *love*. She'd loved Ryan but hadn't thought herself capable of giving her heart to someone else.

Jonas glanced her way. She turned her attention to a box she'd dragged out to look through.

After an exhausting search, the closet yielded nothing useful. "Let's try the living room."

Yet with each room cleared, the hope of finding evidence to identify the person in charge dwindled.

"I wonder if Harley will cooperate to save himself," Jonas suggested after he'd seen her disappointment.

She smiled. "I hope so. I doubt that he has any loyalty to the person who tried to kill him."

"No, Harley's always struck me as the type of person who's only after what is best for him."

Once the final room was searched, the truth became clear. "It's not here," Charlotte managed to get out. "I sure hope we can get Harley to tell us what the key fits." She started for the front of the house when a sound at the back, where Annie had been, grabbed her attention. "Did you hear that?"

Jonas frowned as he started back through the house. "I did."

They reached the back door and Charlotte looked out. Annie was no longer there. "She may have spotted an animal in the woods and gave chase." Before she stepped from the house, she glanced toward the laundry room once more. Something caught her eye. The thickness of the wall was different on the left.

She stopped and pointed it out to Jonas. "There's something off there."

"You're right," he agreed. "Almost as if something has been built into the wall."

She faced him. "We have to break it down."

Charlotte moved to the wall and tapped around. "It appears hollow." She tried the butt of her weapon to smash the Sheetrock. While it worked, it would take forever to get it free. "Did you see any tools in the house?"

Jonas's face brightened. "Yes, in the hall. I'll be right

back." When he returned, he had a couple of hammers with him. "These should work."

Charlotte laid her weapon on the washer opposite them and started swinging the claw part of the hammer. She and Jonas worked together and soon they had a great deal of the wall removed. She flashed her light into the space. "I see something. Hang on." She reached down and grabbed hold of a metal box and pulled it out. "Let's take it to the kitchen where the light is better."

Her hands shook as she carried the box into the kitchen and brought out the key.

With Jonas standing close, she slipped the key into the box, and it opened. She flipped the lid up.

Another ledger was inside much like the one she'd found at the mountain cabin. But this one had names of the people involved in the trafficking ring.

She stood back, amazed at the list of people involved in this.

"Do you see D.A.'s real name?" Jonas asked, looking over her shoulder.

Charlotte began flipping through the pages when a noise nearby grabbed her attention. She looked up and the ledger fell from her hand in shock.

"Phillip?" Phillip Hollins, the county's district attorney, stood in the entrance of the kitchen with a weapon drawn on them. Suddenly everything fell into place. D.A. They'd been looking at the two letters as initials, but it wasn't the leader's initials but his job title.

A sad smile spread across Phillip's face. "You found it. I've been searching all over for that ledger. Kick it over to me."

"Wait, I've seen you before," Jonas whispered. Charlotte saw the shock on his face. "You're the one who pretended to be Betty's nephew."

The betrayal cut like a knife.

"Now, Charlotte." Phillip's kindly tone from before turned hard and unrecognizable.

She and Phillip had worked on many cases together. She'd testified for him lots of times. He and Ryan were best friends and had been since grade school.

She kicked the ledger over. He slowly squatted until he could pick it up while keeping his eyes and the weapon on them.

"How could you? Ryan was your best friend." Phillip had given the eulogy at Ryan's funeral and all the while he was the one responsible for his death.

Something flittered across his face. Regret perhaps. "Yes, well, it was the hardest thing I've ever had to do. I wish it hadn't had to be that way, but Ryan saw me with the girl. He figured out I was involved. I didn't have a choice."

"You had a choice. You could have turned yourself in, but you chose your life over Ryan's and Michaela's."

He looked at her as if she were talking nonsense. "I couldn't go to prison with people I'd put behind bars. They'd kill me." Phillip stuffed the ledger into his jacket. "Harley—he was such an amateur. I should never have gotten him involved. I figured he'd eventually get us all in trouble."

She had placed Brad's phone in her right pocket. Charlotte stepped a little behind Jonas and brought the phone out enough to press the 9-1-1 keys. She prayed the dispatcher could hear enough of the conversation to realize what was happening and send help.

"We thought D.A. was the initials of a person, but it wasn't. It's your position. Phillip Hollins, district attorney," she said loudly.

Phillip looked at her strangely. "We've been over this already."

Beside her, Charlotte noticed Jonas slip his hand in his pocket where his weapon was. It was their only chance.

Charlotte stepped forward enough to hide the activity from Phillip.

"How long have you been involved in trafficking young women, Phillip? How long have you assisted Harley and who knows how many others in getting off when they were guilty?"

Phillip's face contorted in anger. "I didn't have a choice. Harley told me if I didn't help him stay out of jail, he'd go to the police and tell them everything. He said he had a ledger with everyone's names in it that he'd hidden away someplace safe where it wouldn't be found."

She had to keep him talking. "Why did you go after Michaela?"

Phillip's mouth twisted. "I was there at the party the night Sasha brought Michaela there. She saw me… Michaela knew who I was. I'm not sure why she didn't mention seeing me at the party. And I couldn't take the chance she'd keep her mouth shut." He grimaced. "Sasha screwed up by picking Michaela as one of our girls," he spat. "I couldn't risk Michaela changing her mind and going to the police with my name. So, I followed her for a while. She confronted me—told me she was going to tell the police I was involved. I couldn't let that happen."

"So, you kidnapped her," Charlotte said, trying to draw the conversation out while her heart was breaking at what he said.

"Yes. I brought her up to the mountain. I had it all planned out. I'd make it look like a suicide. Michaela was distraught over her missing friend, Sasha. Only Ryan showed up and tried to save her. We fought and I— He fell off the mountain. It was an accident."

Charlotte's stomach clenched. It was a lie. She struggled to keep the pain in when she thought about Ryan's reaction to realizing his friend wanted to kill him.

"So, you killed Ryan and then made Michaela's death look like a suicide, and you got your buddy at the coroner's office to fudge the truth."

Phillip didn't hesitate to confess to everything, likely because he planned to kill them. But then he stopped talking suddenly. "Hey, what are you up to? You've called someone."

He lunged for Charlotte. Jonas pushed her behind him and whipped out his weapon. Down the road, sirens blared. Phillip fired several shots off before Jonas could get a single one off.

Jonas fell to the ground. He'd been shot.

"Jonas!" Charlotte screamed and grabbed the weapon he'd dropped. She fired once. The shot struck Phillip's chest. He hit the floor. Charlotte quickly removed his weapon and felt for a pulse. He was still alive. But right now, all she could think about was she might be losing Jonas.

She dropped down beside Jonas. He stared up at her with fear on his face.

Charlotte unbuttoned his jacket. Blood covered his shirt near his stomach and was quickly spreading. "It's going to be okay," she whispered and grabbed a towel from the counter and placed it against the wound. "Hold on. Help is coming." She grabbed her phone from her pocket. "Dispatch, are you there?"

"I'm here, Charlotte," Ruby answered immediately. "Help should be there soon."

"I need medical attention, as well. Two gunshot victims."

"They're arriving, as well. Hold on."

Charlotte dropped the phone beside her and kept pressure on Jonas's wound. Soon the sirens stopped out front and the house was breached by law enforcement, including Wyatt.

Wyatt ordered men to action. "We need EMTs in here now!"

Two medics ran into the kitchen. One knelt beside Phillip.

"I've got him," Vince, the lead paramedic, assured her as he gently pushed Charlotte out of the way and he and his partner went to work on Jonas.

Jonas's eyes closed as he lost consciousness.

"No." Charlotte covered her mouth with her hand as tears filled her eyes. She couldn't lose him.

The medics worked quickly to get Jonas ready to transport.

"I'm going with him," Charlotte told the two EMTs as the gurney was raised and they headed for the front of the house.

"Go, we've got this," Wyatt called after her.

A second ambulance arrived and two more EMTs took over working on Phillip.

Jonas's gurney was loaded into the ambulance and Charlotte climbed in along with Vince. With lights strobing, they rushed along to Elk Ridge Memorial.

Jonas looked so pale, and he still hadn't regained consciousness.

"He's lost a lot of blood," Vince told her. He hung an IV and packed and bandaged the wound.

They raced down the road and whipped out onto the county road leading to town.

Once they reached the city limits, Dennis, the driver, turned onto the exit for the hospital. As soon as they reached the hospital doors, Vince hopped out and Charlotte followed. Soon, a wealth of medical personnel greeted them, and Jonas was escorted to the ER for examination while Vince ran down his vitals and explained what happened to the attending.

"The bullet is lodged inside. It appears to have nicked his spleen," Vince told the doctor.

Within minutes of the confirmation, Jonas was on his way up to surgery. Charlotte rushed along beside the team. She didn't want to leave his side.

Once they reached the operating room floor, the nurse stopped her. "I'm sorry, deputy, but you'll have to wait here."

Charlotte stopped and watched as Jonas was pushed through the swinging door.

The nurse smiled. "I promise I'll let you know the minute we have word."

It would have to do. "Thank you."

The nurse disappeared behind the doors and Charlotte paced around the waiting area, too worried to sit.

She was making her dozenth or more lap around the circle she'd created when someone stepped from the elevator. It was Wyatt.

She hurried toward him. "Is there word on Phillip?"

"We had to remove his spleen, but he'll be okay."

Charlotte bent over relieved. "Oh, thank goodness. We need him to cooperate." She hugged Wyatt. "Thank you."

He patted her shoulder. "We still have a long way to go to uncover all the players, but thanks to the names in the ledger, it won't take long. You were right about the coroner. He's one of the names listed there. My men are on their way to arrest him now."

She tried to take it all in. "That's unbelievable. And Elliott? He tried to claim he was working undercover."

"Yeah, well, his name is in the ledger, too, and I have a suspicion he's going to back off of the claim soon enough."

She remembered where she'd hidden Harley's phone and told him about it. "How many girls have they taken through the years?" Charlotte couldn't take in the amount of destruction these people had caused.

"We aren't sure, but I have a feeling the first ledger you recovered will tell us. And Harley is screaming he wants to talk. He'll be able to fill in some blanks."

"As long as he doesn't get a lower sentence because of it."

Wyatt assured her he wouldn't. "What's Jonas's prognosis?"

Charlotte swallowed deeply. "He lost a lot of blood, and the bullet nicked his spleen. They're going to have to remove it. Hopefully, there won't be any additional internal damage." Getting those words out was hard.

"He's in good hands." Wyatt looked her in the eye. "Something happening between you two?"

Charlotte wasn't ready to talk about it. The realization she'd fallen in love with Jonas was still too new.

"Never mind." Wyatt held up his hands. "It won't be like Ryan, Charlotte. I have a feeling Jonas is going to be okay." With another pat on the arm, Wyatt left her to the self-realization that, despite her attempts to deny it and cling to the past and her guilt over Ryan, that part of her life was over. Ryan had loved her, but she couldn't bring him back.

She turned toward the double doors. Her future was in there, fighting for his life.

Please God, don't let him die.

When the exhaustion of running for their lives caught

up with her, Charlotte found a chair close by so she could watch those double doors. And she sat and kept her focus on them and the future waiting for her.

After several hours, the same nurse who'd stopped her earlier came out and Charlotte leaped to her feet.

"How is he?" Charlotte frantically searched the woman's face. When it broke into a smile, everything in her body relaxed.

"He's going to be okay. He made it through the surgery. They removed his spleen but there's no other signs of damage. As soon as he's moved to a room, I'll come get you and you can see him."

Charlotte clutched her arm. "Thank you."

Every inch of her body rejoiced in the knowledge she had the chance to tell Jonas how happy she was to have met him and how much she prayed he felt the same way.

Jonas opened his eyes. The world around him was fuzzy. He blinked until shapes became objects and he realized he was in a hospital. The last moments before he collapsed flashed through his head. That man was going to shoot Charlotte. He'd pushed her away but hadn't been able to stop what happened. The pain had dropped him to the floor. He remembered her leaning over him telling him he was going to be okay.

"You're awake."

Jonas turned toward her voice. Charlotte was seated beside him holding his hand.

"Hey," he managed in a voice that was below a whisper. It didn't matter because her smile was all he needed.

"Hey yourself." Her smile was the best thing he'd seen in a while.

She told him Phillip had been arrested. Then someone knocked on the door and Jonas's attention reluctantly left her.

Sheriff McCallister stood in the doorway. "I heard you were awake." He came inside and stopped beside Charlotte. "It's good to hear you're going to be okay. When you're feeling better, I'm going to need both your statements."

Jonas nodded. "How are the women? Betty?" He felt responsible for his neighbor and the victims.

"Fine," Wyatt said. "I'm certain Betty's relieved her time with Harley is over. He had her terrified to do anything on her own." Wyatt shook his head. "She told me he forced her to break off all family relationships. Did you know she has a sister who lives in Idaho?"

Jonas was surprised by that. "No. I assumed her family was all gone."

The sheriff shrugged. "She called her sister and she's going to stay with her for a while."

Jonas was relieved. "I'm glad to hear it."

Wyatt's expression turned grim. "Harley is talking. He implicated Phillip in both Ryan's and Michaela's deaths, but then you both knew as much since Phillip pretty much confessed to the murders in front of you. With the ledger, we have the names of the people involved and the arrests are happening right now. Locating the women won't be as easy. They're spread out across the country—probably others are in different countries. Harley was able to give us the names of the contacts in those other locations, and we're reaching out to law enforcement in those cities." He shrugged again. "I'm hopeful."

Despite what they'd gone through to identify the victims, those young women who were forced into a life of prostitution were changed forever.

"Well, I'm heading back to the station. I'll stop by

in a few days and get both your statements." He nodded to Jonas and clamped Charlotte's shoulder briefly before leaving.

Jonas couldn't take his eyes off Charlotte. Now that she had the truth, he couldn't imagine the thoughts going through her head. "How are you doing with all this?"

She reached for his hand once more. "I'm at peace," she said, surprising him. "I always wondered if Ryan's death was really an accident or if Michaela didn't kill herself. Now her parents can have the truth about what happened. I hope the truth will give them some measure of closure." She stopped as if to gather her thoughts. "It breaks my heart to think Ryan had to die at the hands of someone he trusted, yet both Phillip and Harley will pay for their crimes. I guess that's some small comfort."

He thought about losing Ivy. Charlotte had someone tangible to blame for Ryan's death. But for Jonas there was only him.

She clutched his hand tighter, and he focused on her face. "For the first time since Ryan's death, I have hope for the future." She was smiling and he couldn't look away. It was as if the weight of the world had been lifted from her.

"Why do you have hope?" he asked without looking away and prayed he would be part of it.

"Because of you," she said softly. "I'm so grateful God brought you into my life, Jonas." She leaned closer. "We both have a chance at happiness…together." She waited for him to speak, but he was incapable because she'd just told him she wanted to be with him. And no words could have brought more joy. "I finally realized guilt has no place in the future. I love you, Jonas. But if you stand a chance at moving beyond Ivy's death, you must find a way to forgive yourself. Neither of us can rewrite the past, but together, we can have a future filled with happiness again. We can step out of the shadows of the past and walk in the light." She looked so vulnerable as she waited for him to answer.

Tears filled his eyes. He wanted to hold on to her hand and step into that future with her. "I love you, too. And I'll do everything in my power to make our lives together happy."

And he would. Ivy was his past. Charlotte—this beautiful woman had helped him see the past couldn't be changed. He was ready to let go of his guilt once and for all and embrace Charlotte's love because the future, well, it was wide-open.

EPILOGUE

Eighteen months later...

"Are you sure you want to put the house up for sale?" Charlotte asked him once more as they finished packing the last of his things into her SUV.

He knew she worried about him wanting to return to the Amish ways, but that wasn't who he was anymore. And he was finally happy with his life.

Jonas smiled at the woman who was now his wife. He reached for her hand and touched the simple gold wedding band she wore.

They'd married in a small ceremony at the church he'd started attending with her. Abram was there as his best man. Jonas had invited Ivy's parents and he'd been thrilled when they'd come. They were making small steps at repairing their relationship.

Lainey had stood up for Charlotte. Most of those who attended were law enforcement. In the months since the ordeal with Harley, Jonas had become friends with them all.

"I'm sure." He leaned over and kissed her tenderly. He loved her so much. She was the blessing from *Gott* he never expected to receive.

A few weeks back, Jonas had reached out to a realtor in the area and discussed putting his house up for sale.

He'd long since moved the cattle and his mare, Sandy, to Charlotte's ranch. Jonas was glad Sandy had returned to his place the day after she'd run away from the river.

"It's time." He wrapped his arm around her waist. Since Harley's arrest and upcoming trial, Betty had the house they'd shared together leveled. The property had sold recently. Jonas was happy to see Betty moving on. She'd stopped by with her sister, and she looked like a different person.

He and Charlotte had learned that the place Harley claimed was his in the mountains actually belonged to Phillip. They'd used it to transport the women through the mountains and into a waiting vehicle that would take them to the next stop along the line of the trafficking chain. But Harley had gotten greedy and begun trafficking stolen electronics along with weapons without his partners knowing. Harley's deceit and incompetence was the reason he'd been targeted for death.

Jonas and Charlotte stepped from his old house and into the sunlit day. At times, it was hard to imagine the terrible things they'd gone through in these woods.

Since their escape, Lainey and Abram had formed a close relationship that had become a burgeoning romance. Lainey had confided in Charlotte that she wanted to become Amish so she and Abram could wed. During one of her visits to the ranch, Dottie told them she could see the change in her granddaughter, and she was happy Lainey had found someone to love.

While Jonas was fully embracing the life of an *Englischer*, he'd told Charlotte he wanted to track down the owners of the Christian camp and buy it with the proceeds from the sale of his place. He wanted something good to replace all the ugly things that had taken place there.

His plan was to open a camp for troubled teens to come for healing. Perhaps even for some of the women who had been abused by Harley and his crew. If he could use his skills as a former Amish man to teach young people how to do things with their hands, he'd be pleased. Abram had volunteered to assist, and Charlotte was all on board, as well.

"I still can't fathom it's been over a year," Charlotte murmured and turned to face him. "So many wonderful things have happened. I barely remember the bad anymore."

He brushed back a strand of hair from her face. Something was on her mind and his heart clenched. "Is everything okay?" Charlotte's troubled face reminded him of all that he stood to love, like he had with Ivy.

A smile spread across her face. "Yes, everything is fine. More than fine. I've been trying to find a way to tell you something for a while."

He froze, and she quickly assured him it was good news.

"I'm pregnant, Jonas. We're going to have a baby." She studied him closely. "How does that make you feel?"

He'd made so many mistakes with Ivy during her pregnancy. Jonas had vowed if *Gott* gave him another chance at being a father, he would be there beside Charlotte every step of the way.

"Happy," he managed while tears filled his eyes. "I'm so happy. You make me so happy." He drew her into his arms and held her close. This woman who had changed his life for the better. "I love you, Charlotte. So much."

She pulled away and smiled up at him. "I love you, too. And I'm so happy." She went back into his arms, and he stared into the distance at the Root Mountains, arrayed in their early fall shades of golds and oranges.

The crispness in the air held a hint of the winter to come. For the first time in so long he looked forward to what each day brought. He was no longer existing day to day, going through the motions of what had to be done. He was living. Really living.

"Let's go home." He kissed her forehead.

Charlotte held his hand as they covered the distance to the SUV where Annie waited for them.

Jonas held the door open for Charlotte, then got in and petted the dog who was like family to him—she went everywhere with them.

"When?" he asked, and she looked over at him. He'd been content to let her drive although he had recently gotten his license.

"In six months." She smiled. "My next appointment is soon."

"I want to be there." He wanted to be part of everything.

She smiled and squeezed his hand as if she hadn't thought differently.

Jonas sat back in his seat and watched her maneuver the SUV away from the house that didn't hold any good memories. She turned toward the ranch, which had been in her family for years, and toward their future. They'd made many good memories there already. And, with the arrival of their child, he couldn't wait for what would come next.

* * * * *

Dear Reader,

In an instant, life can change. When solid ground disappears beneath our feet, we can lose hold of the things that seem important. Yet no matter how bad our circumstances get, if we trust God, He will see us through it all. Sometimes, it takes shaking ourselves free of what we think is best for Him to take us down the path He knows is right for us.

That's what happened to Charlotte and Jonas in *Deadly Mountain Escape*. Both suffered great losses in their lives. The pain of those wounds have left them frozen in the past.

Then, an unexpected call sends Deputy Charlotte Walker on a rush to find a missing friend where she ends up almost dying at the hands of a human trafficker.

But thanks to Jonas Knowles, who had a bad feeling about his neighbor, she and her friend Lainey are saved. With the help of Jonas, Charlotte and her K-9 partner Annie embark on a frantic race to save young women from a human trafficking ring operating in the county. In the process, they unravel the secrets of a year-long mystery and end up finding love again with each other.

Like Charlotte and Jonas, sometimes our plans shatter around our feet, but with God's help, everything turns out according to His perfect design.

Many, many blessings,
Mary Alford

LETHAL MOUNTAIN PURSUIT
K-9 Search and Rescue • by Christy Barritt

After witnessing several murders, Natalie Pearson narrowly evades death but knows the killer is still out there...searching for her. And even a remote cabin in the Smoky Mountains can't keep her safe. Now she must trust Detective Andrew Moore and his K-9 to find a killer determined to silence her.

KIDNAPPING COLD CASE
by Laura Scott

Ten years ago, forensic artist Jacy Urban escaped her abductor with no memory of that night. Now the kidnapper has returned, and Detective Cash Rawson is there to rescue her—again. Can Cash help her remember what she's forgotten...before the assailant succeeds in taking their lives?

UNDERCOVER COLORADO CONSPIRACY
by Jodie Bailey

When Staff Sergeants Thalia Renner and Phillip Campbell pose as a married couple to unmask a crooked adoption ring, attacks on their lives make them wonder if their cover has been blown. But the truth is more sinister...and the consequences could make them both victims.

MISSING IN MONTANA
by Amity Steffen

Forced off the road while biking, forensic accountant Holly Nichols is sure of one thing: someone wants her dead. She has no choice but to accept help from her high school sweetheart, but even Seth Montgomery's family ranch doesn't stand a chance against criminals who will stop at nothing to remain hidden...

PROTECTING THE LITTLEST WITNESS
by Jaycee Bullard

After her brother-in-law is imprisoned for murdering her sister, Etta Mitchell will do anything to keep her five-year-old niece—a potential witness—safe. But when they're targeted by relentless killers, Etta must rely on her ex-fiancé, Steven Hunt, for protection, to untangle the mystery behind her sister's death...and to stay alive.

DEADLY TREASURE HUNT
by Sommer Smith

Sheriff Caldwell Thorpe is investigating his wife's homicide when her cousin, Jayde Cambrey, arrives on the island of Deadman's Cay—drawing the predator's deadly attention. Believing it's the same person who killed his wife, Caldwell vows to protect Jayde. But can they find the truth before time runs out?

ROGUE WARRIOR: GREEN TEAM

"So much action that the reader scarcely has time to breathe."
—Newgate Callendar, *The New York Times Book Review*

"Liberally sprinkled with raw language and graphic descriptions of mayhem, *Rogue Warrior: Green Team* is the literary equivalent of professional wrestling."
—*Detroit Free Press*

ROGUE WARRIOR: RED CELL

"In a field of wanna-bes, Marcinko is the real thing: combat veteran, killer SEAL, specialist in unconventional warfare."
—Sean Piccoli, *Washington Times*

"A chilling, blood-and-guts, no-nonsense look into clandestine military operations told like it should be told. It doesn't come more powerful than this."
—Clive Cussler

ROGUE WARRIOR

"For sheer readability, *Rogue Warrior* leaves Tom Clancy waxed and booby-trapped."
—Richard Lipsyte, *Los Angeles Times Book Review*

Photo by Roger Foley

ROGUE WARRIOR®
SEAL FORCE ALPHA

RICHARD MARCINKO
and JOHN WEISMAN

POCKET BOOKS

New York   London   Toronto   Sydney   Tokyo   Singapore

This book is a work of fiction. Names, characters, places and incidents are products of the author's imagination or are used fictitiously. Operational details have been altered so as not to betray current SpecWar techniques.

Many of the Rogue Warrior's weapons courtesy of Heckler & Koch, Inc., International Training Division, Sterling, Virginia

POCKET BOOKS, a division of Simon & Schuster Inc.
1230 Avenue of the Americas, New York, NY 10020

Copyright © 1998 by Richard Marcinko and John Weisman

Originally published in hardcover in 1998 by Pocket Books

ISBN: 0-671-02052-8

First Pocket Books Export Edition printing September 1998

10 9 8 7 6 5 4 3 2 1

POCKET and colophon are registered trademarks of Simon & Schuster Inc.

Cover art by Franco Accornero

ROGUE WARRIOR is a registered trademark of Richard Marcinko

Printed in the U.S.A.

The Rogue Warrior **Series by Richard Marcinko and John Weisman**

Rogue Warrior
Rogue Warrior: Red Cell
Rogue Warrior: Green Team
Rogue Warrior: Task Force Blue
Rogue Warrior: Designation Gold
Rogue Warrior: SEAL Force Alpha

Also by Richard Marcinko

Leadership Secrets of the Rogue Warrior
The Rogue Warrior's Strategy for Success

Also by John Weisman

Fiction

Evidence
Watchdogs
Blood Cries

Nonfiction

Shadow Warrior (with Felix Rodriguez)

Anthologies

Unusual Suspects (edited by James Grady)
The Best American Mystery Stories, 1997 (edited by
　Robert B. Parker)

There are three strategies for victory, those being the Water Strategy, the Earth Strategy, and the Fire Strategy.

—General T'ai Li'ang, *The Li'ang Hsi-Huey* (374 B.C.)

THE *ROGUE WARRIOR®'S* TEN COMMANDMENTS OF SPECWAR

- I am the War Lord and the wrathful God of Combat and I will always lead you from the front, not the rear.

- I will treat you all alike—just like shit.

- Thou shalt do nothing I will not do first, and thus will you be created Warriors in My deadly image.

- I shall punish thy bodies because the more thou sweatest in training, the less thou bleedest in combat.

- Indeed, if thou hurteth in thy efforts and thou suffer painful dings, then thou art Doing It Right.

- Thou hast not to like it—thou hast just to do it.

- Thou shalt Keep It Simple, Stupid.

- Thou shalt never assume.

- Verily, thou art not paid for thy methods, but for thy results, by which meaneth thou shalt kill thine enemy by any means available before he killeth you.

- Thou shalt, in thy Warrior's Mind and Soul, always remember My ultimate and final Commandment. There Are No Rules—Thou Shalt Win at All Cost.

Contents

Part
One

THE WATER
STRATEGY

Chapter

1

THE PILOT, WHOSE NAME WAS ARCH KIELLY, BLINKED THE cargo bay lights twice, then twice again, to signal he was descending to thirty thousand. Once there, he'd crack a hatch, depressurize, then lower the C-130's ramp. That was so we could jump at twenty-nine thousand five hundred—the minimum height we'd need to carry us to within striking distance of our target.

I was so preoccupied with checking the cargo straps on the assault craft (it was tied down astride the double-tracked rollers) that I got caught pants-down inattentive when Arch turned the interior lights off. He did that for a perfectly good tactical reason: so no one would be able to see anything untoward from the western shore of Borneo, five and a half miles below, just in case anybody happened to be looking in our direction, which was, of course, up.

So, I was blindsided (literally) by the sudden blackout. Then Arch the fucking pilot did something else I hadn't remembered he was going to do (although he'd told it to me in simple declarative sentences during the preflight briefing): he banked sharply to starboard as he brought the plane

3

onto a due north heading. Surprise. Doom on Dickie. Which is a polite way of saying in Vietnamese that I was being fuckee-fuckeed. One second I was checking the quick release harness on the ICRRC, an acronym that stands for Improved Combat Rubber Raiding Craft for those of you who aren't familiar with SpecWarspeak. The next, I'd lost sight of everything and everybody else as the plane's interior went completely lightless. It was like, *WTF?*

Then he plunged the nose earthward, dropped the right wing about forty-five degrees, and knocked me completely off balance. I rolled around in the dark like a fucking pinball SEAL, caromed off a bulkhead, got turned around the wrong way (is there any right way in these situations?), tripped over the rollers, lost my balance, and went skidding face first into one of the hard-cast, H-shaped, reinforced aluminum mounting beams that support the plane's forward seating module. It was like, *slip, s-l-i-d-e, SMACK—whaap.*

Oh, that *smarted.* Belay that. It fucking *hurt.* Instant agony. My oxygen mask was knocked askew. My goggles were spun halfway round my head. My helmet strap cut off my air. Now, those of you who know me at all, know that I have a unique relationship with pain. In actual point of fact, I have an existential relationship with pain. By this, I mean that I see pain not as a vague, generalized physiological concept to be explored; not as a cryptic, enigmatic problem to be analyzed; but as a real-time, essential, individual challenge; a subjective, personal confrontational *experience.*

Pain is an ordeal; a physical encounter to be lived through, relished, and explored, *crack* by *smack* by *whaap.* My pain exists so I can demonstrate to you, my constant and gentle readers out there, that I am inexorably . . . alive.

Which is probably why that precise, painful, and even Heideggerian instant was exactly the second the C-130's crew chief—who was waiting for his cue—received said signal from the pilot and cracked open the port side hatch. I heard a Perot-size giant sucking sound, and felt the accompanying tremor as the Hercules lost pressure and its interior temperature dropped about 106 degrees in four and a half seconds. Oh, fuck me very much one more time! Was I ever inexorably, existentially, alive.

I struggled to readjust my helmet, mask, and goggles, but the environment wasn't making things easy for me. One problem: it was dark, remember? Another problem: I was wearing a shitload of equipment, and it was difficult to move quickly since I kept catching my straps, loops, lashes, or laces on one of the 130's numerous interior hooks, hangers, pylons, or braces every time I tried to shift my body position.

You do not, after all, jump out of an aircraft at twenty-nine point five thousand feet to go kill bad guys wearing nothing but skivvies, sneakers, and a K-Bar knife. Everything you plan to use, you must carry with you. And when your operational plan calls for a thirty-mile parachute ride followed by a ten-to-fifteen-mile boat ride, followed by who-the-hell-knows-what, you have to carry enough for contingencies. Contingencies, hell—there's the omnipresent Mr. Murphy to worry about, so you have to go out of the plane loaded down with more junk than you'll find in the Brigade fucking Quartermaster catalog. And things get even more knotty, intricate, complex, when you are operating, like I am, in the black. (No pun intended. What I'm talking about right now are black—as in untraceable—ops.)

Which is why I wore a wet suit (generic, French-made) covered by your basic black Nomex flight coveralls (German manufacture). Over those sat a UDT-style life vest (also in basic black), as well as a Brit Royal Marine CQC (that's Close Quarters Combat) vest equipped with class-III body armor and a flotation bladder, not to mention pockets that held twenty or so pounds of lethal goodies that ran the gamut from plastique (in this case an RDX-rich Czech Semtex) and Bulgarian pencil detonators to a point-and-shoot digital electronic camera (it produces bits-and-bytes computer images on a three-and-a-half-inch disk rather than using conventional film), and half a dozen extra magazines for my pistol, each of which contained vintage East German–manufactured frangible Plus-P load ammo.

From the starboard side of the padded pistol belt around my waist was suspended the ever-fashionable ballistic nylon tactical thigh holster containing a Portuguese knockoff of a Heckler & Koch USP 9mm semiauto pistol. The compartment usually reserved for a spare magazine held a suppressor for the pistol. Suspended from my waist's port side and cinched around my left thigh sat a ballistic nylon mag-holder for six thirty-round magazines (filled with the same Kraut ammo that was inside my pistol mags), so I could reload the suppressed HK MP5-PDW I would be carrying. My belt also held a canteen of water, a pouch holding a pair of small but powerful bolt cutters (British), my first-aid kit (also French), and a K-Bar assault knife in a Kydex sheath. I've already told you about the oxygen mask (Japanese) and helmet (Israeli). I don't think I mentioned the O_2 bottle, navigational chest-pack, and radio.

My normal weight is in the 220-pound area. If there'd been a scale on this flight, I'd have weighed somewhere in the 270 range. And I wasn't even three-quarters loaded up yet. The point of all this inventory description is to illustrate that there were a lot of possibilities when it came to the "materials that catch on protuberances" category.

I noticed that my fingers were going numb under the Nomex gloves. Now, I don't care whether you've jumped from thirty thousand feet once, or whether you've done it a couple of hundred times like I have: when they depressurize the fucking plane, it gets real goddamn cold, real goddamn fast. Even with the coveralls and the quarter-inch-thick neoprene foam wet suits below 'em, we were suddenly in a d-d-d-deep freeze.

I could sense my guaranteed fog-proof Bolle combat goggles frosting over on the outside, which would have made it hard to see the O_2 connector in front of my nose—if I could have seen anything in the blackness. I stumbled through the plane until I found an oxygen outlet. I identified it by Braille, fondled the nozzle, shoved it *sans* foreplay into the female connector, and (unlike the president) inhaled as deeply as I could.

Nothing happened. I sucked again. Nada. I tried a third time. *Bupkis.* This particular oxygen outlet wasn't working. But no O_2 at thirty thousand feet is a course of action frowned upon in every one of the military's field manuals and instructional course materials—not to mention the long list of personal do's and don'ts I carry in my Slovak brain.

So I fought my way aft in the darkness, found a second nozzle, and rapid-switched. Of course, *that* one was screwed up, too. It was right then I realized that my old and constantly consistent nemesis, Mr. Murphy of Murphy's Law fame, had stowed away for the ride.

I yanked the tube connector out of the plane's oxygen supply and shoved it into the O_2 bottle strapped to my chest along with the altimeter, compass, large digital readout watch, Magellan GPS module, and secure radio. I inhaled, and was rewarded with a lungful of oxygen. At least I'd be breathing when we went off the ramp. Of course, after that, things might get sticky. There were twenty minutes' worth of air in the bottle strapped to my chest. We were jumping at twenty-nine-thou five hundred. The estimated descent rate given the air temperature, crosswinds, humidity, and load, was eighteen feet per second. You need oxygen until you pass below ten thousand feet. Well—this was combat, and in combat we might get away with a twelve thou ceiling.

Okay, *you* do the math. Twenty-nine five thou minus twelve thou, divided by eighteen feet per second, gives us approx 972 seconds (I'm talking fast because I'm using up oxygen) which, divided by sixty, comes to just over sixteen minutes of air. So if we jumped in the next three minutes, I'd be hunky-dory. If not? Sayonara, Dickie—it would be hypoxia city.

You say you don't know about hypoxia? Well, lemme explain. The condition is a manifestation of pulmonary insufficiency. That's a twenty-dollar way of saying that your blood ain't gettin' enough oxygen. The manifestations include cerebral vasodilation, and changes in sensorum ranging from confusion to narcosis. In the kind of two-bit plain English I understand, this polysyllabic soufflé means that if I jump from too high an altitude I don't get enough oxygen in my brain (that's the cerebral vasodilation stuff), and I can also experience (here come the sensorum goodies): confusion, drowsiness, sluggish reaction time, loss of muscle control, blurred vision and a confused, almost drunken thought process. Bottom line: if something goes wrong, I can kill myself because my reaction time and sensory perception mechanisms will be off-kilter. Not a favorable condition for the old Rogue Warrior to be in.

Arch turned the emergency lights in the cargo bay on, and everything was all of a sudden bathed in dim red. Now I could see again. There were eight of us making the jump tonight, a HAHO—that's High Altitude, High Opening—insertion, which would take us on that aforementioned thirty-mile airborne parasail, followed by the ten-mile boat ride. And all that—*that* was going to be the easy part. Because after our half-the-fun-is-getting-there fun, we'd have the second part of the good time. To wit: assaulting a ship whose crew was augmented by *zhongdui*—Chinese naval commando reconnaissance units—who were, the intelligence reports surmised, probably as well trained as we were. *Zhongdui* notwithstanding, we'd take the ship down and send it to the bottom before they could get any message to the outside world that they'd been attacked.

Not that executing any of the above would be a problem. Not with the merry band of hop-and-pop shoot-and-looters I had with me tonight. Tonight, I was traveling with *Warriors.* Over there, Duck Foot Dewey ran a second swipe of Russian duct tape around his magazine pouch so it wouldn't come open midair and leave him *sans* ammo for the suppressed HK submachine gun secured to his chest. Just to his left, Gator Shepard checked the tape that wound around the tops of his Adidas GSG-9 tactical boots. The shock of jumping out of a plane can rip your boots right off. That's not a good idea when the outside temperature's about fifty below zero, Fahrenheit. Lose your bootie like that and you get to play "This Little Piggy Froze Solid."

Next to Gator, Half Pint Harris fondled his swim buddy Piccolo Mead's rucksack, pulling on it hard to make sure it wouldn't separate when the chute opened. Hunkered down just across the aisle from Half Pint was Chief Gunner's Mate Eddie DiCarlo—I call him Nod, as in Wynken and Blynken—taking a long and loving last look at his suppressed Heckler & Koch MP5-PDW before he stowed it in the padded scabbard that would ride on his right thigh. Leaning against the bulkhead just aft of Nod was Master Chief Nasty Nicky Grundle, whom I'd rescued not three weeks ago from a drab training assignment in Hawaii. Nasty's web gear was being checked over carefully by his new swim buddy, a former UCLA linebacker named Boomerang, the only West Coast surfer-puke in my current group of shooters.

Boomerang (he pronounces it "Boom-rang") had earned his nickname during BUD/S. Had he ever. The first time he went through training, he broke his ankle the fifth week. So they held him back until the next cycle. The second time around, he broke his collarbone at the end of the sixth week. This time they tried to wash him out. But the sonofabitch refused to go. He kept coming back for more. And the third time through, he graduated at the top of his BUD/S class—with two broken toes and a cracked rib.

I'd tell you more about Boomerang, but I see that Arch the pilot just blinked the red lights three times. And that whining noise you hear? That's the sound of hydraulics. The sonofabitch is lowering the ramp. And over there, the crewmen are unfolding the tracks so the ICRRC package—specifically the Kevlar-reinforced rubber assault craft, engine, fuel bladder, communications package, and assault gear, all lashed together in one ingenious, parachutable bundle—can roll right off the end of the ramp.

Arch blinked the lights thrice again. That was the get-ready sign. The next signal—the green jump indicator—would be roughly five minutes from now.

Shit—I wasn't ready to go-go-go yet. That was on the one hand. On the other hand, there was that old Rogue Commandment that had to be observed. You know the one. It goes, "Thou hast not to like it—thou hast just to do it."

And, there was much "it" to do. So, I scampered up to the cockpit, gave Arch a thump on the shoulder, a hearty "fuck you, cockbreath," and an upraised middle finger to show how much I cared.

Arch handed the controls to his copilot and swiveled in his chair. "Fuck you, too, asshole," he said through his mask. I could see the smile in his cobra's eyes. "Just stay in one piece, huh?"

I nodded. "I'll try."

He extended his big, gloved hand. "If there's ever anything else I can do—just call. I'm in the book at Kadena—there are lots of Kellys, but only one spelled my way, with an *ie.*"

"How come?"

"We come from the Cuban Kiellys. Grandpa was a Rough Rider who stayed behind. Over the years, the spelling got changed."

I grinned behind my mask, took his hand and clasped it. "Well, Kelly with an *i* and an *e,* don't make any fucking offers you don't mean."

His eyes grew serious. "I never do." Arch swiveled, settled back behind the wheel, made sure he had his feet firmly on the pedals, then nodded to his copilot that he was assuming control.

I plugged my Magellan into the navigator's satellite data display. His radar had our target ship on the screen. It was some 125-odd miles from our current position, traveling due north at a steady six knots an hour.

What was our current position? Well, we were over water now—the South China Sea to be precise—west-northwest of Belitung Island, about 200 miles south of the equator, and 110 degrees east longitude. FYI, we'd flown out of

Guam eleven-plus hours ago on this here MC-130E Combat Talon aircraft, which had been custom painted for us in a dull, black radar-defeating stealth paint. The craft itself bore no identifying markings whatsoever. Neither did anyone in crew. Even so, I can tell you (don't breathe a word of this, okay?) that the plane—as well as its crew—came from the Air Force Special Operations Command's 353rd Special Operations Group, First SpecOps Squadron, based at Kadena Air Base, on Okinawa.

I'm not usually a big fan of the Air Farce. But these guys knew what the fuck—they were pros. So far as I was concerned, Lieutenant Colonel Arch and his aircrew could fly me A³, which stands for anyplace, anytime, anywhere. He was the type you wanted on a mission like this one. He'd get the job done, *sans* complaint, no matter what it took. I'd known that the moment we'd met: he had the look of a stone killer in his eyes, and he'd never said anything that wasn't in the affirmative.

Once we cleared Guam, we'd climbed quickly to our cruising altitude, the Combat Talon's operational ceiling of thirty-three thousand feet, and headed south by southeast on a route that would take us just under four thousand miles. We skirted Palau, cut a wide swath past Mindanao, refueled from an unmarked tanker over the Makassar Strait, then flew due west over the Borneo jungle before turning north for our final approach to the target. We'd stayed away from radar sites and flown (we hoped) between Russian, Chinese, French, and Israeli satellite passes. We'd maintained strict radio silence. This mission had to be fucking stealth all the way.

I stared through the pilot's windshield. It was the perfect operational milieu: there were no lights to be seen anywhere. I turned away, plugged my Magellan into the naviguesser's console and pulled the latest information from the navigator's forward-looking radar into my own. Then I plugged into the EWO—that's Electronic Warfare Officer—console, and dumped his target information into my own unit, too. That way, I could set a heading after we'd jumped—a course that would bring us down exactly where we had to be. The info loaded, I punched a series of commands into the unit and watched as it responded properly.

Then I turned the Magellan off, waited fifteen seconds, switched it on again, and repeated the cycle. I see you waving your hand out there. You say what? I'd just checked the GPS once, and I was wasting time? Hey, bub—remember the old Rogue's Eighth Commandment. Thou shalt never assume. So I didn't. I double-checked to make sure that the information I'd transferred was stored properly, and that it was displayed the way I was going to need it displayed. I peered down at the screen. Everything was copacetic. Now I knew there was at least one thing Mr. Murphy couldn't screw with tonight: my Magellan system.

The navigation and target info elements secure, I slid down the ladder rails, found the remainder of my own web gear, pulled it on, double-checked all the straps and Velcro closures, shrugged into my reserve chute, then attached my weapons scabbard, rucksack, and all the other miscellaneous goodies necessary for the night's activities. I punched the display screen of my Magellan and called out the coordinates of our target ship to my shooters so they could program their own GPS units. When I got "OK" signals (and a chorus of "Fuck you very much, Skipper") from everyone, I clambered astride the assault craft and clipped my harness straps to the big, black thirteen-cell Vector assault chute I'd ride tonight. I pressed my thighs up against the Kevlar-reinforced rubber.

"Hey—does that feel good, sir?" Nasty Nicky Grundle shouted. If his voice hadn't been muffled by the oxygen mask he wore I would have sworn that he'd spelled *sir* with a *c* and a *u*.

I nodded affirmatively, then did a pretty passable Rin Tin Tin humps Lassie against the gunwale. Ooh—it *did* feel good. Still laughing, Nasty and Boomerang released the tie-downs and began to slide the ICRRC package aft, holding it steady with a pair of safety straps secured to a pintle in the forward cargo area while I waddled behind, looking not so much like your generously endowed Richard as a fifteen-foot rubber-cocked Dick.

I hand-signaled the guys to circle wagons and watched as Gator, Nod, Half Pint, Duck Foot, and Pick flanked the ICRRC, then began to edge slowly aftward, their progress hampered by the hundred-plus pounds of equipment that each man carried.

I looked up to see the air crew chief's face, obscured by oxy mask and goggles, waving Boomerang and Grundle off. They gave the crew chief a thumbs-up, backed away from the ICRRC, and joined the other swim buddies. Seamlessly, they were replaced by two crewmen whose coveralls were crisscrossed by long yellow nylon safety harnesses secured to the aircraft's bulkheads.

We moved aft until we came to the ramp hinge. There, the crew chief signaled a halt. I looked down. There was nothing to see—only blackness and the void. I raised my eyes and looked out horizontally, and saw a constellation in the moonless night. The Southern Cross? Perhaps. Who knew. Certainly not I.

And then the two green lights came on and blinked twice. I drew my right hand across my throat. The crewmen nodded and unhitched the safety lines. I put my whole weight against the ICRRC, screamed a heigh-ho Silver and a hearty "Fuck-you" as I r-o-l-l-e-d it toward the void, tossed the crew chief the bird, and lumbered off the ramp, pulled by the weight of the assault craft.

Normally, I like to throw a hump and watch the plane disappear behind me. But tonight that was impossible—jumping attached to the ICRRC meant a static opening—that is, with the chute's line attached to the plane—and it came real fast. Some invisible giant hand grabbed me by the nuts and slammed me up against the gunwale of the ICRRC two or three times, then took me by the helmet, tried to twist my head in a complete three-sixty like something out of *The Exorcist,* gave up, and finally slapped me up against the boat face first half a dozen times so I'd feel VMA—very much alive. Then, as suddenly as it had started, it was over, and, the ICRRC hanging under me, the descent smoothed out.

I retrieved a red-lensed minilight from a pouch on my chest, tightened its lanyard loop around my wrist, then checked the steering lines and risers to make sure there were no tangles. I counted cells and saw thirteen. The chute appeared to be in textbook perfect condition. Compass heading was north-northeast. I put some of my weight on the steering line and swung the chute twelve degrees to the right, sending the ICRRC and me due north. Altitude was twenty-nine six and falling. I heard flutter around me and looked for the seven other canopies. Nada. Well—it wasn't cause for concern. After all, they were jumping with dark chutes and without lights.

Besides, every man with me tonight had made hundreds of HAHO jumps. They knew they had to key on the infrared strobe lights strapped to my ankles. And if they missed the IR lights, or the strobes died, each man had a Magellan GPS unit on his chest. And if their Magellans crapped out, and they missed my strobes, they'd have a very, very long swim.

But this was no occasion to dwell on failure. In fact, failure is a word I do not recognize. I have only one way to deal with my life, and with my missions: I attack, attack, attack.

And so, I rolled my head back and looked up at the stars. There are times when Warriordom is perfect—and this was one of them. Believe me, there are few experiences as exhilarating, energizing, or invigorating as jumping out of a perfectly good aircraft at an excessive altitude in order to initiate a mission that will stretch one's physical, mental, and operational capabilities way past the 100 percent mark.

And this Mission Impossible would certainly stretch our operational capabilities. We had been tasked by the powers that be (in this case the White House) with carrying out a stealth-quiet component of national policy. As long as I have a couple of minutes here, let me give you some of the background.

According to those solons in charge of things back in Washington, it is crucial to keep our relations with China on an even keel these days. First of all, China has the potential to become a superpower—and you play politics with superpowers differently from the way you do with other nations. Then there is the economic factor. China, you see, is one of our biggest overseas trading partners. From oil companies, whose investments in China total billions of dollars, to American telecom corporations, where tens of thousands of jobs depend on their selling equipment to the Chinese, to industrial machine toolmakers who hope to modernize Chinese plants, to toy manufacturers who buy cut-rate goods there and sell them at top-dollar prices here, China is important to the American economy. How important? Our trade deficit with China was more than fifty billion smackeroos last year. That gives the Chinese a lot of *crout*.

And, of course, there is also the Machiavellian ingredient. During the Cold War, China was our way of keeping the Soviets off guard. That was one of the major reasons Richard Nixon resumed relations with Peking back in 1972. If the Sovs had to keep a million Red Army soldiers on the Manchurian border, that was a million fewer potential adversaries for NATO to face in the West. Today, there may be no more Soviet Union. But the Russians still want to expand their sphere of influence—and one of the most pragmatic ways to keep them bottled up is to employ the Chinese trump. But these days, Peking—which is now spelled Beijing—is a much harder—and wilder—card to play.

So much for history. Now let's look at the current situation. One problem we are facing is a recent rapprochement between Moscow and Beijing—a potentially dangerous political situation because it means that they could coordinate policy to work against the United States. Another complication: the Chinese are finding new ways to flex their political and economic muscles. They've just taken control of Hong Kong, which adds billions of hard currency dollars to their economy. And they're looking for new ways to expand their influence in Asia and elsewhere, all across the Pacific Rim.

One way the Chinese have done so is through weapons. They are the number two weapons exporter in the world—second only to us. Moreover—and more dangerous—the panjandrums in Beijing haven't bothered to act within "conventional" borders. Over the last year, they have started shipping nuclear missile components (a clear violation of U.S. nonproliferation laws as well as the nuclear non-proliferation treaty they'd signed not two years ago) to Pakistan, Libya, and Iran.

Now, it has been obvious to me for some time that the Chinese have decided to use their new-found position and clout to squeeze the United States whenever possible. The problem is that we have not pushed back.

Let me pause here long enough to give you a theory about international relations. It is a concept propounded by Colonel Arthur "Bull" Simon, the Warrior who led the famous 1970 raid on the Son Tay prison in North Vietnam and who, in retirement, was hired by Ross Perot to rescue Perot's people in Iran, back in 1979.

"Bull" used to preach to us SpecWar youngsters. "If history is any teacher," he'd growl, "it teaches you that when you get indifferent and you lose the will to fight, some other sonofabitch who has the will to fight will take you over."

Those are words we should all take to heart. But "Bull" Simon's real-world experience wasn't held in very high esteem by most of those in the current administration. Our latest national security adviser, the newly installed Director of Central Intelligence, and the secretary of state are all practiced in the fine (and cowardly) art of appeasement. You—yes, you out there. You *what?* You want an example of appeasement?

Okay. At the most recent Sino/American ministerial (a ministerial is when our secretary of state and their foreign minister get together and palaver), SECSTATE hesitatingly—almost apologetically—brought up the matter of the slaughter of students at Tiananmen Square, the use of prisoners to make consumer goods, the torture of political dissidents, and the persecution of Christians.

The Chinese foreign minister slammed his palm on the table and said, quote, "The allegation that anyone died at Tiananmen is a lie. Your other assertions are also without basis in reality."

And what did SECSTATE do? SECSTATE did nothing. SECSTATE swallowed hard. And did nothing. The exchange made all the nightly news programs. I felt sickened when I saw it.

And that wasn't the worst. The worst was that the matter of nuclear smuggling was never even brought up. The fact that SECSTATE lacked the *cojones* to confront the Chinese upset me. I was even more upset when I learned from a very good source that our secretary of state had evidence to the contrary in her briefcase. But instead of using it, she sat there and said nothing.

Officially, therefore, the United States had no reaction to China's provocations. More to the point: our secretary of state has requested that the Chinese consider a schedule of summit meetings over the next three years, the first one to take place in six months. The Chinese have taken SECSTATE's request under advisement. Dammit, we didn't set the agenda—we simply made a request.

What did SECSTATE's disastrous performance tell the Chinese? It told 'em we weren't serious. It indicated we didn't have backbone, determination, or guts. It demonstrated weakness. And weakness is something that should never be revealed—not to other people, and certainly not to a nation like China, which is intent on creating a hegemony in its part of the world.

On a clandestine level, however, I am happy to report that not everyone in the administration assumes the same puppylike, belly-exposed, all-four-feet-in-the-air position that our secretary of state, the CIA director, and the national security adviser seem to adapt so regularly.

It had taken three weeks or so, but the president had

finally been convinced (browbeaten may be a more accurate word, but I wasn't in the room) by the Chairman of the Joint Chiefs and SECDEF—the secretary of defense—that Beijing couldn't be allowed to operate unchallenged, especially when it was selling weapons of mass destruction to states that sponsor terrorism directed at the United States.

Indeed, after carefully working his way around the State Department, the CIA, and the NSC chairman, SECDEF actually convinced the president to sign a national security directive that authorized covert military action if it could be proved without possibility of error that the Chinese were in substantial violation of the nonproliferation treaty. SECDEF argued that by acting covertly—by leaving State, CIA, and even the NSC out of the loop—diplomacy could proceed unabated. The president could still hold his regularly scheduled summit meetings with the Chinese—smiling warmly, acting nicey-nicey at the state dinners, but still let 'em understand that we weren't going to be pushed around.

That was where I came in. As you know, five months ago, the JCS Chairman, an Army four-star and lead-from-the-front warrior named Crocker, had me detailed to his office as his ASR—that's Attack SEAL-in-Residence. I'd gone after a bunch of no-goodniks in Moscow and the Middle East (you can read all about it in *Rogue Warrior: Designation Gold*).

Now, my cage had been unlocked once again. The deal was simple: roughly six weeks ago, FORTE satellite surveillance had detected what appeared to be a shipment of nuclear missile components. It tracked them on a long, meandering odyssey from a location deep within China to the Chinese coast. There, after a two-week period in which the missile components were moved from warehouse to warehouse on an irregular schedule—it appeared the Chinese were trying to confound surveillance, which they must have suspected, by trying to play a version of those street-corner shell games. Anyway, the components were finally loaded on what appeared to be a freighter named the *Nantong Princess,* which was moored in Shanghai harbor. The vessel sailed before any HUMINT—that's HUMan INTelligence—could verify the FORTE's assessment.

But the United States knew for certain the ship was not a commercial craft. That fact had been determined by National Security Agency SIGINT (SIGnals INTelligence) monitoring of its shortwave radio broadcasts, as well as its ELINT—ELectronic INTelligence—and TECHINT—TECHnical INTelligence—capabilities. And we knew that it was making a series of stops all around the Pacific Rim, starting in Pusan, South Korea, and ending at Karachi, Pakistan. Further investigations by No Such Agency, the Defense Intelligence Agency, and a couple of other alphabet soup groups that I'd go to jail for ten years for just mentioning, confirmed BRD—that's beyond a reasonable doubt—that the *Nantong Princess* was in fact a military vessel, manned by Chinese naval personnel augmented by *zhongdui* naval recon forces, and therefore a legitimate target for yours truly.

Since Chairman Crocker and I are not only on a first name basis (he calls me "Dick," and I call him "General") but also see the world eye-to-eye when it comes to taking action, he had asked me to come up with a tactical operation plan to make the freighter and its nuclear shipment disappear, but give the Chinese absolutely no opportunity to blame the United States.

Six hours after he'd made his request, I'd shown up at his office with precisely the kind of KISS (that's Keep It Simple, Stupid) operation I like the best. I'd take a small group of men, carry out a covert assault on the *Nantong Princess* in an isolated area during its leg from Jakarta to Singapore, and send it—and its cargo—to the bottom.

And the Chinese? Oh, they might have their suspicions. But I would leave not a trace of evidence to link the U.S. of A. with anything that might happen in the South China Sea. After all, the shipping lanes between Jakarta and Singapore are known to harbor pirates. The waters are filled with sharks. Ships have been known to disappear without so much as the well-known trace. *That* is known as deniability.

The plan I laid on the Chairman's antique desk wasn't a new one. In fact, it was one I'd taken off the shelf from my Cold War days and adapted to the current requirements. The Cold War plan called for a concentrated electronic bombardment of the target vessel to cut off all communications. I wouldn't have that luxury—I'd have to sever the comms myself. The Cold War plan called for a quick extraction by chopper. I'd modified that element, too: we'd extract by submarine. We'd have a beacon and would be able to summon it into the area once we'd completed the sensitive portion of our mission. And the old plan was paid for out of funds supplied by the Department of Defense's Special Operations budget. This one would have to be black funded. To do that, I suggested that the Chairman funnel some of the $50 million in Russkie money I'd sluiced off to him not three months ago, when my old friend Colonel Avi Ben Gal of Israeli Army Intelligence and I stumbled onto a couple of dozen of Moscow's secret bank accounts, during an operation we'd staged in Paris and the Middle East. The bucks (they were Swiss francs, but it would be simple to convert 'em) were easily accessible, no one would ever be the wiser—and best of all, we wouldn't cost the U.S. taxpayer even a single tax dollar. The man actually footing the bill would be Viktor Grinkov, a nasty, unscrupulous, greedy piece of work who currently ran the Russian interior ministry. It was his money—and he had made it clear through a series of backchannels he was upset at us for purloining it.

I laid the OPLAN on Chairman Crocker's desk. He indicated for me to Park It, then donned half-glasses and began to read. When he'd finished, he asked me half a dozen pointed and specific questions, listened as I expanded on the elements he'd queried, then asked me to wait outside while he made a call on the secure phone that sat at his left elbow.

Four minutes later he'd cracked the ornate wood door himself and beckoned me inside. "I like the funding part," he said, smiling. "SECDEF does, too." He paused. "There's only one element I'd like to change," he said.

I'm always open to suggestion if it makes the OPLAN better. "General?"

"I want you to exfil differently. The submarine commander should have no idea where you've been or what you've been doing. So change the pickup position by at least sixty or seventy miles—more if you can, even if it means taking on an additional fuel bladder. I don't want any submarine's log giving out the relative position where your goddam target went down."

I thought about it. Made a lot of sense. Gave us more deniability—and kept the sub's CO out of the loop. "Can do, sir."

"Good." He tossed my op-plan at me—I caught it one-handed—then pointed his thumb and index fingers in my direction in his trademark "Colt .45" fashion and said, "Then, go get 'em, Dick." Then he added the qualifier. Here is the Rogue Warrior's First Law of Covert Operations: There is always a qualifier.

Unlike most, this one was simple but direct. "Don't fail, don't leave any pecker tracks, and don't get caught," is what the Chairman told me, his face serious.

So, as is usual in my life, there was going to be no wriggle room for error. I had to stage my assault in a totally stealth fashion. I had to take over the ship before any message could be sent out. And I had to neutralize the whole fucking crew. That is a politically correct way of telling you I wasn't going to be taking any prisoners tonight.

Don't look so shocked. War is not nice. And this, no matter what you might think, was war.

Back to the business at hand. After all, there was work to be done—to wit, I had to guide us to the second phase of the mission and set us down ten nautical miles due south of our target. I pressed the switch on the Magellan GPS unit that sat next to the altimeter on my chest pack. The screen illuminated, but I saw no information. No distance to target. No heading. No latitude. No longitude. No nothing.

WTF. I pressed the on/off switch again. And again, the display came up blank.

Let me pause here for just a few seconds to explain the kind of unkosher pickle I was in.

Looking for a single ship in the South China Sea can be a problem *if: if* you are coming from the air; *if* it is night; *if* the ship does not want to be found; and *if* you do not know where the fuck you are relative to the target. Am I making things plain enough for you?

Yes, I had a compass. I could steer north, south, east, and west. I had an altimeter. I knew how high I was. But without the Magellan, which gets its signals from a GPS, or Global Positioning Satellite, I had no way of knowing where I was in relation to the target. I had no course to follow. No glide path to glide along.

My men had Magellans. But I couldn't use their units to help me because we had no way of making contact. Sure I was carrying a radio—but it and all its gear was stowed securely in my chest pack, and there was no way to use it. More to the point, even if I pulled it out and set it up, my guys' radios were in *their* chest packs.

Now, both you and I know that the Magellan was working just fine not ten minutes ago. But that was then and this was now and I was being screwed with by Mr. Murphy more than I wanted to be.

Okay. Let us be logical here. The batteries were working. That I knew because the screen lit up. But the antenna obviously wasn't working. *Why* wasn't it working? I stared at it and tried to be logical. And in staring, I had an epiphany. Y'know, as my old shipmate Doc Tremblay has told me more than once, sometimes I do have fartbeans for brains. The goddamn thing wasn't working because I'd forgotten to plug the antenna, which was located in my helmet, into the unit.

I reached inside my flight suit, brought the connector wire

out, plugged it securely into the Magellan's base, and turned the power on once again. Bingo. Full display. Now, perhaps, it *was* time to sit back and enjoy the ride.

Six thousand feet and descending through thickening clouds. My oxygen had barely lasted through fifteen five, and by the time I'd cleared ten five I was feeling the effects of hypoxia. That is to say, I felt sluggish and drowsy, my muscles wouldn't react very quickly, and my vision was blurred. What's the problem? The problem was that I wasn't making the turns I had to, when I had to—and I was therefore drawing all of us off course.

I fought my body with my body—tried to regain control over myself. But I wasn't having any luck.

Fuck it—I yanked on the right steering line and went into a tight, corkscrewing turn that dumped me fifteen hundred feet—from just above eleven thou to nine thou five—in just under a minute. It worked—the thick air was like a slap in the puss. I was back in control. I caught a thermal, gained a little altitude, and checked my instruments to see how much I'd screwed up.

It wasn't as bad as it could have been. Despite my problems, we'd made progress—some tailwind action had brought us farther along the track than I'd anticipated. That was good—the less distance we had to travel on the water, the better off we'd be. I looked down toward the choppy surface a mile below my boots. Like the Pacific, the South China Sea is an unpredictable, often nasty place. And that's when you've shipped out in something that's measured in the hundreds of tons. Our craft was less than twenty feet in length. It was powered by a single, although powerful, outboard motor.

There was a change in the sound of my parachute. Have I ever explained that you can tell from the way the air passes the foils what your chute is going to do? Well, you can. And from the way things currently sounded, I was about to pick up some crosswind.

I looked up—not much to see. Then, suddenly, the

ICRRC and I were yanked to port. Jerked hard. Crosswind, hell—that was a fucking wind shear. I pulled hard on the steerage lines and risers to bring us back around. No response. I hung on the lines with all my weight. Still nothing. Then I looked up and realized that one of the outer cells had buckled.

That was bad juju. Very bad juju. That is an understatement. You do not want your chute to buckle and collapse, because the chute is what keeps you from hitting the water at about 120 feet per second. And hitting water at 120 feet per second produces the same nasty result as hitting concrete at 120 feet per second. Am I making the point to you through ironic use of numerical repetition? Good. I think the Naval Special Warfare technical term for the condition I am describing is: "go splat."

I was not fucking about to go splat. Not tonight, anyway. I used the ICRRC as a platform, hoisted myself up, stood on the gunwales of the fucking boat, grabbed a handful of the starboard-side risers, and began to hoist myself up them, as if they were a climbing rope. That maneuver sent us into a spin—corkscrewing the ICRRC and me down at an accelerated speed.

But it also filled the leading edge of the canopy and the stabilizers with air. I could fucking feel the difference.

Now all I had to do was reverse the spin. How to do that? Let go the risers and drop—letting my harness absorb the shock—would probably work. I released my grip and dropped. As I hit—hard—I perceived that I'd made an ever-so-slight miscalculation about the weight factor and its consequences. You—the asshole laughing out there— you're ahead of me, aren't you? *You* realized I hadn't factored in the weight of the ICRRC, and so it wasn't my harness that bore the brunt of my six-foot drop, but my nuts—an eye-crossing, testicle-squeezing jolting kick that left me feeling like I'd be singing falsetto for the next couple of weeks.

I checked the compass and worked the steering handles to bring me back to a correct heading. That done, I began my final approach check, as I was under three thousand feet now and descending rapidly toward the water's surface. I heard the flutter of other chutes and looked around to see one, two, three, four shadows closing up behind me. I hoped the rest of my crew was there. But there'd be no way to tell until we all hit the water.

And then it was on us and things happened all at once. The water had what looked like a three-foot chop—more than I would have liked, but not as bad as it could have been. I cut the ICRRC package away at twenty-five feet. It dropped like a stone but landed right side up and ready to go. Then I released my combat rucksack so it wouldn't drag me down like a sea anchor when I hit the water.

Suddenly, instead of coasting the last four yards to the surface, I soared skyward. The big cargo chute caught a gust of air and, unfettered by the weight of the ICRRC package, began to lift me up and away. Shit. Fuck. I was at about ten yards—and sixteen, maybe even eighteen miles an hour—when I cut away. I dropped like the proverbial goddamn thrown stone. Which is to say, I slapped against the choppy surface face first and careened forward like one of those rolling bombs used by the World War II Dam Busters. My left foot caught in my rucksack line, which caused me to ball up and soar ass over teakettle, then flatten out and smack the surface in a painful belly-whopper. The momentum flipped me twice, then—somehow, I saw what was coming—I managed to grab half-a-lungful of air before my hundred-plus pounds of equipment sank and dragged me below the surface.

I struggled against the weight, my legs scissoring and my arms windmilling. Maybe it's the fact that I come from a down-and-out coal mining town in Pennsylvania, but I wasn't enjoying a lot of upward mobility right then.

Time to get serious: I grabbed the inflate tab of my CQC vest and yanked it. There was a satisfying *hiss,* the fucking thing filled with air, and I fought my way up, spitting seawater as I breached the surface like a goddamn killer whale.

I sputtered, and cursed at nothing in particular, then started to flail toward the ICRRC, which bobbed in the two-and-a-half-foot chop perhaps a 150 yards away. By the time I reached it, my lungs were heaving and I was sweating into my wet suit despite the fact that the water temperature was in the low seventies. Believe me, it is not easy to swim, even with a flotation device on, when you're lugging half your body weight in soggy equipment.

I lashed my rucksack to the gunwale hand-lines and cut the umbilical cord that secured it to my harness. Then I inflated my UDT vest to give me more buoyancy, then began the laborious process of removing the craft's drop package, so we could turn this useless lump of reinforced rubber and Kevlar into an assault craft.

The weighted pallet was first. I sliced the nylon netting with my K-Bar. The pallet sank away just as it had been designed to do. Next, I carefully sheathed my knife (I've seen people slice through rubber raiding craft during the boarding process before, and I wasn't about to do that and turn myself and my men into shark feed tonight), grabbed the closest hand-line, pulled myself up, muscled over the gunwale, heaved myself into the boat, and performed one of my more improbable rolls onto the floorboards, which is to say I managed to land face first and smack my nose— *thwap-slap*—against the forward thwart cleat.

WTF. Or, as the long-suffering, hard-working chain-smoking dweeb editor is so fond of misstating, "no pain . . . no pain."

I shrugged out of the CQC vest and secured that, too. I was about to begin my boat equipment check solo when Nasty Nicky Grundle's size twelve paw grabbed the hand-line, and he heaved himself over the gunwale with a grunt, and a friendly, "Fuck you very much, Skipper."

My extended middle finger told him that he was number one with me, too.

Nasty shrugged himself out of his equipment and secured it. Then he began to unbolt the 155-horsepower outboard motor that lay on its side, secured to the floorboard. He was about halfway done when I heard splashing and looked up to see Boomerang, Gator Shepard, Nod DiCarlo, and Half Pint Harris sidestroking toward the ICRRC. About twenty yards behind them, Duck Foot and the Pick played catch-up. That was eight out of eight. We'd be at full strength tonight.

I found the engine mounting brackets and motor bracket in their compartment and fitted them into place on the ICRRC's stern transom. Then I reached down and helped Nasty steady the outboard. He took the driveshaft, I held the cowling, and we lifted in unison—the goddamn thing was a heavy mother, too. Carefully we slid the motor over the engine mounting brackets, attached it to the outboard bracket just behind the transom, and tightened the clamp screws firmly.

Boomerang freed the thirteen-gallon fuel bladder from its stowage cradle in the bow, humped it aft over the two thwart tubes, and began to secure it in position adjacent to the engine. Thirteen gallons was one point nine times the amount of gas we needed to get to our target, and then to our final extraction point. Despite that huge safety margin, if there had been room on the ICRRC I would have brought a second fuel bladder with us. Things go wrong: bladders can leak; fuel gets used up faster than you foresee; or maybe Mr. Murphy decides to put in an unscheduled appearance. Bottom line: gasoline is something you don't want to run out of in the middle of a goddamn ocean.

My other merry marauders tied their rucksacks to the hand-lines, clambered aboard, then set about making our minicraft into a seaworthy man o' war. They didn't spend a lot of time talking to one another—they just Did the Job. That is common in units like mine. That is to say, units in which the men have worked together for so long that they don't need to speak, they simply converse in a kind of nonverbal, body-language shorthand.

Suddenly it began to rain. The sort of slow, steady,

drenching rain common to the tropics. The hair on the back of my neck stood up as I sensed a shift in the surface wind. Just another couple of Murphy elements to factor into the morning's events. I glanced at the luminous Timex on my wrist. It was just past 0100. I knew that sunrise was at 0650. By then, the *Nantong Princess* had to be in two pieces, sitting on the bottom in seventeen hundred feet of water.

Chapter

2

0127. UNDER MOST CONDITIONS, THE ICRRC IS RULED TO BE A tremendously seaworthy craft. The operative word in the previous sentence is *most*. I could tell that tonight was going to be an exception to the rule. We were overloaded by perhaps three hundred pounds—which meant we rode precariously low in the unruly, growing chop and huge arythmic swells. We were being buffeted by crosswinds, which were compounded by the rain squalls. The motion under way was not unlike the worst of the old-style roller coasters: long climbs as the waves swelled, followed by kidney-shattering drops into the troughs. You know those seventeenth-century Japanese woodcuts, with the stylized ocean waves that look like claws, waiting to rake a boat to shreds? Well, those artists knew WTF they were depicting. It is not a pleasant sensation to look up and see waves hovering ominously twenty-three feet above your head. I'm talking about waves that are about to crash over—and into—your tiny fucking craft. Oh, yeah, we were taking on enough water to make baling a mandatory and full-time operation.

The op-sked—which as you have probably already figured out stands for operational schedule but could tonight also stand for optimistic schedule—called for us to maintain the ICRRC's top speed of eighteen knots over the whole run to the *Nantong Princess.* Eighteen knots minus the *Nantong*'s six meant we'd be able to close on her within an hour and a half.

Of course, the ocean does not always cooperate. Right now, for example, despite the fact that I was running the outboard at full throttle we were barely making eight knots. According to my Magellan, the *Nantong Princess* was eighteen nautical miles due north of us, cruising at a steady six knots. Our net forward progress—by which I mean our closing distance—therefore, was a miserly two knots an hour.

Have I told you that fucking sunrise was at fucking 0650? Have I mentioned that by then I had to have fucking sunk the fucking Chinese ship? Have I explained that the *Nantong* fucking *Princess* was eighteen fucking miles ahead of us and that we didn't fucking have nine fucking hours of fucking sailing time? Am I making my emotional state clear to you? Good. I always like to be clear, unambiguous, explicit, precise, direct.

0214. The rain stopped as suddenly as it had begun, and we picked up seven knots of speed. I checked the Magellan. Now the Chinese ship was sixteen and a half miles ahead of us if its pace had remained steady. That gave us just over two hours to close the gap. Maybe the window of opportunity hadn't closed down on us—but the bottom rail was resting on our fingers, metaphorically speaking.

0249. The engine coughed, sputtered, and died. After I finished a pretty passable imitation of my old platoon boss, Chief Gunner's Mate/Guns Everett Emerson Barrett, whose ability to tweak the F-word into a string of compound, complex run-on sentences containing all its known mutations is legendary in Naval Special Warfare, I settled down and began to try to see what the problem might be.

We checked the fuel line from the bladder. It was unobstructed. There appeared to be no extraneous water in the engine or exhaust system. Then I opened the cowling. Mr.

Murphy had somehow loosened one of the spark plugs—it sat dangling at the end of its wire. Nod dried it off, sprayed it dry with compressed air, and pressed it home. Half Pint played the part of snipe—pumping fresh gas into the line, priming the engine, adjusting the choke, then finally yanking the starter cord. The engine coughed, sputtered, then erupted into a welcome, throaty growl, Nod shut down the choke, tweaked the throttle, and we Tally-Ho'd.

0317. We progressed through the swells at sixteen-and-a-half, seventeen, seventeen-and-a-half knots. The Chinese freighter was only six or so nautical miles ahead of us now. We couldn't see it, but it was almost as if I could sense the fucking thing out there—waiting.

0331. We pulled within two miles. As the ICRRC crested the swells, we began to see the *Nantong Princess*'s underway lights twinkling in the distance. Not every time we crested, but every fourth or fifth time. It was enough to prime our sense of anticipation.

0340. We started to feel the ship's wake under the ICRRC's floorboards. That really told us we were getting close. I could see a change come over my men. Before, they'd pretty much kept to themselves, staring out at the water, each man lost in his own thoughts. The wake, which meant that action was close at hand, brought them out of their individual reveries and made them come together as warriors.

Boomerang and Duck Foot, my lead climbers, checked out the rolled caving ladders and the collapsible painter's poles they would use to snag the ladders in the freighter's rail. The rest of the group ran weapons checks, locked and loaded, and secured their combat gear. Gator attached a hundred-foot nylon line to the boat's bow ring. We'd have to secure the ICRRC to the freighter so we'd have a way to extract once the scuttling charges had been placed and armed.

0355. The wake was much reduced now—it was as if we were dead-heading. And then, all of a sudden, we were on her. Somehow, it always happens like that. One instant you're out there—all alone. The next, you come on your target—wham.

The fantail loomed ghostlike in the darkness—a fucking modernistic skyscraper topped by a railing. We could feel the power of her screws now, and we got the blast of heat from the *Nantong Princess*'s discharges. Her name, in yellow Chinese and English letters a foot high, spread out above me like a gap-toothed smile.

I was wet. I was cold. I was tired. And I hurt like hell. But my whole body ignored the whole nasty package. Why? Because I'd just gone into automatic, preaction sensory overload.

No, I am not bullshitting you. I am not giving you some kind of Warrior pseudo-psychobabble. This stuff is real, folks.

Before you go into battle, several things happen to you. Your breathing gets shallow. Your legs may feel a little shaky. Sometimes there's a slight feeling of nausea. And you always experience a huge adrenaline dump.

Those who haven't gone into battle before try to fight or even deny these signals. But those of us who've been there many times let our bodies take the lead. What we are experiencing is the same temporary queasiness every great actor or tenor feels before he goes onstage; the same knot-in-gut feelings pro football players get before the Super Bowl, or tennis pros undergo at Wimbledon. So I let my heart race. I allowed my breathing to go shallow. I felt the bile rise in my throat. And then, as quickly as it had come over me, the wave of sensation faded, subsided, evaporated. I knew my body and my soul were ready for any challenge— and I prepared to go to war.

0358. In the world of commercial shipping, the *Nantong Princess* could not be considered a big vessel. It looked like your everyday tramp steamer—perhaps 250, 260 feet in length, with a beam of 35 feet or so. We're talking about a displacement here of somewhere close to 2100 tons.

But from where we sat on the water, she looked like a fucking behemoth. We eased up close and pulled alongside. Nod was at the throttle, working hard to keep us even with the dark steel plates. That's a lot harder than it might seem. You're in a tiny craft that is fighting the ocean. The ship also creates its own currents—a contrapuntal situation in which the sea pulls you in one direction and the shock waves caused by the ship pull you in another. So your craft moves forward, sideways, and backward simultaneously.

You, there. Yes, you—the one with the thick glasses, the plastic pen protector in your pocket, and your hand flapping like a fuckin' pennant in the wind—you say what I've just described is impossible according to the laws of physics? Listen, bub—if you haven't been there, then S^2 (look it up in the Glossary) and keep reading.

The good news was that we had the power to move at eighteen knots so that keeping up with the ship, which was going at six or so, wasn't a problem. Keeping our ICRRC in an even course, however, was something else.

Now, you are probably wondering how we could make our approach so brazenly—we were perfectly visible in the open sea, after all, and our outboard was roaring at full throttle. The answer is that ships make a, well, shipload of noise. The turbines that drive the engines roar. The ship itself rolls and moans and groans. And there are large numbers of decibels of ambient noise: the screws churning, the bow cutting through the water, the sound of the waves and wind. All of these elements served to mask our approach.

Moreover, we were on a small, dark craft. And frankly it is hard to see anything at night, especially on the ocean, and especially if it is just before 0400, when most of the folks on board are asleep, and those who aren't, aren't at their top form. To see us you would have had to: 1. be in precisely the right place at the right time; 2. be looking for us; and, 3. be the winner of this week's fuckin' lucky club. Get the point? Good.

0401. I gave Nod a thumbs-up. He brought the ICRRC in close to the ship's low, port side amidships rail. Boomerang and Duck Foot extended their painter's poles with the caving ladders attached, reached up, and tried to hook the rail. This is more difficult to perform than describe, because the ship was moving in one rhythm, we were moving in another, and there is a current that flows alongside the ship that has its own syncopation. There is a Naval Special Warfare technical term for this continually mutating chain of events. It is called entering the FUBAR Zone. Entering the FUBAR Zone can be lethal.

See, when the rail was low enough to hook, we were too low by three feet to hook it. When we were in the right position, the rail was four feet above where we could reach because the ship was riding a different set of swells than we were.

Did you know that you cannot take over a ship if you can't get aboard? Well, I was learning this basic fact of warfare here and now. I waved Boomerang and Duck Foot off. I needed three more feet of height.

I hooked a thumb in Duck Foot Dewey's direction. "Get up on Boomerang's shoulders and try it from there—JUST GET UP THE FUCKING LADDER AND DO IT NOW!!"

"Roger, Skipper." Duck Foot clambered onto the forward thwart, then stuck his leg over Boomerang's shoulder.

"C'mon, dude." Boomerang helped Duck Foot straddle his neck. That was the easy part. Standing up was something else. Remember, we were bobbing up and down, and in and out, and side to side. There was pitch and there was yaw. There was roll and there was heave.

Swaying like a fucking drunk, Boomerang struggled to his feet just as the ICRRC hit a bad swell. "Fuuuck—" He went over sideways, launching Duck Foot ass-over-backward, toward the gunwale. Nasty and I made simultaneous diving tackles. I got hung up in the caving ladder—split my lip, smacked my nose, and missed Duck Foot completely. But Nasty grabbed him by the boot just as he was s-l-i-d-i-n-g overboard.

I spat blood and slammed Nasty on the shoulder. "Nice shoestring, asshole."

Nasty grinned and patted Duck Foot's balaclava'd forehead. "Aw, Skipper, I'm kinda used to having him around.

He's so cute and small—it's like having my own fuckin' hamster."

Duck Foot smacked the big SEAL hard enough to bring tears to his eyes. "And fuck you back very much, too," he said.

0402. No time for small talk—we were vulnerable down here, and if we didn't get up the goddam ladder soon, we were going to be visited by Mister Murphy. Duck Foot hoisted himself on Boomerang's shoulders. He snagged the rail on the second try, secured the hook, and started up the caving ladder. Gator and Pick covered him with MP5s.

One of the reasons my men and I pump a lot of iron is that climbing a caving ladder while boarding a ship under way calls for humongous upper body strength. The ladder itself is made of stainless steel cable, with titanium rungs. The fucking thing swings like a goddamn pendulum, and each increment is painful. Climbing a caving ladder is hard enough when you're doing it in training. But in combat, when you are carrying weapons and other equipment, it is a motherfucker.

I could see the strain on Duck Foot as he made his way inch by painful inch. But he never stopped. The sonofabitch just kept moving until he'd reached the top. Then he looked down, saw that he was covered, and he rolled over the rail.

This is the most vulnerable time. The man on top is unprotected, and if a crewman decides to come out on deck for a smoke, there can be trouble. But for once, Mr. Murphy decided to stay in his bunk. By the time Duck Foot unsheathed his MP5, Boomerang was already pulling his long frame up the caving ladder.

Two men on top—we weren't home free yet, but we were a lot better off than we had been ninety seconds ago. Duck Foot lowered a rope and I tied the second caving ladder to it. He pulled it up and snagged a scupper. Pick and Half Pint scampered up—one went fore, one moved aft. Now we had some fucking firepower up there. Gator and I went next. He had the coil of nylon line that was attached to the ICRRC's bow ring.

I grabbed the cable side rail, slid my boot onto the highest rung I could reach, and pulled myself upward. Fuck me—that *hurt*. By the fifth rung I knew I was in the midst of a very existential experience.

0409. Nod, wheezing and sweating, rolled over the rail and collapsed in a heap, hyperventilating. I gave the kid a few seconds to catch his breath. While he dry-heaved I stared down at the water. Two dozen feet below us, the ICRRC bobbed alongside in the current.

0410. We were forty-fucking-five minutes behind the op-sked I kept in my head, so it was fucking time to go to fucking work already.

I gave hand signals and we split into two prearranged groups. Yes, I know just like you do that we were all wearing radios, and we all had wire lip mikes and earpieces so we could communicate securely and quietly. But you don't want to use a radio unless you absolutely positively have to. Radios are particularly Murphy prone. They develop static and crackle at the most inconvenient times. They spontaneously spout loud feedback. And if you press the transmit button and you happen to be close to a TV set or another radio, you can often give your position—or at least your presence—away because your transmission will leak and "print" on that other set. That was why, according to my op-plan, we'd maintain radio silence until the last possible minute.

Okay—Nasty, Boomerang, Half Pint, and the Pick, my Red Squad, headed aft, toward the stern, where the interior ladderway to the engineering compartment was located. They knew their way because they'd studied detailed satellite photos and memorized their route. Simultaneously, Gator, Duck Foot, Nod and I—Blue Squad—would take down the bridge.

It's about to get busy, but let me explain a little bit here about boarding and neutralizing tactics. Your primary objective in any ship-boarding operation is to capture the bridge. If you are in control of the bridge, then you are in control of the entire ship. The EMERGENCY STOP control is always located on the bridge—which means you can bring the vessel to an absofucking complete stop. The captain's quarters are generally close by, too. So is the comm center, the radar room, and—often—the officers' quarters as well.

That is the up side. The down side is that there's likely to be more action—even at this hour—in the vicinity of the bridge than anywhere else aboard the ship. The current NAVSEA (NAVal SEA Systems Command) operational manual for what in SpecWar we call VBSS/H, which stands for Visit Board Search and Seizure operations against potentially Hostile shipping platforms, calls for a minimum of four shooters and two backup shooters when assaulting even the smallest ship's bridge. The assault force generally has an eight-shooter unit in play, plus at least one heliborne sniper uuit.

Cautiously, we moved forward along the weather deck, toward a ladder that I knew from the same series of satellite pictures led to a passageway just off the bridge where the *mo-sin-tin-shang* had his station. *Mo-sin-tin-shang* means radio operator in Chinese.[1]

---

[1] Yes, I know I'm not consistent about using the officially approved, Beijing standard, *Hanyu Pinyin* phonetic transcription spelling that the Chinese Communists foisted on the world some years ago. But you see, the Chinese Communists aren't very nice or moral or honorable people. And despite the fact that this administration has decided to pussyfoot around that fact and grant them most favored nation trading status, the Chinese government uses slave labor to produce goods it sells abroad; it condones torture; it is one of the most repressive governments on the face of this planet; and it clandestinely sells weapons of mass destruction to unstable regimes all over the goddam globe. That makes the Chinese more than a potential adversary in my book. They are a fucking threat to my country. So there's no way I'm going to play their game—not politically, or militarily. And there's no way I'm going to follow the spelling and pronunciation rules imposed by these totalitarian assholes. Besides, I'm the fucking Rogue Warrior, and I can fucking do what I fucking want.

Now, the SIGINT guys at No Such Agency had provided me with good, but not complete, intel. By that I mean, I knew which passageway I had to be in to neutralize the radio operator—but not which precise compartment the *mo-sin-tin-shang* worked in.

0412. Up the ladder. At the top were two companionway doors side by side. I picked the forward-most one—the one closest to the bridge—reached down, and tried the handle. It was unlatched. I lifted the lever slowly, released the catch without a sound, and moved inside.

The lights were dim, but I could make out six louvered wood compartment doors lining the narrow, puke yellow passageway. Unlike the clean sea breeze outside, the air in the passageway was stale. I wrinkled my nose and inhaled. The unpleasant mélange was a fetid mixture of cigarette smoke, sweat, garlic, BO, and Chinese grunge. Obviously, this crew didn't spend a lot of time policing their quarters—or themselves.

We moved slowly and deliberately. I had the point, my suppressed MP5 in low ready, my finger indexed alongside the trigger guard. Behind my right shoulder I could sense Nod's submachine gun. His field of fire complemented my own—and protected my left flank. Behind Nod came Duck Foot, his eyes scanning left-right, right-left as he moved cautiously, MP5 at the ready, breaching shotgun in a quiverlike sheath across his back. Gator Shepard brought up the rear, his back almost touching Duck Foot's.

My first concern was the radio room. We had to silence the ship—cut it off from the world. I checked the doors. None had any lettering. That told me these six compartments were probably officers' quarters.

Damn—this was going to knock us even further off schedule. I used hand signals to tell Gator and Duck Foot to deal with the six compartments while Nod and I continued onward. Gator's head went up-and-down once, Duck Foot gave me a single thumb-up and Nod and I moved off.

No, it wasn't a Good Idea to split my force in two. But

guess what—I had no choice right now. The satellite pictures I'd seen told me my gang of eight was up against three dozen or so Chinese. And experience has taught me that satellites don't always give you an accurate picture when it comes to personnel counts. After all, they can't gather the crew on deck for a yearbook photo. They shoot a series of images over a period of time, and then the intel weenies who insist they know how to make sense out of pigeon entrails tell me what they think they see.

So you tell me three dozen, mister intel-man, and I'll tell you I'm gonna add 20 percent—maybe even a few more points than that—to your guesstimate. So far as I was concerned, we were up against five-to-one odds, minimum. That meant each of my men and I were going to have to carry his own share of the operational weight—plus the extra heavy five-to-one ratio SOS—which as you can probably figure out, means sack o' shit.

Now, things weren't as bad as they might seem. The general rules of maritime room clearance—the ones I was talking about a few paragraphs ago—were written for two-man, not four- or six-man teams. Why? Because with the exception of such areas as the bridge, the crew lounge, the mess deck, and the engineering sections, most of the compartments aboard a ship are tiny. Try to put four or six men inside at one time and you'll probably end up shooting your swim buddy.

That was the up side. The down side was that we were going to have to deal with each compartment as we worked our way to the bridge because I didn't want anyone nipping at our heels. That's a general rule of all tactical teams: you never leave an unsecured area behind you. It may take more time—but your men stay alive.

0413. The end of the passageway was either a T or an L— it was impossible to tell from my present position. Didn't matter now, anyway—too much to do first.

I took the left side, so I could see forward, and cut the pie, moving so as to protect myself as I came around. Glanced back—it was a dead end. No doors. No hatches, no passageways.

Moved into the passageway to my right, now. Step by step—heel, toe. Heel, toe. My eyes scanning, MP5 in low ready. Trigger finger indexed. Breathing steadily so I wouldn't hyperventilate.

Three doorways on my port side—nothing to starboard.

Behind me—where Gator and Duck Foot were—I thought I heard the *crack-knuckle* sound of their MP5 hammers falling in three shot groups.

First door. Nothing. Second door—Chinese characters on it. I looked down at my left hand where I'd inked my clib sheet. The characters didn't match. Third door. Three characters in bold strokes. I checked. Double-checked. They matched. I searched for hinges and saw none—which meant the door opened inward.

My eyes told Nod which way I was going, and what he had to do.

Nod gave me a single affirmative nod of his head and backed away, toward the first of the three doors. He'd take down each room, one by one, while I dealt with the communications shack.

I dropped, peered under the door, and checked for illumination. There was weak, blue-green light coming from the room.

I rose. Held the MP5 in place against my shoulder with my right hand. Left hand on doorknob. S-l-o-w turn.

It was unlatched. I nudged it inward, slow but deliberate, until I got it a third of the way open.

From the doorway I could see three targets inside—three *mo-sin-tin-shang*s.

Immediate threat—the *mo-sin-tin-shang* hunched in front of the old-fashioned green-on-black computer screen, behind a desk/console to my left. He was awake and alert. And he was in close proximity to a bank of buttons and switches that I didn't like the look of at all.

Secondary threats—the other two, who were sacked out

catching z's on the lumpy lower racks of two small messy bunk bed units bolted to the bulkhead on the opposite side of the compartment. One was in skivvies and an aged yellow T-shirt. The other slept in a puke green uniform that looked like pictures I've seen of Korean war–era marine utilities.

I slid inside, my MP5 up, my sight picture forming nicely. This, my friends, is what it's all about—all the pain of getting here; all the wet, and the cold, and the unwelcome presence of Mr. Murphy—none of that fucking matters anymore. Why? Because it's *Show time,* ladies and germs.

Maybe it was the movement—maybe he sensed me the way people sixth-sense threats. Computer-man swiveled in his chair. Reached for something lying on the computer table.

Time freezes in situations like this one—to the participant everything takes place in slo-motion (or, in this case, slo-*mo-sin-tin-shang*-shun); almost like freeze-frame photography. And yet, things happen so fucking fast—no time even to think, just *react* and *do.*

Didn't waste a millisecond—I sight-acquire-fired. Caught him midreach with three of my frangible 147-grain no-name hi-shock bullets right in the head. He went down as if he'd been mule kicked. Hit the desk face first—what was left of his face, that is—clattering the keyboard and knocking what he'd been reaching for—a small semiauto pistol—off the desk into a corner.

One down. I kept moving, closing space between me and Threats Two and Three. You never stop moving; never give up any space. Don't allow the opposition any edge at all. They were moving now—shifting from sleep to wake at the strange sounds.

You can sleep through almost anything if you're accustomed to it. Trains running next to your bedroom window, barking dogs, you name it—if it happens regularly, your brain programs itself. That's why folks who can sleep through a goddam hurricane hear people breaking into their houses—because the sounds of the break-in play differently on that piano they keep in their subconscious.

So what happened? Threats Two and Three came up from their bunks as if they'd been hit with a jolt of electric current. Talk about your dropped-jaw stare. Well, I must have been a fucking sight, too—blood from my split lip running down into my balaclava. All in basic black *sans* pearls, and MP5, up, aimed, and ready to go-go-go.

Left-side bunk rolled out onto the floor. I saw where he was going: the ladderback chair where a pistol belt hung. I stitched him with two three-round bursts and he stopped moving. Now the right-side bunk man—the puke green utilities—moved. He was reaching for something wedged above him.

Had to stop him quick. Fixed his chest dead center in the bright Trijicon night sight front blade and squeezed off a three-round burst.

Nothing. The hammer fell, but no shot. The sound of that hollow *click* rang in my ears louder than a fucking flash-bang explosion.

Fuck me. I racked and tapped and ratcheted the action just like I'd done more than a thousand times in CQC training sessions. An unfired shell ejected—another one went into the chamber and the bolt slammed closed. I squeezed the trigger. *Click.*

I saw the *mo-sin-tin-shang* in the bunk doin' the loco-*mo-sin*. He realized I was doomded—as in doom on me—and he obviously wanted to help the situation along. I dropped the MP5 and launched myself at him—a full-bore, horizontal lunge that took me across the seven feet of compartment—to strike him in the throat, keep the sonofabitch quiet, and keep him away from whatever it was he wanted so badly.

I managed to grab Mr. *Mo*—after all, in situations like this you should be on a first name basis—by the Adam's apple—his call for help was squelched into a silent gulp—

but he used my momentum to carry me—*slam, wham, damn*—Slovak noggin-first into the effing bulkhead.

Talk about seeing fucking stars—it was July Fourth, New Year's Eve, and fucking Coronation Day all at once. My head was dingdonging like the goddam bells of Saint Paul's. My eyes were crossed from the pain of sudden, traumatic neck compression—and that's *my* neck we're talking about, not his.

This guy must not only have studied the martial arts, but he'd also read Sun Tzu, because he sure followed the old bastard's advice for winning, which goes, "When your enemy is weak, become strong."

First he clawed at my eyes. Neck pain be damned—I pulled back and his fingers missed. But he still raked my face and scratched the hell out of it. Then he set about tearing the balaclava off my head—got it about halfway, wrapped his hands around the material, and tried to apply it as a tourniquet to my throat—no doubt to staunch the blood from my split lip and lacerated face.

When Mr. *Mo* realized that it wasn't working—that was after I managed to bring my knee up into his nuts hard enough to make him gag—he tried to remove my right ear with his teeth while he struggled to lay his wily (or wiry, take your choice) Oriental hands on—now I could see it—the nasty-looking stiletto that was wedged in the springs of the bunk above his own rack.

I'm not big on stilettos—unless I'm the one wielding 'em. So it was time to change the venue. Now, I am a big chap, and I outweighed Mr. *Mo* by at least sixty or seventy pounds. But since we were rolling around in a tightly restricted area—namely his bunk, which was maybe six feet by a foot and a half, and he was a persistent little rodent, he had the immediate advantage. Plus with every wriggle, writhe, and wrestle, he was moving closer and closer to the damn pig sticker.

Oh, there was also the noise factor. Frankly, I not only had to kill this sonofabitch—I had to do it quickly, and without letting him make any more fucking noise than he already had made.

Time to get serious. I wrapped him up with my arms and legs and rolled us both off the bunk, landing on top of him with all my weight. That did two things. First, it took him away from his weapon. Second, it knocked the wind out of him—at least long enough for me to work my left forearm under his neck and try to crush his windpipe.

He fought back, but he was losing strength and I was gaining it. Frankly, some of that is size, some of it is diet, and some of it is the fact that I wanted to kill him *mo* than he wanted to kill me—in other words, simple Froggish determination.

Reached with my right for the K-Bar. Wrestled it out of its sheath and brought it up. He tried to fight it away, but I was on top of him and his arms were pinioned. Slammed the blade into him just under the rib cage, and cut upward in a twisting motion, toward the lungs and heart, until he stopped struggling.

Rolled off him. Took his head in my hands and twisted sharply to break his neck—just to make sure he'd stay down.

Clambered onto hands and knees, sweating and out of breath. But no time to rest. Too much still left to do. This was the effing radio shack—there was still the whole goddam bridge to worry about.

First, I had to disable the commo gear. I lurched over to the console and gave it a quick once-over. There was the usual ship-to-shore shortwave shit. Oh, the writing was in Chinese, but the equipment is universal.

Then there was some other stuff that you usually don't find on commercial freighters—like the scrambler fax, the military model SATCOM receiver, and the ultra–high-frequency comms unit.

I disabled them all. Cut every goddam wire in the room, too. Then I edged back into the passageway. After the rest of my work was finished, I'd come back and collect all the papers, logbooks, files, and other sundry intelligence I'd observed.

0415. Nod was nowhere to be seen—and the passageway doors were all shut. I edged up to the nearest one, cracked it open, and peeked inside. One T-shirted, skivvy-clad body was sprawled facedown on the bed. The nicely placed group of bullet holes in his side told me he wasn't going to be waking up. A second corpse with an equally small three-bullet pattern in the dead center of its chest stared at me with uncomprehending eyes from the deck, and I slid the door closed, impressed with Nod's work. I was glad to see that he'd been spending time at the range.[2]

I got just about halfway down the short leg of the L, when Gator Shepard's face appeared peeking around the corner.

He hand-signaled, his left thumb and index finger making a circle. That meant everything was cool—unless he was Brazilian, in which case he was calling me an asshole.

I decided to accept the American interpretation. Nod silently materialized behind me. He is v-e-r-y spooky that way. "How many down?" I mouthed silently. Gator showed me eight fingers. Nod displayed four. That meant we'd dealt with fifteen so far—that left another thirty or so.

I wiped the blood from my face, rearranged my balaclava, stuck a fresh magazine into my MP5, and quietly racked a round I hoped hadn't been fondled, groped, or otherwise disturbed by any of the Murphy clan into the chamber.

---

[2]Now, that may sound cold. But different people see things in a different light. I remember running into my old friend Bert Hickman, a marine sniper, small weapons expert, and internationally ranked skeet shooter, on the day Egyptian President Anwar el-Sadat was killed by a group of fundamentalist assassins. It happened, you'll remember, as Sadat reviewed the October War memorial day parade in Cairo. I was heading for the gym to blow off some steam; Bert was coming from his daily workout. We passed one another at a trot. "Whaddya think about Sadat?" I called to him, shaking my head in disbelief.

"Great hit, great hit," said Bert, never stopping.

0416. Gunfire erupted from somewhere in the stern as we cleared the last of the passageways prior to entering the bridge area itself. *Okay, ladies and germs, that will end the stealth portion of our show this evening.* It was time to go to full-auto, kick-ass rock-and-fuckin'-roll.

No need for radio silence anymore. I pressed the transmit button on my radio. "Sit-rep?"

Boomerang's voice came right back at me. "Got us a lively little firefight here, Boss Dude—"

"Where's here?"

"Forwardmost section of the engine room."

Fuck. "Bad? Anybody down?"

There was a pause. "Nah—we're all okay—brought down six of them, too, before they started shootin' back. But it's gonna slow us down some."

That was bad news. After the engineering space, Nasty, Boomerang, Half Pint, and Pick had to deal with the security contingent, the crew's quarters, and the mess deck. Yes, I know that they had a demanding assignment. Yes, I know that under normal circumstances a full sixteen-man platoon would be employed. But y'know, there are times when you have to operate full-tilt boogie with what ya got on hand. That's how it was right now—and besides, I'd put those four shooters up against any full goddam SEAL platoon anywhere, anytime, anyplace. I winced involuntarily as a burst of gunfire ricocheted in my radio earpiece. "WTF, Boom'rang?"

The motherfucker actually laughed into his mike. "Hey, Boss Dude, I'd love to talk some more but it's gettin' busy here—we gotta go and play some games with these assholes."

Yeah, well I was about to have my own mitts full. I waved at Nod, Duck Foot, and Gator—"Let's *move* it."

No time for subtlety now. Three doors between us and the bridge hatch. They were metal, not wood; they were solid, not louvered—and each of them had one line of Chinese characters stenciled on a rectangular plate above the transom. These obviously weren't everyday living quarters but VIP accommodations or something like that.

I kicked the first door in. Dark compartment, two tables and maybe eight, nine, chairs—blackboard with Chinese writing on it up against the wall. I licked the MP5's 110-lumen bright white Sure Fire combat light around, sweeping the bulkheads, corners, floor. All clear.

As I searched behind DNO—that's Door Number One, but all you *Let's Make a Deal* fans out there probably knew that already—Nod and Duck Foot hit the second door, and Gator went for the third. As I came out of mine, a burst of automatic weapons fire knocked Gator from his doorway. He kind of exploded out and away as rounds cut holes through the metal. He landed with an ominous thud on his back in the passageway.

I moved to where he lay on the deck, grabbed him by the collar of his CQC vest, and dragged him out of the direct line of fire. A second volley of shots came through the compartment door, and I threw myself on top of Gator as the rounds ricocheted up and down the hallway—didn't want him getting any more hurt than he already was.

"I'm okay, Skipper." Gator rolled onto his side to dislodge me.

"Hold it, will you?" I held him down and ran my hands over him until I was satisfied that there were no holes, and no signs of blood. I rolled off him and pulled him to his feet. A third volley came through the door, sending Gator flat on his belly.

"Shit, the cocksucker surprised the hell outta me again." He hunkered down and picked up his weapon. "I can take care of this, Skipper. You keep going."

No way. There was more than one man in there, I could tell from the volume of fire. Besides, I wanted all my men in one piece and didn't need any goddam bad guys nipping at my heels. More—these assholes really wanted to keep us out of their compartment. Even in the height of battle, that made me inquisitive about what might be inside. I motioned toward the door. "Duck Foot—"

"Yo."

I pointed at the shotgun scabbard on his back. "Kill that fucking door!"

Duck Foot pulled his breaching gun—a cut-down Remington 870P Magnum, with thirteen-inch barrel and built-in standoff device—out of the scabbard strapped to his back. The weapon was loaded with five Def-Tec TKO frangible slugs. The TKO is made of powdered zinc—it disperses on contact. But before it disperses, the fucking stuff will disintegrate the hardest lock cylinders, hinges, or reinforced dead bolts.

Duck Foot scurried to the right side of the door, careful to crawl under the bullet holes so his movement would be masked. I stood well to the left side of the door frame, protected by the heavy bulkhead. I pulled a frag grenade from my vest, yanked the pin, and held the spoon down firmly, then gave Duck Foot a single nod of my head.

Duck Foot put the tip of the standoff device between the door handle and bolt assembly, then pulled the trigger. *Whaaaam*—the metal buckled—but the door stayed where the fuck it was.

The explosion was answered by gunfire. Fuck—a long burst of automatic fire came through the door and bounced around the metal passageway bulkhead like goddam pachinko balls, sending all four of us to the deck yet another time. I brushed a sharp sliver of copper-coated lead from my CQC vest. I saw that something had cut through the ballistic nylon of my tactical holster. Bummer. But on the bright side, I'd managed to screw with Mr. Murphy by not losing physical control of the grenade.

My delight was interrupted by Duck Foot's scream. "Oh, goddam—" he shouted.

I looked over. He'd caught a couple of ricochets. One sliced him across the lower arm. The other caught his left cheek like a scalpel pass. The fucking thing about bullets is that when they hit metal, they flatten out and they get real sharp—especially if they're copper-jacketed in the first place. They can do some nasty damage.

Obviously, he wasn't too bad off. Because bleeding or not, Duck Foot thrust the shotgun around and blasted the lock again. This time I sensed motion—so I kicked the door, and as it opened five, six, seven inches, I softball-pitched the frag grenade inside—hard enough, I hoped, to bank it off an interior wall or two and take it back into the center of the room.

Despite the insulation provided by the door and bulkhead, the fucking concussion blast was potent enough to shake us up and send pieces of shrapnel into the door. I hoped it had done more damage to the assholes inside.

It was time to see for ourselves. Gator kicked the door in. It opened wide. Firing from a kneeling position, he hosed a long burst from right to left through the thick smoke, washing the compartment down with his MP5.

No response.

He flicked his Sure Fire on. The bright white light reflected off gray/mustard/black opaque smoke. As it dispersed, I could make out a body. It was wearing the Chinese version of BDUs—in other words combat clothes—and a bulletproof vest. Vests, however, are little protection against frag grenades in small, metal-walled compartments. Next to the corpse was a mangled AK—the weapon had taken a heavy hit from the grenade blast, too. Another body, also in combat gear, with a machine pistol in its motionless hand, lay sprawled near the first.

There was no movement. But I had to make sure no one was playacting. Cautiously, I made entry, approaching with MP5 at the ready position. I kicked the weapons away from the corpses. Then I swept the corners of the room with the light and MP5's muzzle. The beam picked up something and my finger tightened on the trigger. It relaxed when I saw two more bodies. They lay partially concealed by a small wood desk. I approached, kicked the pistols away from their motionless hands, then made damn sure they were dead.

Now I focused on what the hell all these stiffs had been so desperate to keep us away from. There was a humongous fireproof, six-foot-tall, three-foot-wide, three-foot-deep combination-lock document safe strap-welded to the far bulkhead, right next to one of the compartment's two well-used, metal-frame single beds.

This was probably the intel compartment—or maybe it was where the political cadre lived. Either way, there was no time to waste on it now. Our cover was completely blown, as they keep saying on *NYPD Blue,* which meant we'd lost tactical surprise, and we were gonna have to grind out the rest of the mission against full opposition. I punched the transmit button on my radio: "Let's move-move-move—we gotta get to the bridge."

Oh, Dickie could see that this was going to be a long fucking morning.

Chapter

3

WE SECURED THE SHIP AT 0453, ENGAGED THE AUTOPILOT, AND dropped the *Nantong Princess*'s speed to a leisurely five knots. The crew had totaled thirty-eight, including a security force of six *zhongdui,* who had actually turned out to be *zhong*dweebs. Despite the fact that they carried the very best equipment the Chinese manufactured—everything from their bulletproof vests, to their small arms, to the flame retardant uniforms they wore were domestically produced—they'd lacked the will to fight. That, plus the fact that we'd taken them completely by surprise, and they hadn't been very well trained in emergency battle reaction procedures. The ship's company had suffered the predicted 100 percent mortality rate. My own injuries were much lighter. Duck Foot was going to need eight or nine stitches on his cheek and an equal number on the fleshy part of his left forearm. Half Pint lost the tip of a finger—he had no idea how he'd done it, but his fucking TAC glove was soggy with blood—and he was never again going to tell me I was Number One by tossing me the bird. From now on, all he'd be able to muster was that I was Number Two-thirds.

We wrapped the wound as best we could, and I told him that his new assignment during the extraction was to play the role of chum. That's not as in *buddy,* but as in *shark bait.*

Me? I had my usual complement of postcombat dings and dents, but there was nothing a couple of generic aspirin, a healthy dollop of Bombay Sapphire, and a soak between a pair of warm thighs couldn't cure in a jiffy. And oh, yeah—Nasty'd managed to turn his ankle as he dropped down a ladderway into the engine compartment. You ask what he turned it into? He turned it into instant pain. We splinted him with some metal shelf strap from the ship's machine shop, taped it securely, and gave him the radio handle "Hobble Grundle."

I sent Hobble, Gator, Duck Foot, Half Pint, Pick, and Boomerang down into the hold to check the cargo and start placing charges. Nod DiCarlo, whose background includes hefty doses of covert work and psy-ops in such picturesque locations as Panama, Iraq, Lebanon, and Bosnia, joined me for the intel sweep. I extracted one of the two watertight duffels stowed in my vest. Eddie plucked one from his.

In the way that you see things for the first time after looking at them forever, I saw as I smoothed out the creases that the duffels had been manufactured in China. Now, is that poetic justice, or ironic justice?

We began with the bridge: the *Nantong Princess*'s log, her radio frequency plot, master navigation chart, and complete file of maps—they all went into the bag. By the time we cleared the master's cabin, followed by the first mate's compartment, Nod was grumbling, "Yes, sir, no, sir, two bags full, sir." And he was spelling it—emphatically—with a *c* and a *u.*

Two bags full? Yeah—there were probably a hundred pounds or so of papers, books, and other miscellaneous items in the duffels. We probably took too much—I mean, I even stripped the dogtags off the *zhongdui* corpses. But it's hard when you don't speak the language—and where the *Nantong Princess* was going, we wouldn't have a second chance. Besides, I'd rather err on the side of complete than incomplete.

Proud as Blackbeard or Long John Silver with my booty haul, I left Nod to deal with the second mate's compartment, mess deck, and radio room, pulled the second duffel from my vest, and made my way back to the cabin where the big safe was located. The *zhongdui* corpses held nothing of interest for me except their ID cards and wallets. I noticed that each of the corpses bore a small, blue tattoo of a malevolent dragon entwined around an anchor. They'd had the work performed on the backs of their hands where thumb and forefinger came together. I took pictures of the tattoos to add to my intel files. The two Chinese officers—they be ossifers, har, har, har, because they be dressed like 'em, laddie—had no papers on them at all. Nothing in their wallets except Chinese, Korean, and Japanese currency, along with a bunch of Singapore fifty-dollar bills. Nothing in any of their pockets, either—other than:

1. one soggy (yecch!) handkerchief;
2. two ballpoint pens; and,
3. two packs of Marlboro cigarettes and a pair of cheap butane lighters.

But neither was holding any sort of ID card. Nor did either wallet contain a driver's license, or any of the other government-issue identification/credential/documentational detritus you normally find in military/official wallets. That made me suspicious. People who wear uniforms, especially officers, always carry some kind of official paperwork to show who they are, who has to salute 'em, and indicate where they can and can't go. The lack of IDs and other paperwork told me they were on a covert mission of some kind. I snapped their portraits with the digital point-and-shoot camera. We'd wash the images through a DIA computer and see if they'd piqued anyone else's interest.

I went through the cabin inch by inch. The closets held a

spare set of permanent-press uniforms, two sets of anonymous civilian trousers, cheap belts, and extra nylon shirts. Nothing inside the shoes. No hidden compartments in the closets—I ran my fingers carefully over all the walls and seams. There were two imitation leather briefcases. I turned 'em upside down. Out of one fell a crumpled sheet of notepaper with Chinese (Japanese? Korean?) writing. It went into the duffel. The other held detailed city maps of Pusan, Jakarta, and Singapore. I unfurled each one and looked to see if there were any marked locations thereon. It is a fact, folks, that even the most intelligent of intel officers will once in a while mark a map of an unfamiliar city with the location of an upcoming secret assignation, thus giving folks like me a big step up when it comes to setting up an ambush in order to hunt and kill way beyond my normal bag limit of bad guys. These maps may have been well used—the stress tears on the seams betrayed that little infobit—but there were no markings. They went into the duffel anyway.

I found nothing under the thin, lumpy mattresses (or inside 'em, either). The desk was bare. I checked under the faux-Naugahyde desk pad. Nada. Checked the single drawer and found half a dozen Korean girlie magazines, two well-used *Playboys,* and a couple of computer printouts written in Chinese characters. The printouts went into my duffel bag.

Obviously, the safe held everything of importance. Now, if Machinist's Mate First Class Stevie Wonder had been along on this mission he could have had fun cracking it. But the goofy-looking ex-marine wasn't around. He was back in Washington, taking the chief's exam. They only give it once a year these days of downsizing and limited promotion opportunities. And despite the fact that he hadn't studied for the test—he'd been too busy giving me a hand in the Middle East to do any serious book work—there'd been no way I was going to let him come play shoot-and-loot with me when he should be working a number two Dixon Ticonderoga down to a nub on multiple choice and essay questions so he could win a long overdue promotion to E-7.

Hey, whether the Navy knows it or not, the Navy needs chiefs like Boy Wonder—and I wanted to see him promoted. So he was there, and I was here, and there was this goddam gray steel security safe to be cracked and peeled like a *li'tzhou*—which is how they said chestnut on this vessel.

I used my Sure Fire to examine the safe carefully. You don't want to play with something that might be booby trapped, and if this had been my safe, it would have been booby-trapped.

But then, not everyone is me. And there was no sign of spooky-dirty-nasty-nasty in the vicinity.

So I began to do a methodical TTB—top to bottom—exam. The lock was your garden-variety, military/government issue combination lock—you know, the kind that go *"right four times past zero to thirty-two, then left three times to eighteen, then right twice to fifty-nine, then left to zero—and open, sesame."*

The CLIQ—combination lock in question—was mounted on an escutcheon plate that measured about ten inches square. To the left of the CLIQ, a single handle would work the door's locking bolts once the tumblers had been released. The door itself was recessed into the body of the safe. Looking into the recess, I could see the door assembly had been fitted with fireproof gaskets.

In the old days, you'd crack one of these babies by playing with the combination—listening through a stethoscope or electronic eavesdropping device as the tumblers fall into place uno by uno. But that takes time—and sensitivity. And time and sensitivity are two qualities I don't have a lot of. And so, eschewing foreplay, I extracted a can of explosive foam out of my CQC vest, screwed the plastic nozzle into place, and very carefully sprayed a thin stream of foam around the circumference of the combination lock so that the sticky foam seeped behind the face of the dial.

Then I stuck a Chicklet-size wad of Semtex explosive at the bottom of the dial, right at six o'clock. I inserted a fifteen-second nonelectric firing assembly device into the plastique, activated the damn thing, and got my Slovak ass out of Dodge, into the passageway.

When the smoke cleared, I went back inside. The CLIQ had been blown clear across the room. I ratcheted the handle left to right, the locking bolts released, and—open fucking sesame—the door swung wide.

I started at the top shelf. There was cash—thirty, maybe thirty-five, two-inch-thick bundles of Uncle Sam's well-used hundred-dollar bills. I stuffed the money into my duffel. It's nice when the Chinese decide to help us pay down the national debt, don't you think?

There were three thin ledger books. These went into the duffel, too, as did half a dozen thick file folders crammed with papers.

But it was what I found on the third shelf that made me gasp. There were two ring binders, each about an inch thick. The covers were white, with a one-inch-wide diagonal orange stripe running bottom left to top right. Each binder was emblazoned with the seal of the United States Department of Defense. One binder had the words NUMBER ONE, the other was labeled NUMBER TWO. Each bore the notation:

> TOP SECRET
> SKYHORSE
> BIG BROTHER
> TECHNICAL MANUAL

There is a common literary phrase for my reaction as I picked the fucking binders up as if they were red hot—which, in a sense, they were. It is: *holy shit.*

Let me digress here just long enough give you a short primer on classification. Despite what they do in Hollywood and on the TV, or regardless what mumbo jumbo nonsense some of the espionage/military/techno/spook novelists write in their books, there are three—and only three—security classifications for documents and projects.

- There is CONFIDENTIAL. ("Material which requires protection and the unauthorized disclosure of which could reasonably be expected to cause damage to the national security.") Confidential materials are flagged with a blue tab.
- There is SECRET. ("Material which requires a substantial degree of protection and the unauthorized disclosure of which could be reasonably expected to cause serious damage to the national security.") Secret materials are flagged with a red tab.
- And there is TOP SECRET. ("Material which requires the highest degree of protection and the unauthorized disclosure of which could reasonably be expected to cause exceptionally grave damage to the national security.") Top secret materials are flagged with an orange tab or a yellow tab, depending on which department or agency you work for.

That's it. Full stop. End of line.

Now, in order to further protect information from unauthorized disclosure, the top secret classification is often accompanied by either a code word designation, or by utilizing a systemic organizational approach known as compartmentation.

Let's define code word first. Simply put, code words are cryptonyms used to identify sensitive intelligence data, or programs. For example, in the 1960s, No Such Agency and the Navy ran a joint top secret program to eavesdrop on Soviet military communications by having SEALs plant listening devices on the telephone cables that ran across the bottom of the Gulf of Finland, just outside Leningrad harbor, from the Soviet naval base at Sosnovyy Bor, to the military regional headquarters at Zelenogorsk. That top secret program was referred to by the code words Ivy Bells. This one was obviously called Skyhorse.

Next comes compartmentation. In Navyspeak, compartmentation is (and I'm gonna quote directly here, but because of security considerations I can't tell you what I'm quoting from): "The establishment and management of an organization, network, system, or project so that information about the personnel, internal organization, or activities of one component is made available to any of the other components only to the extent required for the performance of assigned duties." So it is altogether possible to have code word clearance to one part of a compartmented project, but be segregated from the rest of it. In other words, you might be cleared to know about Skyhorse, but not another compartment of Skyhorse, which has an even more closely-held series of code words.

Got it? Good. Because you're going to have to know all this stuff cold in just a few pages.

Okay, now, here am I, standing aboard a Chinese freighter, in front of a Chinese document safe, and I am holding in my hands, three top secret, code word classified technical manuals for a project that is so sensitive that even I have been compartmented completely out of it. Talk about irony.

I grabbed the binders, laid them out on what was left of the desk, and scanned. Shit—it all looked real enough to make me very, very nervous. What made me even more nervous were the highlighted sections, most of which had notations, handwritten in Chinese characters, in the margins.

Now, I'm going to tell you a little bit about the Big Brother project. I can only tell you a little bit because that's all I know.

In the past, you may have heard me refer to the concept of C^2W.[3] Today, that C^2W system has been expanded and improved into something they're calling C^4IFTW, a mouthfilling acronym that stands for Command, Control, Communications, Computers, and Intelligence For The War-

---

[3] C^2W, pronounced sea-square-w, stands for Command and Control Warfare. It is when you combine operational security, deception, psychological warfare, and physical destruction in order to deny, influence, degrade, and destroy enemy command and control capabilities.

rior.[4] C⁴IFTW is an integrated system that allows folks like me to enjoy real-time information on the battlefield without having to go through layer upon layer of intel weenies, staff pukes, recalcitrant middle-level managers, and other bureaucratic impediments to my mission.

With C⁴IFTW I can plug in, download, and get the info I need—everything from real-time pictures, to target designation, to thermal imaging, to satellite-assisted maps—delivered when I need it. That technology is available to me, as a SEAL commander, right now.

But that's not the whole picture. C⁴IFTW is a compartmented program. SEALs like me get to see the most basic form of the system. But way up the ladder is a highly developed version of C⁴IFTW, which—because even the code word cryptonyms are classified—I've only heard about and couldn't until right now confirm is the Big Brother project, which as I have just learned was codenamed Skyhorse.

According to the current RUMINT,[5] Big Brother employs many elements of the old C²W system. Which means, if I've been hearing the urinal gossip right, I can not only get tactical intelligence, but I can also screw with my enemy's phone and radio capabilities, fuck up his radar and other imagery, and destroy his own command-and-control capabilities. Best of all, this Big Brother C⁴IFTW fits into suitcased-size packages (two of 'em, I gather from the manuals in front of me now), can be run by battery power if necessary, and totals no more than a hundred pounds in weight.

Or at least, that's what they're saying. Me, I have no idea, because as I told you I'm not fucking cleared to know about

---

[4] You guys think I'm making this up, don't you? Well, I'm not—you can find C⁴IFTW in the United States Department of Defense's current *Dictionary of Military Terms,* a publication of the Joint Chiefs of Staff.

[5] RUMor INTelligence.

Big Brother, although it now appeared that the Chinese weren't under the same goddam restrictions as I was.

I began to skim the manuals. It didn't take me very long to realize that the fucking system was more powerful than rumor had it. You could, very easily, take over a goddam country—at least a small to middle-size one. Places like Saudi Arabia, or Kuwait, Guatemala, Honduras, Cuba, or Syria would be simple. Germany, France, or even Russia would be tough—but perhaps not completely out of the question.

Using Big Brother you could tap into everything from secure military communications to local air traffic control, to police band radios, cellular phones, and shortwave broadcasts. Monitor—hell, you could fucking broadcast over the air on radio and television if you wanted. You could monitor telephone networks—even calls on the new digital phones. You could program the fucking target and acquisition radar on ground-to-air and ground-to-ground missile systems. You could command and control military aircraft and do target assessments as well as any goddam AWACS aircraft. You could broadcast secure comms by covertly utilizing secure transponders on NSA satellites— or French, Brit, Israeli, Chinese, or Russian intelligence birds, for that matter. There is a SpecWar technical term for the capabilities of what I was looking at. It is: *Fuuuuck*in' incredible!

My reverie was rudely interrupted by Nasty's urgent growl in my earpiece. "Skipper, you better get down here fast—"

"Where are you?"

"Aft cargo area—the second athwartships compartment."

I climbed down one staircase and three ladders, and worked my way aft. I could see that the men had done a thorough job of searching the cargo. Every box, carton, crate, chest, and container had been opened and examined. I stepped over a pile of porcelain lamp bases. It occurred to me it was a good thing we'd hit the ship now—because it was more than three-quarters empty. It would have taken us a goddam week to sort through everything if we'd done the takedown just after it had left Shanghai. But secure in the knowledge that the missile components were still aboard from FORTE scans—not to mention solid intelligence that the Chinese had arranged to sell missiles to the Pakistanis—we'd let it cruise through the busier sea lanes, preferring to take the ship down during the most isolated portion of its voyage. So the *Nantong Princess* had unloaded cargo at Pusan, Korea, Yokohama, Japan, and several other ports.

They'd discovered the missiles quickly. There were six large missile containers; the selfsame housings our crateologists had said contained medium-range strategic missiles. The huge wooden containers were mislabeled, of course. But a box that holds a missile looks just like a box that's been built to, well, hold a missile. I saw that the nuclear warheads were packed separately, in precisely the same way we ship our own nuclear missile warheads.

Those were the missiles I had expected to find. What surprised me were the six French-manufactured GLCMs—Ground-Launched Cruise Missiles. The fucking Chinese hadn't even bothered to conceal 'em—they were packed in the same sort of tactical watertight containers that I use to transport my ordnance when I'm operating maritime. The containers were all marked with Chinese characters.

I scratched at my beard. I knew the Paks weren't interested in Cruise missiles; they already had hundreds of them, courtesy of the former Soviet Union, North Korea, and France. No, the Paks had bought medium-to-long-range strategic missiles from Beijing. But what we had here were half a dozen medium-range tacticals whose range was no more than 500, perhaps 525 miles. And they were French, not Chinese. Where the hell had they been going?

Well, there was no time to answer that question because it was only one of many I had to deal with. I was equally perplexed, for example, by the crates of Russian AK-47 assault rifles, concealed inside rough wood containers

marked in English, EXPORT—Zelinograd Machine Tools/
MVD. The letters MVD were disturbing. MVD, friends,
stands for *Ministerstvo vnutrennikh del,* which in English
translates as Ministry of the Interior. From my recent
experience in Moscow, I knew that MVD was the former
Soviet Union's most corrupt government agency. It was
involved in everything from the smuggling of nuclear technology to drug peddling.

But that's another story. Let's get back to my search. I
opened more than a dozen boxes of Soviet Army surplus
SKS semiauto rifles concealed in crates labeled as toys from
the Moskva Toy Company. There were cartons of various
caliber Tokorev and Makarov pistols whose cartons identified them as mushroom soy sauce. There were similarly
camouflaged cases of twenty-year-old Soviet claymore
mines and grenades, as well as roughly two and a half tons
(!) of Semtex plastic explosive, packed in easy to handle and
conceal ten-kilo (twenty-two-pound) blocks, and four to five
tons of Bulgarian, Russian, Ukrainian, and Czech surplus
ammunition, carefully wrapped in thick black plastic,
packed on pallets, and labeled as pig iron.

Cruise missiles? Russian weapons? Eastern-bloc ordnance? This wasn't making much sense. The Chinese sell
more than a billion dollars' worth of these very same goods
every year—so why the hell would they be buying and/or
shipping Russkie stuff when they have literally tons of the
very same materials sitting in warehouses in Shanghai and
Guangzhou? In point of fact, over the past decade China
has been included pretty high up on the world's Top Ten
Weapons Dealers list. Remember? Last year they were, as
the old *Billboard* magazine might have put it, number two
with a bullet.

The "toy" and "machine tool" crates were all stencilled
in Cyrillic. I ran my hand over the rough wood of one of the
crates we'd cracked open. I don't read Russian, but I
understood enough to realize that the stencil read: "Crate
Number 15 of 15." I peered at the weapons inside, then ran
the numbers on my mental tote board. The crates of

"machine tools" and "toys" contained enough small arms and munitions to supply a small army or a large guerrilla force for more than a year from the look of it. And I was examining only a small portion of the total shipment. Don't forget: we'd hit the *Nantong Princess* late in its cruise.

"Pull a bunch of serial numbers off these things," I told Gator. "Let's see if we can find out where they came from."

Y'see, even then, even that early in the story, the situation just didn't compute. There was something hinky about this deal. And the nettlesome truth was that I had no idea what said hinkdom might be. But I realized looking another four yards down the athwartships compartment there was no time to stop and smell the cordite right now.

Why was there no time? Because I saw it wasn't the nukes or the weapons Nasty had called about. It was the two Haliburton aluminum cases—each about the size of a big Pullman suitcase—equipped with integral casters and combination locks.

Nasty was hunkered near one of the cases. He'd picked the locks and opened them flat, like clamshells. The insides were made of thick black foam, hollowed out to hold the contents: a bunch of sophisticated, black-box electronic devices. Some had small screens. Others had dials and buttons. He'd pulled the contraptions out of their numbered foam repositories, spread them out in a semicircle around him, then laid the neat, bundled, color-coded wiring in a separate pile so he could take an informal inventory.

I bent down to take a closer look. There were nine component modules in one case, and twelve in the matching one. Each piece was marked PROPERTY OF THE UNITED STATES OF AMERICA in small letters. I saw two softcover black books the size of combat Bibles sitting in one of the suitcase's rigid foam cutout compartments. I plucked one of them from its nook and opened it. The title page carried a serial number. The frontispiece bore the globe, torch, and satellite-track logo of the Defense Intelligence Agency. Above the title was the word "SECRET." The text, printed in eight-point type, was a comprehensive listing of satellite frequencies and orbital data—ours, and everyone else's, too. I'd seen one of these before on the desk of my old friend Tony Mercaldi. Merc had referred to it as his satellite cheat sheet. I riffled through the book quickly, then started to examine everything else that was packed in the cases.

I looked over each piece of equipment, although there was really no need. I knew what we'd found—a Big Brother unit with all its technical manuals. It was an absofucking-lute intelligence disaster for the United States—and that is a goddam understatement.

Boomerang picked up a radar-defeating unit that could turn a plane, or a small boat, into a stealth craft at the flip of a switch. The box wasn't much bigger than your average Watchman. Boomerang examined the module very carefully. He looked up at me and inclined the rectangular box in my direction. "Hey, Boss Dude, seems to me we got ourselves some real evil fuckin' stuff here. Downright nefarious, in fact." He giggled in that perverse, son-of-a-beachy way only California surfers can. "I sure hope we get to play with it."

Chapter

4

0634. WHILE NOD TOOK DIGITAL PICTURES OF THE CARGO—
more evidence for the Chairman and secretary of defense—
I set up the Big Brother's secure piggyback SATCOM unit
on the *Nantong Princess*'s flying bridge and broke radio
silence. Yes, I knew I was dangerously behind schedule. And
yes, I knew I was acting contrary to my mission directive.
And yes, I knew that I'd probably piss some people off.

But that's part of what Rogue Warriordom is all about.
When you suspect that your country is in jeopardy, you
have to act. Decisively. Right now. And you have to be
willing to suffer the consequences of your actions.

But as you know, there are very few consequences I
haven't already suffered. Besides, I wanted to know WTF
was going on—after all, it isn't every day that, whilst on
board the ship of an adversary nation, you come across a
piece of the most sophisticated equipment your country
produces. So, before we extracted and I sent this ship and its
cargo to the bottom, I wanted answers.

Now, at times like these, it might have been nice to have
had one of the Chinese *ts'ing-po kwan-koon*—that's intelligence officers—on whom to perform a little *suen-man*,

65

which is how they say interrogation in these waters. But as you already know, the *Nantong Princess*'s company took 100 percent casualties, and there was no one to *suen-man*.

So to get answers, I bounced a signal back to Washington. My first priority was calling Chairman Crocker—he had to be told what I'd discovered.

I dialed the secure line on his desk. The phone rang twice. Then a woman's voice answered. "Sixty-eight twenty-four."

The extension number was right. But the voice was unfamiliar. I waited. She repeated the number. I asked, "Who is this?"

"To whom am I speaking?"

There was no way I was going to tell her who I was. "I'm calling for Chairman Crocker."

"He's unavailable. May I take a message?"

"When will he be back?"

"Much later." I heard her hand cup over the receiver, and there was silence for a second or two. Then the voice came back at me. "Who *is* this?"

She was probably trying to run a trace. It was time to go. "I'll call back," I said, and hung up.

Now, you probably want to know how the Chairman could be out of touch when there was a critical mission in progress. The answer is twofold. First, my mission was covert, not clandestine. During *clandestine* missions—like the abortive Tehran rescue mission led by my old colleague and friend Charlie Beckwith—the entire Joint Chiefs sit in their situation room and bite their nails until they learn what had happened. But *covert* missions aren't supposed to be happening at all, and any undue attention might attract unwanted suspicion. And so, the Chairman was following his regular schedule—whatever it might have been—and certainly didn't bother to sit by the phone.

In fact, he was not expecting to hear from me until I was safely aboard the submarine that had been sent to pick up an anonymous SEAL unit engaged in a need-to-know training exercise.

But I still needed help—and advice. So I tried another secure telephone. To be precise, I dialed the secure phone that sat on the left-hand side of the desk that belonged to my old DIA compadre, Anthony Vincent Mercaldi. Merc and I have played games together since Christ was a mess cook and Saddam Hussein wasn't trying to build nukes. If there was anybody who'd know WTF, or not raise any waves asking around if he didn't, it would be the Merc. I made the call to Tony the same way I'd called the Chairman: by sneaking aboard the handiest No Such Agency SIGINT bird (the project designation for this one is code-worded Tracee Wink, and that's all I'm going to say unless you all have the same security clearances I do) and stealing a free ride.

How'd I do that, you ask?

Well, first I found the satellite's general location by checking the handily supplied DIA book of frequencies, trajectories, and orbit paths. Then I set the transponder frequency on which I wanted to broadcast into the six-pound Big Brother transmitter unit. While I did that, Duck Foot unfurled the unit's sixteen-inch metallic satellite dish, which looks like a tiny umbrella blown inside out by the wind.

We eyeballed the predawn sky and held the dish at a sixty-degree angle, pointing due north. Once Big Brother located the transponder, it automatically attached itself to the signal like a hooker sucking cock or a gigolo sucking clit (that's a little bit of EEO irony for any of you politically correct readers out there), caromed it nicely off the NSA/Australian station at Pine Gap,[6] and straight back

---

[6]Pine Gap is located approximately eleven and a half miles southwest of Alice Springs, in the remote, dry-as-a-bone geographical center of the Australian outback. It was first built in the late 1960s (more construction was added later) and resembles a lunar colony in a 1950s sci-fi movie. The buildings are all single-story preformed concrete units. Dozens of radomes hold dish antennas. Other receiving devices pluck SIGINT information from the skies and also capture Soviet (and now Russian) and Chinese telemetry information from missile tests, as well as monitor the French, whose nuclear test zone was north of Australia in Tahitian waters. Pine Gap is staffed by between four hundred and five hundred permanent personnel, as well as a few dozen specialists, who rotate in and out depending on changing mission requirements.

through the SIGINT designator at Vint Hill Station just north of Manassas, Virginia, and on to the Pentagon.

It was just before 1900, one day earlier, on the tenth floor of the DIA building above the Washington Metro stop at Clarendon, Virginia. The phone rang twice, the signal as clear as if I was calling from the next office.

Merc's voice answered. "Mercaldi."

"It's me. We gotta talk. I've come across a real big brother of a problem and I need information about that big brother real fast."

There was a stunned pause on the other end. Then he growled, "What the fuck, Dick, you're not cleared."

"I may not be fuckin' cleared, but I have the fuckin' thing here in fuckin' front of me." I even quoted to him from the effing technical effing manuals, and read him the effing print-order numbers on the effing DIA effing satellite guides.

"Whoa—I don't think you should say any more right now," Merc cautioned.

"Why not?" I told him on what equipment I was transmitting and heard him suck air in disbelief.

"You're shitting me."

"Now, would I do something like that, especially from where I am right now?"

"Where are you?"

"I am somewhere," I said. "And that's all I'm gonna say."

That shut him up. Then he asked for a description of the suitcases. I heard him making notes. Then I asked if he knew how all this here equipment came to be outside the control of the government of the United States.

Merc said simply, "I have no goddam idea at all, but you can believe that I am going to find out."

"Yeah, well if you do, try to do it without leaving any signs pointing in my direction."

Merc saw the logic in that. No sense letting anyone know any details. Especially when it was too early in the game for IFF, which is MILSPEAK for Identification, Friend or Foe. At which point, the pleasantries completed, he told me to finish my goddam work, get my goddam team together, and haul my goddam recalcitrant SEAL posterior to safer territory. "You *are* going to exfil from wherever the hell you are, aren't you?"

I told him that his irony wasn't appreciated, and that in a few hours we'd be in a better location from which to call him. In truth, my team and I were scheduled to have departed some half an hour ago. "Contact me as soon as you've secured after exfil," Merc said. "I'll have answers for you, Dick. I promise."

1012. I could fill you in on all the painful details of our extraction, but I can encapsulate the previous three and a half hours by saying simply that it was a very irksome experience for all of us. We sent the *Nantong Princess* and its cargo of missiles and weapons into fifteen hundred feet of water. We salvaged more than two hundred pounds of intel materials—more than we might have had to, but then since I don't speak or read Chinese, I couldn't tell what was valuable intel, and what was common trash. So I schlepped it all—at least as much as fit in our four watertight duffels—before our explosive charges broke the *Nantong Princess*'s spine in two, and we sent her to the bottom.

Anyway, the duffels, plus the Big Brother suitcases, filled the ICRRC to overflowing once again. Which, in turn, sat us dangerously low in the water. Which also meant that we had to proceed at a safer, slower, and hence less fuel-efficient rate than we'd planned to be doing.

Which meant—are you beginning to comprehend the situation here? Right: we blanking ran out of blanker-blanking gasoline two motherblanking miles from our blankety-blank-blanking rendezvous point, and sat bobbing like a blanker-bleeping cork for half an hour until the blanking submarine commander decided that since we weren't blankin' moving anymore (he could see us clearly on his bleeper-blanking state-of-the-art radar) and since we were signaling regularly—even, perhaps, somewhat frantically—on our Official United States Navy SEAL Mark 4 Mod-3 homing device, he might (yawn, stretch) just as well c-r-u-i-s-e over and pick us up.

Now you might want to know why he didn't move as soon as he sensed our predicament. The answer to that question has two parts. First, since he had no idea what our mission had been (remember—he had simply been assigned to pick a SEAL unit up at a predetermined spot in the middle of the ocean), he probably felt no urgency to come and scoop us out of the water because perhaps sitting and bobbing up and down like a fucking cork was part of our OPLAN (Operational PLAN). Second, and perhaps even more important: coming the extra two miles wasn't on his checklist. And as you all know, nuclear submariners don't do diddly-squat unless it is on their checklists. And so, after our kidney-perforating journey, we sat and heaved (and pitched, and moaned), and tossed, and rolled while he sat, and sat, and sat, watching us through his camo-spotted periscope.

1021. Aboard the USS *Scorpion*. Before we went below, we pulled ourselves out of our assault clothes and deep-sixed most of them over the side, too. We'd been zipped in those wet suits for almost a full day. There are, as you can imagine, no built-in toilet facilities in 'em. So we were pretty goddam ripe. (And that, as the famous old Sino-detective Charles Chan might say, is a velly *flagrant* under-statement of the facts.)

In fact, I asked the chief of the boat—he is the sub's top enlisted man—for a hose to be brought topside so that we could clean ourselves up. At first, he'd balked; there was no hose denoted on his clipboard. But after one delicate whiff of *moi*, he was only too willing to comply, whether the fucking thing was down in black-and-white or not.

1030. I showered properly, changed into a set of bor-rowed blue coveralls emblazoned with the submarine's logo and a name tape that bore the word VISITOR, and made my way to the conn. The CO was there, hunched over a huge nautical chart. He was a compact, muscular guy, built like a punt returner or running back. He let me stand around as he finished drawing a line on the clear acetate atop the paper, then looked up and extended his hand in my direction.

"I'm Dave Brancato. Nice to see all youse guys safe 'n' soun', Captain," he said in an accent that took me back to the North Jersey days of my ute. Then he cut to the chase. "Sorry about not coming to get you sooner," he said matter-of-factly. "I guess I screwed up. So whadabout some hot cawffee?"

I thought about a wry, Roguish response. But to be honest I was beyond mix-ups right now. If I wanted to fret, there were things a lot more consequential to fret over. Besides, it wouldn't do me any good to complain. First of all, this was his boat, not mine. Second, like I just said, there was too much to do.

"Apology accepted," I said, shaking his hand. "And since you probably don't carry Bombay Sapphire, coffee'd be just fine." I paused. "Look, Dave, I'd like to get my guys fed, patched up, and bunked down—they've been on their tootsies for a couple of days. But I need your radio compartment all to myself because I have to get on a secure backchannel line to Washington ASAP."

His bull neck moved left-right and his expression turned to frown. "No can do, Captain."

Y'know, I do not like to hear the NCD words, which is exactly what I told Captain Dave.

"That's not what I meant," he said. "We're talkin' capabilities here, not will ya/won'tcha." He explained that *Scorpion* wasn't equipped for backchanneling. His particular sewer pipe was one of the older boats in service, and the comms package hadn't been upgraded yet. Probably never would be, he said bitterly, because *Scorpion* was scheduled for decommissioning in about eighteen months. You want to know why? Why don't you tell them, Captain Dave.

"Sure, Dick. It is because, thanks to this president, the Navy's environmental appropriation has tripled, while its war-making capabilities have been halved."

So, instead of the latest generation satellite burst transmitter and other high-tech goodies, the *Scorpion* had only the circa 1993, William Jefferson Clinton LFM (Let's Fuck the Military) budget cutback model, a *vox odious* radio/telecom system known as AUTODIN, for AUTOmatic DIgital Network. No bells. No whistles. No frigging backchanneling capabilities, either.

If I used AUTODIN, every one of my sensitive syllables would have to be caromed back to Washington through the cryptovault at the Navy's Pearl Harbor SUBOPS—SUBmarine OPerationS—message center. And any message that moves through a cryptovault can be steamed open, as they say in the "flaps and seals"[7] trade, and copied. Thereafter, it can be examined at leisure by the folks who run the message facility, or turned over to No Such Agency, or even, in some cases, to the local CIA or State Department gumshoes.

I told Captain Dave, *"non vorrei per tutto l'oro del mondo,"* a piquant, North Jersey Italian way of saying I wouldn't touch his AUTODIN with my ten-foot dick. No, I had to transmit to Washington without creating a ripple—or an echo.

That capability was nestled comfortably inside my Haliburton aluminum suitcase. All I needed was fifteen minutes of surface time, and the run of Captain Dave's bridge undisturbed by lookouts or any other sundry personnel save my own men. I wanted to run Big Brother's satellite uplink in private, although I obviously wasn't going to say anything to Captain Dave other than that I vanted to be alone.

---

[7]"Flaps and seals" is the intelligence term for the tradecraft of covertly opening, reading, copying, and then reclosing someone else's mail.

"Heey, I know that. I watch the classic movie·channel when we're in port. Greta Garbo, right?" Dave Brancato grinned. "Well, privacy ain't no prob if you don't mind a little cool salt spray frizzin' your French braid."

First priority: Chairman Crocker. I made the connection, but the same female voice answered, "Sixty-eight twenty-four."

I disconnected. Sorry, ma'am, but I like to do my explaining person to person, not through intermediaries.

I called the Merc. From whom I got very little satisfaction when I finally got hold of him—after three attempts and five hours. He'd swept DIA's computer network and come up dry. Then he'd gone into the Pentagon's net. Nothing there, either. So he called an old contact at Motorola, whose skunkworks (which is a kind of generic spook way of describing Motorola's clandestine operations division), held the contract for Big Brother.

Merc learned nothing until he gave up the numbers on the DIA satellite guides. Then he was told that the particular unit he was talking about had been part of a black project and Motorola couldn't say any more unless Merc could recite the proper code words—which, of course, Merc couldn't do. End of discussion.

Merc paused, and I heard him clap his hand over the receiver, as if someone had stuck his nose into the office. Then he picked up again: "So I figured maybe, it being technology, they'd know something about it at DITSA."

DITSA is how we in the defense establishment pronounce the acronym for DTSA—the Defense Technology Security Agency. They're the folks who make sure we don't send the wrong technogoodies overseas.

"So I called a guy we've known forever—you know the crazy Armenian."

Did I ever. His name is Ron Mardigian, and he's a stand-up guy. I'd done a lot of business with him over the years. "I know of whom you speak," I said.

"Well," Merc continued, "then you know how weird things must be, because he gives me this big song and dance about the fact that we're almost total strangers and why the heck am I calling him about this. And then he says, 'I really can't talk to you on the phone. Come on over for a face-to-face,' he says. And we're talking on our scrambler units, Dick—we're already on fuckin' secure phones! Then he says to call him from a pay phone but don't use the one in the lobby, and don't use any names."

That was strange. "And so?"

"So I jump the Metro to the Pentagon Annex. And I used a pay phone in the station, and I called, and told him, just like he axed me to, 'It's me—I'm here.'

"So Ron, he actually friggin' whispers, *'Go up the escalator and wait.'* And six minutes later the crazy motherfucker shows up wearing this Great White Hunter hat—you know—the ones with the big wide brims—and sunglasses, and he grabs me by the collar, and drags my butt down the street."

Mercaldi paused, as if he was checking the connection. Then he began again. "Now, first I figure he's just being your normal secretive paranoid Armenian, y'know. But then I realize he's really *spooked*. I mean he is *scared*. So I ask him what the fuck, y'know? And he says, 'Look, if we're gonna talk about this I want to do it far, far away from all prying eyes and microphones and all the other, more subtle observational devices we both know about.'

"Then he pats me down. For chrissakes, Dick, he fuckin' pats me down to see if I was carrying a goddamn wire. And then, when he's satisfied I'm clean, he grabs me by the lapels and says, 'Okay, who's this for?'"

I interrupted. "You didn't tell him anything—"

"I told him it was for a friend in the navy," Tony said.

"'A friend.' That's all you said?"

There was a pause on the line. "Well, I said it was for a friend who was a SEAL," Merc admitted. "But, Dick, there are a lot of SEALs."

Right. But not very many of us would be asking about Big

74

Brother. And not many of us have known Mardigian the paranoid Armenian for fifteen years, either. "So what did he tell you when you said a SEAL?"

"He rolled his eyes and said there was no way he could help me, because if my friend was the same friend he was thinking of, he worked for the Chairman, and this wasn't a matter for the JCS. He takes me by the friggin lapels again, and whispers, 'From what I can see, the JCS was locked out of this one. Hundred percent.'"

Goddammit, Mardigian knew exactly who Merc had been talking about. My cover was blown. "Merc, *c'mon*—"

"Hey, Dick, what's done is done, okay. But I kept at him. I really leaned on the sumbitch. Played the old friendship angle for all it was worth."

"And?" I was getting inpatient.

"It took almost an hour, and we must have walked two miles, but DITSA-man finally gave me something. He admitted they had a file on the Big Brother deal."

Here is a fact of intelligence gathering. It is that once you get your foot in the door, or put your nose under the tent, or insert your dick in the—well, just fill in whatever portion of the anatomy makes you feel good—it's easier to get the rest of you inside. "So you pressed him some more, right?"

"Bet your ass. And a half mile later, you know what he says? He tells me—lemme give this to you just how he said it—'So,' he says, 'a special delivery orange-tab pizza comes over from the National Security Council. Extra-extra large, with all the toppings.'

"Okay, I can play along, so I ask precisely what toppings were on it. 'Oh,' he says, 'it had your National Security finding, it had your CIA spook-work, it had your No Such Agency tag, your presidential memo, yadda-yadda-yadda. All code word. All compartmented.'"

The Merc paused. "So I asked him to let me have a slice, y'know? And he says, 'Forget it, it's too hot to slice.' Then he tells me never ever to bring up the subject of this particular pizza, especially at my shop."

"You ask him why?"

"Bet your ass I did. He goes back into pizza code. Tells me it has something to do with a 'new recipe.' Something to do with China and the Russkies—and the dough's been reformulated without any DOD help at all. Then he says, 'Besides, it's already in the oven over at the White House. Been baking for some time from the look of the paperwork.' And that was it. He wouldn't go any further. Told me to keep my nose out of it, and don't bother to call him for any more information."

"Do you have any idea who's behind it?"

"No idea whatsoever," Merc said. "For all I know it's one of those hush-hush freelance things they're doin' so many of these days. From the way the Armenian was talkin' I know it's got a presidential priority, and that it's probably being handled out of the NSC adviser's shop."

"Can you poke a little further?"

"Fuck no." Merc's voice took on a suggestion of alarm. "I may have poked too far already. I think I'm hearing clicks on my phone I never heard before. And I'm starting to see the same people following me—and we're only talking about the last six, eight hours here, Dickie. I'm gettin' as paranoid as Mardigian, and paranoid like that ain't where I want to be. So I think this is one of those F-two[8] situations, y'know?"

I came away from my conversation with the Merc even more confused than I had been before. You see, my entire military career has been built on a foundation of what you might call core values (in the marines they probably call them Corps values). One of the most basic of these is that you do not give aid and comfort to your enemy.

Under that aid-and-comfort rubric, I for one would certainly put giving away one's most sophisticated technology. Now, if anyone would know WTF, it would be Chairman Crocker. But until he picked up his own fucking secure

---

[8] File and forget.

phone, I wasn't about to say a word. I'd grab a combat nap—then try him again.

In the meanwhile, I was just plain old-fashioned confused. Why, you ask? Because here I sat, with hundreds of pounds of documents I couldn't read, and two suitcases containing state-of-the-art techno-goodies, and I had no effing idea what was going on. You can therefore understand my befuddlement.

Now, the good news was that I had a three-and-a-half-day cruise (we were headed back to Guam, from where we'd fly home) during which I would have some uninterrupted time to probe, assess, and—hopefully—unravel these conundrums while I called Chairman Crocker's office in the hope that he would answer his own goddam phone. The bad news was that for the next few days I wouldn't be able to act, except by remote. That was troubling, because as you know, I tend to be a hands-on sort of person.

I dropped from the sail into the conn, manhandled the Big Brother suitcase along the narrow passageways to my quarters, stowed it with its mate, then climbed into the rack for a combat nap.

I don't think I'd managed to close my eyes all the way when a rude set of knuckles rapped a smart paradiddle on the bulkhead outside my compartment.

"Come—" I rolled over, sat up—and slammed my head against the ceiling as the sub surged forward in rapid acceleration. The blow brought tears to my eyes and a hiccough to my "Yo—"

A bespectacled first-class stuck his close-cropped head into the compartment and tried not to react to the look of anguish on my face. But he was stifling a huge smile when he said, "The CO requests your presence in the conn, Captain Marcinko."

Gingerly, I probed my now-tender forehead with callused fingertips. There was probably going to be a fucking lump the size of a chestnut.

I lay back on the tiny rectangular rubber foam widget that passes for a pillow on sewer pipes and listened to the insistent throb of tom-toms between my temples while I tried to focus my eyes on my watch dial. Holy shit, I'd been asleep for eight hours. Some fucking combat nap. I groaned and rolled out of the rack. "Tell him I'm on my way."

"We just received this—ooh, *that* looks real nasty." Dave Brancato stared at my forehead and shook his head sympathetically. He held the message out to me between two thick fingers. "I'm already doing a steady forty-two knots, so I guess we have about three and a half hours until the chopper comes from Singapore for you."

I looked. I read. I groaned. There are times when despite the best of intentions to continually be innovative, clichés say it all.

This was one of 'em. Because today there would be no rest for the weary. Now, I probably shouldn't tell you precisely what the message said because it was classified top secret. But I can give you all gist a hint.

My cruise to Guam was being interrupted, courtesy of CINCPACFLT—Commander-IN-Chief PACific FLeeT. He, in his four-starred wisdom, was TADing me (TAD, you'll remember, is a navyspeak acronym for Temporary Additional Duty, although SEALs refer to it as Traveling Around Drunk) to Yokosuka, the huge joint American-Japanese navy installation near Yokohama.

Once there, I would (I think I'm all right quoting directly here): "advise, counsel, and offer crisis management assistance at the specific and immediate request of Japanese National Police Inspector Toshiro Okinaga, to the HN (host nation) tactical response forces during the ongoing critical and time-sensitive crisis environment currently taking place at Yokosuka's sole fast-food franchise location."

Would you like me to translate that into English for you, folks? Okay. It means that CINCPACFLT wanted my butt in Japan so that I could help a Japanese National Police SWAT team take down a bunch of tangos who had taken a bunch of U.S. Navy personnel hostage at the Yokosuka Navy base McDonald's.

How had CINCPACFLT learned that I was aboard the *Scorpion?* The answer to that question lies far above my pay grade. But I would venture to guess it had something to do with the secure communications facility that is run out of the office of the Chairman of the Joint Chiefs of Staff; a comm unit that can instantaneously connect him with anyone, anywhere in the world.

That being the case, why had the Chairman and CINCPACFLT interrupted the last leg of a sensitive and critical mission to TAD me Japanward? Good question— and if we hadn't been under way at flank speed, I would have gone into the sub's sail with my handy secure transmitter and asked Chairman Crocker that precise question.

But that was impossible. Captain Dave had his orders on paper. And remember what I told you about submariners— they do not change things that have been written on paper.

Now, as to why I was being sent to Japan, the answer is kind of complicated, so bear with me for a few paragraphs of what the old editor calls literary explication, will you? And no, don't go skipping this stuff, because it may turn out to be significant a little further on.

First, the Navy's rapport with JMSDF (the Japanese Maritime Self-Defense Forces) has always been good. So, given the opportunity, CINCPACFLT will go out of his way to help his Japanese counterpart.

But that relationship alone would not have been enough to cause CINCPACFLT to send me humping and thumping to Yokosuka. He acted because of political considerations. You see, putting the Navy aside, our relations with the Japanese were for a while in what might be called a shambles. Moreover, that condition was caused mainly by the United States, not the Japanese.

You want specifics? Well, for one, the Japanese were outraged when it turned out that my colleagues over at

Christians In Action (you probably already know that's what we SEALs call the CIA) knew of, but didn't bother to warn the Japanese about, the Aum Shinrikyo cult.

You say you don't remember the Aum Shinrikyos? They were the no-goodniks who placed canisters of the nerve agent Sarin on five subway trains in Tokyo back in 1995, killing twelve and injuring another fifty-five hundred. Well, it turns out that the CIA knew that Aum Shinrikyo cultists had been testing Sarin as well as Tabun and other deadly chemical-biological agents at a ranch they owned in Australia. They even knew that the Aum Shinrikyos had been able to build an explosive delivery device for their Sarin gas, and that they'd managed to smuggle it from Australia to Japan.

But here's what: Langley never bothered to pass any of the above information to its Japanese counterpart, the intelligence agency called the Cabinet Research Office, better known as Naicho. Naicho was notcho happy.

Then there was the matter of our American military personnel raping that twelve-year-old schoolgirl on Okinawa. The Okinawans overreacted (not without provocation, I might add). They tried—unsuccessfully—to evict all Americans from their island. That is not the kind of relationship you want when it's strategically imperative to keep our air bases and other military installations on foreign soil.

And so, to help bolster the harmony between *Amerikajins* (that's us gringos) and *Nihonjins* (that's the Japanese), a memo went out twenty-two months ago over the signature of the previous White House national security adviser.

Let me show it to you in its entirety. And please remember that the acronym POTUS stands for President Of The United States.

MEMORANDUM

THE WHITE HOUSE
WASHINGTON

SECRET

UNCLASSIFIED WITH REMOVAL OF TAB A

To: Secretary of Defense

From: NSC Adviser ~~MfS~~

Subject: U.S.-Japanese military cooperation

       1.   POTUS directs immediate implementation of the American-Japanese Protocol formulated at December's Japanese-American Protocol RIG meeting.

       2.   All GOJ requests for assistance in the areas of crisis management, risk assessment, and counterterrorism are to receive a Priority One designation from the DOD and all of its related agencies.

       3.   SECDEF will devise, develop, create, define, and execute a Doctrine of Jointness that will allow the United States Government and the Government of Japan to bolster their mutual goals and objectives, as defined by the JAP RIG.

       4.   Refer to E.O. 1297/b-2 [TAB A], for specific guidance on implementing this policy directive, including key areas of bilateral cooperation, and unilateral initiatives.

SECRET

As I said, that memo was written twenty-two months ago. Today, there is a new national security adviser in residence in the West Wing of the White House. His name is Matt Thompson. After less than half a year on the job he considers himself the Metternich of the twenty-first century, and he is vehemently opposed to any strategic cooperation with the Japanese because it might interfere with the pro-China direction in which he has single-handedly moved our foreign policy.

Now, I am not one of your political creatures. I don't make foreign policy—I'm only the animal who carries it out. And so I'm not as current on these things as I might be (although I can guar-on-tee you that by the end of this book I'll be as up to speed as any NSC adviser, columnist pundit, or talking head on TV news). But I do know a few details. Like the fact that Matt Thompson is an old friend of the president's. By old friend, I mean they were college room-mates. And so he, more than most in this administration, has the ear of the commander in chief.

From what I've read and seen, the NSC adviser has been pushing a policy that tilts the United States away from its traditional Pacific Rim allies—countries like Japan, Australia, Singapore, the Philippines, and South Korea—and inclines it firmly toward Beijing. His reasoning? Well, an op-ed in the *Asian Wall Street Journal* a few weeks ago opined that the administration was wisely and shrewdly acting the way it was in order to reverse China's current policy of rapprochement with the Russians, after an es-trangement that has lasted more than a quarter of a century.

A Sino-Russo alliance, the article argued (it was written by some retired State Department suit turned consultant), would "disrupt the vital balance of power so fragile today on the Pacific Rim." And so, to neutralize this new Moscow-Beijing partnership and preserve harmony and tranquillity, the United States would have to shift itself out of its old, confrontational stance and develop a new and much more symbiotic relationship with China. It certainly looked to me as if our NSC adviser was receiving his operating instructions from the op-ed page of the fucking *Asian Wall Street Journal.*

And now, as Paul Harvey says, comes the other side of the story. You see, despite his close relationship with the president, Matt Thompson's wasn't the only opinion represented in the administration. The secretary of defense and the Chairman of the Joint Chiefs of Staff had their own points of view, which they argued both forcefully and publicly.

While it wasn't Chairman Crocker's style to write op-ed articles, he did do interviews from time to time. And whenever he was asked, he said he believed that our strategic relationship with Japan was just as vital—perhaps even more vital—to American interests as our economic relationship with China. He told anyone who would listen that he believed the United States could not afford to lose its bases there.

For his part, SECDEF loves giving interviews, and he's good at it. And during each one, he never lost the opportunity to make the point that with the Philippines gone, America has no ability to move quickly without our facilities on Japan and Okinawa. Whenever he testified before Congress, he invariably reminded the Armed Services Committee members that American weapons makers—whose workers vote—receive a goodly chunk of the $44 billion Japanese defense dollars spent annually.

SECDEF is also a veteran of the kind of war of attrition politics in which you chip away at your opponents. To explain that in real English, it means that an orchestrated series of leaks has been trickling out for the past couple of months, each one detailing an embarrassing tidbit relating to Matt Thompson's China policy and each one chipping away at the president's approval rating. And since we have a president who governs by poll, not conscience, I can report that SECDEF has been able to persuade the president not to act precipitously. Which means—for the present, at least—that DOD has managed to maintain its steady course with the Japanese, despite considerable public bitching, moaning, whining, and sniping from NSC Adviser Thompson's office.

That's the background. So, the political trenches being

dug the way they are these days, when CINCPACFLT gets a request from the Japanese, he probably calls the chief of naval operations, who calls Chairman Crocker, who says, "You bet—act on it pronto."

Why? Because CINCPACFLT knows that by doing so he will make his boss, the chief of naval operations, happy. For his part, CNO is ebullient because he knows that when he does anything that pisses off the NSC adviser, he is going to make the JCS Chairman and SECDEF euphoric.

Amazing how politics works, ain't it?

Anyhow, that's part one of the equation—the political factor. Part two—the personal element—is that I was summoned because it was my old friend Toshiro Okinaga who'd requested my assistance forthwith and chop-chop. Tosho was now, as you can see, an inspector, which is the equivalent of a one-star general, with the Kunika. Kunika is a special action unit of the Japanese National Police. It is in charge of all Japanese counterterrorism operations these days.

Some more background is probably in order here. Not so very long ago, I led the life of a peripatetic teacher, a *ronin*, wandering the globe inculcating students in the deadly arts of Warriordom—specifically proficiency in counterterrorism—to all who would listen (and who had the right security clearances).

Among those with whom I interacted was one Toshiro Okinaga. At that point of life he was a sergeant in Kunika, although he'd managed since then to just about take over the fucking organization. Tosh's English is frawless—the result of four years at Notre Dame (B.A. in political science), then another two for his M.A. in criminology, at the University of Indiana.

But I didn't like him because he spoke like me, chased pussy in his spare time like me, and could match the most energetic young SEAL pup Kirin Ichiban beer for Kirin Ichiban beer over a long night of pub crawling, like me. I wasn't fond of Tosho because he could use polysyllabic words to impress the bureaucrats and draw flowcharts diagramming risk assessment possibilities that influenced legislators. I admired Tosho—and liked working with him—because the man was a Warrior, a real samurai, whose dedication and commitment to improving himself and his men's abilities to make war never ever stopped. He also understood that you never ask your men to do anything that you won't do or can't do. And so, yes, Tosho was a superb pistol shot. And, yes, he was a seventh-degree black belt who knew the difference between dojo martial arts and down-and-dirty-on-the-street fighting. And although he hated heights, he'd learned to fast rope from choppers, rappel down the sides of skyscrapers—and even jump out of perfectly good aircraft. He trained with his men, always pushing them further than they thought they could go.

And when things got real, he was the first one through the door. He volunteered for the tough assignments and the high-risk operations, and because of his dedication to sweat-in-training, he'd seldom lost a man in battle. But perhaps most important is the fact that Tosho has never stopped thinking like a sergeant, even though he now wears the equivalent of a star on his collar. And so, thinking like the sergeant he once was, he'd put in a call for me, because just as I have a Safety Net of chiefs to help me through the rough spots, Tosho has a safety net of counterterrorism shooters to help him through major crises. Frankly, I'm honored to be at the top of his short rist.

Still, Tosho's crisis couldn't have come at a worse time. To be honest, the last thing I needed right now was any kind of diversion—moreover, one that could end up being time-consuming. No, what I wanted was a smooth cruise to Guam, a fast flight back to CONUS—the CONtinental US—and a long investigation to discover WTF was going on *in re* the matter of Big Brother technology, all those Russkie weapons, and the Chinese.

That was on the one hand. On the other hand, part of the responsibility of being a Warrior—an important part of the informal Code of the Warrior—is that you do not let down a fellow Warrior when he asks for your help. And so, I woke my men and gave them a sit-rep. Bottom line: I'd go to Japan. They'd go home.

Did I suffer abuse because they had not been invited to join in the festivities? Hey, is my dick big?

Oh, yes, they complained. Oh, yes, they protested. And when none of those techniques proved persuasive, they sulked, and glowered, and grimaced, and threatened. That's the way it is when hunter/killer shoot-and-looters are denied their fair share of hunting and killing and shooting and looting.

But to be honest, they had a two-part mission equally critical to my own. First, I tasked them with getting the Big Brother equipment back to Washington without attracting any notice. After all, no one, with the exception of Tony Mercaldi at DIA, knew I'd taken possession of the Haliburton suitcases and their contents. And I wanted to keep things that way.

Second, they'd have to start snooping and pooping, which is the SEAL way of saying they'd start making quiet inquiries about what we'd found—and who was responsible. In the same way SEALs recon hostile territory all over the world, my men would go to work as soon as they arrived back in CONUS. They'd check the lay of the land. They'd make studies and observations. They'd look for signs of hostiles—and identify 'em when they found 'em. And then, when I got back, they'd report what they'd discovered to me.

Chapter

5

I WAS SNATCHED OFF THE *SCORPION'S* DECK BY A PAVE LOW chopper's winch line just after 1500 and flown to Singapore. There, I caught a C-20A, which is the early 1980s, no-frills, military version of the Gulfstream III, for the hop to Yakota air base. We landed with nothing in the fuel tanks but fumes. But we landed. From Yakota I jumped a Navy Bell 212 and touched down a few minutes later on the VIP chopper pad at Yokosuka.

I didn't like what I saw as we came in. You could see swells of heavy, black smoke blowing across the expanse of stowage sheds, bunkers, and fuel tanks that ring the Yokosuka installation. Closer in, base traffic was Gordian-knotted—marines and SPs frantically waving at frustrated drivers. Things were worst as I flew over the wide road leading to the knot of "creature comfort" stores, which included Yokosuka's McDonald's—a hub of activity for sailors and visitors alike. We came in at about eight hundred feet, and from the numbers of police, medical, and fire equipment I saw on scene, I knew the news was not going to be good.

Tosho was waiting for me as I bounded through the hatch,

sitting on the fender of a navy gray HumVee, waving at me with the balaclava he'd pulled off his head. He hadn't changed since I'd last seen him—still the same compact little Japanese fireprug, although he'd gone a bit more gray up top. He was wearing black coveralls tucked into GSG-9 boots, a Point Blank bulletproof vest, and the kind of Velcro-rich close-quarters combat tactical rig that cops call SWAT-wear. On his thigh, I could see the butt of an old SAS-type Browning High Power pistol peeking through the ballistic nylon holster flap and thick nylon restraining strap. The narrow band of skin around his eyes—the only part of his face that would be unprotected by either Nomex balaclava or protective eyewear—was blackened from soot, giving him the bizarre appearance of a Japanese Panda in SWAT gear.

Whether the news was going to be good or bad it was still wonderful to see him again. I grabbed him around the shoulders and gave him an old-fashioned Slovak bear hug and a warm "Fuck you, asshole!"

He grappled like a sumo wrestler, slapped my arms away, wrapped me up, held his wide stance and—*"Roguee-sahhhnng!"*—lifted, taking me clear off the ground and spinning me around. He dropped me back onto what the Kennedys might call terra firmer, stepped back and squinted, jut-jawed at me. *"Kon-nichi-wa, Gaijin*—Welcome back, Dick—I just wish it was under better circumstances."

I didn't have to ask for a sit-rep because by the time the Navy Hummer had brought us the five hundred yards to the hostage site, I could see for myself what had happened. My old nemesis Mister Murphy had happened.

I jumped out of the Hummer, stepped back, and looked around to get my bearings. I knew this site—which is probably one of the reasons Tosho had called for me. I'd brought Red Cell here during its heyday, and Tosh and his guys and me and mine had played games at this very same Mickey D's. I'd been the baddie, and Tosho and his shooters had learned how to take down an American-style fast-food restaurant, with its huge reefers, walk-in freezers, open kitchen, and big storage areas.

They were just about to open a bunch of McDonald's in Tokyo and other Japanese cities back then, and Tosh had wanted to see the best way to deal with potential problems. It makes sense, doesn't it? The more you know about the sites you're going to have to deal with, the more effective your response can be.

Well, Tosh knew all about McDonald's—and exactly how to take 'em down with minimal collateral damage. This McDonald's was a charred shell. Shards of nominally shatterproof glass lay everywhere—they'd exploded out, so I knew the blast had been huge and had originated from inside the site. There was little that remained of the still-smoking interior. Forensics crews poked and probed through the debris, looking for body shards. The Kunika shooters in their black Ninja gear sat in tight knots, talking quietly among themselves. Across the way, a company of shell-shocked Marines in combat gear was being debriefed. A row of fire-blanket-covered bodies—some of them still smoldering—lay on the ground. I looked at Tosh and frowned. "What the hell happened, Tosh?"

"It was a *Jibaku*—they suicide-bombed the place." His expression showed the anguish he was feeling. "I tried to wait for you, Dick—told the navy not to push." He shrugged helplessly. "But Admiral Gray—he's the base commander. He overrode me."

That made no sense at all. "Why the hell did he do that?"

"You want the real reason? It's because CNN was broadcasting live, and he was afraid of appearing indecisive, so right on camera he ordered the marines to take it down. I thought his PAO[9] was going to shit."

"You mean MERF did *this?*" I knew the commander of the Marine Emergency Reaction Force based half an hour north of Tokyo—a hell of a Warrior named Shellhammer. He would never have screwed up so badly.

---

[9]Public Affairs Officer.

"No, the MERF wasn't getting here fast enough for the admiral, so he used what he had on hand—the base guards."

"What about you and your guys?"

"I told you, Dick. CNN was on scene. Broadcasting live, by satellite, back to the U.S. The tangos had sent out a list of demands—"

"About?"

"Islands, Dick."

"Islands?"

"The Senkaku islands. There are eight of them—uninhabited, rocky islands. They lie south of Okinawa, just to the northeast of Taiwan—and they're claimed by both China and Japan. The Chinese call them the Diaoyus."

"What the hell does this have to do with anything?"

"It has to do with oil, Dick. Huge fields of it, according to the American oil companies. Japan has to import all of its oil. If we developed the fields just off the Senkakus, we could expand them into something comparable to what the Brits did in the North Sea."

"And the Chinese want to do the same thing."

"Sure they do. Which is why ASDF[10] is always running surveillance flights. We've got E-2Cs overflying the islands on a daily basis."

"What's the American reaction to that?"

"Until recently, it was just fine. After all, if the Chinese took the Senkakus, they'd be within easy striking distance of Taiwan. We're talking two hundred, two hundred fifty miles maybe."

"So, what the hell precipitated this clusterfuck, anyway, Tosh? Seems as if the United States has no overt involvement here."

"It's a little complicated." Tosho shifted his weight before continuing. "See, America has always been neutral on the subject of the Senkakus," he said. "Your government has

---

[10]Air Self-Defense Force.

always referred to them simply as 'the eight disputed islands.' But last week, the White House spokesman began using both the Chinese and Japanese names, which made real headlines here and caused Beijing to go ballistic. The Chinese position has always been that no matter how the dispute went, the islands were always to be called by their Chinese name. The terrorists' first demand was for the United States to apologize, and either resume its policy of neutrality or refer to the islands by their Chinese name alone."

"So this wasn't a group of Japanese?"

"Oh, they were Japanese, all right. Maoists, no less—they call themselves the Red Seeds, and they support China." He paused. "Inscrutable, aren't we?"

He scratched under his CQC vest collar, found something that was bothering him, discarded it, then continued. "Besides, it didn't matter who the hell these tangos were. There was no way the admiral was going to let Kunika control the situation—not with the White House watching and some West Wing idiot on the cellular to him." Tosho wiped at the sooty ring around an eye with the back of a gloved hand. "That would have been . . . un-American," he said bitterly. "Not in the John Wayne tradition." Tosho was full of nasty surprises today.

"The White House?"

"Somebody from the national security adviser's office was watching the CNN broadcast. Whoever it was called Admiral Gray directly—actually got him on the cellular and demanded a sit-rep. The admiral started to explain that things were under control. Then he told whoever it was that you were on your way here to help us handle the situation— that you knew the base from your Red Cell experience." Tosho's face darkened. "From what I heard of Admiral Gray's side of the conversation, things got bad. The White House staffer obviously told him to move it—*right now.*"

"Didn't he object?"

"Not from what I heard. He just stood there, nodding

'yessir, yessir, yessir' into the cellular. And the point that was being made, Dick, was that the White House wanted this thing over and done with before you got here." Tosho wiped at the grime on his face. "Oh, man, talk about screwing with the chain of command. It was inconceivable—"

Actually, it wasn't inconceivable at all. During the Somalia crisis, one of the president's closest public relations advisers regularly called the SpecWar Ops Center in Mogadishu and countermanded the on-scene commander's orders. He got away with it for two reasons. First, most White House reporters didn't believe his actions were significant enough to report, even though said adviser's orders probably caused the deaths of several Rangers and Delta troopers. Second, the adviser was much too good a source—he was extremely close to the president and first lady—to be trashed in public. There is, you see, a journalistic technical term for White House reporters without sources close to the first family. That term is *unemployed*.

"Damn it." Tosho nodded in the direction of the charred shell that had once been the base McDonald's. His thumb hooked toward the medical technicians loading bodies. "Talk about your textbook clusterfucks."

I walked over and took a closer look at the corpses. Three were still covered by blankets. I lifted the edge of one, then another—and saw the charred remains of a child, her tiny form frozen in pain. Oh, Christ—there had been kids inside. And now they were dead. It angers me to see children murdered and fuels my rage against those who perpetrate such deeds. It hurt even more to know that these were Navy children—they were my family. They would be avenged. I would find out which schmuck at the White House caused this and I'd deal with it—on *my* terms.

I stepped back and examined the scene critically. I saw where it had gone wrong from evidence that I could read like a fucking primer. The Marines had staged over there— well within sight of the McDonald's back door, not to mention the security camera that was mounted above it.

Then they'd come around the corner and charged straight ahead, like the fucking Light Brigade, in a keep it stupid, simple, frontal assault. And while they'd been trying to toss flashbangs that couldn't penetrate the tango-resistant windows McDonald's installs overseas, and making a lot of ambient noise in the process, the terrorists calmly murdered the nine American and three Japanese hostages, then blew the McDonald's up—themselves included.

This is what happens when some equivalent form of Grade-A, Extra-Large, ruby red, government-inspected sphincter—e.g., the WHA, or White House Asshole—is allowed to commandeer a situation about which he has no knowledge, no background, and no ability. Then you have your C²CO idiot[11]—COs like Admiral Gray, who don't have the balls to tell that WHA to get fucked unless he has a piece of paper in his hand signed by the commander in chief. So they kiss ass, say, "Yes, sir," and end up getting people killed.

And then you know what happens afterward? Said C²CO spends considerable time and energy trying to lay the blame on the poor schmucks who got stuck holding the short end of the stick because of all those bad orders, flawed intelligence, and institutional stupidity. Please be so kind as to allow me to pause here just long enough for a brief Rogue Rant. Okay? Thanks.

Y'see, there is an unfortunate mode of thinking prevalent among so-called leaders these days. That trend can be summed up in three letters, CYA, which as you probably can guess, stands for Cover Your Ass. CYA means that officers care more about their careers than they do about their men. There is an old Marine Corps tradition that in the field, officers eat only after their men have eaten. There is an old Navy tradition that officers are responsible for the welfare of their men—totally responsible. Most of today's

---

[11]You will remember that C²CO stands for Can't Cunt Commanding Officer.

officers don't give a damn about their men. They want to put in their eight hours a day, then retire to the golf course or the real estate office or the PC so they can check their stock portfolios.

Well, this is a situation I cannot abide, and lately, I have taken to acting, rather than bitching, when I come across it. And so, I looked around to see whether Admiral Gray was in attendance so that I could have five or six choice words about the sanctity of the goddamn chain of command with him before I pounded his pencil-dicked pus-nutted C^2 ass into the yellow Jell-O that he was. Yes, I knew that he wore a star and I didn't. But there are times when that Just Don't Matter—and this was one of 'em.

Tosho saw the Roguish, stop-me-before-I-kill-again look in my eyes, knew me well enough to realize what I was contemplating, and backed me up against the Hummer with his very solid forearm. "Bad idea, Dick—what's done is done."

Maybe yes, maybe no. Between Admiral Gray and whoever had called from the White House, a dozen people had been needlessly killed today. And believe me, I'd find some way to even the score. But in the meanwhile, I had to make tracks for Washington. There was a lot to be done, on a number of fronts, and this untimely diversion had postponed what I knew was a more critical, and long-term, issue.

"Okay, Tosh, you're right. Why not just take me to Narita, and I'll grab a plane for Washington."

Tosho dropped his arm. "Actually, I wish you'd stay a little while longer, Dick. There's still work to be done."

I wondered aloud what that was. Things at Yokosuka seemed pretty much over. "Fact is, Tosh, you didn't need me here at all."

"Not for this fiasco. But since I've discovered who's responsible, I thought you'd like a piece of the action when I go in to clean 'em out," Tosho said, guiding me toward a black Ford Bronco that had windows tinted as darkly as any Florida drug dealer's, and a roof that sprouted half a dozen kinds of antennas.

I looked back toward the charred corpses. I thought about the dead children. I thought about Admiral Gray. "You've got yourself a deal," I said. "I'll get a later flight."

Tosho cracked a grim smile. "Good." He opened the right-hand driver's door and stepped onto the running board. "Just before my shooters and I arrived here, my intel people intercepted a *saishotanchishingo*—that's what we call a whatchamacallit"—he fought for the English words and smiled when he came up with the right ones—"a minimized radio signal, between the hostage-takers at McDonald's and a control post. We were able to locate where the signal came from. It's a warehouse northwest of here."

"And?"

"And I had the place checked out—discreetly. By the time things went sour at Micky D's, I was pretty certain that what we'd come across was one of the Red Seed's headquarters."

"One?"

"They work in cells—just like the Japanese Red Army did. Compartmentation. It makes us have to work harder digging 'em out. Anyway, there were three *saishotanchishingo*s in all. It was enough to tell us this was the place where they staged for this nasty little exercise. It's—" He looked at my apprehensive expression and answered the question I'd been about to ask: "No—believe me, this was a piece of intel I had no intention of sharing with Admiral Gray."

He stuck his thumb toward the opposite side of the Bronco. "So come aboard, sailor. Given the way things were here, these assholes are probably gonna try to scamper soon, so we have to hit 'em, hit 'em before they do."

I clapped Tosho on the back with the flat of my hand. "So—'lay on, Macduff—'"

Tosho jumped right in. "'And damn'd be him that first cries, 'Hold, enough.' Shakespeare, right? *Macbeth.* Fifth Act, final scene."

I hate the kind of people who can go on *Jeopardy* and win, don't you?

Tosho climbed behind the wheel and slammed his door shut. I opened the passenger door and started to get in when I realized there was someone in the rear seat.

I paused, but Tosh didn't give it a second thought. "Dick, this is Alixe Joseph. Alixe—Dick Marcinko."

I pulled myself up, swiveled my arm over the seat back, and offered my hand. "Hi."

I got a firm, dry handshake in return. "Hi yourself. I'm Alixe Joseph."

There was what might in pre–politically correct times be called a pregnant silence in the vehicle. I turned back and took a look. Alixe Joseph was an attractive woman in her midforties. She had an oblong, impish, yet cherubic face, set off by the kind of low-maintenance frizzed hair that isn't so much styled as it is shampooed, blown dry, and left alone. She was wearing a black, double-breasted, Italian hand-finished blazer and narrow-legged matching trousers, and a soft, ivory-colored silk blouse with a high cossack collar and pearl buttons.

The presentation in toto was a woman's version of those Princeton or Dartmouth bespoke-tailored alumni who do not pass GO, who do not collect $200, but proceed directly to the foreign service exam, or meander over to Langley to be fluttered,[12] then backgrounded, vetted, and cleared as TS/SCI[13] spooks. The only difference is that the male version is usually completed with fancy striped shirts from some stiff-upper-lip shirtmaker on Jermyn Street in London and the requisite loud, veddy English wide tie, instead of the hand-stitched, pearl-buttoned ivory silk tunic worn by Ms. A. Joseph.

But, she bore indeed all the other outward paraphernalia of senior spook or diplodom. She had a sensible, under-

---

[12]That's CIAspeak for polygraphed.
[13]Top Secret/Special Compartmental Intelligence clearance requires the Agency's most comprehensive background check.

stated steel-and-gold Rolex on her right wrist. The top of a vermeil Montblanc fountain pen for writing all those fifty-dollar words peeked discreetly behind the raw silk poof atop her blazer's narrow breast pocket. She was probably wearing old-fashioned shoes, too—the kind of $350 Ferragamo flats that woman diplomats, spooks, and Wall Street lawyers all favor.

I leaned over and snuck a glimpse. Yup.

"So, Alixe," I said, "do you work with the Christian brethren and sethren at Langley, or with all those foggy bottoms over at State?"

She laughed—and her blue eyes twinkled when she did. That was a good sign. "Neither," quoth she. When she saw the puzzled expression on my puss, she added obliquely, "But I quick-checked you out in my shop when Tosho requested your presence on-scene, and Tony Merc says to say, hi—and that he'll vouch for me."

For one of the few times in my life, I was struck dumb. I know hundreds of DIA gumshoes—and svelte, stylish Alixe Joseph was decidedly not type casting. I was impressed, and said so.

"I'm part of a new program," she said by way of explanation. "It's compartmented (isn't everything these days?). But we can talk about my component-specific element. I'm part of DHS—for Defense HUMINT Service."

I'd heard RUMINT about DHS. It had been created last year at the new SECDEF's direction. The nice thing about having an ex-senator running the Pentagon is that he has friends on Capitol Hill who actually believe that the armed services should be used for more than playing traffic cops in Bosnia, pretending to be social workers in Haiti, working like Boy Scouts during forest fires in Montana, or killing goatherds on the Mexican border. Activities such as preparing to make war, for example. Well, SECDEF believes in being prepared for war, and he used all his connections on the Hill to further that belief. And so, DHS got itself a three-year program, all quietly appropriated and advance funded.

The monies had been slipped into funding bills that the president didn't dare line-item veto, either.

I told her what I knew. She cracked a smile and made with the fifty-dollar words. "Oh, was *that* fortuitous—it means that our money is impregnable, locked in by Congress, and no matter how he tries, Matt Thompson and his White House mafia can't touch us."

And why would he try, I asked?

Because, Alixe explained, much of DHS's mission was to penetrate the huge Chinese intelligence apparatus that had been expanding all across the Pacific Rim ever since the death of Deng Xiaoping. She was based in Tokyo, worked out of the embassy. But her AO lay from Korea in the north to Indonesia in the south, and her job was to develop agent networks that would help us learn what Beijing was up to, as well as keep an eye on everything else that might affect America's defense stance on the Pacific Rim.

It was a formidable assignment. She must have had a hell of a background to get it, too—although she was spook-usual in her discreetness about what she'd done before.

What she did say was that her job was, these days, being made more difficult because of a political dispute between the Pentagon (read SECDEF) and the White House (read NSC adviser Matt Thompson). It was no secret that the NSC boss wanted the Pentagon, particularly DIA, to keep its nose out of anything having to do with his unique brand of China policy, a China policy that would be supported solely by the CIA's findings.

Of course, Alixe added, the new DCI just happened to be Matt Thompson's old buddy from Yale. They'd even worked together at the same left-of-center think tank in Washington, and they saw eye-to-eye when it came to dealing with our potential adversaries. Can you say "appeasement"? It appeared that they certainly could—and did, on a regular basis.

Now, let me step aside here for a minute and recap because Matt Thompson, whom I have never met, is becoming irksome. First, he advocates tilting our policy away from

Japan and toward China. Now, I believe we need to have an even-handed policy. Japan, after all, is a potential adversary in the economic sense, and we must maintain wariness. Though vigilance is one thing, jettisoning the Japanese, which is what he'd like to do, is something else altogether. And now I learn that he had been lobbying against DIA's HUMINT-gathering operations, one of the most important of which is focused on China. Not good. We've learned in the past that CIA estimates can be absolutely wrong. Like the ones Langley did just before the fall of the Soviet Union, which predicted that communism would be the dominant system in Russia right through the twenty-first century.

So—let me put this in Roguespeak—fuck Matt Thompson. What the hell does he know anyway? He's just another goddam academic who'd never bothered to hump his ass out into the field and lay it on the line. I told Alixe Joseph that any HUMINT capabilities at DIA were positive steps so far as I was concerned.

She nodded in agreement. "Especially because DIA's always been prohibited from recruiting agents and running nets—CIA would never let it happen." Alixe Joseph pointed her thumb and forefinger in my direction in a strangely familiar gesture. "That was true until Chairman Crocker and the new SECDEF came along. They did some heavy lobbying—convinced Congress to come up with the money and provide us some political juice. The problem is that CIA isn't doing the kind of job we need. You know the problems we faced during the Gulf War."

Did I ever. Here is some RUMINT for you. Hank Trott, the self-important CIA supergrade assigned to coordinate intelligence with Norm Schwarzkopf's staff, never even went to Riyadh. He stayed safe and sound back at CENTCOM headquarters in Tampa, Florida, playing tennis and swimming laps. When the commander of Schwarzkopf's J-2[14] complained, Langley grudgingly sent a working

---

[14]The intelligence directorate of Schwarzkopf's joint staff.

group overseas. But they sent it to London, not Saudi. Go figure.

Well, ever since, DOD has been trying to break into the HUMINT business so it can provide military field commanders and the Joint Chiefs with the kind of intelligence that warriors need. And I'm glad to see it has finally succeeded—even though I could have used folks like Alixe Joseph years and years ago.

"Anyway," Alixe Joseph continued, "I set up shop out here last year. They gave me embassy cover—POLAD[15] to the defense attaché to be precise." She pursed her lips. "Sometimes I think it would have been easier working NOC.[16] The way the embassy keeps trying to insert itself into my business is unbelievable. Anyway, things are complicated." She brightened. "But Tosho and I have managed to keep ourselves busy." She slapped him on the shoulder. "Haven't we, buddy?"

Blue dashboard light flashing, Tosho nosed the Bronco around the traffic, moving slowly toward Yokosuka's main gate. "Alixe got here just as the Chinese took over in Hong Kong," Tosh said. "Since they did, there's been a lot of new activity all over Japan—none of it good."

"Certainly, the Chinese have been expanding their intelligence activities here," said Alixe Joseph, continuing Tosh's thought in a way that told me they'd been spending a lot of time together. "That would be natural, given the power struggle after Deng died. Problem is, the hardliners in Beijing—and they're the ones who control the security and intel operations—are flexing muscle. They've been actively recruiting agents, and I think they've even been smuggling weapons—although we haven't found any concrete evidence of it yet, have we, Tosh?"

"Nope," he said. "But I pulled Alixe into the loop today because the group that blew up the McDonald's is Chinese

---

[15]POLitical ADviser.
[16]nonofficial cover.

sponsored. I'd hoped to have one or two for us to interview." His face grew grim. "No such luck."

Alixe's expression told me she was still optimistic. "Maybe we'll still get the opportunity," she said.

"How does Beijing insert its intel apparatus?" I asked. Frankly, I'm not a China expert, and I was glad to run into someone who could explain.

"They use students, journalists, businessmen—anyone who comes in contact with outsiders on a regular basis." She pursed her lips. "In Hong Kong, they used Xinhua— that's the New China News Agency—to infiltrate more than six hundred agents into the territories in the eight months before they took over. And remember what happened after the last Brits pulled out—it wasn't pleasant."

Tosho picked up: "For the six months before the Brits left, the Hong Kong bureau of Xinhua was run by a guy named Li Chimen. But if Li is a journalist, then I'm one, too."

"What he really is," said Alixe Joseph, "is a colonel in the People's Liberation Army." She flipped open the leather secretary that sat next to her on the Bronco's seat, retrieved a series of black and white three-by-five surveillance photos, and handed them to me.

I peered down. Li was a tall, lean man with a long, angular face, with prominent cheekbones and a cruel, thin-lipped, aristocratic mouth above which sat the sort of pencil-thin mustache common to villains in the sorts of World War II war movies currently in vogue on cable TV. I studied the photographs. Li was always dressed impeccably. His demeanor was properly military—he stood erect and straight. But I could make out something of the panther to his stance, too. I sorted through the photos until I found a close-up and I could get a close look at the dark, penetrating eyes below the visor of his PLA hat. The man was a shooter. I could see it in his eyes. I handed the pictures back to Alixe. "What's his story?"

"Li's background is special forces—a real operator from what we've been able to tell. My defectors tell me he ran infiltrations into Taiwan and the coastal islands—he's *zhongdui.*"

"A naval special commando—"

Alixe's head came up, her expression showed surprise. "You know the term?"

I wasn't about to explain. I shrugged her question off. "SEALs like to stay current on the opposition."

She accepted the justification. "Anyway, according to current RUMINT he's also worked covert programs in Libya, Sudan, and Tehran, too—probably helping them set up training camps for who-knows-what kind of organizations. These days he's got a new assignment: assistant to the director of *Er Bu*—"

"That's how the Chinese say 'Second Department'—of the PLA's Military Intelligence Department," Tosho interjected.

Alixe Joseph steadied herself as Tosho jumped the curb. "We call it the MID."

The big Ford threaded the needle between a pair of parked police cars, pulled back onto the roadway with a thwump, drove through the main gate, and accelerated toward Highway 16, which I knew led from Yokosuka northeast, skirted the harbor at Yokohama, then proceeded due north to central Tokyo. "Li does most of the dirty work for another real sonofabitch—a major general named Zhu Linfan." She retrieved the leather binder again, flipped it open, found the page she wanted, and tapped her well-manicured finger atop a newspaper photograph of a round-faced, cold-eyed Oriental in PLA uniform. "Zhu was the colonel who stopped things cold at Tiananmen Square back in 1989. He was the enforcer for Chi Haotian—the one-star at Tiananmen who went on to become defense minister. Zhu was Chi Haotian's top thug—Li is his."

Tosho turned his siren on to speed things up and had to shout to make himself heard. "Anyway, about a year ago, Li turned up as Xinhua's bureau chief in Singapore. After three months there, he was 'posted' to Seoul. Guess what: after two months in Seoul, he went to Jakarta to spell the bureau chief there for a month. Then it was back to Beijing for three or four weeks of 'editorial meetings'—and then, bingo—he turns up here in Tokyo as Xinhua's bureau chief."

Alixe Joseph interrupted. "Not just shows up, Tosh—remember?" She slapped the back of my seat. "It was like he had a goddam press agent. Three articles in the *Asian Wall Street Journal* trying to debunk the Xinhua-espionage angle. A series about Li on NHK—that's one of the local TV networks, Dick."

"Don't forget about the love tap in *Asahi Shimbun* business section," Tosho said. "It amazed me that nobody bothered to do any digging on the guy. Where are all those alleged investigative journalists?"

I grinned. "The operative word there, Tosh, is *alleged.*" I dimly remembered reading the *Journal* articles at the time. But something else jogged my memory, too. "Weren't they written by the same piled-higher-and-deeper asshole who's been writing about China and Japan lately?"

"Asshole is right," Alixe Joseph said. "His name's Bentley Brendel. Retired out of the State Department about fifteen years ago. James Baker hired him back as a consultant on China policy during the Bush administration—right after Tiananmen. He lasted two months, then he jumped ship. Bush's policy was too hard-line, I guess."

"But he still flaunts his Republican creds," said Tosho. "The man has no shame."

Alixe Joseph continued. "Then Warren Christopher's people hired him during the first Clinton administration—gave him an office on the seventh floor at Main State, and a deputy assistant secretary's title. He stayed about a year."

So Bentley the DAS was a political chameleon. I mistrust animals who change color—or sides. "What's he do now?"

Tosho grunted. "From the look of it he mints his own money."

His comment brought a bitter smile to Alixe Joseph's face. "He's put together a consulting firm that handles Asian business deals," she said. "But all he really does is deal with Beijing. You want to build a cement factory in Guangzhou? For the right price Bentley will get it done. You want to open a soft drink factory in Shanghai? You go see Brendel Associates. But bring your checkbook." She shook her head in disgust. "What peeves me so much is that he's considered *the* expert on U.S.-China relations. I mean, he testifies up on Capitol Hill. There are rumors he even still consults at the White House—although when I checked through channels about it, I was told he may have come in once or twice to help the NSC adviser out, but he wasn't on the list of NSC consultants—and he hasn't been issued a White House pass."

"But he still has lots of friends in high places," said Tosho.

"He's certainly made my life more difficult," Alixe Joseph said. "I was sent here to work with the Japanese. Like I said, ever since Li Chimen arrived, there's been a lot to keep Tosho and me busy. Beijing is probing, Dick—they're testing our capabilities; hunting for our weaknesses."

"Any luck hitting back?"

"I'm running two networks here, and a couple of others elsewhere, that are producing some results," she said, animatedly.

"Enough to take a chunk out of Li Chimen?"

"Not yet," she said. "But I'm starting to nip at his heels. I know that because I lost one of my better doubles[17] just about two months ago—and I'm pretty sure Li was involved."

She went on, "But it's tough. Building networks takes time, and coddling, and money, and I'm not being given a lot of those things these days." Her expression grew dark. "And, y'know, it seems as if every time I try to take some countermeasures, or Tosho attempts to get proactive, some supergrade at State, or the Agency, or the White House, starts screaming and yelling about 'disrupting the vital

---

[17]double agents.

balance of power' in the region." She shook her head. "Well, that phrase is something that Bentley Brendel manages to work into almost every article he writes, too."

I knew that. I'd seen the phrase in the *Asian Wall Street Journal* article on Sino-Russkie-American relations. She looked at me intently. "Some coincidence, right? Hey, Dick, you and I both know that *that* sort of 'coincidence' seldom happens in our business."

I nodded. She was right.

"Well," Alixe continued, "I have another 'coincidence' for you. Seven weeks ago, right after my double was murdered, Li Chimen said, 'Sayonara, Tokyo.' He's moved on."

"And not back to Beijing, either, I'm willing to bet," I said.

Tosho grinned. "That's the kind of bet they taught us not to take at Notre Dame," he said. "No, Li was 'promoted' again. He's been appointed Xinhua's interim Washington bureau chief."

Tosho's assembly point was well away from the target—a warehouse in an industrial zone just north of Suginami-Ku. The warehouse was under discreet observation by a platoon of Kunika's best sneak-and-peekers. All the roads going in and coming out had been blocked. But Tosho's infiltration route began more than two miles away, in a quiet, uninhabited area. That showed sound planning.

There is one crucial element of a tactical-team mission that often escapes the planners: the approach. Whether you are staging a drug raid, executing a high-risk warrant, or rescuing a hostage from a bunch of tangos, if you fuck up the approach, the chances are that you will FUBAR the operation. Most often, the approach screwup occurs because the staging area for the raid is too close to the target, the bad guys hear you coming long before you hit the door, and they either destroy the evidence, kill the hostage, or blow themselves—and you—to the well-known smithereens.

SEALs regularly practice this SpecWar stratagem. Indeed, our staging often takes place hundreds of miles from our actual insertion point. But many cops do not. So I was glad to see that Tosh's shooters were far enough away so that their preparations weren't going to attract any unwanted attention.

On the drive over, Tosh had made a long phone call, rattling in machine gun Japanese to someone in his office. I saw the results when I showed up: a full set of combat gear, size Extra-Extra Rogue, was waiting for me. A tall, lanky kid in black BDUs, rappelling belt and harness, body armor, thick fast-roping gloves tied to his belt, and a balaclava bunched around his neck, held out a tactical holster in which sat a Glock 19 with night sights. "Hey, Captain Marcinko—remember me?"

I pulled the pistol out, opened the slide to make sure that it was unloaded, and locked the gun open as I looked carefully, examining the angular face, the Marine haircut, and the uneven smile. He was familiar—but he'd changed his appearance since I'd seen him last. "Yoshioka, right?"

He shook my hand. "You got it, man. It's been a while."

Indeed it had. Yoshi was one of the Kunika shooters who'd helped me secure a load of stolen Tomahawk nuclear missiles from a lunatic-fringe right-wing no-goodnik named Hideo Ikigami.[18] Back then he'd been a long-haired punk rocker who favored black leather and motorcycle boots. Now he was as close cropped and gung ho as a Recon Marine. And from the way he'd bulked up, I could see he'd been working out on the weight pile regularly, too.

I let the Glock's slide go forward and tried the trigger action. It was nice and smooth—staged well, and had about a five-pound pull. I sight-acquired-dry-fired a few times to get the front sight picture embedded in my brain and my subconscious. If you can visualize the correct sight picture

---

[18]If you want to read all about it, you can go out and buy *Rogue Warrior: Red Cell.*

in your head, then you'll always hit your target, because you won't have to waste time trying to remember the right sight picture when you're in combat and the bad guy is shooting back at you.

Yes, I know it sounds very Zen. Well, there's nothing wrong with that—we're in Japan, aren't we? And besides, the technique works, which is all that counts. Hey—don't skip this part because, as the old chiefs used to say, you will see this material again in a few pages.

Okay. You start with the pistol at your side. You bring it up as if to fire, and you align the sights. You memorize that front sight picture. Really *visualize* it. Burn it into your brain. After as many repeats as necessary, you try the same exercise with your eyes closed. When the gun comes up into the same position whether your eyes are open or closed, you are ready. I practiced the exercise a dozen times more with my eyes open. Then I closed my eyes and brought the pistol up to its combat position. I opened my eyes. The sights were perfectly aligned—fucking sight picture was *there*—embedded in my subconscious. I repeated half a dozen times with eyes closed—and came up with a perfect sight picture each time. Now I knew that whatever I pointed the pistol at, no matter what the conditions were, I'd hit.

Next, I fieldstripped the gun to check it over. It was in perfect shape, so clean you could eat off the fucking thing. I looked at Yoshi. "This yours?"

He smiled. "Right on. Sweet little puppy, ain't it?" He handed me five seventeen-round magazines and two fifty-round boxes of Hydra-Shok 147-grain ammo. "I brought an MP5 and four loaded mags for you, too, Captain. Just let me know when you want them, sir."

The "sir," just in case you were curious, was spelled with an *s* and an *i*. Polite kid, huh? I loaded all the magazines and gave Yoshi back the surplus bullets—except for one, which I saved for later use. Then I climbed out of my blue submarine coveralls and pulled on a black Nomex jumpsuit, then shrugged into the Class-III CQC modular bulletproof vest, and strapped on knee and elbow pads. (That was a real luxury. We Froggish types don't generally get to wear pads. We are, after all, maritime creatures—amphibians—and it is hard to swim in knee and elbow pads.) The Velcro belt came next. To that, I attached my tactical holster, knife sheath, bolt cutter case, and two double magazine holders, into which I stuffed the Glock mags (mag number five went into my pocket, along with the spare round). On the vest's Velcro strips I hung my radio case, grenade containers, and flashlight lanyard.

I stuffed the pair of extra-large, soft leather-palmed Nomex gloves into a thigh pocket and secured the flap. Losing your gloves before an assault is a no-no. I hung the helmet they'd given me off my tactical holster. It was a Japanese large, which was still slightly small for my Yankee-size head and I saw no need to put it on until absolutely necessary.

Finally, I retrieved the last of the Glock magazines and shoved it into the pistol, pointed the muzzle in a safe direction, cocked and locked the weapon, dropped the mag, topped the mag off with the round I'd saved, reinserted it into the butt, and slid the Glock into the tactical holster. I secured the flap, checked the strap, then ran a second Velcro strap over the top and secured it, too. Hey—I've been there, and it ain't a Good Thing when your Glock drops out of its holster after you've flipped upside down on a rappelling line because you wanted to be able to quick-draw and so you didn't secure the fucking gun tight enough, then Mister Murphy got hold of it, and yanked it out.

I tugged at my Velcro as I watched Tosho, who was lovingly double-checking the Browning before he restowed it. "Y'know, sometimes I think it would have been easier to be one of those Roman centurions. All they had to worry about was their chest plate, a helmet, a short sword and shield, and those stupid-looking leg protectors."

"Oh, you would have made one hell of a centurion," Tosh said. "No—better—you'd have made a world-class gladiator, real Coliseum material." He saluted me in the old, straight-armed Roman fashion. "Hail, Penis Erectus, omnipotent warrior."

I saluted him with my middle finger. "May the God of War be with you my old and trusted friend, all-powerful Flatulence." I stretched and yawned. "Speaking of which, when can we get this circus maximus under way, Flat, my man? I've gone almost twenty-four hours without killing anybody."

Tosho tapped the transmit button on his radio, muttered something into his wrist mike, listened for an answer, and checked the watch on his left wrist. His face turned serious. "Thirteen minutes, Dick," he said.

Chapter

6

Since we've got a little time on our hands, folks, let me talk a bit about what's gonna happen here. You can label this particular kind of operation whatever the local nomenclature happens to be—because whether you call it a SWAT op, a Delta hit, or a SEAL Team Six shoot-and-loot, the dynamics are basically the same. We are talking here about a special operations unit action against a fortified position. To succeed, all the elements must be delivered in one swift punch. Only that way can relative superiority, or RS, be achieved.

What's RS? It's when a small but dynamic attacking force wins out over a larger but more conventional force. The most critical elements for gaining relative superiority are: one, time, and two, violence of action. In other words, the longer you take to hit your target without decisive, dynamic action, the more prolonged your area of vulnerability—or AV—becomes, and the more chance there is that Mr. Murphy is gonna take advantage of the situation. And if he does, he will move you and your men directly into the FUBAR Zone, which is a Bad Place for you all to be, because the FUBAR Zone is where you get dead. And listen up, out there: do not forget any of this RS and AV stuff because you're going to come across it again in a few hundred pages and there'll be a quiz.

I see you. Yeah, *you*—the one slouching in your chair with the Nike ball cap on backward and the hand lolling in the air. You *what?* You want me to stop speaking in generalities and give you some specifics? Hey—let's all say this together, shall we?—*"Fuuuck you,* asshole!"

Okay, okay—it was a good observation despite the fact that you look stupid with that hat on backward.

So, here is a specific. When we assaulted the *Nantong Princess,* our PV, or point of vulnerability, occurred at the precise instant of our insertion onto the ship. That is, at the point we transitioned from the ICRRC, clambered up the caving ladder, and rolled over the ship's rail. If we'd been observed right then, we might have been repulsed. Why? Because we were stretched thin. There was only one ladder. There were a limited number of angles from which to fire defensively. And most important, there was no way to achieve violence of action and overwhelm the crew.

So we acted dynamically; remember how insistent I was that we all GET UP THE FUCKING LADDER—NOW! Because once we'd gone over the rail and had enough men up there to achieve our critical mass on deck, there was no way the crew could stop us. We'd overcome our area of vulnerability quickly. Thereafter, *we* controlled the situation. Why? Because we enjoyed the element of surprise. Moreover, our speed, ingenuity, and violence of action gave us the advantage, even though the *Nantong Princess's* sailors outnumbered us almost five to one. *We could not fail.*

Here, Tosho had tried to provide his force with as many tactical advantages as he could so that they could achieve relative superiority quickly.

- He had real-time photographic surveillance—television cameras with long lenses—that showed him any movement around the location's exterior.

- He'd obtained a set of plans for the warehouse's interior.
- He was using thermal imagers to try to pinpoint the locations of the tangos inside.
- He had obtained good intelligence on the size of the opposition—there were no more than a dozen of 'em in there right now.

But it wasn't going to be an easy op. After all, they had automatic weapons, and possibly they also had biological or chemical agents, which is an element that all tactical teams should factor into their assault equations these days.

CW/BW agents cause problems. The possibility means that the assault force should wear gas masks at the very least—and full protective gear at the most.

Now, it is hard to stage a tactical op when you are encased in CW/BW gear, which is some of the most cumbersome clothing ever invented. So, Tosho had made an executive decision today: we'd wear the masks, but not the coveralls. I saw no signs of grumbling from his troops. That told me they were M^3s, which as you can probably guess stands for massively motivated motherfuckers.

The assault force would strike in two waves. One wave would fast-rope from choppers and come down from the roof. Simultaneously, the other would go through the front door—preceded by a huge garbage truck equipped with a monster snowplow.

Operational security would be maintained by a secondary, larger force of Kunika shooters backed up by national police. They would seal off the warehouse and set up an unpenetrable cordon sanitaire. Tactical security would come from the five sniper teams Tosho had deployed. He had four static two-man teams, and one airborne unit.

I walked over to where Tosho was running the numbers one last time with his assault team leaders. Alixe Joseph stood out of the way, her arms crossed, playing FOW— which you can probably guess stands for Fly On the Wall. From the engrossed look on her face she obviously spoke fluent Japanese as well as Chinese because, ever the exemplary spook sponge, she was absorbing every nuance.

The shooters were working from a two-by-three-foot surveillance photograph over which a sheet of clear acetate had been laid. I couldn't understand the Japanese characters Tosho was writing with an erasable marker, but the numbers, arrows, lines, *X*s and *O*s that gave the acetate the look of a football coach's playbook made perfect sense to me.

Tosho finished palavering, then looked over at me. "See anything you'd change?"

I looked intently. The one weak spot was entry—it was a big fucking warehouse, there were lots of areas to clear, and the assault team was only forty-six men. "I'm worried that they could hole up inside—especially if they've built a safe room or some other fortified area."

Tosho nodded. "Concerns me, too. We have blueprints, but these guys have occupied this place for a year and a half now, so they could have built stuff we don't know about." He tapped the acetate with his pointer indicating the two roof doorways. "That's why the chopper teams have to be so fast—catch 'em before they have a chance to do anything nasty." He paused. "So, where do you want to be, round eyes?"

I pointed at the roof, too. "I've always liked starting at the top," I said.

Tosho gave me a thumbs-up. "You want it, you got it." He machine-gunned some Nippon at his troops, and there was laughter from behind the balaclavas.

Yoshioka clapped me on the shoulder. "You're with me, *Gaijin*," he said, handing me a suppressed MP5, eight loaded magazines secured in pairs for quick reloading, a fistful of nylon handcuff restraints, and five Def-Tec No. 25 flashbangs. I stuffed everything into the appropriate pockets and pouches of my CQC vest. But I wasn't fully loaded up, yet: Yoshioka pointed to a Go-Bar sitting on the ground. "That's yours, too."

I picked the heavy steel bar up off the asphalt and hefted

it. "Yeah—solid." Was it ever. Go-Bars are thirty-inch-long steel rods with a heavy pry bar on one end, and an adze and pike on the other. There are few doors that can't be induced to open with a little help from these twenty-pound puppies. I adjusted the strap to fit my extra-large *Amerikajin* frame and slung it over my shoulder.

It felt good—reassuring, in the way that two-handed swords and stout-shafted maces felt reassuring to knights about to go into battle. *"Suki-desu.* I like it, Yoshi," I said. "Let's move."

Mister Murphy arrived shortly after takeoff. There were twelve of us crammed into an old Huey UH-1H (actually it was a Bell 212, but they're really quite similar), and the aircraft seemed wobbly and unstable as we lifted off and hovered while the pilot struggled to find the proper trim. Frankly, I prefer heavier craft, like Pave Lows, which can hold a large assault team and its equipment comfortably. But I wasn't overly concerned because our flight time wasn't going to be very long, high, or complex. The assault sequencing was KISS-simple. The ground contingent would smash the front door; we'd fly in just as they were hitting it, our chopper noise covered by the street-level entry and distraction device explosions. The pilot would hover above the roof. We'd fast-rope, hit the rooftop doorways, and swarm down in two groups—clearing hostiles as we went— and meet up with Tosho's shooters somewhere in the middle.

Have I mentioned that Mister Murphy's stowed away on this flight? I have. Good. Have I told you how I knew he was aboard? No? Well, let me explain.

The pilot had just angled the nose down and we'd started what was to be a two-minute flight to insertion. In each hatchway, port and starboard, one of the Kunika shooters readied the coiled sixty-foot fast-ropes and prepositioned the Heli-Vac arms that would allow us to put five men down each rope within six seconds.

Yoshi patted me down while I did the same to him. Every piece of equipment was secure—and exactly where it was supposed to be. I was third man in the starboard stick, with two shooters in front of me to secure the rooftop. Then I'd hit, run to the doorway, pry it open with my Go-Bar, then follow as the number-three man as we made our way downstairs.

I snugged the helmet chin strap, then opened my thigh flap pocket, pulled my gloves out—and saw Mr. Murphy giving me the finger.

What's the prob, you ask?

The prob, bub, is that I was holding a pair of first-class, soft leather-palmed Nomex gloves.

So?

So, Nomex gloves are great for shooting, and since they are fire resistant, they are terrific if you work on an aircraft carrier flight deck, or fly a chopper. They are so form fitting that wearing 'em you can pick coins off a table. Now let me tell you about fast-roping gloves. Fast-roping gloves are made from three- or four-ounce cowhide. They are like a quarter-inch thick, with heavy burn pads on the palms because, when you throw your ass out the hatch, you are moving at about thirty miles an hour as you careen down the rope. That makes for friction. Friction makes for heat. And while Nomex is flame-proof, it ain't heat-proof.

But there was no time to worry about Murphy. The chopper banked sharply to port. Yoshi slapped me on the shoulder. "Ready, Dick—"

I nodded and slapped the shoulder of the man in front of me.

And then we were above the warehouse. Below, I heard the first explosions. The floor plates of the Huey shuddered, Yoshi screamed "Go!," and I threw myself onto the rope.

It was the very sort of descent that makes me know how much I am indeed alive. I came down in a heap. My palms were fucking smoking, my ankle buckled, I smashed my knee, rolled to my left—and got creamed by the next man in the stick, who fell the last three yards because the chopper, relieved of most of its weight, simply rose like a fucking express elevator, leaving a ten-foot gap between the bottom of the fast-rope and the surface of the roof.

No time to waste. I scrambled to my feet and limped to my assigned door, retrieving the Go-Bar as I went.

I assessed as I moved. Solid steel exterior stairwell door, probably a single panic-bar inside. I crammed the thick pry wedge into the jamb just below the steel lock plate and pulled toward me, as if the Go-Bar was an oar and I was the ferryman on the fucking River Styx.

The door separated and opened outward.

I kicked it full ajar—saw a single flight of concrete steps and metal rail leading down to a landing one floor below. I dropped back to rearrange the Go-Bar and grab my MP5. As I did, the point man went in, his subgun at low ready, its combat flashlight probing the stairwell. The number-two man followed, his weapon pointed over the point man's left shoulder.

My turn. Just as I started around the doorframe, the point man was knocked back by a burst of automatic weapons fire. The number-two fired two long bursts down the stairwell to cover us as we grabbed the point man's CQC vest and dragged him out of the line of fire. There was bright red spilling all over his mouth and chin—oxygenated blood coming back up his throat from a bad neck wound. I pulled him around the doorframe and handed him off to someone behind me.

I backed off too, my left hand patting my vest until I found two flashbangs. Extracted them. Grabbed the first pin, pulled it, reached around the stairwell, and tossed it gently—heard it go *bouncie-bouncie-bouncie,* and then repeated. I didn't hear the second flashbang bounce, but then, that was probably because the first one fucking *exploded.* A hundred and seventy-five fucking decibels. Two point four million candlepower.

I looked at number-two man and gestured, Follow me. I

led the way. The Kunika shooter followed two paces behind.
Through the door. MP5 in low ready. Scan. Breathe. Scan.
Breathe. Then all of a sudden he must have seen something
nasty that I'd missed because he screamed *"Fuhatsu!!"*[19] and
threw himself backward through the doorway like a fucking
circus acrobat. That was when I stopped scanning, looked
down, and saw what he had seen: the second Def-Tec. I
noted with horror it was sitting intact directly between my
two feet. There had been four, five, maybe six seconds since
I'd tossed it—and the Def-Tec No. 25 is constructed with a
1.5-second fuse. Obviously, not this one. This one had been
put together by Mister Murphysan.

Well, fuck me too much. I flung myself headlong down the
stairwell—which is, of course, precisely the instant the
goddamn thing exploded, its blast adding to my speed as I
hurtled down the stairs. Oh, that hurt. Yes, the Def-Tec No.
25 is a very nasty, even spiteful object when it misfires.

This was not a Good Thing. I reached out and tried to
catch the railing, but I couldn't get hold of the fucking thing.
Finally caught hold of the rail, flipped like an easy-over egg,
and came down on my bad ankle. Well, not quite. I actually
landed on my foot. But I was immediately back in the air
again because my foot had in fact come down on the
cylindrical, heavy-gauge steel casing of the now exploded
flashbang. The aforementioned casing had, of course, been
aided by Mr. Murphy or one of his fucking relatives, and
hence had beat me to the landing. It was like stepping on a
fucking roller skate—my foot went out from under me, my
legs lifted higher than my goddamn shoulders, and I shot
down the next flight of stairs, flailing as I went.

It occurred to me as I was hurtling downward that the
fucking Go-Bar on my back would not feel very good if I
landed on it. So, borrowing a technique from HALO work, I
jerked my shoulders (cracking every one of my goddamn

---

[19]Japanese for "That's a misfire!"

vertebrae in the process) and executed a half-roll. That helped stop my momentum, although I was still carried down onto a landing, where I rolled up against the door in a noisy heap. First things first: I pushed back from the door and pulled what was left of my gas mask off. The damn thing had cracked in two during my fall, and two of its straps had separated. It was useless. Then I reached up and back, and pulled the Go-Bar strap around my neck so I henceforth could carry it sideways—a less hazardous position for Dickie's health and kidneys in general.

Unhampered by my weight, the door to the landing cracked open. I let go the Go-Bar and reached to scoop my HK up. Oops. It is said that Heckler & Koch's MP5 submachine gun is virtually indestructible. The operative word here is *virtually*. As I rolled onto my hands and knees and scrambled for my weapon, I discovered that my fall had bent the goddamn barrel—not much, but enough to render the fucking gun inoperable.

And that was the good news. You want to know about the bad news? It is that my unintentional forward progress had put me two flights of stairs in front of everybody else on my assault team. But don't worry—I wasn't alone. I had company. He was large, and he had a long, long quasi-Samurai ponytail (and ugly horse's ass face to match), and he had me in the fucking sights of his AK-47, which was pointing straight down at me from the doorway.

Remember what I said at the beginning of the chapter about RS? Remember the phrase violence of action? Good. Well, since there was no time to think, I took my useless MP5 by the barrel and batted his weapon. It wasn't a goddamn home run shot, but the stock of my subgun caught the front of his muzzle and foul-tipped it up and away just long enough for me to launch myself at him.

First I hit him with the door—he was standing in the frame—and rocked him back. But not as much as I'd have liked. He brought the folding stock of the AK down on the point of my shoulder, which hurt like hell and knocked me off balance. But he must have liked my company because as

I fell backward, he grabbed my web gear and pulled me out of the stairwell, his free hand raking my face as he yanked.

Well, this fucking Yankee wasn't going home. I slammed the bottom of his chin with the meaty part of my open palm. That rocked him back a giant step. As he reeled, I hit him squarely in the chest with my forearm.

Big mistake. He was wearing body armor. Plate body armor. Hard plate body armor. My whole arm went numb, and he took advantage of the momentary lull to try and smash me across my hard Slovak head. But he telegraphed: I saw the blow coming, reached through the door, lunged up, and grabbed him by the long hairs.

A word of real-world, life-experience caution here. If you have lengthy hair like I do, make it a cardinal rule to wear a balaclava over your ponytail, or a knit cap to keep your dreadlocks under wraps, because they be an inviting target of opportunity for somebody like me who (sorry, Mom) don't fight fair.

I wrapped his ponytail around my hand and pulled hard. His head came crashing down—right onto my raised knee. There was a satisfying *crunch* as his nose broke. (Well, it was satisfying to me, anyway.) I smashed his face down twice more—*whomp, whomp*—to make sure he'd have a hard time breathing from now on.

But the sumbitch wasn't downed yet. He put his shoulder into my gut and pushed me into the doorframe like I was a tackling dummy. I felt my back go all Rice Krispy—that's snap, crackle, and pop. Then his hands came up, grappling for the Go-Bar, which was hanging athwart my chest.

I tried kneeing him in the nuts, but he was having none of that—his arms pressed while his hands searched for the steel Go-Bar rod.

He found it and started to exert pressure, pressing it like a goddamn barbell slowly up my body, moving inexorably toward my neck.

I broke free and used a forearm blow to stagger him back—God but he was a solid motherfucker—but I rocked him just enough to catch the Go-Bar with my left hand and twist it downward. The thumb is the weak link here, and while he was bigger than I and outweighed me by thirty to forty pounds, I was better conditioned, stronger, and—this is the significant factor—more determined.

So I pushed, and I twisted, and I wrestled, and I took the fucking bar away from him. Well, not away, but at least it was I who controlled it—not he.

I jerked the bar vertical, with the pry blade under his chin. He didn't like that at all, which he indicated by slapping the bar forward six inches and smacking me straight in the face with it.

My helmet took the brunt of the blow—it was knocked flying.

But now the sonofabitch only had one hand on the bar.

I torqued it away from him, kneed him in the balls to back him up flat against the wall, reversed the Go-Bar's ends like a fucking baton twirler, held it like a bat, and using every bit of force I could muster, I swung the six-inch spike up, up, up, slipping it under his left armpit just beyond the body armor and slamming it home toward his lung area.

You look dubious out there. Well, bub, lemme tell ya, the spike on a Go-Bar will puncture a steel door, and tangos are much softer targets than steel doors.

The look on his face told me I'd hurt him bad. But he still wanted my ass. Even as he went down, he was clawing my face, pulling my web gear, trying to wrestle the pistol out of my tactical holster. Fuck it—it was time to put him away for good. I yanked out the Go-Bar (oh, he didn't like that at all), reversed it, drew it back, and then slammed him hard upside the head with the steel shaft, splattering brain and bone in a nasty Rorschach pattern on the wall. He capsized, rolled over, and slid onto the deck. Sayonara, asshole.

He wasn't the only one. I just about collapsed from exhaustion just as the "train" of Kunika shooters passed me, moving to clear the stairwell and hallway. There was the sudden pressure of a hand on my shoulder. I knelt, as drained as an empty beer can, trying to catch my breath and slow my pulse. I looked up and saw Yoshioka. His face was tinged with the sort of concern youngsters feel for old farts. "Hey, you okay, Cap?"

"Affirmative," I wheezed, sucking air. I must tell you in all honesty that this sort of exercise is a young man's game, and I am not as young as I used to be. I breathed deep, hoping to stifle the pounding in my brain and chest. "You keep your men moving, Yoshi, I'll catch up with you."

Twelve minutes after entry, Tosho declared the site secure. The op hadn't been a total success, even though the score was Kunika 15, Red Seeds 1. First, the shooter on my assault group who'd been hit in the throat had died—he'd taken a burst right through the carotid artery, and by the time the medics had got to him he'd lost more than half the blood in his body. And another of Tosh's boys was going to spend a couple of months in the hospital with a cast on his leg—he'd been hit twice in the thigh and the bone was badly shattered. Second, there were no survivors. One Red Seed had been taken alive, but he'd died of his wounds within minutes. Two more had committed suicide. They were obviously a determined, committed bunch.

Tosho debriefed his assault team on site. It was good procedure to do while their memories were still fresh, and besides, the area would be free of interlopers for the next few hours while the police brought in investigators and forensics personnel. As the shooters discussed things, talking with their hands like Italians, or fighter pilots, I watched Alixe Joseph make her way through the debris, methodically poking through the rubble, opening crates and boxes, looking for evidence.

I followed suit, digging, probing, searching the detritus, too. Yes, there were nasty things inside those crates— bomblets, weapons, and ammunition, too. There were cellular phones and electronic equipment. There were uniforms, too—Japanese Defense Force uniforms, as well as dozens of sets of the distinctive coveralls used by Tokyo's power company and electric utilities workers. Tosho was going to have his share of headaches over this group, but he'd obviously hurt 'em bad with this hit, because they hadn't had time to divvy the stuff up and hide it in small lots. Tosh had discovered the mother lode.

That may have been great for him, but to be honest, my heart wasn't in my work. I was antsy. I wanted to go back to Washington. There were things to do, important matters had to be attended to. I had Big Brother on my mind. And I wanted to settle the score with the anonymous (but not anonymous for much longer) asshole at the White House who'd ordered that C²CO, Admiral Gray, to commit his Marine guards, which got the McDonald's hostages killed. Besides, my hands were singed, my face was sore, my ankle throbbed, and there wasn't a bottle of Dr. Bombay Sapphire to be found anywhere within two kilometers.

And then, as often happens when you're not really looking, something caught my eye. On a pallet on the far side of the second floor was a rough wood container. Stenciled on the outside was the legend EXPORT— Zelinograd Machine Tools/MVD.

Oh, we've seen that name before, haven't we? That's right—it was aboard the *Nantong Princess*, on the crate that held Russian AK-47 assault rifles. Which brought to mind the fact that the log on the *Nantong Princess* had listed Yokohama as one of the ship's ports of call. I took my Go-Bar and pried the container open. Can you guess what I found inside? If you said *totsugekijin*, which is how Tosho refers to assault rifles, you'd be right on the old yen.

I reached for the pad and pen that were stowed inside my CQC vest. I wanted the serial numbers off these suckers. We'd check to see if they were part of the same shipment we'd scuttled on the *Nantong Princess*. And once I'd finished copying, I'd fine-tooth-comb this whole fucking place to see if there was anything else of significance I'd missed. I've told you this in the past, but it's important enough to repeat: no matter how hard the bad guy tries to cover his tracks, he always leaves some evidence behind.

Well, I wasn't going to leave this warehouse until I'd found a new shard or two to take back to Washington with me. There was a dangerous pattern emerging here, and I wanted to unravel it.

Who the hell is that out there shouting, "What pattern, what pattern?" Wait—I see him. It's that dweeb editor again. He's running down the hallway, waving his goddamn blue pencil around, complaining that I'm making too much of a jump; that it's too soon to talk about patterns.

Yo, ed, since this is a Rogue book, let the Rogue get a few words in edgewise, will ya? You will? Good.

Okay, let's look at what's gone on recently.

- *Item:* The Russkies and the Chinese, habitual and historical adversaries, have recently formed a very public alliance with each other, to the detriment of the United States.
- *Item:* To counteract this new Sino-Russian alliance, United States policy in the Asian region has undergone a disastrous sea change. We seem to be abandoning Japan and the rest of the Pacific Rim, and throwing our support (both overt and covert) to China, offering the United States as an alternative to the Russkies.
- *Item:* This current policy is exactly the one recommended by an ex-State Department official and consultant, who is currently making loads of bucks helping the Chinese put trade deals together. Happenstance? Coincidence? You tell me.
- *Item:* Big Brother, one of America's most state-of-the-art tactical military communications packages, turns up on a Chinese freighter. My quiet inquiries indicate that the U.S. package is there with White House approval. Happenstance? Coincidence? You tell me.
- *Item:* The Chinese are buying Russkie military equipment—paying off the Russkie Ministry of the Interior—and covertly shipping it all over the Pacific Rim. Where is that stuff ending up? Well, from the look of things, some of it ended up right here in the Red Seeds warehouse. And guess what—the *Nantong*

Princess had less than one-third of its cargo still aboard. It had made half a dozen stops before we scuttled it.

- *Rhetorical Question:* how many warehouses from Pusan to Jakarta are currently filled with smuggled Russkie ordnance, courtesy of the Chinese government? And here's another rhetorical question: who were all those weapons and other lethal packages intended for? Tangos? There are enough of 'em around these days. Fifth columnists? That's a possibility, too. Homegrown insurrectionists? There are half a dozen so-called movements of national liberation currently simmering all over the Pacific Rim.
- *Item:* Alixe Joseph and Tosho—both of whom are fluent in Chinese and knowledgeable about Chinese intel ops—had described an increased level of hostile military intelligence and pro-Chinese terrorist activities in Japan after the arrival of Li Chimen to run the Xinhua bureau. Happenstance? Coincidence? You tell me.
- *Item:* Li Chimen, a SpecWarrior-turned-intelligence agent (and bona fide DIA-certified thug), whose previous posts coincide with all the *Nantong Princess*'s ports of call, is currently headed for Washington for a short-term assignment. Happenstance? Coincidence? You tell me.

Now, my old rabbi and mentor, the late warrior CNO Admiral Arleigh Secrest,[20] taught me that intelligence isn't something that you should look at piecemeal. "Base thine actions neither on the factoid nor the infobit, lest ye step in nasty poop on the road to victory," he growled at me. "Seek ye the big picture, examine every small detail by placing it in context. And when ye hast developed a pattern of action,

---

[20]You can learn why he's the late CNO by reading *Rogue Warrior: Green Team*.

therein shall ye find the answer to your problem—and the path to triumph."[21]

And so, dear editor (and devoted readers), if you will look over the above information carefully, if you will try to see each element as part of a larger whole, then you—like I— will conclude that there is something very . . . hinky going on.

Do we know precisely what that hink is? No—not yet. But I am absolutely certain of two things. First, whatever is going on bodes no good for my country. Second, I am going to find out exactly what *is* wrong, and put a stop to it.

---

[21]No, CNO Secrest didn't really talk like that. I am simply employing a literary device to make you readers hearken back to the Ten Commandments of SpecWar, the teachings of General T'ai Li'ang, and other elements of these *Rogue* books, so that you will see how the Rogue mind works—always free-associating, making connections, and looking for patterns.

Part Two

THE EARTH STRATEGY

Chapter

7

IT WAS SNOWING LIGHTLY AS MY PLANE TOUCHED DOWN AT Andrews Air Force Base just outside Washington. Did you know that a recent federally funded survey indicated that the average driver in the national capital area spends the equivalent of two weeks per year stuck in gridlocked traffic? Have I ever pointed out that whenever it snows, even just a dusting, the normally sluggish Washington road system becomes even slower and more congested? Have I alluded to the fact that despite half a dozen messages left on the Rogue Manor answering machine and at the Alexandria, Virginia, apartment shared by Gator Shepard, Boomerang, and Duck Foot Dewey, I hadn't been able to confirm that anybody would be coming to pick me up? Have I ever told you that when it snows, it is virtually impossible to find a taxi cab?

Well, then perhaps you will be able to calculate the roguish blackness of my mood after forty-nine hours of flight-slash-delay, riding in steerage class—i.e., sleeping on a splintery wood pallet and pissing into a tube—on a Military Air Transport Service priority zero cargo flight. Its Flying Dutchmanlike odyssey took me from Tokyo to

Sydney, Australia, meandered through Hickam Field, Hawaii, stopped for fuel at Nellis AFB just outside Las Vegas, Nevada, and detoured to Montgomery, Alabama, to deliver some C^2 general's personal household belongings, before finally setting down at Andrews right at the height of the evening rush hour.

Now, my forty-nine hours had not exactly been wasted. I'd had a lot to think about as I plucked pallet splinters from the Rogue butt. Before I wheels-uped, I'd made a handshake deal with Alixe Joseph and Tosho. I'd given them the rough outline of my nasty-pattern theory (*sans* the Big Brother stuff of course). They thought it made sense enough to agree to work the problem as if it was a real-world situation, not an intel squirrel's scenario, and to sit-rep me on a regular basis.

Alixe Joseph even gave me a bunch of bon voyage gifts: there was a file containing her eval of Li Chimen, accompanied by English-language news clips and photographs. There was a second file, enumerating the probes that she believed the Chinese had made in Korea, Japan, Singapore, and Indonesia since she'd arrived in the region. From the look of things, they had been concentrating on each nation's various warfare capabilities. In Japan, for example, there had been attempts to recruit agents; there had been probes of Japanese Defense Force installations. Most troubling, there had been a push to obtain materials dealing with Japan's technological infrastructure—its power grids, telephone networks, and transportation and air traffic control networks.

She let me read—but wouldn't give me—a third file. In fact, she cut the code word designator from the top sheet before she even let me see it, but I caught a peek as she snipped (I'm naturally nosey). The result: I learned that all her HUMINT materials bore the compartment label Weather Gable.[22] A very pissed-off Alixe swore me to

---

[22]Like most American intelligence organizations, DIA uses computers to assign code words. It is done that way to prevent the opposition from coming up with a formula that would allow them to figure out what the files deal with if they can decipher the code word designators.

secrecy on the subject of her compartment designator, and I promised—Warrior's Code honest—not to tell anybody what I'd seen, or what it meant.

Anyway, I scanned those two pages carefully before giving them back. They were dynamite; they bore a few of the latest results of her HUMINT-gathering networks. The Chinese were actively recruiting Koreans, Malays, Filipinos, and Singaporeans, among others. And not just any sort, either. They were looking for disgruntled former cops, bitter, retired soldiers, and other cynical, bored, or just plain crooked security types—the exact same sorts of renegade malcontents that are actively recruited by the outlaw groups that often call themselves militias in the good old U.S. of A.

Alixe Joseph watched the expression on my face as I read her materials. I looked up. "Have you shared any of this with Tosho?"

"Not yet," she said.

"Maybe you'd better, given what we found at the warehouse today."

She considered the suggestion and finally nodded her agreement. "Will do," she said. "In fact, I'll ask him to check the background of the tangos he took down today and see if they fit the pattern." She paused, her hands on her hips. "Look, you're the counterterrorism expert. What do you make of it all?"

What I made of it all was that the Chinese were putting together a series of paramilitary fifth columns, all across the Pacific Rim, and that we'd better watch our butts.

She'd nodded. "That's what I've been trying to hammer home, too. But my memos just seem to disappear into the void back at headquarters."

My look told her what I think of bureaucrats. "Well, *I* think it's a good premise. Stay in touch—let me know what you guys come up with."

* * *

So, during the flight, I'd hunkered over a legal pad and—Hey, hey, hey, what's that ruckus out there? Oh, it's that bleeper-blanking reader again—the one in the dumb-looking worn-backward ball cap, interrupting my train of thought to wonder aloud why I had to take such a long, circuitous flight home when there are at least half a dozen direct and nonstop commercial polar-route flights from Tokyo straight to the States every day.

You want to know why I just didn't jump one of those? It's another good question, despite the dumb ball cap, so I'll explain.

Y'see, it helps to have a passport and other forms of personal identification with you when traveling on commercial flights. In fact, the security personnel at airlines insist on it these days. But I had no passport. Fact of the matter was, I had no IDs at all. Nor money (except for the two twenty-dollar bills that Alixe Joseph kindly pressed into my hand just before I left). Nor anything else, not even a wallet. I didn't even have the correct time: the goddam cheap allegedly waterproof East German dive watch I was wearing had gone *mausetot*[23] shortly after we'd hit the South China Sea.

And where *was* everything you ask? Well, my worldly possessions had all been left behind in a Navy safe on Guam before we'd set off to hunt the *Nantong Princess*. You do not go on a covert mission carrying a fucking passport, an ID card, a Visa, AMEX, or any other sundry items that might serve to identify the origin of your corpse should something untoward happen during said covert mission.

Happy now? Yes? Okay, then back to our narrative. We taxied (and taxied, and taxied) to what had to be the most distant arrival position on the tarmac. Finally, the engines were shut down, the ground crew chocked the wheels and opened the hatch. I clambered down the ladder onto terra

---

[23]That's Kraut for dead as a doornail.

firma, tossed the bird at the Alabama-based flight crew that was performing its postlanding check,[24] and slogged, frigid in my borrowed Kunika lightweight Nomex flying suit, across the slushy macadam. I trudged wearily past the trio of huge, well-illuminated hangars where the presidential aircraft are stored, in the direction of the squat terminal building three hundred yards away. The terminal was barely visible in the freezing drizzle beyond a low chain-link fence. I knew there was a pay phone inside, and I'd try to raise someone to come and get me. If that didn't work I hoped I'd be able to beg, borrow, or steal, and believe me, in my mood all three were equal possibilities, a ride home from a ground staff Samaritan.

As I drew within a hundred yards of the fence, I saw what looked like two yuppie scum sphincters. They were swathed in brightly colored goose down and patterned, knit ski caps—holding a long paper banner. You've seen 'em, those seamless sheets you can print out on a computer to celebrate a birthday or anniversary. Who the fuck are they expecting, I wondered.

The closer I mushed through the slush, the more distinct the letters became to my tired Rogue eyes. The sign read: WASHINGTON WELCOMES DICKHEAD.

And the yuppie scum? Well, holding on to one end of the banner, complete with his trademark wraparound shooting glasses, was the world-class operator I call Stevie Wonder,

---

[24]When I come back in my next life, I'm gonna come back as an Air Farce MATs pilot. That way I can get paid without having to work. There had been five—count 'em, five—changes of air crew over the course of this flight. SEALs perform under incredible physical and mental strain at warp speed for goddam weeks at a time. These guys' shifts could be counted in fucking *minutes.* Shit, the Air Force has better union rules than most fucking commercial airlines. (It is also, incidentally, the only uniformed service that issues regulation umbrellas to its male personnel. God forbid that a drop of water should fall on a pilot's *kop.*)

even though his real name resembles neither Stevie nor Wonder. With his free hand, he was waving my wallet and car keys at me. And on the other end of the banner, swathed in a bright red parka and Oakley baggy surfing shorts, his bare feet in plastic flip-flops, stood Boomerang, an SES (look it up in the Glossary) on his Huckleberry Hound face and a spare down jacket under his arm.

"Yo, schmuck," Wonder bawled in his New Yawk accent, "How many times do I have to tell you? Never stay on the fucking C—that's the goddam local. You gotta change at Forty-second Street for the A train if you want to make any fuckin' time."

I gave each of them a big abrazo. "Good to see you guys."

Wonder looked at my banged-up face. "I see you've been keeping yourself very existential," he said.

Boomerang threw the spare parka over my shoulders and wiggled his bare foot to shake loose some slush that had lodged between his toes. "We better make tracks, Boss Dude. You have a command performance tomorrow at the Chairman's office—zero six-thirty. They've been on the horn all fuckin' day asking WTF you were."

"Merci, trouducs," I grunted gratefully, calling them shits-for-brains, which as you know by now is a term of endearment in Frog Frogspeak. "But if that's the case, why the hell are we still standing here with our fingers up our bung-holes?" Hell, even though I'd been working nonstop on the flight I knew there was still a shitload to do before I'd be locked, loaded, and ready to see the Chairman. I shrugged into the parka and stretched long and hard, all the better to work the cramps, cricks, crimps, and kinks out of my aching joints. Stretching didn't work, of course, and I knew there was gonna be no time for a sauna, or (morer & betterer) a soak in the Rogue Manor hot tub between a pair of warm thighs, either. Oh, doom on Dickie—this was about to become a long, long night.

* * *

I was sitting in the Chairman's anteroom by 0612 the next morning, in pressed dress blues, my French braid tied off neatly with black parachute line, my metal polished and my black shoes spit shined, poring over the current issue of *Navy Times*. Between my knees, one of the waterproof duffel bags I'd used aboard the *Nantong Princess* sat squat and heavy on the polished marble parquet. I'd had exactly seventeen minutes of sleep—the briefest of combat naps. But I was absofucking S&P (look it up in the Glossary): all showered, shaved, and Right Guarded. More to the point, I was fucking *prepared* for making *WAR,* which word, as you should know, is the acronym for We Are Ready.

Now, being ready for WAR is a large part of what being a SEAL is all about. Remember the Rogue Warrior's Fourth Commandment of SpecWar? Let me refresh your memories so you don't have to waste my time turning to the front of the book to find it.

The Fourth Commandment goes, "I shall punish thy bodies because the more thou sweatest in training, the less thou bleedest in battle." Well, that commandment applies to your paper wars in the Pentagon as well as it does to your blood-and-guts struggles on the battlefield. The Warrior is always prepared, always more prepared to do battle than his adversaries. The Warrior also knows that sometimes you can't just out-kill your enemy—you have to out-think him, and you have to out-perform him.

To make these points during training, our Frog tadpoles are pushed way beyond any level of stress they may have encountered in their lives before. They are deprived of sleep but still must be able to think clearly. They are deprived of food but still must be able to operate at their physical peak for days on end. And they are deprived of warmth but they still have to make it all the way through. They learn, often the hard way, that they are a part of a team, platoon, boat crew—a *unit*. And they come to understand that if the *unit* does not succeed, then the *man* most likely will fail, too. But at the core, the center, the nucleus, the root of it all, it is each man alone who must summon up within himself the courage, the stamina, and the pure guts to go on until he has completed his assignment.

Because the lucky tadpoles who survive this anvil of pain, anguish, despair, and agony will, through their suffering, have come upon one of the central epiphanies of Warriordom, which is: You Must Go On. The Warrior does not give up. Ever. No matter how tired, or cold, or fatigued, or stressed, THE WARRIOR WILL COMPLETE HIS MISSION. There is no demand too great, whether physical, psychological, strategic, or tactical. There is no exigency that cannot, and *will not,* be overcome.

That is why when I select men for my teams, I do not necessarily select those who can breeze through the qualification tests like gazelles. I want men like Boomerang—grunt-and-bear-its who, if they fail once, just keep trying and trying and trying until they succeed. *They* are the ones who become the real Warriors because they have been endowed with the hearts, souls, and the boundless, persistent, uncompromising, indefuckingfatigable gritty determination of Warriors.

Thus endeth the lesson.

And so, as tired as I might have been, I worked the same way tadpoles do during Hell Week at BUD/S—which is to say flat out, and balls to the wall. I wasn't alone either. My guys had been going full-tilt boogie since they'd returned, and they'd come up with some nuggets I could use. But I wanted more. So I sent Stevie Wonder to the Navy Yard, where he knew of an Intelink terminal he could, ah, borrow, and had him siphon off as much classified material on our relations with China and Russia as he could lay his pernicious paws on. I rousted Tony Merc out of his warm bed in Oakton, dispatched him to DIA headquarters, and had him print out as many of the agency's reports on current Chinese intel operations as he could be persuaded to give me.

I laid every piece of paper we'd assembled out on the

floor, sorted everything twice, separated thrice, then sifted once. That done, I shuffled the whole package thoroughly, then dealt each "card" one more time.

Thomas E. Crocker, General, United States Army and Chairman of the Joint Chiefs of Staff, walked through the door at 0621, followed by two aides. I knew the first of 'em, a tonsured, straight-leg Mick colonel named O'Grady, whose round, rimless glasses gave him the look of the old-fashioned parish priests I used to altar-boy for in New Brunswick, New Jersey. O'Grady had worked for the Chairman for more than fifteen years. The second aide was new: a woman in her midthirties (and a civilian to boot) dressed in a dark blue pantsuit. I almost double-taked. Although she wasn't wearing the lapel pin common to DOD security, I could see the faint outline of a pistol at waist level. But she wasn't part of any security detail: the Chairman's personal top secret document case was chained to her left wrist.

I stood, saluted, and greeted the Chairman by his first name. "Keeping banker's hours these days, General?"

I was hoping Chairman Crocker would crack the hint of a smile. But he didn't. He didn't introduce me to his new aide, either. He just looked back in the general direction of his retinue and barked, "You folks wait here. I won't be long."

Then he pointed his right index finger at my chest, jerked his thumb over his right shoulder, and intoned First SEAL Roy Boehm's two-word definition of leadership.

"Follow me," he said, abruptly about-facing.

I can take orders from a real leader as well as any man, and the Chairman comes under that category, so I followed General Crocker across the wide second-floor hallway, past the reception area with its flags and Marines in dress blues, to an anonymous doorway secured with a cipher lock. The Chairman blocked my view with his broad shoulders, hunched over the lock, and punched in the combination. The lock opened. Then he turned the doorknob, swung the door wide so that I could muscle the duffel through, and beckoned me to precede him inside.

I went through the door into a SCIF, which stands for Sensitive Compartmented Information Facility. SCIFs are safe rooms—they can't be bugged, either by the opposition, or by a fellow agency that might like to learn what's on your mind when you think you're not being overheard. This was the Chairman's SCIF. It wasn't the only one either: each of the joint chiefs has his own SCIF these days. That should give you some idea about the growth of institutional paranoia here in the Pentagon since the arrival of the Clinton administration.

Chairman Crocker shut the door behind us, then shook it to make sure that it had closed properly. He pointed to one of the half dozen molded plastic chairs that sat adjacent to the three-by-five-foot Formica table, and indicated that I was to Park It.

I Parked It, the duffel between my feet.

He perched on the edge of the table, looking down at me. His expression was not especially friendly. "Remember what I emphasized to you before this most recent exercise began?" he asked. He didn't bother waiting for an answer, so I guessed the question must have been rhetorical. "I told you not to leave any pecker tracks," he said.

He paused just long enough to grab a lungful of air. "Goddammit, Dick, right now my friggin' message pad looks like the friggin' bedsheet from a friggin' California gold rush whorehouse."

He cracked his knuckles and edged closer, staring down at me intently. "Hell has been breaking loose around here over the past couple of days, and it all seems to have to do with you. First, somebody over at the White House called SECDEF's office to complain that you and some idiot from DIA were making loud inquiries about a program that's so fucking classified that even I don't know all the compartments. Then yesterday, somebody else at the White House told NSC adviser Thompson that the reason the hostage rescue at Yokosuka got screwed up was that you'd muscled your way in—and he went and fucking tattled to the fucking president. Result? My goddam butt got boondockered by the CINC before I could set him straight. Then there are all kinds of inquiries coming from the NSC about your being tasked out of this office—which is something that only you, me, SECDEF, and the president are supposed to know about. And as if all of the above wasn't enough, I got blindsided by your old pal Viktor Grinkov, who wants a quiet, off-the-record meet in Rome to talk about the fifty mil we siphoned out of his offshore accounts—and SECDEF says I actually gotta go talk to him. And that's only the beginning—"

I know it is considered rude for those of us who wear mere eagles on our collars to interrupt folks who wear four stars on theirs, but this was one of those times when it was necessary. "General," I said, "I wasn't able to reach you from the *Nantong Princess,* or the *Scorpion* and I certainly wasn't about to leave a message with whoever was picking up your secure phone. And the Grinkov thing's important, I know, but I really think you'd better take a look at a few things I brought back from overseas before you finish reaming me my new asshole."

One of the things I admire about Thomas E. Crocker, General, USA, is that he has never suffered from the HICs—head-in-cement syndrome—that affects so many of our senior officers these days. The man is willing to listen. He may fire your ass when he's heard your side of the story, but you will have had a fair hearing.

The Chairman raised his hands in mock surrender, growled, "Okay, Dick, you have your say, then I'll finish mine," and vacated his perch on the table.

I unzipped the duffel bag, retrieved a handful of manila file folders on which I'd written numbers, and carefully laid six piles of paper out on the table for inspection. Then I unbuttoned my blouse, retrieved two sheets of xerographic bond from my inside pocket, unfolded them one by one, smoothed them out, and placed them on the table under the

Chairman's intent gaze. They were, of course, photocopies of the Big Brother technical manual cover pages.

I watched General Crocker's eyes go wide. "Where the hell—"

"They were in a document safe aboard the *Nantong Princess*," I interrupted. "So, General, how's about you let me give you the fuckin' show-and-tell that's kept me awake for the last couple of days."

Chapter

8

AFTER JUST OVER AN HOUR-LONG MONOLOGUE FROM ME, IT WAS his turn. There was no more chastisement, either. I sat back and listened as General Crocker spoke from the half dozen legal-pad sheets of neat handwritten notes he'd made, ticking off the problems and flagging the political minefields as he saw them.

Tick One was that he believed, as I did, that the Chinese *were* on the offensive—indisputably—both on the Pacific Rim and, more ominously, here in the United States. One didn't have to be cleared top secret to know it, either: it was obvious, he said, to anyone who reads newspapers or watches television that Beijing is working hard to expand its political and economic influence.

He went on to point out that there was nothing wrong with that, either. We Americans do the same thing overseas. But, the Chairman added, the Chinese weren't just trying to sell us toys, shoes, diesel engines, and knitted goods. They were buying influence inside the White House and on Capitol Hill. They were infiltrating agents of influence inside our government. And they were trying to penetrate our high-tech and defense industries, much as the old Soviet Union had done during the 1950s, 1960s, 1970s, and 1980s.

And the new Chinese dragon enjoyed some advantages that the old Soviet bear had never had. There were, for example, tens of thousands of Chinese students in American colleges pursuing graduate degrees in everything from nuclear engineering to physics—and the FBI had determined that more than 10 percent of them—some willing, some not—were being used by Chinese intelligence as spies.

China was also America's largest trading partner, which gave it clout in the marketplace, not to mention in the White House. But the administration seemed willing to ignore the fact that Chinese were using their leverage to seek illegal goods and services. There had been half a dozen Silicon Valley employees caught selling restricted information to Chinese agents in the last five months alone. And the Chairman said he knew of at least a dozen cases over the last two years in which Beijing had managed to infiltrate American defense-industry corporations. The companies had been targeted because they built the sorts of missile guidance components the Chinese were still unable to manufacture.

There was also intelligence gathered by DIA's HUMINT project. In contradiction to the CIA's current assessments (assessments that the Chairman noted bitterly were being kept from him by the director of Central Intelligence) DIA's own reports indicated that the Chinese were out there prowling and growling aggressively—covertly supplying weapons to pro-Chinese movements all across the Pacific Rim. His information dovetailed very neatly, he said, with what I'd uncovered on the *Nantong Princess*.

It even made sense. Freelancing—that is, the White House clandestinely pursuing foreign-policy goals without informing the other branches of government—is commonplace. The Clinton administration did it when, with the president's permission, the NSC adviser allowed Iran to sell arms to Bosnia. During the Reagan years, Oliver North freelanced most of the Iran-Contra affair. During George Bush's presidency, he allowed a clandestine counterterrorism program to be freelanced out of the vice president's office.

But all those freelance affairs had two elements in common. One: the man in charge—i.e., the President of the United States—knew about 'em and sanctioned 'em, and, Two: they all worked (more or less) to the U.S.'s advantage.[25] Here, someone had convinced the president to give away our most capable technology, but get nothing in return. Moreover, the Department of Defense and Joint Chiefs had been entirely frozen out of the process.

So, when you added what the Chairman knew and what I'd discovered—the Russian arms, the missiles, and the Big Brother materials—to the fact that one of Beijing's nastiest intel honchos had just been transferred to Washington, it was clear that something pretty nefarious was going on, and someone close to, or perhaps even actually inside the government, was helping Beijing achieve its goals—to the detriment of the United States. Hopefully, Chairman Crocker said, some hint of that would be found in the duffel bags of papers and other goodies I'd brought back from the *Nantong Princess,* all of which he said he'd have translated ASAP.

That brought us to Tick Two, which was that no matter how we—that is to say he and I—may have felt about the situation, we were still MILPERS, or MILitary PERSonnel. And in the United States, MILPERS come under civilian

---

[25]The counterterrorism program during the Bush years bore fruit in April 1997, when Peruvian troops, many of whom had received their initial hostage-rescue training from a team of American experts back in the 1980s, rescued seventy-one of seventy-two hostages from Tupac Amaru terrorists at the Japanese embassy in Lima.

authority. The Jeffersonian bottom line: we don't allow either kings, or juntas, in the U.S. of A. Which meant that we MILPERS aren't allowed to take matters into our own hands, no matter how strongly we believe that someone, probably someone in the executive branch, might well be selling the country out.

No way. We would have to go through channels, which meant reporting what we knew to SECDEF, and letting SECDEF convince the president that he should change course, and turn the matter of who was giving the Chinese aid and comfort over to the Justice Department for investigation.

Which brought us to Tick Three: which was that we couldn't report diddly-squat to anybody right now. Oh, we—that is to say, I, and now the Chairman—had doubts, apprehensions, misgivings, suspicions, and intuitive concerns. But there was no hard evidence of wrongdoing. No obvious traitor. No mole. Ergo, nothing indisputable to take to SECDEF.

Which was followed hard by Tick Four. In order to convince SECDEF of anything, we (that is to say yours truly) would have to obtain said aforementioned hard evidence. Which brought us back to Tick Two: we were military personnel, and we weren't supposed to conduct investigations of the executive branch. (Do you sense a certain circumscriptive quality to General Crocker's recitation? I certainly did.)

Then, having thoroughly ticked himself off, the Chairman proceeded directly to point out the political minefield flags.

Flag One was that no matter what the fucking rules said, I'd probably have to do some sneak-and-peeking of the sort that could end me up deep in PIG SHIT, which is to say, a Penal Institution with Guards and SHiv-Inflicted Tattoos.

That brought us directly to Flag Two. Let me put this flag in Chairman Crocker's words, because he is a four-star general and I think you should be exposed to the way a four-star general talks when he is in a bug-proof room. "Use extreme fucking caution, Dick," is the precise phrase he employed. That made sense: if I created waves; if anyone got wind of what was going on before I obtained any hard evidence of wrongdoing, malfeasance, or other nefarious behavior, we would both be out of jobs. Clandestine military investigation of the government is an act frowned upon these days. Discovery of my activities would bring us directly (Do Not Pass Go; Do Not Collect $200) back to Tick Two and Flag One—and bury us both in PIG SHIT, and you already know what *that* acronym stands for.

Flag Two was followed by flags Three, Four, Five, Six, Seven, Eight, Nine, and Ten. I won't take the time to go into them now, but you should know that for someone who, like the book jacket says, obeys no rules, I was being handed a fucking list of do's and don'ts almost as long as my *szeb*.

Flag Eleven was that I was going to have to distance myself from the Chairman's office for the duration of this little exercise. Now, *that* flag made sense for any number of reasons. What were they, you ask? Well, let me cite just two for now, so we can climb out of this literary narrative section of the book and get back into some fuckin' action.

First, any Navy captain walking in and out of, or phoning in and out of, the Chairman's office on a regular basis draws attention to himself—and attention was something that I didn't want, or need. Second, General Crocker had mentioned that there'd already been discreet inquiries from someone at the NSC regarding my being tasked out of his office. That was Bad Juju. And third, we'd managed to keep the *Nantong Princess* mission a secret so far, and I didn't want to jeopardize a successful mission.

So OPSEC (OPerations SECurity) would be a primary concern. Oh, I don't mind taking risks, but I also don't like my rogue butt compromised. And yet I still had to maintain contact with Chairman Crocker on a regular basis.

Obviously, if all evidence of my rogue persona was going to be exorcised from the office of the Chairman, what we needed was a cutout. I suggested we repeat a system that had worked once before: I'd keep the Chairman sit-repped through a one-star admiral named Kenny Ross, a submariner I'd worked with before who had been detailed to the Chairman's intelligence staff a while back.[26]

That, the Chairman said, was a no-go. It was Ken Ross who had fielded the NSC call about my activities. Whoever it was over at the White House making waves (that's a Navy technical phrase, y'know) knew about the association between Ken, the Chairman, and me.

"I've got a better idea," Chairman Crocker said. At which point he picked up the secure telephone that sat on the conference table and punched in a series of numbers. He didn't identify himself, but simply barked, "Joe, come on over to the SCIF, would you, please?"

Less than half a minute later, I heard the cipher lock on the outside of the door being punched. The door opened, and a young woman walked in, the same one who'd been chained to the Chairman's briefcase. She closed the door behind her, leaned against it to make sure it had sealed properly, then stood at attention. "General?"

Chairman Crocker pointed his right thumb and index finger first in her direction then mine. "Jo—Joanne Montgomery, this is Dick Marcinko. Dick, this is Jo."

I rose and extended my hand. "Hi. Dick Marcinko."

She gave me a strange look as she took my hand with a firm grip and pumped up/down once, formally, in the Eurostyle. "Hi, Dick Marcinko, I'm Joanne Montgomery. We've talked on the telephone."

"Jo's a White House Fellow," the Chairman was saying. But I wasn't listening. Of course I'd heard that voice before—I'd heard it on the fucking secure phone asking me if I wanted to leave a message.

I grinned and got a grin from her in return. And then, with that particular circle closed, I refocused on what Chairman Crocker was saying. He was saying, "Joanne's

---

[26]You can read about it in *Rogue Warrior: Designation Gold*.

been with me for about six weeks now, functioning as my special assistant. Learning all about the Joint Chiefs."

I know about White House Fellows. The program dates from 1964, and it was designed to nurture future leaders; indeed, General Colin Powell, former U.S. Senator Tim Wirth, and the ex-inspector general of the U.S. Department of Transportation, Mary Schiavo, had all been White House Fellows. Generally, about a baker's dozen are selected each year from more than a thousand applications. Roughly two-thirds come from the private sector. The rest of 'em are midlevel government, both civilian and military. Each fellow gets to serve for a year as a special assistant to a high-level government official.[27]

Joanne Montgomery was one of the government selectees. How did I know that? I knew it because while all White House Fellows must undergo a security clearance, non government people—even fellows—aren't allowed to carry weapons inside federal facilities. And she was packing, remember?

"Where are you from?"

"State—Diplomatic Security Service."

"Joanne was the agent who saved our ambassador to Burundi's bureaucratic butt last year," General Crocker said, exhibiting his usual diplomatic form.

I remembered reading DIA cables at the time. The ambassador had been on a trip up to the Rwandan border to inspect some refugee stations. On his way back to Bujumbu-

---

[27]Fellows write speeches, help review and draft proposed legislation, answer congressional inquiries, chair meetings, conduct briefings, and otherwise assist high-level government officials. They are assigned to work with senior White House officials, Cabinet secretaries, or other deputies. In the past, Fellows have worked for the Vice President, the White House Chief of Staff, the national security adviser, the Attorney General, and the Director of Central Intelligence. If you're interested, you can find more information about the White House Fellows Program on the Internet at *http://www.whitehouse.gov/WH/WH_Fellows/html*.

ra, the Burundi capital, the two-car motorcade, a lead vehicle and the ambassador's limo, was ambushed about halfway between Ngozi and Muramvya by a group of rebels.

The ambassador's driver—an FN[28]—froze in panic. The DSS agent sitting in the front seat of the car, one J. M. Montgomery to be precise, had swatted the driver out of the way, thrown the vehicle into reverse, executed a tactical maneuver known as a bootlegger's turn, and sped away to safety. The agent's rapid reaction not only saved the ambassador's life, it also allowed the lead car, which held three more DSS agents and the CIA station chief masquerading under political officer cover, to escape unharmed. It was an act of heroism for which the secretary of state had personally awarded the agent the Department's Medal of Valor. "You're Agent J. M. Montgomery."

She nodded. Y'see what preconceptions can do to you. I'd always assumed that Agent J. M. Montgomery was a man. That's because I hadn't followed my own SpecWar Commandment—the one that says "Thou shalt never assume."

---

[28]The official designation is Foreign National. Let me say right here that the logic of allowing an FN inside your embassy where he/she becomes privy to policy decisions and other sensitive matters has never made any sense to me. The reason for having 'em is that most of our diplomats, spooks, and other officials don't speak the fucking language or understand the modus vivendi of the country they've been posted to. And so they need FNs to do their business for 'em—dealing with the natives in the visa section, running interference with the local authorities, helping diplomats get everything from driver's licenses to finding apartments. FNs also work as chauffeurs, cooks, maids and butlers, and maintenance workers. But allowing an FN that kind of proximity to diplomats and that kind of access to the embassy gives foreign intelligence services a real leg up when they want to spy on us. I thought for a long time it was just me who was being paranoid. Then I discovered that the Russians don't allow FNs to work for them. Neither do the Chinese. The Israelis have only a very few—and they segregate 'em. Ditto the French, and the Brits. Does that tell you anything?

And it wasn't the fact that she'd won a medal that impressed me, either. I'm not impressed by medals, not the way they're handing 'em out these days. No, what registered loud and clear is that Agent J. M. Montgomery hadn't had to think—she'd been ready to *act*. She'd obviously prepared for what she was going to do beforehand—and when ye olde *merde* hit the *ventilateur*, she Just Did It. That, friends, is Warrior behavior.

General Crocker pointed toward one of the plastic chairs that ringed the conference table. "Park it, Jo," he said. "We've got a crisis situation here and I need a volunteer for hazardous duty—and I do mean hazardous." He paused and waited for a reaction from her.

The even smile that spread across her face as she sat herself down was both radiant and reassuring. "Can do, sir."

It made more operational sense for me to work out of Rogue Manor, my two hundred acres of snakes and lakes that kind of sidles up to the Marine base at Quantico, than it did for me to sit anywhere at the Pentagon. But before I could do any prowling, growling, sneaking, or peeking, Jo Montgomery and I had to set up our own OPLAN (Operational PLAN), OPSEC, and OPCON—OPerational CONtrol—procedures. It was already close to 1100, and I suggested that we do our plotting over an early lunch. We then spent some minutes negotiating food types.

As you know, I am a snake eater. That means, I will eat anything. Literally. Others are not so easily satiated. So Joanne ruled out Mexican and Ethiopian on aesthetic grounds. I vetoed French because there was nowhere decent close by. She ruled against Vietnamese because she'd eaten Vietnamese twice in the past three days, and Japanese because she said the food was boring. We finally settled on Chinese. It was a happy and unanimous decision because we both picked the same restaurant as our First Choice.

We left the Pentagon separately. I walked to the white,

F-250 pickup that I'd parked in the Pentagon's river entrance lot, threaded my way out, and headed south along the GW Parkway. I passed National Airport, then suddenly shifted lanes, pulled onto the right-hand shoulder, backed up rapidly, and swerved into the airport entrance. I sensed no incongruous movement behind me—except for a guy in a van who'd thrown me the bird when I cut him off. I circled the airport, weaving in and out of the traffic lanes. I drove into the huge parking structure's front entrance, whipped across it, and exited out the back, adjacent to the airport's south entrance. There, I cut across six lanes of traffic and slipped out the back door, ran a red light on Route 1, then pulled off into a quiet residential neighborhood and made a wide, slow, four-block circle while leisurely checking my six.

Then, confident I was not being trailed, I pulled back onto Route 1, drove north, and worked my way back onto the GW Parkway using an excruciatingly complicated series of vehicular maneuvers that involved, among other things, running westbound for three hundred yards on an eastbound exit ramp. (After all, you can never be too safe or too secure, right?) Safe, secure, and solo, I sidled north past Arlington National Cemetery and the Iwo Jima Memorial, slid onto Route 50, took the Rosslyn exit, then slipped up past the CIA's spook house on Fort Meyer Drive, skidded onto Wilson Boulevard, and strung my way through the light traffic until I passed Highland Avenue. Then I turned left, went around the block, came back, drove two blocks, turned left again, and parked well off the corner. I traded my double-breasted uniform coat for a sweater (all the gold braid and ribbons often attract unwanted attention), pulled on a pair of unlined leather gloves, then walked north and west oblivious of the January chill, past a series of one, two, and three-story buildings housing an ethnic cornucopia of stores that ran the gamut from Thai, Cambodian, Peruvian, and Jamaican groceries, to Vietnamese jewelers, Indian tailor shops, Afghani and Pak rug stores, Japanese sushi bars, and Chinese herb dealers.

I hadn't been through the neighborhood in a while, and I didn't like the developments I now saw. What had once been pristine walls now bore the kind of angular, spray-painted gangsta-cool turf-marking graffiti that has become common to urban areas all over the country. The stores, too, showed signs of increased crime: metal grilles behind the plate glass windows told me that the shopkeepers were afraid of smash-and-grab robberies. Almost every store except the groceries had PLEASE RING BELL TO ENTER signs. Another bad omen. I grew up in a neighborhood of small businesses—and small businesses thrive on walk-ins.

I cut through a small, potholed parking lot that sat between a Salvadoran meat market whose boarded-over window was evidence of a recent break-in and a now-closed Italian restaurant and turned into the unpaved alley that would shortcut my route by three-quarters of a block.

I hadn't gotten more than fifty yards—I was, in fact, picking my way through a muddy section of alley between two Dumpster containers, moving v-e-r-y carefully so as not to ruin the perfect spit-shine on my shoes—when the hair on the back of my neck stood up.

There was nothing overt. Nothing had happened—*nothing*. And yet, some primordial instinct buried deep in my subconscious (it was probably located right behind the pussy detector) took over, and my body told me that things were not right.

Oh, I know, you're going to accuse me of macho Warrior psychobabble right now. Well, bub, here's the truth: when you have been in the field for as long as I have and you have had as many close encounters of the fatal kind as I have, you will appreciate the fact that my antennas have been honed by years of nasty, brutal, sometimes painful experience.

Besides, I always carry myself in what might be called condition yellow. That is, I am perpetually alert. I am constantly aware of my surroundings, and I am quite capable, thank you very much, of responding quickly and lethally to perceived threats without providing any indication to my adversaries I'm about to do so.

So, I didn't stop. I didn't hesitate. I didn't do anything to show that I was now aware of any danger. But my body had subtly shifted its attitude—and so had my brain. Without having to think, I'd shifted into condition orange—in weapons terms, I was locked and loaded, but the safety was still engaged.

It came off when a salt-and-pepper team[29] of teenaged assholes stepped out from behind the Dumpster ten yards ahead of me.

TNO—Thug Number One—held out his arm like a traffic cop. "Yo, my man, hold it up." He was dressed in an oversize, baggy quilted cotton tunic, three-sizes-too-large jeans held up by a clothesline belt, and sported the requisite baseball cap. (Worn backward, of course—what *is* it with people these days?) Around his neck hung a pair of the sort of heavy gold chains favored by cocaine-tooting pro football players and/or pimps, and the $150 NBA-style high-top sneakers I have come to think of as mugging moccasins. My friends on the local SWAT team call 'em felony flyers.

I kept moving, my course steady. My left hand had already emerged from my trouser pocket. The spring-loaded collapsible baton I always carry was extended, and it was concealed from view in a reverse grip that shielded it against my arm. Had TNO seen it? Not a chance. I could read him like a fucking primer, and he was too busy already counting the money in my wallet to pay any attention to anything else but my right hip pocket.

The arm extended once again. "Yo—*hey*, my man, I'm talkin' to you—"

TNO did have an irritating manner. But I wasn't going to let it affect me. My pace was still constant; obviously I was

---

[29]That's copspeak for a team of malefactors composed of one white scumbag and one black scumbag, although in today's politically correct (and gastronomically diverse) atmosphere it could mean one white scumbag and one green scumbag, or one white scumbag and one red scumbag, or, well—you get the idea.

lost in thought. No threat. No eye contact. No War Face. I let the distance seep away. Ten yards, nine, eight, seven, and six—*that* was when he began to shrug his quilted jacket to the side so he could reach toward the sloppy waistband of his oversize trousers and withdraw the pistol I just knew he had. Which was precisely when I accelerated, covering the last five yards in about three-quarters of a second, and smacking the shit out of him with my baton.

Oh, TNO wasn't expecting *that*. He was expecting me to pull up. Stop. Let him proceed with this mugging unfuck-inghampered.

But that wasn't what happened. What happened was that I *turned*—rolled into a dervish spin like a gold-medal hammer-throw Olympian to give myself an extra measure of deadly, tight-as-a-fucking-spring kinetic energy—my baton unsprung, punched round like a goddam baseball bat from its concealed position, and, using every ounce of power my hand/wrist/arm/shoulder/torso/back/hips/thighs/legs could muster, I—*whaaaaap*—slashed him across the face, opening a deep, nasty-looking laceration that ran from behind his ear right down to the corner of his mouth. Then I reversed my swing and butt-stroked him, smashing the baton's pommel into his zygomatic arch (for those of you who haven't read *Gray's Anatomy* lately, the zygomatic arch is the thin bone at the outer corner of the eye, and let me tell you, it's a painful fucking place to get hit).

The blow sent him spinning to the ground—where, from the sound of it, I broke at least three of his ribs when I scuffed my perfectly spit-shined, steel-toed uniform shoe on his cheap jacket as I roundhouse kicked the stupid sonofa-bitch into next fucking week.

No time for any more follow-up, however, because TNT—that would be Thug Number Two—had decided that since I was being uncooperative, his assistance would henceforth be required. But like most inexperienced male-factors, he hadn't had a lot of background in the fine art of dealing with unwilling participants in street muggings. So, like his partner in crime, he, too, was now fumbling for his weapon—which, obvious greenhorn that he was, he'd stowed in the deep pocket of his own high-waisted, low-crotched baggy clown pants.

What was this, the fucking gang that couldn't draw straight? I caught him on the tip of his elbow with the baton. Oh, that brought a delightfully anguished expression to his face. Instinctively, he grabbed at the boo-boo. *Whap*—I hit him in the other elbow. He looked at me, his eyes fucking crossed in pain, and dropped to his knees. He looked up at me as if to say WTF?, but I was in no mood to give out answers during this particular little CQC seminar. So instead, I picked him up by the scruff of the neck and the necktie belt on his stone-washed baggies and ran him face first into the corrugated metal of the Dumpster. When I dropped him I saw that he'd lost all his front teeth. *C'est dommage, non?* Right—*non.* Let's just think of it as a Roguish form of attitude adjustment.

I rolled the now-inert TNT over, pulled his pockets inside out, and found a cheap, nickle-plated .25 caliber pistol. The other thug—also out cold and definitely in need of medical attention—had a Smith & Wesson 9mm semiauto. I unloaded both, tossed the rounds in the nearest Dumpster (a Rogue rule of thumb: unless you are in absolute extremis, never—*never*—use other folks' ammo), pocketed the pistols, then retraced my steps to the truck and stuck the 9mm Smith under the front seat.

Has something significant about the above incident occurred to you? It certainly did to me. What is it, you ask? Well, it occurred to me as I made my way back toward the restaurant that this was the first time in six fucking books I've had an altercation that hasn't been interrupted in some devious way by my old nemesis, Mister Murphy, or any of his goddam family. I mean, I didn't head-butt anybody wrong and knock myself out. I didn't smash my own hand into the wall. I didn't trip myself up, go *splat* in the mud, and ruin my clean, pressed uniform. What made all of the above bad news not good news was, one: TNO and TNT were such obvious fucking greenhorns; and, two: nobody, not Wonder, Nasty, or Boomerang; not Tosho, Avi Ben Gal, or Mick Owen; *nobody*—not even that fucking dweeb editor, who delights whenever I smash myself up—was around to watch as things went blankety-blankety-blank-blank-bleeper-blanking *flawlessly.*

I mean, I'd just creamed the shit out of those two in a goddam vacuum. Gentle reader, where oh where's the justice in this world?

That was all on the one hand. On the other hand, I have lately learned how to take "yes" for an answer. And lemme tell ya, a greenhorn sphincter can kill you just as easily as an experienced asshole. It's just a matter of luck and Mister Murphy.

Twelve minutes later—and just over half an hour behind schedule—I marched past the pair of white marble Shao-Li dogs guarding the entrance to the Hunan Number One restaurant. I pushed the door open and let my eyes grow accustomed to the darkness. I'd been coming to this big, anonymous place for more than a decade, and I was still unknown by the staff. I was just another happy, hungry Big Pink Ghost.

The red frocked wallpaper and mirrored back walls, 1950s lava lamps, and genuine imitation Naugahyde upholstery reminded me of the Chinese restaurants of my youth in North Jersey. But that's where the similarities ended. Hunan Number One's cooking was none of your oughie-gooey chopped-up suey, limp-as-a-dead-man's-dick lo-mein, or red dye number three glazed sweet-and-sour pseudo p-p-p-porky pig. Despite its name, Hunan Number One served only top-of-the-line Hong Kong-influenced Cantonese food. Like what? Well, there were your tiny, steamed pork spareribs in delicate black bean sauce. And shrimp wrapped in lotus leaves, then steamed with black beans and fresh ginger slivers. There were fresh clams in black bean sauce. Do you get the idea that they used a lot of black beans here? Well, you're right. But that wasn't the whole story. There was also real duck soup, complete with gelatinous duck feet for Republican political consultants to suck on. There was crispy chicken roasted in a salt shell. And broccoli stems steamed in salty oyster sauce. And camphor-and-tea–smoked roast duck. Like I said, top-of-the-line Cantonese food: simple, and delicious.

The restaurant was already half-filled with early lunch-timers. There was your smattering of Pentagon types in uniform. There were your Arlington pencil pushers from the consulting firms and Beltway bandit offices, and there were your Chinese families, sitting at the big round tables with the lazy Susan servers, out for some good home-style cooking.

Joanne was there already, looking the way a reproachful teacher regards a tardy student as I made my way toward the table. She was sitting off to the left in the rearmost booth, her back up against the back wall. It's hell when two operators have lunch or dinner and there's only one seat whose back is to the wall.

Well, the booth was plenty big for two. But since the back wall had a mirror that allowed me a good view of the room without being too obvious, I stood, hovering like a chopper in admin approach, while I decided where to sit. My behavior brought a knowing smile to her face. "Make you nervous to sit with your back to the window?"

"Bet your ass." I dropped onto the banquette opposite her. "Sorry I'm late—I got held up."

"But you left the office before I did."

"No, I mean I got *held up.*" I palmed the .25 caliber automatic, slipped it under the table between us, and dropped it on her lap.

She hadn't expected that. "What the—?"

"I told you, I got *held up.*"

Her eyes told me that I'd actually shocked the hell out of her. She laughed out loud, looked down to examine my memento, then slipped the little pistol into her jacket pocket and looked at me with an expression that registered somewhere between respect and incredulity. "Thanks for the souvenir, I guess."

"Not at all." I swiveled and beckoned the closest waiter. *"Fuwuyuan."* Waiter. He was hovering in a matter of seconds. I surveyed the bare table, then ordered a beer. *"Piju, quing,"* I said, asking for a beer and exhausting my conversational Chinese. I looked over at Jo Montgomery. "You want one, too?"

"I don't drink . . . alcohol," she said in a mock Transylvanian accent, pausing the same way Bela Lugosi paused in the movie *Dracula* when he was asked if he wanted a glass of wine.

She peered up at the waiter. *"Ch'ing wo yao beizi ching-cha?"*

"Sheh-sheh," the waiter nodded, obviously impressed, and bustled off.

"What was that all about?"

"I asked him for a cup of green tea, and he said, 'thank you.'"

I was impressed, too. "Where'd you learn your Chinese?"

"From my mother."

"Your *mother?*" Agent J. M. Montgomery looked like the archetypal gringo to me, complete with a soft, quasi-southern accent I couldn't place.

She read my quizzical expression. "My grandparents were missionaries. Momma was actually born in China, in Soochow. Nana and Pop—they were my grandparents—sent her back to live with her sister Odessa in North Carolina just before Pearl Harbor. Don't forget—the Japanese had invaded China long before they attacked us, and things got bad quickly. Momma was only eleven then, but of course she spoke fluent Mandarin. She'd had a Chinese *ama*—that's a kind of nurse—and she'd actually learned Chinese before she'd learned English."

"Did your grandparents make it back after war was declared?"

Her face clouded. "No, Nana and Pop were executed by the Japanese as spies in 1943. I really don't know how Momma made it through that without a lot of psychological damage. She still doesn't talk about it much. But she did survive. She's a strong woman, Dick, very, very strong. Anyway, sometime back then she developed the habit every night before she went to bed of speaking Chinese to herself. I guess it was a way of staying close to her parents. And also, she kept telling herself that one day, she'd go back—see where they'd lived, and where they'd died. So, every single night of her life, Momma has said her prayers in Mandarin. And then she recites something else she knew as a young girl, a phrase, a greeting, something. Over the years, she taught me a few words, too. Just a little bit." She paused long enough to crack an uneven smile. "Enough to get me in trouble."

"Did she ever go back—close the circle?"

"Actually, yes she did, ten years ago. And she took me." She grinned as she remembered. "I got my divorce—and my master's degree from Tufts—the same week. I had six weeks free before I joined State. Momma had made all the arrangements in secret. She really surprised the heck out of me. We were there for eighteen days."

"It must have been wonderful."

Joanne's gray eyes misted slightly. "It was better than wonderful. Because I saw China not as it was—which was gray, and dusty, and filled with people whose faces didn't reflect much happiness at all—but through her eyes. I saw China as it must have been when Momma lived there. She remembered so much, Dick, so many details about places, and the history of the country, and stories about the people she'd known. And all of a sudden I realized what she'd been doing all these years when she spoke her Mandarin every night. She'd been *remembering*. Forcing herself to hold on to things so she'd never ever forget them. Doing serious memory work." She paused and laughed at herself.

I didn't get it. "What's so funny?"

"'Memory work.' Momma's maiden name is Memory. Mary Fay Memory. The Memorys come from south-central North Carolina, south of Fayetteville, north of Laurinburg. That's where I grew up, in a log cabin in the middle of a big pine forest just outside a one-street, three-church town called Wagram."

She paused as the waiter set his tray down and placed a pot of tea and a cup in front of her, and a bottle of Xingtao beer and a water-stained glass in front of me.

When he'd finished, she said, *"Sheh-sheh."* Thank you.

I did the same, adding (in English, of course) that we'd wait to order. I poured my beer, inclined the glass in her direction, and said "Cheers."

She poured steaming tea for herself with a steady hand, lifted the cup, said *"Gombay,"* and drank. "Good tea." She set the cup down. "Okay, Dick, that's enough about me—now it's your turn. How the heck did someone whose French braid is as long as yours end up in General Crocker's SCIF, anyhow?"

We finished three pots of tea, a six-pack of Xingtao, and a baker's dozen plates of dim sum, the Chinese equivalent of Lebanese meze, Spanish *tapas,* or Italian antipasti, by the time we'd exchanged life stories. And I'd been right in my assessment: Jo Montgomery was an operator. Behind the master's degree from the prestigious Fletcher School of Law and Diplomacy, and the fluency in three languages, and the ten years of real-world experience, lay the soul of a Warrior. She was always looking for ways in which to improve her proficiency. Yes, she'd been to the State Department's management leadership seminar and had taken courses at the Foreign Service Institute. But she'd also been to shooting schools from Gunsite to John Shaw's Mid-South Academy. She'd taken classes at Heckler & Koch, and cross-trained with the FBI's Hostage Rescue Team. She'd learned tactical driving at Bill Scott Raceway in West Virginia and the Scotti School in Lakeland, Florida.

Which brought us to what she'd done in Rwanda. I asked a rhetorical question to which I already knew the answer: "What you did was more mental than physical, because you'd prepared yourself—war-gamed, right?"

She slapped her chopsticks onto the plate, reached across the table, and high-fived me. "You are only the second person in the whole world to have ever said that to me," she said. "And you're so darn right."

I wondered aloud who the other was.

"Tony Blauer. A Canadian martial arts instructor I met a couple of years ago when three of us from DSS got sent to his dojo in Montreal. We went to study Chu Fen Do."

You could see by her animation that she'd liked the course. She retrieved her chopsticks, snagged a "potsticker" dumpling, dipped it in salty hot chili sauce, popped it into her mouth, and tried to speak.

Except the hot sauce obviously got in the way because her face grew flushed, and I could see beads of perspiration form on her forehead.

She watched me watch her. "Hey, if you're not sweating, you're not eating, right, Dick?" Without letting me get a word in edgewise (or any other way) she swallowed a quick mouthful of tea to wash the potsticker and hot sauce down, then continued. "Tony's one of those instructors who preaches that technique can only get you so far, that it's attitude that makes the difference in the real world. We use him—so do a lot of law enforcement agencies. State likes what he does because he teaches mental exercise, psychological preparedness, as opposed to strictly physical combat stuff. Face it, Dick, my job isn't like yours. SEALs are supposed to break things and kill people. We're not. We're essentially defensive types. Our mission is to keep our folks alive."

"So what did he do?"

"He made us work hard at being constantly aware of our surroundings. I guess you could call it antenna-honing. He made us go out on the streets and play 'What If' games. What if those three no-goodniks over there attacked us? What if that car was going to scoop up your principal? What if you're on an elevator and a guy grabs you from behind? How would I defend? How would I react? How would I protect? In essence, what he did was teach us to war-game all the time. Real obvious, right? Keep it simple, stupid." She drained her tea and answered her own question. "Right, but there aren't a lot of people who teach like that. So anyway, there I was driving up the road to Bujumbura, and I was war-gaming the whole time. What if there's a roadblock . . . what if the driver freezes . . . what if they have RPGs . . . what if, what if, what if. When it all actually happened, I don't even remember thinking—I just *acted*. I'd done the mental stuff. The physical was easy."

She was right, of course. That's why I always insist on saturation training. By saturation, I mean You Do It until you don't have to think about it—it all just comes naturally. Shooting? You have to hit that three-by-five card b-bang—two shots—whether you are hung out or hung over, hyperventilating, or hypothermic. Chute fucks up and you're HAHOing at twenty-five thousand feet? You have to know what to do. If you guess at it, you're gonna be dead—which won't do Dickie any good on the mission.

Now, having just preached all of the above, let me make another important point. It is that you cannot just Do It and let it go. You have to spend as much time on the mental aspects of Warriordom as you do on the physical. Yes, shooting is a frangible physical skill, and the more you practice the better you will become. But remember what I explained to you a few pages back about visualizing the front sight picture before you shoot? That's the mental part. And you can spend almost as many hours working on it—concentrating, focusing, fixating on that visualization—as you do working on the range itself. When it all comes together, you will know exactly where that sight picture is going to be under any circumstances. In a dark stairwell, going over the rail of a ship, climbing an oil rig—or sight-acquire-firing as you go through thick smoke and your target is only a shadow among many shadows. But you know you will hit him, because you have, one: shot hundreds of thousands of rounds and, two, because you and the weapon have become one physical and mental entity. You become the ultimate weapon—and you cannot fail.

Then, having pretty much exhausted the life-story stuff, we lingered over a last duo of dim sum—spareribs baked in black bean sauce, and steamed broccoli stems stacked neatly as Tuscan cordwood in oyster sauce, and worked out our operational planning. She'd already pored over most of the materials I'd brought to the Chairman's office in the SCIF. She'd read through the reports carefully, committed the photographs to memory, and asked intelligent questions.

So when it came to an OPLAN, things were actually pretty KISS. Whenever I had something to report to the Chairman, I'd page Joanne. She'd call that number within two minutes, and we'd set a rendezvous. If she had to get hold of me, she'd call Rogue Manor and leave a message from Lucy Memory. I'd call her pager, and we'd repeat the process outlined above.

Yes, I know it wasn't very sophisticated. But simplicity is always the best way. Or, as Roy Henry Boehm, Lieutenant Commander, United States Navy and godfather of all SEALs, used to preach in his Zenlike fashion, "Look, asshole, a straight line is always more efficient than a maze when you're trying to get from point A to point B."

What the lieutenant commander means is that the more intricate things get, the more chance Mister Murphy has to insinuate himself into your operation—and the more chance there is that you will screw up. So we kept it simple, stupid, just like Roy would have wanted.

* * *

Our operational planning finished and our life stories told, it was time to go to work. I pulled my wallet out. Joanne already had a twenty in her hand to cover her share. I protested—after all, I make more than she does—but she insisted: we'd go Dutch, or we wouldn't go at all anymore. Sometimes you just have to take "yes" for an answer. I was about to wave a fist above my head to summon the *fuwuyuan* when I saw Joanne's whole body stiffen. I dropped my hand and looked up, into the tinted mirror.

It was like looking into one of those fun house distortions, because what I saw couldn't possibly be for real: a five-by-five in a generic, badly cut, and even worse-fitting gray pinstriped suit. What's a five-by-five you ask? A five-by-five is the SEAL technical term for an S_3FA—that's a short, shit-filled, slovenly, fat asshole. Anyway, this S_3FA was currently waddling into my field of vision, marching splayfoot up the aisle toward our booth. His baggy trousers, which he hitched once, twice, thrice, in the three yards of travel I could follow, cut a belted smile under a humongous belly. His blue button-down shirt was wrinkled, and either *it* was soiled or the mirror was. His tie—askew—was gravy and/or sneeze stained. You pick it. Around his neck was one of those long steel ID chains that look like lamp pulls. The chain looped down, like a monocle sash, and disappeared into the left side of his suit coat—probably buried in his shirt pocket. Clasped in the chubby fingers of his chubby left paw was a Nokia cell phone very much like the one filled with plastic explosive I'd recently used in Lebanon to disassemble a nasty, corrupt, immoral piece of work named Werner Lantos.

With a heavy wheeze the S_3FA dropped two banquettes away, literally inhaled all four glasses of water on the table, belched twice, then mopped his neck with a greasy handkerchief. It may have been thirty-six degrees on the street outside, but even in the Hunan's dirty mirror I could see the perspiration shine on the back of his head.

Then I saw what had made Jo Montgomery react so

strongly. Following the five-by-five and just coming into view in the mirror was a six-foot-plus, long-faced, thin-lipped Chinese man in a dark blue raglan-sleeved cashmere overcoat that came almost to his ankles. The garment's fluid drape and smooth, graceful sweep gave him the sinister look of a malevolent Mandarin as he made his entrance, gliding with the confident, catlike, spare moves of a seasoned point man. Watching him, you just knew that his footsteps would be silent as an apparition's.

As he drew closer I could make out nuances: thick black hair, combed straight back and slightly gray at the temples. Thin mustache. Under the coat he wore a band collar shirt, and his neck showed the kinds of muscling that betray constant and consistent PT. I picked out the details of his face. It was lined and cruel; his eyes were dark and penetrating. Of course Joanne would react—it hadn't been two hours since she'd stared at his picture to commit it to memory. It was Li Chimen.

Chapter

9

I OBSERVED, FASCINATED BY THE SHEER ATHLETIC SUPPLENESS OF the man, as Li effortlessly shrugged out of his coat, punctiliously folded it in half lengthwise, measured the seams and edges to ensure that everything was precise, then punched the armholes, so that the coat could be rolled over onto itself once again without leaving the faintest hint of a crease in the fabric. As he did so, even in the mirror, I could see something sticking out of the deep inside breast pocket of his coat—and the hair on the back of my neck stood up again, the way it always does when something is very, very wrong.

What I saw was the very, very top of a manila folder. But that wasn't what had made all my systems go to battle stations. What made the klaxon horn sound was the fact that even though the mirror was dirty, I could discern the corner of the top of the folder was tabbed in bright visibility orange. Whatever was in that folder was top secret material. And Li Chimen had no business with it.

Then everything disappeared from my line of sight as Li folded the coat crosswise, laid it carefully on the banquette next to him, lowered his body, and slid onto the seat. His face was obscured by the bulk of the S₃FA's broad shoulders and bull neck.

But not before he caught me looking at him.

Instinctively, I wrenched my eyes downward. Oh, fuck me. Oh, doom on Dickie. It's bad tradecraft to get caught peeking at the fucking opposition. It is worse tradecraft to get caught peeking at the fucking opposition and then to tell them, with a gesture so goddamn operatic in scale it could have been performed by Caruso at La Scala, that yes, you have been caught peeking.

Here is a real world lesson. If you are ever out on a surveillance, and the object of that surveillance happens, because of your stupidity or inattention, or simply because Mister Murphy is standing at your side, to catch your eye, do not, I repeat, DO NOT abruptly turn away, shift to avoid eye contact, or modify your behavior by ONE IOTA. You must not hedge, evade, dodge, shuffle, or sidestep in an obvious manner. Because if you do, your opponent will realize that you are attempting to keep tabs on him, your role will be compromised, and you will be out of the game.

Now, what should I have been doing? I should have been war-gaming the situation, not gawking at Li Chimen, mesmerized as it were, by his entrance. I should have been saying to myself, *Okay—if he looks at me, I'm going to maintain eye contact, then slowly, s-l-o-w-l-y, slide back to my conversation with the obviously attractive young woman with whom I am having lunch, so that Li will think that, like any normal folks, I glance up when I perceive activity in the mirror, then, satisfied everything's cool, I go back to my own fucking business.*

Jo looked at me, concerned. "What's up?"

What was up was my fucked. Oh, yes, even the Rogue Warrior fucks up from time to time. I kept my eyes on the table. "I'll tell you later—outside."

She started to react. I stopped her. "Don't, not yet."

Now she really was puzzled. I looked over at her. "Jo—what's happening over there?"

She looked up, innocently inquisitive, as if searching for the waiter (see, *she'd* been war-gaming even if I hadn't. I told you she thinks like a Warrior), but long enough to take a discrete glance over my shoulder and down the room. Then she focused back on me. "The fat guy's turning to look at you." She paused, raised her head a little—as if responding to something amusing I'd said. "Now he's turning back. Shaking his head."

I could hear the dialogue in my mind, playing out like a little movie.

Li Chimen leans forward. He's a pro, and his antennas are always up.
LI: Well, do you know him?
S₃FA: *(Turns. Looks.)* Nope—never seen him before. And believe me, I'd remember a French braid like that. Nice piece of ass he's with, though.

Hey, hey, hey, out there, don't get the wrong idea. That's the S₃FA talking, not me. And it wasn't that Joanne isn't attractive—she is. And under other circumstances, I might have done something about it. But we'd been assigned to work together, and let me give you the Warrior's most basic social code. It is that in a working relationship there can be no room for anything but work. If that tenet is broken, shit will happen, missions will be compromised, and all the juju will be bad.

Moreover, while my desire for pussy is second to no man's, I believe that any officer or noncom—man or woman—who takes advantage of a command situation to get laid is a traitor to the uniform he or she wears, and the tradition of Duty, Honor, and Country for which that uniform stands. No exceptions.

That's why I have always believed in absofuckinglute equal opportunity: do the job and I will like you and respect you. Do not, and I will fuck you over and transfer your ass as far away from my command as it is possible to do. That's how I want to be treated—and it's the way I have always treated those under my command.

Indeed, I'm am proud to say that *I* have always treated everyone alike—let's say this together, shall we—*just . . . like . . . shit.*

Okay, so much for my Roguish social mores. Let's get back to the situation at hand. By purest happenstance we'd been in the right place at the right time, and I'd caught a glimpse of something that I wasn't supposed to see. Maybe Mr. Murphy'd decided to come over to my side for once. Maybe he hated the Chinese. I didn't care. However things had come about, I was going to take advantage of them. That is part of Warriordom—being fluid enough to know when to take "yes" for an answer.

So—we'd been about to split. But there was no way I was going to do that now. I wanted a closer look at Li Chimen, and more to the point, I wanted to know who the S₃FA— the man who'd probably passed Li the top secret folder— was. Of course, I couldn't do both. Not unless they left together.

I looked down at the table surface again so that no one in the room could read my lips and only Joanne could hear what I was saying. "The Chinese guy has a TS doc on him," I mouthed quietly.

That was all I had to say. Jo nodded. "Got it," she said. "We'll stake 'em out."

Jo ordered us another round of tea and beer, we paid the waiter—it is bad tradecraft to get left behind because the opposition has paid its check and you're still waiting for yours—tipped him well, then sat and plotted.

Jo was parked closer than I was. She'd found a spot just down the street. I was at least three to four minutes away— and that was at a dead run. Certainly, I was far enough away to make pursuit impossible if we all left the Hunan at the same time. The answer, of course, was for us to leave as they were in the middle of their meal, then regroup outside.

And if their lunch came to an abrupt halt and they left before we'd had a chance to set up? Well, there is a SEAL technical term for that circumstance. It is: doom on us—we'd be fuckee-fuckeed.

We were too far away to hear Li's conversation. Which was just fine with me, because it meant they were too far away to listen to ours. Just after their entrées were served, Jo and I nodded at each other. She rose. I helped her into her coat—blocking the view so that no hint of pistol betrayed itself as her suit jacket parted—then let her precede me toward the front door. As she passed Li's table, she paused as if to reposition her handbag—*good war-gaming there, Jo*—which let me get a good look at him, and see what else besides food might be sitting on the table.

Li was older than he'd appeared in the mirror—in his mid-fifties, perhaps. But he was lithe and muscular in his expensive Italian suit of ministerial gray, set off by a well-tailored black silk band-necked shirt. He gave me a quick glance but no more, then went back to his conversation. Li spoke in an uncommonly deep voice; his tone was robust, the timbre unique. But no matter how singular his voice may have been, the gist of what he was saying was completely lost on me, because he and the S₃FA were speaking in lapid-fire Chinese. I mean full-tilt boogie Norinco belted 7.63-by-54 machine-gun ammo Chinese.

We pushed through the front door, kept moving until we were past any possible sightline, then stopped. I looked at Jo. "Catch anything?"

She shook her head. "Not really. He was speaking in a dialect I've never heard before."

"Nothing at all?"

She scratched the side of her head. "I mean, I got a couple of words—something, something, something, *quickly*. And then something, something, something *recovery*. Or it may not have been *recovery*, but something else. Fact is, Dick,

I'm not fluent the way Momma is, and don't forget—the Chinese she taught me is Chinese from the 1930s or even before that."

Such are the pitfalls of real life. Unlike all those pogue-Rogue TV movies, where your superheros stumble on the nugget that allows them to save the damsel, wax all the bad guys, save the world for democracy, and do it all in one sixty-minute hour (less sixteen minutes of commercial time), this was real life. And while I may have just laid eyes on the bad guy of our current little melodrama, I had no idea who his companion was, or WTF they were up to—except that secrets were being given away.

My first reaction was to call the Manor and call out the troops. That was impossible, of course—they were more than an hour out of town. So it would be just Jo and me. We set up in an alley that ran perpendicular to Hunan Number One's front door, about 150 yards north of the restaurant. Jo, in her green late-model Volvo with Maryland plates, faced east. I parked my pickup across the street opposite her car, facing west. She would take fat man. I'd follow Li Chimen. We could even stay in touch, as both of our vehicles were equipped with cellular phones that had the all-important hands-free feature. Were our comms secure? Absolutely not. But they were all we had. You generally don't go out to a get-acquainted lunch with secure comms.

We sat, engines idling, for another twenty-five minutes, phones connected. Why did we do that? Because Mr. Murphy was in the neighborhood, and I didn't want him screwing with the connection once we'd started our surveillance.

I could hear classical music playing in Jo's car. I had my radio turned off and spent the time thinking—war-gaming the hunt that was about to begin. Then, as is often the case, our solitude was interrupted by an uninvited guest: the ubiquitous Mister Murphy. (See—I told you he was close by.) First, Joanne's phone went dead. I knew it died because the music stopped. I looked across the street and gestured

WTF. She paid absolutely no attention to me. That was because she was too busy, all hunched over, trying to restart her car. And from the way she was moving I could tell that the Volvo was not responding. Which, of course, was the very instant that a humongous white Cadillac limousine with Washington, D.C., vanity plates that read WODE right-turned off Wilson Boulevard, pulled past the Hunan Number One, then K-turned, and glided to a smooth halt right in front of the pair of white marble Shao-Li dogs.

The right front door opened, and a tall, athletic kid in a double-breasted blue Armani suit that didn't quite hide the well-developed shoulder muscles and pecs pulled himself out, cell phone in his left hand, scanned the street once perfunctorily and, deciding that things were okeydoke, opened the rear right-hand door.

At which point, smooth as any Secret Service or DSS op, Li Chimen and our S_3FA emerged from the Hunan's front door and swept into the car. Kid Armani slammed the rear door closed, disappeared into the front seat, and the limo accelerated, cut across Wilson Boulevard, performed a quick and efficient left turn, and disappeared from view.

I pulled out of the alley into the street, tapping the horn and waving at Jo. I could see her lips moving, telling the car what she thought of it as she ran, handbag flapping, in my direction.

She hit the running board like a pro. I was moving at fifteen miles an hour or so by the time she pulled herself into the cab. "I swear," she said, breathing hard, "I'm going to take the meritorious service bonus that's sitting in my FARA credit union account, march straight to a car dealer, and put it down on a Mountaineer or an Explorer. I've had it with these damn foreign cars."

I recently told you about the quality of traffic flow in the greater Washington, D.C., metropolitan area. Just in case you were speed-reading and are fuzzy about what I said, "abysmal" may be one valid, though understated description. But for once, the sorry state of metrogridlock was working in my favor. I followed the limo's course—and discovered much to my delight that it was stuck in a construction zone traffic funnel just about opposite the Courthouse Metro stop. We were only three blocks behind our target. I cut across two traffic lanes, and threaded the needle between a cement truck and a police car. Indeed, one of the wonderful things about a full-size pickup truck is that you sit way above the other traffic and maneuvering becomes much, much easier, especially when one has, like I do, heavy ram bumpers fore and aft, as well as a huge trailer hitch that extends (just at radiator height on most cars) a full eighteen inches behind the thick stainless steel bumper. I glanced over at Joanne. "And now, *voilà*—the back door."

I right-turned onto a side street, then immediately swung left into the wide, empty alley that paralleled the street I'd been on.

At the next intersection I peered left. Traffic was still not moving. So I ran another block in the alley, then left-turned, waited out the Honda ahead of me, then slowly right-turned back onto Wilson.

"Cool moves, Dick." Jo backhanded my shoulder hard enough to leave an impression. "Can I use your phone?"

"Sure."

She picked it up. Squinted. "Is is analog or digital?"

"Digital."

"Good. Mine's analog and anybody can listen in." She punched in a number and pressed the "send" key, waited, then said, "It's Joanne. I need you to check a DC plate for me. Yes, District. A vanity plate: Whiskey, Oscar, Delta, Echo."

We sat in silence as she waited, the receiver pressed to her ear. Then she said, "Thanks. Yeah I miss you, too."

I looked over at her. "Old friend?"

"We worked on Secretary Baker's detail together. He's a terrific guy. Reliable." She smiled. "He runs our training division now. Best of all he has access to the Virginia State Police computer. That car"—she indicated the white limo we now sat half a dozen vehicles behind—"belongs to one Bentley Brendel, Incorporated."

"The five-by-five?" He sure didn't look like any former diplomat or world-class lobbyist. When Alixe Joseph had described what he did and how effective he was, I thought he'd be one of those tall, smooth operators—the kind of 40-longs whose photographs always appear in society magazines with the daughters of venture capitalists on their arms. Well, you've seen this guy—he looks like a fucking fat toad, doesn't he? I mean, we're talking Jabba the Cunt in a bad-fitting suit.

Of course, I've been in the trade long enough to know not to judge by appearances. It's what you do, not what you look like, that is important to me. And what old Bentley had done was to pass a verboten folder to a Chinese intelligence agent. So far as I was concerned, that was enough to justify my tacking his scalp to my lodgepole.

I checked our position. We were far enough away to escape their attention, but close enough to make sure that both our targets were outlined behind the tinted privacy glass. I squinted. They were both present and accounted for. All we had to do now was shadow 'em.

Which didn't present me with much of a problem. I am speaking here, incidentally, in the automotive, not the surveillative, sense. Once clear of the one-lane construction zone, the Caddie proceeded down Wilson, cut right, and swung onto the parkway, cruised onto the Roosevelt Bridge, then meandered up onto E Street and worked its way north on Seventeenth. No problems there. The snag occurred when the limo pulled to the curb outside the Old Executive Office Building just below G Street, Bentley Brendel got out, and discretely patted the left side of his suit coat. Let me halt the action here long enough to tell you a fact of real life and tradecraft. It is that no matter how well we are schooled in the black arts, we often slip up by being human. Watch men as they come out of restaurant booths—they'll pat their wallets to make sure they've not dropped them. Well, here, Bentley was simply doing the same thing. He wanted to make sure he had his little package. So he tapped the folder, folks, giving himself (and me) a sure sign that it was there. The S_3FA pulled *his* bulk through the door, wheelied and waddled south, head lowered against the chill wind, walking quickly along the tall, nineteenth-century wrought iron pickets that guard the Old Executive Office Building. Half a minute later, Li Chimen emerged from the limo and headed north, slouching toward Pennsylvania Avenue.

One can not simply abandon one's vehicle on Seventeenth Street directly outside the Old Executive Office Building. The United States Secret Service Uniform Division, which is tasked with providing security to the OEOB, which is how it's known to us Washington insiders, is shall we say . . . sensitive about such things as car bombs, and hence tends to frown on abandoned vehicles parked anywhere near the OEOB. I use the word *frown* here ironically, because anything that gets abandoned outside the OEOB is generally T&B'd by the Secret Service.

What's T&B'd, you ask? T & B stands for towed away & blowed to the well-known smithereens. Furthermore, I couldn't flash the lights, hit the horn, cut across the oncoming traffic, and park in that no-parking zone I'd spotted on G where the worst they could do was give me a $200 ticket, because flashing of lights and honking of horn make a Roguish spectacle, thus attracting attention to *moi,* which would not help my ongoing practice of professional surveillance tradecraft.

At least Jo could act. "I'll take Bentley," she said. She let the S_3FA pass us, moving in the opposite direction, checked his position in the rearview mirror, and satisfied he was safely past us, cracked the door open.

"Where do we link up?" she asked, one foot on the running board.

"The Hunan," I said. "Eighteen hundred hours. We'll get your car started."

I got an uneven, sheepish grin in return. "Y'know I forgot all about *that* little problem." She hovered on the running board. "Thanks." Then the door slammed shut and she was gone.

I turned my attention back to Li Chimen. He was almost at the corner now. I had a decision to make. If he crossed Pennsylvania Avenue, I'd be stuck way behind him. If he turned right or left he'd be out of sight in a matter of seconds.

There was a momentary pause on the oncoming traffic. I pulled the wheel left, gunned the truck, and cut through the single line of cars, pulled to the curb—wheels on the sidewalk, shut the ignition off, jumped out, flipped the alarm system on, and cantered back around the corner, searching for Li's blue cashmere coat.

It was nowhere to be seen. I dashed to the corner, wheeled, looked around.

I saw him a hundred yards away, gliding down Pennsylvania Avenue, moving parallel with the White House fence, directly across from Lafayette Park.

The light was red but to hell with the traffic. I cut across Seventeenth Street at a run, slowing down as I passed through the antiterrorism barriers that sit at each end of the White House's section of Penn. I jogged past the entrance to the Old Executive Office Building just in time to see Li disappear into the Secret Service gatehouse that sits astride the northwest gate of the White House, directly opposite Jackson Place.

I stopped and watched, my nose pressed to the wrought iron pickets like any twelve-year-old tourist's. Li walked inside the security checkpoint and was immediately passed through. Then he marched up the long, curved black macadam driveway that leads toward the West Wing— the offices that house the vice president, the national security adviser, and the White House chief of staff among others. He disappeared into a doorway of the one-story building that links the West Wing to the White House proper.

Whoa—a fucking Chinese spook gets admitted into

the West Wing of the White House? WTF was going on here?

WTF, I discovered when I met Jo Montgomery at 1800, was that Li Chimen had a press pass. That's right, our adversaries, if they represent a valid journalistic entity (and Li certainly did, as he was the duly accredited Washington bureau chief of Xinhua, the New China News Agency), can get themselves admitted to the White House much more easily than any loyal taxpaying American citizen can. In fact, during the Cold War, all sorts of KGB types meandered in and out on a regular basis because they were bona fide representatives of *Pravda, Izvestia,* Novosti Press Service, Gostelradio, and half a dozen other "official" Soviet news media.

Now, it seemed, Li was doing the same thing. Of course, the press is kept segregated at the White House. I learned that they are confined to the pressroom and cannot wander the halls unaccompanied to seek out sources and do random interviews. Even the fifty-foot trip to bill signing ceremonies in the Rose Garden are closely monitored by the Secret Service and the White House press-office staff. Moreover, since the place is swept for bugs daily, it is not likely that a listening device can be planted during a photo op in the Oval Office. So the fact that Li had a press pass wasn't troubling in the cosmic sense.

No, much more disturbing was the nasty fact Jo developed. Which was, that Bentley Brendel, the selfsame former State Department official and current lobbyist who has been writing all those op-ed pieces in the *Asian Wall Street Journal,* pushing his own brand of China policy, and—as you have seen—passing state secrets to a Chinese spy, also had a White House pass. More significant, so far as I was concerned, was that he held not a permanent pass, but a *T* pass. The *T* stands for *temporary.* It told me that Bentley had not undergone a security clearance to obtain it, even though that *T* pass obviously gave him access to NSC,

DOD, NSA, and other classified materials.[30] Equally disturbing was the fact that the lobbyist had been given a hideaway office on the second floor of the OEOB (that's the Old Executive Office Building, the old War Department building that sits inside the White House complex). I surmised he had a hideaway office not a public one because he wasn't listed in any of the building directories, and his name hadn't been provided to the White House telephone operators. I knew all of this because I'd checked—I called 202-456-1414, which is the White House's main switchboard number, and asked for Mister Bentley Brendel, please. Quoth the White House operator: "I am sorry, sir, but I can find no such person listed in the current telephone book, or any of my addenda."

I also learned that Bentley Brendel met regularly with the NSC adviser, and had access to NSC research on the Pacific Rim. Jo had developed that tidbit from a Secret Service agent she knew named Ty Weaver, a guy she'd first met at the Beltsville, Maryland, range used by both DS—the Department of State's Bureau of Diplomatic Security—and the Secret Service. Anyhow, she'd run into Agent Ty by the southwest gate, which is where she'd followed Brendel.

They caught up with each other and traded shop gossip, and it turned out that he—along with the rest of the Secret Service's PPD, or Presidential Protective Detail, was pissed

---

[30]You will remember that in the first Clinton administration, more than a hundred of the political appointees working at the White House held temporary passes for more than a year. That was because they had not complied with regulations that require all White House staffers to answer questions about their finances and background (including drug use) in order to obtain an FBI security clearance. Without it, they were denied permanent passes—even though they had access to classified materials. Why did that happen? Well, there were allegations of drug use as well as other . . . irregularities. If you're interested in learning more on the subject, you might try the book *Unlimited Access: An FBI Agent Inside the Clinton White House,* by former G-man Gary Aldrich.

off because "that fat little fuck," which is how Ty referred to Brendel as the S₃FA waddled toward the OEOB, had a *T* pass (which as I have noted means he hadn't gone through his security investigation, remember?).

"So?" Jo had asked, all innocence.

"So," she reported later, "Ty says that even though the pass is temporary, Brendel uses it to bring bunches of off-the-books, late-night visitors into the compound—even into the Oval Office—to demonstrate his access and his influence."

Now that *was* another nasty piece of news. But there was more. "One group was even speakin' freakin' Chinese," Ty'd told her. "They turned out to be military officers."

Jo asked him what happened.

"The detail that was on duty that particular night complained to the SAIC,[31] who went to Porkchop when they were one-on-one and raised a stink," Ty said, using the Secret Service's radio shorthand code for the president. "So the president said he'd check it out. Then, before you know it, Sunburn[32] is bitching at the Secret Service for getting in the middle of policy decisions. He raised holy hell, even showed up at West One[33] and threw a shit fit. He actually threatened to get the SAIC's ass canned.

"So the SAIC went back to Porkchop, and the friggin' president wimped out—whined that day-to-day China policy was Matt Thompson's department, not his. Told my boss that anything this Brendel guy wants, he gets, because that's the way Matt Thompson wants it—and Brendel's been of great service to the country. SAIC told us bottom line is we can't say a damn thing, even if we believe security is being

---

[31]Special Agent In Charge.

[32]All top White House staff have Secret Service radio code names. Sunburn is NSC adviser Matt Thompson's. The First Family's code names all begin with the same letter. These days, the president is code-named Porkchop, the first lady's handle is Pickle, and first daughter is Princess.

[33]West One, for West Wing One, is the Secret Service's White House command center.

compromised. I tell ya, Jo, the freakin' lobbyists own this damn White House and everybody in it."

Let me take the time for a small digression here. Yes, I know that you may think what I've just told you seems farfetched—i.e., that someone who is probably the paid agent of a foreign government has access to the White House, and to our national security secrets. Well, it has happened before—remember all those contacts with people representing all sorts of foreign interests during the 1996 presidential campaign? Some of those folks actually had government jobs and top secret clearances. Frightening, ain't it?

Okay. I told Jo to pass her infobits to Chairman Crocker, tell him about the orange-tabbed folder I'd caught a glimpse of, and for God's sake stay in touch with Ty. He was a valuable source, so far as I was concerned, a pair of eyes and ears right in the middle of things. I added that if we needed to contact each other she should call me as we'd prearranged. Meanwhile, I'd go to work.

The look on her face told me that she wanted in. But we both knew that was impossible. She was the cutout in this scheme, not one of the operators.

Chapter

10

Two quick points of information. First, the Pentagon's official definition of counterintelligence is: "any activity initiated, or information gathered, in order to prevent, block, obstruct, impede, or restrain any espionage, sabotage, or other intelligence collection efforts performed by (or on behalf of) foreign governments, organizations, or persons." Second, according to the NAVSOF—NAVy Special Operations Forces—doctrine under which I conduct my SEAL business, I am permitted to use deadly force while within CONUS (the CONtinental United States) *if*, when I employ said deadly force, it is, let me quote again: "To protect the security of nuclear weapons, and/or the security of other combat-system sensitive defense technology the loss of which would cause irreparable harm to the National Security of the United States."

Now that you've heard the highfalutin' twenty-dollar words, let me put the gist of the above paragraph in language that you and I can understand. I sat my guys down and told them the clock was ticking and we were after a traitor—and a spy. I added that we were operating in the black, and if we got caught, not only were our careers over, we'd probably be sent to prison. I added that if anyone wanted out because this op might place his whole career in jeopardy, it was okay with me. I don't mind putting my four stripes on the line when I believe the goal is worth it. But it's not my way to force anyone else to do it. I wanted only volunteers—and I'm happy to say that every single one of my merry marauders stepped forward and said, "Daddy, Daddy, please take me!"

The personnel issue decided, I told the men that things would probably get serious in the near term, and because of that, we would all start carrying weapons immediately. That, too, was a career-affecting decision. Navy personnel are not permitted to carry weapons whilst in CONUS except under extraordinary conditions, and then only when approved all the way up the chain of command. Well, since I seemed to be the entire and self-contained chain of command on this little stealth venture, I decided to approve all weapons requests—starting with *moi*.

There was, incidentally, substantial personal significance to this particular command decision, which is why I did not make it lightly. I am, you will remember, a convicted felon. Being such, I am forbidden to possess firearms. But I am also a sworn officer in the United States Navy, and in that official capacity, I can, and I often do, carry whatever kind of weaponry I may need to get the job done. Of course, trying to explain NAVSOF doctrine to some Washington, D.C., Metro cop—i.e., that I was a Navy officer on official duty—if said officer were to catch me dressed in civvies and with a locked, loaded, and suppressed submachine gun, in a city whose weapons laws are the most restrictive in the United States, would be, shall we say, a challenge.

When one is on assignments like this one, one do not carry a letter from the Chairman of the Joint Chiefs of Staff that says, more or less, "Dear Mister Police Officer, please let this nice Roguish fella do what he wants because he works for me." One be out on one's own—and if I got caught, it would be up to me to get myself off the old hook.

Despite a temper tantrum that would have done Maria Callas justice, Wonder would remain out of play for this entire little exercise. His job was to remain stuck at a desk (curled up in an overstuffed chair, actually), doing his homework. They give the chief's exam only once a year in these days of downsizing and forced early retirements, and in his specialty—machinist's mate—less than 8 percent of the candidates are selected. I wanted him to get a goddamn perfect score. If he didn't get one, he'd remain a first-class for another friggin' cycle, or be up-and-outed with no course of appeal.

Nasty Nicky Grundle was going to be out of action, too. His ankle hadn't just been sprained aboard the *Nantong Princess*—it was friggin' broken. The s.o.b. was going to be laid up for a month minimum. That left Gator, Half Pint Harris, Duck Foot Dewey, the Pick, Eddie "Nod" DiCarlo, and Boomerang available. To round out the squad—I like to work with even numbers because then everybody gets a swim buddy, and swim buddies are the two-man nucleus from which all UDT and SEAL activities derive—I made a call down to the amphibious base at Little Creek, where the playful party animal I call the Rodent was marking time at Special Boat Unit Two.

An hour later Rodent (real name Dave in case you keep track of these sorts of things) was heading toward Rogue Manor in his bright red Bronco at what the *PO*-lice usually refer to as a high effing rate of speed. It seemed that he had sixty days of unused annual leave time available, and a very accommodating CO named—well, maybe I'd better leave the CO out of it. There still are a few unit commanders who don't deserve the C²CO label, and I don't want to fuck up this one's career by saying a proper *merci beaucoup* and letting the world know whom he be.

I broke the troops up into two four-man teams. Half Pint and Pick, Gator and Duck Foot were assigned to Li Chimen. Li had gotten a good look at me and I didn't want to spook the spook—at least not yet. That left Rodent, Boomerang, Nod DiCarlo, and me to cover Bentley Brendel.

Boomerang, who owns a perfectly restored 1978 750-cc Hondamatic rice rocket,[34] volunteered for motorcycle duty. I accepted. Bikes are efficient in city traffic—remember all the trouble I had trying to park my pickup truck on Seventeenth Street? I did—because I now had a $200 ticket as a souvenir of *that* particular excursion.

I sent the guys out on a preliminary foray within hours after I got back to the Manor. I wanted a site survey of Bentley Brendel's offices, which were located in his home, a pair of renovated row houses just off the C&O canal in Georgetown. I wanted other site surveys on Li Chimen's residence—wherever it was—and his office, too.

Boomerang and Rodent sped off in the Rodent's Bronco. Half Pint and the Pick took my F-250, while I hit the computer, logged on to the Internet, and did some serious research on one Bentley Brendel. After six hours I grabbed a combat nap. Then it was back to work. There were a lot of hits about him, and I wanted to read them all. When I finished the public stuff, I accessed some other, more restricted materials. Those, too, proved interesting. You see, despite my Roguish, off-the-cuff wild-man, seat-of-pants hop & pop & shoot & loot persona, I am a very orderly person who does a lot of research before he goes into battle. Don't let the Rogue act fool ya.

By 0940 the next morning, my lethal Leprechauns were back, sipping strong coffee, and delivering the news.

The news, according to Boomerang, who, being senior man, had overseen the target assessments, was that Li Chimen lived by himself in a three-bedroom apartment in one of the high-rise condos near Ballston and worked out of

---

[34]That's biker shorthand for a fast, maneuverable motorcycle of Japanese manufacture. Yes, I know that on the one hand, the Hondamatic 750 weighs about 700 pounds and isn't the fastest, most maneuverable Jap bike on the road. On the other hand, you have never seen Boomerang ride. He handles the effing thing like a goddamn Kawasaki 500.

a Rosslyn, Virginia, office building located not four blocks from the Hunan Number One. That explained why he'd still had the top secret memo in his coat pocket when they'd arrived. He simply hadn't had enough time to read it all before he and Bentley went back to their respective offices.

The Xinhua bureau was a six-room suite with a steel door, cipher locks, and an electronic security system that relayed its signals straight to the Chinese Embassy on upper Connecticut Avenue. Xinhua had three identical BMW sedans parked in the secure garage, nine floors below the offices. The cars were watched by a staffer. The office, too, was manned twenty-four hours a day.

Boomerang's assessment was that we could crack Xinhua's bureau anytime we wanted. Cipher locks, after all, pose no real problems if you've had the right kind of training, which we have had. The problem would be getting in and out without killing whoever was inside.

Problem indeed. There are rules about these sorts of things. The FBI, which handles domestic counterintelligence, tends to frown on SEALs who shoot-and-loot in downtown Arlington, Virginia. I didn't think the Chairman would look kindly on it, either.

Boomerang continued his monologue. "An' I got some good news and some bad news on the five-by-five's place."

The good news, he reported, was that there are only so many ways of coming and going in Georgetown, which limits the target's access and egress to and from his base. In this particular case, our bull's-eye—Bentley—lived on Thomas Jefferson Street, a narrow, one-way northbound street that ran between K and M Streets. "That very selfsame fact," Boomerang said, "is also the bad news, Boss Dude."

Why was that bad news, you ask? Well, it is hard to remain anonymous very long in such confined areas. Oh, we could have used a surveillance van (if we'd actually had one). You've seen 'em on the cop TV shows with their darkened windows and video cameras, parked across from the target's house. And in real life, the FBI even used a stakeout RV to videotape the crooked congressmen they caught taking bribes when they pulled the ABSCAM sting back in the late 1970s.[35] But here's what: unless you're a congressman (most congressmen tend to have less brains than a pet rock), surveillance vans become obvious, especially to anyone with any intelligence background, after only a few days on-site. I mean, if you lived in a nice neighborhood, and suddenly a beat-up panel van started parking directly across from your house every day, wouldn't you get suspicious? Bentley Brendel certainly would, because he was a pro. And because he was a pro, watching him would be more than a chore—it would be real hard work.

Now, as you all know, I am not opposed to hard work. But the more I thought about a static surveillance the more I decided that it was a bad idea.

Why, you ask? Well, first of all there were the numbers. A static surveillance is terrific if you are the FBI, and you have a hundred counterintelligence agents, twenty-five assorted vehicles, plus a chopper or two or even a plane, as well as a bunch of other miscellaneous assets, like C^3—that's Command, Control, and Communications—vans, to put into play. I had four men, and my total assets consisted of three cars, my F-250, Rodent's Bronco, and a rice rocket. Full stop. End of story.

Now, let me state for the record that any four of my guys are equal to any hundred FBI agents, even the heroes of ABSCAM. But that's not the point. Point is, I suddenly realized that my job wasn't to *surveil* Bentley Brendel and Li Chimen—it was to *hock* their *choinik* as my Israeli friend

---

[35]The FBI targeted crooked congressmen with ABSCAM—for AraB SCAM—in 1978. They set up a bogus Saudi sheik in a town house on fashionable W Street Northwest, where they videotaped the congressmen who promised him their votes and influence in return for cash bribes—*baksheesh* in Arabic. Seven congressional *bakshitters* were convicted.

Avi Ben Gal might say, using an old Yiddish phrase that translates loosely to "rattle their teacup."

In other words, I was going to force Bentley and Li to commit themselves before they were ready. That is one of the key distinctions between conventional thinking and unconventional thinking. In conventional warfare, you tend to play out the chess game in the act/react mode.

Here, I was going to provoke my enemy into acting prematurely. And by doing so I would surely destroy him.

The key to this operation was Bentley Brendel. Why? Because he was the inside man, the one with access, influence, money, and clout. When I did my *hock*ing, he'd nudge Li's *choinik* for me—and I could make the two of 'em tumble and smash.

I was just working out how to do my rattling when the phone rang. Now what's the significance of that, you ask—phones ring all the friggin' time, right? Yeah, they do. But this one was the unlisted phone I keep all for myself. Nobody has the number, not Chairman Crocker, not even Stevie Wonder.

I let it ring half a dozen times, then plucked the receiver off the cradle. "Marcinko—"

"Captain Marcinko, this is the White House operator. Please hold for Admiral Prescott of the National Security Council."

Now, those of you who've been through this historical litany before may skip ahead to the italics below if you want. But you new guys, listen up, because as the old chiefs used to say, you will definitely see this material again. Okay, here's the backstory: Rear Admiral (Upper Half) Pinckney Prescott III has been the bane of my existence since I commanded SEAL Team Six and he was the commodore and grandee panjandrum of NAVSPECWARGRUTWO (NAVal SPECial WARfare GRoUp TWO). He's the asshole who once disapproved my request for extra boot laces for my men. Yes, I am serious. He thought they were an extravagance because we tied our boots with knots not bows and cut them off. I tried to explain to Pinky (these were the days when I actually took him seriously) that when you jump out of a plane at thirty-nine thousand feet your boots can separate from your feet if they are not knotted tightly. Pinky, who hates to jump from more than thirty-five hundred feet (and does it only to keep up his SEAL qualification so he can earn his precious hazardous duty pay for jumping), would have none of my argument.

That gives you a sample of the way he thinks. Now, as to his personal history, Pinky the Turd, as I like to call him, is the son and grandson of admirals. Pinky da foist was foisted on the Navy because, as a pseudoaristocrat from a Philadelphia Main Line family *sans* benefit of trust fund, he had to make a living. So they sent him to Annapolis. Little Pinky (that would be Pinky Deuce) followed in his daddy's black shoe steps twenty-five years later, and—as if to prove the Peter Principle once and for all—Pinky III, aka the Turd, Annapolis '72, brought up the rear. Luckily for the nation, Mrs. Pinky the Turd, the former Harriet Lickadick Suckacock of Blue Balls, Pennsylvania, was spayed some years back and hence has whelped no offspring. Anyway, somehow, after Annapolis, Pinky managed to survive BUD/S training and become a SEAL. Well, let's be honest. He wears the same Trident I do. But he's never been in combat. He's never led men from the front. He's never done anything in the military but fight paper wars, which makes him the epitome of the Can't Cunt officer—a lard-assed worthless pencil-dicked pus-nutted shit-for-brains turd-bucket staff puke. Am I making myself like clear yet? Good—then we can get back to the business at hand.

The fucking White House? The fucking National Security Council?

And then it fucking hit me. Pinky had crowed not three months ago that he was about to be appointed to a White House job. I'd dismissed his boast, written it off as hyperbole, which as you may know is also the name of one of the world's most famous Hollywood agents. But he'd been telling truth. Well, fuck me. (And *that*, friends, is precisely what he was about to try to do.)

He dropped the phone just as he came on the line—I could hear the receiver clattering all over the floor, and Pinky, all flustered, whining and bitching and moaning as he tried (and tried) to retrieve it.

Fact: it is hard to sound like an Important Person when you've just flubbed your entrance. But he tried. After all, Pinky is very trying. The only problem is that when P-P-Pinky gets flustered, he t-t-tends to stu-stu-stu-stutter.

"D-D-Dick," he said, sounding more like P-P-Porky fucking Pig than any naval officer ever should, "this is Pinky P-P-Prescott."

In response, I held my receiver out horizontally by its coiled cord and let it bounce onto the slate of my office floor like a fucking yo-yo. Even at that distance I could hear his howl of protest. I bounced it once again for good measure, caught it one-handed, brought it back to speaking position, and growled, "Sorry P-P-Pinky." I wasn't apologizing when I said that—I was simply describing him.

"G-G-Goddammit, Dick, I am an admiral. Don't mock me," the Turd brayed. I could just see him sitting behind his big desk, all pissed off. I do truly like it when Pinky is pissed off.

"Oh, I truly am so sorry, sir," I said, saying the last word slowly and distinctly so Pinky would know I was spelling it with a *c* and a *u*. Then I waited to see what the sonofabitch wanted. I wasn't about to give him any help at all, either.

"You will report to my office first thing in the morning," Pinky said imperiously. "You are causing grave and profound problems for this administration, and I plan to put the brakes to you right now."

Y'know, sometimes, when the fucking lightbulb goes off it can almost blind you. There was like this big flash in front of my eyes—all of a sudden I realized who the fuck had called Admiral Gray in Japan and ordered him to hit the McDonald's with a team that was unprepared.

Do you remember that Tosho told me that the assault had been ordered when Admiral Gray mentioned my name to the person calling from the White House. That remark, which I'd found puzzling at the time, now made perfect sense.

If I had been in the room with Pinky at that point I would have throttled him, consequences be damned. But I wasn't. All I could do was respond audibly, and so I fired a salvo that must have burned the hair off his fucking jug ears. I told him that, so far as I knew, he wasn't a blankety-blanking part of my blanking chain of command. I told him where he could fold his bleeper-blanking order and stuff it where the sun don't shine, *sans* benefit of K-fucking-Y jelly or any other unguentary blanking lubricant.

For some reason, Pinky didn't appreciate my response—not that it mattered one rusty F-word to me whether he did or he didn't. I heard him huff, and puff, and try to catch his breath so he could blow my house down. But as we all know, Pinky is more wuss than wolf. And, more to the point, he is a bully and a coward, and since he was in no position to bully me, he chickened out by kind of hiccoughing twice, stuttering something-something-something about something-something else (it all sounded so indistinct he might have actually put his hand over the mouthpiece to keep me from hearing).

Then he tried to hang up on me. But he dropped the fucking receiver again, which gave me the chance to Boehm him instead, by hanging up first. What's Boehming? Boehming is the present participle of the verb "to Boehm," a verb derived, as you can probably guess, from the last name of that sneaky, malevolent, lethal man o'warsman, Lieutenant Commander Roy Henry Boehm, USN (Ret.), the godfather of all SEALs. Boehming is when you go out and fuck some fucking fucker before the fucking fucker can go out and fuck you.

So, having Boehmed Pinky, I was feeling pretty good about the encounter for the next eight, or perhaps even nine minutes. That was when the other phone on my desk—the one whose number everyone knows—rang. I picked it up and got my own hirsute earful of Thomas Edward Crocker, General, United States Army, and Chairman of the Joint Chiefs of Staff.

"Dick, goddammit to hell—"

"General, you know what I like about you? It's the great sex. You always engage in so much foreplay before you start to fuck with me."

He had to laugh. Which stopped his verbal hyperventilation and calmed him down. But the unruffled gist he delivered was the same as the message he would have administered had he been Roto-Rootering my sphincter at warp speed.

He kept it simple, stupid and simple, declarative. Dick be nice. Do not kill Pinky. Go see him. Find out what he has to say. Keep me informed.

I began to object.

General Crocker was having no objections. "Dammit, Dick, think of it as recon," the Chairman interrupted. "I am juggling a bunch of balls right now and I need to know what's going on over there, because SECDEF and I have been shut out."

"But—"

"Don't give me 'but.' Remember what SEALs did back in Operation Desert Storm. Just before we committed to the attack, they went in quietly from the sea, reconned Kuwait City, and got the lay of the land. They didn't get to kill anybody or break anything. But we learned a hell of a lot from the information they brought out, information that saved a lot of lives. Sometimes you have to come and go and not let on what you're about."

Point taken. I am a merry marauder. I like to maraud, which is a little-used verb meaning to loot, pillage, burn, & plunder.[36] But my natural appetite for such activities must

---

[36]*Maraud*, in case you didn't know, is derived from the Middle French term *un maraud*, which means . . . a *rogue*. Incredible the way these things come together, ain't it?

sometimes take a backseat to the priorities of the mission. And the mission here was to bring back some HUMINT about what was going on inside the National Security Council; to see what damage had been done, and by whom.

"You're right," I said. Of course he was right. To rattle Bentley Brendel's teacup, I'd have to get myself inside the White House. That might have been a problem—until, that is, the Turd summoned me inside the gates.

The Chairman, obviously relieved, started giving me hints about what I should look for. But I wasn't listening. In fact, my mind was racing. Unconventional warfare means doing the unexpected—winning through surprise, and speed, and violence of action. Unconventional warfare means keeping the opposition off balance.

Well, although there was no way I'd tell General Crocker about it, I was about to go on the offensive. And I'd start by yanking on da Turd's leash and seeing where he led me. My instincts told me that the Turd would lead me directly to Bentley Brendel, and from there, it would be a short trip to Li Chimen.

Oops—there was silence on the line. Obviously, the Chairman had stopped talking.

That made it my turn. "I'll get the job done for you, sir," I said obliquely, telling the truth without divulging any of my own Roguish, UNODIR specifics.

"I'm glad to hear you see things my way," the Chairman said. "And Dick?"

"General?"

"Remember—it's the White House. No weapons."

Chapter

11

THERE IS SOMETHING SPECIAL ABOUT GOING TO THE WHITE HOUSE. I don't care who you are; I don't care how much of the world you have seen, or what you have experienced. Passing through those gates, walking or driving up that black macadam driveway and entering through the North Portico doors is something very, very extraordinary. It is equally as special to go through the tourist entrance opposite the Treasury Department, or come through one of the five appointments entrances for a meeting in the West Wing, Old Executive Office Building, East Wing, or residence. No wonder: the White House is a heady place—an icon that represents the United States as a nation.

It is a fact that presidents can awe even the most powerful folks in the nation simply by asking them over to the White House for a little tête-à-tête in the Oval Office, a friendly coffee in the basement library, or an overnight in the Lincoln Bedroom. In fact, this current president raised more than $10 million for his last campaign by doing just that.

But even the president's cynical attempts to turn the White House into a money-making bed-and-breakfast cannot dim the place's significance or its message. Sure, the commander in chief may be a schmuck, but sooner or later, said schmuck will be gone. The White House will remain. Why? Because Sixteen Hundred Pennsylvania Avenue is *America*'s house. More than the Capitol, or any other public building in the Washington area, it represents the very core, the hub, the nucleus, of our unique, American form of democracy. Within its heavily guarded, sensor-laden perimeter resides the spiritual energy of Washington and Adams, of Jefferson, and Lincoln, of Eisenhower, and Kennedy (the president who caused SEALs to be created by Roy Boehm back in 1961), and of Roosevelt and Reagan.

I defy you to pass onto the White House grounds without experiencing a huge, patriotic emotional rush. And I believe that holds true whether you are a tourist, a visiting head of state—or a SEAL captain like me, whose sense of Duty, Honor, and Country is stirred deeply whenever I am there.

It doesn't matter who the president is, either. It's the office that you respect—not the man. As First SEAL Roy Boehm told John F. Kennedy when the president summoned Roy to Blair House, "I didn't vote for you, sir—but I'd die for you."

At 0855 the next morning I presented two forms of identification at the very same southwest gate of the White House where Bentley Brendel had led Joanne not twenty-four hours ago—and got sent around the block for my troubles. Seems that these days the southwest gate is only for those august personages who are important enough to hold White House creds. The rest of us mortals have to use the basement entrance of the Old Executive Office Building, which is located on Seventeenth Street, to get to our appointments.

I didn't need the hassle. I'd been up most of the night.

There is a thirteen-hour time differential between Washington and Tokyo, and I'd been on the horn to Alixe Joseph and Tosho, getting intel dumped, sit-repped, and generally *se mettre au courant,* which is how they say brought up to speed in Paris. Since I didn't have any secure phones at the Manor, I'd used the Big Brother equipment. I can report to all you taxpayers out there that it works as well when it's connected to conventional phone lines as it does when you uplink to a satellite. This is one covert program you got your money's worth out of.

Anyhow, what I learned was disturbing. There had been an increase of clandestine Chinese activity all across the Pacific Rim in the past forty-eight hours. Specifically, there had been antigovernment riots in three Korean cities— twelve dead—a power outage in the Indonesian capital of Jakarta, and a general strike in Tokyo.

I already knew that Beijing had recently increased political pressure on Singapore, Indonesia, Japan, and Korea to join it in a pan-Asian trade, defense, and political organization that would be in effect a combination of the G-7 industrial countries and NATO. The Chinese foreign minister had not a month ago visited his counterparts in Tokyo, Jakarta, and Seoul. He'd been rebuffed. So now, they were striking back.

Alixe, who sounded uncharacteristically agitated and preoccupied, said that it was obvious to her that the Chinese weren't going to take *bu*—no—for an answer, and had ratcheted things up a couple of notches. Couple of notches, hell—they were beginning a campaign of covert operations designed to force things their way. "There has been a definite increase in the number of scrambled transmissions coming out of Beijing," Alixe told me. "Something bad is going on."

That comment made my internal warning light (it's the selfsame one that sits behind my pussy detector) go off. "Hold on." I ran for the digital camera, removed the disk, threw it into the computer, brought up the images I'd taken on the *Nantong Princess,* and scanned them into a file, which I then double-encrypted using DIA's basic shareware encryption program. Yes, I have it on all my computers. "I'm faxing you three pages, double encrypted."

"What're the keys?"

"First key are the first five letters of the first word and the last three letters of your two-word compartment. Second key is your favorite brand of shoe—you were wearing 'em when we met."

I heard her laugh heartily. "You're very observant, Dick."

Four minutes later, Alixe said, "I think I know those faces. Let me do some digging. I'll get back to you as soon as I've got something concrete."

Then I told her about Bentley Brendel's White House pass—and his access to classified material. I heard her gasp.

"That is truly disturbing news," she said, not telling me anything I didn't already know. "Look, Dick . . ." She hesitated, as if searching for the right words.

"What's up, Alixe?"

"We're secure, right?"

"Top of the line."

I could hear her take a deep breath. "In the last six hours, three of my best . . . ah, sources, have been eliminated."

Now I understood her unsettled tone. "Who were they? How did it happen?"

"That's not important. What's important is that they weren't connected. Three sources, three cells. They were operating independently of one another." She exhaled in a *whoosh.* "Remember when I told you there are no coincidences in our business?"

"Roger that."

"Well, there's a leak somewhere, Dick, and I can't do anything about it from here."

"I'll keep my eyes open," I said. "But it's way outside my AO."

"I know. But frankly, you're being out of the loop makes you someone I can talk to. You're not connected—perhaps *you* can see the pattern. Maybe I'm too close."

"I'll keep my eyes and ears open," I promised. "Meanwhile, you keep your head down. And call Tosho if you need protection."

The uniformed Secret Service officers behind the desk in the foyer scrutinized my military ID and Pentagon pass, looked me up and down twice, watched v-e-r-y closely as I walked through the metal detector—and when I failed the test, hand-searched me. I surrendered my collapsible baton and the short knife that most folks think is a belt buckle to an agent whose nameplate bore the moniker Moldea, took my receipt for the toys and my visitor's pass, ran the magnetic strip on the back of the pass through the electronic scanner, then proceeded down the narrow corridor toward the stairwell.

Yes, the OEOB has elevators. Good ones, too. But I always prefer to walk. Pinky's office was on the south side of the third floor, we SEALs do our PT wherever we find an opportunity, and walking up four flights of stairs seemed like an opportunity to me.

I—what *is* it? Sorry for the interruption, folks. It's the dweeb editor again, gloating because he says he's caught me in an inconsistency. Four flights of stairs. And Pinky's office is on the third floor. Yeah—but I walked into the basement entrance, remember? Seems to me that the editor had better start reading these manuscripts as closely as you-all do.

Okay. I chugged up the stairs. At the third floor I turned left, then right, walked down a long, marble-floored corridor lined with piles of cardboard Port-A-Files. I saw to my horror that many of them were marked CONFIDENTIAL, or SECRET.

I have spent most of my career doing work that is classified—and most of that work will remain undescribed, because to tell you anything about it would compromise what I did and how I did it. I may be called a Rogue, but lemme tell you, I have a healthy respect for secrets—and I know how to keep 'em. Moreover, I do not like to see secrets splashed all over the front pages of the newspapers.

Yes, I realize that journalists argue that the public has a right to know, and under that right-to-know rubric they often compromise our national security, damage our ability to conduct intelligence and military operations, and impair our relations with our allies. Furthermore, I defy any journalist to show me where in the Constitution, the Founding Fathers talked about the public's *right* to know. Oh, we have a First Amendment, which guarantees freedom of expression. But freedom of expression does not constitute a "right to know." Face it: there is no *right* to know. Now, I do feel that the press has a responsibility to report, educate, and enlighten, so that the electorate can make informed decisions on national policy.

But this business of spilling secrets has caused people I know to die unnecessarily, and operations I have been a part of either to be called off, or fail. So I do not like the wholesale spilling of secrets. Thus, when I see crates of documents marked SECRET sitting unprotected in corridors, stored in Port-A-Files, not document safes, I get worried. It tells me that, so far as the current administration is concerned, protecting secrets is not a priority. Of course, if the current administration was interested in protecting secrets, it wouldn't allow any lobbyists to hold *T* credentials and bring military officers from a potential adversary nation into the White House complex after hours. Thus endeth the sermon.

I threaded my way south, into a third corridor, which, I noted, was being scanned by a series of TV cameras mounted just below the high, ornate ceiling. The doors in this passageway, antique, heavily oiled wood six-paneled doors with ornate brass knobs, each bore the legend ENTER THROUGH 385 on cardboard signs mounted alongside the doorjambs. Below was another strip of cardboard on which sat an arrow, pointing in the direction in which I was proceeding. I marched another ten yards until I saw "385" printed on the cardboard, wheeled left, and turned the knob.

I walked inside a small, narrow office crammed with filing cabinets and document safes. Two old wood desks holding desktop computer terminals sat one opposite the other in the center of the room. The desks looked like they belonged to grad students in the final throes of dissertation writing: each was piled high with miscellaneous memoranda, news clips, books, maps, and other research materials. Power cords and telephone lines ran haphazardly across the threadbare wall-to-wall carpet. A dusty laser printer, wired through a three-position data transfer box, sat atop a two-drawer document safe.

I closed the door behind me. The office was empty except for a late-middle-aged woman behind the rearmost desk, a desk so neat and orderly that it looked out of place in the chaos that surrounded it. She was half-standing so she could see me over the piles of files, miscellaneous boxes, not to mention her own humongous computer screen. She waved at me. "Captain Marcinko?"

I nodded.

She worked her way around the maze of office stuff and took a couple of steps in my direction, her hand extended. "Come on back and wait with me until Admiral Prescott's ready for you. I'm Avenir Reynolds—his assistant."

I extended my own hand. "Nice to meet you Ms. Reynolds."

"Avenir—Avenir, please."

"Sure." I slalomed over the paper berm and desks piled high with bureaucratic detritus toward her desk. I stopped as I caught sight of the aged, creaky-looking straight-back wood chair that sat dead center in front of her schoolmarm's desk. It was so decrepit that it would probably buckle under my weight. "If it's all right with you, I'll stand."

"He might be a while."

"It's okay—I don't mind standing." Of course he'd be a while. Keeping me waiting was SOP for Pinky. He thinks it gets me on edge; knocks me off my timing. But all it really does is give me more of a chance to Boehm him.

Avenir straightened her perfect bun, took a close look at her creaky chair, then looked back at me with a bemused, quasi-motherly expression. "Why not sit at *his* desk and have a nice hot cup of coffee while you're waiting."

Sit at his desk? That meant he wasn't around. Would I like to sit at (read rummage through) Pinky's desk without him in attendance? Hey—does the pope speak fifty-seven languages?

"Why, that would be just terrific," I said, a huge, playfully Roguish smile spreading across my face.

"Good," Avenir said. "This way." She started toward me.

I headed toward the door to my left—the one that led to all the adjoining offices—so she could take me to Pinky's office suite. Instead, she stopped halfway down the narrow office, in front of one of the pair of scarred, timeworn oak bureaucrat's desks. "Here we are," she said, smiling with a civil servant's professional bemusement at the incredulous expression on my face. "Yes, *this* is Admiral Prescott's desk."

As I've just said, the desk was piled high with papers, newspaper clips, photocopies, and messages. A brown paper bag, carelessly torn open, served as a place mat for a half-eaten bagel half schmeared with cream cheese. Next to the bagel that bore Pinky's capped tooth marks was a teacup filled with coffee so dark it looked solid. A circa 1982, four-line push button telephone sat to the left of the teacup, just in front of the fourteen-inch computer screen with the Navy SEALs screen saver going full speed. Pinky's dirty-lensed half-glasses sat carelessly dropped on the smudgy keyboard.

Now, you are probably asking yourselves WTF right now. I mean, Pinky is an admiral, and admirals, one would assume, always get classy quarters in which to work.

You are correct in your assumption. In most places a two-star anything would get a big office and a great view. But then, this was the White House, and the perk of just being able to say where you were calling from when you make phone calls or give out your address is the equivalent of a Pentagon fourth-floor, E-ring office suite, with a view of the river and the Jefferson Memorial, which is precisely what Pinky had given up when he came to work over here.

Avenir pointed to a straight-back oak chair that looked even creakier than her own, stood back, and crossed her arms like a nanny. "Just make yourself comfortable." Now, I wasn't about to rifle Pinky's desk under Avenir's watchful gaze, and almost demurred the sitting bit once again. But when I looked between the bagel and the coffee, southeast of the keyboard and northwest of the two-week-old *Time* magazine, and I saw precisely what was on Pinky's desk, I double-clutched, threw myself into gear, and changed my mind about the chair—and the coffee. All of a sudden I wanted to get as close to that desk as I could.

Fifteen seconds later I was perched precariously in the straight-back chair, exchanging pleasantries and making small talk with Avenir as she produced a delicate bone china teacup and saucer from the neat and orderly credenza that sat behind her neat and orderly old desk, and poured me a healthy dose of overcooked black stuff from a coffee maker so old it must have been bought during the Johnson administration. The Andrew Johnson administration.

From the way she bustled around, smiling coquettishly and burbling, I could see my company made her happy. Pinky probably treated her like a nonperson—sat all day in the same room and never spoke to her except to bray an order, or bitch about a mistake. He tends to act like that with secretaries, assistants, and other low-ranking facto-tums who don't wear as much gold on their sleeves as he does.

And so, while I sat there, my legs primly crossed at the ankles, chatting with Avenir Reynolds about the weather, and the Navy, and what being a SEAL was all about, I was taking copious mental notes on what I saw on Pinky's desk. From the messy look of things, and the number of requests he'd been tasked to fill, Pinky had been working his scrawny behind off lately.

And most of what he was doing was in the classified area. He'd left a trio of thin orange-tabbed document folders sitting on his desk, fanned out like king-size playing cards. The way the labels were written indicated they'd been sent over from DIA. The code words Weather Gable printed across the orange tabs told me that inside were copies of Alixe Joseph's raw HUMINT reports, printed out on what I call TS/SCI paper.[37] That set off a nasty bunch of bells and whistles. I looked closely at the middle one, which had a crease down its center, betraying the fact that it had been folded then smoothed out. *That* little piggy had been to market.

A yellow Post-It with a line-drawing cartoon of a computer wonk attached to the top folder read: "Pinky, pls get these three rpts back ASAP. My ass is going to be shredded if the boss finds they're gone." The note was initialed "H." I'd find out who the hell H was, because this was exactly the kind of leakage that can (and, in fact, had just) ended with some of Alixe Joseph's agents being eliminated by a bunch of UNPs—unknown nasty parties. Now, I knew how the leakage had occurred. Pinky had given the folder to Bentley. Bentley had passed it to Li Chimen, who'd read it, and handed it back. But Li'd folded it and stuck it in his pocket so he could finish reading it after lunch.

Here is a real-world lesson, folk: careless use of intelligence materials gets people killed. It's happened before. When the Israelis distributed the raw intel reports from

---

[37]TS/SCI paper, as it's come to be known, is specially formulated so that if it is put in a Xerox or other brand of photocopier, it will not duplicate. It was put into use shortly after the American spy and traitor Jonathan Pollard allowed one of his Israeli control officers to duplicate 360 cubic feet of TS/SCI documents on a copier. Don't ask me how TS/SCI paper works—I don't know. All I know is that it *does* work.

their paid spy, Jonathan Pollard, some of the documents found their way into the hands of the KGB, the old Soviet intelligence apparatus. By carefully analyzing where the raw data had come from, the Sovs were able to track down the sources we had used to collect our intelligence. They neutralized—murdered—those sources, and our intel flow dried up.

Alixe Joseph was working under embassy cover. That may have given her diplomatic protection. But she still wasn't bulletproof. And her field agents—the Japanese, Chinese, Malay, Filipino, or other FNs working in her networks—obviously *they* weren't bulletproof, either.

Pinky had compromised them merely by showing these Weather Gable files to Bentley Brendel. And Bentley? He had signed the agents' death sentences by showing the files—at least one of 'em, maybe all—to Li Chimen.

I was so angry—furious with Pinky for being so fucking stupid, and with Bentley Brendel for being such a fucking traitor—that I had a hard time keeping myself under control. But maintaining control, friends, is what being a Warrior is all about. And so I channeled my anger, transmogrifying it into energy, and determination, and willpower—and I kept my eyes moving.

From reading the contents of the most accessible of the half-dozen or so White House memoranda (all tabbed top secret and each one addressed "TO: RADM P. Prescott III, FROM: BB"), I surmised that Pinky's most recent assignment had been to check out any possible incident that might have taken place recently in the South China Sea, which involved the United States Navy.

How did I surmise that? Because this is how the MIQ (which stands for Memo In Question, and pronounced MEEK) began:

Pinky—Imperative you track all USN movements over the past fourteen days in two quadrants. The first is bordered by 105 and 110 degrees East Longitude, and 0 and 5 degrees South Latitude; the second is 122 to 124 degrees East Longitude, and 24 and 26 degrees North Latitude, and get results to me soonest.

I'm counting on you to deliver the goods, just like always. Go get 'em, tiger!

I had no idea what Pinky had been looking for in the second area of operations—the one just north of the Tropic of Cancer. But I knew the first one all too well. It is the quadrant that includes the Belitung Straits, which is where my very own SEAL Force Alpha had begun its infiltration route that resulted in the scuttling of the *Nantong Princess*. The sonofabitch was trying to track *me*—except he didn't know that critical infobit.

So, how had Pinky gone about it? Well, from da Turdlike chicken scratches on his note pad and the scrawled telephone numbers and area codes I could make out, he'd done it by calling every one of his Annapolis schoolmates stationed at PACFLT—PACific FLeet—and CINCPACFLT in Hawaii, and asking if they'd picked up any RUMINT about clandestine or covert activities in the South China Sea AO. He hadn't found out anything—and I am pleased to report that he is too stupid about these things to have bothered to check with any other military commands— like, for example, the Air Force—specifically, the Special Operations Command's 353rd Special Operations Group, First SpecOps Squadron, based at Kadena Air Base, Okinawa.

But he had of course used an open line when he'd called his pals—it said so on his phone log sheet. Which meant that every fucking Chinese, Japanese, Russian, Korean, and Australian intel squirrel with access to COMINT, SIGINT, or TECHINT[38] had listened to Pinky's request for information, and started their own snooping.

---

[38]COMmunications INTelligence, SIGnals INTelligence, and TECHnical INTelligence.

Obviously, Pinky's pals had produced for him, although they'd come up dry. There were half a dozen blue-tabbed (Confidential) transmissions from CINCPACFLT headquarters on his desk. I scrunched the chair closer, smiled over at Avenir, kept talking, and began to read as much as I could:

No USN activities currently reported in any of the specified AOs.

read one.

No OPLAN in effect for the specified AO during the time frame outlined.

read the second.

SUBOPS reports USS *Scorpion,* operating outside specified AO, retrieved NAVSOC[39] unit commanded by Captain Richard (NMN) Marcinko, after unspecified training mission.

read the one just below it. I'd have loved to see the fourth, but I'd of had to shuffle the pages around, and I wasn't about to alert Avenir to my activities by being overt. The Chairman had wanted me to supply him with HUMINT about what was going on here at the NSC. And HUMINT he would get: the NSC, it seemed, was trying to spy on the Navy.

Okay—I see you out there. You're asking how I could do all that reading when the pages on the desk were upside down. Well, bub, reading upside down may be a rapidly disappearing art, but it is nonetheless a capability that is important to industrial spies, intelligence officers, journalists, and other assorted snoops—including *moi.*

But I didn't learn it in spy school, or at some black-arts seminar. I was taught how to read upside down and

---

[39]NAVal Special Operations Component forces.

backward some years ago by an old-time newspaper typeset-
ter and proofreader named Neil Shine, who was in charge of
printing up the St. Ladislaus of Hungary newsletter at my
parish back in New Brunswick, New Joyzey, when he wasn't
setting type for a couple of dozen other publications in the
storefront print shop he ran in the neighborhood. See—in
the days before computers, they set type in hot lead on Rube
Goldberg machines called Linotypes. You read your page
proofs in trays of solid lead letters that were cast by the
Linotype, then set into rows of lead print. The words were
set upside down and backward, so that when the molds
formed from them were rolled through the press, everything
came out right side up.

Anyway, as a teenager, I worked for Neil Shine for a
while—I delivered packages, cleaned up the used lead,
helped him remelt it so it could be cast again, and—ulti-
mately—helped him proofread copy. It took him some
time, but he managed to inculcate me in the mysteries of
reading upside down and backward closely enough to catch
typos, misspellings, and punctuation gaffes on the trays of
type that lay haphazardly all over the place. It is another
instance of learning something that you think has no
significance as a kid, only to find that in your later life, it
pays off—and pays off well.

Now I can go into an office and sit, talking to you, and all
the while, be reading and committing to memory every
fucking memo you have on your desk. It is an art that has
saved my Slovak butt more than once. And now, perusing as
I sipped my overcooked java, pinky extended from the
undersize china cup's handle like a fucking society dame, I
realized WTF: having been tasked with checking incidents
in the South China Sea, and knowing that I had been in the
neighborhood, Pinky had set about finding out WTF I had
been doing in the same area he'd been tasked to research.

From what I could make out, he wasn't having much luck.
They'd even tracked down the *Scorpion*'s CO—a radiogram
from Captain Dave Brancato routed through the SUBOPS
message center at Pearl Harbor reported where he'd picked

me up. But, Dave's message continued, he had no idea where I'd come from, or what I'd been doing, except sitting out of gas and bobbing like a cork for half an hour. That, and we were so foul smelling that they'd had to hose us off before they took us below.

God bless the Chairman for insisting that we exfil as far as possible from where we sank the *Nantong Princess*. We'd been worried about the Chinese—but his planning had saved us from Pinky.

There was a message from CINCPACFLT which confirmed that he had put out a search for me when my presence had been requested by the head of the Japanese National Police's counterterrorism unit.

Marcinko was located through office of CJCS. The request was routed through CNO. There was no prior contact by Pearl [Harbor] and his reasons for being in the AO described above are unknown.

CINCPACFLT added that his command had dispatched a chopper to retrieve me at such-and-such a position, and a plane to pick me up in Singapore and take me to Tokyo. End of story. And there was an E-mail from Admiral Gray, the base commander at Yokosuka, stating that he had no idea where I'd arrived from—that, in fact, I had not even had the courtesy to check in with him and report my presence on his hallowed territory.

Finally, a curt note from General Crocker's J-2 (Intelligence Staff) admin officer stated that Captain Richard NMN Marcinko had been temporarily assigned to the Intelligence Staff of the Office of the Chairman and that his duties were nobody's fucking business but the Chairman's, so piss off.

Basically, Pinky was drawing a blank so far as I was concerned. That was the good news. The bad news was contained in the smoothed-out but still obvious vertical crease on that Weather Gable folder. The first thing I'd have to do as soon as I got out of here was call Alixe Joseph and tell her that she—and her nets—had been blown to the opposition. No wonder she was losing people. Damn—she'd have to make arrangements to shut everything down quickly, before Li's people rolled them all up—if they hadn't already been.

My planning was interrupted by the intercom on Avenir's desk. It was Pinky, braying, "We are ready for Captain Marcinko now," and she could show me down. The look that flashed on Avenir's face as she listened to him caterwaul betrayed what she really thought of her boss. But she smiled professionally, rose, smoothed her dress from the lap out, in the way that matronly women of a certain generation so often do, then beckoned for me to follow her.

She led me back into the hallway. We marched back to the stairwell, went down one flight, turned left at the landing, then a quick right, and walked down a long, spotless corridor. Avenir stopped in front of a beautiful, well-preserved rock maple paneled door that must have been installed when the OEOB was known as the War Department. There was no sign adjacent to the doorjamb. Avenir reached under the collar of her blouse, retrieved a single key on a long steel chain, slid the chain over her head, put the key in the lock and turned it until the door opened, then dropped the chain and key back over her head.

She opened the door for me then stood back and indicated that I should go inside. "Please, go right on in, Captain," she said, the slightest tinge of loathing in her voice. "They don't like to be kept waiting."

I did as she requested. She gently closed the door behind me from the hallway side. I heard her footfalls tap-tap-tap decrescendo, fading into the distance.

So, this was to be a solo appearance. Well, that was fine with me—you know how I like the limelight, especially when I am filled with rage. I paused and looked around. I was in a small foyer that had an ornate plaster ceiling twelve feet in height. A nineteenth-century oil painting of the *Bonne Homme Richard* sat on the right-hand wall, mounted over a Chippendale side table; a huge photographic vista of the Washington region was hung opposite the oil. Next to the door towered an old-fashioned coat stand and umbrella rack. The rug on the floor was Aubusson, and antique. I'll tell you what: the effing secretary of the navy doesn't have as nice a foyer outside her office.

Straight ahead sat a pair of ornately carved wood doors that must have been nine feet high. I examined the frames. The big hinge pins indicated that the door opened outward, that is to say, in my direction. I took one doorknob with each hand and quietly tested 'em, rotating the doorknobs. They both worked just fine.

I took a deep breath, preparing my body, my mind, and my soul for deadly combat, exactly the same way I would if I'd been about to jump blind into hostile territory from thirty thousand feet. I was about to begin Show Time—and a flawless, deadly performance here was just as important as it had been aboard the *Nantong Princess*.

But here, I didn't need any cues written in Chinese characters on the hirsute palms of my hands. I didn't need suppressed weapons or assault knives strapped to my CQC vest. My anger at what was being done to the Nation was my motivation, and I'd brought the most deadly offensive weapon I know to this encounter—*moi*.

And, no—I didn't plan to take any prisoners here, either.

I twisted the polished handles, waited for the latches to clear, then swung the big doors outward toward me.

(*Enter the Rogue, upstage center.*)

I froze in the doorway for effect—and to focus on the threat. That was a mistake: I was almost overcome by the view. I looked, transfixed, across the huge, ornately furnished office, behind the antique leather-topped mahogany partners desk, to the five eight-foot-high-by-three-feet-wide windows, beyond which the North Portico of White House and its grounds lay in well-manicured splendor. To my left was an Empire-style sofa, covered in red, green, and blue vertical striped upholstery. The sofa was flanked by two leather club chairs, and the grouping was completed by a Queen Anne coffee table. Arrayed behind the desk were the flags of the United States of America, and the deep blue, gold-fringed standard bearing the presidential seal. Some hideaway office, huh?

I refocused my attention. Pinky the Turd was sitting at attention in the club chair facing the windows, twisted around like a corkscrew, looking wonderfully, delightfully (to me, at least) ill at ease. Behind him, sitting regally at the partner's desk, wedged tightly—even uncomfortably—in the high-backed, Supergrade, black leather and mahogany judge's chair because of his girth, was the S₃FA, aka Mister Five-by-Five, aka Bentley Brendel. He recognized me and my French braid at once from the Hunan Number One. His eyes went wide, then as quickly as he could counterreact, he fought back his emotions and neutralized his expression. But not before I saw what he'd done. Yeah—I'd caught him in bad tradecraft just the way Li Chimen had caught me.

And his attempt to conceal passed me the same sort of unintentional message I'd given Li. You see, there was no reason for him to hide the fact that, by happenstance, we'd run across each other in a restaurant. Except, of course, if he had something to hide. Like, for example, the folder he'd passed to Li Chimen.

His response noted and filed away, I finished my scan. Standing to my right and just behind Bentley's chair was the same baby-faced security boy who'd picked him up at the Hunan Number One yesterday. Kid Armani was wearing another seventeen-hundred-dollar suit—this one an Oxford gray with pinstripes. His White House pass had a big *V* on it—which told me he wasn't a Fed, but a rent-a-cop. That meant he wasn't packing heat—or any other weapons, either, because (being a visitor) he'd had to go through the same metal detectors I had. That information, too, was noted and filed.

So much for the tableau bit. Time to go to work—after all, lives were at stake. I stepped through the doors, swinging them closed as I did so, and peered over toward Pinky.

I am pleased to report that he looked dreadful. Since Pinky never works out, his uniforms have always hung loose on his wimpy, skimpy frame. At the White House, the uniform of the day is civvies. And as bad as Pinky looks in uniform, he looks worse in a suit. First of all, the sonofabitch is cheap, so he tends to buy his clothes at Filene's, or at one of those rubber-stamp factory outlet stores that line Interstate 95 between Washington and the North Carolina border. Second, since Pinky seldom wears civvies, his suits don't fit very well either.

As the Turd scrambled to his feet, I saw that he was even more badly attired than usual. He may have been wearing the sort of blue pinstripes favored by NSC staffers, but since the cheap suit was more polyester than wool, it hung on him like a goddam plastic shower curtain. You could actually see where the trousers hanger had left rude indentations in the cuffs of his pants. The jacket sleeves were so long they hung way beyond his hairless knuckles. There was a full half inch of air between his off-off-white shirt collar and the skin of his scrawny neck. His tie looked like a reject from one of the gauntlet of pushcart vendors on Connecticut Avenue who sell the clip-ons favored by bartenders and off-duty Metro cops. Believe me, it wasn't a very pretty picture—something that brought newfound joy to my Roguish heart.

Oh, and there was more: his hair, which tends to cowlick when he's tense, was standing straight up in a full Dagwood. A second cowlick, on the far right side of his head, protruded obliquely, as if he'd stuck his finger in an electric socket. That told me he was under severe stress. And from the awkward, stilted, downright uncomfortable look of things, all the stress was being administered by Bentley Brendel himself.

The fat man leveraged himself out of the big chair and came around the huge desk, waddling in my direction, his huge thighs chafing, his left hand rubbing the sparse hair on his balding head as he moved. He was working in his shirtsleeves—a well-worn white Oxford button-down shirt to be precise. He wore the same gravy-stained tie he'd sported at Hunan Number One. His light gray pinstriped trousers, which had been cut to give him four or five inches of spare room at the waist, whose baggy cuffs hung three inches above the shoelaces on his well-worn, down-at-the-heels brown cap-toes, were held up by a pair of cheap red elastic clip-on suspenders.

The whole combination resulted in a bizarre, absurd, even ludicrously cartoonish Homer Simpson look. In fact, compared to Bentley Brendel, Pinky the Turd's sorry sartorial résumé looked like Beau fucking Brummel's.

But I'll tell you what: this Bentley had the silver-cloud voice of a fucking Rolls-Royce salesman. It was a voice you just knew made *money;* the same come-and-get-it-while-you-can timbre as fucking game show announcers, auction house shills, or fly-by-night tent preachers. "Bentley Brendel, special consultant to the president for National Security Affairs and Diplomacy," he oozed.

Then his demeanor—and the timbre of his voice—changed. The smoothness disappeared, replaced by nasty, ugly, aggressive reverberations. "And it disturbs me that I've been hearing an awful lot of troubling things about *you,* lately, *Dick,"* he snorted, extending his trotter vaguely in my direction.

Chapter

12

HE CAME TOWARD ME MOVING QUICKLY FOR A MAN OF HIS
weight. No way was I going to let him take the offensive. I
closed the distance between us and took his hand in a
firm—and by that I mean *f-i-r-m*—read viselike—grip. His
eyes betrayed the considerable pain I was causing him, but
otherwise he covered himself pretty well. Since I wasn't
especially glad to meet him, I said, "Dick Marcinko—I've
read some of your op-ed pieces and I disagree with 'em."
Then I let go.

Kid Armani stood, his arms crossed like a fucking statue,
missing the whole thing. I glanced over at Pinky. He knew
me—and what I'm capable of. From the look on his face I
thought he was going to piss on himself.

Brendel snatched his wounded hand away, turned, and
scooted back to his desk, where he dropped into his high-
backed chair and peered imperiously at me. "Take a seat,
Dick," he said, his voice completely drained of any pretext
of courtesy. "Admiral Prescott and I have a series of
questions for you that will have to be answered."

Oh, did he indeed? "Thanks, but I'll stand, *Bent*ley."

Now, you're probably asking why I started our relationship off the way I did, instead of playing along, then sandbagging him later. Two reasons. The first is because I didn't have any goddam time to waste—I wanted to get back to the Manor and alert Alixe Joseph about the leak to Li. Second, it would have done me no good at all to delay the inevitable. Not tactically; not strategically—and not plot-wise, either. Remember, I was here to rattle his teacup, not look good.

Besides, tadpole, always remember the words of that great Chinese tactician General T'ai Li'ang, who wrote in 374 B.C., *"Always treat the enemy as if he is the enemy, because the enemy will invariably treat you that way."*

Makes sense, doesn't it. Take this current situation. Bentley Brendel knows exactly who I am—or at least he thinks he does. He's already talked to Pinky about me. And if he is as good as I think he is, he's realized that Pinky is a schmuck, and he's done some outside research as well. Which means he already knows that I don't much care for guys like him.

So to ensure that I, not he, controlled the situation, I proceeded by following the Rogue's way of doing business—dominating the situation from the get-go. The pain I'd just caused him defined our relationship—which was antagonistic. It told him that *Ich versucht den Lebensnerv zu treffen*—which is how I go for the jugular in Deutschland.

General Li'ang doesn't make sense to me, Master Marcinkosan. What about Sun Tzu? Sun Tzu wrote that deception is the key to victory. And General Li Chung, the eighth-century war master who told his disciples, "Feint left, move right; feint right, move left. Hint advance, then maneuver rearward; hint retreat—then advance and decimate."

What's your point, tadpole? Sun Tzu doesn't dismiss direct action—*if* the timing is right. Neither does Li Chung. Besides, General Li'ang isn't ruling out deception as a course of action—he is simply telling you that you should always treat an enemy like an enemy, whether you deceive him or not. And besides, in this particular case, as I've just explained, deception wouldn't help at all.

Why? Because I'd studied this guy. Despite the slovenly appearance, he was a diplomat—and an effective one, judging from everything I'd read. And what did that mean? If experience was any teacher (and it is a great teacher, believe me), it meant that he was a talented negotiator. And diplomats have found that when you are negotiating, you are not taking action—*versucht den Lebensnerv zu treffen*—you're responding to the latest set of positions.

But I wasn't here to negotiate. I was here to make him act precipitously—to go against everything he had ever been taught and learned during his long diplomatic career. To do that, I had to stun the sonofabitch—rock him harder than he'd ever been rocked before. And I wasn't going to do it by playing nicey-nicey. So I put my war face on. It was time to do battle with this fat fuck and roll him like an ugly dumpling.

Brendel looked over at me. "As you will, *Dick.*" He gestured somewhere in Pinky's general direction, as if to cue him. "Admiral Prescott . . ."

Pinky cleared his throat. I could see his Adam's apple bobbing up and down. "There's a p-problem," he began cautiously.

"Well, t-tell me about it—maybe I can help," I said, his obvious discomfort making me smile.

Pinky's face flushed. "D-Dammit, Dick, don't *do* that." He fought to regain whatever composure he thought he might have had. "Look, Dick," he began, struggling to keep his stutter under control, "we are currently in the midst of some very delicate negotiations with the C-C-Chinese, and—"

Brendel's short pudgy fingers slapped the surface of his desk. "This administration's dealings with the Chinese, whatever they may be, are not within Captain Marcinko's purview, Admiral." The fat man glared in my direction. "There have been some disturbing military-originated developments in the past few weeks; developments that are not in America's interest." Brendel turned to face me directly. "I know that you work directly for the Chairman of the Joint Chiefs of Staff," he said. "And in that capacity, you must know that the Chairman has opposed the administration's China policy whenever and wherever he has had the opportunity to do so."

I said nothing.

Brendel's tone sharpened. "The Chairman is wrong. He may be a good soldier, but he is no politician. And it is politics, not military science, that must govern our relationship with China."

Now, my friends, I knew, and you should, too, that this S_3FA is JPW—just plain wrong. Without a tough military policy, potential adversaries like China will run roughshod over us. Remember Colonel Art "Bull" Simon's advice about nationhood. But I wasn't about to say anything—yet. I was still here to learn what this broad-beamed butt-fuck was all about.

Bentley's silver tones rolled on. As they did, something on the credenza behind the S_3FA caught my eye. It was an ornately designed antique silver-hinged double-picture frame. On one side, sat the full-frame image of Major General Zhu Linfan—Li Chimen's boss. It was warmly inscribed *To Bentley Brendel, who has done so much to bring our nations together*. On the other side, sat a sheet of velum. Printed on its ivory surface in elaborate calligraphy, were the following lines:

> All warfare is deception.
> So when strong, display weakness;
> When weak, feign strength.
> If your target is nearby,
> Make it appear to be distant.
> Only thus will you achieve your objectives.

I knew those lines. They were from Sun Tzu's seminal book on strategy, *The Art of War*—and they were the same words of advice I had taken to heart many times over the course of my career.

I shifted my focus back to the five-by-five. "That is why," Brendel was saying, his voice growing louder and more insistent, "we want to know where you have been, and what you have been doing on the Chairman's behalf."

"Now, why would you want to know that?" I asked rhetorically.

"That is not for you to know," he answered imperiously. "This administration does not answer to the military—it is the other way around."

"Do you speak for the administration?"

He smiled self-contentedly. "I do."

It was time for the old Rogue wake-up call. My eyes locked on the S_3FA's. "I'd like to see you produce that in writing, you fat fuck."

Guess who blinked—and it wasn't me. "I do not have to show you anything," Bentley Brendel finally said, his teeth clenched.

"Oh, it's not that you won't show me anything—it's that you *can't* show me anything." I pointed toward the walls of the S_3FA's office. "You know what's not hanging here?" I asked rhetorically. Bentley Brendel gave me a blank look. So did Pinky.

"There is no fucking presidential commission on the wall," I said, directing my comment to Pinky, watching his eyes grow wide.

Now, it is a fact that each and every assistant and special assistant to the president has on his/her/its wall a large sheet of velum, on which, in fancy calligraphy, is printed said appointee's presidential commission. That's the document that makes the appointee official.

But Bentley didn't have a presidential commission. All he had was his fucking fancy art, and his impressive collection of photographs, and the goddamn quote from Sun Tzu.

I jerked my thumb toward the wall. "Bentley," I said, "you don't fucking have a piece of paper. You're here, but you're off the books." I paused. "You don't even have a fucking security clearance."

Now that remark surprised the hell out of Pinky. Because Pinky da Turd, *le grand zero*[40] that he is, knows how the system works. Pinky understands there must always be a piece of paper to show exactly where one fits within the chain of command. Pinky knows that *sans* a security clearance, there can be no access to sensitive materials. Indeed, if anyone understands the concepts of chain of command, and written, stamped, and approved security clearances, to the bureaucratic cross of a *t* and the pen-pushing dot of an *i*, it is Pinckney Prescott III, Rear Admiral (Upper Half), United States Navy, staff officer, bureaucrat, and professional apparatchik.

"A word to the wise, Pinky," I said. "If this special consultant can't produce a current TS/SCI, I wouldn't be showing him anything more than the daily newspaper clips—because if it gets out that you've been sharing DOD's operational secrets with him—and believe me, Pinky, I'm gonna look into that matter very, very closely—I don't see any promotions in your future."

Judging from the panicked look and white pallor on Pinky's face, I'd just put him between ye olde rock and ye olde harde place. Not my problem. He'd fucked things up. Now it was payback time.

From the comic book, my-top-is-about-to-blow look that was roiling across Bentley Brendel's kisser, I'd knocked that motherfucker back a pace or two, too. Time for another jolt.

I tossed my thumb in Brendel's direction. "Hey, Pinky, guess who he had lunch with yesterday." I didn't wait for an answer. "The top Chinese spook here in Washington. Name: Li Chimen. Rep: nasty. Maybe you should go back to your office and check out the name with your pals at DIA."

Pinky peered over at me with a blank expression on his

---

[40]That's how they say zee beeg asshole in *française*.

face. I guess I hadn't been clear enough, or specific enough, or maybe I was talking too fast. Whatever the case, he wasn't picking up his cues. Well—I'd get back to him in a minute. I looked over at Brendel. "You clear your meeting with Li with Buzzard's Point,[41] *Bent*ley?"

I didn't wait for the S₃FA to respond. "And, by the way, what was in the orange-tab folder you gave Li?"

Brendel looked at me with murder in his eyes. "I gave him no such thing," he said evenly.

Itsy-bitsy problem here, folks. First, I'd seen the evidence—the folder in Li's pocket, and the creased folder on Pinky's desk. Second, no matter how controlled his tone or modulated his voice, his eyes—murder look and all—gave him away. Recent psychological experiments at two universities and the National Institute of Health here in Washington have proved that micromomentary shifts in eye focus—that's a fancy way of saying REMs, or rapid eye movements—often indicate mendacity. Let me put that in SEAL technical language: liars are prone to being shifty-eyed assholes. And this asshole was definitely shifty-eyed. He was giving off lots of REMs as his pupils darted quickly side to side, and up and down.

Since I was in an EEO frame of mind—which means as you know that I will treat everyone just like shit—I looked back toward Pinky and let him have a second salvo, too: a barrage that would get his scrawny behind out of the office so I could have a few words in private with this corrupt, overweight asshole.

I faced Pinky and spoke slowly. "If I were you I'd go back to your office and start checking documents," I said. "See whether or not one of those orange-tab folders—the very one you gave old Bentley here yesterday morning—is creased. Because that's what I saw in Li Chimen's pocket." I

---

[41]Buzzard's Point is the location of the FBI's Washington Field Office and the headquarters for all FBI counterintelligence activities in the nation's capital.

watched as every fucking bit of color drained from the Turd's face. "Pinky, I think you have been passing TS/SCI information to someone who doesn't have a clearance— something that might make your pal over at DIA, Mister H, awfully nervous."

"Holy c-c-c-cow," Pinky stuttered. One thing about the Turd is that you don't have to tell him something bad twice *if* you are speaking slowly, and *if* your lips are moving distinctly, and *if* his whole fucking career is on the line.

The Turd lurched to his feet, wrenched himself toward the double doors with all the grace of a Krameresque pirouette, struggled with the knobs until he finally got the doors open, and careened out of Brendel's office, a panicked, primal squeal coming from deep in his throat.

I walked to the doors and closed them. That left Bentley, Kid Armani, and me. So far as I was concerned, it was about to be serious *choinik-hocking* time.

I crossed back to the desk, put my palms on the smooth leather, taking just enough time to read the number on his private line and commit it to memory, and leaned toward Brendel. "You're dirty," I said.

Brendel flicked a finger in my direction. Kid Armani came around the big chair toward me, his iron-pumping arms coming up into play. I didn't wait—my right arm snapped out and I caught the youngster in a viselike grip, my right thumb and forefinger crushing his throat and larynx, my arm lifting him half an inch off the floor. *Surprise*, asshole—don't fuck with SEALs.

I drew him close. His eyes were bugging. His face was turning blue. "Sonny," I stage-whispered, "it is time for you to take a hike." I squeezed just a tad tighter. "Got that?"

His head moved up/down, up/down.

"Good." I released my grip just in time to see Bentley reaching for the phone. I swatted his pudgy hand away and pulled the receiver cord out. The S₃FA started to protest. I reached across the desk and smacked him across the face. "You're garbage," I said as he howled in protest.

He put a fat hand up to his cheek. "You'll pay for that."

He pushed his big chair backward to stay beyond my reach. I started to move toward him when I sensed something behind me.

It was Kid Armani, trying to get back into it. He'd heard me, but he just hadn't listened. I tell ya—kids these days, they just don't listen. I feinted left with my eyes—his eyes followed. I jigged right with my body—his body followed. That's when I caught him *slam* with a sucker punch that lifted him six inches off the floor. He came down in a heap and didn't move.

I turned back to Bentley. "Worse, you're a liar." I came around the desk, crowded him up against the window and hit him again, across the face, half a dozen times. Not hard enough to hurt him—but more than hard enough to provoke him. Go ahead—check your psychology books: you will see that folks like Bentley dislike physicality of most any sort—especially when they are the ones getting pummeled.

"This is how I deal with liars, Bentley," I said as I struck him. He tried to wriggle free, but he couldn't because I'd trapped his legs between my own. He struggled, but he couldn't do a fucking thing—I towered above him, slapping his face at will with both my open palms.

Finally, I stopped. I scowled down at him. He cringed and hid behind his hands. I saw fresh circles of sweat as he ducked behind raised arms to ward me off in case I resumed my assault. I stepped back and sat on the edge of his desk.

"This is Chairman Crocker's doing," he wheezed. "You work for him—I know that. He is trying to scuttle our China policy. He sent you here." Brendel looked up at me with undisguised hatred. "I will see both of you in hell for what you've done," he said.

I returned the gaze. "Chairman Crocker didn't send me, *Bent*ley. I came here on my own. But I'm more than willing to bet that you get sent to hell a long time before we do."

I rose, turned my back, and moved upstage, stepping deliberately over Kid Armani's inert form, walking slow as a fucking bullfighter who's just scored a clean kill. I gave

Bentley my back as I strode toward the double doors. I opened them, then turned slowly toward the seething lobbyist. "You'd better get a lot more careful, *Bent*ley," I said as I eased the doors of his hideaway closed, "because I know you're a fucking traitor and I'm gonna be watching you very, very closely. Until, that is, I decide to kill you."

Now that I have a moment as I'm making my way back to Pinky's office, let me explain what has just happened. Many years ago, when Roy Boehm, the godfather of all SEALs, was in Vietnam, he was forbidden by the can't-cunt four-striper to whom he ostensibly reported to engage the enemy in battle. "You are here to advise, and to train, and to observe," he was told. "So advise, train, and observe—but under no circumstances are you to engage the enemy."

If you believe that Roy would ever pass up an opportunity to engage the enemy, I have some oceanfront property to sell you. It is located on the beach just outside Mesa, Arizona.

So, how did Roy solve his problem? He simply took his advisees so far out into the boondocks that they ended up way behind Viet Cong lines. Then he arrayed them up in an ambush position. Then he had one of his men make enough noise to attract the enemy's attention. At which point the VC attacked, giving Roy the opportunity to strike back hard and kill 'em. Moreover, when he got back to headquarters, he could truthfully report that while, yes, he had engaged the enemy, he had done so only because his men had been "overrun" by Mister Victor Charlie, and they'd had to fight their way out.

Well, I was about to use the same tactic here. But first, I had Pinky da Turd to deal with.

Pinky was down on his hands and knees as I came through the door of his office, his ass wriggling like a dog's as he searched frantically for something on the frayed rug under his desk. Avenir was nowhere to be seen.

"Lose something, Pinky?"

221

He reacted to the sound of my voice, and startled, jumped up and cracked his head on the desk hard enough to send him back onto the floor.

He came back up cautiously, his eyes wide. His mouth was a mask of fear. His voice crescendoed into a panicked moan. *"Dick—I didn't know.* I didn't know. He's the one I've been reporting to. He has a big office. The NSC adviser's always calling him—*I didn't know."*

The sorry fact of the matter is that he probably didn't know. Pinky is not an evil man—evil in the sense that he would betray his country. Unprincipled? Sure. Machiavellian? Of course. Unscrupulous? You bet. Scheming and manipulative? *Bien sur.* But not in the traitorous way. All Pinky ever thinks about is getting himself another star. That's probably what got him into trouble in the first place. Bentley had played da Turd for the fool he is. He'd probably been too busy kissing Bentley Brendel's huge ass to check the guy out.

But I wasn't about to let him off the hook. "Who the fuck is 'H'?"

"Who?" Pinky pulled himself to his feet and dropped into the chair behind his desk.

"Mister *H*—the asshole who sent you these." I tapped the Weather Gable files with my index finger.

"I can't tell you, Dick—he'd absolutely kill me. It was done as a personal favor."

I advanced on the desk, put both hands on it, and leaned into Pinky's quivering face. "You'd better worry more about me killing you than him," I said. "You've already compromised a lot of work—not to mention a whole bunch of lives—and if you don't get with the goddamn program and help me with the motherfucking damage control, I'm gonna disassemble you piece by fucking piece."

He looked up at me and saw I was deadly serious. Then he buried his face in his hands and gave up the name. Just as I'd thought, it was one of his fucking Annapolis mafia. Don't they learn anything there besides how to cheat on tests, assault female middies, and deal drugs?

Sure—they're taught it's all right to leak the nation's secrets—under certain conditions. Condition One is to make sure the person to whom you're leaking is a fellow member of the Naval Academy ring-knocker's club. There is no Condition Two.

I stood over Pinky like an impatient headmaster while he laboriously typed out a memo to the file, spilling his guts, single-spaced, onto a thick page of White House memorandum velum. Yes—that's *typed*. I had him use a typewriter because I didn't want to leave any electronic fingerprints where Bentley Brendel—or anyone else—could get their hands on 'em. It took him three tries—and too much fucking time—to get the words just the way I wanted 'em composed. I shredded the drafts. Then I photocopied the finished page and had him sign and date each copy. Then I slipped them both into my suitcoat pocket.

The sight of his career disappearing into my 46 long really panicked him. "But what about *me*," Pinky whined.

I looked down at the sorry sonofabitch for whom I wasn't sorry at all. " 'What about you?' *Fuck* you, Pinky. You're dog meat."

Chapter

13

IT WAS SNOWING LIGHTLY WHEN I GOT BACK TO THE MANOR, just after 1300 hours. There was a message from Alixe Joseph to check my computer for an encrypted file. "I hope the information helps," her voice told me. "Use the same numbers that you gave me, Dick. Talk to you soon. Sayonara."

I turned the machine on, decrypted the file, and read. First, Alixe had identified the pictures I'd sent her. Seems that I'd killed two of Beijing's top electronic warfare specialists—a pair of one-star generals, both American educated. I scratched behind my beard. What the hell they'd been doing on the *Nantong Princess* I had no idea. I read on. The situation, Alixe wrote, was getting hotter in Japan, Korea, Indonesia, Singapore, and the Philippines. *"Dick—if I had to bet, I'd say all these areas are feints to keep us off balance."*

Her point of view made sense to me—remember if you will the Sun Tzu quote in Bentley's office. In fact, so far as the Chinese are concerned, deception is a central element of warfare. General Chun Li is the tactician who wrote three books of verse about deception more than two thousand years ago. Sun Tzu's earliest (and mostly forgotten) work, *The First Principle of Victory,* is a short polemic on the subject of deceit.

I assembled the troops and put us on a war footing. I called the Chairman's office to give Jo a sit-rep to pass on. It wasn't all going to be good news, either. On the one hand, the memo I'd wrung out of Pinky gave us the leverage we'd need to take my findings to SECDEF—and, I hoped, get Bentley Brendel's big, broad, bad butt tossed out of the White House and straight into a Justice Department investigation. On the other hand, everything was still pretty circumstantial, and I had the unpleasant intuition that SECDEF wasn't going to act on it until we'd made our case airtight.

Whatever I believed was moot: the Chairman was out of town for the afternoon, giving at West Point what the morning papers had described as "a major policy address about America's military readiness." I asked to be patched through. But the factotum who answered the phone in the Chairman's office refused. I wasn't on General Crocker's list, he said.

"Then please connect me to Joanne Montgomery."

A pause. Then: "I am sorry, sir, but you are not on Miss Montgomery's list, either."

Of course I wasn't. When we'd made our OPSEC plan, we'd kept me off to keep me stealthy. I dialed Joanne's pager number. I waited five, six, seven minutes. There was no response. Frustrated, I sent Boomerang, Nod, and the Rodent into town along with three of the Big Brother components. They'd tune in to Bentley's offices at the OEOB and the Georgetown town house, and see what they could learn, now that he'd been properly spooked. I dispatched Duck Foot, Half Pint, and Pick to Rosslyn with some more of our electronic goodies to get a handle on Li Chimen's activities. Then I used the scrambler phone module to get on the horn to Tokyo and contact Alixe Joseph at the secure receiver at her apartment.

No luck there, either. I switched phones and dialed her pager number, then Joanne's again. When I didn't hear back from either one in fifteen minutes I called AMEMB[42] Tokyo. The switchboard operator rang Alixe's office. There was no answer. I left a message for her to call me as soon as possible.

I was a little concerned. Belay that. I was very concerned. So I woke Tosho up and (we were on one of the Manor's regular—i.e., nonsecure—lines), filled him in as best I could *in re* the last six hours' developments. It didn't take much until he started connecting the right dots—he is, after all, a perceptive asshole with a Notre Dame degree. He told me he'd do what he could, starting immediately.

I was about to dial the Chairman's office again when Duck Foot called. He started to tell me something, then the signal faded, dissolved into static, and the phone went dead. I hung up.

Thirty seconds later the phone rang again and I plucked the receiver from its cradle. "Yo?"

"Li's on his way to Dulles," Duck Foot reported. "He jumped a cab outside his office. Traveling light—just a carry-on and a briefcase. We're six cars behind him on the Dulles access road. What do you want us to do?"

"Stay on his tail," I told him. "Let me know what he does—where he goes."

"Roger-roger, Skipper."

Six minutes later the phone rang again.

"Yo, Boss Dude—it be Boomerang."

"Dica."

"The S_3FA's grabbed the shuttle to New York. Should we go with him?"

"Negative." I wanted everybody to stay close by for the time being. "Just make sure he gets on the plane."

"Ten-four."

I dialed Joanne's pager number again. This time, she

---

[42]AMerican EMBassy.

called back within ninety seconds. "Sorry about the delay. I got your pages but I couldn't get to a phone."

"I have to see the Chairman—now."

"We're still at West Point. A reception at the superintendent's quarters."

"As soon as you get back, then."

"Hold on, Dick." She put her hand over the receiver. I heard muffled words. Then Jo came back on line. "The Chairman says that we should follow the procedure he set up for us."

There are times for procedure—and there are times to ACT. This was one of the latter. "Jo—I gotta see him."

The tone of my voice must have convinced her. She cupped her hand over the mouthpiece. Ten seconds later she said, "Meet us at Andrews at sixteen thirty. We can talk in the car on the drive to the Chairman's residence."

"I'm on my way."

1725. I was waiting on the tarmac as the Chairman's Gulfstream taxied to a halt in the thickening snow. I'd trucked in with Gator, who'd left more than an hour earlier for Fort Meyer, which is where the Chairman's residence is located. He'd pick me up there. While I waited, I called the Manor. There was a message from Duck Foot. Li had caught an ANA flight to Tokyo. He'd done some checking and discovered it connected with a flight to Beijing.

The hatch opened, the stairs dropped, and General Crocker's sinewy, wide-receiver's frame was framed by the craft's narrow doorway. He paused, his eyes searching until he found me. Then he called "Dick" and waved me over.

I jogged toward the plane, reached out and shook his hand as he bounded down the stairs. "Glad to see you, General." He looked tired. Exhausted, in fact. "How was the flight?"

"How was the flight? The flight was goddamn miserable, was how the flight was," he growled, as if he was talking to himself. "Turbulence all the way—I'm lucky there was no coffee. If they'd had any coffee, I'd be wearing it. Then goddamn C-SPAN carried my speech live, so I guess I'm in hot water with the White House again. Probably a whole damn passel of reporters already calling my house asking when I'm going to resign. Then we had a damn weather hold that kept us circling for"—he checked the big stainless steel chronometer on his left wrist—"almost an hour. And tomorrow I have to leave for that"—he caught himself— "damn meeting across the pond—plus the trip to NATO South they tacked onto it—at zero dark hundred, although why the hell they—" He stopped muttering to himself in midcomplaint and refocused his attention. "Sorry to have kept *you* waiting, Dick."

The Chairman's big midnight blue Cadillac limo slid to a gentle halt just in front of us, and the driver, whose blue blazer's breast pocket bore the Chairman's seal, came around and opened the right rear door. I started to stand aside, but General Crocker put his hand on my shoulder and pushed me in first. I took the left side of the big, wide seat. Then he stood back so Joanne could clamber inside.

She shrugged. "It's okay—I'll ride shotgun." She opened the right-hand door and settled herself in. Finally, the Chairman pulled himself through the door, dropped into the right rear, took a sheaf of document folders from the driver, and switched on the reading light as the door closed.

He pulled on a pair of half-framed reading glasses and scanned the folders quickly, shuffling them as he perused. By the time we cleared the main gate at Andrews, he'd stuffed the reading glasses back in his shirt pocket, and the folders were sitting next to his right thigh.

Joanne shifted in her seat belt, swiveling so that her arms came over the seatback and she could hear better. General Crocker looked over at me with an expression that could only be called intense, pointed his thumb and index finger in my direction in his trademark Colt .45 gesture, and said, "Okay, we're all yours. What's so urgent?"

I fired for effect from the very first round. Between the drive and the flight delay, I'd had plenty of time to put my thoughts together, and I wasn't about to waste the Chairman's time. But before I tell you what I told him, there is one ancillary infobit you should recall.

What is it, you ask?

Well, as Alixe Joseph explained earlier—and you *were* paying rapt attention, weren't you?—you will remember that Chinese intel ops are traditionally very broad, but not very deep. By that, I mean, they may send five thousand students overseas for intelligence-gathering purposes. Each student has only a small bit of responsibility. Kind of like using eight thousand people to dig a twelve-mile trench. Each digger shovels only the ground in front of him or her. That kind of way of getting the job done is prevalent in totalitarian societies, which resemble a pyramid: an excess of cannon fodder at the bottom, and a few well-fed, rich, self-important key players at the top.

So, while the Chinese may employ hundreds of thousands of agents on the info-digging front, the collation of those many spadefuls of information—and their refinement from rough intel ore to golden intelligence—takes place back in Beijing.

In fact, because of the way the Chinese system works, nothing ever takes place that hasn't been dictated by Beijing Central—Er Bu headquarters—a seven-story building that sits opposite a park on Huangsi Road, about five kliks from Tiananmen Square.

Big deal, you say. Knowing how the Chinese intel system operates is all very well and good—but it doesn't help because you still don't know when Beijing is going to act.

Not so. Remember that framed quotation in Bentley Brendel's hideaway office? I do—and I believed that Zhu Linfan did, too. And those lines of Sun Tzu's were the key to this tactical problem.

Let's look at the big picture. Let's examine the Chinese game plan.

- *Item:* there were all those Chinese-sponsored political donations during the last presidential campaign.
- *Item:* there was all that pressure on American trade—

all those former secretaries of state, whose law firms, consulting businesses, and corporations did billions of dollars' worth of business in China.

- *Item:* there was the misguided political belief—amplified by such agents of influence as Bentley Brendel—that by currying favor with the Chinese we could lure them away from any alliance with the Russkies.

That was the overt stuff. Then there was the covert.

- *Item:* the use of students, journalists, visitors, and others as intelligence operatives.
- *Item:* the leaks of classified materials provided by Bentley Brendel and perhaps others in positions of power.
- *Item:* there were all those tango cells that Alixe Joseph had identified—cells of disaffected former military types, prepositioned from Pusan to Jakarta. And what did each of those tango-enriched locations have in common?

The common factor was Li Chimen, Er Bu's Number One Son, who'd visited each and every one of the target areas in the short period before the well-known *merde* hit the well-known *ventillateur.* Li's most recent assignment had been Washington—and now he'd skipped. My guess was that he was returning to the Er Bu nest in Beijing. And if that proved to be true, then the Chinese were about to act.

"Okay," Chairman Crocker said, "let's say for the moment that I accept your reasoning. The question is where." He turned toward me. "If CIA knows anything, it certainly isn't saying anything." His face took on an expression of distaste. "They froze us out a long time ago. Now, I sent all your materials to DIA—but they haven't been able to make sense of 'em, at least not yet. So, what do you have to say, Dick?"

The answer, I told him, lay in Sun Tzu's words of wisdom; the words I'd seen in Bentley Brendel's office:

> If your target is nearby,
> Make it appear to be distant.
> Only thus will you achieve your objectives.

I was convinced that the Chinese were engaged in an artful feinting spell right now; a ruse that would conceal their true objective. What that objective was, I hadn't yet figured out. But I believed it wasn't Japan, Korea, Indonesia, or Singapore that we had to worry about. That was where the activity was going on—so, we had to look elsewhere.

What targets of opportunity did that leave? It left Russia. Unlikely. Despite the new alliance between Moscow and Beijing, Russia hadn't pulled its troops off the Manchurian border—more than a million men were still poised on China's border. Moreover, even given the current state of Ivan unrest, the Russkies were still capable of inflicting massive damage all across China if war broke out. They had the nukes, the air force, and the troops. So far as I was concerned, that ruled out the Russkies.

There was Vietnam. The Paracel Islands, near which there may be a huge untapped oil field, are claimed by Vietnam. But the Chinese already controlled the Paracels. That ruled out a Chinese move against Vietnam. Why fix something that ain't broke?

Which left only one viable target so far as I was concerned: Taiwan.

If you will go back with me to the *Nantong Princess*, you will recall that the missiles that surprised me were not the ones that the Paks had bought. They were the ground-launched Cruise missiles with conventional warheads. At the time, I had put 'em out of my mind. I should not have.

I took a map of the South China Sea out of my briefcase. On it, I had circled Taipei as ground zero, and drawn a radius of five hundred miles around the nationalist capital. "I think the Chinese are going to hit Taiwan from somewhere in that area, and I think they're going to do it soon," I told the Chairman.

"But they could hit Taiwan from the mainland easily enough," General Crocker said. "Why go to the trouble?"

"Because it gives them deniability," I insisted. "Or at least it did before . . ." I flicked my eyes toward the back of the driver's head. "Y'know—when I went overseas recently."

"Deniability?"

"That's why they had the suitcases—the ones I brought back." I wanted to say more, but I wasn't about to here or now. I'd finish my monologue in the den of General Crocker's house, where I could speak without being overheard. I knew that Big Brother would have given the Chinese the capability of mounting a stealth attack against Taiwan.

General Crocker nodded, rubbed at his face, and peered out into the darkness as the big car steered gently through light traffic, around the cloverleaf leading to the I-395 expressway, which in turn would take us across the Fourteenth Street Bridge and the GW parkway. "Look—without going any further, I think you have enough circumstantial stuff for me to brief SECDEF. And I'll order CID to take a real hard look at that Li Chimen guy and Bentley Brendel, too."

"Too late, General," I said. "Remember: Li skipped. My guys were following him. He caught an ANA direct to Tokyo at 1700. Used an official Chinese government passport when he went through the gate, too." I paused. "And Bentley Brendel caught a shuttle to New York City. I don't know what he's up to, but I'd bet he was about to take the well-known powder."

The Chairman interrupted. "So, you think—"

"I think that they're going to do whatever they're going to do pretty soon now. I think—"

"Dick—" Joanne interrupted.

I looked up and saw a concerned expression on her face. "What's up, Jo?"

"Look, maybe I'm being paranoid, but I think we've picked up a tail."

I leaned forward. "Why?"

"Same pair of headlights have been following us all the way from the main gate at Andrews."

The Chairman frowned. "Are you sure? It's snowing like hell."

"They're halogens," Joanne said. "They have this bluish tint. They stand out—and besides, the traffic's been real light."

I swiveled and peered out the rear window. "Beemer—about a hundred fifty yards back?"

Joanne nodded. "Yup."

I was instinctively troubled that it was a Beemer following us, but for the life of me I couldn't figure out why. No matter—I reached forward and tapped the driver's shoulder. "What's your name, soldier?"

"Crawford, sir. First Sergeant Billy Crawford—they call me Rommel."

"Rommel?"

"'Cause I drive this here tank of a car like the freakin' Afrika Corps barreling through the freakin' Sahara Desert, sir."

"You E&E qualified, Rommel?"

"Roger that, sir."

I reached over and secured General Crocker's seat belt. He started to protest, but I was having none of it. One of the things you don't want is bodies flying all around the interior of a car while you're attempting to evade and/or escape a nasty situation.

I tapped the driver's shoulder again. "Rommel—are there any arms aboard?"

"Negatory, sir—we're not allowed to draw weapons these days."

Of course they're not. In these politically correct times, military personnel spend more time in sensitivity training than they do on the range. Guards at the entrances to most military installations are not allowed to carry loaded magazines in their weapons. And God forbid that the Chairman's Army driver stows a 9mm or a shotgun in the car. Oh, heaven forfend. Weapons are a manifestation of the sort of incipiently aggressive behavior that might be misunderstood by the panty-waist touchie-feelie generation X-ers over in the White House as aggressive, tough, warlike . . . perhaps even *military,* and therefore completely unacceptable.

The Chairman leaned forward. "Maybe you should call Washington Metro and let them handle this."

Joanne gave her boss an Are you out of your mind? look. "No way—I'm gonna call the Park Police." She plucked the mobile phone from its cradle and dialed, then turned toward the Chairman to explain. "Metro's response time can be as long as half an hour—we never call on 'em. Besides, we're already on the approach to the Fourteenth Street Bridge. Park Police has jurisdiction from here until we get inside Fort Meyer, General."

I rapped the back of First Sergeant Billy Crawford's headrest with my knuckles. "Just keep it nice and steady so we don't spook anybody. But Rommel, you keep your fucking eyes open, okay."

He looked up into the rearview mirror so he could see my face and nodded energetically. "*Jawohl*—yes, sir, Captain."

The concern on Joanne's face lifted momentarily. "I've got the op center on line." She identified herself as a DS agent and gave her ID code, then quickly described our situation, route, speed, ID'd the car she thought was trailing us, then rang off. Quickly, she dialed a second number. "I'd better let DOD police know what's up, too."

As she dialed, I tapped her shoulder. "You carrying?"

She patted the purse at her feet. That made two pistols in the car.

The big Caddie slowed briefly as the driver started to make his turn onto the northbound George Washington Parkway. "Yo, Sergeant—"

"Sir?"

"Go south, then backtrack onto one-ten. Let's see if this guy really is following us."

Rommel accelerated and veered onto the southbound exit, then hung a quick right that took us back the way we'd come. But instead of crossing the bridge again, he swung sharply onto a narrow access road that would take us alongside the Pentagon's north parking lot, north toward Memorial Bridge, swing west just past the Iwo Jima Memorial, and head straight into the back gate of Fort Meyer.

The Beemer stayed with us through the first turn, then it dropped way back. I strained to see through the rear window, but I'd lost sight of it. There was only the curtain of white, and the darkness beyond the glow of our own head and tail lights.

I like to know where my enemy is. "Slow down, Rommel. Let's see if he shows up."

Crawford braked, and I unbuckled my seatbelt, turned and peered through the rear window glass. Nada. Then, as we came out of the turn, I could pick out the familiar bluish lights above and behind us on the cloverleaf. "They dropped back."

Joanne tossed me a quizzical look. "Strange."

"Maybe not." I pointed at the Pentagon, all lit up and looking beautiful in the snow. "Maybe because we were getting too close to home, now."

She swiveled and faced front again, scanning the road ahead of us. "I hope so."

Rommel came out of the tight turn, and—carefully, because there were obvious ice patches on this little stretch of road—checked his six, then eased onto the single, narrow northbound lane. On one side of us lay the huge Pentagon parking lot. On our right, the shoulder dropped away precipitously. Just below the snow-covered gravel, the land descended into a shallow gully through which ran a small, winding creek that emptied into the Potomac somewhere north of National Airport.

The fucking van came from nowhere. I mean *nowhere*. It

was a dark van anyway, and it was running without any lights, and it must have been idling in the Pentagon lot access road, because that's the only direction we weren't paying attention to.

He closed in a flash and hit the Caddie in the left-hand rear quarter panel—*whaaaam!* From the impact he must have been doing about fifty. I knew what he was doing. He was trying to ram us over the shoulder and knock us into the creek.

Sergeant Billy Crawford aka Rommel *did* have E&E training. Instead of panicking—jamming on his brakes— he accelerated. He fishtailed like crazy for about a hundred yards as he applied steady pressure to the gas pedal. Then the big Caddie found its footing, and Rommel muscled his way into the opposite lane, our metal grating against their metal.

The van man didn't like that at all. The sonofabitch backed off, then came at us again—*whaaaam*—into the rear bumper. The impact threw me across the width of the Caddie, bounced me over General Crocker, and smashed me into the door header face first, opening a nasty cut at the corner of my right eye.

I fought my way back, seeing fuzzy stars as I tried to shift my body across the wide seat. As I scrambled, my peripheral vision—bleary though it was—picked up movement behind us. Y'know, when things like this happen, they always seem to happen in slo-motion. First, I sensed something happening behind the van's windshield. Then, as my brain synapses started to work properly, I saw the shotgun barrel come over the van's dashboard.

I screamed "Motherfucking gun—" yanked the Chairman out of his seat belt, rolled him onto the floor, and threw my body over his just as the van window exploded outward, the Caddie's rear window exploded inward, and we were all showered with hot glass fragments.

"Oh, shit goddam it—" Rommel Crawford screamed, his left hand grabbing at the back of his neck, "I'm hit, I'm hit—"

"I've got the wheel, I've got the wheel." That was Jo-anne's voice, loud and clear, from wherever she was hun-kered in the front seat.

I looked up long enough to see a curtain of blood running down the back of Rommel's neck. Then the van smashed the bumper again. The impact was hard enough to make my teeth hurt.

We were losing speed. You can't lose speed—but if you do, you'd better make the tango stand off. I raised myself off the floor enough to clear my P-7 from its holster, stuck my nose up, and looked back over the trunk.

The van was accelerating again—six yards and closing. I popped up. Saw two faces in the jagged frame that had been the windshield—round-faced, fucking targets with knit caps and ballistic glasses. Van Man One and Van Man Two. I tried like hell to find my fucking front sight and squeezed off two two-round bursts—ba-*bang,* ba-*bang*—and nearly deafened myself in the process. It may be busy here, but let me impart to you a morsel of SpecWar trivia anyway: shooting a pistol in an enclosed space is hard on the old Rogue eardrums.

Hard—but necessary, because even though I hadn't killed the sonsofbitches my shooting forced them to drop back a few precious yards. I snuck a peek and saw Van Man One hunch over the wheel and start coming up on us again. I rolled onto the seat to give myself a more stable platform and, kneeling, double-tapped twice more.

No, I *didn't* hit them this time, either.

Look, despite what you have seen in all those Hollywood movies and TV shows, it is hard to shoot from one moving vehicle into another with any precision, especially when you're in pursuit, or being pursued. There's lots of motion, there's lots of vibration, and it is nigh on impossible to get a decent sight picture. Not to mention the fact that the folks in the other vehicle are also shooting at you. All of the above tends to make the process difficult. It is even more difficult if you are armed with only a pistol. Indeed, that's why shotguns and submachine guns are the most effective weapons during car chases—with them, you can spray and pray, and if you're lucky, some of your shots will find a goddam target.

I rolled out of sight and reloaded. There was one round in the pipe, eight in the new mag, and eight in the mag sitting in my windbreaker pocket.

That's seventeen rounds, folks. Not enough for this kind of exercise.

Another fucking shotgun round came through what was left of our rear window. I heard Joanne scream, "Goddammit!"

I had to put these motherfuckers on the defensive. "Sergeant—can you drive okay?"

Rommel's voice was real shaky, but the kid came through: "Yeah—yeah. Sure I can."

"Put the goddam pedal to the metal, son—get us fifty feet of clearance, then brake like hell—make 'em hit us dead center—our rear bumper."

I pounded the back of the seat with my fist. "Joanne— you stay with the Chairman. No matter what, you stay with him."

She was obviously speaking through clenched teeth. "Got it—"

I could tell from the way he was moving under my legs that General Crocker didn't like being out of the action. But he had no choice. He was the fucking protectee—and things were gonna stay that way.

"Rommel—okay—hit it *now*. Get the fucking lead out!"

I raised myself high enough to shoot twice. We'd progressed past the Pentagon now and were coming up fast on the Memorial Bridge turnoff. Crawford must have stood on the fucking gas pedal because the big Caddie reared up on its hind legs and took off.

Van man followed—gaining on us, gaining on us, gaining on us, gaining on us. I screamed, "NOW—hit the fucking brakes NOW!"

God bless all sergeants. The goddam limo swerved,

fishtailed, then straightened out—just as the fucking van closed on us.

It was Van Man who panicked. He must have been going sixty-five when he hit his brakes—and one of the fucking icy spots on the road at the same time. The goddam van swerved, whipped around, caught itself on the low pavement edge, flipped twice, and rolled into the gully on its roof.

"Brake, brake, brake." I was reaching for the door handle even before Rommel managed to get the big car stopped. I yanked and pushed. The fucking thing was stuck. I yanked and pushed harder. Nothing.

"Shit—" I rolled my shoulder into the door. Nothing moved.

Well, fuck it. The goddam car was going to need body work anyway. I shoved the P-7 into my belt, lay on my back, raised my legs, and kicked the fucking window out. Then I pushed myself through—ripping something or other on a shard of glass stuck in the frame.

I slammed my fist twice on the roof of the Caddie. "Rommel—get this fucking car the fuck outta here—I'll catch up with you." The Chairman would be safe back at Fort Meyer, in a protective cocoon of DOD police and MPs.

I waited for Rommel to move. As soon as he'd started to pull away and the big car disappeared into the snowfall, I retrieved my pistol from my waistband and started across two lanes of snow-covered pavement toward the shoulder where the van had disappeared. I wanted those motherfuckers. I wanted 'em bad.

So bad that I didn't see the asshole in the Jeep Cherokee who, determined to Keep Going No Matter What, nearly smacked my Slovak butt into next week as he drove past, eyes fixed straight ahead in an "I don't wanna know what that mean-looking individual with the French braid and the gun is doing on the parkway" expression, at a steady forty.

I crested the shoulder. I was facing the Potomac, which lay about three hundred yards beyond and below the roadway. The van had skidded from my right to my left, hit the low curb, then—from the look of the ragged track it had gouged out of the earth—it had flipped and rolled, the momentum carrying it into a grove of saplings that bordered the stream some sixty yards from where I stood.

The fucking thing was smoking. Two of the wheels were still turning. The impact had popped the passenger side door open. I saw no movement inside.

I started over the crest toward it, hit an icy patch in the darkness, and tumbled ass over teakettle, pitching and bouncing like a fucking pachinko ball as I caromed off trees, and rocks, and who-knows-what-the-fuck-else. I came to rest upside down about fifteen feet from the van. I straightened my legs and rolled over onto hands and knees, checking myself from the ankles up for bruised and-maybe-even-broken bones. The quick verdict: I was sore as hell—and I'd probably get a lot sorer before too long—but there was nothing broken.

In the kind of panicked flash you get when you wake yourself up from a nightmare all sweaty, I suddenly realized that I'd been checking myself with both hands. You want to know what the significance of that was?

Okay—if I was using both hands, then where the fuck was my pistol? It had been knocked out of my hand when I'd tripped. I felt the ground around me. Nothing.

Onto hands and knees again, feverish fingers probing the snow all around me. Where the hell was the goddam weapon. This is why they put lanyard loops on pistols such as the P-7, which are intended for military and police use. It is a no-no to lose your weapon. But lanyards are not your typical SEAL equipment—although I sure wished I had one right now. But wishing wasn't getting the job done, so I kept crawling, moving in rough circles, retracing the random path I'd followed when I'd ass-over-teakettled from the road.

I searched about ten yards of hillside when I realized I was wasting everybody's fucking time—especially mine. I regrouped and patted myself down to see what I had on me. Not much. The folding knife I habitually hook on my trouser pocket had disappeared. I'd left the collapsible baton back at the Manor. I wasn't carrying my favorite sap—a flat, black leather job filled with six ounces of bird shot. The only blip on my radar was the Gerber Multi-Plier that sat on my belt adjacent to what was left of my right kidney.

I retrieved it. The Multi-Plier is a handy little pocket tool whose hollow steel handles encase a pliers, a file, two screwdrivers, a church key and—more to the point here, two blades—a traditional pocketknife, and a blunt-tipped serrated blade. I selected the serrated blade, then dropped the pliers, locking the handles so the fucking thing wouldn't collapse and cut me off at the knuckles.

Gingerly, now, I worked my way up to the van in a careful approach. Came up from the rear as stealthy as a crafty fucking dacoit. Put my ear to the back door panel. Heard nothing—no breathing, no moans, no scratching.

So I crept forward in the dark, moving slowly toward the wide-open passenger door. Tried to catch signs of movement by using the rearview mirror, which had been twisted grotesquely by the impact.

But it was impossible to see anything inside the van's black interior from my angle. Maybe they'd both been tossed into the rear by the impact and the ensuing rocking-and-rolling. But maybe *ils font le mort*—which is how they play possum in le Frog-speak, and were waiting to gig me before I could gig them.

No time to take chances. I backed off so I could circle wide, then come in from the opposite side. No sense walking into a trap.

I crept to my left, and worked my way along a narrow line of saplings to the bank of the creek, dropped down, broke through the ice crust, and sloshed into the knee-deep water.

Was it cold? You bet. But so what. I didn't have to like it—I just fucking had to do it. Besides, the white heat of my rage over these two assholes who'd nearly killed the Chairman was more than enough to equalize things. Yard by yard I worked my way back, moving southward—downstream, toward the crushed, smoking vehicle.

Thirty feet from it I saw something in the darkness. Cautiously, I moved closer. Pulled myself out of the creek and up onto the snowy bank. Ten feet away lay one of the van men. He—what was left of him—was sprawled facedown on the ground, arms and legs akimbo. I drew closer to make sure he was dead.

Was he ever. His skull had cracked like the well-known melon from impaction against a large and sharp rock. His blood and brains formed a nasty Rorschach in the snow.

I rolled him over and patted him down for ID—or anything else I could get my hands on. He wasn't carrying a fucking thing. No wallet. No keys. No ID. No labels in his clothes. Nada. *Klum. Blee.*[43] I checked him for a watch. He wasn't wearing one. But he did have a tattoo on the back of his hand: a dragon intertwined with an anchor. The artwork looked vaguely familiar but my woozy brain couldn't place it.

I dropped his arm when I heard sirens in the distance. That was a fucking welcome sound. I could use the cavalry right now to help sort things out. I started back, toward the van. I hadn't gotten two yards when the hair on the back of my neck stood up. I stopped. I held my breath. And then, that same basic, instinctive, visceral intuition that has kept me alive all these years grabbed me by the goddam figurative lapels and tossed my hirsute ass three feet to the right—*now.*

I tucked and rolled—just as a fucking nasty ninja in a knit cap came hurtling past me, the long tire iron in his hand whistling past my Roguish right ear.

He was moving like a fucking bull in a ring—it was all

---

[43]*Klum* is nada in Hebrew. *Blee* means *sans* in Hebrew. Avi Ben Gal taught me those words.

charge; no cunning, just raw, naked, kinetic energy. The sonofabitch wanted me *dead*.

Yeah, well get in line, chum—so do a lot of others. *Ole!* My roll took me out of reach, and Van Man's momentum carried him past me, right toward the creek. I tried to play picador and stick him with the blade as his muscular back slammed past me. I missed. But I wasn't about to wait for him to charge again. I went after the motherfucker before he could turn and whip that big piece of steel anywhere near me.

I caught him still on the fly—hit him with my shoulder and smacked him hard into a big tree. He turned, grunted, wriggled out of my grasp, and brought the tire iron around, its angled knob striking at my head. I deflected it with my right forearm—I saw the damn thing coming and reacted in time to blunt the main force of his swing.

I said the main force. But not the whole force.

Let's use another sports metaphor. Van Man had tried for a home run—but all he got was a bunt.

However, I don't think I have to tell you that even a bunt hurts like hell when it connects with the radius bone. There's no padding anywhere to cushion the blow. I saw dots and stars in front of my eyes. I went numb from my shoulder to my cuticles.

But that wasn't the bad news. The bad news was that the shock of tire iron on forearm made me drop my Multi-Plier into the creek.

Oh, shit. Oh, doom on Dickie. Do not pass "GO." Do not collect the two hundred fucking dollars. Take Mister Murphy by the hand and proceed directly back to square one.

My friends, I must tell you truth and say you sooth: I *hate* fucking square one.

So, I wrenched myself free and grabbed at the hand holding the tire iron with both of my huge paws before he could swing it again. He tried to knee me in the balls, but he missed—I'd already worked my way inside and he couldn't muster his leg properly. Now that I had both hands on the tire iron, I used it for leverage. Remember, I'm the fella who presses 450 pounds, 155 times, every morning rain, snow, sleet, or sunshine, at Rogue Manor's outdoor weight pile.

This felt like the 152nd fucking rep. Every part of my body burned. But slowly, inexorably, I worked the shaft up, and around, adjacent to his left temple. His eyes shifted when he saw what I was doing, and there was a look of panic as he realized that he couldn't stop me. I popped him twice—a quick & dirty *wham-wham*—upside the head.

Now *he* was the motherfucker seeing dots and stars.

But Van Man was a wiry little asshole. He clawed at my face, smacked the meaty part of his palm into my nose—geezus, that *smarted*—then grabbed for the iron so he could return the nasty favor I'd just done him.

This was going on too long. I wrapped him up; took the tire iron and raised it high—out of his grasp—and while he struggled and flailed for it, I brought it down—hard—between his shoulders, directly at the spot where his neck joined his spine.

That stunned him just long enough for me to career us both to the right, and tumble us down into the creek.

Now here is some more sooth. I am a SEAL. I can survive very nicely, thank you very much, in the cold and the wet. He wasn't—and couldn't.

We spun into the water. Yes it was scrotum-shriveling frigid. But I was white hot enough to stay fucking warm and toasty while I hoped he'd freeze up—both literally and figuratively. I popped him with the tire iron, which loosened his grasp on the fucking thing. Then I took him in a headlock and rolled us both underwater.

Oh, he didn't like that. But instead of struggling like most folks—which is exactly what I wanted him to do because he'd lose his air and die—he worked at me methodically, his fists and legs punching in that rapid Spetsnaz-like syncopation of two hundred blows a minute, fought his way to the surface, caught a quick breath, came back with more energy than I thought he had left, wound up, and slammed me hard in the solar plexus with his elbow.

That took my breath away—and knocked us both back up onto the scrubby, frozen bank.

Now he grabbed the initiative—swung around, made a spear of his hand, and chopped at my throat with it. It was a glancing blow, but it caught my Adam's apple and it hurt like hell. Then he rolled on top of me and squeezed at my throat with both his hands. I came up between his arms, broke the hold, and swatted him across the ears.

I must tell you that it did very little to improve my situation. Van Man was better then I'd anticipated. We grappled for advantage—neither of us was able to get it, either. Then he hit me with a shoulder like I was a tackling dummy. But not in the direction I'd have expected: the motherfucker was trying to slide me back down, down, down, into the cold creek.

Geezus—*he was trying to get me underwater.*

My left hand still held the tire iron. I used it like a riding crop and hit him on the outside of his leg—right at the knee joint.

That brought him up short. He whispered a sweet nothing in my ear—while trying to remove it from my head with his teeth.

But it gave me an opening. I brought the iron up, around, and over the top of him. His hands tried for it once more—wrestling and twisting desperately. He got one hand on it, but I wasn't about to give up control. Then I held him close, and, screaming, we rolled off the bank.

I grabbed a breath just as we dropped under the water's surface again. In the blackness and the cold I was able to wrest the tire iron out of his grasp, and work it into my right hand. We surfaced. I pushed off—my legs kicked free of the slippery sonofabitch—and I thrust the tire iron backward, swinging it like a club, catching him in the mouth.

He never stopped. Just spat teeth and came at me again, his face a bloody, determined mask. I never give up ground—or water—so I lunged at him—cutting the distance between us; making it impossible for him to take the offensive. He drew back—feinted to his left. But I was watching his eyes, not just his body, and I didn't buy it— which meant that instead of swatting where he wasn't, I was able to whip the tire iron around and smack his lower right arm with all my strength. I heard the brittle *snap* that told me I'd shattered both of the bones halfway between elbow and wrist.

Oh, *that* brought him up short. But it didn't stop him. He charged again, his wounded right arm hanging useless while he flailed toward my face with his left claw. I put the pointed end of the tire iron between us like a bayonet. Then, as he drew within half a yard, I brought my arm back, and body-punching like a goddam steam engine piston at full throttle, I screamed, *"Yaaaaah!"* and impaled the nasty little motherfucker on the tire iron's wide, chisel point.

He screamed, too—although it came out like a fucking gurgle—as I worked the steel shaft into his body cavity about two inches below his sternum, and lifted him up, up, up. Now his ass belonged to *me*. My war face was the last thing this asshole would ever see.

Oh, but Van Man was a wiry little fuck, and he tried to pull the shaft out of his body, but he had only one good arm, and besides, I outweighed him by eighty or ninety pounds. I held him away from me, thrust him back, and down, and pitched him into the creek. He started to come back. I gigged him with the point of the tire iron again—then used every ounce of my energy to pin him to the bottom. I stood on him, pressing on the tire iron's head, holding him firmly underwater until all the life went out of him and he stopped struggling.

My whole body was shaking. I sank to my knees, threw up what seemed like a gallon of creek water, reached down and grabbed Van Man's corpse, struggled toward the bank in a desperate half-crawl, pulled myself up as far as I could manage, and collapsed facedown, dry-heaving my guts into the snow. I could feel myself getting hypothermic—losing control of my body; slipping into a drowsiness that could kill me if I didn't keep moving. So I kept going. I rolled Van Man over and began to search him. Like his partner, he carried no ID, no labels, no nothing—except the same fucking tattoo on the back of his hand.

As the hypothermia washed over me and I began really losing it, I had the kind of epiphany reserved for the dying: I realized where I'd seen the goddam dragon and anchor tattoos before. They were on the *zhongdui* corpses when we'd taken down the *Nantong Princess*. Then everything went black.

I don't have any idea how long I lay there, but the next time I remember anything I know I heard sirens. I cracked my eyes open. Suddenly I was aware that there were lots of flashing lights in the neighborhood. But I was still too fucking tired to pay any real notice.

Then a bunch of hands grabbed at me roughly and rolled me over. Lights shone in my face. I was patted down and handcuffed, then dragged by my arms up to the roadway and pushed into the rear of a DOD police car. I wasn't about to protest—they had no idea who was a good guy and who wasn't, and I'd have done the same thing in their place.

Indeed, they pulled me out, took the handcuffs off, and wrapped me in a blanket after they got a good look at my ID card. I gave the cops as accurate a sit-rep as I could, adding that I'd lost my duty pistol, and that when they found it, could they send it over to the Chairman's office. Then I asked to be driven to Fort Meyer—Quarters Six. The Chairman's residence. The OIC made a quick phone call, nodded in the affirmative to a grizzled sergeant, and I was handed off to a DOD security officer.

He, a two-striper in dark foul weather gear, helped me clamber into his vehicle. He climbed in, started the car, and turned the heater fan up full blast. I sat next to him, shivering. He flipped the interior lights on and with professional detachment peered into my face. "Geezus," he pronounced, "what fucking meat grinder have you been through?"

I gave him a playfully Roguish look. "Y'know, I could tell you," I said through chattering teeth, "but then I'd have to kill you, too."

Two and two began to equal four pretty quickly. Joanne called her contact at Park Police and learned that a unit had stopped a Beemer belonging to Xinhua in the vicinity of the Pentagon six minutes after she'd placed her call to them. Two occupants. No reason to hold 'em—and they were let loose. The wrecked van had been stolen earlier in the day— about one and a half hours after my meeting with Bentley Brendel. The deceased occupants were Chinese—Chinese *sans* IDs. It would take forever to check 'em out—*if* they could even been checked out at all. Except: I knew that they, like Li, were *zhongdui*.

That was why Van Man had tried to pull me underwater. He'd been as comfortable there as I. He just hadn't been as good at his job as I'd been at mine.

I asked General Crocker if there was any way we could check Bentley Brendel's phone logs without making waves. The Chairman gave me an upturned thumb—and called in a big chit from an old colleague. He secure-dialed the colonel who ran WHCA (the White House Communications Agency) and had him check the phone logs. There had been a call from the Old Executive Office Building to Xinhua's Arlington offices three minutes after I'd left Bentley Brendel's hideaway suite. It had lasted two and a half minutes.

But Li Chimen was on his way to Tokyo—and even Tosho couldn't even shake him down when he arrived because he was traveling on an official passport and had to be treated as if he was a diplomat. Even so, I put in a call to Tosho. I wanted to see whether he'd found Alixe Joseph— and I wanted him to have a heads-up *in re* the matter of Li Chimen. I tried him without any luck at Kunika headquarters. When I dialed his home, the phone rang twenty times and I hung up.

Okay—the next question was spelled *B-e-n-t-l-e-y*. Joanne called Ty Weaver, her Secret Service agent pal, and gave him a heads-up about the five-by-five. He put her on hold while he called the FBI to secure Bentley's office, then came back on line and said he'd get on the horn to a fella named Forbes, an old contact of his at the Customs Service in New York.

Six minutes after Ty Weaver hung up, Special Agent in Charge Forbes was on the phone. Joanne sit-repped him in simple declarative sentences, and as soon as she was finished, Forbes put the word out through his airline network to locate one fugitive S_3FA yclept Bentley Brendel. It didn't take him long to discover that the SIQ—that's S_3FA in question—had caught an Air France flight from New York to Paris. Smart move on his part: we couldn't call the flight back because it was sovereign and French once it had left the runway at Kennedy.

I put Tony Merc on the case. Merc's friends at AMEMB[44] in the City of Light traced Brendel to a connecting flight out of De Gaulle Two. Destination: Beijing. Bentley was on the run, too. I guess I *had* rattled his fucking teacup.

I sit-repped everything I knew to Chairman Crocker. He rubbed at his twenty-two hundred shadow with a broad hand, and nodded. "That fits," he said cryptically, then disappeared into his study to use his private comms unit and brief SECDEF.

On the domestic front, there was good news and bad news. Let's deal with the upside first. It turned out that Rommel Crawford hadn't been hurt too severely. He'd absorbed a glass frag in the neck, and he'd be sore as hell because they'd cut and stitched him to get the fucking glass shard out. But he'd be okay. Not-so-good news was that Joanne had taken a trio of shotgun pellets in the upper arm. The medic's diagnosis: wound trauma and minor nerve

---

[44]Remember, that's the acronym for AMerican EMBassy.

damage. She wouldn't be lifting any weights, shooting any pistols one-handed, or even working on a computer much for the next month or so. But she didn't complain—and she insisted on staying on the job.

Meanwhile, it was important to keep the lid on while my men and I did as much digging as we could. The Chairman's limo had disappeared long before any TV camera crews showed up. So, after that short and secure conversation with SECDEF, the Chairman's office put out a short press release stating he'd been involved in a minor, weather-related traffic accident on the way home from Andrews. He was unscathed, the release said, and would maintain his schedule.

Which meant leaving for NATO at 0930 the next morning, with a private stopover in Rome—the schedule said he was paying a courtesy call on the ambassador, but in point of fact Rome was where he'd meet with Viktor Grinkov. Which brings me to the bad news, which I received at 2335, sitting in an overstuffed club chair in the formal living room of Quarters Six.[45]

I was wearing a borrowed set of coveralls and a pair of half-a-size-small, two-widths-too-narrow boondockers, and well into my third Doctor Bombay Sapphire on the rocks, which meant that I was almost warm and able to feel my fingertips, when General Crocker interrupted my recuperation. "Dick—I want you and your men with me when I leave tomorrow for my meeting with Viktor Grinkov. There is a lot at stake here—more than you might understand right now. Frankly, I don't trust him. He's damn mad about the fifty million we took,[46] and I'd feel a lot safer if you and your people were watching my six for me."

---

[45]Quarters Six, a huge red brick house that sits on Grant Drive in the center of Fort Meyer, is the official residence of the Chairman of the Joint Chiefs of Staff.

[46]I've mentioned this sluiced money before. It belongs to the Russian Minister of the Interior, Viktor Grinkov. I took it from him. To see how I did that, you'll have to read *Rogue Warrior: Designation Gold*, which has recently been released in paperback.

I had a hundred reasons why that wasn't a good idea. Like the fact that I was making palpable progress here in Washington—and that if I should be going anyplace it should be to Tokyo, to work with Tosho and Alixe Joseph on cracking the Chinese operation that was, I was convinced, about to break wide open somewhere near Taiwan.

But none of my hundred reasons outranked General Crocker's four stars. He even put his "request" to me in words I understand perfectly: "Dick—you do not have to like this assignment. You just have to do it."

And I *was* willing to do it, not like it—until Tony Mercaldi called for the second time in two hours.

I took his call in the Chairman's study. I hoped he had more news on Bentley Brendel. But he didn't. He was edgy. Nervous. He hemmed and he hawed until finally I broke in. "Merc—just spill it, okay? WTF—Did mister five-by-five disappear altogether?"

"Dick—" He stopped cold again. There was an uncomfortable, tormented quality to this performance, which was very unlike Merc. I did not like the way things were going at all.

"Merc?"

"Yeah?"

"You're covering something. I've known you long enough to know." I paused. "C'mon—spill."

I heard him swallow and breathe in. "Alixe Joseph is dead—she was shot to death six hours ago."

I was standing when he said it. I sat down—hard. No time for feeling. I'd grieve later, in private. Right now, I wanted the facts so I could run with 'em—and obliterate the motherfuckers who'd murdered Alixe. "How, Merc. How?"

"Like I said, shot. It was staged to look like a Yakuza hit, but we know better."

"Where?"

"Right outside her apartment. She had the keys in her hand. She was hit from close range in the back of the head. Three shots from a twenty-two, from what I've been told." He took another deep breath. "It's still pretty sketchy."

"Who?" I wanted to know. I wanted to go find 'em.

Merc sighed. "We're still working on that—assembling the reports."

That's the thing about fucking intel squirrels. They are always assembling, or distilling, or refining, or processing. But they're never fucking *acting*. Well, a DIA officer had been killed—and it was time to go to war. "Fuck, Merc, get off your ass." I was pissed. I was angry. I wanted somebody's fucking head on a pike. "Goddammit, Tony—she was vulnerable. Her nets were being rolled up by Li Chimen's goons. She told me that—and she told it to you, too. But from what I can see you guys did nothing to protect her."

"Hey—come off it, Dick." Merc's tone was vehement. "That's a load of bullshit. First of all, she knew the risks. She was a professional—like you, and like me. Second, we beefed up her security as much as was feasible—given her mission. But she was a goddam HUMINT officer—not some computer analyst. HUMINT officers can't work from inside a friggin' cocoon. She had to move. Get around—*operate*. You know that as well as I do. But we did what we could."

He stopped long enough to catch his breath. "Look— Dick, we did some things. I'm not about to tell you what on an open line. But we are making progress on this. Do me a favor. Cool down. Call me back later—on equipment we can talk on—and I'll fill you in. I promise." The phone went dead in my hand.

I wandered back into the living room. General Crocker took one look at my face and shifted gears. "Dick, what's wrong?" The tone of his voice was evidence of the concern he was feeling.

I told him what was wrong—and why my men and I had to go to Tokyo, not Rome. There was a murder to solve. There were bad guys to eliminate. There was—

That's as far as I got. The general was having none of it. His face grew red. He rose and pointed me toward a chair. I sat. He stood over me. There would be no goddam

UNODIR operations, he said—none whatsoever. We were scheduled to wheels-up for Rome at 0930. Sharp. And my blanking men and I would blanking be there. No blankety-blanking excuses. I would coordinate with the motherblanking RSO[47] in Rome. His name was Olshaker. Olshaker was up to blankety-blanking speed about the meeting, although he had no blanking idea what it was all about.

General Crocker's language was like a slap across the face. I'd never heard him talk like that before. On he went, sounding like a grizzled DI barking at a wet-behind-the-balls recruit. No bleeper-blanking missed plane. None of my blankity-blank-blank bleeper-blanking Rogue blanking behavior. This was a goddam command blanking performance, he growled—and *he* was the blanking one in bleeper-blanking *command*.

You do not argue with generals. Not when they're talking like that. I saluted, and gave him an "aye-aye, sir." But I must tell you that my heart wasn't in it.

---

[47]Regional Security Officer.

Chapter

14

ROME WAS COLD AND WET WHEN WE TOUCHED DOWN AT *zero zero e un quarto*—which is 0 dark hundred in anybody's language. Most flights arrive at Rome's big international airport at Fiumicino and take the autostrada directly into La Bella Roma. For better security—always keep the bad guys guessing—we changed the flight plan over Genoa, notified AMEMB Rome by secure comms, and flew into the smaller airport at Ciampino, sixteen miles southwest of the city.

Despite the weather, the hour, and the last-minute shift of plan, the American ambassador, the DCM, and the embassy's chief military attaché were all waiting like pensioners at the bottom of the rolling stairway as the plane's hatch was popped open. It was proper protocol to Welcome The Chairman, and they were going to follow protocol no matter what the hour—or the weather. I peeked through a window and saw that each principal had his own soaking-wet, pinstripe-suited FS[48] factotum holding a huge umbrella to

---

[48]Foreign Service.

254

keep said principal's consequential self dry. I tell you, when you live your life as a junior-grade, still-wet-behind-the-demarche diplomat, it ain't just a job, friends—it's a fucking adventure.

While the Chairman strode out the front door and played the PE role—that stands for proper emissary—I dropped out of a rear hatch directly into a puddle and squished my way toward the five embassy limos parked on the tarmac.

As I strolled over, a tall, thin prematurely gray dude in a double-breasted 44 extra long with a dark microfiber raincoat thrown over his shoulders in zee Continental style, pulled himself out of the shotgun seat in the first Caddie. He hunched his shoulders against the insistent drizzle, ambled in front of the hood, looked me up, looked me down, then smiled and extended his arm. "You must be the Dick Marcinko look-alike they promised would be traveling with the Chairman. I'm Olshaker, the RSO."

"Ciao, Olshaker, *molto piacere*—nice to meet you." I took his hand and shook it. "What's the drill?"

He pointed toward the last three cars in line. "Those are yours. Serviced 'em yesterday in our own shop, and they haven't been out of our sight since, so I don't think there are any bombs aboard. They've got partial armor—reinforced windows and door panels, but nothing underneath. I'll show you where the panels are, so if you have to shoot through the doors you can do it without the rounds coming back on you. You've got two sets of radios per car. One of them's a dual-channel, it goes car-to-car, and direct to the embassy ops center. Plus, there's a cellular."

"Va bene." I wasn't about to say anything, but I'd brought two sets of radios with me, too—and those were the ones we'd be using. There's an old sailor's creed that goes, Never piss into the wind, never eat at a place called Mom's, and never, never, never use another man's comms—unless you want the sonofabitch to listen in to what you are saying.

But you had to admit, he was thorough, was Olshaker the

RSO. I put on a grateful face. "I can work with that. Drivers?"

"Yup," Olshaker said, dryly. "Three. One for each car." He cracked the hint of a smile. "And even though I know you Navy guys like to do your own driving, I'm gonna saddle you with my DS jockeys, because unless you're all named Tuzzolino or LaBrusciano, and they speaka the Italian with a Romano accent, I figure we know the city better than you do—especially if you have to haul some real heavy ass at high speeds through these narrow damn streets."

Well, that made sense, too—I didn't want any FN drivers handling the Chairman's car, and I knew that DS—that's shorthand for the State Department's Bureau of Diplomatic Security—runs its personnel through a twice yearly defensive driving course. *"Benissimo,* Olshaker—terrific."

He pointed his long jaw toward the aircraft, where my guys were offloading. "You need any help with your stuff?"

And let him see exactly what I was carrying? No fucking way. "Hell, no—I've got seven horny youngsters who've been cooped up for the last nine and a half hours with nothing to do but clean weapons and sharpen knives. They need to burn off some excess energy or they're gonna kill something right here."

Olshaker nodded. "Well—if there's anything else you need . . ."

"There any pussy handy?"

"Not close enough to do either of us any good." He'd never even blinked. I liked this asshole.

"Then I'd like to get sit-repped."

He rubbed his face. "Not a whole lot to say. Russkies came in yesterday—delegation of three: Grinkov and two military types. Probably special forces from the way they were built and moved—all wearing civvies. They flew in on Alitalia, so they're obviously trying to travel in mufti."

So Viktor was traveling light. Only two bodyguards—probably former Spetsnaz **Alpha Unit** types who currently worked for the Ministry of the Interior in OMON, the

MOI's SWAT team. Well, I'd come up against 'em recently, and they were second-rate. "That's manageable."

"Not really." Olshaker's face went grim. "They were followed by a second security team—of forty. We're talking goons, man, real goons." He noted the concern on my face. "They came in on Aeroflot, nine hours after Grinkov—as if we wouldn't notice." He shook his head. "How damn stupid do they think we are? Anyway, they brought a lot of shit with 'em—automatic weapons mostly."

"Are they looking to hit us?"

"My gut tells me, yeah. I'd say a hit from motor scooters—like the old Red Brigades used to do. They weren't staking out your hotel as of twenty-three hundred hours, which tells me they aren't gonna try something frontal. But I'd be real careful moving around town."

For 'not a whole lot to say,' Olshaker was giving me a real earful. "Anything else I should know?"

"Not much—the three Russkateers spent today in the Via Condotti buying up half the friggin' city, according to the Langley gumshoes who were shadowing 'em. Where they get their dough I have no idea—but they sure do spend like it's going out of style."

"Where are they staying?"

"Grinkov and his two pals have a big suite that takes up the whole top floor of the Grand Palace—it's the place that looks like a friggin' Sicilian wedding cake. Sits between the Piazza della Repubblica and the Piazza San Bernardo— near the main railroad station."

"Goons, too?"

"No friggin' way. Not at three million two hundred fifty thousand lire[49] a night. No—the goons are all six to a room at the cat house—that's what we call the Hotel Katty, which is about five blocks from the Grand, and about one-eighth the price."

"What about our Italian brethren?"

---

[49]Two thousand bucks, more or less, these days.

"SISMI?"

"Yeah, that'll do for a start." Yes, I see your flapping hand out there, wondering WTF. *Si*, I will explain. SISMI (pronounced *seize me*, and rhyming with *please me, tease me*, and *greeze me*), is an Italian acronym that translates into full-length English as the Service for Information and Military Security. It oversees all of the political, military, and economic intel ops for the Italian government. It also handles counterintelligence and assumed the counterterrorism portfolio about five years ago. SISMI operates out of the Ministry of Defense on the Via Twenty September.

You *what?* You want to know how many people work for SISMI? What are you, trying to give me a fucking test to see whether I'm as up-to-date on this shit as the publicity releases claim I am?

Okay—fuck you back: according to the most recent classified CIA analysis, SISMI has about three thousand full-time employees, plus an equal number of agents, snitches, informers, and other assorted scuzzballs. They are scattered throughout Italy, Europe, the Middle East, and North Africa. Happy now? Can I get back to the fuckin' action now? Oh, I *can?* Well, *fuuuuck* you.

Olshaker nodded in the *affirmativo*. "Yeah—they were on-scene when Viktor arrived, so I guess they're on his case, too. Probably bugged the hotel room by now. But SISMI's going to stay hands-off when shit hits fan. The Russkies are about to close a big deal with Fiat to build car plants, and the Italians don't wanna rocka da boat."

If they'd bugged the Russkies, they'd probably bugged our rooms, too. The Italians like to do that sort of thing—it makes 'em feel Machiavellian. Did it matter? Not really. I'd come prepared. I slapped Olshaker across the back. "Well—what about getting this sideshow on the well-known *strada*. The meet is scheduled for zero ten hundred tomorrow." I glanced down at the big-watch-little cock timepiece on my thick, hairy wrist. "Sorry, that's ten hundred *oggi*—today."

Olshaker gave me a double thumbs-up, turned, and hand-signaled two of his Caddies to move toward the pile of boxes my guys had piled near the plane's aft hatchway. "Stow your gear and we'll roll the wagons," he said. "You're headed for the Grand Flora."

He pulled a sheet of paper out of his pocket and unfolded it to reveal a well-drawn map of Rome's center. The one-way streets were all marked clearly; the best routes had been highlighted in bright yellow. "Usually, they put you Pentagon folks up at the Ambasciatori"—he put a long index finger on the paper—"because it's right across from the embassy. But"—he slid his finger north an inch and a half—"we've moved you up the Via Veneto to the Flora. It's a smaller place—it's also got a nice driveway we can get a car up to. The entire building is illuminated all night because it sits right opposite the Borghese Gardens and the old Roman city wall. Besides, we can cover the Flora more easily because it has only two ways in—the front door and the service entrance—and two ways out."

He folded the map and handed it to me, then turned ninety degrees and pointed through the misty rain. "See over there? That's four *carabinieri* cars. They'll be running interference for you guys on the drive into the city."

"What about you?"

He perused my meat-grindered face and abraded knuckles. "Hey, from what I hear, you can take care of yourself pretty good. Me, I'm gonna run the boss and the DCM back in my cars. Then I'm going back to my flat, and grab a warm shower and some hot pussy. I got me a long-haired dictionary waiting there—she's got a real nice set of vowels, too—and I want to improve my vocabulary tonight."

"Well fuck you very much, Olshaker—I want your life."

0028. We pulled off of the tarmac and threaded our way through the airport, flanked by the quartet of Alfa Romeo sedans (each of them containing a trio of *vigilantes*—sub-machine-gun toting, *Carabinieri Nazionale* tactical officers in black combat fatigues and a dour driver), and motorcaded north, east, then north again. Soon we'd shifted from the airport road onto the Appian Way, our blue flashers illuminating the gates of the stone quarries, brick factories, and tourist restaurants that currently line the two-thousand-year-old route.

We came into the city southeast of the Forum, then took a circuitous course that more or less followed the old city wall, until the Alfas dropped back and allowed our limo to pull into a narrow driveway on the top of the Via Veneto, just opposite the Borghese Gardens and the *muro antiqua*— the old Roman wall. Heeey . . . *ecco:* the Grand Flora. Across the wide street, just closing for the night, was Harry's Bar. Also across the street were two Alfa sedans, each occupied by a pair of well-turned-out SISMI greezemes, trying to look inconspicuous. Yeah—right. Somebody should tell 'em that (a) smoking is bad for you; and, (b) if you do smoke, it is hard to look inconspicuous if you drop a dozen or so butts right outside the window of your car. It's like a fucking sign that says, "Yo—look at me—I'm on a stakeout!"

0112. I got the Chairman tucked into his second-floor, front-of-the-hotel, two-room suite and left Gator and Half Pint (and their suppressed MP5-PDWs) in the living room, and Nod DiCarlo and Rodent (and *their* suppressed MP5-PDWs), in the bedroom to baby-sit. Yes—that was correct. *In* the Chairman's bedroom.

Oh, General Crocker protested. Oh, he bitched. He wanted my guys down in the lobby or out in the hallway— just like the three pairs of young, energetic DS agents Olshaker had assigned to augment our SEAL security force. And did he try to countermand my order? Hey, do I have a big dick? But I would have none of it. He'd commanded me to protect him—and I'd do it. But I'd do it (let's all sing this together just like Ol' Blue Eyes, shall we?) *m-y-y-y w-a-a-a-y.*

0121. We turned out all the lights in our four rooms, made a big and noisy show of going beddy-bye—just in case anybody happened to be listening to the SISMI transmitters we'd discovered by using our Big Brother equipment. I'd disabled the pair in Chairman Crocker's suite, but left the single mikes in our rooms alone. So, yeah, as that old *briccone,*[50] Machiavelli, might have said about the Flora, *I muri hanno orecchi*—da walls hava da ears. Then, as prearranged during the long flight from Andrews, we quietly changed into our work clothes in the dark.

Work clothes, you ask?

Yeah. Basic black—*senza*[51] benefit of pearls. BDUs, which as you know stands for those oxymoronic Battle Dress Uniforms I like so much. Soft nylon ropes. Carabiners. Rubber-soled climbing shoes. Suppressed sterile[52] handguns and a pair of MP5SD's. Sharp knives with blackened blades. FLIR[53] enhanced night-vision devices. My pocket-size digital camera. Nondescript, crushable hats stuffed into pockets. All to be hidden under the dark nylon raincoats that we'd tied around our waists for the time being.

0134. We used our secure radios to coordinate our exit. I pressed my transmit button four times—*stic, stic, stic, stic*—and received three double-*stics* in return. Everybody was ready to move.

Our rooms—which adjoined one another—bracketed the Chairman's suite. The tall, narrow windows, *con vista sul parco*—with a view of the Borghese Gardens—faced the hotel's northern side. We were directly opposite the old Roman wall, just east of the Porta Pinciana. Below my window ran the Via Campania.

Stic-stic. With lights extinguished and secure radio earpiece securely stuffed in my hairy Slovak ear, I turned the cremorne bolt, cracked the French-door window of my

---

[50]A *briccone* is a guinea Rogue.
[51]Without.
[52]Untraceable. In this case, we were carrying suppressed Tokorevs I'd picked up in Moscow, and a pair of Czech CZs.
[53]Forward Looking Infra Red.

room, and crept out onto the narrow balcony. Slowly. Deliberately. Without making any silhouette. I peered through the wrought iron railing. The street below was deserted. I raised my head until I could sweep the street left/right, right/left with my night-vision monocular.

Nada. No traffic. No pedestrians. No SISMI baby-sitters either. I double-clicked. Although I didn't hear anything, I knew that three other French windows were cracking open.

I counted to twenty, then began my move. Tonight I was point man. First, I tested the rail—I've had the perverse pleasure of these things giving way in the past—then after I found it stable, I eased myself over the wrought iron, stretched out full length, and plunged noiselessly, dropping two meters onto the floor of the next balcony below, landing on the balls of my feet. I hunkered down, caught my breath, and waited.

No reaction—on the street, in the park, or from the room inside. I pressed my transmit button twice. *Stic-stic.* As I glanced up, five bodies rolled over the rail, hung, and dropped, one by one, soundlessly, to the balcony on which I crouched. I waited for three thumbs-up. I got two—and a big hairy bird from Boomerang.

Okay—one more once. Over the rail. Down to the next balcony. Stop, look, listen. I clicked my transmitter—let's do it all again.

Avanti! Duck Foot dropped silently, his landing was a modified tumbler's tuck-and-roll. Boomerang came down, light as a fucking Nureyev jeté. The Pick came down hard—he landed with a grunt (and got as nasty a surfer's look from Boomerang as if he'd wiped out). I waited. We hadn't called attention to ourselves, so it was Over The Rail time again. I tested the rail—it was solid, Jack—and rolled over the top. This was the big one—ten feet at least to the pavement below. I stretched myself out full length, and was just about to let go and drop onto the sidewalk, when I heard *Stic-stic-stic-stic-stic* in my ear.

I froze, my big Frog feet dangling three meters above the pavement. I risked a look groundward. Geezus fucking Christ—a goddam creature out of a Fellini movie (or a Bonnard painting) hove into view.

And what was it, you ask?

From where I was hanging, it looked like a little Italian *fungo*—that's a mushroom. By that I mean a short, squatty guy, complete with a huge, flowing cape and a big, floppy fedora with a wide brim. He stopped dead in the water right below where I hung, and the *figlio d'un cane*—that's a guinea sonofabitch—stood there and lit a fucking cigarette. Didn't he know that smoking could be bad for his health? Especially if I landed on him and broke his fucking neck.

I shifted my attention to more pressing matters. Like the fact that my hands were coming loose from the railing. This was not a Good Thing. Time to regroup. I used the rail like a pull-up bar, and—my fingertips leaving fucking impressions in the goddam paint—I hauled myself up, up, up three, four, five, six, seven painful inches. It is hard enough to do fingertip pull-ups when you are programmed to do 'em. When you haven't set your body attitude properly, they become nigh on impossible. My damn muscles were on fire. The sinews in my arms were so tight I could hear 'em popping. I grit my teeth—I'd have loved to grunt and groan right then but I couldn't allow myself to make any fucking noise—and raised myself another four inches. It was barely enough to allow my left knee to hit the balcony lip, gain a fraction of traction, and take my hundred-plus kilos of body weight off my fingertips. More or less stable now, I clenched the rail with my left hand, slipped my right arm over the top like a grappling hook, and held on, rivulets of sweat running from my face down through mustache and beard, trickling down my neck and cascading into my black BDUs.

Finally, after an eternity—Rome is the eternal city after all—he moved on, sauntering away into the darkness. I released my grip, lowered my body, and dropped like a fucking stone onto the concrete—a move that did not do a lot of good for my already tender ankle and previously banged-up knee. This was turning quickly into a very existential sort of night.

0139. We shrugged into our raincoats to cover our assault gear, pulled on our hats, then followed the Roman wall for some seven blocks. There, I signaled a right turn onto a narrow side street. I pulled a map from my thigh pocket, unfolded it, shone a red-lensed light on the heavy, water-proofed surface, and diagrammed the routes I wanted everyone to take to our final assembly point.

Plans made, we broke into three groups so as to attract zero attention. I proceeded down a winding thoroughfare lined with narrow, five- and six-story houses that held stores on the ground level and apartments above. Duck Foot and Boomerang turned left, threaded their way through a small piazza, and disappeared into the night. Pick reversed course, heading back the way he'd come.

Nineteen minutes later, we had reassembled on the small piazza a block and a half from the rear entrance of the Grand Palace hotel that I'd pointed out on the map. Now, I see you out there. You're asking WTF we're doing right now.

My friends, the answer is simple. I was about to Boehm ol' Viktor Grinkov before he could Boehm Chairman Crocker. And yes, I realize that the general had forbidden me to UNODIR while we were in Rome. He wanted me to handle his security—and nothing else. Well, to my way of thinking, that's what I was doing right now. Viktor had brought forty tough Ivans with him. They were no doubtski about it shoot-and-looters from OMON.[54] Maybe they'd ambush us on the way to the meet; maybe they'd hit us somewhere else. But I knew, because I'd had recent hands-on experience with these folks, that they were planning something nasty. By preempting Viktor's goons, I was simply doing my job—*i.e.*, protecting the Chairman's valuable butt.

---

[54]The acronym for *Otdel Militsii Osobovo Naznacheniya*, or Special Purpose Militia Detachment, a SWAT team that is run by the Russian Ministry of the Interior.

0207. We moved on the Grand Palace. The hotel dated from the thirties—indeed, it had once been Mussolini's favorite stashing grounds for his mistresses. Unlike many others of the same general period—like the Flora, where we were staying—the Grand Palace hadn't been built in the style of a classic Italian palazzo. Instead, it had been designed in the pseudo-Roman style common to Fascist Italy. Which meant it was a big, ugly box, seven floors in height, with an absurd mélange of rococo trim that included gargoyles, quasi-Corinthian columns, and even a flying buttress or two. There is an architectural technical term for this sort of design. It is: abominable.

But I wasn't concerned with aesthetics tonight. Y'see, I look at things differently than you do. You see a repulsively designed building with gargoyles and columns and go "yuck." I see all those loathsome protrusions, ugly protuberances, and odious projections as keep-it-simple-stupid ways to get in, do my job, and get out, without leaving any telltale signs that I've come a-calling.

0209. I gave Boomerang my night-vision monocular and ran him around the block—the piazza, actually—to do a site survey and target assessment. The kid's a quick worker: he was back in eight minutes with a detailed sit-rep. The SIQ—Suite In Question—was located dead center below the hotel's ornate marquee, seven floors above the sidewalk. The suite had eight windows, five of them humongous double-hung jobs and three narrow casements, all facing the piazza. Two of the big windows, right dead center, were cracked open. So far as surveillance and security were concerned, Boomerang had picked out three cars of watchers—he didn't know who they were—on the piazza. There were half a dozen loiterers in the hotel lobby. And he'd taken a look up at the roof and caught the hint of a cigarette's glow up there. The opposition—and I considered everyone but me and my guys in that category—was definitely present and accounted.

0221. I checked my watch as we began our move in and didn't like what either the big hand or the little hand told me. It was already getting late—which means it was moving toward early morning. Hotels tend to start getting busy very early in the day. No—I don't mean the guests. I mean the employees. The kitchen help, housekeepers, and other factotums generally arrive between 0400 and 0500. That didn't give us much time.

We made our approach from the rear of the hotel, working our way past the empty—and more significantly, unlit—loading dock. A pair of cast-iron drainpipes next to one of the three service entrances led from street level to a small balcony about thirty feet above the sidewalk. From there, I saw that we could climb from window ledge to window ledge, making our way like urban mountaineers, up to the roof.

I tested the pipe—it was solid—took off my raincoat, and tied it securely around my waist. I looked up. Thirty fucking feet is a long fucking climb.

Hey, don't snicker at me. I mean, have *you* ever tried to climb a thirty-foot drainpipe? My suggestion is: don't. It is a nasty and painful activity. There is very little to do except hold on as tightly as possible, and muscle your way up by sheer will and determination, using every molecule of your upper body strength and every ounce of power you can summon in your thighs.

When I ran SEAL Team Six and Red Cell, I expected my shooters to be able to shinny up caving ladders, ropes, and drainpipes. We worked daily to develop our upper body strength. We still do. But since those days, my Roguish body has taken its fair share of dings, dents, nicks, and notches. And—I know you find this hard to believe—I don't climb those caving ladders, ropes, and drainpipes with the same exuberant abandon I did just four or five years ago. Especially when I've just been suspended by my cuticles from a fucking wrought iron railing.

But then, I didn't have to like it—I just had to do it. And since I have always practiced First SEAL Roy Boehm's two-word definition of leadership—FOLLOW ME!—I reached as high as I could, got a good grip on the pipe, wrapped my legs tightly, sprang up—and slammed the shit out of my previously dinged, dented, nicked, and notched left knee as I smacked it hard into the stone wall.

Oh, my friends, that hurt. But I wasn't about to let a goddam guinea drainpipe spoil my evening of fun & games. I just kept going. Didn't look down, didn't look up. Just hugged, and pulled, and hugged, and pulled, and fucking inch by fucking inch I fucking crawled up the fucking pipe.

I'd soaked clean through my damp BDUs by the time I came even with the dark stone of the balcony rail. As I strained to make my final assault, I was taken up and pulled in by lots of strong hands. Wheezing, I caught my breath and looked up to see that, in the time it had taken me to muscle my way up, the rest of my team had scampered upside the other drainpipe and were waiting for me.

"Maybe next time you might consider the elevator, Skipper," Duck Foot said helpfully.

That was something I really needed to hear right now. I pulled myself to my feet. "Fuuuuck you, you wet-behind-the-balls cockbreaths—that was just the beginning. Now let's see how you youngsters do on the serious stuff."

Duck Foot removed his hat and performed a neat little jump-and-bow flourish that would have done a commedia dell'arte performer proud. *"Prego,* Skipper—after you, *per favore, Signore* Beeg Deek."

Chapter

15

0248. I POKED MY BROAD SLOVAK BEAK THROUGH THE FOUR-inch crenellations that saw-toothed the top of the Grand Palace's roofline and took a quick look-see. Yes, I hurt. Yes, I was sore. And cold—and wet from the SEAL-strength sweat that had three floors ago soaked through all my clothes. But I'd done what I'd had to do: I'd brought us up a long, arduous, clandestine route without disturbing any-body—including the infamous *Signor* Murphy who, I hoped, had taken an overdose of sleeping pills tonight.

I paused, then scanned the rooftop using the night-vision monocular I pulled from my top right BDU blouse pocket. Half a dozen yard-square air vents jutted into the night air like squatty monoliths. In the center, the fire stairs housing rose like a miniature saltbox house, the front of its sharply angled top sat nine or ten feet above the tar-and-metal surface of the roof; the rear end dropped down to perhaps three and a half feet. A huge spool, the kind that's used to transport the thickest kinds of electrical cables, sat on its side about halfway to the farthest corner of the roof.

Other miscellaneous detritus—several piles of construc-

268

tion and maintenance equipment—were scattered randomly on the rooftop. A quartet of television antennas completed the bleak landscape. And, *ecco*—there was the rooftop security force. There were three of them up here tonight: a trio of tired Russkies. The Ivan closest to me looked to be almost asleep. His head kept bobbing up and down. It would nod toward his chest, then jerk fitfully up again as he lolled, his back against the fire door, a suppressed Bizon submachine gun—which is how I knew they were Russkies—cradled in his arms.

From where Ivan had situated himself, I knew what he was thinking. He'd assumed that no one could get onto the roof without coming through the fire door—and his body provided the burglar alarm. Well, he'd never read the old Rogue commandment: "Thou shalt never assume."

The other two, in short leather coats, but *senza* hats, were over on the far side of the roof, some twenty-five yards away. Through the green night vision, I saw hot dots of cigarette ends dangling from their lips. They slapped at themselves to keep warm as they shifted their weight in the same shuffle-footed manner centurions, castle guards, doughboys, constables, Secret Service agents, gatekeepers, and other similar security types through the ages have always shifted from one leg to another as they stand lonely watch on cold, dark nights.

One of the sentries turned and pointed down toward the piazza, his arm extending through one of the big, cutout letters of the hotel's marquee sign. The other one followed his gaze, nodding with the same sort of deliberate head/neck movement as one sees with cattle. As they stood, their backs to me, I could make out pistol butts jammed into the center, rear, of their trouser waistbands. Suppressed Bizon submachine guns hung idly from their shoulders. I ratcheted up the power of my monocular and looked at the fire indicators. The guns were on SAFE. I panned up, down, and side to side and saw no radios or other communication devices. Oh, these Russkie pusskie assholes were about to be *mine*.

Not that it was their fault. Let me take a couple of seconds here to tell you a little known fact of the Warrior's life: standing watch is hard. Being a sentry is tough. It is easy to get bored. It is easy to succumb to drowsiness and nod off. It is easy to lose your concentration and your focus.

But the true Warrior *forces* himself to remain alert. The true Warrior fights apathy, ennui, monotony, and inertia with every ounce of his strength—and he remains wakeful, vigilant, heedful, and wary. The lesson here, tadpoles, is that the Warrior never gives in to weakness—whether it is mental, physical, or emotional weakness. The Warrior always remains strong—and so, while the wannabes flunk lunch, the Warrior WILL NOT FAIL.

Now, I am happy to report that most of those who stand watch when my SEALs and I are out-and-about, prowling & growling, sneaking & peeking, or snooping & pooping, are not Warriors. They are wannabes—average Joes, or Paolos, or Ivans, or Rafiqs. You get the picture. They grow weary. They bore easily. And so, in those solitary, lonely, desolate hours between midnight and dawn, they lower their defenses. They give in to their weaknesses. They lose their edge. And that, my friends, is precisely when I attack out of the dark, bringing death and devastation, mayhem and destruction.

I let my body drop below the roofline, catching myself on the eight-inch-wide, finely scalloped decorative shelf four feet below the crenelated roof. I half turned, and hand-signaled to Boomerang, who stood tiptoe on the top of a window frame, six feet under my size ten-and-a-half boots. Like Gaul, the message was divided into three parts. One: there were three unfriendlies up there. Two: I'd deal with 'em. Three: pass the information on. He returned my signal with an upturned thumb. Boomerang reached over his left shoulder, extracted the suppressed MP5SD with ACOG[55]

---

[55]Advanced Combat Optical Gunsight.

night-enhanced sight he'd stowed in the scabbard on his back, and carefully handed it up to me. I took it, clipped it to the lanyard that hung around my neck, then unclipped Boomerang's own safety line from the gun and let it fall away.

I glanced down. My guys were strung out over two floors, looking like black-clad Spider-man imitations as they clung to window ledges and frames, gargoyles, and other outcroppings. Tactically, this was not a Good Thing. Remember when we stormed the *Nantong Princess?* I told you about the AV—the Area of Vulnerability—during a SpecWar operation. If you don't remember, then go back to the beginning of the fucking book and read it all over again, because you need to understand this shit. To nutshell the situation, we were currently too widely dispersed to achieve the kind of violence of action necessary to bring off the mission. We were vulnerable. And it was up to Dickie to makee-makee all better. To put it in Roguish literary terms, Since I was the tip of the spear right now, I'd have to do all the impaling.

Show Time. I pulled my balaclava down over my face, flipped the safety to its semiauto position, held the weapon in my right hand, and leveraged myself back up so that I was crouching just below the roofline.

Carefully, so as not to make a silhouette, I edged up, up, up, ever so slowly, and peered through the crenellations once again. The far-side Ivans hadn't moved. Neither had the closest target, who was still in pseudosiesta by the doorway.

Moving cautiously but decisively, I raised myself up high enough to bring the weapon over the edge of the roof without making a sound. Then I stood, crouched, with my weight on the cold stone lip, brought the MP5 up to my shoulder, and held it tightly.

The sight picture was perfect—the reticle shone bright red in the darkness; my point of aim was directly on the left eye of the snoozing sentry twelve yards away.

I pulled the weapon tighter. Got myself a perfect cheek mold. My finger eased onto the trigger and I began to take up the tiny bit of slack I knew was there. The balance was just as it should be. I inhaled, then partially exhaled, held myself and my weapon steady as the well-known rock, and s-q-e-e-z-e-d off a single shot.

The only sound was the MP5's hammer dropping—and the thud of the motherfucking round as it whacked past my target and hit the fucking metal door with a *clang* much louder than Big Ben's peal—at least that's the way it sounded to me. The somnolent, snoozy Russkie sonofabitch had snored, jerked his head just as I'd pulled the trigger—and I'd missed him entirely.

But now he *was* awake—jolted into battle-stations alertness, bringing the Bizon up, sniffing like a watchdog and scanning the horizon. He began to rise—and as he did, he saw my silhouette, and I saw him see me and react.

It didn't take him but about a third of a second or so to do all of what I've just described above. But there is a phenomenon that often occurs during incidents such as these. It is called tachypsychia, which is a fifty-dollar word that means you appear to see everything going on around you in slow motion. The FBI, which has always had trouble with big-money words, calls it "visual slowdown." But no matter which term you use, it all comes down to the same thing: it is as if time freezes. Tachypsychia often occurs in conjunction with two other psychic phenomena during gun fights, hostage rescue assaults, and other spec-ops. The first (and most dangerous) is tunnel vision. If you do not see the threat, you will get yourself—and your teammates—killed. The second, much less dangerous, is known as auditory exclusion. Simply put, it means that your hearing often shuts down during the extreme conditions.

Now, I have taught myself to counteract tunnel vision by remembering two things. First, I breathe regularly no matter what else is happening. Second, I always keep my eyes scanning left/right, **right/left**, constantly searching for threats.

And so, as time slowed down inside my brain, I saw the Russkie see me; saw him as he struggled to bring the muzzle of the Bizon down and across, more or less in my direction. And because I'd kept my breathing steady and my eyes moving, I also saw that the other two Ivans had turned toward the sound, and one was fumbling with his subgun while the other was reaching around the back of his trousers for his pistol.

My brain may have been in slo-mo. My body wasn't about to waste a millisecond. I snapped the fire selector of the MP5 down to full auto and squeezed off a six-shot burst, catching the closest Ivan in b-belly, c-chest and f-face. It wasn't the neat one-shot, one-kill sniper shooting I'd been prepared to do—but it knocked the sumbitch down and kept him there.

That left the other pair. I raised the muzzle and scanned with the ACOG. They'd disappeared. I murmured "shit" into the lip mike to keep my guys sit-repped about the latest developments, rolled over the ledge, and scuttled to the first of the air vents, some three yards northeast of where I'd come over the top. I worked my way around the yard-square device, then moved to my left, so I could cut off any flanking move the opposition might try.

I'd just taken cover behind a second air shaft when I heard the *thwock* of a body hitting something solid behind me. I swiveled, bringing the MP5 up threatward, when Boomerang's voice hissed in my earpiece, "Yo, Boss Dude—I'm white six and ready to rumble."

"I'm green eight," I responded. "We got two targets— somewhere in black or red I think, and moving this way."

Gibberish, you say? Not at all. Boomerang was telling me that he'd come over the top and was at the rear center of the roof—behind me and to my right. I'd told him where I was, and where I believed the missing Ivans to be. The shorthand terminology comes from something called the Colour Clock Code, which is an assault tool invented by SAS 22 Regiment—the Limey counterterrorist unit currently run by my Welsh shipmate and fellow shoot-and-looter Colonel Mick

Owen. The CCC has been adapted by most hostage rescue units, as well as SpecWarriors all over the world.

I'm a little busy here, but to give you a quick pic, the target area is divided into four quadrants: front one is white, then left quadrant is green; top quadrant is black, and right quadrant is red. Center black is twelve o'clock; center white is six, center green is nine, and center red is three.

"Going red," Boomerang said. That meant he was moving to my right.

"Flanking green," I answered. I moved forward, my MP5 in low ready, scanning and breathing. I'd gone about six feet when I heard Duck Foot quack, "White six going green."

He was coming up behind me. I checked my position relative to the roof—I'd progressed about a quarter of the way to the marquee. I whispered "green eight" into my lip mike and kept going. Another six feet and I heard The Pick's voice: "White six going red."

There is a lesson to be learned here. The lesson is simple: during an op, concentrate on your job—not on anyone else's. I was listening to my men as they arrived. I should have been scanning and breathing—because Pick's last syllable hadn't cleared my earpiece when the fucking air vent next to my face exploded.

I rolled right, then left, then scrambled forward eight or nine yards, launched myself airward, and tumbled over the top of the big wooden cable spool. As I took off, a round shattered the heel of my boot. *Doom on Dickie.* I tucked and rolled, my shoulder slamming off the edge of the rough wood spool, knocking it back and to the side.

The MP5 came out of my hands—and nearly knocked me cold as the lanyard jerked it rudely, the butt end swiveled, followed the lanyard's lead, and slapped the shit out of the upside of my much mistreated haid as I came down in a fucking arms and legs akimbo heap.

Let me rephrase the last portion of that ungrammatical, one-sentence paragraph, so that it is more precise. Came down in a fucking arms and legs akimbo heap—right on top of one of the fucking Ivans.

At least I knocked the wind out of him—and sent the pistol beyond his reach—when I did my crashing. But the interruption didn't distract him for long. He recovered, then started to flail the way Russkies are taught to flail—two hundred blows a minute is what a passing grade during Spetsnaz Alpha Team training requires. This cockbreath must have graduated Phi Beta fucking Kappa by the way he kept it up—slamming and swatting and gouging and clawing while we rolled between the spool and the outer wall like a couple of arcade-game pinballs.

My life was made somewhat more difficult by the MP5, which kept getting in the way as I tried to wrest the advantage from him. Well, what's life without a challenge every now and then. I grabbed the Ivan by the neck and slammed him into the ground. He kneed me in the balls (if he'd connected properly I'd be telling you this as a coloratura). I responded by gouging his eyes. That slowed him down—if only marginally—as he struggled to get his hands on my MP5, and I tried to move him toward the silenced pistol that lay just about a yard beyond my reach.

I say "struggled" because he kept up the fucking Alpha exercises *sans* stoppage. Oh, that playing the punching bag routine gets tiresome. Finally, I was able to wrap my arms and legs around him and smother the blows, while using my elbows, knees, and teeth to do some in-close damage. Yeah—teeth. So far as I was concerned, he didn't really need both his ears.

We rolled left, then right, then left again—back inside the big wood spool, where it was harder for him to maneuver. Why harder, you ask? Because he was on the inside—which left him less room. I jammed him back against the core—I outweighed the sumbitch and was able to muscle him—then, as I held him in place, I reached down into my boot top, retrieved the Gerber stiletto from its sheath, brought it up, and stabbed toward his solar plexus.

He realized what was happening—and he rolled, tossed, and scrambled like a mad motherfucker. One of his hands found my knife arm and grabbed on to it, deflecting my aim. I fought back, stabbed as hard as I could—and buried the fucking blade in the wood.

Now *he* grabbed for it—both hands on my knife arm; his legs flailing, a series of guttural imprecations that no doubt expressed sarcasm about my parentage coming from his throat as we wrestled in the confined space. In the absurd way that things come to your mind when you are in extremis, it occurred to me as we lay there, fighting for our lives, that this guy really needed to use some fucking mouthwash—badly.

Then Mister Murphy actually did something unexpected. He played with somebody else's karma for a change. The goddam MP5's suppressor came into the picture again. Before it smacked me, I was able to grab it with my left hand and, using it very much like my collapsible baton, I slapped Ivan the Terrible Breath *whap-whap, whap-whap,* across the face with it.

Which brought him up short. The muzzle of the suppressor cut him across the eyes, and his hands loosened on my knife arm—didn't entirely free me, but his two-handed grip released just enough to give me some fucking wriggle room. I bit his wrist—that made him let go—then wrenched the blade out of the wood, brought it back, *slammed* it up between us, and—quick, before Mister Murphy could screw with me again—jammed it up-up-up into the right side of Ivan's neck, smashing the dagger's point and quarter-inch-thick double-edged blade through sinew and muscle until I found his carotid artery.

I pushed the fucking knife home, worked the blade around as best I could, then brought the blade down and cut at a ninety-degree angle—parallel to Ivan's jawbone. That got him. The sonofabitch gurgled and thrashed. I held his head down with a forearm, my full weight on his body until he stopped moving. Then I pushed back, rolled off him, and crawled out of the spool. I rolled over and lay on my back, my chest heaving, my lungs burning, and my extremities completely numb. I closed my eyes, and counted to twenty to repress the hyperventilation that was pushing my heartbeat and breathing way into the triple digits—and yeah, if the other Ivan was going to kill me, so fucking be it. I was JPE—just plain exhausted.

I sensed someone approach. I opened my eyes—even my fucking eyelids hurt when I raised 'em—and looked up.

Boomerang's long face appeared over me upside down. "It's all clear, Boss Dude—we're ready to move—that is, if *you* are," he said in a voice untinged by any hint of exertion, but so heavy with irony that if I'd had the strength I would have throttled the wonderful motherfucker then and there.

Gentle reader, there are some times when I hate youth—its energy, its vitality, its . . . youth. And this was one of 'em. I rolled onto my hands and knees, then pulled myself to my feet. Boomerang, Pick, Duck Foot, and Half Pint watched solicitously as I plucked a pair of three-inch-long splinters from the meaty part of my right hand, then pulled another two inches of nasty wood from the side of my left knee.

"You assholes have got to be the world's most outstanding bunch of motherfucking cocksucking no-load shit-for-brained pencil-dicked pus-nutted sphincter-lipped world-class bunghole cockbreaths," I said, my voice displaying the kind of affectionate spirit that told 'em just how much I really do love 'em. I knelt and wiped the blade and grip of my Gerber on the dead Ivan's trouser leg, then replaced the knife in its sheath. "So, now that we've enjoyed the preliminaries, and I've told you how I really feel, let's stop standing around like a bunch of pussy-ass can't cunts and get our real work done already."

See, the thing that makes being a SEAL different from being any other SpecWarrior is that SEALs really do believe that getting there is more than half the fun. I mean—look at us. We'd fucking climbed the outside of a goddam eight-story building, killed us a trio of nasty Russkies, and we hadn't really begun our evening's work yet.

0312. I lowered myself down three yards of soft climbing rope, just under the hotel marquee, parallel to the living room of Viktor's top-floor suite. Carefully, I pulled myself close to the window frame and peered inside. The lights were off—although I saw illumination under two of the three doors leading to the bedrooms.

I swept the room with my night vision. There was no one lurking. And so, moving cautiously, I pendulummed right, then left, then right again, hooked the windowsill with my toe, and pulled myself around until I could raise the window, and slip through.

Stealthy as a fucking panther I dropped onto the Oriental carpet. I released the rope so Duck Foot could make his descent and proceeded into the huge room, my eyes growing accustomed to the darkness. Behind me, Duck Foot dropped onto the carpet. He moved to my left and took a defensive stance, suppressed MP5 up and ready. Right behind him, Boomerang slid through the window.

0314. We moved on the lighted bedrooms first. I stood to the side and allowed Pick to check the door handles, which he did using my FLIR-enhanced night-vision monocular. Neither was locked. We split into two groups. I waited until we were set—then went *stik-stik* into my radio.

Boomerang and Pick opened the doors simultaneously, and Duck Foot and I charged into the target rooms. I went in low, my suppressed pistol ready. Only the bedside lamp was on. Across the room, a big, fat, pusskie-eating Russkie tried to scramble from underneath a lithe, dark-haired hooker (yes, I can report that she was a real brunette), who I could see had been working hard but without results on his long, limp Ivan dickski.

It wasn't Viktor. No matter: I was on him before he could react—swatted him across the temple with the butt of the pistol and knocked him cold. Before the hooker could scream, Boomerang'd clamped a gloved hand over her mouth, and I'd looked her in the eye and raised my left index finger to my lips in the universal sign for *silenzio*.

She nodded vigorously. Boomerang held her steady while I bound her—and the Ivan—with duct tape. No sense in taking chances. We covered them with the blanket, turned out the lights, and moved on.

0317. Duck Foot was already back in the living room, his gloved hand giving me a downturned thumb. I shrugged. "Empty," he mouthed.

That was not good news. The last thing I needed right now was for some fucking partied-out Russkie general to show up, accompanied by who-knows-who.

I hand-signaled Pick to wedge the suite's door. It wouldn't stop a determined assault, but it would slow 'em down and give us some advance warning. Then I turned my attention to the remaining bedroom door.

Since the door opened inward, we stacked outside on the doorknob side. Pick stood opposite me, clear of the door so his feet couldn't be seen underneath. His hand moved toward the knob, grasped it, and tested. He looked at me and nodded once, up/down. It worked.

0318. I waited. Duck Foot's hand was on Boomerang's left shoulder; Boomerang's left hand rested on mine. I felt a solid squeeze, which meant they were ready. I nodded once at Pick, who turned the knob and opened the door.

Except it didn't open. Pick pushed again. He used his shoulder. Nada. The motherfucker'd been locked from the inside.

Goddammit—Pick had examined the other two doors. But he hadn't checked this one out. We were fucked. We'd made noise. For all I knew Viktor was on the fucking phone to his OMON shooters, or the hotel desk, or both. I pushed Pick out of the way, stood back, and kicked the door with the flat of my foot, just below the ornate brass knob.

The latch and frame shattered cleanly—just one *crack* of splintering wood, and I went in, pistol at low ready, my mini assault light up and on. Boomerang was right behind me; Duck Foot on his tail.

I lit Viktor up with the bright, narrow beam. He stopped what he'd been doing and looked in my direction, his pale, flabby arm flew toward his face to cover his eyes from the piercing brightness of my light. He screamed something unintelligible and tried to cover himself and his young playmate with the bedclothes.

Frankly, I was shocked—*shocked*—at what I saw. Y'know, there is a Latin medical technical term for what I'd just caught Viktor doing. But since I'm not a doctor and neither are most of you, I'll use, ah, layman's language. To put it plainly, I had interrupted Viktor as he was in the midst of sucking some serious cock.

Shocked or not, I wasn't about to waste my time—or his. I was on him before he could react. Swatted him down and slapped him upside the head with the butt of my pistol to keep him quiet. His bedmate, who was in far better condition than Viktor, tried to put up a fight. But he was no match for my guys, who had him wrapped up like Tutankhamen's fucking mummy in less time than you can say eighteenth dynasty.

We pulled the drapes closed, then turned on the bedroom lights.

I bound Viktor's arms and ankles, ran a loop of tape around his mouth to keep him quiet, then propped him up atop his big bed. Boomerang, who I must tell you looks very menacing when he's wearing his balaclava, did the same for Viktor's playmate.

There was something familiar about the guy. I pulled a chair over to the foot of the bed. Turned it around so I could put my arms over the rail and sat astride it. Looked closely. He was a tall, rangy, muscular asshole, whose cruel eyes still tried to intimidate even though he'd been rendered harmless. I never forget cruel eyes—and I'd seen this guy's baby browns somewhere before. It took me about thirty seconds to figure it out—after I spotted the key to his identity on the bedside table. A solid gold Rolex President-model watch lay there. The fucking things probably weigh half a pound or more.

I gave Viktor's playmate a Roguish grin and tapped him on the big toe with the same silenced Tokorev pistol I'd taken off one of his men in Moscow. "Colonel Rolex—how's it goin'?" I'd met this bona fide prick in Russia, not six months before, when he'd tried to wax my ass. He was an OMON colonel. He was a big-time OMON hatchet man. He had ties to the Russian Mafiya. And now, I'd just discovered much to my delight that he was also Viktor's main squeeze—make that main suck.

I didn't wait for a reply—Colonel Rolex was gagged in any case—but turned my attention to Viktor.

Now, it can get cold in Rome during the winter. Even so, Italian architecture has never utilized much insulation during construction. The reason is that, while there may be occasional frigid spells, winter in central and southern Italy is generally pretty temperate. And hence, buildings—whether they are apartments, office buildings, or five-star hotels—tend to get downright chilly at night. But you couldn't tell that from Viktor. Vik sat there, sweating buckets, his little Russkie dik shriveled into never-never land. I gave him a critical once-over. Shit—the motherfuck-er had bigger tits than my first three girlfriends back in Lansford, Pennsylvania, combined.

I pulled my balaclava off and shook my French braid out. "Yo, Viktor—remember me?"

He rolled his eyes away and remained silent.

"You wanted to talk to General Crocker about your money, right?"

The *szeb* just sat there and sweat.

"Well, Viktor, he's not here. I am. So let's you and me do some *zapodlo*."[56]

His eyes told me that he wasn't in the right frame of mind to do beez-i-ness.

"Okay—don't say I never asked." Hey—I wasn't about

---

[56] *Zapodlo* is Russian Mafiya slang for business. It's a word that Viktor understands all too well.

to waste my time trying to convince him one way or the other. I pulled the digital camera out of its padded fanny pack, made sure that I hadn't broken it during the night's exertions, flipped the strobe to automatic, then snapped half a dozen images of Viktor and his pal sitting there with his tits and their plumbing hanging out. "Maybe we could sell these to *Pravda*. What about *Novosti*—is *Novosti* still in business, Viktor? Or maybe *Time,* or *Newsweek*—or one of the German tabloids. The fucking Krauts wouldn't bother to mask your poor excuse for a dick, y'know. Or maybe your beloved president would like to see 'em—I'd bet mine would."

That got the motherfucker's attention. He went crazy behind the gag, throwing himself around the bed like a fucking organ-grinder's monkey.

I handed the camera off to Duck Foot. "So, does this mean you want to deal, Vik?"

Now, you may think that I'm being a little heavy-handed here. I mean, I was about to blackmail the sonofabitch— and blackmail isn't generally considered your everyday dignified, well-mannered, genteel sort of behavior. Of course, I'm not your everyday dignified, well-mannered, genteel sort of Rogue, either.

And don't be so fucking squeamish out there. You've read the stuff in the front of these books. You know that there are no rules when it comes to making war. You know that I'll fucking win any way I can. And so far as I was concerned, I was at war with Viktor—and the sooner I was finished with him, the sooner I could move against Li Chimen and Bentley Brendel.

Let me add something else here. War is not a nice thing. It is not neat. It is dangerous. It is bloody. The powers that be keep testifying up on Capitol Hill about how we will make meticulous, orderly, prim and proper war in the next century. They talk about smart weapons and battlefield electronics; about nonlethal munitions that confuse the enemy and thus defeat him. Hey—let me tell you something. That testimony, well intentioned as it may be, is all so much horse puckey so far as I am concerned. Sure, the weapons and the technogoodies will get more sophisticated. Just like laser-guided missiles, and stealth aircraft, and the fucking arsenal ship that they're talking so much about these days, and on-the-ground, real-time C^{4}IFTW materials like Big Brother.

But war will always come down to the grunt in the field, or the SEAL in the water, doing his nasty, messy, lethal job. War will always come down to one simple premise: kill your enemy before he kills you. And no "nice" technology, or "smart" weapon will do the job as well or efficiently as a man with a gun—or his bare hands, if that's what it takes.

It is my unshakable belief that our wars will always be decided by the ability of one man being able to kill another man, face-to-face. It is also my strong belief that when you kill enough of the other guy, you'll destroy his will to fight. When the will to fight is broken, his leaders will capitulate—and you will have won. But the foundation of all war is killing—and tonight, Viktor understood that he was the dead meat.

0323. Boomerang and the Pick moved Colonel Rolex to his own room so that Viktor and I could speak in private. Meanwhile, Duck Foot did his CI[57] number on Viktor's room—and flagged a pair of listening devices. I made sure that Viktor saw them. When he indicated that he had, I turned on the clock radio that sat by his bedside, found a station that played rock-and-roll, and turned the volume loud enough to mask our voices.

Then I sat on the edge of the bed, reached over, and pulled the tape off of Viktor's face. Oh—sorry. That must have hurt, because I took some skin with it.

No, I didn't bother covering him up. I kept him sitting there, nervous, sweating, and cold, with his limp-as-a-corpse's-dick pecker hanging out in plain sight. It's an old psychological warfare game that works well during interro-

---

[57]Counterintelligence.

gation. Most folks become real ill at ease when their plumbing's exposed. I was happy to see that Viktor was one of those folks.

Now, I had three goals to achieve tonight. The first was to make sure Viktor understood that General Crocker was off-limits to OMON—or anybody else that Viktor might hire to wax the Chairman's four-starred behind. Second, I needed information. Remember, if you will, back to the *Nantong Princess.* When we'd boarded it, we'd discovered a cache of arms masquerading as machine tools, all labeled EXPORT—Zelinograd Machine Tools/MVD.

Remember I told you that "MVD" stood for Russia's Ministry of the Interior?

Well, Viktor ran the fucking MVD, and I wanted to know what the hell he was doing selling all those weapons to the Chinese, when the Chinese had more than enough weapons to sell on their own. Matter of fact, I wanted to know everything Viktor knew about the fucking Chinese and their current politico-economic-military strategy.

And third, I wanted to make sure that Viktor and I would enjoy . . . (Hold on a sec. Enjoy is probably not quite the correct word. I don't think Viktor enjoyed a single aspect of *moi.* Something which, under the circumstances, is quite understandable. Therefore, let me rephrase.)

Okay. And third, I wanted to make sure that Viktor and I would *sustain* a continuing relationship over the next few years. Frankly, I don't have many top-level sources of information in the former Soviet Union. Oh, I've met my share of ex-KGB gumshoes, killed my full bag limit of ex-Spetsnaz shooters, and spent more time negotiating with retired GRU colonels than I care to remember. But I lack regular rations of firsthand, top-quality information. The kind that someone at Viktor's level could deliver—if he could be persuaded to do so.

Now to be honest, I'd come a-calling tonight with a dual purpose. My primary goal was to dissuade Viktor from trying anything untoward with Chairman Crocker. But I had a second objective in mind as well. I figured that I could save General Crocker some work, and do some good for the country, by buying Viktor's assistance. After all, I had access to something he wanted: the fifty million simoleans (less what we'd spent on the *Nantong Princess* op) I'd siphoned from his Swiss and other offshore bank accounts. And I had actually been willing to let him have his money back—small chunk by small chunk—in return for the right kind of Grade-A information.

But that quid pro quo shit wouldn't be necessary any more. I had Viktor by the S&Cs—which as you can probably guess stands for short-and-curlies. Literally. See, your typical Russkie tends to be somewhat homophobic. Ergo, male-on-male cocksucking, rimming, and butt fucking are activities that most Ivans just don't cotton to. So Viktor would have a hell of a time explaining away the digital pictures in my camera—even though I hadn't actually caught him in flagrante delicto, which as you probably know is an old SEAL synonym for flagrant sphincter licking.

Just to be sure that he understood the situation, I snapped half a dozen more frames—good quality pictures of him sitting in the bed, trussed up like a porker ready for the oven. Then, like the SEAL Mafiosi I am, I sat on the edge of the bed, looked Viktor in the eyes, and stage-whispered the kind of *bricconesco* offer he simply couldn't refuse, right into his P-P-Porking the P-P-Prick ear.

Chapter

16

0623. WE PULLED OUT WAY BEFORE FIRST LIGHT. AT 0456 I coitus interruptus'd Mark Olshaker (it sounded to me like I'd caught him in the middle of the idiom "to fuck the brains out of" with his long-haired dictionary). I let him catch his breath, then arranged for a security detail to replace my men *immediatamente*. He wheezed, groaned, then rolled out of the sack (all the while describing my choice of timing in a series of ornate, extravagant, and thoroughly unprintable Italian terms), checked his laptop and his emergency call-up sheet, and told me he could assemble an eight-agent crew of top-rated shooters to be on site by 0600. That was perfect—it even gave me about half an hour of Murphy time.

Next, I rapped quietly but insistently at Joanne's door until she answered groggily, handed her two sealed envelopes to give to the Chairman, and told her we were leaving. That remark certainly helped cut through the painkillers and wake her up enough to start lobbing questions in my direction. But I wasn't about to answer any of 'em. Frankly, the less she knew about my plans, the better for us all.

My first note to the Chairman was pretty KISS, too. It explained to General Crocker that his meeting with Viktor had been canceled, and that I'd update him on all the details back in Washington. Meanwhile, I wrote, I'd completed the assignment he'd given me—*i.e.*, securing his butt during this leg of the trip. And so, as I considered my job in Rome concluded, I had other priorities to see to—like dealing with whoever had murdered Alixe Joseph. So unless otherwise directed, *sayonara*, General, I'll see you back at the Pentagon in a few days.

Yes, it was an abrupt, brusque, curt note. Some might even have found it impertinent. But it did the job. And since I am not looking to receive an admiral's stars—my captain's scars still look damn fine to me—I don't mind sometimes cutting a corner or two (or three or all four) in the bedside manner department.

The second message was neither short nor abrupt. It was a memo that detailed my thoughts about what the Chinese were up to, based on the intel materials I'd seen from the *Nantong Princess,* and the information I'd been able to gather, assemble, and analyze over the past few days—including some pearls of wisdom I'd gathered from Viktor earlier. I suggested that the Chairman might like to speak directly—but securely—with his counterparts in Korea, Indonesia, Singapore, and the Philippines, so they could crack down on the Chinese networks that Li Chimen had built. I added that I believed that time was crucial, as Li's clock—actually, it was more of a time bomb than a Mickey Mouse watch—was ticking away.

I closed by telling the Chairman that I was acting in what I believed were the best interests of my country—and that I'd take whatever lumps might come my way when I got back to Washington. But I emphasized that those lumps were to be mine alone—my men were to be considered blameless.

Good News/Bad News department: the good news was that we had valid diplomatic passports, which would help us to travel with the two lockboxes of lethal equipment we'd brought with us from Washington. The bad news is that when you carry diplomatic passports and boxes of weapons, ammunition, and explosives, you need visas from the countries to which you are going.

I called Tosho, pulled him out of a meditative, postworkout sauna, a nefarious offense for which he called me a larger and more grotesque variety of unprintable things than Olshaker had. (Small sociological point: Olshaker's and Tosho's different reactions really tell you volumes about the way diverse cultures function, don't they?) Anyway, Tosho arranged for us to be vetted at the Rome airport by Japanese consular officials. He kept me on hold while he worked his magic. After eight minutes of silence, he came back on line. We would fly JAL from Fiumicino. Unfortunately the only flight he could get us all aboard was a GG— remember, that's a local train—which had stopovers in Riyadh and Delhi. Bottom line: it would be a minimum of twenty-two hours before we'd wheels down at Tokyo. But those twenty-two hours would at least be spent flying first-class—something that would give my men a chance to grab a series of long, restorative combat naps between sessions of sushi and Ichiban, and games of saki-to-the-stewardess. The long flight would also give me time to come up with an OPLAN.

Because, y'see, although I was certain that the Chinese were about to attempt some form of offensive, and I was convinced that their strike would be directed at Taiwan, I still wasn't certain about which direction it would come from. They were about to act. But where? I believed the answer to that quandary was to be found at the start of this story. Yes—at the very start. Every molecule of my instinct, every element of my operational experience, told me that the solution lay at the beginning of my current odyssey. We'd discovered the answer aboard the *Nantong Princess*— we just hadn't known what to look for at the time. The *Nantong Princess* was the linchpin of Li Chimen's little exercise.

And so, while my men slept and played, I worked. I scoured DIA's translations of the materials I'd brought back with me to see what Tony Merc's people might have missed. I cross-checked Viktor's political insights about the Chinese with materials I'd been able to get my hands on. Then I went back and pored over every one of my own notes. I reconnoitered the maps and charts; I double-checked the intel reports, and reassessed the target assessments. I reread all of the files I'd brought with me. And after sixteen hours, groggy from lack of sleep, I was no further along than I had been in Rome.

Part of it was Alixe Joseph. The white heat anger I'd felt at her murder still gnawed at my guts. But you cannot allow such things to sway you, or you will not focus properly on the threats you have to counter and the problems you have to solve. Oh, there is a positive way to use rage—I'd used my rage constructively after one of my SEAL Team Six plankowners, Cherry Enders, was killed taking down LC Strawhouse's oil rig in *Task Force Blue*. His death kept me going when my own resolve began to waver. And I'd used rage to help give me the drive to find those responsible for the murder of my godson Adam in *Designation Gold* and take my revenge on them all.

But here, I realized that I was pushing the edge of the emotional envelope. I wanted Li Chimen and Bentley Brendel—but I had no way to get my hands on them. They were in Beijing. And so I sat, goggle-eyed and burnt out, thirty-nine thousand feet above the Arabian Sea, trying to make head &/or tail of the *Nantong Princess*'s ship's log, and its messy navigation charts.

Nothing made fucking sense anymore. We were sitting here, captives of time and space. In five and a half hours we'd arrive in Japan—and I hadn't the foggiest fucking idea what I was going to do there. Frustrated, confused, angry, and punchy, I locked everything away in my huge briefcase.

I ordered an Ichiban beer. The word means number one

in Japanese. Ichibans come in tall, twenty-two-ounce bottles. I watched as the obi'd stewardess poured it out into my proffered glass (we were in first class, after all). When she'd finished, I didn't just gulp it down. Instead, in pseudo-Japanese fashion, I passed the glass under my nose, smelling the hops and the malt, appreciating the perfect shape of the foamy head, and allowed my fingers to savor the coolness of the glass—as if I were participating in a classic tea ceremony. Then, I drank slowly, *feeling* the beer as I swallowed it, letting the liquid release my tension and give me energy.

I pressed the recline button. My seat slid back and the leg rest raised itself. I lay supine, the cold glass of beer in my hand, and let my mind drift off and free-associate. It is a truth: sometimes, *not* thinking produces more valuable results than thinking.

Oh, I see you, snickering among yourselves, pooh-poohing the above two paragraphs.

Well, tadpoles, listen and learn about the real world. When I was still a wet-behind-the-flippers Warrior, Roy Boehm, the godfather of all SEALs, took me aside and whispered (growled and croaked, actually) some sooth into my shell-like Slovak ear.

Quoth Roy: "I am fuckin' convinced that there are times when the fuckin' Warrior simply cannot fuckin' deal with fuckin' problems in the Western way, by which I mean, taking a heads-on, literal, straightforward approach to military problem solving. No, Dick—what you sometimes gotta do is take the Oriental approach. Use the discipline of Mindfulness. Let everything be everything, and in equal degrees of being."

Oh, I hear you: *Master Marcinkosan is engaging in Asian psychobabble. Master Marcinkosan is trying to lay some new and inscrutable form of strange Oriental manure on us.*

Listen up, tadpoles. Roy Boehm went through fucking BUD/S *twice*. The second time he did it he was *forty-two* fucking years old. Let me tell you something: you will fucking pay **attention** and **respect** to anybody who has the brass balls to go through BUD/S at the age of forty-two, because it's more than any of you can do.

More to the point, the philosophical nucleus of what Roy told me makes perfect sense to anyone who has devoted his entire adult life, as Roy did, and as I have, to the art of making war. And even *more* to the point: Roy's advice has made me a better Warrior; it has allowed me to kill vast numbers of my own enemies efficiently and mercilessly, just the way it helped Roy kill vast numbers of *his* own enemies, efficiently and mercilessly.

In retrospect, Roy managed to teach us tadpoles a great deal about the Asian mind, despite our recalcitrance at the time. He knew the region. He'd delivered weapons to Filipino guerillas during WWII. He'd been to China back in the late 1940s; his first tour in Vietnam came while President John F. Kennedy was still alive. And Roy was— still is—an inquisitive little Frog. And so, by the time he decided to take me under his flipper he'd studied it all: Taoism, Confucianism, Buddhism. He'd read so much Sun Tzu, Ssu-Ma, Fudo, Huang Shih-Kung, T'ai Li'ang, and Wu Tzu that he'd begun to sound as fucking inscrutable as they were, sitting like a fucking BWB—that's a Buddha with beer—going on and on about concepts such as "endless interaction" and "mindfulness." We, of course, were young, foolish, and resisted his advice. He sometimes had to pound it into us—literally. "Physical inculcation" is what he called it. We referred to it as mucho fucking pain.

But the simple fact is, the sort of Asian thinking Roy preached really works if (a) you study hard, and (b) you let it just wash over you. So just S^2—that's sit the fuck down and shut the fuck up in case you don't feel like going to the Glossary—and learn something.

Okay, let's start with what Roy calls "that heads-on, literal approach," which is common here in the West. The Army's Field Manual 100-5, *Blueprint for the AirLand*

Battle, states the Principles of War in nine simple terms.[58] They are a valuable resource, so let me quote them to you.

1. *Objective.* Direct every military operation toward a clearly defined, decisive, and attainable objective.
2. *Offensive.* Seize, retain, and exploit the initiative.
3. *Mass.* Concentrate minimum essential combat power to secondary efforts.
4. *Economy of Force.* Allocate minimum essential combat power to secondary efforts.
5. *Maneuver.* Place the enemy in a position of disadvantage through flexible application of combat power.
6. *Unity of Command.* For every objective, ensure unity of command under one responsible commander.
7. *Security.* Never permit the enemy to acquire an unexpected advantage.
8. *Surprise.* Strike the enemy at a time or place, or in a manner, for which he is unprepared.
9. *Simplicity.* Prepare clear, uncomplicated plans and clear, concise orders to ensure thorough understanding.

There is nothing wrong with these principles—in fact, some of them come very close to paralleling the Ten Commandments of SpecWar. But the very codification under the important-sounding rubric Principles of War has the potential to make them restrictive, confining, and limited so far as I am concerned.

Here is a second Western example. All SEAL missions are currently divided into seven phases. There is premission,

---

[58] The original *Principles of War* were first published by the U.S. Army in 1921. They are derived from the work of British Major General J.F.C. Fuller, who developed a similar set for the Brits during WWI. It was General Fuller, incidentally, who first formalized the concept of KISS—Keep It Simple Stupid.

insertion, infiltration, actions at the objective, exfiltration, extraction, and postmission. Each of those seven steps is broken down and analyzed; moreover, each one is currently diagrammed and flowcharted. Today, statistical analyses of virtually every mission are generated by computer, allowing holographic simulations to be run by the senior mission planners before a single SEAL is permitted to go anywhere or do anything. The formulations derived are precise and meticulous. They are conscientious, and explicit—just like the Principles of War. But they, like those nine principles, also can be restricting.

Here is a third example. The SpecOps theory of relative superiority (you should remember it because I told you it was important to do so earlier in the book, and I'm not going to take the time to restate it here) was created in a way that allows it to be diagrammed on a chart. In point of fact, flowcharts, graphs, computer-generated models, and statistical-type diagrams have become a large part of what SpecWar is all about these days.

But, as Roy told me so many, many times, things cannot, and—more important—*should not,* always be diagrammed, programmed, graphed, charted, or codified. Sometimes, he insisted, things must just be *felt;* sometimes they must simply be *sensed.*

Listen, for example, to how the great swordsman Fudo described the tactics of winning in his 1648 seminal work, *The Sword.* Fudo wrote:

> Some teachers insist that in combat, your eyes must focus on your enemy's sword in order for you to succeed in killing him. Others say no—follow your opponent's hands and you will prevail. Still others teach you to watch your opponent's eyes, or his face; to focus on his hips, or his feet. All of these are wrong. What you must do is to sense your opponent in much the same way the archer senses the flight of the arrow before the arrow is loosed, or the painter senses the stroke of his brush,

before the bristles touch the paper. The true archer does not have to *see* the center of the target; he can sense it perfectly in his mind. The great painter does not have to use a compass in order to draw a perfect circle. That perfect circle already exists—a vision inside his head. What they do is to translate their visions to the target and the paper. In the same way, you must never fix your eyes on any one thing, but must perceive the whole world around you as you engage in battle. If you fight in a manner that is consistent with that all-encompassing vision—adjusting, compensating, and harmonizing as you do combat—you will never fail.

I remember the day Roy first read that passage to me. He finished, slapped his empty beer can down on the kitchen counter, grinned at me (he has big white teeth, and he has always looked a little bit like Freddie, the malevolent, Dixie-cupped, dynamite-holding, cigar-chomping UDT Frog mascot when he grins), put his big, wide nose right up to my big, wide nose, and growled, "Now, try to diagram *those* fucking tactics, you asshole."

And so I reclined the seatback, closed my eyes, and replayed everything that had taken place aboard the *Nantong Princess*. Played it all like a fucking videotape, in my mind. Occasionally, I stopped the tape and reran a section. I played things in reverse. I shuffled events. I looked at the problem as if it was a holograph—examining it from top, bottom, and side-to-side. Then I free-associated—let my mind play games until I forced myself to recall every morsel, pseudofactoid, and partial infobit of picayune, inconsequential, and meaningless intelligence I'd absorbed since we'd taken down the *Nantong Princess*.

Yes, friends, despite the fact that I love to hop & pop & shoot & loot, a great part of Warriordom is mental, not physical. And the mental part is just as demanding—if not more so—than the physical.

After two and a half hours of Ichiban and free association, I unlocked my briefcase, pored over the contents, and extracted three items: a page from the *Nantong Princess*'s ship's log, the ship's chart of the South China Sea, and my notes from a conversation with Alixe Joseph. I looked them all over carefully and saw on those sheets the information I had been looking for, but previously had been unable to detect. All of it was right there in front of me. And it was so fucking simple that I had to be right.

Part
Three

THE FIRE
STRATEGY

Chapter

17

TOSHO AND A SHORT, BESPECTACLED JAPANESE IMMIGRATION official whose shiny black sharkskin three-button suit with all three buttons buttoned, white long-pointed collar shirt, and narrow black silk tie gave him the look of a type-casting Nisei William Mollis agent, were standing on the mobile platform as it wheeled up to the 747's fuselage. Tosho looked exhausted. He stood off to the side, his arms crossed, his foot tapping impatiently, his face grim.

He gave me a cursory abrazo and my guys an off-handed *Kon-nichi-wa* before he led us all down a steel stairway onto the tarmac, toward a pair of black Ford Broncos with smoked-glass windows and lots of radio antennas. The plane's huge cargo hatches were already open—and our luggage and the three big equipment lockers we'd brought with us were being unloaded from their own container, which sat separate from the others. "I had your stuff specially tagged in Rome—easier and faster that way," Tosho explained abruptly. I watched as the immigration man took our passports, laid them out on the hood of one of the Broncos, peered through his thick-rimmed glasses at each picture and, satisfied that us was us, inserted small sheets of paper atop our visas, stamped every sheet neatly, restacked the documents in the order he'd received them, and returned each with a polite bow.

I'd seen the same thing done once before. In the days before there was any sort of Middle East peace, the Israelis used to slip a sheet of paper into my passport and stamp it, instead of leaving a permanent mark inside my passport. That way, when I traveled to such places as Saudi, or Kuwait, Oman, or Algeria, those countries, still in a technical state of war with Israel, would accept my passport.

Puzzled, I accepted my passport and lowered my head to return the official's courtesy. *"Domo arigato*—thank you."

Immigration Man bowed even lower. *"Doo-itashimashite*—you're very welcome."

We took the expressway back into the city, crawling the last twenty kliks or so through exhaust-heavy glidlock. Tokyo traffic was even worse than I'd remembered—it made Washington in the snow look good. Tosho drove in silence, his jaw clenched, looking like some kind of Japanese bulldog. He habitually played country music on the Bronco's cassette deck, singing along volubly with Garth Brooks, or Mary Chapin Carpenter. Today, there was nothing but silence. I wondered what was bothering him but knew enough to leave him alone when he was in one of his solitary black-brack moods.

Our two-vehicle caravan made its way along the Tokyo Expressway Number 1, exited just above Yurakucho Station, threaded through traffic behind the Imperial Hotel, took a turn onto Uchi Sai Wai-Cho, and finally came up behind the Nippon Press Center. Half a block on, Tosho veered into a narrow alley and pressed a button on the Bronco's overhead console. Fifty yards in front of us, a huge, reinforced steel vehicle barrier painted yellow and black lowered itself into the ground. I peered up through the windshield and made out multiple surveillance cameras on mechanical gimbals. We bumped across the lowered steel barrier. Tosho stopped far enough beyond it to allow the second Bronco to clear, then tapped his siren and flashed his lights twice. The antiterrorist device raised itself with a loud, hollow *clung,* after which, a pair of massive metal doors sixty feet beyond our front crash bumper retracted, allowing the two Broncos entry into the huge, multilevel garage taking up the first two floors of the windowless, six-story building that I knew served as Kunika's headquarters.

We parked the vehicles and locked them. Tosho led the way, chugging up four flights of stairs at a constant double time, never breathing hard. He quick-marched us past a trio of security checkpoints, returning the guards' salutes with hasty waves of his hand, and wheeled into a long corridor off of which dozens of Kunika officers worked in cramped cubicles that looked to be a lot smaller than the hot tub back at Rogue Manor—not that I'd had the chance to enjoy that or any of the Manor's other amenities, lately.

He swung left at the corridor's dead end, opened the door to what looked to be a small conference room, beckoned for us to enter, then when we'd all done so, he closed the door with the back of his broad shoulders and turned the deadbolt lock.

Now that ve vere alone, Tosh looked over at me—and the look wasn't especially friendly. "What the fuck, Dick?"

What the fuck indeed, gentle reader? Do I have such an ineffable effect on people that they habitually tend to greet me in loving terms and affable sobriquets?

I looked back at Tosho. "What the fuck what the fuck, Tosh. I have no damn idea at all what you're so fucking steamed about."

Tosho withdrew a sheet of paper from the inside pocket of his jacket. "Try this," he said, handing it to me.

I looked. I read. It was a confidential fax to the head of Kunika from the chief American defense attaché in Japan, and written at the behest of the Chairman of the Joint Chiefs of Staff, requesting assistance in finding and detaining one Captain Richard No Middle Initial Marcinko and seven of his enlisted men, who, the fax continued, were currently engaged in the commission of an unauthorized action with regard to the recent death of an American Embassy official, and hence presumed to be somewhere in the area of the Japanese capital.

"Guess who got the assignment," Tosho said. "And when Boss-san finds out I'm the one who let you into the country, I'm gonna be toast."

"I don't plan to be here long," I said. "Maybe he won't find out."

"He finds out everything," Tosho said. "That's why he's Boss-san."

All of a sudden, Kunika headquarters didn't seem the best place to be. "So why bring us here, Tosh?"

"To be honest, it's the one place nobody'll be looking for you. As you can see, the Americans think you're here to shake the city up trying to find whoever killed Alixe. DIA's got gumshoes staking out her place—and a few other locations, too."

Actually, I had a pretty good idea who'd killed Alixe Joseph—had her killed is a more accurate description— and he wasn't within a thousand miles of Tokyo. Which is what I told Tosho.

"You mean Li Chimen," Tosho said. "Yeah—I think he's dirty, too. But he came through on a diplomatic passport and we couldn't touch him. The sonofabitch is back in Beijing."

"I think he's already out—or close to it, and without his diplomatic creds," I said.

That got Tosho's attention. "Out? Where, in Tokyo?"

"Not quite," I said. "South of Tokyo. I'm about to check it out and take him down." I wriggled my eyebrows in Tosho's direction. "You speak Chinese. I happen to have an opening for somebody who speaks Chinese. So—you wanna come along for the ride?"

For the first time since we'd arrived, I got a warm smile and an eager grin. "Hey, *Gaijin-san,* I'm supposed to 'find and detain,' ain't I? I guess that means I have to keep you in rine-of-sight until I put you on the prane for Washington. If that means I gotta deal in some second-rate, third-world language like Chinese for a while, so be it."

Now I see a bunch of you folks out there, scratching your heads, and starting to ask all those reader-type questions that always seem to start 'What the . . .' and 'How the . . .' Don't worry—you're not the only ones. My favorite dweeb editor's just stabbed out his cigarette and started to reach for the ol' blue pencil, because he thinks he's caught me in a string of inconsistencies. Okay, I'll take the time to elucidate here and now, because once we get going in the next action sequence, things aren't gonna let up until the very end of the book, and I don't think I'm going to have much time to stop for these literary asides and 'splain things to you.

- *Item:* I know where Li is going to strike. He is going to strike in the Senkaku Islands. How do I know that? I know it because the Senkakus are noted on the ship's charts I took off the *Nantong Princess*. Now, there is no reason for them to be noted on said charts—unless the ship was going to stop there. But why would the *Nantong Princess* stop at the Senkakus? After all, we all know that the Senkakus are uninhabited islands—and there are no port facilities.

The reason the *Nantong Princess* was going to stop at the Senkakus was to offload cargo.

Offload what, you ask? Missiles, friends. Missiles. And two electronic-warfare officers. And Big Brother.

- *Item:* There were half a dozen French-made GLCMs[59] aboard the *Nantong Princess*—but no launchers.

---

[59]Ground-Launched Cruise Missiles.

That told me the Chinese had already prepositioned the launchers.

- *Item:* The cruise missiles aboard the *Nantong Princess* had been stored in watertight containers. That told me they'd be dropped over the side as the ship passed the island and stored underwater until it was time to launch. Then they'd be brought up and deployed. But since I'd scuttled the *Nantong Princess,* the Chinese were going to have to bring missiles with them when they came.

I'd tossed another lench into the plot as well when I'd wasted that pair of one-stars aboard the *Nantong Princess.* The ossifers I'd killed were Li Chimen's EW—electronic warfare—officers. They were the guys who would have run Big Brother.

That was another major piece of the puzzle now in place. Big Brother was one of the keys to this plan. I'd spent my time worrying about how the Chinese had gotten their hands on the system. What I should have been doing was trying to figure out how the fuck they'd use it—where it fit into Li Chimen's plan.

Well, by letting my mind wander in that ineffable, enigmatic, inscrutable, abstract, Zen fashion just as Roy had taught me to, I had done just that. Big Brother was an extremely versatile system. It was, in fact, fully capable of functioning within the three capabilities our Pentagon planners have given to electronic warfare. Does that sound like incomprehensible bureaucratic Navyspeak? Let me illustrate what I mean in language you can understand, given our current scenario.

- Big Brother could initiate EA—an electronic attack—which would degrade and destroy Taiwan's capabilities to resist a missile attack.
- Big Brother could provide EP—electronic protection—which would neutralize and thwart all Taiwanese capability to retaliate against Li and his missiles.

- And Big Brother could provide ES—electronic warfare support—by enabling Li to listen in to the Taiwanese command-and-control communications networks and silence them at will.

But I had scuttled the *Nantong Princess* and its cargo of cruise missiles, and, even more significantly, absquatulated with his Big Brother system. That had to have made Li's OPLAN a lot more complicated. It also opened up his AV—that Area of Vulnerability, which exists during the first, precarious stages of all SpecOps. And when it did, when Mister Murphy-san was doing his worst to crusterfuck Li Chimen, I'd be waiting—to take advantage of the situation.

Okay, okay—I hear you. You want to know how I'm so sure that Li will be on-scene. That's easy. It is because I know that Li Chimen tends to be a micromanager. And how do I know it? I know it because he has never, so far as I can see, delegated any important job to anyone else. He set up his own ops in Singapore, Jakarta, Hong Kong, and Tokyo by going there himself and supervising. And when someone—Alixe Joseph—started nipping at his heels in Tokyo, he went straight to Washington to find out who it was—and neutralize the threat. So, now that the well-known *merde* was about to hit the well-known *ventilateur,* I knew Li would want to keep his dirty hands on the switch.

And if all of that isn't enough for you, try this: Li Chimen is a SpecWarrior officer; a Chinese SEAL. A shooter. Like me, he leads from the front. No, friends—Li Chimen will be on the scene.

And so will I—I have a score to settle with the cockbreath.

Chapter

18

As you know, I've always believed that getting there—
wherever *there* might be—is more than half the fun . . . not
to mention more than half the pain. The fun (and pain) I
was currently contemplating would consist of somehow
moving ourselves and our equipment about a thousand
miles south of Tokyo, then dropping onto a rocky, uninhabited island, and setting up an ambush that would annihilate
Li Chimen and his forces—and do all of it without alerting
the Japanese, the Americans, or the Chinese to our plan.
Hey—piece of tofu, right?

Absofuckingrutely.

But first, we had to achieve that first thousand-mile leg.
How to do it? We'd steal a plane. I contemplated hot-wiring
a commercial jet at Narita, but discarded the idea as
impractical. First of all, boosting a commercial jetliner
would attract unwanted attention. Second, someone—read
moi—would end up having to pay for the damn thing. And
even though these books have made me several dump
trucksful of money, I still have a problem shelling out the

kind of petty cash that JAL or ANA's lawyers would demand for one of their 727s or DC-9s.

That left the military—to be precise, the United States Air Farce. Now, stealing an airplane from the USAF is actually much easier than you might think. There are no ignition keys to worry about, and the sky cops who are in charge of security at most Air Force installations spend more time reading girlie magazines or surfing on the Internet than they do actually watching all those billions of dollars' worth of equipment sitting idle on the tarmac. To be honest, the toughest part of stealing from the Air Force is making sure that you have adequate fuel—*and* that you can get your hands on it. The Air Force takes more precautions with its gas pumps than it does with its aircraft. They generally put locks on their gas pumps—which is more than they do for their airplanes.

So, with evening coming upon us quickly, I was ready to head straight for the nearest Air Force base, when Tosho, who had been scanning the radio, came up with a better idea. "Let's go south right now," he said. "They're looking for you from Akita to Kobe—a real full-court press. Why push our luck?"

I was delighted to hear Tosh include himself in my little group of merry, marauding miscreants. "South? Atsugi? Yokosuka? Where?"

"Actually, I was thinking about Okinawa. There are what—thirty or so U.S. bases there—lots of places to borrow a plane. It's more than halfway to the Senkakus— which means we can take something smaller than a C-5." He pointed toward my crotch. "Despite what you may imagine, *Dick,* sometimes smaller is better—because that way we attract less attention, *Gaijin-san."*

I have always liked the way Tosho thinks, and I told him so in Roguish style.

He responded by extending his thick middle finger in my direction. "You're always Ichiban with me, too, Dickhead."

I rapped my scarred knuckles on his desk. "So—how do

you propose we get to Okinawa without attracting attention?"

"Aren't you the one who's always talking about 'Keep-It-Simple-Stupid'?" he asked. He didn't wait for me to answer him. "So, I'm gonna keep it simple. I'm planning to fly commercial," Tosho said. "Want to come along?"

Sure I did. But there were all sorts of people out there looking for us. I posed Tosh a simple question: how do you get nine armed and dangerous fugitives aboard a commercial flight?

He gave me such a simple answer that he sounded like Roy Boehm: "Easy, Dick: you go as nine armed and dangerous . . . policemen."

Sound puzzling? It's not—it's as KISS as Tosho said it would be. How? Well, Okinawa—and some 160 smaller islands—are all a part of Japan's forty-seventh prefecture, which gave Tosh all the operational authority he needed. He picked up the phone and dialed one of the three interisland airlines. He identified himself, asked for the government service desk, and then proceeded to rattle machine-gun Japanese into the phone. Six minutes later, he turned to me, a big, wide grin on his face and an upraised thumb on his right hand.

"I told 'em I have a training team that has to scramble immediately. We're booked on a flight at nineteen hundred," he said. "Now—lemme get on the horn to Okinawa and make sure we'll have the right kind of transportation waiting at Naha."

1858. We drove three big black Kunika Broncos right onto the tarmac, unloaded under the gaze of the ground crew—not to mention the passengers, their noses pressed to the windows—and humped our equipment up the steel steps of the rolling gate and through the hatch into the DC-10's first-class section. Tosho did all the talking. The rest of us, in black SWAT coveralls, thigh-holsters and Glocks, web equipment, balaclavas, Bolle goggles, Nomex gloves, and kilos of Velcro, did all the schlepping. Yeah, we probably looked like a bunch of exceptionally un-Japanese Japanese—but as long as we kept our *gaijin* mouths shut, no one would be able to prove anything one way or the other.

1909. Our crates, cases, and bags were seat-belted securely into twelve aisle seats. We took window seats and strapped ourselves in just as the wheel chocks were yanked and the tug began to push the plane back from the gate.

1939. We reached cruising altitude thirty-two thousand feet over O Shima island. According to the schedule, we had ninety-six minutes until touchdown. Tosho shooed the stews—oops, sorry, please excuse the political incorrectness—*the flight attendants* out of first class—an act that earned him dirty looks from Boomerang, Rodent, Gator, Duck Foot, Nod, and the Pick, and a "you're number two-thirds with me" gesture from Half Pint. Then, curtains closed, he waved his index finger in the classic circle the wagons move and said, "Okay, gents, time to change clothes—let's all get civilian."

2115. We sat patiently—curtains still closed—until the plane had emptied out and the flight crew and stews had disembarked. Then we picked up our gear and trundled it down the portable stairs and into a pair of waiting Nissan vans.

I looked them over in the airport's amber sodium light. Perfect. The vans had seen better days—they looked like well-used family transportation. Lots of small dings and scratches, but well maintained and clean. One was tan, the other maroon.

If you want to stay anonymous, friends, don't be driving some kind of transportation that makes you stand out in traffic. Cops, MPs, and other sundry law enforcement types tend to notice flashy cars the way hunters see deer in the forest. They don't see the whole deer—just a flash of white tail or a movement that shouldn't be there. Same principle applies here. Drive a red Testarossa or a fancy gold Jeep Cherokee Laredo with mirror-tinted windows, or a Bronco brimming with radio antennas and it'll catch a cop's eye not because he's looking for that specific car, but because it stands out in the normal traffic flow.

We stowed the goods. Tosho clambered into the driver's seat of the tan van. I rode shotgun. Duck Foot, Half Pint, and the Pick rode with us. Boomerang took the wheel of the maroon van, with Nod at shotgun, and Rodent and Gator squeezed into his backseat. Tosho turned the engine over and gunned it a couple of times. Running with only our parking lights on, we convoyed across the tarmac, paralleled the main taxiway, and exited the two-meter chain-link perimeter fence through the gate that led to the airport's fuel farm.

When we'd cleared, Tosho pulled onto the shoulder and turned toward me. "Okay, Cisco—I got us this fuckin' far. Now it's your turn. What's next?"

That was a good question. Frankly, I had no idea what was next. I mean, we were here to steal a plane from the military. So that meant heading for an air base. Uncle Sam's Misguided Children had one at Camp Butler—which is headquarters for III MEF, or the Third Marine Expeditionary Force. But Marines tend to be possessive about their aircraft. They actually do mount decent security. The Air Farce, on the other hand . . .

I looked at Tosho. "Go north, Pancho," I said. "Head for Kadena."

2321. We skirted Naha with its congested streets and all-night tourist bars, and drove north on a multilane freeway running parallel to the coastline, passing klik after klik of the USG—U.S. Government—issue razor-wire fence that denotes military installations, interspersed with knots of fast-food restaurants, pachinko parlors, used-car lots, and beer halls. Even this close to midnight, the road was chockablock full of traffic moving from pachinko parlor to beer hall to McDonald's. Tosh eased into a garishly lighted gas station just outside Kozo, a town from which you can just about spit—and hit the razor wire secured to the top of Kadena's perimeter fence line. I looked inside. The convenience shop was filled with late-night shoppers buying Orion beer and Baggies of Japanese snacks.

I'd come up with a plan, which I shared with the guys. The drill would be simple: we'd abandon the vans in town, break onto the base through the fence line—we're talking miles and miles of fence line and there are lots of places to sneak through it without attracting attention—take whatever we could lay our hands on, fill it with fuel, and haul butt. The Pick would get us off the ground,[60] then fly us over the target. When we were ready to go out the hatch, he'd turn the plane due east so it would run out of fuel over the open sea, secure the controls, and we'd all HALO onto the island.

I swiveled toward Pick. "What do you think—they've got a bunch of Hercules here that're always ready to go. C-9s too—for all the damn CODELs[61] they get."

"I-ee," Tosho grunted. "Stay away from the big stuff. Too complicated. You'll need a tug to move the damn thing—and most of the 130s are probably on a working flight line."

Pick wrinkled his nose and shook his head, too. "Negatory. Tosh is right: smaller's better, Skipper. Finding enough fuel for a fuckin' C-130 or a C-9's gonna give us problems—not to mention towing it over to the damn fuel farm without attracting every sky cop in the area. I think we should look for a C-12. It's got the range and it doesn't have a very big signature."

I know when to take "yes" for an answer—so I did. Besides, the Japs ran E-2C ELINT flights over the Senkakus—and I didn't want any stray pups sniffing at our sphincters. Yeah—so long as we're not talking about my cock, smaller might be better. I turned to Tosho and pointed

---

[60]As we demonstrated in *Rogue Warrior: Red Cell*, Piccolo Mead can fly anything from a C-130 to a fucking Buckeye powered parachute.
[61]CONgressional DELegations.

toward the road that led to the air base. "Hey, Pancho, let's go shopping."

We'd just turned onto the road when it hit me. "Whoa—stop—hold it up." I smacked Tosho on the left arm hard enough to make him wince.

He brought the van to a screeching halt so quickly that Boomerang nearly rear-ended us. "Now, what is it, Dick—"

"You have phone change?"

Tosho snaked around in his seat belt until he was able to work his hand into his right trouser pocket and wiggle his fingers.

I watched the crotch of his pants dance. "Are you playing with yourself or getting me the goddam phone change?"

Tosho shot me a knowing look. "Both, asshole." He extracted a handful of coins and handed me six of them. "These should do." He looked at me quizzically. "So, what's up?"

I opened the van door and eased out into the cool night air. "I'll let you know in a few minutes—if things work out."

I was back in eight minutes. Tosh looked at me inquisitively. "What's up?" he asked.

"We wait here."

Six minutes later a mirror-waxed, black vintage Corvette coupe wheeled up to the gas station and pulled in front of the van I was sitting in. Lieutenant Colonel Arch Kielly, dressed in pressed coveralls, hoisted himself out of the cockpit and sauntered over, a shit-eating grin on his face. He wore mirror-polished boondockers and gold-rimmed, tinted glasses that shaded his dark, killer's eyes. The yellow, 353rd Special Operations Group unit patch with its winged black-and-blue panther stood out against the sage green, flame-retardant material of his coveralls.

"Long time no see, you asshole," he said, his arms extended wide so he could give me a *fuerte* abrazo.[62]

---

[62]That's how Cubans hug one another.

I jumped out of the van and hugged him back. "Fuck you, too, Arch. Thanks for coming."

I made introductions. Well—sorta. He already knew my guys, so I gave Arch a thumbnail on Tosho. The pilot was obviously impressed. And I explained to Tosh that Arch and I knew each other from a previous mission we'd both been a part of. Arch picked up the cue flawlessly. "Just think of me as your government-approved taxi driver," he explained.

Then Arch turned to me. "So, what was so fuckin' important that you couldn't come over to the house, drink a case of cold Orions, and explain it there?" he asked.

When I told him in general terms what I needed, he leaned back against my van, arms crossed. His eyes went wide. "Shit, Dick, when I say 'call on me anytime for anything you need,' you really do take it literally, don't you?"

"Hey—what are friends for, if not to ruin each other's careers." Now, I may have been flippant just then; the situation, however, was anything but—and that's what I told Arch.

"It's that important?" Arch scratched his broad chin.

I shook my head. "It is, Arch." I gave him a quick sit-rep about Li Chimen and Bentley Brendel. I provided a timetable, and related what I believed to be the consequences of inaction. Arch looked as if he'd heard it all before. Then I told him about the murder of Alixe Joseph.

Arch's expression grew intense and the color drained from his face. "I had a friend who was in the same kind of trade," he said. "I knew him as Brian Williams—although we both knew that wasn't his real name but a professional alias, just like Alixe Joseph wasn't your friend's real name. Anyway, we'd been to the War College together, and afterward, well, we ended up working on the same real tight-hold joint project—you know the kind of thing I'm talking about. I was back in the States. Brian, he was out there all by himself. No backup. No protection. Bottom line: he was betrayed—and he was killed. And it's always outraged me that the people in charge forbade me to do anything to avenge him, or go after the scumbags who had him killed—although we all had a pretty good idea who they were at the time." He paused and stood there, remembering. His cobra's eyes went misty. "He was *alone,* Dick. He died alone—and in very great pain."

I understood only too well what was going on, so I let him take his time. "You know," he finally said, his voice heavy with emotion, "people like Brian, or your friend Alixe Joseph, they're the real heroes—the ones the late director of central intelligence Bill Colby once referred to as the gray men of intelligence gathering. I mean, Dick—you and I, we can draw weapons, and we can go out and use 'em on the bad guys. Oh, sure—we may put ourselves in harm's way. But we're given the means to defend ourselves and kill our enemies before they kill us. The ROEs[63] under which Alixe operated didn't allow her to use anything like the stuff we can put our hands on. No guns. No missiles. She had to work out in the open. Undefended. She was vulnerable." He paused, overcome with emotion, and bit his lower lip. Then, after a few seconds, he continued. His voice was low, but its tone was resolute. "Look, if this scumbag Li was the one who had her killed, then I'm in—all the way. Anything I can do to help you put these cocksuckers in the ground, I'll do—pedal to the metal."

0012. We followed Arch onto Kadena—letting him precede us by six or eight cars so that the guard at the gate wouldn't link his Corvette with our vans. Yes, we just drove onto the base. I stowed Tosho on the floor, and the rest of us round-eyed devils rolled our windows down and waved at the bereted guards as we cruised past. The technique had worked during my days at Red Cell—and it still works now. It distressed me to see that some lessons don't ever get learned. I also noticed that the guards' pistols had no magazines in their butts; the M-16s stowed inside the gatehouse were unloaded, too. Neither do others.

---

[63]Rules Of Engagement.

We parked the vans in the darkest corner of the BOQ parking lot[64], and changed back into our basic black outfits once more. I knew there are so many transients at a base the size of Kadena, that the sky cops hardly ever take notice of new vehicles. So we had at least twenty-four hours before anybody would ask WTF. Just to be on the safe side, Gator extracted the slingshot and Baggie of ball bearings he habitually carried in his fanny pack, and shot out the three closest security lights.

Arch cruised by, his headlights out, gave our location a critical once-over, and me a thumbs-up. Then Pick jumped into the 'Vette and took off with him. They would recon the plane, get charts, and check on fuel. Before they left, Arch handed me a map of the base from his glove compartment. Using it, I sent Boomerang, Nod DiCarlo, and Half Pint Harris to the rigger's loft to cumshaw us our parachutes from the sport-jumping club's locker. Gator, Rodent, and Duck Foot were dispatched to find enough webbing to secure our gear for a jump. And Tosho and I stayed behind to load magazines, and guard the equipment.

0019. Mister Murphy paid a visit, in the person of an Okinawan rent-a-cop.

I saw him coming before he saw us, and shoved Tosho onto the floor of the van. "Shhhh—"

The rent-a-cop Took Notice. He turned in our direction and marched toward the van. He was a wizened little guy in a bad-fitting uniform. A huge flashlight hung off his belt, and a time clock weighed down his left shoulder. He extracted the flashlight, brought it up, and shone it at the van.

I stepped out, closed the door, and moved in front of him to block his view. *"Kon-ban-wa."* Good evening.

He looked past me, bowed slightly at the waist, and painted me with his light. *"Ohayo gozi-masu."* Good *morning.* He went on tiptoe so he could look inside the van.

---

[64]Bachelor Officer's Quarters.

He was a nosy little guy with a creased, round face and a gray, wispy mustache. He walked up to me, looked me up, looked me down, looked me side-to-side, and finally peered right up and into my face. His mustache twitched like antennae. Slowly, he drew his tongue across his lower lip, letting it come to rest in the far right corner. *"Amerikajin,"* he finally said.

"Hai," I answered. Yes. "Captain."

He bowed. *"Kon-nichi-wa."* Greetings. He paused. He perused me again. I think it was the full beard and French braid that caught his attention. "ID paper please?" he asked.

His accent was so thickly Japanese that I could literally shrug the question off, my arms opened wide in the universal gesture for, I don't understand what the fuck you're saying.

He repeated the question. I had two choices right now. I could show him something, in which case he might go running off and ask someone about the *Amerikajin* with the French braid and it would be doom on Dick time, which as you know is the way of telling you in Vietnamese that I'd be fuckee-fuckeed. Or I could jump his bones, tape him up, and leave him where he'd be found in a couple of hours—and I'd be long gone. I knew that he couldn't be allowed to see Tosho—or the rest of my merry band of murdering marauders. Most of all, I couldn't let him learn about Arch Kielly, who was due back any minute, now.

So, I started to reach into my back trouser pocket, as if to withdraw my wallet. Instead, my left arm whipped around to knock the flashlight out of his hand and wrap the old guy up.

Except that by the time my big Slovak fist arrived at the spot where he'd been holding the flashlight, it grabbed a handful of air. Simultaneously, my arm was pulled forward, my body was yanked off balance, flipped like the proverbial flapjack, and I came down—hard—wham on my back on the fucking macadam of the BOQ parking lot. Who was this guy—the fucking star of those *Karate Kid* movies?

I rolled over onto my hands and knees, and groaned. The old watchman stood there, waiting, his face as impassive as an Oriental Sphinx. He waited until I'd pulled myself to my feet, bowed slightly from the waist—never taking his eyes off of me—and repeated his request: "ID paper, please."

I brushed myself off. Okay—so he knew Okinawan karate, or judo, or whatever the martial art flavor of the island happened to be. But guess what—I know that stuff, too. So I feinted left and watched as Old Guy watched me. I feinted right and watched. I saw where his eyes were moving, and I knew what I had to do. No, my response didn't include killing. I didn't want to hurt him, after all— just put him down long enough for me to bind and gag and stow him, so we could get on with the night's work.

Time was a-wasting. I feinted again—then, my feinting spells over, I went for his legs. Here's a fact: take a man down onto the ground and grapple with him, and all those wonderful holds and throws and kicks and the other sophisticated third-degree black-belt techniques he's mastered at the dojo are just about useless.

I dove, stretched out like a cornerback reaching out to shoestring tackle a wide receiver with the ball. But the sonofabitch stepped aside like a toreador and—*ole!*—as my body shot by him, he tapped me on the back of the neck with the butt of his flashlight. Not enough to do any real damage. But quite enough to let me know that if he'd wanted to, he could have broken my Roguish neck.

Once again, he stepped back and bowed. "ID paper, please."

What could I do? I bowed—keeping him in focus all the time while he did the same to me—and reached for my wallet. Which was when Tosho, moving like the real-life ninja he is, caught the old guy from behind, buckled his knees, and fell on him, his bulk pinning the watchman to the ground. The two of them rolled around like kids on a fucking playground, with Tosho stage-whispering—desperation creeping into his voice—"Stop the sidewalk superintendent shit and Get The Fucking Duct Tape, Dick—"

0032. I'd just finished stowing the night watchman in a phone booth sixty yards from the BOQ when my rigger's loft cumshaw crew returned with long faces. They'd found enough altimeters, wrist compasses, and miscellaneous web gear for all of us. But we were two MC-5 chutes short—MC-5s are the seven-cell Paraflite RAPS—Ram Air Parachute Systems—that we SEALs (as well as Recon Marines and Army Special Forces) normally use for HALO or HAHO operations. There were a bunch of MC3s—the old, round chutes that are used in static-line drops. But they'd rejected 'em and instead rooted around until they'd found a tandem—an old, military nine-cell Vector, to be precise, which had obviously seen more than its fair share of use. I examined the damn thing and wondered aloud if it had even one more hop in it—especially a blind jump in which the air conditions, ground conditions, sea conditions, and potential hostile conditions were all unknown.

Boomerang hefted the big, dark pack. "No prob—I'll jump this thing with Nod here, Boss Dude," he said, thumping Ed DiCarlo on the shoulder. "It's so cool."

"Cool, hell—I *hate* it when we jump tandem," Nod complained. "You gotta understand, Skipper, he's impossible. Always trying to fucking backseat drive. 'Steer right.' 'Steer left.' 'Flare now, brake now.' I swear, he's worse than my wife."

0047. Arch Kielly and Piccolo Mead drove up in a regulation USAF Hummer with a truck body on it. They jumped out and Arch began tossing our stuff into the boxy rear of the vehicle. "C'mon, c'mon." Arch's tone was urgent. "I found the plane—a C-12 just like you wanted. C'mon—get your stuff packed and we'll drive over. You guys can stow your gear while I locate a fuel truck."

Hey, maybe Mister Murphy had finally gone to sleep for a few hours. The C-12 is small enough so that we wouldn't need an APU—that's one of those four-wheeled, electric-driven auxiliary power units you see running around airports—to jump-start its dual Pratt & Whitneys. Arch could flip the switches, play with the chokes and throttles—in other words, do whatever magic that pilots do—and we'd be on our way. It was great news, and I burbled with enthusiasm. "Where is it? How long until we get there? What's the configuration? Where's the nearest runway?"

Arch interrupted his packing long enough to point vaguely over his shoulder into the darkness. "It's that-a-way some, just past the chop shop." He resumed stowing goodies, pausing long enough to look at me standing there, asking questions. "C'mon, Dick—get the lead out. What the hell difference does it make what where when why how? We have a plane. So, let's just get this fucking gear put away ASAP and get our asses over to the fucking thing."

He had a point. Warriors do not ask superfluous questions or burble like five-year-olds. Warriors do the job. I buttoned lip and started stowing.

Chapter

19

0053. WE JAMMED OURSELVES INTO THE HUMMER LIKE CLOWNS in one of those half-pint circus cars (to be totally honest, a bizarre, even outré similarity could probably be argued, given the absurdity of our current situation). Arch hit the ignition switch, the diesel gurgled to life, and, *sans* headlights but *avec* running lights, we chugged across Kadena like a squat tug cutting through a harbor. We passed some of the administration buildings, drove behind some huge stowage facilities, and skirted the humongous hangars and maintenance sheds. In the distance I could make out red landing lights and blue-lighted taxiways, as well as the dim lights in the "cab"—the air base's main control tower. Every few minutes, we could hear the roar of jet thrusters reversing as a plane came in to land, or the high-decibel sounds as a fighter took off into the moonless night sky with afterburners on full.

But Arch kept us well away from the active portion of the base. He drove slowly so as not to attract attention, easing past the darkened warehouses, stowage sheds, and outbuildings. He cut across the road maintenance facility with its dump trucks and graders, and skirted the recycling collection area, making his way around Kadena's seemingly endless perimeter, until—after what I thought was an interminable trip—we came upon the VIP terminal, approaching on a little-used service road that came up on the terminal's blind side.

We swung wide past the darkened structure and stopped, bathed in soft orange light from the sodium lamps on twenty-foot poles. Arch got out, opened a double-wide gate, pulled the Hummer onto the tarmac, and then rolled the four-foot-high chain-link fence closed behind him. He cut the engine and the lights, jumped out, did a little courtier's bow—the kind you see in the sorts of Tyrone Power/Linda Darnell movies they tend to show on AMC—and pointed to a half dozen aircraft in a neat line, chocked directly behind the low, neutrally painted building, and facing toward us. "Your transportation waits without, my liege," Arch pronounced.

It was too good an opportunity to pass up. "Without what?" I asked.

Arch's face went elastic. "Hey—I thought this was action-adventure, not Abbott and Costello."

0105. Gator used his slingshot to extinguish the three closest security lights, which allowed us to work in semidarkness. First, we changed clothes once again, back into the black SWAT stuff Tosho had given us. We strapped on our web gear and our side arms, our CQC tactical vests, thigh pouches, and other sundry lethal items. Then it was time to pack the aircraft.

I took my flashlight and peered inside. The plane had been configured as VIP transport. My beam illuminated six plush reclining chairs, a walnut wood desk console, a galley, with full bar—and very little damn space for our pile of lethal goodies. Doom on Dickie—fuckee-fuckee me. We were going to have to reconfigure the damn cabin before we could load out. I turned toward Arch. "You carrying a wrench with you tonight?"

Arch went through the Hummer's toolbox, then shook his head. "Negatory."

"Anybody else?"

The silence was absolutely deafening. I sighed and reached for the Gerber Multi-Plier on my belt—fuck! It was gone! I was going to have very existential fingers before the night was over.

0135. We began to load our gear a full thirty minutes behind the schedule I kept in my brain. Even with the seats and desk console removed, it was going to be a tight fit.

We were delayed even more when Arch reported that he couldn't find a topped-off fuel truck that was unlocked. The pilot took Duck Foot—and Duck Foot's set of lock picks—with him and disappeared into the night on foot. By the time they drove back, it was another quarter hour we should have been airborne.

Now, you may be wondering just why I was so intent on getting going quickly. First of all, since we were borrowing an aircraft, it would be easier to stay out of sight in the dark. Second, if by some chance Li Chimen and his crew had beaten us to the Senkakus, we'd have an easier time with them—and they a harder time with us—if we hit at night. But from the way things were progressing, it was gonna be light—or almost light—by the time we jumped. And third, the more time we took now, the less time Arch would have to get the plane back to Kadena unnoticed.

0154. Arch topped off the tanks and sealed 'em. He pulled the crib sheet out of the document folder and ran the preflight check with Pick. Then he did a solo walk around, pulling the wheel chocks as he did.

0157. He settled into the left-hand seat and adjusted for back and forth and side to side and up and down and pitch and yaw and whatever the fuck pilots adjust their seats for, until he was comfortable. I scrambled forward and watched as he and Pick played with the switches and dials, talking that fucking pilot-talk that nobody ever understands or makes sense of. I guess they were satisfied with themselves, because Arch's head turned, and he said, "Good evening, ladies and gentlemen. My name is Arch Kielly and I'll be your pilot tonight. We'll be following a southerly route over the beautiful South China Sea—"

Impolite though it might have been, I interrupted. "Yo, Arch." I didn't need a monologue—I needed to get our asses in the air, and that's what I told him.

"What's your point?" Arch got himself comfortable, and hit what he had to—and the port engine grumbled, growled, and snarled into life. When Arch was happy with what he heard, he kicked the starboard engine in, watched as his revs climbed, adjusted the prop pitch to just where he wanted it, then eased off the brakes and started a slow roll.

"Okay, gents, we're on our way," he said, stating the obvious. He steered us away from the VIP apron. We began to pick up a little bit of speed as we taxied off into the darkness.

I realized what Arch was going to do. The C-12 may not be a STOL—Short TakeOff and Landing—aircraft. But it can hustle its airframe skyward pretty damn quickly. So Arch was going to roll us out to a deserted taxiway at the very edge of the field, and sneak us right into the sky before anybody noticed.

Except he didn't do that at all. In fact, he flipped on what had to be every single one of the C-12's running lights, as well as its taxi/landing headlights. And he wasn't heading anywhere near the perimeter, but taking us directly toward the long line of red, orange, and blue lights that I knew designated Kadena's main taxiways and active runways.

One minor, niggling question occurred to me. It was this: how the fuck did Arch think he was gonna use a fucking runway? Hey, Kadena has multiple active runways. To use them, you've gotta get cleared by the control tower, especially since the air base is operational twenty-four hours a day, and if you just fucking go for it there is a very good chance that you will get yourself creamed by an F-15, or an F-16, or a C-5B, or—well, you get the idea.

But so far as I knew—and this knowledge was based on my own firsthand experience—it is generally hard to get clearance from a control tower when you are stealing the fucking aircraft. Being an inquisitive kind of Rogue, I posed that question to Arch.

"Hey, Dick, go back and close the drapes," he said by way of an answer. Who the fuck had he studied Q&A with, Roy Henry Boehm?

Puzzled, I stood up and turned to do as I was asked. Without warning, Arch gunned the engines, increasing our speed. He fucking knocked me clean off my feet. I careened back into the cabin, smashed snout first into one of the Big Brother suitcases, bounced off the adjacent bulkhead, then reversed course and landed in a heap at Boomerang's feet.

His long face peered down at me. "Awesome English, Boss Dude. What do they call that—a massé shot?"

"Fuck you, cockbreath." I found my footing, and my handkerchief, and blew fresh blood from my throbbing nose. What was it with Arch? Did he like to play STR— Smack the Rogue—every time we fuckin' flew together?

My eyes still teary from the blow my nose had sustained, I peeked through the porthole. We were moving past a series of hangars well illuminated by the warm, orange-tinged light of sodium lamps. A pair of black, stealth-painted C-130s sat outside one of the hangars, guarded by half-a-dozen dark-uniformed individuals with automatic weapons.

"Hey, fellas, that's where we keep the plane you rode in," Arch shouted toward the rear, oblivious of my newfound pain.

I stowed the hankie and continued into the fuselage. "Let's close the fuckin' drapes," I barked.

Drapes? Well, actually they were more like opaque curtains. But each window had a pair, stretched between two horizontal rods. That way, the VIPs could nap on the way to their destination. I slid curtains across the first of the four pairs of round windows, and watched as Gator and Rodent pulled the rest shut.

I headed back toward the cockpit. "Done, Arch," I said.

"Now, will you please keep the fucking speed stable and answer the fucking question?"

"Pick—get the hell off the flight deck until we're airborne," Arch replied by way of an answer. "And Dick—you keep out of sight, too."

He didn't wait for a reply. Instead he plucked the pilot's headset from its rest, slipped the cups over his ears, adjusted the microphone to sit just below his lower lip, and turned the comms system on.

I hunkered down well below the window line and behind the cockpit doorway and watched as he played with the radio dials and the keypad, punching in a series of frequencies. When he'd done that, he hit his transmit button. "Tower—Beech Two-Two-Three-One-Lima."

Tower—WTF?

"Repeat—Tower. This is Beech Two-Two-Three-One-Lima, Lieutenant Colonel Kielly, requesting taxi and takeoff clearance for a nonscheduled night navigation and evasion exercise."

There was a fifteen-second pause as Arch waited for an answer. "That's KILO, INDIA, ECHO, LIMA, LIMA, YANKEE," he replied, using the phonetic alphabet to spell his name. "Three fifty-three special ops wing. Yes—that's right. I'm nonscheduled. I have to work out a specialized approach for something upcoming." He grinned vaguely in my direction. "I think they bought it," he said excitedly. He clapped a hand to his ear so he could listen more easily. "Affirmative, tower." Another pause. Arch nodded positively. "Sure thing. Can do."

He dropped our ground speed and veered the C-12 gently to the left. "Confirm: Taxiway Tango-Papa-One-Six to Runway Romeo Three-Three. Hold and wait for flight path and takeoff clearance." He paused. "Affirmative. Thank you, tower."

He waited another thirty seconds, then hit the transmit button again. "Tower, Beech Two-Two-Three-One-Lima." He paused. "Affirmative. Mission profile has me turning the squawk off after I'm feet wet. Yes—affirmative: I will fire up the squawk prior to final approach, ETA three hours."

The C-12 coasted along the taxiway, its headlamps probing the darkness. Arch gave the plane some additional throttle as he approached the runway we'd been assigned. He turned the aircraft perpendicular to the runway and braked, bringing us to a full stop. He looked out over the wings to make sure his flaps were in the correct position, did a final cockpit check, then turned toward me. "We're ready to go," he reported.

Arch's attention was diverted by the radio. "Affirmative, tower," he barked. "Beech Two-Two-Three-One-Lima standing by." Arch turned toward where I was crouched in the cockpit doorway. "We have to wait for a pair of planes coming in—a flight of F-16s, I think."

From out of the black, an F-16 roared in front of us at an altitude of fifty feet, its engine screaming. Arch tapped his headset. "Say again, tower—say again." He lifted his head in my direction. "I can't hear worth shit with that engine noise."

The second fighter roared in. Arch was shaking his head, as if there'd been a malfunction. But obviously, nothing was wrong because he didn't wait for further clearance but jammed the throttles and bounced the C-12 forward, almost smacking me into the doorjamb as he did so.

"Hang on." Arch gunned the aircraft, launching it crudely and rudely to the right. The props were at full pitch, and we lurched down the runway, fishtailing a little bit for the first two hundred yards until Arch could steady the plane.

He was gaining speed when the runway lights went dead on either side of us. "I think somebody in the cab[65] just realized I'm not cleared to be flying this here plane tonight," Arch shouted. "Well—they're too fuckin' late, right?"

He checked the airspeed and, happy with what he saw,

---

[65]Remember—that's the main air-traffic control facility.

eased back on the wheel. We slipped into the night sky. "Say again, tower, say again," he said into his lip mike. "Sorry— say again, tower—I can't read you. I'm going radio silence now. I'll catch you on the flip side." He swiveled toward me and grinned. "Yeah—right."

We were climbing steeply now, banking into the darkness. Arch retracted his gear, trimmed his flaps, then waved Pick up from the rear and pointed him toward the right-hand cockpit seat. "You get yourself settled in," Arch said. "I'll hand it over to you once we're clear of Kadena airspace and I've put this thing where they won't be able to find us." Pick dropped into the copilot's chair and locked the armrest down. "Hang on," Arch growled, "I'm about to see just how much punishment this airframe can take."

He banked sharply left, then right, as he continued to climb steeply. Then he heeled over to my left, and kicked the fucking plane into a balls-to-the-wall dive.

My gut knotted, just like it does every time I ride a fucking state-of-the-art roller coaster, and I slammed Arch on the shoulder. "Fuckin' A, Arch—great!" I braced myself against the cockpit door and watched the altimeter roll backward as we roared groundward. I could see whitecaps through the front windshield.

Arch whipped the nose around, and we leveled off at two hundred and fifty feet. "Fun, huh?" he asked. He didn't wait for an answer. "Okay—we're feet wet," he continued—but heading northwest. "Now—let's start the disappearing act."

He hit the squawk switch, which killed the IFF—Identification, Friend or Foe[66]—transmitter.

---

[66]IFF uses electromagnetic transmissions—pulses—to which similar equipment carried by friendly forces automatically responds. IFF keeps you from shooting down your own (or allied) aircraft. Some aircraft have an IFF/PI, which is an IFF with a Personal Identifier, so that a specific aircraft—SECDEF's, for example, or Air Force One—can be distinguished.

"Now they'll have trouble spotting us." Arch played with the radio frequency buttons, and listened to what was going on. "Even so, they're scrambling something to come after us," he reported glumly.

So much for leaving Mister Murphy on the ground. But we weren't without resources of our own. "Boomerang," I shouted, "weren't you the asshole who wanted to try out the radar-defeating module in that suitcase we brought with us?"

0244. Enveloped by Big Brother's electronic shield, we were invisible. Don't ask me how the fucking thing works because I don't know. All I do know is that I was able to listen in to the pilots of the F-16s that had been sent to find us and escort us home, and the kind of language they used wasn't even fit for *this* fucking book. This damn equipment was *good*. We flew on in total darkness—no exterior lights, no interiors either. Pick kept our altitude at two hundred feet, plus or minus fifty, holding the C-12 steady above the mild chop below.

Back in the cabin, we parceled out the equipment by Braille and secured everything so it was jumpable. You cannot jump holding on to a three-hundred-pound steel crate, for example. And so the explosives, claymore mines, minigrenades, and other goodies I'd brought all the way from Washington via Rome got repacked in ballistic nylon bags and Velcro'd to our CQC load-supporting SEAL combat vests, or H-harnessed inside combat packs or aviators' kit bags. The guys looked like Michelin men by the time they were all suited up and ready. I played jumpmaster, checking each man's toggles and straps; making sure that the Velcro tabs were tight, and that all pouches would remain closed during our jump. It is hell when you're upside down in the air and you see all your ammo fall out.

Arch Kielly squinted at the shadows as we set up for the jump. "It has occurred to me," he said, "to ask how the fuck you guys are ever going to get back once this little exercise is over."

"Arch, if I knew that I'd tell you," I said. I hadn't gotten that far in my planning yet.

He shrugged. "Maybe I should come and get you."

It was a wonderful gesture. But it was impractical, and I told Arch so. He was going to have a hell of a time explaining what he'd done—and I didn't want to make things any worse for him than they already were.

"I guess you're right," he said grudgingly, sounding disappointed. He headed back toward the cockpit and the controls so Pick could douse his face with cammo cream and get his gear on.

0252. Pick and I were the last ones to make ready. I undid all the straps on his RAPS then let him shrug into the harness container. I held it steady as he pulled it high onto his back, threading the chest strap around his jumpsuit. Then he fastened his leg straps, pulling each one tight and securing the loose ends. As I held his pack in place, he adjusted his main lift webbing straps and tightened the horizontal adjusters. He stood straight, threaded the waistband through its buckle, and cinched it as tight as he could. He jumped up and down—that was hard for Pick because he's a tall sonofabitch and his head barely cleared the C-12's bulkhead—and, happy with the way the chute rode, stowed all the excess webbing so it wouldn't flap around during decent. Satisfied, he gave me a thumbs-up. I checked him once again—stuffing a loose web end I discovered into his waistband, then pronounced him good to go.

Pick held my chute for me while I strapped myself into it. Once it was secured, it was time to load up. Now, we SEALs are normally issued combat packs—either medium or large, depending on the mission requirements—which come with sets of webbing specifically designed to be attached to your front, or to your rear. The packs positions allow you freedom during your freefall so that you can maneuver your body and not kill yourself. We, however, were jumping with cumshawed equipment. That meant we had no combat packs. Instead, we had an unlikely assortment of ballistic nylon duffels, helmet bags, and carryalls with which we'd have to make do.

We would also be hampered by the sheer amount of equipment we'd be jumping with. Listen up—this is important. The Ram Air parachute has a more or less constant speed. By that I mean you travel at twenty-five to thirty miles per hour during descent. But that descent rate is calculated on a maximum load of 360 pounds of suspended weight.

Okay, let's run tonight's numbers. I'm a big s.o.b., somewhere in the 220 range. My MP5 and its eight loaded forty-round mags, plus my USP pistol and its six loaded fifteen-round magazines, come to about twenty-seven pounds. That's almost 250. My jumpsuit, vest, boots, belt, web gear, first aid fanny pack, and other assorted accoutrements add another twenty-seven pounds, eight ounces. That brings us up to 275. The parachute system—the RAM chute, reserve, and the packs, cables, and straps that come with 'em— weigh just over forty pounds. That's 315. Then there are the miscellaneous goods—ranging from two one-quart canteens, knives, and ropes to bolt cutters—that weigh about fifteen, sixteen, maybe even seventeen pounds per man. That takes us into the 325–326-pound range. Each of the Big Brother suitcases weighs seventy-five pounds. And our claymores, explosives, detonators, grenades, and other goodies added a total of 350 more pounds to the total. That's 500 more pounds of weight to be divided among eight chutes—62½ pounds each. The weight of the bags we were going to carry everything in added another fifteen pounds to the total—two pounds per chute. That's more than thirty pounds above the limit for which the chutes are designed.

Thirty pounds is not a lot of weight, you say. I'll tell you what: *you* carry a fucking thirty-pound sack of potatoes around for a few days and then tell me if you've changed your mind. And it's a shitload of weight when you're jumping. Combine thirty pounds of excess weight and an old, worn chute (or one that's been partially destroyed by saltwater landings) and the opening shock can destroy a cell or two. Result: you burn in. Or, if the chute has a malfunction and you've got to cut away and deploy your reserve chute—and you're well below the five-thousand-foot safety altitude—that thirty pounds can make a big difference then, too. But we would jump with the additional weight because tonight we had no choice.

That's another element of tonight's jump: the difference between training and balls-to-the-wall combat. Training jumps have safety officers on site; they always use lots of flares to mark your landing zone; there's constant monitoring of the ground wind speed. (According to the latest training manuals, "peacetime ground wind training limits will not exceed eighteen knots.")

Tonight, I had NFI—no fucking idea—what the ground level wind speed was. And frankly, I didn't care either, because we'd jump no matter what the velocity might be. Ocean chop? It didn't matter. The only thing that mattered was getting down and killing as many of the enemy as could be done. We had the murder of an American intelligence officer to avenge. And we had the Nation's security to protect. So no matter what the price was, I'd pay it. I'd pay it so that we would not fail.

0301. Arch turned on the radar and the plane's GPS system long enough for us to get a fix on our target. We were approaching from the north; our ETA was seventeen minutes. "Hang on—I'm climbing to ten thou for the release," Arch called out. The nose of the aircraft rose sharply, and the pitch of the props changed.

Tosh eased his way forward. Together, we used the Big Brother scanner to check for radio transmissions from the biggest of the islands—the only one with sufficient land mass to plant missiles. There was nothing emanating from the island. That was a piece of good news: it meant that we'd be arriving before Li Chimen. Tosh took the scanner, stowed it in the improvised combat pack that hung between his legs, and made his way aft. He was jumping third in this stick.

Boomerang signaled that we were still clear of surveillance. I gave him an upturned thumb. He would monitor until the last minute, then switch off the Big Brother module and stow it just before he and Nod jumped their tandem chute.

0313. I worked my way up and down, checking everyone's gear one last time, securing errant straps and making sure that all the flaps and seals were closed tight. As I checked, I peered into each of my men's faces. Their skin was dark with cammo cream, but all of their eyes were bright, and their War Face expressions were resolute. They'd come to play—and to win. There was no mistaking it.

Now let me digress for just a couple of minutes here to tell you a few things that are very, very important to me. First—and most significant—there is something euphoric about commanding such men as these Warriors. It is a thing that fewer and fewer officers ever get the chance to do, these politically correct days when manager-officers flourish and warrior-officers are shunned.

But, when you come to the old bottom line, isn't *war* what the military is supposed to be all about? So far as I am concerned, the military is not about getting money for college, or learning a trade, or getting an education, or feeling good about yourself. Those may all be peripheral aspects of being in the military, but they're not what the military is about. And here comes Point Number Two: which is, that at its core, being a sailor, or being a soldier, or being a Marine, is about being a warrior. It is about *MAKING WAR*. It is about Duty, Honor, Country. It is about breaking things and killing people. It is about spit and polish. It is about blood and sweat. It is about training, and discipline, and the sort of internal fortitude—the old guys like Ev Barrett and Roy Boehm call it GRIT—that keeps you going when your body and your mind want to lie down, roll over, and quit.

The folks in charge today—all too many of 'em—seem to have forgotten what the military is all about. They spend their time designing new sorts of missions; missions that make our sailors and soldiers and Marines into cops, or tree huggers, or social workers. Shit—our military spends more money these days on fucking recycling and environmental fucking protection than it does on goddamn bullets. So the fucking grunts may be perfectly accomplished when it comes to stacking old fucking newspapers in bins, and sticking plastic fucking bottles in the right colored containers, but they haven't learned how to fucking shoot straight, or clear a jam in their fucking rifle under battlefield conditions, or bring down an enemy tank with a LAAW, because there's no money for live ammo and realistic training anymore.

So let me tell you something, friends: we don't need any more fucking bureaucrats, or any more fucking apparatchik systems analysts, running our military (as has been the case with all too many of our recent Chairmen of the Joint Chiefs of Staff). We need kick-ass officers. Real leaders. Men like Tom Crocker, who is a Warrior in the tradition of Grant, Sherman, Pershing, and Patton; Nimitz, Halsey, Stilwell, and "Chesty" Puller—all officers whose men would follow 'em to hell. Those true American heroes, blooded by battle, their mettle forged on the anvil of war, were all willing to take chances—and risk lives—in pursuit of victory and defense of democracy. It is a hard thing to give an order that you know will result in casualties. But that is what being an officer is all about. It is about taking charge. It is about being responsible. And there is another thing, too: being an officer is about living Roy Boehm's two-word definition of leadership. Being an officer is about the words "Follow Me!"

And so, as I looked in my men's eyes, I realized that I was, once again, being given the greatest gift any officer can ever receive. I was being given the rare opportunity, the sacred responsibility, of leading Warriors into battle. There is no more fulfilling feeling a man can ever have. Thus endeth the sermon.

Chapter

20

0317. TEN THOUSAND FIVE HUNDRED FEET. ARCH SLOWED THE airspeed to just over a hundred knots. Then he turned on his systems. He scanned his screens and peered at the GPS readout. "Good luck," he said. He extended a gloved hand in my direction.

I took it with a firm grip. "Thanks for everything, Arch. You know . . ." I struggled for the right words. This Warrior had put his career on the line for me and my men.

He turned and looked at me. "Hey—forget it. You'd do the same for me, asshole, right?"

No doubt about that. "A³, Arch—anyplace, anytime, anywhere." I released his hand, struggled aft, and hooked myself into the last of my gear. Then I cracked the hatch and stowed it securely. The wind screaming past the aircraft was deafening. I adjusted my goggles, stood in the hatchway and looked down, the slipstream slapping at my face. Ahead and below I could make out the narrow chain of islands in the darkness. I stood to the side, so that Gator and Rodent, my first two jumpers, could stand ready in the door, and peered forward into the darkened cockpit. Arch held a flashlight in his right hand, its beam pointed vaguely in our direction. When he extinguished it, we'd go out the door.

The beam went out. I slapped Gator's back and he threw himself through the hatch. Rodent followed. Then Tosh, Duck Foot, Pick, and Half Pint. Boomerang and Nod waddled up to the hatchway in their big tandem rig—and stuck halfway through it. Their equipment had wedged tight in the hatchway and wouldn't move.

There was more—I saw that one of the equipment bag straps had come loose and wrapped itself around the hatch hinge plate. I reached under my chute waist strap, extracted my Spyderco folder from its horizontal belt pouch and sliced through the strap. Then I took hold of the ballistic nylon bag that was causing the logjam and shoved against it, using every ounce of my body weight to get the fucking thing moving. When it finally pulled free—and went out into the slipstream—it yanked Boomerang and Nod right with it. They disappeared into the void with a fast-fading "Hoo-YAAA!"

Time to go—I threw Arch a salute, followed it with the hairy bird, and jumped last.

I never saw the aircraft disappear—I was too centered on the jump itself. I went through the hatch and jumped, swiveling as my feet cleared, to position myself groundward. My body was in what I like to call "the hump"—back arched, arms and legs akimbo. I fell six hundred feet like that, my arms and legs extended, knees bent, my feet higher than my shoulders—a perfect example of what they call "the stable free-fall position" in the ops manuals.

It was perfect until the strap holding the improvised combat pack between my legs decided to separate and the pack came loose, yanking my legs around and skewing my body. Thus altered, my aerodynamics were unfavorably transmogrified and detrimentally metamorphosed in a negative manner. That's the Navyspeak way of saying that the fucking pack threw my big Slovak butt into a nasty, upside down, right-hand spin—the kind of spin that makes jet fighter pilots puke.

I reached down to resecure the broken strap. Big mistake. Did you know that extending the arms in an uneven manner during free fall will cause the parachutist to execute a turn? Well—you know it now, and so did I. I'd extended both arms to reach toward my combat pack. I was now spinning so unevenly that my eyes began to roll back into my head. This was an HFS—one hard fucking spin—which is a maneuver they don't teach at jump school. Belay that. I'd gone way past "spin." I was all the way to "corkscrew." Put all your emphasis on the last syllable, please.

This was not a good thing. From here on, I was vulnerable for a rough-and-tumble time—which was something I didn't need. Moreover, all this pitch-and-yaw shit was not doing my brain any good. It was like being inside a fucking tumble dryer.

Time to makee-makee better. I brought my arms back to what's known as the "Delta" position—arms about a foot from my sides, palms down—like a swept-wing fighter. That stabilized me out of the spin—which left me only the nasty loose pack to deal with. Look, Ma—no hands: I used my thighs to work at the combat pack, worming it with my knees until I had it centered once more. And they think they know fucking spin control at the White House.

Woozy, I checked my altimeter and compass. GNBN.[67] The GN was that I was stable again. BN: my current heading was 165 degrees from where I should have been going. Of course, where I should have been going was a guesstimate. Oh, there is a formula to calculate the HARP—or High Altitude Release Point—for HALO missions. To do this, you take the aircraft speed, the average wind velocity at jump altitude, the average wind velocity and direction at each two-thousand-foot interval from the exit to the opening altitude, factor in the forward throw as

---

[67]If you're too dense to figure this one out, you can look it up in the Glossary.

you exit the aircraft, and the free-fall drift, and *voilà:* the HARP you will need to land on the proverbial dime. Believe me—the textbooks say it's all mathematically precise and can be worked out to within a few centimeters. Yeah—well I know better. In a vacuum, things might go as planned. But you don't jump in a vacuum.

Tonight, for example, there was no information about the wind speed after we left the plane. No poop about its direction, either. To use the technical language of parachuting, we didn't know fuck all. And so, we'd have to feel our way down—use our intuition; our instinct—based on the experience of the thousands of jumps that each of us had made over the years. That's why I have always insisted on saturation training. The more experience you have, the more you know, the easier it will be to take evasive action when Mister Murphy sticks his ugly face into your business.

I turned my head and shoulders slightly to the right to execute what's known as a slow body turn. As I drifted left, I kept an eye on my compass until I'd hit my original bearing. I was back on track. Where I was in relation to the rest of my group I had no idea—but at least I was heading toward the Senkaku chain, and not toward the China coast.

The altimeter read 4500. Yes, I know that in the ops manuals that's five hundred feet below the MCA, or minimum clearance altitude, for air training operations. But this was the real thing, not some training exercise, and we would pull at 2500 feet above the island.

3100 feet. I could see waves breaking against the craggy shoreline. This was going to be a very chancy fucking landing.

2700 feet. I reached for the big rip cord handle. It wasn't there. Oh, it was definitely Doom-on-Dickie time.

With my right hand, I reached up, tried to locate the rip cord housing, and felt for the cable—which should have been protruding—and felt, and felt, and felt. Nada. Nothing. Bupkis. I started to barrel roll—fuck me—and brought my left arm up to counter my right. That kept me stable. If, that is, you believe that falling toward the earth at a rate of a 180 feet a second is a "stable" activity.

2400 feet. I found the cable end and worked my thumb and index fingers around it. Except that I was wearing gloves. And when you're wearing gloves it's hard to grasp hold of the inch-long end a fucking eighth-inch-diameter steel cable in the best of conditions, and this was not the best of fucking conditions but the worst of fucking conditions because I was free-falling at a high goddamn rate of speed while strapped to a shitload of equipment—and I didn't want to make myself any more unstable than I already was.

1900 feet. I worked my fingers up past the swage balls, along the cable end, as feverishly as any fucking freshman ever fingered pussy—except this goddamn cable was slipperier than a slurpee, hormonal, sixteen-year-old cheerleader humping in heat in the back of a van. But I kept at it, pushing the rip cord housing aside as I did.

1680 feet. I *felt* it. Oooh—it felt good, too. I wrapped the cable once around my index finger—which gave me some fucking purchase. And then I pulled—HARD. Nothing happened.

1500 feet—and the ground moving up real, real fast. I pulled HARD again.

1200 feet. The fucking chute deployed—breaking my free fall by standing me upright as the big Ram Air slammed open above my head. It was like—wham! My velocity dropped from 180 feet per second to zero. My head snapped back almost breaking my neck; my eyes bugged from the pressure the straps were placing on me. And yes, friends, all of that kinetic energy of Dickie and every single ounce of his equipment being brought up short, was centered on the triple-reinforced canvas strap that cut right across my right nut. It was all excruciatingly existential enough to make me cross-eyed for a few seconds.

But only a few seconds. There was stuff to be done. I checked to make sure all the cells of the chute had deployed properly. They had. I grabbed the toggles and steered right, then left—and moved as I wanted to. I brought the toggles to shoulder level and applied half brakes. My descent speed and angle changed, just the way they should. Okay—the controls were working. I couldn't quite see the ground, so I checked my altimeter. Four hundred feet and descending at a rate of nineteen feet a second—faster than I might have liked—but then I was carrying a lot of excess weight. The wind was at my back, and I toggled left so that I could fly my downwind leg, then come back into the wind for my final approach and landing.

300 feet. I knew I was awfully low for this downwind leg, but some things can't be helped. I unsecured and lowered my combat pack and the supplemental equipment bags so that my landing would be softer—hitting the ground still strapped to all that equipment is not good for the jumper's health. I felt to see that my weapons were stowed tight and right. They were.

180 feet. Shit—I hadn't paid attention to my position and I'd drifted much farther offshore than I should have been. I craned my neck. The breakers were more than half a mile to my rear and off to my right, now—and I was being carried offshore at thirty-five, maybe even forty miles per hour.

Why was this happening? It was happening because I hadn't been paying attention and been caught in what's known as a land breeze.

See, during the day, coastal land warms faster than coastal water, and the air above the land rises. The cooler air above the water takes its place, with the result that you get what's known as an onshore breeze. At night, the reverse takes place. The coastal land mass is cooler than the water—and the breezes move offshore. I'd been caught in one of these nighttime thermals.

This was real bad juju. I pulled hard on the control toggles to bring the chute around and come into the wind. RNT—Rule Number Two—of parachuting (it is right up there with Rule Number One, which, as you can probably figure out is always remember to pull the fucking rip cord) goes: always land into the fucking wind. Yes, I know that the dust jacket of this book says that as the Rogue Warrior I obey no rules. But there are a few rules that even Rogue Frogs like I have to obey—unless, that is, we want to croak prematurely.

No fucking way. I yanked on the steering toggle with all my weight. The airfoil reacted—dipping its outer edge into a tight turn. Tight turns are dangerous—especially at the altitude at which I found myself, which was so low that I thought my combat pack was going to catch the water and, acting like a fucking sea anchor, drag me under.

I released the toggles. The airfoil lip caught a big breath of air—and I was lifted up, up, up—two fifty, three hundred, three fifty, four hundred feet.

Now I saw breakers directly ahead of me, perhaps a quarter mile away. I steered toward the shoreline, looking for other parachutes as I descended. None were in sight.

135 feet. Since things were going altogether too well, Mister Murphy decided to fuck with me. One second, I was coming in as smoothly as a goddamn 747 on computer-assisted final approach. The next, I was slapped upside the haid by a nasty patch of wind shear and dropped sixty feet in about a second and a half. All the fucking bells and whistles went off at once. It was like fucking klaxons. The chute stalled, collapsed, and I dropped the last thirty-five feet, feet first, into the water, like a boulder rolled off a bridge.

I barely had time to grab a breath before I was dragged under. The shock was fucking explosive—water is hard when you hit it. My goggles were torn off, my body was ensnared by the nylon lines. Above, the dark parachute shroud descended to entwine and entomb me.

There was no time to think—only act. My right hand clawed at the quick-release toggles on my chute harness and I shrugged out of it and kicked away as best I could, hampered by the equipment packs whose long straps were wrapped around my legs.

My left hand reached for the automatic inflation valve on

my UDT combat vest. I yanked it—and felt an upward surge as the compressed gas was released, the vest inflated, and I was borne surfaceward.

I popped the choppy surface, snorted water like a fucking humpback, rolled onto my back, and sucked big, welcome lungsful of cool air. I looked around to get my bearings. I was about three hundred yards offshore. The vest would keep me afloat. Now all I had to do was pull in that hundredweight of soggy equipment, heave to, and swim. Yes, I am being ironic right now, in case you were wondering.

0332. I pulled myself out of the breakers, deflated my UDT vest, retrieved my combat pack and equipment bags from the surf, shouldered them as best I could, and staggered across the short span of rocky shoreline. I'd been carrying more than a hundred pounds of baggage. Now, everything I had—including my clothes—had been soaked through, increasing the load by what felt like 100 percent but in fact was probably only 50 percent.

And, oh, have I mentioned that it was cold and getting colder? Yes, I know it's the South China Sea. And I know we were just north of the Tropic of Cancer. But the water temperature was only about seventy degrees—and seventy degrees gets cold after a while if you do not have thermal protection—which I didn't. More to the point, the night air was about fifty-six, and from what I could tell there was a ten- to fifteen-mile-an-hour wind blowing across the island. The Roguish bottom line is that I was getting cold, fast. And there was nothing to do about it except keep going.

0340. I'd humped my baggage a hundred yards inland, when I heard something off to my right. I dropped to the ground, released my gear, withdrew the USP from its ballistic thigh holster, and moved forward, staying low and moving silently.

I heard the sound again and stopped. Withdrew my night-vision monocle from its pocket on my CQC vest, stretched out, and scanned. Twenty yards away, his head just as visible over the crest of a low, rocky ridge as it would have been in the midday sun, Half Pint was working feverishly at something. I retrieved my gear and moved in his direction.

When I got closer I saw that he was working on Piccolo Mead, who was lying on his back, his face contorted in pain. Half Pint looked up. "Yo, Skipper—asshole here decided to break his ankle on a rock." He worked on the Pick's left leg, handling it gingerly as he wrapped tape around an improvised set of splints and secured them. Half Pint turned back to his swim buddy. "You probably did this on purpose— thought we didn't have enough tactical problems already, right?"

"You got it," Pick said through clenched teeth. "Hey, Skipper, you have any morphine—if I had morphine I think I could walk once asshole here gets me bound and splinted." He sucked air sharply as Half Pint gently lifted the injured leg and wrapped surgical tape under the arch of his foot. "Oooh, that smarts." Pick shifted his shoulders. "Nurse Ratchett here says he doesn't have any. I think he likes it when I'm in pain."

I felt behind my back to the first-aid pouch that hung above my kidneys, unlatched it, pulled one of the half-dozen Syrettes out, and placed it into Pick's hand. "Go for it," I said. "But don't get a habit, huh?"

I closed the first-aid pouch. "You guys see anybody else?"

Half Pint nodded. "Gator came down over there." He pointed to the south. "And I think Boomerang and Nod did, too."

"Rodent? Tosho? Duck Foot?"

"Oh, we're all present and accounted for—although how we're still alive amazes me." Tosho's deep voice came from my left. He limped into view, followed by the five missing SEALs. "I think we have to talk about your choice of landing sites, Dick. Did anyone ever tell you you're a shitty jumpmaster?"

0410. We split into two squads and recced the island well before first light. It didn't take long—even though this was the only island in the chain large enough from which to launch an attack, it was less than a mile in length, and only six hundred yards or so in width. There were no structures—except for a single burnt-out shack with a wood flagpole lying out front, located on the island's highest point. Vegetation was limited to scrub brush, thistle, sea grass, and the sorts of dwarf trees that thrive in salt air and bad soil environments.

The place was uninhabited, although there were signs—well camouflaged signs but signs nonetheless—that someone had been snooping and pooping recently. All footprints had been obliterated by dragged branches. Wheel tracks had been raked out, then dealt with in a similar fashion. But Duck Foot, the Eastern Shore deer hunter that he is, was able to discern 'em all. I put him on the scent. It didn't take long for him to discover that the tracks led to a series of caches. One cache contained weapons. Another held marine communications equipment—the same sorts of waterproof radios that SEALs use. A third—a cave just off the landward, or southwestern, end of the island, held an eight-meter, rigid inflatable boat—very similar to the one we'd dropped to chase down the *Nantong Princess*—on a wheeled utility trailer. An outboard motor sat on an adjacent pallet, a pair of fifty-gallon drums of gasoline, a siphon, and five fuel bladders on the ground nearby. Now I knew how Li planned to make his getaway.

At 0535 we struck real pay dirt. Duck Foot led me toward a large cave just inshore of the island's southernmost coast. It had been covered with radar-defeating stealth netting. Inside, sat two mobile GLCM launchers. Country of origin: France. You remember about GLCMs. The acronym stands for Ground-Launched Cruise Missiles. I'd discovered six French GLCMs onboard the *Nantong Princess*.

Okay. Now we had everything but the supporting cast—e.g., the bad guys. Which presented me with a certain tactical dilemma, to wit: where the fuck were Li and his people going to land? I mean, we had a whole damn island to cover—and nine people to do the job. Sure, we could booby-trap the arms and comms caches, and disable the launchers. But if we allowed the bad guys to come ashore unimpeded, they could overwhelm us by sheer force of numbers. It would take 'em a lot of time, and cost 'em a lot of KIAs. But in the end, they'd overrun us. And then? Then they'd replace the equipment and procede with their mission, delayed but not deterred.

Unless, that is, we could stop 'em as they came ashore. Remember the principles of SpecOps—AV and RS and all that shit? Well, if we hit Li—hard—just as he and his men were most vulnerable, then we could keep them from achieving relative superiority. We would win—and they would fail.

And when were they most vulnerable?

Just as they were coming ashore is when. But where the fuck would they do that? I assembled the troops and outlined the problem. We sat down Indian-style in a circle. I drew a rough map of the island on the ground, setting pebbles to represent the caches and caves of equipment we'd found.

"What story does this picture tell us—if it does in fact tell us a story?" I asked. I waited for a response—but no one spoke.

Finally, Duck Foot's hand went up. He skewed his face up and pulled on his lower lip. "The pattern seems to be random, Skipper. I don't think it tells us much of anything." He paused and tugged at his lip again. Then he continued. "But the tracks I found—I think *they* speak loud and clear. The tracks tell me that Li Chimen brought everything inland from the same place," he said. He took his K-Bar and inserted it where I'd outlined the island's southern tip. "There," he said definitively. "That's where they're gonna land."

Tosho's round face turned toward Duck Foot. "How are you so certain?"

"Two things. One is that the beach there is all gravel and stone—no sand. So they leave fewer tracks coming out of the water, and those they do leave are easier to disguise." He looked at Tosho. "Didn't you tell us that your people fly

E-2C aircraft regularly over the island to make sure the Chinese haven't pulled any stunts?"

Tosho nodded. "Two Hawkeye flights a day—zero seven hundred, and fifteen hundred. Regular as clockwork."

"Well—the thermal gear on a Hawkeye can't pick up anything on stone." Duck Foot shook his head. "And the aircraft doesn't have infrared capability—it can't track." Duck Foot pursed his lips and set his bulldog jaw. "Nope—that's the way they came."

Rodent interrupted his shipmate. "What was your second point, Ducks?"

"That was the clincher. The track leading from the south coast was the most disturbed one. It was the only track used over and over—the signs were obvious."

Gator snorted. "Obvious? To who? Shit, Ducks, I didn't see anything—not a broken bush or a single fuckin' footprint."

Duck Foot grinned. "Maybe you weren't looking in the right places, city boy."

I looked at Duck Foot and marveled. There are some things that you can teach a man—and there are others that you can't. Duck Foot Dewey was a hunter. He'd been out in the woods since the age of four or five. And the basic tracking skills he'd learned in the woods and marshes of Maryland's Eastern Shore as a kid would keep us all alive here in the fucking South China Sea today. "You've convinced me," I said. I looked around. "So what are we waiting for, assholes—let's get to work."

0642. Tosho translated the Japanese Defense Force E-2C pilot's transmissions, while I tracked the Hawkeye on my Big Brother miniradar. The plane was getting close enough to make me nervous. I put my fingers in my mouth and blew a shrill whistle. "Everybody get your asses under cover—the Hawkeye's due overhead in ten minutes, and I don't want us fucking up in case he's early."

"Early, shmerly." Tosho continued working on the series of detonators he'd assigned himself to wire. "We Japanese are very punctual people. You heard him on the radio, and that little black box of yours plotted his position to within a hundred yards. He said he won't be here until oh-seven-hundred—and he won't. We still have a few minutes."

"C'mon, Tosh—move."

"Look, Mister Dickhead, I know about time. Timeliness is next to Godliness. That's what they taught us at Notre Dame."

"I thought it was cleanliness that was next to Godliness."

"Well, they taught us that, too." His extended middle finger told me I was still *Ichiban* with him.

"Look," I said, "maybe they'll come on time, maybe they'll be late. But I don't want Mister Murphysan screwing with my karma today," I said. "We're getting under fucking cover—*now.*"

1000. The inland booby traps were all set. Duck Foot and Rodent set one series at the arms cache—just in case Li's people made it that far. Gator, Half Pint, and Pick—who hurt like hell but was damned if he was gonna miss any of the fun—disabled the missile launchers so subtly that the Chinese wouldn't realize it until they'd locked, loaded— and hit the "launch" button. Then, just for good measure, Pick booby-trapped the comms. While he played, Nod DiCarlo, Boomerang, Tosho, and I laid out the (blood) red carpet with which we'd greet Li Chimen when he arrived.

Now, when you are setting up an ambush, there are four benchmarks that you must always try to satisfy. First, you want to locate your ambush in a place that will force your enemy into a fatal funnel—a killing zone. Second, you must be able to position your own force so that it enjoys several overlapping fields of fire. Third, you must be able to withdraw quickly and effectively—so that, for example, if the enemy calls for artillery or air support you can haul your butt outta there pronto, Tonto. And fourth, you want to be able to make your ambush site look as if no one has ever so much as disturbed a single twig, so the enemy will walk right in.

Now, as we all know, nothing is ever perfect. The southern end of the island was wide and flat. It was going to be hard to create the sort of fatal funnel you can create on narrow jungle trails, in urban alleyways, or twisted riverine settings. I improvised by setting a series of camouflaged Claymores at each side of the natural landing zone. They would keep Li's force—which was probably going to be much larger than my nine-man contingent—from getting around the sides and flanking us.

We did enjoy good fields of fire. That was because we controlled the high ground. Well, relatively high ground—we were perhaps twenty feet above sea level. We dug our positions out and camouflaged 'em.

It was good—but not good enough. I needed an additional element—something that would really bottle Li up.

I was problem-solving when Boomerang ambled up, holding one of the Big Brother black boxes.

"Whatcha got?"

"Radio transmission override, Boss Dude."

"So, nu?"

He shook the box under my nose and gave me the sort of bemused look computer wonks reserve for folks like me who can't tell the difference between a RAM and a ROM. *"Override,* Boss Dude," he repeated, moving his lips s-l-o-w-l-y and enunciating each syl-la-ble, as if he were speaking to an idiot. When he saw I still didn't get it, he sighed, shook his head, and said, "I can make a detonator out of this, Boss Dude. We use one of the Chinese radios. Wire it with some C-4. Then I use this little widget, set the frequency here"—he showed me where—"and then, when I turn the radio on, the circuits close, the C-4 goes *boom,* and we stir-fry some Chinese."

"Sounds like the same thing we've already got with the Claymores," I said.

"But I'm talkin' *underwater,* here, Boss Dude," Boomerang said. "I can plant the C4 underwater—cut 'em off as they land."

He is a devious child, isn't he? "Do it."

* * *

1134. Tosho, who was monitoring the Big Brother radio equipment, waved me over to the command post he'd dug. He removed his headphones. "There's definitely something going on out there," he said.

"Close?"

"From what this thing tells me, yeah—close. It started out real faint. But over the last half hour, it's been getting stronger. Not constant—but it's like *there,* y'know? Sounds like encrypted stuff. UHF."

I had a pretty good guess what he was listening to. It's the sort of stuff that gets sent from a sub, which is what I told Tosh.

"That would explain the signal strength," he said.

I looked at him. "But no voice transmissions yet?"

He shook his head. "I haven't heard anything yet."

"Keep listening." I started to move off. "Hey, Tosh—"

"Yeah?"

"Can that thing really gauge distance?"

"Yeah, it sure can." He flashed a smile. "You *Amerikajins* are getting real good at this hi-tech samurai stuff."

I bowed low in the classic style. *"Domo arrigato."* Thanks a lot.

He returned the gesture. *"Doo-itashi-mashite."* You're welcome. Then he fitted the headset over the top of his head, adjusted the earcups, and started playing with the digital controls on his black box.

I turned and jogged across the crest of the stone-covered rise down to the water's edge. Boomerang was sixty yards out, facedown in ten feet of water. He had strung his C4 across a fifty-yard stretch of the bottom, burying each charge carefully, then concealing the line between the charges. I shouted at him. He surfaced, trod water, and shook himself like a dog to take the seawater out of his long hair.

"Yo, Boss Dude—"

"How's it coming?"

"I'm done, but I'd like another five, maybe ten minutes. I wanna make double sure my tracks are invisible."

"Yo—*gaijin*—" I turned. Tosho was standing atop the rise, waving his arms. I jogged back up toward where he was standing.

"They're awful fucking close, Dick." He looked down at his equipment. "I'd say five, maybe six miles offshore."

Shit—given the quality of optics these days, a sub's scope could just about pick us out moving on the beach at that distance.

Ready or not, here they come. I turned and hand-signaled to circle the wagons.

Boomerang tread water, his hands on his hips, immobile.

"Boomerang—move."

"But I ain't quite done yet, Boss Dude," he called.

"Oh yes you is." Even at more than a hundred feet, Boomerang could tell from my expression that I wasn't making a request but giving an order. Abruptly, he stroked for the shoreline.

I put two fingers in my mouth and shrill-whistled. The rest of the troops came-a-running. "Company's coming," I said.

Chapter

21

1955. WE SPENT THE REST OF THE DAY WAITING—WITHOUT ANY sign whatsoever of Li's approach. Now, there's some significance to this. When you are laid up in your ambush position, there's no movement allowed. No coffee break to stretch the aching muscles and crack the joints and generally get limber. Hell—there's no coffee, either. You have to remain motionless, right where you have dug yourself in. You stay coiled to spring—ready to GO.

Now, achieving this kind of passive yet kinetically active balance is much harder than it sounds. Just remaining in one position for a long time can be difficult—hey, hey, hey—you out there. Yeah—the one with the dumb expression who just said "bullshit." *You* go out in the woods, or to a park, and secrete yourself for six to seven hours, motionless, your face, neck, and hands darkened by greasy cammo creme, your BDUs soaked by sweat and piss. Then come back and tell me how easy it was.

Because it is not easy. And there was more. I have told you that these islands were uninhabited. That is not precisely true. What I meant is that there were no *humans* here.

But there were more than the fair share of polydactyl creatures, most of the creepy, creepie-crawlie variety, many of them equipped with sharp mandibles and nasty stingers, and the uncanny ability to make life extremely uncomfortable.

And then there were the gnats. Kamikaze gnats. Big, brown, persistent, tenacious, aggressive, blood-sucking critters. The kinds of gnats that get inside your ears and bite you just past the point where you can work a finger up to dislodge 'em. The kinds of gnats that fly into your eye, bury themselves just under your lower eyelid, and squirm around until you are almost blinded.

Last but certainly not least, there was the small but significant matter of drinking water—or, more to the point, the lack thereof. We'd been exercising our bodies. Between the jump, the landing, and the work ashore, we'd been sweating like crazy. But we'd brought only two canteens of water per man: sixty-four ounces. That's not a lot when you have been engaging in strenuous activity, or operating under stressful conditions. It's not a lot when you've been held in one position for almost a full day, and the sun is beating down on your back, and you're dressed in black. A man can go without food for a week if he has to. But water is a definite life-or-death factor in warfare—and we didn't have enough to last more than another few hours.

It occurred to me as I was lying there, that if Li got suspicious—as I might under similar conditions—he could sit offshore for a day or two, checking on things from afar. If he did that, we'd be up the well-known creek *sans* paddle— or anything else—by the time he decided to come ashore.

The evening E-2C had long since come and gone—and we hadn't given ourselves away. Indeed, even though we were packing radios, earpieces, and lip mikes, I'd ordered radio silence—and double-checked to make sure that everyone's receiver had been turned off. I wasn't going to give our existence away by allowing someone with monitoring equipment to listen in as we chatted among ourselves, or leaked signals.

2003. I wanted to know whether there'd been any sign at all that Li and his *zhongdui* were on the move. So I eased from my position and crabbed around to the well-camouflaged position sixty yards below the ridgeline where we'd put our Big Brother equipment.

Tosho and Gator were in charge of monitoring. My hands asked if they'd heard anything lately. I got a negatory head shake from Tosho and a downturned thumb from Gator in response. They weren't picking up anything. Well, they weren't alone: the SpecWar radar that sits inside my head may have been going round and round, but there was nothing on the screen there, either.

I crawled back to my post and scanned the horizon. Nada. I passed Boomerang, who lay prone behind the mound of rock and earth that would protect him from any thermal scanning emanating from the water. He was observing the waterline through the ACOG sight on his MP5. He paused long enough to give me a dirty look. He'd wanted to finish his underwater booby traps, I hadn't let him, and he was still sore at me. Well, I was right and he was wrong. Just because Li hadn't come ashore back then, and still wasn't giving off any signals, didn't mean he wasn't in the neighborhood, prowling and growling.

2109. It was dark, it was quiet—and it had grown comfortable. A dangerous time for Warriors. The kamikaze gnats had returned to base for the night. The air currents had moved offshore, sweeping the day's heat away. And the last-quarter moon shone through partial clouds onto the water's surface, providing us with just enough light to enjoy the wave patterns as they broke gently on the offshore reef.

We lay in our ambush positions in pairs, strung out over sixty yards in a crescent that gave us effective, crossed fields of fire, concealed atop the uneven, scrub-covered ridge some seventy yards above the water. The gentle lapping of the water against the rocky beach was soothing, lulling me and the men into a quiet state of relaxation. This was not good. The white noise and quiet sapped our ability to concentrate on the possible dangers out there. Being uncomfortable—just like pain—can be a good thing: it keeps your senses primed; keeps your body and your mind sharp.

Even though I knew what was happening, by 2110 or so, my eyelids got tremendously heavy, and the thought of grabbing a combat nap was very, very inviting. And then, I don't know what it was—a subtle change in the air currents, or a motion in the water so slight that it was almost (but not quite) imperceptible, but something tripped the sensor wire inside my brain and the fucking klaxon horn screwed in position just below the bullshit detector went off. No—I didn't react outwardly. But even without any discernable movement, I went from passive alert to battle stations in a millisecond.

Then, the hair on the back of my neck stood up. I don't know where this instinctive reaction to danger first came from, friends—but it is a regular, palpable sensation that has kept me alive for years. When the hair on the back of my neck stands up, I know that something or someone that wants to do me damage is close by.

I moved oh, so s-l-o-w-l-y, lowering my head a millimeter at a time until I'd cleared well below the ridgeline. I swiveled to my left and clenched my right hand into a fist, then stuck my thumb out and pointed it toward the ground, silent-signaling "enemy suspected." Six yards away, I saw Duck Foot's eyes move in my direction—the moonlight catching the whites of his eyes. His blackened face bobbed up and down, and he turned and repeated the signal to the Pick, who lay six yards to his left. Pick would relay the signal to Half Pint, who controlled the leftmost field of fire. Then I turned to my right and repeated the sign, passing the word to Nod, who passed it to Boomerang, who passed it on to Rodent, who'd pass it to Tosho and Gator.

2111. I eased my way back up to the ridgeline. Pulled my night-vision FLIR[68] monocular from its pouch and let it

---

[68]That's Forward-Looking InfraRed, in case you didn't remember.

drift left/right/left across the surface of the water. Then I repeated my action, panning slowly, letting my eye grow accustomed to the green-lit fluorescence.

Once again, the hair on the back of my neck stood straight up. *There was something going on out there that was out of the ordinary.* I screwed my eye tighter into the monocular, concentrated, and—goddamn it—lost whatever it was.

Fuck me. That was my fault. Remember your basics from Hunting 101? I certainly hadn't. When you're in the woods stalking deer, you almost never see a deer in its entirety. What you see is a piece of something that catches your eye—a furry ear caught against the vibrant green of a holly bush, or a hint of that flicking white tail, moving in front of the rough bark of a locust tree, or the rapid movement of the deer's head as it senses a predator. The accomplished hunter sees these flashing signs because he is not tunneling. Oh, his vision is like a cone—but it is narrow at his eye, and grows wider and wider as he surveys the forest around him. The neophyte looks at things in precisely the opposite way: his cone is wide at the eye, and it narrows down the farther away it gets.

That's what I'd done here—I'd tried to focus closely on what I thought I'd seen—and I lost it all.

I pulled my eye away from the monocular, rubbed at it, and then tried again. I panned across the water's surface, letting my eye pick up what naturally attracted it.

There—there they were. Something was working against the wave pattern out there. I used the range finder. They were just over 250 yards from shore and coming closer, closer, closer—the infrared painting 'em like a school of fish moving close to the surface as it shifts direction in the currents. I'm not talking about anything big, friends. It was just a touch, a trace, a trifle; only the slightest insinuation of contrapuntal motion out there—the merest *flick* of the deer's tail—but it was fucking contrapuntal motion nonetheless, and I fucking saw it.

I panned again. Now that I'd caught the hint of movement, it was easier for me to pick it up. Yes—one, two, three swimmers, stroking so quietly that they weren't making any ripples, moving just under the surface of the water. They were obviously wearing rebreathers so as not to leave any telltale bubbles. But they couldn't escape the FLIR's half-mile range—or my man hunter's eye. I dropped behind the ridge and my hands relayed what I'd seen. *Stay down,* I told my guys. *Don't let them catch us with thermal imagers or infrared.*

Did I know they had that kind of equipment with 'em? Nope. But I did know that, given the proliferation of technogoodies, even your basic Hizballah terror cell can buy over-the-counter night-vision devices, hand-held GPS monitors, and secure comms. That being the case, why shouldn't I believe that *zhongdui* shooters should-could-would have 'em too? Answer: never underestimate your enemy.

I picked the targets up again. Now they were less than a hundred yards out—stroking steadily toward the shoreline. I used every molecule of my consciousness to pan the night—vision monocular back out where they'd come from—but couldn't pick up on anything. My instinct told me that this was the advance party—and that once they'd secured the beachhead, Li and the rest of the troops would follow.

So, we had to let 'em come ashore. That was fine by me. I hand-signaled orders up and down the line and received affirmative responses.

2119. The waiting is bad enough when there's nothing going on. When you know your enemy is out there, moving inexorably in your direction, I don't care how many times you have gone to war; I don't care how many men you have killed. It is always the same: your breath goes shallow. Your blood pressure and your heartbeat accelerate. There is a slightly oily, queasy feeling in the pit of your gut. Even though your bladder's empty and you couldn't get a straight pin upside your sphincter, you all of a sudden feel the need to take a piss and a dump.

2121. The trio of swimmers stopped about fifty yards

offshore, in waist-deep water. I could see 'em plainly in my night vision now. They dropped their masks around their necks; eased the rebreather hoses from around their necks and secured 'em; squatted to remove their fins, and secured them one by one at the rear of the UDT-type vests. Then they lay back in the water, retrieved their weapons, and checked 'em out.

I studied the men we were about to kill, totally absorbed by what I was seeing. It was like watching a mirror image of ourselves coming ashore in a potentially hostile environment. We have operated against terrorists of various stripe; against Russkie special forces, Libyan Army units, and the Iraqi Republican Guard. But never before against a maritime unit like the *zhongdui*. I could tell by the way they moved that these guys were good. The *zhongdui* we'd gone against on the *Nantong Princess* were second-raters—these guys were *operators*.

Slowly, covering one another, they moved out of the water and up onto the shore. Point man had night vision held to his eyes. He scanned the rocky beach in front of him, searching for any sign of hostiles. Then his vision shifted, rose toward the ridgeline where we were hidden. I held my breath—kept myself absolutely motionless—and watched as he watched me. The temptation to move my eyes as he moved his was absolute—but I fought it. I was going to give this sonofabitch *nothing*.

His night vision dropped to his chest, he retrieved his submachine gun, and the trio moved off stealthily along the beach, toward the path leading to the cave that held the missile launching equipment. They were here to check it out—then they'd call the landing party in.

Of course—Li had to bring the fucking missiles with him tonight. I'd made it necessary when I'd sunk the *Nantong Princess*.

I came off the ridge and silent-signaled my intentions, first to the left, then to the right. When I got confirmation that I'd been received and understood, I removed my CQC vest and web gear, my boots and my socks, keeping only my suppressed MP5—on which I fastened the FLIR—and my knife. Then I worked my way down the inland slope, making my way at flank speed toward the eastern coast— toward the cave concealing the launchers. Tosho, similarly equipped but wearing boots, slipped into my wake.

2131. We got there first—and we got there silently. That's why I'd taken my boots and socks off. The soles of my feet are tougher than the fucking Vibram they're using on boondockers these days. So I run through the woods faster barefoot than you can in boots. But that's not why I do it. My feet are like sensors. I can probe for trip wires and other booby traps more effectively with my ten-and-a-half-triple-E feet than I can with a couple of hundred thousand dollars' worth of newfangled electronic countermeasures gadgetry. So when I need to move, really *move,* I prefer to go the old-fashioned way: barefoot.

And, having stubbed the Rogue toes only once or twice on the way, I'd picked out a trail that allowed us to move fast— but not make any noise. We approached from above the cave's mouth—setting ourselves so we'd be impossible to pick up if the *zhongdui* swept the area surrounding the orifice with their imaging equipment.

2141. I heard the slightest hint of movement below my position and to my left. My body tensed as the trio of *zhongdui* came closer. I had to really work to hear 'em at all—they *were* good—until they came to the camouflage netting. We'd fucked with it so that it rustled more than anybody'd want—and gave their position away.

I waited until the rustling stopped—which meant they'd gone inside to inspect the launchers—then, inch by inch, I began my move.

To my right, Tosho mirrored me.

The pace was excruciatingly slow. My big toe probed the ground. When I felt confident, the ball of my foot followed. Then the arch; then the heel. Sixty seconds to move less than a yard—and I wanted to cover another six yards before these assholes emerged.

There was nothing to do but keep moving. And that's

what I did—my whole body turned into an early-warning system. I put another yard behind me. And a third. In two more feet I'd be in a good position to "cut the pie" of the cave mouth—which meant I'd finally enjoy a decent field of fire. Which is precisely when Mister Murphy stuck his own bare foot onstage. First, I stubbed my big toe on a loose rock and sent it skittering and clattering. Then Mister Murphy booted me in the ass and sent me sprawling down the last eight feet of hillside.

Oh, fuck. Oh, doom on Dickie. I clutched my MP5 to my chest, tucked my shoulder, and rolled as I fell, so as not to hit face first.

I needn't have worried—because halfway down, Mister Murphy flipped me over, and I landed flat on my back, which under other circumstances might have knocked the wind out of me. Tonight, however, there was no chance for that—because as I hit, half a dozen rounds kicked the ground two feet from my right thigh. No gunfire sound, either—just *phhht-phhht-phhht* as they struck the hard earth.

Fuuuck you, whoever you are!—I sprayed-and-prayed the cave mouth while trying to focus on where the hell the threat was coming from—it was just a tad dark, you recall—and received a second barrage from my left.

Yeah—but this time I saw his supressor flash. *He was outside.* This was Mister RSG—the rear-security guy. I rolled away from him, came up looking through the FLIR sight. Found him—he was wedged behind a boulder, his position hampered by his bulky CQC vest and other equipment. I fired a three-shot burst in his direction to keep him off balance. Came up onto my feet. Took cover at the opposite edge of the cave mouth. Was about to draw down on him when I heard the welcome sound of a body collapsing on the ground. Stuck my MP5 around the mouth of the cave and saw RSG facedown—and Tosho's upraised thumb extended for me to see.

One down. That was the good news. The bad news was

that *Zhongdui Er* and *Zhongdui San*—that's how they say *zhongdui*s two and three back in Beijing—were primed to repel boarders—and if I'd been them, I'd have been on the radio at the first sign of commotion.

No time to waste—and no one but me to do the dirty work. I rolled under the cammo netting and into the pitch black cave. Hugged the side wall. Brought the MP5 up so I could see through the FLIR. Swept side to side. Three yards from where I crouched, two heavy four-by-four stowage crates provided meager cover. I crabbed behind the first of 'em, poked my night vision out and panned. Thirty feet in front of me, the missile launchers stood, low and skeletal on their fat pneumatic tires. Behind them, the big crates of auxiliary equipment glowed green against the green phosphor of the lens.

The infra red picked up a white-hot spot at ground level next to the rearmost, right-hand crate. The lens of my night vision picked up the nasty beam as it shot past my head. Fuck—*Zhongdui Er* was trying to laser me. I pulled back— if he hit me in the face with the fucking thing he'd burn my corneas like *cuchifritos*. DOD issues antilaser goggles to all its combat forces these days—including me. But mine were safely stowed, fifteen thousand miles away, back in the duty locker at Rogue Manor. BFH[69] they were, sitting there.

I rolled to my left—the second crate providing cover. Sucked ground and stuck the business end of the MP5 far enough out to get a sight picture. The angle was bad. From where I lay, no way could I hit *Zhongdui Er*—unless he just about stood straight up like one of the fucking paper pop-up targets we use when we borrow the FBI's kill house at Quantico.

Sometimes, as Doc Tremblay says, *entiymah feeshmok*— which is Cairene for the fact that I sometimes have fartbean brains.

---

[69]Big fucking help.

Why do I say that? I say it because we fucking train for this exact fucking scenario. In total darkness. Using the same goddamn equipment I currently had on my Roguish person. Except I hadn't been war-gaming, or thinking, or what the fuck. I'd just been flailing along.

I mean, this was as simple as assembling a Port-A-File.

Fold along the dotted lines to reveal Tab A. I tucked back out of sight and retrieved my knife.

Depress scored portion of cardboard to reveal Slot B. I resumed my prone position and got a sight picture.

Insert Tab A into Slot B. I threw the knife at the left-hand wall.

Like fucking clockwork, *Zhongdui Er* and his laser-equipped subgun and *Zhongdui San* and his semiauto pistol popped up—both exposing head and shoulders, thank you very much. *Zhongdui Er* was right where the crosshairs of my FLIR were zeroed. I stitched him with a three-round burst, and he dropped faster than the automated targets at Quantico. Deader, too. I pulled left, which is where the second commando had shown himself—but there was no sign of him.

Okay—*Er* down, *yi* to go. And no time to waste.

I rolled back to my right, came around the crate, and charged, using my night vision to make my way in the blackness.

The sonofabitch was hunkered down behind the rearmost crate—fumbling in his CQC vest. Fumbling for what I didn't know—but I wasn't about to let him get his hands on whatever it may have been. I charged. He fired wildly down the cave. That did him more harm than good. The muzzle flashes fucking blinded him, and now he shot twice again into the stone roof of the cave. He was still trying to recover when I let go three three-round bursts to make him keep his head down.

He did exactly as I hoped. I vaulted the first of the missile launchers, skirted the second, worked my way around the first crate, and came up five feet behind him.

April fool, motherfucker. I caught him in my sight looking the wrong fucking way—and squeezed the trigger.

There was a very ominous click as the MP5's hammer fell on an empty chamber and he turned toward me, his pistol pointed at my chest. Yes, I see you out there waving your hand, screaming that the MP5 bolt locks back whenever the magazine expends its last round. You are correct. But sometimes even the MP5 misbehaves. Maybe it was all that saltwater. Maybe it was the fact that I hadn't cleaned the fucking thing since before we'd left for Rome. Maybe it was the fact that suppressed weapons need more TLC than your normal submachine gun. I didn't know the reason—and I didn't fucking care. What I did know was that the goddamn gun was no use to me now, and I don't have time to stand here fucking explaining things to you.

Zhongdui San had his War Face on. I could see it through the night-vision sight. I dropped and rolled against the back wall of the cave just as he fired five rapid shots in my direction. My eyes shut reactively and I went into a ball— hoping to absorb only one or two of the rounds that had to impact. He kept shooting—sharp stone shards cut at my head and neck.

Then the gunfire stopped—and he'd fucking missed me. The old Rogue reflexes had come through for me once again. I listened as best I could (my ears were ring-a-ding-ringing from the at-close-range explosions). But through the reverbs I still managed to pick out the hollow sound of a mag dropping onto the ground. Shit—the sonofabitch was reloading.

No fucking way. I shot forward and tackled him around the knees, my subgun clattering to the uneven stone surface of the cave as it danced clumsily on its sling. The MP5's hot suppressor muzzle slapped the side of my face—I felt heat through my beard, but that didn't stop me from body-slamming the *zhongdui* as hard as I could. Then the sling separated and the HK fell away.

I found his gun hand, rolled him to my left, and smashed

weapon and hand on the cave floor. He grunted and tried to bring the gun back across my face. I fought him off and— "*uh*"—slammed his hand back into the ground again. The pistol dislodged and went skittering off in the blackness.

But *Zhongdui San* wasn't giving up. He rolled away, scrambling like a fucking tadpole out of water. I grabbed at his legs. He smashed one of his soft-soled boots into my face hard enough to jar my teeth. I found his ankle and twisted it 180 degrees to starboard. He screamed but kicked again. The blow glanced off my forehead. I saw stars and lost my grip on him.

He came straight for me, his shoulder found my solar plexus, and, grunting, I was knocked backward. He kept at me—our hands grappling, groping, probing for weakness. Then I felt him shift—his right hand shook free of my left, and he turned away slightly as we battled for advantage.

Instinctively, I knew WTF was happening. *The sonofabitch was going for his knife.*

I hate knives. I hate using them as weapons because no matter how good you are, how proficient, how deadly, you will almost always get cut in a knife fight. But I had no choice. I reached for the big Cold Steel blade on my belt— and came up empty. It was gone. I'd used it—tossed it away to draw fire. Fuck me—I guess I could try to beat the sonofabitch to death with my dick—he'd suffer the blunt-instrument trauma known as death by friendly weapon.

Fuck—this was no time for black humor. I wrestled with him in the darkness, feeling for where his hands were going. His left hand had my right hand tied up, and we played fucking fiddly-fingers as we struggled for dominance. He was a wiry little finger-fiddler—and he *was* little, built like many SEALs, who are short and small-framed. But those pint-size SEALs will outlast most five-gallon Rangers when it comes to endurance. And this *zhongdui* may have been small, but he was wiry, and strong for his size. Shit—he was strong for *my* size.

His right hand—knife hand—was behind him. I worked my way down from his shoulder and tried to find it and break a finger or two before things got serious—or dangerous. But I could tell from his position that he'd already drawn whatever kind of knife he had from its sheath, and his wrist was turning, turning, turning, so that he could get the business end of the fucking thing pointed in the direction of my vitals.

Now, let me pause here just long enough to remind you of something I said earlier: when you are rolling around like this on the ground all those fancy moves you've learned in the dojo don't do you fuck-all. This ground fighting shit is down and dirty. Like the Rogue's Tenth Commandment, there are no rules.

I broke my right arm free and smashed his cheek with my elbow. I shattered a bone. I heard it go—and he reacted. But my blow hadn't been effective because he didn't stop working his right arm around—I could feel the point of the fucking knife bite into my left hip. It penetrated and nicked the bone—which sent a spasm of white-hot pain from my leg to my shoulder.

I fought him off, my teeth gritted to keep from screaming. Balled my right hand into a fist, kneed just enough clearance between us so that I could strike across my body, then—*"Fuuuuck you"*—brought my right fist down like a fifteen-pound sledgehammer on his left clavicle.

The shoulder bone snapped—and reactively, he released his grip on the knife, which fell away. I didn't chase after it—and I didn't allow him any recovery time, either. All I could think of was killing the sonofabitch—and doing it soon. I used my bulk to wrap him up, slam him onto his back, and then I leaned into him—my forearm crushing his throat—and pressed with every fucking ounce of fucking energy I could fucking muster until I fucking crushed his fucking Adam's apple and shut off his fucking air. When he stopped struggling, I took his head in my hands and twisted until I'd broken his neck—hey, hey, hey, don't be so fucking queasy. You don't want the opposition reviving and coming after you when you think they've been neutralized. This *zhongdui* s.o.b. wasn't gonna be able to do that.

I rolled off his corpse and worked my hands around, trying to find my MP5, and *Zhongdui San*'s pistol and knife.

A blinding beam of light penetrated the cave's blackness. "Yo, Dick." Tosho's voice came from behind the light.

I tried to pull myself to my knees—and rolled over onto my back instead. My fucking hip hurt like hell. "Over here, Tosh."

He came through the cave gingerly, examining the *zhong-dui* to make sure they were dead before he got to me. Then he looked me over—including the blood on my BDUs. "Nicked you, huh?"

"Yeah—but not too bad I think."

"Lemme look." He pulled and poked and un-Velcro'd until he exposed the wound. "At least he didn't nick an artery," Tosho said, his expression tinged with concern. "Hey, guess what—the guy outside wasn't carrying any comms." He directed his light at the two corpses. "And these two don't seem to have any radios, either."

He swung the light around to catch me probing the wound on my hip, slapped my hands away, and before I could react, jabbed me with a tetanus Syrette he'd plucked from his first-aid fanny pack. He retrieved a second Syrette. "Novocaine. That'll keep you on your feet for a while."

I shook my head. "I can do without it—want to stay sharp."

Tosho shrugged. "Up to you, bub."

"You know how much I like fucking pain—how alive it makes me feel." I pulled myself to my knees, then stood up, tentatively shifting my weight onto my injured leg. Oh, yes, fuck, it *hurt*—but that pain would give me an edge. It would remind me why we were here: to avenge Alixe Joseph's murder and checkmate Li Chimen.

But my *will,* not the pain, had to dominate the situation. I focused my whole being on the problem, allowing my body to absorb the pain and diminish its intensity and its hold on me. The weaker the pain grew—the more my mind was able to control it—the stronger I became. When I had conquered it, I was able to stand tall and straight. I rolled my neck and shoulders, working the kinks out. I shifted my web gear around until it was comfortably balanced, then adjusted my BDUs until they were shipshape, too.

It was time to go back to work. "They weren't carrying radios?"

"Nope." Tosho helped me sling the MP5. "But the *zhongdui* outside was carrying these." He pulled an olive drab plastic container holding two foot-long IR lightsticks from his BDU pocket. "That's how they were going to signal the rest of the troops to come in."

I nodded. Then I gave the plastic a second look. "Lemme see that again."

I took hold and examined it in the beam of Tosho's flashlight. "Fuck me."

"What's up?"

"This is American—U.S. Government issue." This didn't make sense. "Lemme see the light."

I took Tosho's flashlight and examined the first of the two *zhongdui* corpses in the cave. It didn't take long for me to see WTF. "Holy shit—"

"What did you find?"

"Something *you* overlooked, Sher-rock."

Tosho approached. "So, nu, Doctor *Rot*son?"

"Look at their uniforms—their equipment."

Tosho nudged the corpse with his toe. Then he saw what I'd seen. "Holy shit indeed." He knelt and started a closer examination. "These guys aren't wearing Chinese equipment."

"Bingo," I said. I fingered *Zhongdui San*'s CQC vest. "This vest is the same one the Royal Marines use." I pointed at the pistol the dead Chinese had carried. "Beretta—a model 92. U.S. Army issue." I rolled the corpse over. "French fins and mask; German web gear." I paused. Let's look at the other two.

It didn't take us long to discover that *Zhongdui Yi* and *Zhongdui Er* were as multilaterally equipped as *Zhongdui San* had been.

Does that tell you anything, gentle reader? It tells me volumes. Remember how I'd outfitted my men when we'd set out to scuttle the *Nantong Princess*? That's right—I'd equipped us with gear that didn't read "This Equipment Belongs to United States Naval Special Warfare Personnel" in bright neon lights. I'd provided my nasty SEAL strike force with the same model British CQC vest these *zhongdui* swimmers had on. We'd carried vintage East German ammo—they were using Czech. We'd worn French wet suits, and Israeli Kevlar helmets. They wore Italian wet suits, hadn't bothered with helmets, but they carried Japanese knives. None of the weapons I'd seen so far—Italian pistols; Belgian submachine guns—had any visible serial numbers.

Well, the main reason to use such sanitized equipment is to confuse the opposition during a covert operation. If you get waxed and your body is discovered, the use of untraceable or varied equipment makes your country of origin much harder to determine. So, when I operate in the black, I never carry USGI,[70] or even American-made equipment, even though that's what I prefer. I mean, I like the Royal Marine CQC vest. It's okay. But the one made by Blackhawk Industries of Virginia Beach is better, more durable, and it weighs less. It was designed by SEALs for SEALs. I could go on, but I think you get the picture.

Okay—fast-forward to the present. Here are three *zhongdui* commandos. They're not wearing the regulation Chinese-issue equipment in which they normally operate (remember, I saw what they normally carry aboard the *Nantong Princess*), but a jumble of foreign-manufactured stuff.

I rolled the corpse closest to me and started working my way through its pockets. "Check for IDs," I told Tosho. "I'm willing to bet you a hundred bucks we won't find anything on these guys—not even a dog tag."

---

[70]U.S. Government Issue.

Six minutes later, I was absofuckinglutely certain that Li was running an off-the-books operation. Oh, perhaps it had been sanctioned by the Chinese government—or one faction of the government. Maybe Li had been unleashed by Major General Zhu Linfan in the same way I'd been turned loose against the *Nantong Princess* by Chairman Crocker. Maybe he'd even been given the green light by Defense Minister Chi himself.

But no matter who'd approved this little operation, I knew in my Roguish heart that Li was operating covertly tonight. The thought made me smile—because if he and his crew disappeared at sea, no one was going to make any diplomatic waves over the vanishing act. Not even one tiny ripple.

Show time. I turned toward Tosho and shook the package of IR lightsticks in his direction. "Well, *I* think it's all clear—don't you?"

Tosho's War Face dissolved into a malevolent grin. "I think it's rock-and-roll-out-the-red-carpet time for Mister Li," he said.

Chapter

22

2235. I'D STOOD ATOP THE RIDGELINE, PARTIALLY OBSCURED BY vegetation, twisted the IR lightsticks, and activated 'em. Tosho'd held one high above his head; I'd held the other. We stood there like fucking Statues of Liberty for three to four minutes. Then we'd planted them high enough on the ridge so they'd be visible guideposts for the incoming force, and got to work.

2252. My FLIR was trained out to sea in the general direction the trio of *zhongdui* had come from. The night-vision unit—it's built by Texas Instruments just in case you wanted to know and order one—has a range of just over a thousand yards—more than six-tenths of a mile—although it can pick up only a man-size target eight hundred yards out.

I didn't have to worry about man-size targets—I spotted the RIBs coming at us as they churned into the FLIR's range. Four of 'em, traveling slowly, inexorably, toward the point of shore that dead-centered between the IR light-sticks.

Tosho was back on the Big Brother equipment. I looked

over toward his position and shrugged, arms out, palms up. "Anything?"

He shook his head negatively. "Either they're maintaining radio silence, or they're not carrying."

I thought about SFA's approach to the *Nantong Princess*. We'd had radios, but I'd made sure they were turned off, too.

Back to the ridgeline. I'd reminded the guys to stay low, below the prying IR that Li was carrying. I'd do all the spotting through my FLIR.

I peeked through the tube and used the range finder. The RIBs were six hundred yards out now—moving clumsily as they tried to maintain a straight line through the crosscurrents and riptides that sent the RIBs skewing off course. Progress wasn't made any easier by the weight each boat was carrying: one cruise missile, and one-two-three-four-five-six-seven men. Twenty-eight of the opposition in all. I could handle those odds. I set the FLIR down. The high clouds had blown out to sea. The sliver of moon provided minimal light and I could make the boats out with my naked eye now.

"What's the range, Boss Dude?" Boomerang hunkered with his hands on the improvised radio detonator.

"Five hundred yards and closing."

He grinned at me. "Cool."

2259. I waited until the boats were just athwart the explosives to give Boomerang the go-ahead.

He was actually giggling as he flipped the switch on the Big Brother black box and the C-4 exploded, kicking water and sand and rock fifteen yards into the air. The detonation was fucking textbook. It caught two of the four RIBs square under their keels. The boats cracked in two and folded like cardboard under the weight of the missiles. The second pair of RIBs were tossed rudely shoreward by the explosions— sending most of the *zhongdui* inside flailing into the churning surf.

I let loose with a series of full-auto three-shot bursts into the floundering *zhongdui* shooters. I hit one, two, three, as quickly and efficiently as if I'd been on a sporting clays range. Hey—what were my guys waiting for, an invitation? "C'mon assholes." Now the rest of the men followed my example, catching the survivors in a murderous cross fire.

But things weren't completely one-sided. The Chinese returned fire—from the water and from the boats. It was haphazard, but a stray round can kill you as easily as a well-placed shot if you're in the wrong spot at the wrong time.

But it was we, not they, who controlled the situation. We'd caught them at the most exposed segment of their insertion—the precise instant when their AV (Area of Vulnerability) was most pronounced. And we were currently taking full advantage of the situation.

I watched through my FLIR as Tosho caught one of the two remaining RIBs broadside and loosed a stream of 9mm into it. He killed one pair of Chinese shooters outright. The surviving *zhongdui* rolled into the water, firing wildly as they went. The second RIB, still untouched, tried to escape our killing zone by heading toward the safety of the rougher but less dangerous shoreline, two hundred or so yards off to my right. I fired at the RIB, hoping to hit the outboard engine and bring the fucking thing to a stop.

After one three-shot burst, the MP5 jammed. "Fuck." I racked, tapped, reloaded, and slapped the bolt forward. Nada. I dropped the mag and exchanged it for a new one, then racked the round out of the chamber and let the bolt fall once more. I looked up, found a knot of targets charging onto the beach, and squeezed the trigger.

Click. Nothing. The fucking gun was not being helpful. Maybe I'd bent something during the fight in the cave. Maybe it was overheated, or dirty—sand and grit are not beneficial to the internal working parts of the MP5. Whatever the case, it wasn't doing me any good now. I transitioned, easing the subgun to the ground, retrieved my USP, sighted just above the heads of the struggling *zhongdui,* and fired. I caught one, knocking him backward into the water. It was a lucky shot—but I didn't give a damn: it had put the s.o.b. *down.*

Fuck—one of the downed *zhongdui's* shipmates swept the ridgeline with machine-gun fire, kicking up huge shards of earth and rock as the belt-fed weapon spat rounds at us.

A rock fragment tore past my cheek and sliced the lobe of my left ear. "Shit." I peeked over the top of the ridge. The survivors were forming a skirmish line—disciplined firing coming at us now—and charging the beach. We'd cut their number by almost half. But that wasn't good enough. They were heading for the weakest side of our position—and if we weren't careful, they'd be able to work their way around our right flank. I ducked as the machine gun stitched our position again.

"Fire the mines," I shouted off to my right, where Rodent hunkered, the small electric detonator for the starboard-side Claymores secured next to him. He was stretched over the top of the ridge, firing down at the beach. "Rodent—*Rodent*—hit the fucking switch *now!*"

Finally I caught his attention and received an upturned thumb. He rolled toward the detonator, shouted, "Fire in the hole," and turned the fat knob.

I ducked and waited for the concussion. Nothing.

I stuck my nose over the ridgeline—and saw the RIB beach itself and the Chinese in it head for cover, firing to give their shipmates still in the water a chance to make it ashore.

"Rodent—fire the fucking thing."

He worked the mechanism again and again, then threw it down in disgust. "It's dead, Skipper—damn thing won't work."

Of course not. The fucking thing had probably had its wiring reversed by Mister Murphy when we weren't looking.

I grabbed my useless MP5 only so I could use the FLIR night sight. Peered through it and saw six, seven, eight, nine, ten Chinese shooters heading for cover, firing at our positions as they charged up the beach toward cover. In the lead, I picked out a tall, lithe figure firing a chunky Styr assault rifle one-handed. It was Li Chimen. He had a smaller, stocky *zhongdui* by the web gear. He was dragging the poor sonofabitch, whose feet were kicking uselessly, as he was hauled across the rocky beach, toward the flank of the low ridge on which we'd dug ourselves in.

I lowered the MP5, brought up my pistol, and squeezed off half a dozen rounds in Li's direction, but all I managed to do was kick up dirt. After all, I was shooting more than 150 yards away—and I was doing it with open sights, in the dark. Without the IR sight, it's hard to shoot effectively at night. You are rendered almost sightless by your own muzzle flash—and the enemy's. Your eyes lose all night vision and you're effectively firing blind.

I picked up the MP5 and caught him again in the FLIR just as he disappeared into the underbrush and rocks, out of my line of sight. He was shouting back toward the beach, trying to rally his troops.

Well, they wouldn't get rallied for very long if I had anything to say about it. I wanted this motherfucker's head on my own personal pike. Pistol in hand I rolled off the ridge top, lunging toward the track that would take me down the back way to cut Li off at the pass. As I went by Pick, he rolled over onto his side and lofted his MP5 in my direction. "Skipper—take this."

"Thanks." I grabbed the weapon, pulled the bolt back, and checked it on the fly, and inserted a fresh mag from the pouch on my left thigh. I patted myself as I loped downhill. I still had two full MP5 mags. One was in the gun. I dropped the USP's almost-empty magazine and pulled a full one from my belt. I had five more—seventy-five rounds. In the pouches of my CQC vest I also carried half a dozen of the mini frag grenades I'd developed some years back. I figured I had enough ordnance to do Li in. And if I ran out, I'd gnaw through the motherfucker's carotid artery if I had to. I'd do anything I had to, to put him down.

I scooted down the hill and zigzagged through a field of large, rough boulders interspersed with tough, thorny bushes, working my way southeast like a broken-field runner. But I wasn't single-minded—wasn't without my early warning system. I hadn't gone more than a couple of hundred yards when I sensed rapid movement behind me. I dropped into the shadows between two boulders, cut behind one and took a different path, going back the way I'd come.[71] I waited until the footsteps passed me, then stepped out, MP5 raised and ready to do nasty business. Nod and Boomerang stopped their forward motion and turned toward me.

I dropped the MP5's muzzle. "What goes?"

"See—" Nod started to explain, but Boomerang cut him off.

"Yo, Boss Dude—just thought we'd tag along. Like, we don't want you having all the fun."

I put a palm on Nod's shoulder. "That right?"

Nod nodded, his head bobbing up and down slowly. "Yup."

I shrugged. "Suit yourselves, assholes." That's what I said as I turned and resumed the pace. But in my heart, I rejoiced to have these two Warriors with me. They had chosen to follow me; they had chosen to risk their lives with me. What greater tribute can an officer receive from his men than to be followed by them?

2307. We worked our way back parallel to the main trail that Duck Foot had identified, but keeping eight to ten yards off. I didn't want to run into any of the opposition in a head-to-head confrontation. I took point—and the right-hand field of fire. Boomerang's 44 long frame followed six yards behind me, his weapon scanning the left side of the trail. Six yards behind him, Nod moved stealthily, his weapon's muzzle scanning left/right. I moved quickly—perhaps faster than I should have—but we had a lot of

---

[71]What I was doing, of course, was following one of the precepts set down in 1759 by Major Roger Rogers, whose Rangers were America's first SpecWarriors. Rogers' Standing Order Number Seventeen goes as follows: "If somebody's trailing you, make circle, come back onto your own tracks, and ambush the folks that aim to ambush you."

ground to cover if we were going to cut these assholes off before they were able to mount a counterambush. We hadn't gone more than three hundred yards when I heard a series of sounds crescendo off to my starboard side. The opposition was close by—and getting closer by the second.

No time to prepare. I silent-signaled "enemy ahead," pointed in the direction they were approaching from, then dropped. Behind me, Nod and Boomerang also disappeared.

The hair on the back of my neck stood up. Now I heard soft footfalls in the darkness as the *zhongdui* came closer. The point man came by, moving carefully, no more than eight to ten yards away. He drew opposite to where I lay, and stopped, as if sniffing the air. I slowed my heartbeat and breathing. Incredibly, I could actually smell the *zhongdui*—he gave off a scent redolent of garlic and onions.

Roy Boehm used to say that when he operated in Vietnam, he always knew where Mister Charlie was, because Mister Victor Charlie used *nuoc mam,* a sauce made of fermented fish heads, on his food. "I could smell the fuckin' enemy," Roy used to say.

Here and now I experienced what he'd been telling me. Point Man moved on. After a twenty-second hiatus, other *zhongdui* followed—precisely how many there were I had no way of knowing, but by counting (or trying to count) footsteps, I guesstimated eight or nine. Things grew quiet once again. We lay in our position for what seemed like an hour but was no more than a minute. And then— incredibly—I heard two voices coming along the same track the *zhongdui* had just passed. As they drew closer, I realized they were arguing, in sotto voce. They were speaking Chinese, so I couldn't understand what the hell they were saying. But one was obviously plaintive—whiny and complaining—while the other was taut, tense, tight, and angry. I'd only heard that forceful voice once before—but its deep tone and uncharacteristically rich timbre had stayed rooted in my brain. That voice belonged to Li Chimen.

There was a sharp exclamation from the angry voice—and then silence. The whiner started to say something. He was interrupted by the unmistakable sound of palm slapping against cheek, and the same angry exclamation, stage-whispered. You didn't have to have a degree in Chinese—I certainly don't—to understand that Li's warrior instincts had kicked in, he'd sensed our presence, and he wanted noise discipline RIGHT NOW.

There was the single muffled sound of something hitting the ground, about six yards off to my left. Then things went absofucking silent.

There are any number of elements here that could be classified as GFs—goatfuck factors. Nod, Boomerang, and I were spread out in a single-file line. We hadn't had enough time to set ourselves into an ambush position—that is to say, facing the enemy in a way that allowed us intersecting fields of fire. We were strung out over somewhere between ten and thirty yards—I had no idea precisely what the spacing was—and we'd allowed the main enemy force to pass us by.

And then, in one of those wonderful Warrior epiphanies, I saw in my mind's eye the framed verse in Bentley Brendel's White House office. You remember it. *What?* You say you don't remember? You'd better take a fucking course in reading retention before the next novel's published. Okay—here it is:

> All warfare is deception.
> So when strong, display weakness;
> When weak, feign strength.
> If your target is nearby,
> Make it appear to be distant.
> Only thus will you achieve your objectives.

Lying on my side, I e-a-s-e-d two of my minifrags out of their pocket, quietly pulled the pins out of the spoons, and lofted the fucking things as hard as I could. I sent one out as far behind Li's position as I could throw it; I tossed the other in the direction the *zhongdui* had taken, hoping to land it near the middle of the group.

The first explosion obviously caught the *zhongdui* by surprise. I knew it because one of 'em panicked: he abandoned all pretense of fire discipline and unleashed his whole fucking magazine at once. Tracer cut overhead from way off to my right.

Doom on you, *zhongdui*. You just told Boomerang and Nod precisely where you are. I heard more grenades, followed by the unmistakable chatter of MP5s, and knew that my pair of merry, murdering marauders were on the case. These *zhongdui* were about to become *zhong*chop-suey.

The second explosion—maybe a second and a half after the first—surprised Li Chimen. I knew that because he tucked and rolled in my direction.

Bad move, Li. Now I knew exactly where he was. I slid the MP5 onto my back, came up, slithered to my left, and caught him from behind, my arm around his neck, the crook of my right elbow shutting off his air, while my left hand tried to hold him in place.

It wasn't gonna happen. Li rolled just far enough to give himself some space—he didn't need much—at which time he used the muzzle of his Styr to hit me hard in the solar plexus.

Yes, I have a rippling washboard tummy because I do my hundreds of sit-ups every single day. But rippling washboard or not, you take a full-tilt boogie hard-ass poke in the solar plexus with the steel muzzle of an assault rifle and I guar-on-tee that it will feel just like you have been hit with a cold chisel driven by a fucking fifteen-pound sledge. Given the physics of the situation, my body doubled over, my arm came loose, and my elbow released his neck. I felt that fucking poke all the way to my eyelashes. Li wriggled away, reversed course, turned to faced me from a distance of six feet—and then realized precisely who the Rogue round-eyes was.

His face became a mask of rage. He bellowed an unintelligible imprecation and fumbled for the Styr.

Bad move. I was on him before his finger could even deal with the safety. I knocked the weapon up into his face. He brought his arm around and slapped it away. I tried to twist the gun—wrap the sling around his throat and use it like a garotte, but the fucking thing was too short. Then the sling unhooked itself from the butt end. I grabbed the Styr and twisted it out of Li's hands by the muzzle and swung it like a fucking baseball bat, slamming him upside the head and shoulders with it.

I connected once or twice, but the Styr is an unwieldy weapon—it's got that goddamn bullpup stock—which makes it easy to shoot, but as a kickass butt-stroker it is a goddamn POS. Finally I slammed the fucking thing onto a rock and shattered it—wasn't gonna give Li the opportunity to use it on me.

He regrouped, backing off slightly.

Another bad move, Mr. Li. Never give up any of your territory, or this fucking Rogue will move into it.

I pressed forward, crowding him. I didn't say a fucking thing—I let my eyes and my War Face do the talking. His hand dropped toward the tactical holster on his right thigh. I feinted with my hands, and as he reacted, kicked him in the left thigh.

It brought him up short—but not short enough. He was still fumbling for the pistol. I tackled him, knocking him backward into a scruffy tree. The fucking tree was dead—it just went *over*—and we tumbled with it, rolling and grappling for position as we did. We were face-to-face—nose to nose. I tried to bite his ear, but he elbowed me away. He clawed at my eyes. I drew back and buried my teeth in his neck. He tried to pull my left ear off. I grabbed his right hand with my left, brought my right hand up and separated the fingers until I had just one—the middle one—then bent it back until it broke.

That got his fucking attention. He roared like a Spielberg

dinosaur. But the sonofabitch didn't give up—he gritted his way through the pain, managed to extract his body from my grasp, caught me with a nasty shot to the ribs, and slammed the base of his palm toward my jaw.

I deflected the blow and struck back with the edge of my hand. My target was the portion of his neck just below his left ear and above his carotid artery. But Li's body wasn't being cooperative—he moved as I swung from the shoulder. The edge of my hand made contact—with the very solid trunk of a tree.

Oh, that smarted. Belay that. It fucking hurt. But there was no time to think about dings because Li was coming back at me—a dervishlike kick that brought his long, muscular leg up and around, and his heel moving toward my face at a tremendous rate of speed.

Since the perception of time has slowed here—it always does during combat—let me explain what's about to happen. Blows such as kicks can be turned against the enemy by using the principle of turning force. Simply put, by changing the direction of the blow, it can be not only deflected, but also turned to your advantage, because you will force your enemy out of position and leave him vulnerable.

Yes I was hurting. Yes I was in pain—and my injured hip wasn't helping much—but that, friends, is when all that training you've gone through over the years pays for itself. All the pain of BUD/S. All the dings from saturation jumps; the hypothermia from cold-water swims and long, frigid nights out in the boondocks, getting rained and snowed on. All the workouts. And the range time. All of those things are what make Warriors able to keep going when others do not. And when you combine the ability to keep going with white-hot rage, the combination makes you unbeatable. YOU WILL NOT FAIL.

And so, pain or no pain, I moved past his linear kick and, as his leg went past me, I smashed the back of his calf with my fist as hard as I could. The blow cramped him—and he went down. I dove at him and hit hard before he could recover—an elbow to the chin followed by a knee to the balls designed to make a eunuch out of him. But he deflected my knee and tried to roll out from under me.

I was having none of it. It was time to put this sucker away for good. My left forearm came down hard on his throat, cutting off his air. My right reached for the USP in my tactical holster.

Li realized what I was doing—and he fought back, desperately trying to counterattack. He clawed and bit and kneed and struck—but I had him and I wasn't about to let go. The pistol came out of the holster. He grabbed at it with his left hand, but it was no use. I brought the fucking muzzle up, up, up, until I wedged it under his armpit. Funny thing about that—it's real hard to dislodge the muzzle of a gun from under your arm without giving the shooter ample time to squeeze off a couple of rounds.

Oh, we were struggling. Oh, we were going at it full tilt boogie rock-and-roll hoochie-koo. But when he felt the gun's ineffable presence up in his armpit, his eyes went wide.

He was mine—he knew it and I knew it. "They're rolling up your networks," I told him, my voice even and low. I kept full pressure on his throat. "Korea, Indonesia, the Philippines, Singapore—they'll all be shut down." I leaned down toward him so he could see my face up close and personal. "They're going to disappear—the same way I made the *Nantong Princess* disappear. But that's not why I'm here."

I let him see my War Face—let him see it good. "Those *zhongdui* you sent to kill Chairman Crocker—they're dead." I cut off more of his air supply. "But that's not why I'm here, either."

I pressed down harder on his neck. "No, I'm here because you had a friend of mine murdered. Had her killed because she was effective."

He tried to spit at me, but he couldn't summon any breath, and the saliva bubbled uselessly between his lips.

"And y'know what they say—do the crime, do the time."
I adjusted the USP's muzzle—didn't want to shoot myself
in the forearm, after all. "It's time to pay, Li—time for you
to pay in full."

He really started to struggle now.

My finger tightened on the trigger. The trigger on the
USP's Variant One has about a twelve-pound pull in
double-action mode. That's not a lot for me.

"Sayonara, Li." I squeezed off a round.

It must have hurt. His eyes went wide—then glazed over
as he struggled. Blood, bright in the faint moonlight,
bubbled in his mouth. He kicked and screamed and fought.
But it was a death throe—I'd hit him where it would kill
him.

Just to make sure, I pulled my forearm back, raised the
muzzle of the pistol, and squeezed off two more rounds.
The first blew his jaw away. The second took a big chunk of
skull when it exited.

I pulled myself off his corpse and struggled to my feet. I
was one tired sonofabitch. I started to holster my weapon—
but heard movement behind me. Brought the USP up. Its
front night sight squarely center-massed on a short figure in
black combat gear.

"Geezus—don't shoot." Bentley Brendel waddled toward
me, his hands raised in surrender.

He came forward slowly. Looked down at Li's corpse.
"Thank God," he said. "You got him."

I said nothing.

"I'll be able to straighten things out as soon as we're back
in Washington," he said.

"You're not going back to Washington, *Bent*ley," I said.

He began to lower his arms. The muzzle of my pistol told
him to keep things exactly as they were.

"What—"

"Alixe Joseph," I said. "You betrayed her. You betrayed
our country."

He shook his head. "No—it wasn't me—"

I closed the eight feet that separated us and slapped him across the face with my pistol. The front sight drew blood. "You're a liar, Bentley." I slapped him again, drawing more. "Worse, you're a traitor." I paused. "I hate traitors."

He started to say something—but I wasn't in the mood to listen. I kicked him and he went down. He rolled onto his hands and knees, scrambling to put some distance between us. He turned toward me, his round porker's face contorted with rage. Struggled to retrieve his pistol from its holster.

Now, I'd actually considered—in passing—bringing the sonofabitch back alive. But then I remembered what my old colleague Colonel Charlie Beckwith used to preach. "Kill 'em all," Charlie said, "and let God sort it out."

Good advice. Advice to live by—and die by. And so I double-tapped Bentley in the head. He went down like the pile of shit he was.

I holstered my weapon and walked over to check the bodies. I knew they weren't carrying anything, but as the old chiefs taught me, never assume anything. In the distance, I heard only the sporadic firing of MP5s—and I knew that my Warriors had prevailed once again. I sat down on the cool ground, put my head in my hands, and worked to slow my heartbeat. It had been one long, fucking day.

0244. We blew the undamaged cruise missiles but left the *zhongdui* bodies where they lay. That would give the Japanese E-2C overflight something big to report later in the morning—and tell the Chinese, who monitored every bit of radio traffic in the region, that they'd fucked up, too. By 0300 we'd rolled the eight-meter boat into the surf, floated it off the trailer, and packed what was left of our gear. We took the *zongduis'* water and some of their weapons. Gator and Rodent had filled all five fuel bladders—more than enough to take us back to Okinawa.

0335. I stowed the last of the Big Brother suitcases, then ran a quick circuit to check the situation on the island. Boomerang and Duck Foot set explosive charges in the caves. I counted heads to make sure we were all accounted for and shooed everyone out to the boat. We helped Pick over the side, easing him into the scuppers. Finally, I made my way into the water and pulled myself over the gunwale.

Nod started the engine. Tosho checked the Magellan GPS screen, punched in a set of coordinates, and set our course for Okinawa. Nod gave us some throttle, and we cut through the rising tide and headed out to sea.

I lay back in the scuppers, bone tired. I watched my men as they re-created the evening's events, their hands moving like pilots describing combat.

By the time we'd lost sight of land, the breeze picked up and the seas became following. On the eastern horizon, the first glimmer of dawn started to rise out of the sea—a hint of vibrant color painting the dark sky. I let my head loll back onto the gunwale, and felt the water's motion; allowed myself to respond to its incredible strength and power. I felt a sailor's sense of absolute belonging. What is perfection, you ask? Perfection is being here—on the ocean, out of sight of land—with my Warriors.

But it was also time to move on. To go home. After all, there was Pinky's retirement to plan.

Glossary

A²: Aforementioned Asshole.

A³: Anytime, Anyplace, Anywhere.

Admiral's Gestapo: what the secretary of defense's office calls the Naval Investigative Services Command (See **SHIT-FOR-BRAINS**).

AK-47: 7.63 X 39 Kalashnikov automatic rifle. The most common assault weapon in the world.

AVCNO: Assistant Vice Chief of Naval Operations.

BAW: Big Asshole Windbag.

BDUs: Battle Dress Uniforms. Now that's an oxymoron if I ever heard one.

BFH: Big Fucking Help.

BOHICA: Bend Over—Here It Comes Again!

Boomer: nuclear-powered missile submarine.

Briccone: (Italian) Rogue.

BTDT: Been There, Done That.

BUPERS: Naval BUreau of PERSonnel.

C-130: Lockheed's ubiquitous Hercules.

C-141: Lockheed's ubiquitous StarLifter aircraft, soon to be mothballed.

C-4: plastic explosive. You can mold it like clay. You can even use it to light your fires. Just don't stamp on it.

C²CO: Can't Cunt Commanding Officer. Too many of these in Navy SpecWar today. They won't support their men or take chances because they're afraid it'll ruin their chances for promotion.

C⁴IFTW: Command, Control, Communications, Computers, and Intelligence for the Warrior.

CALOW: Coastal And Limited-Objective Warfare. Very fashionable acronym at the Pentagon in these days of increased low-intensity conflict.

Cannon Fodder: See **FNG.**

Christians in Action: SpecWar slang for the Central Intelligence Agency.

CINC: Commander-IN-Chief

CINCLANT: Commander-IN-Chief, AtLANtic.

CINCLANTFLT: Commander-IN-Chief, AtLANTic FLeeT.

CINCUSNAVEUR: Commander-IN-Chief, U.S. NAVal forces, EURope.

CLIQ: Combination Lock In Question.

clusterfuck: See **FUBAR.**

CNO: Chief of Naval Operations.

Cockbreath: SEAL term of endearment used for those who only pay lip service.

CONUS: CONtinental United States.

CRACKERS: CRiminal hACKERS—cyberpunk tangos.

CQC: Close Quarters Combat—i.e., killing that's up close and personal.

CQC6: Ernest Emerson's Titanium-framed Close Quarters Combat folding knife favored by Marcinko SEALs. It is currently licensed to Benchmade Knives and available commercially.

CT: CounterTerrorism.

DADT: Don't Ask, Don't Tell.

DEA: Drug Enforcement Agency.

DEFCON: DEFense CONdition.

DEVGRP: Naval Special Warfare DEVelopment GRouP. Current U.S. Navy designation for SEAL Team Six.

detasheet: olive drab, 10-by-20-inch flexible PETN-based plastic explosive used as a cutting or breaching charge.

DIA: Defense Intelligence Agency. Spook heaven based in Arlington, Virginia.

Dickhead: Stevie Wonder's nickname for Marcinko.

Diplo-dink: no-load cookie-pushing diplomat.

DIPSEC: DIPlomatic SECurity.

Dipshit: can't cunt pencil-dicked asshole.

Dirtbag: the look Marcinko favors for his Team guys.

Do-ma-nhieu: (Vietnamese) Go fuck yourself (See **DOOM ON YOU**).

Doom on you: American version of Vietnamese for "go fuck yourself."

Dweeb: no-load shit-for-brains geeky asshole, usually shackled to a computer.

EC-130: Electronic warfare-outfitted C-130.

EEI: Essential Element of Information. The info-nuggets on which a mission is planned and executed.

EEO: Equal Employment Opportunity (Marcinko always treats 'em all alike—just like shit).

ELINT: ELectronic INTelligence.

EOD: Explosive Ordnance Disposal.

F^3: Full Fucking Faulkner—lots of sound and fury.

FIS: Flight Information Service.

flashbang: disorientation device used by hostage rescue teams.

FLIR: Forward Looking Infra Red.

FNG: Fucking New Guy. See **CANNON FODDER**.

Four-striper: Captain. All too often, a C^2CO.

frags: fragmentation grenades.

FUC: Fucking Ugly Corsican.
FUBAR: Fucked Up Beyond All Repair.
fuhatsu: (Japanese) misfire; dud.

Glock: Reliable 9mm pistols made by Glock in Austria. They're great for SEALs because they don't require as much care as Sig Sauers.
GNBN: Good News/Bad News.
Goatfuck: What the Navy likes to do to Marcinko (See **FUBAR**).
GSG-9: Grenzchutzgruppe-9. Top German CT unit.

HAHO: High-Altitude, High-Opening parachute jump.
HALO: High-Altitude, Low-Opening parachute jump.
HICs: Head-In-Cement syndrome. Condition common to high-ranking officers. Symptoms include pigheadedness and inability to change opinions when presented with new information.
HK: ultra-reliable pistol, assault rifle, or submachine gun made by Heckler & Koch, a German firm. SEALs use H&K MP5-Ks submachine guns in various configurations, as well as H&K 33 assault rifles, and P7M8 9mm, and USP 9mm, .40- or .45-caliber pistols.
Huey: original slang for Bell's AH-1 two-bladed helicopter, but now refers to various UH configuration Bell choppers.
HUMINT: HUMan INTelligence.
humongous: Marcinko's dick.
Hydra-Shok: extremely lethal hollow-point ammunition manufactured by Federal Cartridge Company.

IBS: Inflatable Boat, Small—the basic unit of SEAL transportation.
IED: Improvised Explosive Device.

Japs: bad guys.
Jarheads: Marines. The Corps. Formally, USMC, or, Uncle Sam's Misguided Children.

jibaku: (Japanese) suicide bombing.
JSOC: Joint Special Operations Command.

KATN: Kick Ass and Take Names. Marcinko avocation.
KH: KeyHole. Designation for NRO's spy-in-the-sky satellites, as in KH-12s.
KISS: Keep It Simple, Stupid.

LANTFLT: AtLANTic FLeeT.

M³: Massively Motivated Motherfuckers.
M-16: Basic U.S. .223-caliber weapon, used by the armed forces.
MagSafe: lethal frangible ammunition that does not penetrate the human body. Favored by some SWAT units for CQC.
Mark-I Mod-0: basic unit.
MILCRAFT: Pentagonese for MILitary airCRAFT.
MOI: Ministry of the Interior.

NAVAIR: NAVy AIR Command.
NAVSEA: NAVy SEA Command.
NAVSPECWARGRU: NAVal SPECial WARfare GRoUp.
Navyspeak: redundant, bureaucratic naval nomenclature, either in written nonoral, or nonwritten oral modes, indecipherable by nonmilitary (conventional) or military (unconventional) individuals during normal interfacing configuration conformations.
NIS: Naval Investigative Service Command, also known as the Admirals' Gestapo (See: **SHIT-FOR-BRAINS**).
NMN: No Middle Name.
NRO: National Reconnaissance Office. Established 25 August 1960 to administer and coordinate satellite development and operations for U.S. intelligence community. Very spooky place.
NSA: National Security Agency, known within the SpecWar community as No Such Agency.

NSCT: Naval Security Coordination Team (Navyspeak name for Red Cell).

NSD: National Security Directive.

NYL: Nubile Young Lovely.

OBE: Overtaken By Events—usually because of the bureaucracy.

OOD: Officer Of the Deck (he who drives the big gray monster).

OP-06-04: CNO's SpecWar Briefing Officer.

OP-06: Deputy CNO for Operations, Plans and Policy.

OP-06B: Assistant Deputy CNO for Operations, Plans and Policy.

OP-06D: Cover organization for Red Cell/NSCT.

OPSEC: OPerational SECurity.

PDMP: Pretty Dangerous Motherfucking People.

POS: Piece Of Shit.

POTUS: President Of The United States.

RDL: Real Dirty Look.

RPG: Rocket Propelled Grenade.

R²D²: Ritualistic, Rehearsed, Disciplined Drills.

S²: Sit the fuck down and Shut the fuck up.

SAS: Special Air Service. Britain's top CT unit.

SATCOM: SATellite COMmunications.

SCIF: Sensitive Compartmented Information Facility. A bug-proof room.

SEAL: SEa-Air-Land Navy SpecWarrior. A hop-and-popping shoot-and-looter hairy-assed frogman who gives a shit. The acronym stands for Sleep, Eat And Live it up.

Semtex: Czecho C-4 plastique explosive. Used for canceling Czechs.

SERE: Survival, Evasion, Resistance, and Escape school.

SES: Shit-Eating Smile.

SH-3: versatile Sikorsky chopper. Used in ASW missions and also as a spec ops platform.

Shit-for-Brains: any no-load, pus-nutted, pencil-dicked asshole from NIS.
SIGINT: SIGnals INTelligence.
SMG: SubMachine Gun.
SNAFU: Situation Normal—All Fucked Up.
SNAILS: Slow, Nerdy Assholes In Ludicrous Shoes.
SOCOM: Special Operations COMmand, located at MacDill AFB, Tampa, Florida.
SOF: Special Operations Force.
S&P: Spit-and-Polish.
SpecWarrior: One who gives a fuck.
SSN: nuclear sub, commonly known as sewer pipe.
STR: Smack The Rogue.
SUC: Marcinkospeak for Smart, Unpredictable, and Cunning.
SWAT: Special Weapons and Tactics police teams. All too often they do not train enough, and become SQUAT teams.

TAD: Temporary Additional Duty (SEALs refer to it as Traveling Around Drunk).
Tailhook: the convention of weenie-waggers, gropesters, and pressed-ham-on-glass devotees that put air-brakes on NAVAIR.
TARFU: Things Are Really Fucked Up.
TECHINT: TECHnical INTelligence.
THREATCON: THREAT CONdition.
Tigerstripes: The only stripes that SEALs will wear.
TIQ: Tango-In-Question.
totsugekijin: (Japanese) assault rifles.
TTS: Marcinko slang for Tap 'em, Tie 'em, and Stash 'em.

U$_2$: Ugly and Unfamilar.
UNODIR: UNless Otherwise DIRected.

VDL: Versatile, Dangerous, and Lethal.

Wanna-bes: the sort of folks you meet at Soldier of Fortune conventions.

Weenies: pussy-ass can't cunts and no-loads.
WTF: What The Fuck.

zhongdui: (Chinese) Naval reconnaissance commando unit of the People's Liberation Army.
Zulu: Greenwich Mean Time (GMT) designator used in formal military communications.
Zulu-5-Oscar: escape and evasion exercises in which Frogmen try to plant dummy limpet mines on Navy vessels, while the vessels' crews try to catch them in *bombus interruptus.*

Index

All entries preceded by an asterisk (*) are pseudonyms.

About the Authors

RICHARD MARCINKO retired from the Navy as a full commander after more than thirty years of service. He currently lives in the Washington, D.C., area, where he is CEO of SOS Temps Inc.—his private security firm, whose clients are governments and corporations—and Richard Marcinko Inc., a motivational training and team-building company. He is the author of *The Rogue Warrior's Strategy for Success: A Commando's Principles of Winning,* and the four-month *New York Times* business best-seller *Leadership Secrets of the Rogue Warrior: A Commando's Guide to Success.* In addition to his best-selling autobiography, *Rogue Warrior,* he is coauthor, with John Weisman, of the *New York Times* best-selling novels *Rogue Warrior: Red Cell, Rogue Warrior: Green Team, Rogue Warrior: Task Force Blue,* and *Rogue Warrior: Designation Gold.*

JOHN WEISMAN is one of the select company of writers to have both fiction and nonfiction works on the *New York Times* best-seller lists. He is the author of more than a dozen books, including the critically acclaimed novels *Evidence* and *Blood Cries,* and the nonfiction best-seller *Shadow Warrior,* the biography of CIA agent Felix Rodriguez. Weisman's well-received CIA short story, "There Are Monsterim," was part of the 1996 anthology *Unusual Suspects* and *Best Suspense Short Stories: 1997.* He divides his time between homes in the Washington, D.C., area, and the Blue Ridge Mountains of Virginia. John Weisman can be reached via the Internet at jweisman@ix.netcom.com.